THE FALL OF
CADIA

More tales of the Astra Militarum from Black Library

• MINKA LESK •
MINKA LESK: THE LAST WHITESHIELD
An omnibus edition of the novels *Cadia Stands, Cadian Honour,
Traitor Rock* and several short stories
by Justin D Hill

SHADOW OF THE EIGHTH
A novel by Justin D Hill

CREED: ASHES OF CADIA
A novel by Jude Reid

DEATHWORLDER
A novel by Victoria Hayward

LONGSHOT
A novel by Rob Young

SIEGE OF VRAKS
A novel by Steve Lyons

KRIEG
A novel by Steve Lyons

KASRKIN
A novel by Edoardo Albert

OUTGUNNED
A novel by Denny Flowers

CATACHAN DEVIL
A novel by Justin Woolley

STEEL TREAD
A novel by Andy Clark

VOLPONE GLORY
A novel by Nick Kyme

WITCHBRINGER
A novel by Steven B Fischer

VAINGLORIOUS
A novel by Sandy Mitchell

HONOURBOUND
A novel by Rachel Harrison

THE FALL OF CADIA

ROBERT RATH

BLACK LIBRARY

A BLACK LIBRARY PUBLICATION

First published in 2023.
This edition published in Great Britain in 2024 by
Black Library, Games Workshop Ltd., Willow Road,
Nottingham, NG7 2WS, UK.

Represented by: Games Workshop Limited – Irish branch,
Unit 3, Lower Liffey Street, Dublin 1,
D01 K199, Ireland.

10 9 8 7 6 5 4 3 2 1

Produced by Games Workshop in Nottingham.
Cover illustration by Neil Roberts.

See Black Library on the internet at

blacklibrary.com

Find out more about Games Workshop
and the worlds of Warhammer at

games-workshop.com

Printed and bound in the UK.

For Dustin and Mike,
the only friends I'd want when exploring a Blackstone Fortress.

For more than a hundred centuries the Emperor
has sat immobile on the Golden Throne of Earth.
He is the Master of Mankind. By the might of his
inexhaustible armies a million worlds stand
against the dark.

Yet, he is a rotting carcass, the Carrion Lord of
the Imperium held in life by marvels from the
Dark Age of Technology and the thousand souls
sacrificed each day so his may continue to burn.

To be a man in such times is to be one amongst
untold billions. It is to live in the cruelest and
most bloody regime imaginable. It is to suffer an
eternity of carnage and slaughter. It is to have cries
of anguish and sorrow drowned by the thirsting
laughter of dark gods.

This is a dark and terrible era where you will
find little comfort or hope. Forget the power of
technology and science. Forget the promise of
progress and advancement. Forget any notion of
common humanity or compassion.

There is no peace amongst the stars, for in the grim
darkness of the far future, there is only war.

DRAMATIS PERSONAE

+++FORCES OF THE IMPERIUM+++

CADIAN DEFENCE FORCES

Lord Castellan and High Command War Cabinet

Ursarkar E. Creed	Lord Castellan, Lord General of the Astra Militarum
Jarran Kell	Colour Sergeant, Creed's personal attaché
Conskavan Raik	Logistar-General
Audaria Zabine	Supreme Commissar
Marus Porelska	Former governor, slain at Tyrok Fields

24th Cadian Interior Guard

Ignitio Barathus	Colonel
Marda Hellsker	Major, engineer qualified
Ravura	Company Sergeant
Lek	Corporal
Dakaj	Chief Medicae
Suvane	Surgeon's orderly

Kasrkin 27th, Fire-team Gamma

Servantus Glave	Volley gunner
Okkun	Pointman
'Stitcher' Kristan	Medicae
Sergeant Veskaj	Hellgunner, sergeant
Luzal	Hellgunner, vox-operator

Kraf Crime Syndicate

Salvar Ghent   Crime lord

Karle Petzen   Underboss

89th Combat-Pict Recon, Kraf Air Command

Hanna Keztral   Captain, pilot of Avenger *Deadeye*

Lahon Darvus   Lieutenant, armament operator of *Deadeye*

THE MOST HOLY ADEPTA SORORITAS

Order of Our Martyred Lady

Eleanor   Canoness, guardian of the Shrine of St Morrican

Genevieve   Canoness, custodian of Ecclesiarchy lands

Celestine   The Living Saint

THE HOLY ORDERS OF THE EMPEROR'S INQUISITION

Talia Daverna   Inquisitor, Ordo Hereticus

Katarinya Greyfax   Inquisitor, Ordo Hereticus

ADEPTUS MECHANICUS AND ALLIES

Adeptus Mechanicus, Servants of the Machine God

Magos Klarn   Mechanicus representative to Cadian high command

Belisarius Cawl   Archmagos Dominus

Qvo-87   Clone-servant of Cawl

House Raven, Oath-Bound Protectors of the Omnissiah

Neeve Vardus — Baroness, pilot of the Knight Paladin *Cold Iron*

THE MOST REVERED ADEPTUS ASTARTES

Black Templars, Sons of Dorn, Cruxis Crusade

Marius Amalrich — Marshal of the Cruxis Crusade

Mordlied — Castellan, bannerman

Space Wolves, Sons of Russ

Orven Highfell — Wolf Lord, Ironwolves Great Company

Sven Bloodhowl — Wolf Lord, Firehowlers Great Company

Dark Angels, Sons of the Lion

Korahael — Master of the Fourth Company and strike cruiser *Sword of Defiance*

Raven Guard, Sons of Corax

Odric A'shar — Ceremonial Lieutenant, commander of the Company of Brothers

+++LEGIONS OF CHAOS+++

THE BLACK LEGION, SCOURGE OF THE IMPERIUM

Black Legion Command

Ezekyle Abaddon — Warmaster of Chaos, 'The Despoiler'

| Dravura Morkath | the Fortress Child, cup-bearer to Abaddon |
| **Cacadius Siron** | Intelligence chief, formerly of the Alpha Legion |

Chosen of Abaddon

Urkanthos	Lord Ravager (Khorne), Hounds of Abaddon
Skyrak Slaughterborn	Lord Corruptor (Nurgle), Bringers of Decay
Zaraphiston	Lord Deceiver (Tzeentch), seer of the Black Legion
Devram Korda	Lord Purgator (Slaanesh), Children of Torment
Krom Gat	Lord Unifier (Chaos Undivided), Iron Warriors

Local Cadian Allies

| **Yann Rovetske** | Agent of Chaos |

Daemons

| **Artesia Gore-mouth** | Shadow-daemon of Khorne |

+++PERFIDIOUS XENOS+++

NECRON LEGIONS OF SOLEMNACE, NIHILAKH DYNASTY

Trazyn the Infinite	Overlord, Archaeovist of the Prismatic Galleries
Sannet	Arch-Cryptek of Solemnace, companion of Trazyn
The Huntmaster	Game warden, bodyguard to Trazyn

HARLEQUINS, POOR PLAYERS OF THE LAUGHING GOD

Sylandri Veilwalker
Shadowseer, Masque of the
Veiled Path

PHASE ONE

REVERBERATIONS

ONE

Blood and iron.

Iron and blood.

One lay on the other, and within the other. The slick shine of the iron-rich blood – still warm – on the cold surface of the bell. Two related elements, joined in accidental symbolism.

If records were to be believed, the bell had been forged from blood.

It was said that when Saint Gerstahl – the sacred soldier, favoured patron of the Cadian trooper – fell defending the Gate in the centuries after the Great Heresy, acolytes collected his vitae in a crystal reliquary. There it stayed for centuries, a venerated and lucrative relic on the shrine world christened with his name.

Until, one night, Blessed Gerstahl appeared to the cardinal with a message: he must extract the iron from the tarry, coagulated remnants and forge it into a bell.

A bell that would toll when Cadia was in mortal danger.

The cardinal forged the relic as instructed, then took the bell on a tour of the Cadian Gate, purifying world after world with the vibration of its holy resonance. A fortunate choice, since it escaped destruction when the Despoiler immolated the shrine world – and Gerstahl's incorruptible remains – during the Third Black Crusade.

On Solar Mariatus, two million welcomed the bell. Sobbing crowds parted to make a path for the fifty Battle Sisters of the Order of Our Martyred Lady who formed its vanguard. In the Derades Subsector, it was said that its chime healed the deaf and straightened crooked limbs. And on Laurentix, in the Belis Corona System, the populace wailed in ecstasy when it tolled a dozen times without being touched by human hands.

That was when the Black Legion descended upon it, in the opening raids of the Twelfth Black Crusade.

The vanguard had sworn to die rather than surrender their relic. And they fulfilled that oath. Their bodies now lay beneath the cold iron of the bell, some resting in its shadow. Chest cavities blown open, limbs severed from the impact of traitor bolt-shells, their own vitae splashed onto the blood-forged iron. It ran in frozen rivulets down the engraved surface, turning the scrollwork and decorative psalms into channels of gore.

They had saved it, in a sense.

Their stoic defence had given Trazyn time to lock the bell and its entourage in stasis, then spirit it to the archival vaults of Solemnace.

Now it hung, unmoving and fastened in time, among the relics of Cadia past. Gazed upon by the unseeing eyes of general officers snatched from the battlefield, zigzag trench-lines full of Shock Troops and a rank of Chimera variants bisected to show internal detail.

Overhead, a squad of Night Lords Raptors arced through the vaults above a lit display of human eyes.

All of them, artefacts of the Cadian Gate. The ephemera of Abaddon the Despoiler's twelve Black Crusades.

Darkened exhibits stretched across twenty-five square miles, a private gallery of humans, exquisitely arranged to please the historical and aesthetic tastes of the alien curator who'd imprisoned them.

Nothing in the gallery apart from maintenance scarabs had moved in over a millennium.

Which is why the soft *pat-pat-pat* of fluid echoed as far as it did.

It fell from the iron surface of the bell like the first drops of icicles melting on the eaves of a hab. Drip. Drip-drip.

Jewelled drops met the upturned forehead of a slain Battle Sister and stained her pale skin with splashes of crimson.

Pat. Pat-pat.

More drops. Coalescing on her brow, trickling into her open eyes.

Blood moved on the bell's skin, collecting in beads like rain on a window and falling in defiance of the stasis field.

And the bell, without propulsion or force, began to swing.

A hand's breadth at first. A sway. Its clapper moving in a soft pendulum arc too weak to do more than scrape the sides.

Then, the arc widened, the violent motion of the bell flinging droplets of blood to either side, spattering the faces of stasis-locked Shock Troopers. Sizzling on the protective fields of lasgun displays. Swaying wider until the bell went fully perpendicular and the clapper inside dropped, its hammer striking the iron of the bell.

Clang.

One.

The blackstone floor vibrated. A rank of medals swayed, its stasis field shorting out. An organic clatter filled the chamber, the sound of ten thousand jaws – held shut by hard-light holograms – shaken so hard that the teeth rattled.

Overhead, the flight of Night Lords Raptors tumbled from the vaults and into a trench display, snapping bones and crushing lasgun barrels. Neither Traitor Space Marines nor Guardsmen reacted.

* * *

Clang.

Two.

Trazyn, Overlord of Solemnace, Archaeovist of the Prismatic Galleries and He-Who-Is-Called-Infinite, screamed in rage.

'Sannet! What is happening?'

'Unclear,' answered his chief cryptek, his multijointed fingers dancing across phos-glyph panels. 'Unknown resonance. Macro-seismic. Cracking the vaults, releasing coolant. We've lost the Ooliac sand sculptures.'

'Call the restoration scarabs.'

'Not responding,' Sannet answered, data-chains flashing across his ocular. 'Our nodal program misinterpreted the vibration as a re-interment signal. The legion has entered radical shutdown. I cannot rouse them.'

Trazyn cursed the very wheel of the cosmos. The interval between shocks had been only seconds apart, and while mental speech between he and Sannet was near instant, they were running out of time before the next tectonic shudder would hit.

'It's not tectonic, lord,' said Sannet. 'It's coming from the gallery.'

'Where?'

'The Black Crusades wing.'

'That's only two levels do–'

Clang.

Three.

The shockwave shook Trazyn apart, his joint servos spasming and dislocating with the intensity of it.

He evacuated the dying body and rushed his spirit-algorithm

into the network of data-channels in the walls. Found a waiting lychguard he could use as a surrogate. Melted and reshaped the borrowed body into his accustomed form as he ran towards the gates of the Cadian gallery. Waved a hand at the enormous gates in a gesture of opening.

Clang.

Four.

The doors ahead, twice the size of a monolith, blew off their hinges and toppled down at him. He felt them crumple the necrodermis of his cranium like parchment and burst his central reactor before he transferred to another body, sheltered in the lee of a Baneblade.

He sprinted. Waving hands at display plinths, throwing code-signals from his palm emitters. Trying to restart shielding and repulsors, to protect his delicate artefacts.

'No, no, no, no, no, no–'

Trazyn saw the bell.

Trazyn saw the blood.

He slowed his chronosense to take in the swinging relic and its sheets of ruby spray. It was far more human vitae than had been splashed on its surface.

Almost as if the relic itself were bleeding from the pockmarks and scratches where bolt-shells had marked it.

'Sannet,' Trazyn said, casting his visual senses into the data-stream of Solemnace so his cryptek could run analysis. 'The stasis field has failed. Hard restart.'

'The field is active,' Sannet responded. 'Movement should be impossible.'

'Not impossible, warpcraft.'

Trazyn watched in fascinated horror as the bell completed its arc, the blood-forged metal swinging high as the hammer inside dropped like the great mace of a warmaster.

Clang.

Five.

Across the galaxy, past burning stars, teeming worlds and cold expanses of nothing, lay the blasted world of Eriad VI. The Ark Mechanicus vessel *Iron Revenant* hung in its orbit, casting a cruciform shadow on the surface.

Down, down, through the nuclear-blighted atmosphere and crust overrun with ork ravagers. Down in black tunnels of alien scale and curve, stood Archmagos Dominus Belisarius Cawl.

'Nearly,' he said, stretching the word. His eyes squeezed tight, optic nerves rerouted through the visual lenses of the skull probe he'd guided into the bore-hole. The on-off strobe of its ultraviolet lamp – used to map the worming tunnels within the blackstone – was the only illumination. He sensed a data-stream connection. 'Careful, little one. Rise two skull-lengths. Pivot thirty-five degrees right. Ahead four lengths – now, now, now! All ahead steady and open connection! Op–'

The data flooded in, pasting across his vision, unfamiliar glyphs that slid cold into his mind, chill as the nothing of space.

The servo-skull's vision blasted to static, its auditory ports howling in Cawl's augmented brain.

'Damn it!' he cursed, yanking the skull-jack free from his temple. 'Qvo, another probe!'

No response. His programmable servant – cloned from a long-dead companion – was either not listening, or perhaps had reset due to the flood of data.

'Qvo?' He turned. 'Qvo, are you lis–'

He stopped.

The aeldari standing behind his right shoulder had not triggered a single alert in his sensorium net.

She crouched on a cogitator bank, toes together, knees spread wide – an inverted-triangle pose inhuman in its gravity-defying grace.

'The skeins of fate wind tight about the gate,' Veilwalker said, her egg-like mask nothing but a swirl of smoke. The hues of her motley seemed to blaze in the dark cavern. 'Again, I plea – does thy mind now see?'

'Your rhymes are impenetrable nonsense,' he growled. 'It is a necron world, bombarded by the Despoiler during the Fourth Black Crusade. But why would he bombard an empty planet? I cannot fathom why you insisted I come here.'

'More excavation,' the xenos answered, cocking her head, 'will dispel frustration.'

'To hells with your childish rhymes. Just tell me what you want me to know!'

She shook her head, mask gleaming blue in apology. 'You must play your role – the bell does toll.'

'And what, by the blessed reactor, is that supposed to mean?'

Clang.

Six.

'It started an hour ago, canoness,' said Sister Navarette. Even with her daily training regimen, Genevieve could hear that her Seraphim Superior was out of breath climbing the bell-tower stairs.

They should have taken their jump packs.

The Shrine of St Morrican was a large edifice, and the bell-tower one of the tallest buildings in the Kraf Sector – securing the gateway between Cadia Primus and Cadia Secundus.

For nigh a hundred days it had served as a linchpin of the defence, ensuring that the Archenemy forces of the Thirteenth Black Crusade – which had overrun Kasr Myrak to the north – did not break loose into the Kraf Plain.

'It's ringing?' Genevieve asked. 'Are you certain?'

'Without being touched.'

Genevieve bolted up the last flight, emerging into the vault of the bell-tower. And saw her own face, tight-lipped, looking back at her.

'Canoness Genevieve,' said her twin sister, Eleanor, with a formal bend of her head.

It was every bit like looking in a mirror. Ironic, given how different they were. Twin canonesses in twin suits of armour. Only differing in every other way – and the simple fact that Genevieve's recent ocular augmetic replaced her left eye rather than the right.

But when they faced each other, that only enhanced the feeling of looking in a glass.

'I see you are late,' sneered Arch-Deacon Mendazus. 'As was ever the case.'

'If you wanted me here, perhaps either of you could have sent word a miracle was occurring.'

Eleanor opened her mouth to respond.

Then the Bell of St Morrican sounded.

Eleanor crouched under the bell, staring up into the dark interior, and reached out a hand to help the frail Mendazus duck underneath.

The bell moved not, its clapper hung dead at its centre. And yet the great throat reverberated with the thrum of a note struck far away.

Genevieve joined them, the two canonesses and their overseeing priest standing inside the massive enclosure, flesh shaking from the aural assault.

Genevieve touched the curving interior surface. 'It resonates. It trembles.'

'Signs and wonders,' whispered Eleanor, genuflecting. 'It rings without human hand, like its sister, the Bell of Gerstahl. The one that rang in warning of the Twelfth Black Crusade, then ascended to avoid capture.'

'A bit late for a warning, isn't it? We've been fighting the Despoiler's Thirteenth Crusade for nigh three months.'

'It rings in celebration,' said Arch-Deacon Mendazus.

'Celebration of what?' she asked.

He looked at her, scorn on his features. 'Victory, of course.'

Clang.

Seven.

'Cruxis! Cut them down! Do not let the cowards flee!'

On a mound of dead stood Marshal Amalrich of the Black Templars, sword extended in challenge at the traitor drop-ship. The power field of his blade crackled as it cooked off heretic blood.

Castellan Mordlied climbed to the Marshal's side, hoisting the banner of the Cruxis Crusade. Ahead of him, the engines of the traitor transport ignited, washing his armour with a rolling wall of flash-heated air. The engine discharge immolated two hundred Traitor Guardsmen, who had only a moment before been clawing with desperation towards the craft in hopes of evacuating off Cadia. They disappeared into feathery ash clouds that billowed towards the line of black-armoured Astartes converging on the ship.

Mordlied's hearts lifted along with the pennant as the artificial wind caught it, the twin-forked banner lashing in the gust like a dragon's tail. With a two-handed heave, he drove the point of the banner-pole into the top of a wrecked rockcrete bunker and drew his chainsword.

A Traitor Guardsman, his face scarified with a heathen rune, came at him with a meltagun. Mordlied keyed his chainsword and took him at the shoulder, sectioning the heretic like a side of meat.

'Bring it down!' Amalrich shouted, pointing at the rising dropship. His shaven skull was bare, so the pitiful heretics could see the Templar cross branded on his forehead. A las-bolt flickered off his conversion field. 'Let none escape!'

A host of missiles rushed towards the lander, crashing into armour panels and clipping off landing struts. Crimson lascannon beams lanced the bottom of the rising craft, leaving orange trails of super-heated metal and exploding an external fuel tank.

For a moment it appeared to be rising skyward like a sun, slow and drifting on the burn of the lift-nozzles.

Then the engines stuttered, and the ship – wide as two hab-blocks – dropped back to the surface of Cadia.

The explosion washed over Mordlied like the Emperor's grace.

He took the snapping cloth banner in his armoured fist, raised it to his lips, and kissed it.

Clang.

Eight.

Visibility: Six miles, minimal cloud cover.

Altitude: 3,500 feet.

Speed: 1,100 miles per hour.

And diving.

1,613 feet per second.

Captain Hanna Keztral swallowed the Gs. Clenched her teeth against the discomfort. Watched her altimeter spiral like a chrono gone mad. Cut the engines.

'One second,' warned her armament-operator, Darvus.

Keztral tried not to look at the green-brown of the Cadian moors rising up in her Avenger's canopy. The grey skyline disappearing above her helmet lip. She angled the ram-thrust engine upward, ready.

'Two seconds,' Darvus said, alarm rising faster than the ground. 'Kez, it's too...'

Keztral hauled back on the stick, slammed her foot on the ignition. Felt the ram-thruster jackknife their nose to almost horizon level, forward momentum ripping air past their aerofoils in a glorious sensation of lift.

Below, a traitor armoured column streaked towards them like a las-bolt. Just a rust-streak on the blurred green of the passing landscape.

'Fire! Fire! Fire!' she ordered, but it was unnecessary, just the drunk head-rush of circulation returning after the dive.

Under her feet, she could already feel the armament spinning, each black eye of the cylinder firing one after the other.

'Good approach!' Darvus yelled behind her, eye in his telescopic sight. 'Keep steady.'

Enemy fire drilled past. Amber whip-tails of tracer rounds. Red las-beams. Something hard, a heavy bolter round, sparked harmlessly off the armour of the tail assembly.

Avenger strike fighters were fast craft, and a kite like Keztral's *Deadeye* – stripped for speed – was hard to hit without advanced warning.

Warning that Keztral, diving in steep from fifteen thousand feet, didn't give them.

'Spools empty!' yelled Darvus.

Keztral stamped the right pedal and hauled the stick back, rolling them over into a sunward climb. Leaving the enemy column behind – utterly untouched by fire.

'Good captures!' crowed Darvus. 'Analysts back at Kraf Air Command will be thrilled with this film. Rotary picter especially. You hit the approach perfect, Kez.'

'Can you tell where they're headed?'

'That's the best part,' Darvus answered, voice tinny in her helmet vox. 'They're retreating.'

Clang.

Nine.

Major Marda Hellsker swallowed and squeezed the grip of her laspistol.

She had to set an example for her troopers. Show stoicism in the face of the enemy. Not betray her feelings.

She failed, and the smile spread across her features.

Her company sergeant, Ravura, caught the look and grinned. Leaned forward so she could hear him over the roar of the Chimera engine.

'We're going, sir!' he said. 'The front, at long last.'

She looked down the bay at the troopers, swaying in their jump seats with each jostle. Lasguns between their knees. Packs swinging in the overhead netting.

Despite the shadow of their helmet lips, she could see the sparkle of teeth in every trooper down the bay.

'Let's hear you roar, Twenty-Four!' she shouted.

'Twenty-Four, in the war!' they barked as one, then dissolved into a chorus of hoots, howls and cheers.

'Frekkin' finally!' added Corporal Lek.

'Belay that,' bellowed Ravura, without much force. 'Someone needed to keep Kasr Kraf secure. And they gave it to us – because they knew the Despoiler wouldn't dare hit Kraf with the Twenty-Fourth on the gates.'

More cheers, louder this time. Drowning out a message crackling in Hellsker's micro-bead. Good on Ravura, flipping the script on Lek's undermining bullshit.

Spending the war at Kraf had been hard. Not a shot fired in

anger. More killed by commissars than enemy rounds. Discipline fraying with the inability to prove themselves.

And the 24th Interior Guard wanted, so badly, to prove themselves. To be able to look the other Cadians – those who had deployed to warfronts across the galaxy – in the eye. Show that even though they'd drawn the unlucky lot of remaining on-world as a garrison force, they were still soldiers of Cadia.

The buzzing in her ear continued, escalated. Hellsker frowned and pushed it deeper with a finger, waving for quiet.

'What's wrong?' asked Ravura.

'We've stopped,' said Hellsker. 'The engine's cut.'

She banged on the communication hatch until the driver slid it open. Told her what was coming over the vox.

Hellsker bit her lips. Took a moment to compose her face before turning to deliver the news. Keep it short, she told herself. Be stoic.

They were looking at her, expectant, when she turned. Smiles still gleaming under their helmets.

'Message from the front. Enemy is in full retreat. Pulling back to landing fields. The Thirteenth Black Crusade is over. We are victorious. Our orders are to pull back to Kraf. Eject your powercells, make weapons safe.'

They slumped back into their seats, popped cells and stowed them. Pulled helmets down to cover their eyes and crossed arms over lasrifle barrels. Trooper Keska's shoulders trembled, and Hellsker knew he was weeping. Corporal Lek dropped his head back against the bulkhead and snorted an ironic laugh. Udza, her vox-operator, dropped any façade of toughness and leaned forward, burying her eyes in the palms of her hands.

Even Ravura had nothing to say.

Marda Hellsker focused on her breathing, maintaining her neutral expression. Sat down, buckled herself back in her safety harness, and stared at the rear hatch of the Chimera.

For a moment, just a moment, she had thought she'd become a real Shock Trooper.

Through the armour of the hull, she could hear a reverberation.

She realised it was cheering, and slammed a fist on the armoured bulkhead beside her.

Clang.

Ten.

Trazyn could hear the bell's echo even within the hyperspace oubliette.

A thing that should not be possible, but impossibilities seemed to be getting increasingly common.

'I am obliged for the rescue, Huntmaster. But was it quite necessary to *drag* your planetary overlord?'

'My apologies, lord.' The Huntmaster released his grip on Trazyn's clavicle collar. The deathmark's single ocular gleamed. 'The bellow of the beast was approaching. It cannot find us in here.'

'Yes, well.' Trazyn brushed his necrodermis off with his metal hands. The Huntmaster had once been the greatest game warden in the dynasties, but like most necrons, the deathmark was now quite mad. 'I see you picked up Sannet as well. What is the gallery's status?'

'Major damage, lord, cascade failures.'

'When the ringing stops, I want that relic out of here – cast it through the webway portal, let it bedevil the aeldari. But before that, prepare the *Lord of Antiquity* for sail.'

'You,' stuttered Sannet, 'you are leaving Solemnace, lord archaeovist? In such a state?'

'If that bell foretells what I think it does, it means a cataclysm of historic proportions – one that would be most fascinating to observe up close.' He paused, reading damage glyphs. 'The legions are inactivated, I see. What about the galleries?'

'Only the closed collection remains untouched,' answered Sannet. 'Its enfolded dimension seems less affected. The Horus Heresy exhibit, the Terran artefacts, and of course the special acquisition.'

'It will have to do. Get me a complement of mindshackle scarabs. Come, Huntmaster. I daresay there will be game big enough for even you.'

Clang.

Eleven.

'That price,' the captain said, 'is murder.'

'That price,' Salvar Ghent responded, mirroring his pause, 'is final.'

The captain was a Mordian. Off-worlder. Slab-like features with a sharp little moustache. Ghent didn't like him, but Ghent didn't like people in general.

'We have defended this world. You could show some appreciation.'

'I could, I suppose.' Ghent leaned back in his chair, looking at the equipment of the bomb-shattered manufactorum. The building had no roof, casting the desk he'd ordered dragged onto the factory floor in gauzy sunlight. A flight of Lightning fighters darted by overhead, rattling the autopistol he'd laid on the desk. 'How about I show my appreciation by selling you the last ten cases of leolac in Kasr Kraf, so your troopers can celebrate?'

'But the price...'

'If you don't pay it, Cadians will. Leolac is the local favourite. A premium liquor. And a premium liquor demands a premium price.'

The adjunct standing behind the captain sneered. 'Don't play with us, gutter-trash. You're talking to soldiers, not some grubby ganger boss.'

'Sergeant Jollan, let's be civil.'

Ghent, back when he was low enough in the underworld to have such a disrespectful nickname, had occasionally been known as Slide-Eye for the way his gaze seemed to wander like a searchlight, never looking at who he was speaking to. Now, the purple eyes settled on the subaltern.

'So much for Mordian discipline.'

'Keep pushing and I'll show you Mordian discipline.' Jollan laid a white-gloved hand on her glossy leather holster.

'Lass, I know the commissars tell you your life's worth nothing, but don't throw it away over catering expenses.'

'My apologies, sir,' continued the captain. 'Sergeant Jollan is a proud daughter of Mordian. But she is correct – you are trying to cheat us. And I do not appreciate the implicit threat of the pistol in front of you.'

'I see,' said Ghent, raising two fingers.

Four gangers stepped out from the rusting equipment, drum-fed autoguns held at waist height as they advanced.

'Then let's make the threat explicit. Just so you can *appreciate* it.'

'Don't,' warned the captain, as Jollan's hand curled around her laspistol.

'Listen to the captain, lass, you won't win this one,' said Ghent. 'See, we might not wear the skull-and-wings, but we're still Cadians. By the time an intake sergeant spat in your face and told you to stand up straight, we'd been doing live-fire drills from age nine.'

Ghent reached down under the desk, pulled up a blue ceramic bottle of leolac and pulled the cork.

'Now,' said Ghent. 'Shall we toast your victory, and return to the question of price?'

* * *

Clang.

Twelve.

Corks popped, bouncing off the ceiling and landing on the long table. A group of artillery staff officers were trying to hit the chandelier. They cheered as one missile lodged in the hanging strands of crystal, and the lieutenant who'd fired it celebrated by pulling directly off the bottle.

To Colour Sergeant Jarran Kell, it sounded like the hollow pop of mortar tubes.

He walked down the table, passing a group of Vostroyans snare-drumming the wooden surface with their fists. In their centre, a lieutenant worked her way along a line of blue-glowing shot glasses. The Vostroyans burst into a cheer as she finished the last, triumphantly crushing the glass in her bionic fist.

A captain of the Eighth approached Kell singing 'Flower of Cadia', and pushed a flute of sparkling vin into his hand. Kell took it and raised it in a toast, then discreetly ditched it on a sideboard. He picked a cap off the table and deposited it on the head of an intelligence corporal – someone's aide – who lay face down on the table with his arm wrapped around a leolac bottle. His fellows had kindly decorated him with a collection of flatware.

Kell took a right turn and put a hand on the double door-knob, but stopped when he heard the call of, 'Creed! Where's Creed?'

He turned and waved them off.

'We want the Lord Castellan!' shouted another. 'Speech!'

It became a chant then: '*Speech! Speech! Speech!*'

'Soon,' he shouted back, knowing that in an hour, most would be so drunk they wouldn't remember to ask again. 'After the night's work is done – someone has to manage the victory.'

As the cheer rose, he disappeared through the blast-proof doors before it became quiet enough for more demands.

'Those idiots are still at it, I see,' said Ursarkar Creed.

The commander of the Cadian Eighth, saviour of Tyrok Fields, and Lord Castellan of Cadia bent over a desk collaged with documents and maps. Empty sacra tumblers served as paperweights, and an ashtray fashioned from an Earthshaker shell smouldered with half a dozen cigar-butts. The room – so pristine when Creed had moved into it – reeked of tobacco.

'The Archenemy is in retreat, pulling off-world,' Kell answered. 'You told them to enjoy themselves.'

'I said to enjoy it while it lasts, there's a difference.' Creed turned red-rimmed eyes back to the charts. 'I know Shock Troopers can't do anything in moderation, but I didn't mean for them to undermine readiness. This isn't over.'

'So a night of venting heat will be good for morale, *especially* if this isn't over.'

Creed grunted. 'Still, move reveille up an hour tomorrow morning. They can have their fun tonight, but I want them to feel it.'

Kell smirked, the closest he got to a smile, and handed over the data-slate tucked under his arm. 'Report from South Primus. The Volscani are holding on. They don't seem to be running with the mutants and irregular cultist militias.'

'Under all the spikes and blood runes, they're still Guardsmen,' mused Creed. 'That's what makes them dangerous. Any word from Admiral Quarren and the picket fleet?'

'No, sir. But he should have established his blockade at the Eye of Terror by now.'

'Let's hope that I'm being paranoid.' Creed leaned backwards with his hands on the small of his back.

'It's true what the war council says, you know. The forces that hit us were commensurate with previous Black Crusades. Larger, even.'

'Not you too, Jarran.' Creed shook his head.

'It is possible *he* was killed in the Eye, fighting some other warlord.'
He saw Creed's look and added: 'It's happened before.'

'You can't believe that.'

'We picked up signals saying so. Good quality intercepts. Hard
decryptions, definitely look authentic.'

'Tell me this, if this was the main Archenemy attack, where are
the Terminators? Where're the waves of Black Legion, the warp
engines? We've had cultists and mutants, Traitor Astartes in tactical roles, but you're telling me the Archenemy leadership spent
centuries building this force then never landed here in person?'

Through the door, a drunken chorus was singing 'Flower of Cadia'
again, and Creed had to shout to make himself heard over the din.

'No one can explain that to me. Not any of them. Not the Navy,
not the Aeronautica, not Militarum intelligence or the Scholastica
Psykana or the demigods of the Adeptus Astartes. None of them
can tell me the *one Throne-damned thing* I want to know.'

He threw his cigar-butt on the desk in frustration, smearing a
debris field of ash across a chart of the Rossvar Mountains. Then
he slammed both fists onto the desktop and shouted the last three
words:

'Where is Abaddon?'

Clang.

Thirteen.

The ship emerged from the immaterium with a noise like a
child being torn from the womb. A moment of blood, a primal
experience of a creature first feeling the cold air and pull of gravity – sucking atmosphere into its lungs before screaming it out in
pain and confusion.

Except in this case it was not the ship that screamed, it was the material world around it. The very atoms rent apart, bleeding inde-scribable colours.

Dravura Morkath watched through the crystal windows as the vessel she had tamed for her master spilled forth into realspace.

The sudden shock of translation hit the bridge crew, already over-taxed in serving the ancient vessel. Beastmen vomited. One opened its mouth and bit down on its own arm hard enough to fracture it.

A Mechanicum adept at a fire-control station suffered a compound-ing error in his synthetic brain. His logic chains – rerouted so drastically to make sense of the pandemonium of the Eye – jammed as it encountered the silent order of realspace.

He collapsed to the deck, the smoke of frying neural circuits waft-ing from his tear-ducts.

Morkath saw his thoughts as he died, his stream of consciousness surrounding his augmented cranium like the halo on the fresco of an Imperial saint.

All beings thought differently. Some of the beastmen on the bridge projected impressionistic swirls of ink around their heads, full of despair. Others expressed their conscious with jagged-edged panic.

This adept, in his death throes, still thought in the blinking typeface of a cathode screen as his brain ticked down like a dying chrono.

Back to station. I can get back to station, lord. I can...

Pain, so much...

Do I live?

I can...

...still...

...serve...

'Children of the Eye,' growled a voice behind her. 'Not meant for realspace.'

Morkath turned to look upon her Warmaster, ensuring her mind did not search the cloud of thoughts swirling around him like an aura of flame. Her master did not always want her to see what resided there, and neither did she.

Morkath bowed to her lord.

Abaddon. The Warmaster of Chaos, right hand of Horus, Master of the Black Legion and the being fated to kill the False Emperor. The man who had pulled Morkath out of the dark as a child, and made her what she was – though what that was, exactly, remained a subject of whispers.

The Warmaster sat in an ebony throne too large for his enormous frame. What manner of creature required such a seat – one large enough to dwarf the Warmaster, even in his battle plate – was, like so much aboard the Blackstone Fortress *Will of Eternity*, beyond Morkath's understanding.

Yet the space around the Warmaster was not empty. Daemon-things flitted there, darting and howling. Folding in upon themselves in geometric shapes or bursting into flames that devoured their essence as some stray emotion set them ablaze.

Morkath closed her eyes and willed herself not to see the motes of warp-things. To screen them out, and see only the revered face of the being she was lucky to call father.

'The stars are different this time,' he said.

'Different, my lord?' Morkath asked, opening her eyes to see the Warmaster without his shroud of parasitic spirits.

'I remember.' Abaddon's head, twice as large as that of a mortal, did not regard her as he spoke, yet even so, the low rumble of his voice rattled through her. 'I recall how the stars looked when we exited the Eye last time.'

'During the Gothic War,' Morkath said.

'Yes, before we took you in, foundling. I remember where every star was fixed, then. It was the same. The same constellations, unchanging from the first time we exited the Eye to the last. Twelve times, the same starscape.'

'But now they have changed?'

'New stars,' growled Abaddon. 'Different stars. Moving... a fleet.'

'Contacts! Contacts!' bleated a Mechanicum sensory officer. She stood permanently wired into a pit, slick organic cables – bunching and relaxing like the tentacles of an undersea octopod – connecting her exposed cranium with eight psykers floating in fluid sacs. 'Imperial fleet! Bearing eight-two-six. Two thousand five hundred miles distance. Emperor class! Mars class! Vengeance class!'

'Reading ship silhouettes,' intoned Cacadius Siron. He was a former Alpha Legionnaire – now Abaddon's intelligence chief. Before him, projection lasers danced in the air, sketching wire-frame outlines of Imperial vessels. 'Tentative identifications: *Might of the Faithful*, Emperor class. *Final Blow*, Mars class. *Duke Lurstophan*, Dauntless class. *Abridal's Glory*, Gothic class. They are from multiple battlefleets – Scarus, Agrippina, Corona.'

'A combined fleet,' said Abaddon. 'Consolidated due to casualties.'

'Our opening moves must have damaged their fleet assets even more heavily than we estimated,' Morkath said.

'With the remnants split chasing the *Vengeful Spirit* away from Cadia,' added Siron. He seemed ready to speak again, but the Warmaster cut him off.

'Meaning, the Gate is open.'

'To Cadia!' roared a beastman, raising its clenched fists. Across the command deck, crew howled, crowed, bellowed, gurgled, ululated. A thousand mutant throats screaming the elation that came with an achievement millennia in the making. Feet and hooves stamped the decking. 'To Cadia! To Cadia!'

Under the noise, only Morkath heard the Warmaster growl.

'A step,' he said. 'It is only a step. The Crimson Path awaits.'

PHASE TWO

CADIAN VICTORY

ONE

'Holy Throne,' whispered Admiral Quarren. 'How many are there?'

The command deck of the Emperor-class battleship *Might of the Faithful* had observation windows eight hundred feet wide – but the roiling wash of warp translation took up nearly the entire expanse.

By far the largest warp emergence Quarren had ever seen.

But it wasn't the prismatic un-colours of the immaterium that chilled him – it was the splinters of black amidst the unnatural hues.

Ships. So many ships. More than he'd battled so far in the entire Black Crusade – a campaign his force had barely survived.

'Identifications!' Quarren shouted, pulling sensor data via the neural link with his command throne. 'We need to know what to tell Cadia.'

'Report from observation flight Decimus,' shouted a flight controller, pressing the cups of her earphones hard to her skull. 'Long-distance send. Coming in faint… *Terminus Est*. Confirm *Terminus Est*.'

'Throne,' breathed Quarren's executive officer, Rabella. 'I thought it was a myth.'

Quarren waved her quiet, looked to a communications officer with his hand up. 'Speak.'

'Frigate *Steeldart* submits sighting report of a heavy battle cruiser,' snapped the officer. 'Wait. Another one. Destroyer *Voidswift* has sighted probable Murder class. They are unsure due to warp distortion in the superstructure. More... Rogue trader Adolphus Zant aboard privateer *Brigand* reports a... He doesn't know... It's battleship-sized but covered in tumorous growths. Horns. Eyes.'

'More vessels emerging,' Rabella said, sigil lines dancing green across her augmetic lenses. 'Based on silhouettes–'

'Stop. I don't need more.' Quarren saw a stylus rattling on the arm of his command throne, and realised he was shaking, with the ship rattling in sympathy.

He drew a breath, stilled his fibre bundles. Remote-triggered a system flush of soothing dopamine from the racks of phials in his chair.

This was like no fleet he'd ever faced. No fleet anyone living had faced. The greatest Archenemy armada since the Great Heresy.

They would never survive. But survival was not their directive.

Quarren and his picket fleet were the eyes of besieged Cadia. In the event of traitor reinforcements, they were to send a code-word message back to the fortress world. Enemy fleet dispositions, numbers, heading, certain code words indicating the size of the oncoming force.

Shatter Blue meant a fleet of task-force size.

Shatter Green a full fleet.

Shatter Red a crusade-sized armada.

They'd hand the message to the fast-moving frigates, who would tack and make speed for Cadia, relaying the message to the remaining ships of Admiral Dostov's fleet, waiting in ambush in the debris field of the Iron Graveyard.

The hope was that if Quarren fought to the last, and Dostov hit the traitor fleet as it passed through the maze of shattered warships, it might delay the Archenemy sufficiently for Cadia to prepare.

This was easily a Shatter Red.

Quarren put his odds of survival at about ten per cent. When he'd accepted this mission from Creed, he'd known the odds.

He was almost relieved.

Because there was one more code word. A phrase he'd hoped to never utter. One that he, indeed, believed impossible. After all, no one had seen one of the vessels since the Gothic War.

Yet in the stream of return data flashing across his vision, he saw a material that did not map with Imperial or enemy void craft.

'Enhance grid four-seven-gamma,' he said.

When the imagifier specialist did so, an audible gasp swept across the nine hundred men, women and tech-adepts of the bridge.

He unshipped his speaking horn and keyed it to broad-channel dispersal, addressing every ship of the fleet with the words he had hoped never to say.

'Shatter *Black*. I repeat, Shatter *Black*. Escorts, tack and set plasma engines to full. Get minimum three thousand miles clear before initiating warp travel. We don't want localised rifting. Emperor be with you.' Then he cut the transmission and yelled to his bridge crew. 'Don't stand there! Shields ahead full! Load torpedo complement. Fighter wings and bomber crews on deck. Nova cannon to full power.'

'That's...' said Rabella.

'I know what it is,' snapped Quarren. 'All ahead full! Put us between the enemy and our messenger squadron. Weapons, what's the status on those torpedoes?'

'Ready to fire when ordered, admiral.'

'That's a Blackstone Fortress,' Rabella finished.

'Give me a spread,' said Quarren, leaning forward to sketch a rough diagram on a gridded slate-display with his stylus-implanted finger. 'A big one. They're going to try and envelop us and get to the messenger ships. I want them to have to run a gauntlet while they–'

'Incoming!' shouted a scanning officer. 'Incoming torpedoes! Sectors beta-six-nineteen. Beta-six-twenty. Beta-six–'

'Arming defensive turrets,' answered a countermeasures ensign, her hat falling askew in her haste to create a targeting augur. 'Three hundred plus incoming ordnance. Charting interception courses.'

'Fire once the arming servitors are ready,' said Quarren. 'Torpedoes? Loose!'

Three ordnance officers, their metallic craniums connected in a network of drooping cables, rattled off orders in eerily overlapping voices. 'Tube one, launch. Tube two, launch. Tube four, launch. Tube six, launch. Tube three, launch. Tube five… Five reports launch failure. Disarm and dispose. All tubes save five reload.'

The defensive turrets opened up, spraying streams of explosive ammunition that zipped into the black of the void like embers rising from a breaking campfire log. They filled the forward viewers, those amber firebugs, detonating incoming torpedoes one after the other.

Bang.

Quarren lurched in his command throne. Rabella, who had gone to supervise the coxswain attempting to thread the torpedo screen, grabbed a midshipman who'd lost his balance and nearly fell into the pit of sensor crew.

'Hit on starboard fighter bay twenty-four,' reported an engineering chief. 'It looks like…'

Klaxons. Blue dome lights whirling.

'Throne of Terra,' growled Quarren. 'What in the hells–'

'It's the messengers!' shrieked a navigation ensign. 'They've raised Geller fields and are preparing for warp entry.'

'Who's *they*?' raged Quarren.

'Frigates *Veritable* and *Starchaser*. Destroyers *Lavertine*, *Opterion Light*, *Pyrax Orchades*… They got the order and are running.'

'Hail them!' Quarren shouted, as the ship rocked again. 'Tell them that's too close! Don't they know they'll–'

Fifty yards from him, Quarren heard a shriek like the sound of a void-vacuum tearing open a bulkhead. A sanctioned inter-ship communications psyker arched his back in his pit-cage, a fountain of sparking, oil-slick light beaming from his distended mouth.

'Breachers!' Rabella shouted, running across the shuddering bridge, drawing her laspistol.

The psyker's teeth broke outward and spilled to the deck, where they rattled and jumped from a new torpedo hit. He choked rather than screamed now, for within the light forcing itself from him was a bulbous yellow beak, dislocating and snapping his jaw with the violence of its impossible birth.

Rabella and the Naval breachers made it there just as the first wet feathers of the head began to emerge. She fired first, puncturing the tortured psyker through the chest as the troopers blew host and abomination apart with their massive shotguns – silver slugs designed and blessed for the purpose.

'Admiral!' buzzed a tech-priest. 'Warp incursions on decks fourteen and eight. Astropathic choir and Lord-Navigator Carsullus are–'

'Damn them.' Quarren opened an audio channel to hear for himself. Cut it once he heard the chorus of screams from the astropaths' loft. He'd *told* the escorts not to make warp translation so close. Now they'd triggered a mass possession.

This battle was going to be even shorter than he'd thought.

'*Lavertine* is away!' said the navigation ensign, yelling over the boom of shotguns executing another comms-psyker. '*Starchaser* away. *Pyrax Orchades* away...'

'Launch everything,' said Quarren. 'All fighter and bomber wings. Primary target is the Blackstone Fortress. Drive right for it. Ram it if you have to.'

In the kaleidoscopic insanity of the warp rift, he saw a bright point coalescing around the Blackstone Fortress. A bright star within the black one.

Not a star – a beam. A rent in space roiling with the plumage and maws and twisted limbs of the hell dimension, soaked in the unholy shifting light Quarren could hear and taste and feel.

For a moment the light of the immaterium bathed him, until the *Might of the Faithful* – all two-and-a-half miles of length with a displacement of sixteen billion tons – tore itself apart on the atomic level.

The remainder of the fleet, decapitated, drove hard into the battle that would prove the most intense and difficult of their careers. A desperate delaying action. Two million voidsmen sacrificing their lives, and the ships that were both their homes and temples, to give Cadia a chance to live.

The action lasted seventy-seven minutes.

TWO

'So this is a coup, is it?' Creed said, pacing.

Kell had never seen Creed sit down during a war council. He was too animated, had too much energy. He drifted across the room, leaned over maps, puffed and relit his cigar. Now, he walked to the reinforced armaglass window and thumped it with a fist. 'All this time, I thought the Volscani traitors were out there, not in here.'

'Don't be dramatic, Ursarkar,' said Logistar-General Conska-van Raik. In contrast to the Lord Castellan, he was seated, his peaked Munitorum cap tossed casually on an empty chair, flicking through a data-slate that was connected via cable to a port in his temple. 'It's an administrative matter, really. Your appointment as Lord Castellan was an emergency measure, never ratified by the Military Diet.'

'Well then have them ratify it!'

'It doesn't work like that, and you know it,' snapped Supreme Commissar Zabine. In contrast to the oily, casual Raik, she sat bolt upright. 'Under statute sixty-seven-gamma of the Code of Command, any person invested as Lord Castellan during a state of emergency will relinquish that office once the danger is past.'

Creed sucked his cigar, as if considering, then blew a column of smoke in Zabine's direction. 'Well that's the problem, Audaria. The danger isn't past, is it?'

'Mopping-up operations don't require a Lord Castellan. The enemy is broken.'

'All fronts are reporting enemy retreats.' As Raik spoke, his fingers danced along the data-slate. 'Requests for ammunition and fuel have fallen twenty per cent. Combat is tapering off. We're experiencing domestic unrest due to the ration cuts. If we raise civilian rations back to fifty per cent and military to ninety, we could avoid–'

'It's a false retreat. They're baiting us into pursuit. Disbursing our forces so when the second wave lands, we can't coordinate. The Despoiler will encircle us in bits and pieces.'

Raik and Zabine briefly locked eyes.

'What is it? Out with it.'

'Lord Castellan… No, you do it, Zabine.'

'Naval intelligence has confirmed via satellite picts that the *Vengeful Spirit* was part of the traitor fleet that withdrew towards the Eye of Terror. Presumably, the Despoiler is aboard. Admiral Minzet is in pursuit.'

'I have recalled Minzet,' said Creed. 'Or rather, requested that Grand Admiral Kozchokan recall all elements of Battlefleet Cadia and take station around the fortress world. The Despoiler was not on the ship – like the retreat, it's meant to open our defences. Draw our fleet assets away.'

'You beat them, Ursarkar,' Raik said. 'That's the truth of it. The Thirteenth Black Crusade is over. We got hammered. Governor Porelska – Throne rest his soul – was assassinated, you took command, and we've turned the situation around. Be proud. It's been a hard-fought victory, but it's over.'

'Tell that to the poor bastards scrabbling it out in the ruins of Kasr Myrak, or Halig, or a hundred other battle-fronts.'

'That's nothing new,' said Zabine, waving a bionic hand. 'We'll be rooting out holdouts and purging cults for years, decades probably. But large-scale suppressions don't constitute an emergency, not on Cadia.'

'Ah, we are back to the mutiny.'

'It's not a mutiny,' said Raik. 'It is a check on your power. You cannot hold office indefinitely – especially now that the crisis is past. Indeed, there are concerns that you yourself plan a coup.'

'Ridiculous,' sneered Creed.

'Is it?' asked Raik. 'There are units unaccounted for. Whole regiments that came back in the recall that have simply disappeared.'

'It's a big war.'

'The Two-Hundred-and-Eighty-Second Shock Infantry, the Hundred-and-First Armoured, the Eleventh Kasrkin's Air Assault Section – I could go on. According to our records, these units drew six months' rations on your orders then disappeared.'

Creed pursed his lips. Tilted his head, considering his answer. 'It's a very big war.'

Kell took a step closer, judging whether to intervene. Creed was goading them now, and like it or not, the Lord Castellan's war cabinet were powerful people.

'The worry is you're holding them in reserve,' said Zabine.

'So what? All commanders have a reserve.'

'A personal reserve,' Raik clarified. 'To support your continued tenure as Lord Castellan. We have battered, under-strength units – you have a fresh and rested army. And this plan to pull everyone back to Kasr Kraf gives you quite the power centre.'

'I also have questions about these vox-broadcasts,' Zabine piled on. 'The ones where you play "Flower of Cadia" and address the troops directly. Propaganda and messaging falls under the Commissariat's purview. It smacks of an attempt to create–'

'To create what? High morale? A sense that command cares about them?'

'A cult of personality,' Zabine finished. 'To make the troops loyal to you, not Cadia.'

'Supreme Commissar,' Kell said, stepping forward. Decades of serving under Creed had taught him to strategically break conversational flow before Creed escalated things into a shouting match. 'If you wish to be copied on future broadcast messages, I can arrange for that. And Logistar-General, I can provide an itemised list of deployments for any unit deemed...'

Creed waved him quiet. 'Why would I bother with a coup? If I've beaten the Arch-Traitor and driven away a Black Crusade, do you really think I'll need a secret army and personality cult to stay on as Lord Castellan? Hells, I could wave my hands and the troops would insist the Diet invest me as peacetime governor.'

Silence.

Zabine stared. Raik pursed his lips and raised his eyebrows, eyes on his slate.

Creed let out a deep chuckle. 'No answer to that one, eh?'

'You have three weeks,' said Zabine. 'At the end of it, the Military Diet will vote to end the state of emergency and appoint you the Supreme Commander of Cadia.'

Kell quietly clicked his tongue. It was a grand title, but a major step down. The Supreme Commander was the head of Cadia's armed forces, but had none of the governing power vested in the Lord Castellan. The Military Diet – with its representatives from high command, the Administratum, the Ecclesiarchy and Battlefleet Cadia – would no longer be subservient. Creed would be one power among many.

Creed dropped his cigar in the ashtray and bent down over the desk, resting his forearms on it, hands clasped. Looked directly into Zabine's eyes.

'I hope that happens, Audaria,' he said. 'Truly. It would make me the happiest man wearing flak if this is over in three weeks. But it won't be. I can feel it.'

'The data contradicts your feelings,' said Raik. 'All indications suggest the danger is past, and further–'

Detonation. A percussive *bang* close enough to be heard even through the armaglass window. Then another, and another.

Raik ducked low, head disappearing below the edge of the desk. Zabine's hand flew to her bolt pistol.

'See what's going on out there, Kell, will you?' Creed said in a disinterested mumble.

'Mortars?' asked Raik. 'Rockets?'

Kell pulled the heavy blast curtain aside, saw the next shell-burst send a sparkle of incendiaries through the air. Two more explosions, lighting the reinforced blockhouses and kill-zone plazas of Kasr Kraf yellow and blue.

'Fireworks,' he replied.

'Frekk-faced idiots,' swore Creed.

'Illegal,' hissed the commissar. Fireworks were banned on Cadia – too easy for insurgents to remake them into improvised explosives. 'I'll have some of my people out in the city with execution orders.'

'Forget it,' Creed responded. 'We'll ask them to stop in the next broadcast. In the meantime… This city is built to resist orbital bombardment. It can handle a few firecrackers. Are we done here?'

Kell looked out the window of the command spire, down on Kasr Kraf, lit with unauthorised celebrations.

'We have to discuss enemy disposal,' said Raik. 'There are supply routes entirely impassable due to enemy dead. And hygiene is an issue.'

'Burn them,' said Creed.

'But the promethium cost…'

'Burn the heretics' bodies. I won't give up a handful of Cadian earth. Not even to bury them.'

It was a good line. Kell made a mental note to write it into Creed's next vox-address.

An air-burst bloomed over the commercia district, hanging in space for a moment, looking like the red chrysanthus blossoms his mother used to grow in their ration garden. And for a moment, he remembered the smell of spring, when the hearty flowers opened their petals and released their feathery seed-pods to the wind.

Scarlet chrysanthus.

The Flower of Cadia.

Down in the commercia, Yann Rovetske looked up at the sound of the explosion.

He saw the aerial bomb fracture the sky, throwing red sparks across the black night. It lit the street celebration a lurid crimson, making it appear the narrow avenue – and its revellers – had drowned in blood.

And if Yann Rovetske had his way, they would.

He oiled through the crowd. Never rough, never shoving. Nothing to attract attention. A Whiteshield bolted past him, trying to flag down a companion she'd sighted. Rovetske said nothing as the young woman barged his shoulder as she passed.

He did not expect an apology, and didn't get one.

He wore an Administratum tunnel worker's uniform. Everyone on Cadia had a uniform, just like everyone on Cadia had a rank. On his collar were the chevrons of a sanitation-sergeant.

But he was a civilian, and even the lowliest Whiteshield didn't need to apologise when they knocked into him.

Cadians loved to say that they were practical people. That as a soldier-society, advancement was by merit and ability. That there was no caste system on Cadia.

No, instead they had an *understanding*.

It was *understood* that the officer corps of the Shock Troopers was chosen based on education – with those who graduated top-grade from the best cadet academies getting advanced placement. The fact that those academies happened to be in the districts where the old-blood military families lived was immaterial.

It was *understood* that the selection lottery – where one out of every ten troopers was tasked to stay on Cadia and join the garrison forces of the Interior Guard – often just happened to skip those from old lineages. And when it didn't, they often served two years before shipping off-world as an officer or advisor to a fresh unit.

It was *understood* that those in support roles gave up seats in the mess to combat troopers. *Understood* that it was only right and proper that the enlisted got full rations, and low-grade workers only half.

Rovetske's family had been rich. A trading consortium, responsible for bringing in combustible minerals for high-grade explosives. They had money, money enough to supplement their sixty per cent rations as much as they liked.

But money had little use on Cadia. Here, combat and lineage were the trading currencies. And all the credits in the world couldn't buy him respectability, or entrance to an officer-track cadet academy.

So when the Empty Man came when Yann was twelve, offering to train him for paramilitary operations – he gladly accepted.

After all, what Cadian could turn down a chance to fight?

Another firework detonated, washing the milling celebrants a cool blue.

Rovetske took his toolbox through the crowd, past a groundcar selling bootleg raenka out of its rear hatch. Past a group of Mordians doing some kind of circle dance. Skirting aside to avoid a preacher holding aloft a skull, shouting for the soldiers to repent and return to their units.

When the crowd thinned, he walked down a quiet alley – raised a hand to his eyes to preserve the privacy of two corporals kissing – and found the blue door marked with three purity seals.

Number 14, Enfilade Street Beta.

He knocked five times. Paused. Knocked three more.

It opened a crack.

'I came about the pipes,' Rovetske said. 'I heard they've gone bad.'

The door swung open. Inside, a woman with a back bent to one side – from a lifetime of wearing heavy flak vests and packs – held up a kerosoline lantern.

The dim light was barely enough to illuminate her liver-spotted skin. Cataract-misted eyes reflected the gleam.

'They said you would come,' she croaked. 'They–'

Rovetske put a finger to his lips, and with a sure motion stepped inside and pulled the door closed.

'Take me to it,' he said.

'I'm sorry about the glow-globes, it seems they've gone out.'

Typical Cadian hab inside. Rockcrete walls, thick as his arm was long. Rectangular slit windows. A hatch and ladder that, if opened with an arc-torch, led to the flat above. More a bunker than a home.

In the event of city-fighting, this hab could be garrisoned with Kasrkin that would murder any troops trying to use the alley to flank defenders on the main avenue. Ducking into Enfilade Street, it had not escaped Rovetske that the buildings facing down either side of the narrow passage had turret emplacements bulging from their third floors – mount a heavy stubber in each and the little passage would become a kill-zone.

Yet he could see mildew growth on one wall, and the stamped-metal furniture had rust dripping from the rivets. Slovenly behaviour for a Cadian. She'd be fined if the readiness inspectors came knocking.

'Where are you keeping it?' he asked.

'The basement.' The woman ran a dry tongue over withered lips. 'Our people have gathered. We waited. As instructed. Even as others rose. The dreams of Donava the Eye-that-Sees told him it was not time...'

'It wasn't.'

They passed an ammunition locker, bolted to the floor and ready to be filled with munitions. The woman had used it as a sideboard, cluttering it with fading pict-portraits of a trooper, edged in black ribbon. Husband? Son? Impossible to tell.

Bad ventilation. The place smelled of whatever root cellar passed for her larder. An ambient fug of sprouting tubers and old meat.

They passed two foldaway bed racks. Went down a corkscrew staircase, below ground level. Probably a munitions store. Rovetske guessed the roof of the building was meant to be a mortar position.

'When did you receive the blessing?'

'Last night. From Hekuta the Hand-that-Strikes. He said a man would come for it. Someone important, I didn't think...'

He saw her wrinkled-fruit mouth turn down at his uniform.

'You do realise that this is a disguise, yes?'

'Of course,' she said, shoulders relaxing. 'Yes, of course. You don't look like a half-rationer. Too well muscled. I'm a seventy-percenter myself. Pensioned. Or it should be seventy per cent. Bloody Creed.'

'We will bloody him soon enough,' Rovetske said. The number surprised him. It was high. Seventy per cent ration cards rarely went to those outside middle age. Usually a rate that high meant reserve duties, the possibility of being called back up.

That this crone rated seventy per cent foodstuffs meant Creed was more desperate than–

He grabbed the woman, hand clamped around her frail arm, and hushed her. He pressed one ear to the rockcrete.

There was a noise inside the stone, between crumbling and crawling. Creaking, like a steel ship in heavy weather. A burst pipe, trickling through porous rockcrete?

The smell of meat and spice was stronger, nearly choking. Perhaps a sewer main or...

'Venerable lady,' said Rovetske. 'You did not *open* the blessing, did you?'

'Venerable lady! Well, I like that! I'm not–'

He grabbed her by the shoulders, feeling the parchment skin move over her bones. '*Did you open it?*'

'No, not… Not until it told us to.'

'Frekk,' he swore and released her, looking at his hands. Pulled them into the heavy rubbarine plumbing gloves that hung at his belt.

'It wanted us to sing to it. That's what it told the Eye-that-Sees. It is a god, after all. Or at least–'

'How old are you?' he demanded.

'Wha–'

'*How old?*'

'Well, I'm… I'm forty-two, if you must know.'

'Frekk, frekking. Frekk!' He pulled out the rebreather every Cadian carried in a pouch at their hip. Yanked it over his head, mumbling the canticle of obeisance the Empty Man had taught him. Tested the seal as he dropped one hand to the rip-tear pocket on the uniform's front.

'Did we offend?' the woman croaked. As she grimaced, he saw her gums retreating. 'We only did what was asked–'

Rovetske shot her point-blank, the stubber round entering just above one eyebrow and splashing the wall with an entire life's worth of resentments. Before he'd taken a step, it had already curdled and blackened.

Yann Rovetske bolted down the stairs, praying to the lords of ruin that he had not already been too exposed. Cursing himself for not seeing the signs: the rusting furniture, the mildew and scent of fruiting decay.

He came down the stairs, pistol gripped in both hands.

The basement was, indeed, an ammunition store. He could tell that from the shell-lift in one wall, just before the rust that was sprouting from it like frost ate through the supports and dropped it, shattering, to the floor. Steel shelves blackened and twisted in on themselves. Exposed glow-globes in the ceiling were dimming to sickly orange. They began to burst, showering sparks.

But once he saw the people, he couldn't look away.

They stood in a circle, mouths open in an atonal note. Faces locked in ecstatic joy, teeth clattering to the floor in little *tick-tack-tick-tack* sounds as they dropped from greying gums.

The one leading the circle wore a tall headdress made from beaten brass – likely once part of a military band instrument. Through the dripping green oxidation, he could make out an enormous eye covering the face.

He lined his gunsights up on the eye, and every head wrenched in his direction – some pivoting so far he heard vertebrae crunch.

Their violet Cadian eyes, tainted from birth by the Eye of Terror, burned.

And then with a *bang* the rest of the glow-globes went.

He saw them coming in the strobing light of his muzzle flashes. Brief images, like single frames from a pict-reel. Each emphasised by the hammer-blow sound of gunfire in an enclosed space.

Bang.

A man, his Munitorum assembly-line uniform rotting off him, grasping with hands that lost fingers even as they reached.

Bang.

A corporal. Limping from a gash opening like a smile in one thigh. A long-buried hard round rolled out from its previous spot, nestled against the long bone. Shrapnel dropped from his arms.

Bang.

Hands on Rovetske's forearm. A woman's mouth full of worms. '*Ioava vokkh!*' he shouted, invoking protection.

Bang.

A green headdress to his right, the jaw under it already shot away, still waving a staff.

He emptied the magazine, backing towards the stairwell. Sucking and drawing breath through the choking respirator.

Then, nothing.

Rovetske fumbled in his heavy gloves for the lamp-pack fixed to his plumber's helmet. When it snapped on, the light was thin. Later, when he stripped and burned the clothes, he'd find the batteries had corroded so badly that they'd leaked acid onto the helmet's lip.

He tried not to look at the bodies. That was hard, because they lay everywhere. A few swelled and burst as he passed, faces blackening. Others began shrinking in mummification.

Yet, they still sang.

He had seen the Plague of Unbelief before. Even assisted, tangentially, in poisoning the water facilities in Kasr Holn so that the dead would rise when prompted by a catalytic warp ritual.

This was different. It had rotted living people. Aged them. Opened old injuries long healed. Bayonet wounds. Gory tunnels of gunshots. Detached fingers that had been sewn back on after a manufactorum accident.

Not the rot of Nurgle, something else. The ravages of time condensed.

Only the rune pendants sewn under Rovetske's skin had protected him. He could feel them hot against his flesh.

Rovetske moved fast. Crunching over bones and stooping under disintegrating metal shelving to find the thing they had circled around.

A rack of stoppered glass tubes three-inches high. Eight in all. They had originally stood upright in a wire carrier rack like samples from a biologis laboratory, but the steel of it had browned and curled like a dried flower stem, so they splayed in their mounts. One lay on its side.

A pus-like yellow liquid bubbled happily inside the tubes.

Rovetske opened his long toolbox, its interior empty apart from a block of protective foam with eight long indentations and a pair of tweezer clamps.

He used the clamps to lift the phials into their places, glad the Empty Man had sent the dream, briefing him to inscribe protective runes on the inside of the box. Sweat pooled in his rebreather. It itched against his face, the rubber already drying and cracking.

'I am your servant. Your servant. Do not harm me. This place is not your function. I am to convey you. This place is unworthy of you. Please do not harm me.'

A voice in his hindbrain implored him to join the chorus, to sing.

Instead, he closed the box and snapped the clamps down.

When he walked out, the floor was already starting to buckle and swell. Handfuls of rockcrete crumbled away from the walls to expose twisting, rust-furred rebar and disintegrating I-beams.

Stairs gave way beneath his feet as he ran upward, through the decaying hab and out the door.

When he opened it, two troopers were standing outside. The couple.

'What's going on?' said one, his face twisted in concern.

'Sinkhole,' Yann Rovetske said, pulling off his rebreather. 'In the basement. Water erosion. There are still people down there!'

He stood aside.

Rovetske was not a psyker. At least, not in the way average people understood it. He could not pour warpfire from his throat or destroy minds with a look. But when he lied, people believed him.

The two troopers rushed in the door, Cadian heroes that they were.

He closed it on them, yanking it shut even as rust froze the hinges. Then he melted into the celebrating crowd as behind him, Number 14 Enfilade Street Beta collapsed in on itself, and vanished into the ground.

Above him, fireworks burst.

The milling, idiot crowd thought this was the end.

And it was.

In his right hand, the long workman's box swayed slightly on the hinged handle – as if something alive inside was shifting.

Hungry to be let out.

Below the streets of Kasr Kraf, Servantus Glave moved through the dark, confident he was the deadliest thing in it.

He was, after all, a Kasrkin.

His breath drew even and steady through the respirator clamped over his face. His eyes scanned the tunnel ahead, his helmet lenses' low-light veil painting everything a hazy red.

His volley gun's barrel shroud gleamed obsidian black at the bottom of his vision. It stayed steady as he moved, secured to his carapace chestplate by a jointed actuator arm to prevent fatigue and improve accuracy.

'Hold.'

Okkun, on the team's micro-bead channel.

Glave froze. The pointman floated in his peripheral vision, their two locator dots overlapping on the positional map built into the inside of Glave's wristplate. Despite the tension and sweat seeping down his back, Glave kept discipline. Didn't move. Didn't give into the temptation to look. Knew Okkun was kneeling, scanning with the auspex.

'Heightened decibel levels ahead. Could be street noise.'

They waited in the hot, foetid dark.

The drainage tunnel was the width of a two-lane road and roughly as high. Flooding last summer had brought in street trash from above. When the water receded, it left the scum to rot.

Tunnels crossed all of Cadia. A natural consequence of a fortress world that had weathered multiple sieges. New cities built on the ruined defences of old. Water management canals and drainageways to ensure the cities – built of steel and rockcrete – didn't flood during the seasonal rains.

And below that, the true tunnels. The black tunnels. Where long ago, during the Dark Age of Technology, ancient men had quarried out the uncanny pylons that dotted Cadia's surface.

At least, that's what Glave had been taught in the cadet academy. Though during his below-ground work with the 27th Kasrkin, he'd found that the smooth surfaces and odd pillars resembled no Imperial architecture he'd ever seen.

Things, he reasoned, must have been different then.

'Can we move up the support?'

'Patience, Glave,' chided the pointman. 'Getting some bounce off the corner. Not a hard contact, just a little… haze. Mechanical. Could be a cultist infiltration party. Get ready in case of exchange.'

Glave clenched his teeth and let go of the volley gun's pistol grip to flex his hand. It always hurt when overworked, but he never complained. Every Kasrkin was used to pain, internal and external. And Glave could endure plenty of both.

He'd been born unable to hold a lasgun. The fingers of his right hand fused together, little to ring finger, and pointer to middle, so he had a thumb and two double-width fingers. Fully functional for everyday life, but not enough to serve the Emperor.

To do that, he'd need to fit his index finger through a lasgun trigger-guard.

All Cadians needed to be ready for the cadet academy by eight years old. That was the first eligibility screening – and the one that decided whether he'd be a Shock Trooper or a half-rationer at the manufactorum. With his hand, the closest he'd get to a battle-front would be loading pallets of ammunition on a cargo hauler.

Children were rarely fitted with bionics – they grew too fast, and replacing the technology would be prohibitively expensive.

There was surgery, but he risked losing most of his function, and the recovery time meant he'd miss the screening.

Most prospective recruits would've been out of luck. But he was not most recruits.

His father, General Hezkett Glave, had led the 117th Mobile Artillery during the Siege of Santaan, and had parlayed that victory into a position as head of the Advanced Gunnery School. And Hezkett Glave refused to accept that his son was fated to load shells rather than fire them.

He used his pull, and Servantus had been granted provisional acceptance in a mid-level cadet academy – using a lasgun with the trigger-guard removed.

The instructors didn't like it. The cadets either. Every part of the Imperial system emphasised that the individual must be shaped to fit the institution – that the institution would accommodate Glave seemed an aberration.

They thought he was weak, and Cadians were conditioned to sense weakness and savage it.

He responded by being the best. Top marksmanship awards. Exemplary fitness and personal inspection reports.

Then, he discovered boxing. Glave loved boxing. The gloves covered his hand, and he could finally pummel his tormentors and earn praise for it. He'd won district championships, gone to the hemispheric finals.

When he'd turned fifteen and attended a review board to determine his eligibility for induction, one of the instructors who'd persecuted him had actually spoken on his behalf.

The panel questioned him for an hour. Made him disassemble lasguns, showing he could modify one for his use within thirty seconds. Forced him to lift weights and clock running times exceeding the normal enlistment standard.

When it was done, and they came back from deliberation, the

lieutenant-general who headed the board reported that Glave would get his enlistment papers.

'Cadet, your father did a lot to make this happen,' he added, looking down from the raised table. 'You better put a bayonet in the Despoiler himself.'

Glave saluted – and silently swore he would.

Now he was Kasrkin. And no one called him weak.

'It's a contact,' voxed Okkun, securing the auspex to his shoulder webbing and shouldering his hellgun. It was a short-barrelled model, made for tunnel clearance. 'Voices. To the right of the T-junction.'

'Contacts detected,' Glave sent to those behind. 'Moving up to confirm.'

They crept forward, slinking like scavenging dogs amid flood detritus.

Glave stopped ten feet from the right-hand turn and knelt, bringing his volley gun up. Around the corner, they could hear a mechanical *thok-thok-thok*. A cylinder? A generator?

'Ready,' Glave said.

Okkun unshipped the auspex. That was the protocol. A pointman to scan the route, a volley gunner to fill the entire expanse with las-fire at the first hint of trouble. If it was anything they couldn't handle, they were to call the support.

'I see–' said Okkun.

And that's when the man walked into Glave's sights.

He had his belt undone, fingers fiddling with the button of his trousers. Glave might have been able to take him with a knife if he hadn't turned the corner directly into them.

Glave depressed the modified paddle-trigger of his volley gun, unleashing a banshee wail of las-fire that lit the man's startled face.

The burst struck the target centre-mass, blew his ribcage into component parts and carried on into the ceiling behind him.

Cooked blood misted in the air, flash-fried into ashen scabs that washed over Glave from the superheated assault. Standard las-bolts burned holes in targets. The volley gun fired hot enough to create molecular explosions and convert energy to kinetic force.

Okkun dropped his auspex, the fallen hand-unit clacking against the ground as he gripped his hellgun.

Glave had already risen, skirting the falling enemy, sidestepping to bring his stubby weapon around the corner and light it up with a stream of fire that scorched down the side-pipe.

Beyond the glow of the incandescent volley – bright white in his heat-sensor vision – he saw forms further along the tunnel. Indistinct. Moving, dodging. His overcharged las-fire speared through one hunched red blur and sent a piece of it spinning off into the air. Gouts of orange blood sprayed from the wound.

'Hard contact!' he yelled into his micro-bead. 'Fire support! Fire–'

Kinetic impact on his carapace vest. Yellow blinks in the dark. Hard rounds, returning fire.

Glave dropped prone to lessen his silhouette. Squeezed off another burst that took a target's legs off. Gunfire echoed down the tunnel. Slugs cracked through the air above him and chewed bits of rockcrete from the wall at his right, where Okkun sheltered. One round contacted Glave's shoulder guard and kicked it backwards.

'Throne!' shouted Okkun. He switched his hellgun to a left-handed grip and sprayed las down the corridor. 'How many are there?'

'Not enough,' Glave growled.

He tracked a motion blur and squeezed the trigger. Nothing happened. A blinking indicator in his vision flagged a power interruption. He glanced under his arm to see sparks fizzing from the dual cable connecting his volley gun to the power pack on his back. He'd taken a hit. And now, it was giving away his position in the dark.

Something slammed into the crown of his head and his red-tinted heat vision stuttered out. A head hit. He'd been shot in the head.

He slithered sideways, willing his body to work despite the splitting headache. Unaugmented vision dark except for the strobe of muzzle flashes.

Okkun leapt out from his cover, squeezing shots down the corridor one-handed while grabbing Glave by a strap of webbing. Dragging him back into cover.

Okkun was shouting, but Glave could hear nothing but a roar. The floor seemed like it was moving. His disorientation so bad that...

No, not disorientation. The support had arrived.

The Leman Russ Exterminator careened out of the darkness, turret already rotated ninety degrees. It ripped past them, one tread passing six feet from Glave's boots, pulping what was left of the sentry he'd shot. It stopped dead in the T-junction.

Slugs flattened against its armour.

In response, it clicked on its floodlight and filled the tunnels with ballistic fury. One heavy bolter sponson swept right to left and back, twin autocannons on the turret alternating fire in that metallic double-blast that – magnified by the tunnel – felt like hammer-blows. The barrel flare stretched ten feet.

Even enclosed within his helmet, Glave heard nothing but ringing until it was all over, and 'Stitcher' Kristan was halfway through examining him.

'–ard head, Glave,' he said.

'What?'

The medicae's brow furrowed. He snapped his fingers on either side of Glave's unhelmeted head. 'You hear that?'

'Yes,' said Glave. He didn't like being nursemaided. Wanted to stack back up in the file. 'Good enough to serve.'

'Seriously now, I don't want to put you back in concussed. Danger to the team. If you have any doubts, I'd recommend you pass the volley gun off and move to the middle of the file–'

'No.' Glave tried to stand.

Stitcher pushed him back down, using the weight of the bigger man's power pack to his advantage. 'Take it easy. They're still casualty counting. Throne!'

'I know you're trying to help, Stitch. But you don't understand. You're not a soldier. Not really.'

'I carry a hellpistol in defence of Cadia too.'

'You're support,' said Glave. 'Your job isn't to kill heretics, mine is.'

'Well, you already killed your quota today.'

'Not heretics,' said Okkun, walking around the corner. He held a bundle of yellow paper in his hands. 'But traitors all the same. Civilian clothes, mostly. Low-end night-lenses. Autoguns and stubbers. The autocannons ripped apart the machine they were running, but it looks like they were printing these.'

He tossed the handful of yellow paper slips in Glave's lap. They fell like autumn leaves, spilling across his armoured legs.

Glave picked one up between shaky fingers.

'They're counterfeits. Good ones.'

'Underminers,' hissed Stitcher. 'Eroding our defensive posture right from under us.'

It was a ration card. A ration card entitling the bearer to seventy per cent foodstuffs allotment.

And another, and another, and another.

A feast had fallen in Glave's lap.

But there was only so much food. And a feast for some would mean famine for others.

Not all enemies were tainted by heresy – some made do with greed.

THREE

Dravura Morkath had lived her entire life amid grotesque demigods. Beings who knew no fear even before their metamorphosis into fused, flesh-and-armour vessels of the empyric forces. Warriors that could crush her small frame with a single blow.

Yet she was not afraid, for she stood at the right hand of the Warmaster as his architect and cup-bearer, holding in her overlong fingers a chalice fashioned from an immense skull. Legend held that it came from the flesh-twister Bile's facsimile of the primarch Horus, slain by the Warmaster in some unhallowed age.

Just as the warlords of Abaddon's inner circle were his Chosen, so was she. For Dravura Morkath was his conduit to the Blackstone Fortress. The empyric architect who alone could colonise the inert noctilith with the essence of the warp. In fact, she was the very being who had tamed this council chamber, channelling empyric energies into the veins of the dark stone and webbing it in tumorous spans of flesh and pulsing arteries. She knew each breathing surface, had watched the gelatinous clusters of eyes first open their lids and the teeth ringing the doorway emerge from grey semi-organic gums.

Without her, this fortress that birthed her – this *Will of Eternity*, as they called it, though it was far too ancient to carry a name – would be nothing but hostile stone.

No sane warrior would dare touch her.

That was why she feared this warlord – for he was anything but sane.

'Warmaster,' Urkanthos said, kneeling before Abaddon. When he bowed and planted his armoured fists on the deck, his blood-slick gauntlets left smears of red. 'I present to you the False Emperor's fleet, burning in the void.'

He did not acknowledge Morkath; indeed, she was unsure that he had registered her presence at all. Like most transhumans, the Lord Ravager had come to ignore as insignificant any being smaller than himself.

'Rise, my Lord Ravager.' The Warmaster inclined his head. 'Your tribute of blood and wreckage is accepted.'

Morkath saw the pride bloom behind Urkanthos' head in a gory pool, like a head-shot man bleeding out on a marble floor. Even the thoughtforms of his consciousness presented in her vision like blood.

This was why the Warmaster wanted her here – to be his thought-seer. To watch the minds of his lieutenants as he revealed his grand strategy for the conquest of Cadia. And one by one, Morkath had done so. She'd seen the putrid cloud of unconscious around the pipe-vented skull of Skyrak Slaughterborn, the thoughts weaving in and out of the haze like flies. How Devram Korda, Lord Purgator of the Black Legion, plotted in an intricate confessional narration that spooled out like the brushstrokes of a master calligrapher. She saw Lord Deceiver Zaraphiston's three eyes glimpse changing prob-abilities that rattled inside his skull like oracle bones. Finally, there had been the Warpsmith, Krom Gat, former Iron Warrior and repre-sentative among the Chosen of Chaos Undivided, whose mind was an interlocking mandala of gears and wheels.

The Warmaster rarely gathered his Chosen together these days. Too often those councils fell to factionalism or became bogged down in questions, and it was too difficult to compartmentalise information. Better to meet them one at a time, if only so Morkath could better watch their minds.

And watch them she had, scanning for glimpses of treachery. The extreme resonance of the council chamber – so thoroughly conquered by her flesh-workings – amplified her powers of cognitive forensics threefold.

Yet Urkanthos, the master of the Black Fleet, had a mind far more intense than any she had seen this day. It was full of pain and blood.

'Do you know why I have sent for you?' The Warmaster gestured his Khornate champion to his feet with the Talon of Horus.

'To discuss the landings.' Urkanthos rose, the two enormous horns bolted to his forehead curving back like longbows. It was an apt metaphor, since every inch of him was like a drawn bowstring, tight with potential violence. Impaled skulls and heads, some fresh enough to glisten, stared vacantly from his armour's trophy rack. 'I request you grant my Hounds of Abaddon the honour of the vanguard when we scour Cadia.'

'And what makes you believe that you deserve such an honour?'

Morkath tried not to look at the Warmaster. In the presence of others, her eyes were supposed to be cast down in respect. But now, her animal need to understand the brewing conflict betrayed her. Both her eyes – one natural, one replaced with a blackstone orb – flickered up to her master's face.

Abaddon had never forbidden her from reading his thoughts. Indeed, at times she assumed he thought things for the explicit purpose of her reading them. A precious shared mind-connection so she could better serve him.

They were always surface meditations, intentional thoughts. But that did not change their magnificence.

As she looked, she saw the thoughts orbit around his shaven skull like the planets on an astronomical model. An astrolabe of light, angelic in its perfection. It would be the most beautiful mindscape she had ever seen, apart from one thing.

The Mark of Chaos Ascendant on his forehead, ignited there by the warp gods themselves.

Seen through the noctilith orb embedded in her left socket it appeared as the Eye of Terror in miniature, like a bonfire on his brow.

Morkath turned away, like a child who has tried to look at the sun.

'Why would I deserve it?' Urkanthos growled. Drops of dark arterial crimson spattered in his fading halo of red, his rising fury manifest as his Butcher's Nails sensed a confrontation and bit deep. 'I am the master of the Black Fleet. The victory is mine. Never has a fleet of the True Powers, any fleet, destroyed such a large Imperial force so quickly. I have annihilated–'

'Annihilated?' The Warmaster's question silenced Urkanthos. 'Several cruisers made warp translation before the opening salvo. Even now they are en route to warn Cadia of our approach. You call that annihilation?'

'It is an unstable warp route, Warmaster, and the daemons are in pursuit.'

'We do not rely on daemons, Lord Ravager.' The venom in the Warmaster's voice nearly manifested in the air. 'They are tools, not brothers to be trusted.'

'We could not catch them, the picket fleet had prepared their flight before emergence, and they entered warp space far earlier–'

'Excuses.'

'You ask the impossible!' Urkanthos roared, daggers of pain lancing from his head as the Nails bit deep. He took a step forward. 'No mortal could do–'

'Hold, brother.'

No mere command, that word. It came from the depths of the

endless pit, with cold winds howling between each syllable. Darkness deepened around Abaddon as he spoke, and Urkanthos froze mid-stride, his own shadow seeming to flinch at the sonic force.

Even the fortress itself gave a thin howl.

Morkath saw that Urkanthos, champion of Khorne, was afraid. He hated being afraid – his mind coiled defensively at the emotion, and Morkath wondered if long before his remaking as a Space Marine that fear had been the centre of his violence.

The Warmaster laid an armoured gauntlet on Urkanthos' breastplate, a restraining, calming gesture. And when he spoke again, it was with a soft understanding utterly alien to the unholy command he'd just uttered. 'I ask the impossible, brother, because if I do not ask the impossible, we cannot do the impossible. You have served well, but do not demand my favour.'

'I… apologise… Warmaster,' Urkanthos said, gritting his teeth against the spur of the Nails.

Morkath looked closer, thinking she glimpsed a figment around his head then. One connected to his shout that no *mortal* could do what the Warmaster asked.

Angron. The face of the daemon primarch had slipped across the surface of his mind. Interesting.

'You are fresh from battle, and your Nails bite deep. It is forgotten. But you are right, I have called you to discuss the landings.'

The Warmaster stepped away, and whatever force held Urkanthos let go. He shook his great horned head, centring himself.

'There will be no landings, or at least not as you imagine.' The Warmaster stepped to the viewing platform, turning his back on Urkanthos without concern to look at the whorl of the Eye. As he stepped close, the fleshworked walls quivered in fear at his presence. 'That is what I have told the others. Scouring Cadia is not our purpose. We will destroy it.'

'If not me in the vanguard, then… Korda?'

Devram Korda was the Lord Purgator, a Slaanesh devotee whom Urkanthos despised. Morkath could see suspicion coiling in his bloody thoughts like a water snake.

'We will break Cadia with the *Will of Eternity*.'

'My Warmaster, I do not understand.'

'Our ruse has worked – we have bluffed the servants of the False Emperor. They think the campaign is over, that we have wasted our strength and are defeated. Siron's spies tell us that on the surface, the servants of the Corpse-Throne are leaving their fortress cities to pursue our retreating forces, and their Naval screen has left to chase the *Vengeful Spirit* and *Planet Killer*. They are out of their strongholds, exposed, open to orbital bombardment.'

Urkanthos said nothing, but Morkath saw his bloody thoughts coagulate with the discomfort of the conversation's direction.

'The strength of Cadia is in its kasrs, its fortress cities,' continued the Warmaster. 'Those we shall destroy with the *Will of Eternity*, one by one. This will leave the enemy without headquarters, supply centres, communication hubs or fall-back locations. They will have nowhere to return to. Meanwhile, orbital bombardments will kill the field armies. There will be a limited landing to protect Krom Gat and his war machines, which will demolish the pylons. That is how we will break Cadia.'

'It is strategically sound, Abaddon. Clever. Cunning. But dangerous. The gods will not like it. The Powers gave you the *Vengeful Spirit* and *Planet Killer* as gifts, yet you use them as diversions and give the glory of the killing blow to this xenos construct.'

'I care nothing for glory, only victory. And the Powers did not give me the *Vengeful Spirit* and *Planet Killer*, Urkanthos, I took them. Remember – we do not serve the Powers, they serve us.'

'But–'

'I did not rebel against an Emperor who acted like a god simply to pledge to entities that claim to be gods – did you? These are old thoughts reasserting themselves in you, from before your rebirth in black and gold.'

'Yes, Warmaster. But should the fortress fail...'

'Do not wish for this battle, Lord Ravager. Cadia is but a step. Break it, and we forge the Crimson Path. Create a rent in space from which the Imperium can never recover. You crave the honour of Cadia? Imagine landing on Terra.'

The Khornate warrior nodded, teeth clenched.

'The fortress,' he growled. 'I suppose that is why *it* is here.'

That was when Morkath learned that she had not escaped Urkanthos' notice. For he looked at her directly then, his hatred so intense it unwisely drew her eyes into his.

And when they met, her mind fell tumbling into the black portals of his pupils.

Morkath saw through the butcher's eyes, and she saw *red*.

A crimson haze of spurring pain. A hot spike deep in her brain meat that demanded murder.

The Butcher's Nails. The torture implant that Urkanthos had, somehow, lived with for millennia.

This was not what she'd wanted. She'd been attempting to pierce the deep-running veins of thought. Possibly glimpse the subconscious. But this was full thoughtstream merge and memory contamination. A recall dream.

In it, Urkanthos was before the great double doors of a chapel, his armour slicked in blood.

The blood did not all belong to the pathetic cultists who had sacrificed themselves guarding the chamber within. Some was from his own Hounds of Abaddon, killed in this fool's errand aboard the blackstone monster.

Thirty years they had been doing this. Thirty years since capturing the *Will of Eternity* in the Gothic War, spent trying to tame the depths of the noctilith beast. He would not be here at all, except the Warmaster had chosen him – and he wanted to show Abaddon he was capable.

'Open it!' shouted the Warmaster, carving through the malnourished devotees who tried to stop him.

Morkath braced herself for what she'd see next.

Urkanthos grabbed the double doors and threw them open so hard, the blackstone tracks sparked as they slid into the walls.

Inside was an armoured sanctuary. Defaced aquilas and statues of the primarchs covered in pulsing sacs of organs and tarpaulins of veined skin. Blackstone cables, woven through with warpflesh, wrapped the statuary and candle racks like roots infiltrating an ancient jungle temple.

Sacrificial victims lay before the altar. Whatever was in here, they'd been worshipping it.

Nothing moved, for a moment.

Then Urkanthos detected movement behind the altar. His ballistics cogitator pinged a target. He snatched up his pistol and fired, exploding a baptismal font full of tarry ooze.

'What have you found, old man?' growled Hekksha. He was not one of the old breed, but Urkanthos liked him. A killer through and through.

'Small animal. Fast. Maybe a genestealer.'

They had found stranger in this damned fortress.

Another blur of movement. Both warriors fired, shattering an organ so the pipes toppled like felled trees, contacting the flagstones with a chiming musical clang.

'Come out!' shouted a voice behind – Abaddon. 'We will see you!'

And incredibly, it did.

At first, Urkanthos believed it to be a massive vermin. A hunched scavenger, perhaps an exotic alien. But that was only because what the creature actually was appeared so unfathomable that he did not recognise it until it raised its wax-pale face.

It was a child, dressed in rags and black hair matted. She was perhaps six or seven, though so malnourished she might have been as old as ten.

One eye was a brilliant violet, the other a sable orb.

The black eye was not natural, but a false blackstone one recently implanted. A starburst of poorly healed incision lines showed where the devotees of the fortress – now dead thanks to Urkanthos – had implanted it.

Dravura Morkath knew, as a mind-scanner, that not everyone saw her the same way. To crew who feared her, she was a twisted monster, but the transhuman Astartes generally looked on her almost as a pet.

But still, it was strange to see herself as a child.

Hekksha laughed. 'A dangerous beast indeed, lord. Let me.'

Hekksha's bolt pistol snapped up with a speed Urkanthos could only see due to his enhanced visual acuity. The instinct to slaughter civilians ran so strong in Hekksha that he did not hesitate – he had killed children before and believed he would do so again.

But the child Morkath moved her right hand an instant before he raised the weapon, her young mind seeing Hekksha's intention before his brain sent the signal to do it.

Morkath saw her tiny fingers spear upwards through the air.

Noctilith spikes drove up from the floor like a wave smashing upon rocks. They speared through Hekksha's abdomen and split armour plates. He fired his pistol high, taking the face off one of the primarch statues behind the child Morkath. Before he could adjust his aim, a final spike impaled his chin and exited the crown of his helmet.

Another Hound of Abaddon stepped through the door to the sanctuary shouting, levelling his boltgun.

Morkath's tiny hands snapped together in a clap.

The sliding double doors slammed closed on the Chaos Space Marine, severing both arms at the elbow.

Urkanthos tracked the blurred shape of the child, firing. Shells detonated on the floor and altar.

He dashed towards an organ where the child Morkath was taking cover – not realising that she had intentionally drawn him that way, into the cables that lay coiled on the floor like the ropy body of a strangling serpent.

One wrapped him, and he toppled hard on his face. Rubbery cables entangled his right leg like a strangling vine. He fired into them, shots sparking off his power armour. But another cable struck viper-like from the floor and feelers wormed into the pistol's action, jamming it. More pinned his axe to the floor. One, thick as his gauntleted fist, constricted his neck.

He no longer saw red. Now he saw deep crimson, the rage almost too powerful.

But then it ebbed, because the red began going grey at the edges.

'Stop! Stop, child!'

In whatever consciousness remained after the adrenal bombardment, Urkanthos recognised his Warmaster's voice.

Abaddon strode ahead, weaponless. He had disconnected the Talon of Horus and laid it on a stone pew. Put his daemon blade aside.

Urkanthos could hear the sword whispering in protest.

The Warmaster of the Black Legion strode forward slowly, hands raised.

'We do not wish to harm you.'

Urkanthos attempted to protest, managing only a strangled choke. Not harm her? *Not harm her?* One brother was dead, perhaps two. And he wished to forgive the bitch?

A grate banged. Bare footsteps on blackstone, padding up behind the half-destroyed altar.

Abaddon knelt, though doing so still made him taller than most human mortals. 'Come, child,' he said, gesturing with a gauntlet.

Glittering eyes peered from behind the altar. In the ceiling vaults, cables slithered in distrust.

Urkanthos' vision was black at the edges now. Black as the noctilith stone.

'Come,' beckoned Abaddon, with no sense of hurry. 'Let me look at you.'

The girl slunk out. She was painfully thin, the shadow of her bones visible beneath the translucent skin. She did not walk like a human, but crossed the floor crouched and ape-like, using her hands as additional points of support.

'Beautiful,' said Abaddon. 'Let us talk. That is why you were made, I think. To communicate.'

The girl seemed to cock her head, as if listening, then approached slowly.

Urkanthos struggled, furious in his abasement.

'Release my man,' said Abaddon. 'He was only trying to defend me.'

The child turned her strange eyes towards Urkanthos and gave a low hiss.

The cable around Urkanthos' throat gave a last constricting jerk, then released and slithered into the shadows. He gasped, sucking in the acrid, life-giving air. Coughed blood.

'Thank you.'

The child babbled. 'An-keew. An-keew.'

'Come,' said Abaddon. Working slowly, he unshipped one massive gauntlet and held his bare hand out to the child.

She hesitated, reached for the enormous hand, then pulled her fingers back.

Abaddon did not react, holding steady until the skittish girl laid her hand in his. He enfolded it, gently, as if taking a fledgling dropped from a nest.

'I am Ezekyle Abaddon, the Warmaster. What is your name?'

The girl said nothing.

Urkanthos cursed in Nucerian, mewling through his damaged voice box. Calling her every foul name he could think of until the profanity descended into oaths.

'I will kill you, *dravura morkath*. You will die in pain, *dravura morkath*.'

Trapped in the memory, she leaned forward looking at herself. This was the moment she wanted to see.

'He is right, you know,' said Abaddon. '*Dravura Morkath*, that's you, isn't it? It means Fortress Child.'

Morkath saw the child she once was blink, only barely understanding. The young girl opened a mouth full of noctilith teeth, gums criss-crossed with the scars of implanting, and responded with a mewling gurgle. 'Maaraukaaaaath?'

Until this time, she had spoken to none but the worshippers who venerated her, and to the fortress. A parent that need not christen her.

But this was the moment she, Morkath, was given a name.

And the moment she met her father.

'Are you certain you are not injured?' asked the Warmaster. They were in his private study, a turret room piled high with tomes and scrolls.

The room with the greatest voice-shielding on the *Will of Eternity*.

'It was nothing,' Morkath answered. The fleshwork on one wall of the study had weakened in translation, the Blackstone fighting the colonisation and reasserting its neutral warp-polarity. She pressed her palms to it and opened herself, pouring empyric energy into the stone to charge it, so the webs of flesh lost their grey pallor and plumped. 'An accidental intake of past events. Urkanthos has never got over our first meeting...'

'I was there. You are recovered now, let us move on.'

'Yes, Warmaster.'

'How did you find the council? How much did they lie?'

'They are mostly truthful,' she told him. 'Korda wishes to concoct a new serum that he believes will make you even more powerful. Increase your reaction time.'

'I will not take it.'

'He plans to dose you. At the victory feast, when all is concluded. During the ritual challenge-toasts, he will poison you with a blessing that will enhance your senses, drawing you closer to Slaanesh.'

'A blessing cannot be given, Morkath, only accepted.'

'I do not understand.'

By way of answering, he held his right gauntlet out and Morkath unfastened it, hefting the great piece of armour. It was as heavy as a good-sized anvil, and with its fingers extended spanned the width of a human breastplate. Morkath drew a deep breath as she took the weight on her blackstone-sheathed bones, bending her knees as she set it on a plinth.

'The Four have tried to shower me with blessings,' said Abaddon. 'And if I had accepted...'

He held out his great hand, unblemished, each finger big around as a spear's shaft. As he flexed it, the knuckles cracked and popped.

'...I would look a great deal different. Skyrak. Urkanthos. Korda. Krom Gat. That is what you get when you accept gifts. The Powers have remade them in their own image.'

'You have only accepted the Mark,' Morkath nodded. 'And that mark is that of all the gods, not one.'

'Even so, this' – he tapped the Mark – 'cannot become who I am, or else I will be lost to it. Like Horus. The last time we nearly destroyed the Empire of Lies. One must wear the crown without becoming it, and always be ready to take it off.'

Morkath's heart ached for him then, for this being who carried such a burden on his noble shoulders. She nearly reached out for his great hand to lay a comforting touch on it, wondering if she should speak the words she'd waited centuries to say.

She knew that if she did so, he would respond. She could see as much in his whirling thoughts.

But their great endeavour was in process, and he had no room for emotion. After Cadia, Morkath swore, they would be honest with each other. She would call the Warmaster what he was to her, and he would respond.

They would give a name to this bond.

She would call him father, and he would call her daughter.

Was that what he was thinking, as he stared at her? Was he on the precipice of the same admission?

'Dravura,' he said. 'Tell me what Urkanthos thinks of – other than blood.'

'He worries Korda is undermining him. It may turn to blows.'

Abaddon grunted. 'It may. Is there anything else?'

He gave her the luxury of thinking about it.

This was the reason he retained her. Her usefulness. An inherent ability to let him balance the powers and interests of his lieutenants. Men who were loyal to him, but also being directed – with or without their knowledge – by the warring forces of the empyrean. It was a bitter irony that her father felt deep as bone.

To keep his coalition together, he must deal with the strongest among the factional leaders of the Black Legion. But especially of late, the strongest were also riddled with corruption. Consciously or not, they could not help but try to usurp and undermine one another, upsetting the balance of the Legion. Each tried to win the greatest victory, attract the greatest favour from the Warmaster, in hopes of personal elevation by their god and enticing Abaddon down their patron's path.

But aboard the Blackstone Fortress, their minds were open to Morkath. Their plots and fixations on display to manipulate and frustrate.

'We must watch Urkanthos,' Morkath said. 'There will be enormous slaughter on Cadia, and that will only empower him.'

'That is why we're using the fortress,' said the Warmaster, dismissively. 'So no one god can claim the credit. To keep balance in victory.'

'Perhaps,' Morkath said. 'But when he said no mortal could do what you asked, he thought of Angron.'

The Warmaster paused amid turning towards a chart, his drifting attention recentred. 'Angron? Do you think he seeks ascendency to daemonhood?'

'I cannot say for certain. But Angron has been in his thoughts of late. It was not the first time.'

'Gods of the warp, imagine wanting that. To be yoked like a grox to a patron. Ten thousand years later, and Angron is still a slave-gladiator – but this time owned by a god. A daemon prince would unbalance the council, swing it to Khorne. Yet another reason to avoid grinding sieges on Cadia. We cannot let Urkanthos spill too much blood, but if we restrain him, his Hounds of Abaddon will revolt.'

'The *Will of Eternity* will bring you victory.'

'If not, it will be a landing. And in that case I dare not hold Urkanthos back.'

'But, my lord, to deploy him risks giving him victory. And in that case, you might as well invite the Blood God onto the council table.'

'It is a contingency. And that is the job of a Warmaster. To have contingencies – even bitter ones.'

Morkath looked at him then, and took in a sight she had never witnessed before.

Her father, the Warmaster, was seated in a great chair. Thoughts circled his head in orbits of cosmic symmetry. But for just a moment, the golden cycles and rings flared, the planetary bodies of thoughts and beliefs gleaming jewel-like.

For the barest instant, it was not a planetary system that floated above his head.

It was a crown.

One so heavy, he strained under the weight.

FOUR

Major Marda Hellsker sat in the chair with a valise across her knees, trying to keep her back straight. Her spine still felt bent out of shape from the jerky Chimera ride back to Kraf, but she refused to look slovenly while sitting beside her colonel.

Especially not in front of the Lord Castellan.

She heard a chuckle to her left. There, two tankers from the 35th Armoured Shock – captains by their bars – sat on a long bench down the hall. They were looking at something behind her. She turned to see what was funny.

Only after glancing down the empty hallway did she realise it was her.

'Ignore them,' said Colonel Barathus. His own eyes were straight forward, and he spoke overloud, so they could hear. 'We didn't make it to the battle-front, true. But it was *their* job to clear the Kraf Road for us to get there. Sloppy work, that. Heard it went six days behind schedule.'

One of the captains shot up, but the other pulled him back. Unlike Hellsker, Barathus had a combat badge, and he was a colonel. Rank still counted for something.

They drifted further down the hall, chatting while looking over their shoulders.

'They're jealous,' said Barathus. 'You're going to meet the Lord Castellan. General Saxka left those two outside once they were done bringing in her maps.'

Hellsker smiled. She couldn't believe she was about to meet Creed. Ursarkar E. frekking Creed.

She had followed dispatches on his career since she was fifteen, long before he'd become famous. One of her instructors at the academy had served with him in the Eighth, and tipped her off early that he was a man to watch. She'd read his short treatise on the use of combined arms against irregular cultist forces, and during advanced battle school had wargamed several of his more famous actions. She'd listened, breathless, to each broadcast during the war. Even now, the strains of 'Flower of Cadia' made her stand taller.

'Do me a favour, Marda.'

'Sir?'

The knob to their left turned, the sound of voices finally breaking through the soundproof door as General Saxka and her command staff emerged, still calling over their shoulders and laughing about a parting joke.

Hellsker shot up to attention, snapping a clean salute.

Barathus rose slowly next to her, reseating his cap and greeting Saxka with a more casual salute, paired with a friendly nod.

'Just try to remember that Ursarkar Creed puts his trousers on one leg at a time.'

'What does that mea–'

'Turn to face,' he said, and she complied without hesitation. Barathus adjusted the formal engineer braid on her chest, and brushed brick-dust off her shoulder. 'He's just a man, Marda. Not a legend. And if you look at him like that, like you're doing now, he won't respect you. Act like you're worthy of being there, because you are.'

'Colonel,' prompted an adjutant from the doorway, and in a moment of utter surrealism, Hellsker saw it was Jarran Kell.

Barathus nodded, as if he hadn't seen Kell in propaganda picts, or on the back of the lho-stick cards packed with their ration of smokes. 'We'll not keep the Lord Castellan waiting. Stay on my shoulder, major.'

'Static defence,' Barathus said. Even below his silver moustache, Hellsker could see the scorn. As if he'd swallowed vinegar thinking it were wine. 'After a hundred days of sitting, doing nothing as Cadia burned, you're assigning my Twenty-Fourth to static defence at some nowhere pass?'

Hellsker couldn't believe what she was hearing, much less what she was seeing. Barathus, her colonel, was questioning orders – arguing with Ursarkar E. Creed.

She was still reeling from the uncanny feel of being in the room with the great man – who was simultaneously everything, and nothing, like she'd expected.

Just as in the posters and vids, Creed eschewed the formal capes and epaulettes of his office – instead wearing a Combat Dress Alpha uniform, where standard fatigues were highlighted with removable signs of status like his crimson chest-braid and sash. His scandalously wrinkled greatcoat lay over the back of a high chair stacked with papers. His diagonal scar, crossing his forehead to split his eyebrow and end on his cheek, was if anything more prominent and dashing in person.

But he looked tired. Tired and impatient. Red-rimmed eyes and bad skin, his cheeks mottled with razor burn. His nose was slightly pink, with river deltas of veins sketched across it. The funk of amasec, cigars and body odour suffused his office – a mix Hellsker found extreme, despite her lifelong habituation to barrack-room smells. She suspected the armaglass windows could not open for safety reasons, and that Kell's attempt to keep things squared away could only do so much.

Even now, Kell stealthily cleared a half-eaten plate of fried-meat rolls, leaving only the untouched bowl of vegetables.

'You're disappointed,' Creed answered. 'But—'

'Disappointed! It's a damned insult. I know we never got along as cadets, but do you need to take it out on my command?'

'They're uniquely suited to—'

'To static defence? Because they're Interior? They're Throne-damned Shock Troopers. Trained in assault. They have excellent ratings in simulated battles. Better than some off-world regiments you've sent against the Archenemy. Give them a chance, and they'll stand next to any damned unit on the line. *Any damned unit.*'

The interruption was so alien to the chain of command, so impertinent, that for a moment she covered her embarrassment by looking down at the map.

At the Delvian Cleave. A remote pass carved in the Rossvar Mountains they'd been assigned to garrison.

As a static defence force. A duty Cadian commanders offloaded to Whiteshields and half-trained planetary militias, while the real troopers took on assault roles.

She looked up, throat burning, a hint of Barathus' own rage in her eyes.

'It needs defending,' said Creed, voice rising. 'And your Twenty-Fourth Interior is best suited. You have an engineer company. Alpine training. Enough rotations in the mountains that your troopers can handle the elevation. It's not personal.'

'No, of course not,' Barathus sneered.

'This is a strategically vital route. Maybe one of the most important pieces of geography in the current war.'

'Don't do that. Don't try to—'

'Barathus—'

'—control me with my sense of duty, I'm not—'

Creed picked up a leather-bound tome and slammed it onto the map table. Hard. Loud enough to echo.

'You'll hold that pass and like it, you arrogant son of a bitch,'

Creed roared. 'I'm the frekking Lord Castellan of Cadia, not your old schola-chum. That's your pass. *Your pass.* And if you don't want it, maybe I'll have you shot and let her do it.'

His eyes flicked briefly to Hellsker, appraising.

Barathus opened his mouth, closed it again. Looked down at the map, his hands in fists by his trouser seams. 'My apologies, Lord Castellan... There is no excuse.'

'No,' said Creed, his shoulders relaxing. 'No there isn't. But Barathus, I'm not lying to you. This has to be done. And it must be done well. It might be nothing, I confess – if we're lucky you'll see no action. But if we're unlucky it's going to be a hell of a fight.'

Creed dragged the map of the Delvian Cleave off the desk and shuffled across the room to a chart board. Pinned it up behind a plastek sheet. 'Come over here, let me show you what's at stake.'

Barathus drifted in behind the Lord Castellan. Bending as Creed – nearly a foot shorter than him – marked the elevation map with Xs and arrows. The two murmured, back and forth.

Hellsker had not been invited. But Barathus had said to act like she deserved to be there, so she went.

She'd gone two steps when the hand clamped over her bicep. Hard, muscled. It felt like a bionic, but when she looked, she saw it was flesh.

Jarran Kell was holding her back.

'Not now, sir,' he said.

'Excuse me, colour sergeant. I'll thank you not to touch an officer.'

Kell gave an apologetic nod, but didn't remove his hand. 'My apologies, but the Lord Castellan's conversations are confidential.'

'I'm his executive officer, I need to know the tactical situation. If he's wounded or killed...'

'The colonel will brief you later. Besides, Barathus is a proud man, and he's being humbled. He won't appreciate a witness.'

'I don't think it's your prerogative to decide–'

'Hellsker, of the Twenty-Fourth. Didn't a Colonel Revvan Hellsker command the Twenty-Fourth Shock Infantry? Before its redesignation as Interior, I mean. Your father?'

'My uncle.'

'That's his sword on your hip? Looks like it's seen the wars.'

'He bequeathed it to me, that and his plasma pistol.'

Kell nodded. 'Bad luck, drawing that deployment. No one wants to face the Great Devourer. But still, who could ask for a better death. To fall battling a monster, hand to hand...'

'The colonel needs me.'

'Of course,' he said, and released her. 'Deepest apologies.'

Hellsker turned to see that Barathus and Creed had finished speaking. Kell, she realised, had detained her just long enough.

Barathus straightened and gave Creed a salute.

The Lord Castellan returned it, then dropped it to an offered handshake.

'I'm relying on you, Barathus. We all are. Remember – if they come, do not give them a single step.'

Barathus nodded, and Hellsker noticed how wax-white his face was. How sweat glistened in his thinning hair, despite the chill of the room's atmosphere conditioners.

Hellsker fell in behind him, quiet and straight-backed, until the door closed behind them.

'Colonel? What did he say? Was he serious about those orders, or just blowing smoke up our arse?'

'Marda.' Barathus swallowed. 'I hope it's the latter. I really do. Because if it's not, we're in serious trouble.'

Salvar Ghent's morning ritual was dependable as the dawn bugle call. By 0600 hours, he was dressed and staring down from his window, listening to his underboss Karle Petzen recite the daily commodity prices.

'Amasec for one hundred and twenty credits,' said Petzen, following the ledger lines with his finger. 'A pound of seared grox flank, real, two hundred. Pound of omni-meat, eighty. Glucose sweetener, ten credits per packet.'

'Ten?' Ghent turned away from the window; his dish of caffeine clinked as he laid it down on the porcelain saucer. 'Not seventeen?'

'The Munitorum found a vault full of it, were expecting it to be replacement lasgun barrels.'

Ghent nodded, turned back to the window to look down on Kasr Kraf's Recreation Plaza. 'Pull it off the market until the price rises to twelve.'

Petzen made a note, kept reading.

Caffeine, sixteen credits per ounce. Stub ammunition, sixty-seven per box. Raenka, ninety per bottle.

Salvar Ghent was living in the fat times. The victory times. The celebration times.

Salvar Ghent was *rich*.

Soldiers had the best ration rates on Cadia. While manufactorum workers and Munitorum clerks – fifty- or seventy-percenters, mostly – often used their meagre pay to purchase extra foodstuffs at the public exchanges, soldiers got fed enough that they could splash out for fast pleasures.

The general fallback to Kraf had been excellent for business. Paymasters had caught up with the troops and were issuing back pay. The fools in flak wanted to celebrate.

An ideal situation: war-time prices combined with an excess of money and the celebration of new peace.

Even now, not yet an hour after the dawn bugle, Kraf's Recreation Plaza was full of soldiers threading from one fleshpot to another. In the morning light, you could barely see the red lanterns.

Ghent saw who went where. Studying. Watching. Listening to the soft strains of the Vostroyan Orchestral playing over the vox.

'We have one issue, our ration card manufactorum. The one in Second District. The authorities hit it,' said Petzen.

'I thought our provost chief in Second District was paid off?'

'He was. It wasn't the mil-provosts. They were Kasrkin. Looking for heretics we think. Ran into us instead.'

'Poor bastards.'

'They killed them with a tank.'

Salvar Ghent engaged in a rare display of eye contact, trying to discern if Petzen was joking. When he saw his lieutenant's expression he added, 'Poor, *poor* bastards. Did they evacuate the plates?'

'The what?'

'The plates, the master plates for printing cards. Did they recover them?'

'No, machine was chopped to pieces. Heavy bolter rounds, mostly. Autocannon.'

Ghent clicked his tongue. 'Cadia can't kill something without overkilling it. That'll be a problem.'

'Rationing was ending, I thought?'

Ghent shook his head. 'If that were happening, we'd see an influx of military surplus on the under-market. Proteyn bars. Camp stove promethium. Vitamin tablets. Spools of uniform fabric. Munitorum clerks would start skimming and offloading. None of them are doing that. They've got orders to continue conserving resources. We need that printer up and running again. This war isn't over, and that means the ration-card market is far from done. Food allowances will get cut again. People will be hungry. Where there's hunger, there's profit.'

Petzen closed the book. 'Red light establishments are doing well. Maybe instead of the press...'

'I trade goods, not people,' Ghent said, his eyes sliding over the plaza. 'It's simpler. Ration tins can't walk away. Besides...'

The brass-cased civilian vox-unit went to static, the orchestrals dying, and 'Flower of Cadia' came over the airwaves. A maudlin tune, Ghent had always thought – but at least it was an instrumental, without the mawkish lyrics of remembrance and sacrifice.

'He always breaks in when they're playing good music, did you notice that?' observed Ghent. 'Some oompah military march or a sergeant calling daily exercises, he's nowhere to be seen. But once a bow touches a string, there he is.'

'Probably doesn't want to interrupt the popular programmes.'

The last blaring notes of the song ended.

'*Soldiers of Cadia,*' came Creed's voice.

'He sounds scratchy, nasal,' said Ghent. 'He's let the cigars and Arkady Pride get to him. Clearly *his* rations aren't being cut.'

'*–know that you have given much. And it grieves me to ask more – but more is required. I have today received word that a picket ship has returned into far-system orbit. We cannot be sure, and I ask you to rein in speculation, but it is possible it carries news of another strike towards Cadia.*'

Ghent's slippery gaze made eye contact with Petzen, held it for a moment, then slid away again.

'*It is also my sad duty to report that St Josmane's Hope has been destroyed. The incarceration world was overrun by the Plague of Unbelief, but I have been assured by the surviving provost-wardens that every Cadian, both jailers and jailed, fought the Archenemy to the last cellblock.*'

Pause.

'*On to war dispatches. Outside Kasr Halig, the crew of super-heavy Shadowsword…*'

'That would explain why our contraband shipments to St Josmane's haven't been able to find a transport,' said Ghent, talking over the war news. 'Probably destroyed weeks ago, and definitely not in some heroic last stand.'

'You think he's lying?'

'He's an officer, of course he's lying. But never mind that, there's an opportunity here.'

'In a destroyed world?'

'St Josmane's Hope was a parts producer. Convict labour. The only place in-system that produced the Type Sixty-Seven-Gamma rotational joint clasp.' Ghent spread the finger and thumb of one hand to make a C-shape. 'They're about this big. It's what allows a tripod-mounted weapon to freely traverse on the ball joint. Auto-cannons, lascannons, heavy bolters, that kind of thing. It's a part with a high breakdown rate. Very saleable. We have six containers of them waiting in warehouse eight-eighty-one. Give it three days for the Munitorum clerks to get desperate then start making approaches. Do it quiet. Charge them one hundred and fifty per cent of standard price. Not double. If it's double they'll run to the commissars.'

Petzen nodded. They went quiet.

Creed was wrapping up, the strains of 'Flower of Cadia' beginning to swell behind his voice.

'I assure you, my comrades,' he said, *'that I will not allow the Despoiler to break this world.'*

Ghent snorted. 'Cadia was broken long before the Despoiler got here.'

Kell opened the door to Creed's war room as softly as possible, ignoring the silent, hand-wave protestations of the vox-specialist. The man pointed at a red light outside the door, the one by a sign that read *BROADCASTING*.

I know, mouthed Kell. *I know, damn it.*

'I assure you, my comrades,' Creed said, pausing, as Kell's script told him to. His chart table was partially cleared, the glasses, plates, books and rolled-up maps temporarily moved aside to accommodate an enormous vox-pickup array, its microphone heads the size of frag grenades. 'That I will not allow the Despoiler to break this world.'

The broadcast conductor nodded and dropped his hand.

An assistant in a clunky plastek headset turned a knob, raising the volume on 'Flower of Cadia'.

'My soldiers,' Creed finished. 'I am proud to say that whatever awaits, we will overcome it. Cadia stands.'

The strains of music crescendoed, and the director motioned to the vox-officer crouched below the pickup array on the desk. The young woman threw a lever, then yanked three cords. Pulled down her muffled headset.

'Clear,' she said. 'Off-air.'

'What do you think, Kell?' Creed grunted. He held out a hand and one of the vox-officers passed him a tumbler of amasec, then placed the artillery shell ashtray – its cigar still burning – on his desk. 'I thought it was... What? What's wrong?'

Kell shook his head. 'We need to clear the room. Vermilion-level clearance only.'

'We'll be quick,' said the conductor, bending over an equipment case. 'Five minutes.'

'Now.'

'But, the equipment...'

'Out!'

He used his colour sergeant voice. The one all drill sergeants knew. Projecting so the words landed like hammer-blows on the brain. Like his breath itself had mass.

Cadians feared few things as much as a sergeant's displeasure.

In seconds, the room was clear. Kell heard the door engage, felt the privacy field and sound dampeners spool up.

'What is it?' asked Creed. 'Have we identified the ship?'

Kell took the data-slate from under his arm. Placed it in front of Creed. It was a Tier-Alpha, its blue-tagged case indicating that it carried top-grade encryption.

'The ship is the *Pyrax Orchades*, a destroyer from Battlefleet Scarus. A messenger from the picket fleet.'

'Just one? Are others inbound?'

'They barely made it themselves. Their starboard-side is torn open, exposed to the void. They took seventy per cent casualties getting here. There were two others that didn't survive warp translation. There were... warp-things that boarded the ship. Can't get a good description. Whatever it was ripped the cladding from the reactors. What's left of the crew has terminal rad-poisoning – only one officer, an ensign, is left.'

Creed puffed his cigar, not realising it had gone out. Kell could see ash fall from the end as his hand shook. Others might have interpreted it as fear, but Kell knew it was adrenaline. 'Does he have a sighting report?'

'He wanted to make it in-person, as the captain ordered. Too sensitive for the vox. They transferred him to a medicae facility on one of the orbital defence platforms to stabilise him, but his vitals dropped and he entered cardiac death.' Kell nodded at the data-slate. 'Thankfully, they got a high-grade slate to him in time. Had to shock him twice with the defibrillator to bring him back. Only on the third time was he lucid enough to be recorded.'

'Have you watched it?'

'No. Not yet.'

Creed opened the leather cover of the slate and selected the vid file. Kell moved behind his shoulder.

A face filled the screen. For an instant, Kell thought he was unusually old for an ensign, then he realised the man's skin had been so rad-burned it was wrinkling and sloughing off like the peel of a rotten fruit.

His lips, split up to the bottom of his sunken nasal cavity, bled as he whispered.

'It's distorted,' said Creed. 'Poor quality. Can't even hear him.'

'He's inside a plastek hazard suit, the medicae team couldn't transfer him otherwise. If we raise the volume.'

Kell reached forward and turned the volume wheel until they could hear the words issuing from the man's destroyed lips.

'*–out of the Eye… They came… So man…*'

His eyes drooped, closed. A tone sounded, and in the background, voices. Yellow plastek-shrouded hands entered the frame and spiked a syringe into a medicine port, hit the plunger.

The ensign gasped, eyes flying open to show the dilated pupils narrowing to pinpoints at the rush of stimms.

'*SHATTER BLACK,*' he rasped. '*SHATTER BL–*'

He gagged, the word bubbling in his throat. Kell could see his Adam's apple working up and down under the wrinkled skin.

Then he opened his mouth as if to scream, and nothing emerged but a stream of inky blood.

The screen went black.

'Call the war council. All of them – Astartes, Sororitas, no exceptions,' said Creed. 'And start the sirens.'

FIVE

At dusk, a choir sang across Cadia. Voices raised in a tone of danger, mechanical and foreboding. The sound echoed through streets as labourers and soldiers hastily cleared them. It keened high across empty moorlands and fens. Howled through remote observation posts and listening stations in the snow-capped mountains.

Far out on the Caducades Sea, missile boats blared the note across a cold, rolling ocean. The dim forms of their crew, barely visible from afar, rushed to their stations to contest any orbital landing.

It came from the trumpet-shaped throats of the crisis sirens – each a rectangular box with three bugles sprouting out its sides. An object so ubiquitous on Cadia, that in the kasrs people gave directions based on them.

To get to the commercia, walk three sirens north and turn left. Then walk two sirens.

The sirens did not all trigger at once. The signal went out from Kraf and spread, so that often units in the plain would hear the keening over the horizon and know they were about to hear the same on their voxes.

'And this part?' asked the bell-ringer.

He tapped a black box wired onto the very powerful – and very illegal – high-gain vox-set.

'That's the key loader,' said Yann Rovetske. 'Try not to touch it.'

Rovetske and the bell-ringer crouched low, trying to stay below the sight-line of neighbouring spires. Behind the bell-ringer was a dizzying vista, the whole inner defensive works of Kraf West sprawled below, looked down upon by the chapel tower of St Jaeneth of the Redoubt.

All that crucial infrastructure and defence network, laid out like a tactical map.

Only the Ecclesiarchy was allowed to build this high on Cadia. Any other structure had to be defensive in nature. The towers on their left and right contained massive laser arrays, pointed skyward.

Rovetske slid a plastek-protected booklet to the bell-ringer. 'To operate it, take this key list. Look up the proper position for the tumbler switches, based on the date and hour. Set the toggle switches.'

Rovetske yanked a rectangular cartridge out of the vox-set, exposing the network of metal pins on its interior. Demonstrated how they shot out or retracted in differing patterns as he threw the binary toggle-switches on the unit's face.

'When the key is set, insert it.' Rovetske slotted it home. 'And your message will be encrypted. Remember to change frequencies every three hours, and don't leave it broadcasting or–'

The vox bleated a sharp howl. Rovetske switched it off.

'What was that?' asked the bell-ringer, spooked.

Around them, the sirens rose in a wail.

'That's the sound of your Warmaster calling, soldier.'

Soldier. The word hit the bell-ringer hard, and he held out his right fist – born with a club, precluding him from service – for Rovetske to shake. One of the many cast-offs that made Cadians so easy to radicalise and recruit.

Popular wisdom held that Cadia was a hotbed of recidivism due to its proximity to the Eye, but in Rovetske's experience, the unrelenting martial culture manufactured about as many rebels as it did soldiers. He never had to work hard, just had to tell these alienated, oppressed civilians they were worth something.

Rovetske reached out and shook the man's hand, seeing the tears in the Cadian's eyes.

'I live to serve,' said the bell-ringer.

Genevieve found her in the Chapel of the Lost Commandery, kneeling before the altarpiece and reciting from her book in a whisper.

'Eleanor.'

Her sister continued to murmur. Speaking the names of the lost Sisters who had been called to defend Cadia fourteen hundred years before, but had diverted to suppress an uprising on Chandry – and were never seen again. A shame so great that it had led the Order of Our Martyred Lady to station a permanent presence on Cadia.

'*Eleanor.* The sirens have started. And I've received a summons from the Lord Castellan.'

Eleanor stopped reading, sighed, and marked the page with a ribbon. 'As have I, canoness.'

'There is to be an urgent war council at Kraf.'

Eleanor kissed the book and hung it from her belt, then made the sign of the aquila before standing. 'We must have a representative there. Failing to appear would compound our Order's shame.'

'When shall we leave?'

Eleanor nodded. 'Soon. But would it not be better if I went, and you stayed at the shrine? After all, I am the keeper of the sanctum and its relics, you are the defender of Ecclesiarchy lands outside the wall – should both of us go, it would leave the sacred space undefended.'

'I was invited.' Genevieve suddenly felt foolish, standing in her freshly lacquered armour, its damage from a hundred days of conflict hastily buffed out.

'Yes, I know. But Arch-Deacon Mendazus insists we cannot leave the lands without a canoness, and between the two of us, it is I who handles the strategic concerns, is it not? While you are more front-line warrior.' Eleanor's nose wrinkled. 'It is probably best if we play to our strengths.'

Then she left the chapel, leaving Genevieve alone with the muffled echo of the call to war.

The sirens wailed through the Delvian Cleave, the sound twisting weirdly and muffled in the snowbound canyon of the pass.

'You hear that?' asked Hellsker. She pulled at the officer's scarf she'd wound around her throat and ears. Looked over her shoulder at the bleak mountain road they'd chewed up with their line of Chimera transports. They'd been riding hatches-open to better see the terrain, and she had to strain to hear over the growl of the transport's engine. 'Is that what I think it is?'

'Can't be,' said Company Sergeant Ravura. 'It's the engine covering the stops. Probably two longs and a short, chemical alert somewhere down on the Kraf plain. If it were a general stations call it would be one long–'

The siren tower to their left cranked up, starting high before settling into a rising and falling wail that filled the canyon.

Ravura turned to her, a smile on his chapped lips. Said something.

'What?' Hellsker asked.

He leaned close to her ear, cupping his leather-gloved hands and shouting. 'I said, Twenty-Four, in the war!'

Castellan Mordlied rammed the spiked adamantine butt of the banner-pole through the tank commander, pinning him to the Leman Russ' armoured cupola.

The heretic mewled, his rune-carved skin turning even whiter as splashes of blood lapped the banner-pole from his burst heart. He clawed at the impaling shaft, cursing Mordlied in the name of his false gods.

Mordlied stepped on his face, tracked a target, and fired a single bolt-round. The mass-reactive shell struck a crewman scrambling out of the rear escape hatch, a live battle cannon round in his hands. Clearly attempting to trigger it among the demigods assaulting his armoured company.

Around him, the lieutenant's fellow Black Templars butchered the tank column. To his left, an Initiate pressed his flamer to the vision slit of an immobilised Chimera. When he fired, Mordlied's auditory enhancers detected muffled screaming before the ignited promethium burned all the oxygen, stealing the crew's breath.

To his right, Marshal Amalrich carved into a looted Taurox with his power sword then gripped the ragged metal of the cut and tore off the vehicle's door. A Sword Brother standing just off the Marshal's left shoulder fired two rounds inside the carved-open transport, paused, fired once more then moved on.

The column had been retreating when they caught it, already broken by a flight of Avengers who had dived down and riddled it with armour-penetrating rounds from their rotating cannons. Those wrecked vehicles had choked the roadway and slowed the traitors, allowing the Cruxis Crusade to come upon them close.

An alert in Mordlied's vision. Encoded and classified vermilion-plus. Data spooled and a red-lined Templar cross rotated as his helmet's cogitators filtered it through the decryption key.

As banner-bearer, Mordlied was the Marshal's herald. All outside communications came through him.

The document unlocked. He scanned it, eyes darting back and forth.

'Marshal,' he voxed. 'We are requested at war council. And advised to pull back to Kraf and prepare for a fresh assault. High command believes the Despoiler to still be incoming.'

'*So it goes,*' answered Amalrich. In the distance, Mordlied could see the Marshal plant his ceramite boot against the burned shell of a staff car and shove it aside. *'These are dregs. I want a finer vintage of enemy.'*

'Did it work?' Creed asked.

'Indeterminable,' Magos Klarn buzzed in response. The mandible claws at the end of his mechadendrites clicked with nervous strain. 'The apparatus functioned, though it exceeded safe parameters. The concentrated psychic force drawn from the sources was able to transmit, but whether the message was sent in full cannot be determined.'

Klarn saw the Lord Castellan's snarl of disapproval.

'It is the best I could do, under the circumstances.'

'You have done all I asked. We'll simply live in hope, I suppose.'

Klarn realised he had misinterpreted the Lord Castellan's mood. With his one semi-organic eye, he tried to discern the expression Creed was transmitting as he searched the chamber with his haunted, black-rimmed eyes.

When he looked around, Klarn realised Creed's expression was not disdain, it was a physical reaction. A response to the smell. Klarn's own olfactory organs had long been replaced with an atmospheric sensor that conveyed the air's chemical components, but not its scent.

The scent of burning flesh and liquefied human protein.

Most of Cadia's dedicated astropathic choirs had died in the initial assault, succumbing to a massive empyric pulse that overwhelmed their brains, burning out neural pathways and melting their eyes. Klarn suspected it was a stratagem – meant to prevent Cadia from calling for reinforcements.

Which was exactly what they were doing now.

With the astropathic choirs depleted, Creed had to improvise. He'd taken sanctioned psykers from regiments, convinced an Inquisition vessel to give up its human cargo, and pressured the Navy to hand over as many as they could spare. He'd ordered the provosts to open the jails and execution-centres, sending any inmates who'd been imprisoned due to psychic manifestations.

Now all of them, the cooperative and the coerced, were dead. Most had burned like candles, the warpfire energies bursting their skulls in a licking flame of indescribable colour. Others had bellies distend until they burst, letting forth horrible tiny creatures that Klarn's servitors washed with flame before they could grow from their flopping, larval forms. The unluckiest had become temporary hosts for daemons, who struggled and died, themselves unable to handle the vast psychic backwash of the transmission.

All of that energy, pulsing through Klarn's transmitter to convey one message.

'*All forces,*' repeated Creed, as if reading Klarn's thoughts. '*Cadia besieged. Despoiler comes. Make haste.* Eight words. That's what they died for.'

'Now we must hold out long enough for it to matter.'

'On that note, magos, do you…?'

Creed trailed off, looked over his shoulder. He had left even his colour sergeant outside.

'There are naught but servitors here.'

'Do you have any hope of success?'

'I do not hope, lord. Hope is the refuge of those whose faith in the Omnissiah is weak and their calculations imprecise. I have divinatory percentages.'

'And what do they say?'

'The null-array is ancient, and our understanding of it only partial. Adepts of my order last encountered the warp-beam of a Blackstone Fortress in the Gothic War. But the information they shared on its capabilities was collected in combat, which rarely makes for good data. If the null-array can counteract the beam, it may protect Kasr Kraf, but beyond that I cannot speculate. Still, we will need a miracle.'

'That is your best estimate, then. A miracle.'

'Thankfully,' Klarn buzzed, 'the Omnissiah works in the realm of miracles.'

SIX

'That, is what we know,' said Creed, his voice amplified by the vox-pickup in front of him. 'Our latest update suggests the Despoiler is one day from Cadia.'

Kell looked across the semicircular table he'd laid out for the war council. He'd managed the room's setup himself, with a protocol expert from the Administratum advising the seat placement. You didn't want to make a mistake right off the landing ramp. Sitting the Space Wolves next to the Dark Angels, for instance, or the Cadian high command delegation further from Creed than the Navy. Indeed, it had been a difficult balancing act. Only the magnanimity of Magos Klarn giving up his seat made it work – a move that was proper since he was giving testimony, and did not biologically require a chair.

'Let me go over it again,' said a towering warrior with a black line tattooed across his face.

Kell keyed the vox-speaker that he'd affixed to his formal carapace armour. 'The chair recognises the honourable Wolf Lord Sven Bloodhowl, of the Firehowlers.'

'My thanks. If you tell this tale right, the war we have fought – with all its hardships – has been a mere foreboding. And the Great Traitor, the Despoiler, Abaddon…'

Several members of the war council gasped at the name, and Bloodhowl paused to spit on the floor before continuing, to dispel the ill luck. His saliva sizzled on the decking, releasing a twist of smoke.

'This filthy creature has brought a Blackstone Fortress which can annihilate us without him setting foot here.'

A woman, her angular face nestled deep in a hood, raised her hand. As she did so, one sleeve of her crimson robe fell away, revealing the sable greave of her power armour.

Two things surprised Kell: her relative youth given her position, and the fact that the seat next to her was empty.

'The chair recognises the revered Canoness Eleanor, of the Order of Our Martyred Lady. Keeper of the Shrine of St Morrican.'

'According to the chronicles I have studied, the Despoiler took *three* fortresses during the Gothic War, did he not? And by combining their arcane ordnance, they destroyed a sun. Are we sure there is only one?'

'If I may?'

'Chair recognises Inquisitor Talia Daverna of the Ordo Hereticus, Chief Inquisitorial Legate of the Cadian Gate.'

'It is unlikely they possess more than one.' Daverna was a tall woman with powerful arms and broad, muscular shoulders. Shoulders that, in the bawdy slang of the Cadian barracks, were said to belong in a flak vest. Born in Kasr Derth, she wore an officer's greatcoat in a manner calculated to show that despite the rosette, she was one of them.

Kell found her both intimidating and monstrously attractive.

'The Despoiler only escaped Battlefleet Gothic with two activated Blackstone Fortresses,' she continued. 'The third was reclaimed by a Navy boarding party. Since then, prisoner interrogations – supported by remote viewing and the Emperor's Tarot – suggest that he gave one to the Red Corsairs. Possibly some kind of payment for services. Our best assessment is that only one remains in his possession.'

'Faith shall shield us.'

'Chair recognises venerated Marshal Marius Amalrich of the Black Templars, leader of the Cruxis Crusade.'

Of all the transhumans sitting around the half-circle, it was Amalrich that Kell found the most unnerving. Pale-skinned and towering in his black ceramite shell, a few whisker-like scars around his eye sockets marked where his eyeballs had been scooped out and replaced with high-grade augmetics that glowed solid amber.

He was also the only representative in the chamber who still carried arms – his bolt pistol and power sword fixed to his armour with heavy chains. A bannerman stood behind, unmoving as a statue.

'Thankfully, we have technology in addition to faith,' responded Creed. 'Magos Klarn, you may reveal our countermeasure.'

'Chair recognises Magos Klarn.'

'Ever since the Gothic War, my predecessors in the Mechanicus have known the Blackstone Fortresses and their unique warp-based weaponry have been a threat to the Cadian Gate. In the millennia since, we have put considerable resources into developing an array that harnesses Cadia's natural defences as a way of diffusing the warp-beam.'

'You speak of the pylons, magos?'

'Affirmative, Lord Castellan,' Magos Klarn said, bowing. 'Whether by a quirk of geology or a remnant of the Dark Age of Technology, it is thought that the pylons have some stabilising effect on the warp. Our hope is to turn this passive attribute into an active defence. We can shield Kraf, and perhaps the plains surrounding it.'

'What do we expect the Despoiler to target with the warp-beam?' asked Bloodhowl.

'He's going to hit the kasrs.' Creed said it matter-of-factly, brooking no argument. 'The fortress cities have always been key to Cadia's strategy. We've spent thousands of years hardening the positions and training to defend them. Eliminate the kasrs and we are an army without bases, logistical centres, command-and-control. But Kraf, unlike the others, has the null-array. It's why I picked it as our rallying point. And that is what I would like you all to do – rally here. Join the pullback, and make your stand on the walls of Kasr Kraf.'

A pause as everyone took the information in.

'Unacceptable,' said Eleanor.

'Why?'

'It is our duty to guard the Shrine of St Morrican. Am I to decamp to Kasr Kraf and watch as our precious shrine is defiled?'

Kell leaned down and whispered to Creed, reminding him of the empty chair.

'What about your sister, then?' Creed continued. 'Her role is in the mobile force, yours is defensive.'

Eleanor's mouth made a tight line. 'I am empowered to speak for both of us.'

'At least the Holy Sisters deigned to come at all,' Bloodhowl snapped.

Kell decided not to follow protocol. Instead, he looked across to the seat laid out for Master Korahael of the Dark Angels.

The master's helm flickered and rolled. An imperfect holo-image of his head and chest was projected from a base unit so that he looked like the heroic busts in Administratum buildings.

'*Is that a slight, Wolf?*' the master answered. His voice came through hollow, partially due to the connection, and partially because he had not removed his helm. '*We are still aboard the* Sword of Defiance. *It would be improper for the ship's commander to leave it in this state. Enemy infiltration is a constant threat, and we are labouring to get the weapons systems fully operational to serve as air defences. It is no small feat to bring a wrecked strike cruiser to operational status.*'

'Your work is appreciated,' said Creed, trying to break the tension. 'But do you need the full complement? Can none be spared to defend the walls of Kraf?'

'*Spare?*' sneered Korahael. '*No, I do not have any warriors to spare. And I thank you not to speak of us like shells in an ammunition tin. We are not yours to spend, Ursarkar Creed.*'

Kell saw Creed's jaw wire tighter. Remembered how in his last medical review, the oral chirurgeon had warned him he was wearing down his teeth.

'I apologise, Master Korahael. It was not my intention to cause offence, indeed, my concern was just the opposite – defence. We will need reinforcements to man the walls. I have the Militarum, I have a commitment from the skitarii, and I have a collection of Adeptus Astartes from various Chapters – a combined force of remnants and casualties have sworn to serve on the wall.'

'And we will fight to the last,' said a pale Astartes in night-black ceramite.

'Chair recognises Lieutenant Odric A'shar, of the Raven Guard, elected commander of the Company of Brothers.'

A'shar shrugged, a half-smile playing across his pale, languid features. 'I'm done. That was all I had to say.'

'We appreciate that deeply, lieutenant.' Creed nodded. 'They are sorely needed. It is true that I have troops, but exactly what kind of troops? The Despoiler will hit us with the full might of the Black Legion. That means Traitor Astartes, strange engines, perhaps even warp abominations. We need survivable, power-armoured infantry to counteract – the Adepta Sororitas, the venerated Astartes. Units that do not tire. Now, who among you will help me? Who will defend Kraf?'

Silence.

'Shall we go around?' asked Creed. 'Canoness Eleanor?'

'Chair recog–'

Creed gestured for quiet, and Kell snapped off his vox-hailer.

Eleanor shifted, put her hand up even though the room had turned informal. 'We are sworn to defend the shrine. This sacred duty cannot be altered by mere military necessity.'

'Very well,' said Creed. 'Master Korahael? Will you lead your Dark Angels to fight on the walls of Kraf?'

The holo-projection fizzled and popped, refocused. *The* Sword of Defiance *is too valuable an asset to abandon. You will see the strategic wisdom of this once its guns are run out and it opens fire.*

'You will be vulnerable to the warp cannon,' argued Creed. Kell could see sweat prickling on the back of his commander's neck. 'You and Canoness Eleanor will be exposed, possibly outside any null field we will deploy. Vulnerable to orbital bombardment.'

'I have chosen my ground,' said Korahael. *'Just like you have chosen yours at Kraf. The* Sword of Defiance *is a worthy defensive strongpoint, we can prevent Kraf from being fully surrounded.'*

'And you can hide any of your precious secrets,' growled Blood-howl. 'Is that not so, Korahael?'

'My Wolf Lord Bloodhowl,' Creed said, turning, 'your Firehowlers will assist us, surely? Or your brother Wolf Lord Highfell and his Ironwolves?'

'The Wolves of Fenris never refuse a call, Lord Castellan.' Bloodhowl leaned back in his chair. 'But the Ironwolves are not warriors of foot. Their warfare is that of the ranging pack – a wall defence is not the place for them. Before I came, Jarl Highfell told me that he plans to raise his banner in the ruins of Kasr Jark, and will oppose the enemy landings like an ice wyrm – striking and encircling from his cave. It will prevent the Archenemy massing forces to the north. If you need armour, why not the Knights of House Raven?'

'The baroness is already moving east to engage Legio Vulcanum,' Klarn replied. 'The heretek Titans of Vulcanum are approaching Kasr Kraf from that direction, and will be here within days unless countered. With our Titan forces committed in Cadia Primus, and unable to redeploy, House Raven is the only option. They cannot serve on the wall.'

'I will take the wall and hold it,' interrupted Marshal Amalrich. 'Instruct my crusaders to disburse themselves amongst the men. We have seen on the maps an outer defensive work called the Martyr's Rampart, is that correct?'

'Yes,' Creed answered. 'On the southern sector.'

'That will be ours.'

'Very well, that is a start,' said Creed. 'We have A'shar and his company on the western wall, the Cruxis Crusade in the south – Wolf Lord Bloodhowl, you answered only for Lord Highfell, would you do me the honour of taking the north?'

'I think not.' Bloodhowl grinned, his canines sharp with sly mischief. 'I think instead I shall do something else.'

'And what is that?'

Kell could hear the strain in Creed's voice. Imagined the supreme effort his commander must be making to keep his temper.

'I think I will solve all our problems. I will board the *Will of Eternity*, kill Abaddon, and use his thick skull to sharpen my axe blade.'

The room went quiet.

'Was that a jest, Wolf Lord?' Creed said.

'It was not,' Bloodhowl rejoined. 'Not a jest. Not at all. The *Firemane's Fang* is the only war vessel in Cadia's orbit, the Navy has' – Bloodhowl waggled his fingers – 'gone away. Chasing the *Vengeful Spirit*. Not yet returned. We will board the *Firemane's Fang*, run it through the enemy fleet and into range of the *black fortress*.'

He demonstrated with his hands, bringing them together in a T-formation.

'Fire… What is the word in Gothic…?' He paused, asked another Wolf behind him something in Fenrisian, then nodded at the answer. 'Just so, boarding craft. We will use boarding craft, storm the fortress, and destroy it from the inside before it arrives to Cadia. Like we did with St Josmane's Hope.'

'It's a risky venture,' Creed warned. 'Desperate. You're right, the Josmane operation was successful – but a Blackstone Fortress is no prison planet. We don't know its schematics or how to effect catastrophic sabotage as we did with the Josmane plasma grid. It could mean throwing away your Firehowlers for no gain. And I doubt there would be enough of them – you have only fifty-eight warriors now, yes?'

'Which is why I would need additional forces. Perhaps numbers from Lieutenant A'shar? Some Cadians?'

'Lieutenant A'shar's force has been committed, to the western wall..'

'I will have to ask my brotherhood,' said A'shar. 'I am not their commander as such. I lead them in battle, but I cannot tell them where to die. That is not part of our compact. Many of them lost brothers to the Archenemy in the initial attack, and will likely relish a chance to strike back. I must at least present them the option.'

'If the Adeptus Astartes are committing,' buzzed Magos Klarn, 'the Mechanicus will answer as well. I offer a full maniple of skitarii. They will be needed to understand the technical aspects of the fortress and how best to sabotage it.'

'And what about Cadians?' asked Bloodhowl. 'How many are you willing to pledge, Creed?'

Kell knew Creed's dilemma.

On one hand, it was a gamble. And gambles rarely paid off. It would be committing men and resources to a risky action with small chance of success. The loss of any Astartes would be keenly felt.

And yet...

It would give the troops hope. And in the wake of the sirens, hope was in short supply. News had leaked about the irradiated ship and destroyed fleet. You could feel the choking fear in every street and wardroom. Creed had, Kell suspected, oversold the possibility that the null-array might work as a viable countermeasure. But if the strike force succeeded...

'You have my support,' Creed stated. 'And the remaining strength of the Cadian Thirteenth Regiment. Go. Take your swords to that heretic fortress and break it. Let the void spill into its shattered core. Emperor speed you. Council adjourned.'

At that, a chorus of junior officers and subalterns cheered and clapped. Knuckles thumped tables around the semicircle, those of the power-armoured Astartes sounding loud as drums.

Creed stood, adjusting his jacket with a soldierly flourish.

When he'd turned towards Kell, he whispered, 'I brought them here to take their troops, and the sons of bitches took *my* troops instead.'

At 1100 hours, sergeants stormed the reserve barracks, bellowing at the troopers of the 13th Shock Infantry as they lay recuperating in their racks.

That was Corporal Evra Sark's first clue something big was going on.

There was no hesitation. Sark was a veteran, and both she and the rest of Zeta Squad had been conducting make-ready drills since they were children.

They strapped on their kit, kissed aquila pendants, formed up in a line by their bunks, then jogged down the central aisle of the hangar that served as their billet. At the end of the aisle a quartet of armoury officers had the weapons lockers already open, snatching the corresponding Kantrael-pattern lasgun from each numbered slot in the squad lockers and slapping it into a palm as each called out their weapon.

'Zeta, Seven.'

A tossed rifle, a catch.

'Zeta, One.' A chainsword experimentally revved before it was handed over.

'Zeta, Two.'

A flamer and tank hefted into Trooper Vemmis' waiting arms.

Sark called for Zeta Nine, and caught the rifle, looping the strap over her shoulder as she ran to the rockcrete parade ground.

Outside was the regimented chaos of a marshalling. Squads fanning out of their lines to arm up at open ammunition crates. Discarded pressboard boxes, empty of las-cells and hard rounds, tumbling in the wind.

'Grenades!' yelled a supply corporal. 'Two each! We are short! Share and share alike, companions! Satchel charges for engineering and demolitions specialists *only.*'

'Squad troopers designated Three, Six and Nine!' roared another supply sergeant, this one with a bionic eye and leg. At his table of crates, troopers were reluctantly loading lasrifles into padded crates.

Sark, as Zeta Nine, hustled over.

'Turn in your lasgun here. You will be carrying shotguns for this mission. Close-quarters work. Butcher's work. Soldier's work. Troopers Three, Six, Nine, get one shotgun, two boxes of cartridges and a bandolier!'

Sark turned her beloved las in, threw a bandolier over her shoulder and started loading it. She was pushing the third cartridge into the stiff woven loops of the ammunition belt when the shell bent. Sark held it up for the sergeant.

'These cartridges are shit. They're the cheap ones with the cardpaper shell. Don't you have any plastek ones?'

'Munitorum sends me what they send me, killer,' the supply sergeant responded, and by the apologetic note in his voice, she knew that he'd seen the steel plate that had replaced her left cheek. 'Best get on and form up. Finish kitting out in the transport.'

'Promethium?' asked Vemmis, his bulky fuel tanks only half-shouldered.

'After embarkation, son,' the sergeant responded. 'You'll be shipboard in sixty minutes and fuel up then, that's all I know.'

Sark swore and shoved the half-empty box of cartridges in her musette bag, then sprinted to join her squad in formation. A line of Chimeras were pulling up to the readied squads, dropping their rear hatches to six inches above the rockcrete so they could keep moving as the Shock Troopers clambered aboard.

She arrived just in time to hop on at a slow jog, turn, and offer a hand to Vemmis with his bulky flamer.

He nodded his thanks, but said nothing until they plopped, gear-laden, into the fold-down seats of the Chimera.

'Hey.' Vemmis jerked his chin at the shotgun. 'Where the hells are we going that you need that?'

'Orbital defence platform?' Sark guessed.

It wasn't until forty-five minutes later, when the back hatch dropped again, that they realised they were in for something extraordinary.

The growl of the armoured column had obscured the crowd noise. It washed into the troop bay all at once, along with the drifting snowfall of rose petals and paper streamers.

Sark raised her eyebrows high, looked at Vemmis.

He shrugged.

When they stepped out of the Chimera, two servo-skulls splashed them with spotlights while a third – a propaganda-capture unit with picter-lenses fixed in its sockets – swept its gaze over them. Soldiers of every regiment on Cadia cheered and applauded, the sounds of individual voices and hands overlapping into a general din.

It was a troop review, leading up to three fat transports.

A banner in a grandstand full of Vostroyans read KNOCK IT OUT OF THE SKY. A Mordian military band played a conjoined medley of the old hymn 'Death is Mine Instrument', 'Sayeth the Throne' and 'Flower of Cadia'.

A Tallarn reached out from the rope line and passed Sark a small bottle of clear alcohol, and she wondered how the Desert Raiders could possibly have ended up here.

'Frekk me,' said Vemmis. 'The frekking Astartes are here.'

Sark looked and scoped a patchwork company marching into the right-hand transport's ramp. She snapped her gaze to the transport on the left, and saw the adept-soldiers of the Machine God boarding in arcane geometric formations.

'Look at that,' she said, elbowing him.

Vemmis didn't move. His eyes were glued to a balcony halfway up a spire.

'It's him,' he whispered.

'Who?'

'*Him.*'

Sark craned her neck to see what he meant – made out a squarish head crested with silver hair. A hulking coat around the shoulders. And next to him, a tall man holding the battle standard of the Cadian Eighth.

'Oh hells,' she said, with reverence and fear. She kissed her fingers, and touched the picture of Saint Gerstahl painted on the rear of her helmet, so he'd watch her back. 'I think we're going to the Blackstone Fortress.'

'Why the Thirteenth?' Kell asked. 'What got them this… honour?'

There was no worry of being overheard. The pickup mic in front of them was not yet live, and after the assassination of Governor Porelska at the Tyrok Fields, even subalterns were kept at a distance during public events. A triple-layer conversion field sizzled the air around them, sniper teams lurked on every rooftop around Kraf's central marshalling ground, and half a dozen fire-teams of Kasrkin were concealed in the shadowed vaults of the balcony – out of sight, but ready to intervene.

'They're down to sixty-two per cent of original strength,' Creed murmured. He lifted his hand in valediction as a propaganda-cherub circled them, capturing the gesture for later broadcast. 'Troops usually need a rotation off the line after taking a beating like that – they're on the edge of combat effectiveness. We probably wouldn't have rotated them back in unless we were desperate.'

'In other words, we can afford to lose them.'

'We can't afford to lose anyone, Jarran.'

'You know it could work.' The wind dropped, and Kell waved the banner of the Eighth to keep it from falling limp. 'We could have faith.'

'Faith. Everyone wants me to *have faith*. High command wants me to have faith in their structure. The Church wants me to have faith in the Emperor. Klarn wants me to have faith in the damned Omnissiah, and now you want me to have faith in, what? The Emperor's Angels casting dice?'

'So why make a spectacle of them if they're not coming back?'

'Because, our war council this morning was a failure. A total failure. I don't have an army defending Cadia, I have half a dozen independent forces all pursuing their own interests. But maybe if we do this' – he swept a hand at the crowd – 'they'll get used to working together. It's worth losing the Thirteenth, even the Astartes, if the symbolism sinks in.'

'And if it doesn't?'

Creed pulled at the lapels of his coat. Wound the red braid of office holding it across his chest tighter. 'If it doesn't, then we're groxmeat. And I'm forever remembered as the man who lost Cadia.'

Five minutes later, Creed gave his address.

Two hours later, the embarkation complete, provosts cleared the landing pads and the transports lifted to the *Firemane's Fang*.

By the time it started to get dark, the turquoise afterburn-rings of the ship's engines were already starting to fade in the night sky. Lost in the unholy stain of the Eye of Terror.

SEVEN

'I tasted your call,' the voice said. *'Urkanthos, you have slaked my thirst. Why do you summon me?'*

Urkanthos pulled his razor-tipped gauntlet from the Naval voidsman's chest, the ribs giving way with a wet crack as he squeezed the human heart in his fist. It still beat, as though it were an animal trying to struggle free of his grip.

Urkanthos tore it out and threw the corpse on the mound in front of him. It was chest high. An offering to raise the daemon.

He'd felt it enter him. Its slippery, hot essence passing by the back of his neck. A sensation Urkanthos had never grown used to.

He dropped the heart in the casket with the others, where the electrical stimulation of arc-coils kept them thumping, so the pile of organs continued to pulse and heave. He knew better than to speak to the daemon before the full sacrifice was complete – or else it might take more than Urkanthos had willingly given.

When he had made the pact with it, it had wanted his soul. When he refused it that, it had wanted his body. But he was no second-born, making his body a tabernacle to a foreign daemon. Urkanthos was too cunning for that – he did not want to host a daemon, he wanted to ascend to daemonhood.

But he had to give it something. Something connected to him. A thing that, while it was not part of him, was inextricably his.

'Artesia Gore-mouth,' Urkanthos said. And the name brought with it the taste of iron. 'There is work to be done. Cadia lies open to us.'

Urkanthos steeled himself before turning towards it. Even after a decade, it felt *wrong*.

The sodium lighting threw his shadow stark on the bulkhead before him, sharp and dark. A perfect silhouette.

Apart from the mouth.

Where his mouth would have been was a grinning gash, a flowing trickle of blood running from it where it said: *'Cadia. We have heard. Abaddon's desire finally fulfilled.'*

The voice enraptured and repelled him. It was female, or at least presented itself as such, though Urkanthos was too canny to trust in what shape it took. Ragged lips, like the edges of a saw-wound, pursed as if offering him a kiss.

'Your desire too, the red desire.'

The bloody mouth smiled so wide it reached the edges of his helmet's shadow. As it did, more vitae splattered out onto the decking. *'The True Gods will not allow it. As the bearer of the Mark, Abaddon stands at the centre of the Great Game. Each god wants him, yet also cannot let the others have him. None wish him to succeed without their help, and he refuses to pledge to one.'*

'The Warmaster intends to use the fortress to destroy Cadia, denying the gods a victory. But should Khorne deliver Cadia for the Black Legion, Abaddon would be indebted. It would tip the table of the Great Game. It is our best chance. But I will need power. *Much* more power.'

'Offer me your body. Sacrifice more than this thin shadow and I can deliver all you wish. Joined together, I can make blood taste unto you like wine. Your lips will know Cadian from Valhallan by the bloom of its flavours.'

'You speak as though I were a Slaaneshi devotee, enthralled by my senses.' Urkanthos turned, the joints of his semi-organic armour squelching on the sheets of gore that had begun to curdle and go tacky. With his last victim fallen, he could feel the Nails beginning to bite again, like pointed screws turning behind his eyes. 'Blood is blood. And Khorne does not care from whence it flows.'

'Wrong, my liege, all blood is not equal. Sanctified blood, that Khorne loves above all. If you let me into your mouth, your nose, your eyes, I could show you...'

'Enough! You are goading me. Persist and you will be banished.'

'I could offer you so much.'

'Let us discuss what I can offer you, Gore-mouth. You are a bloody shade, tempted and bound, and that's all you will be.'

The entrapped daemon gave a wet, purring growl. Spine teeth, like those of a deep-sea fish, unfolded from the red gash.

'But the bigger the man, the bigger his shadow.'

He stepped away from the wall, backing up to the lights behind him, growing his silhouette large as a Dreadnought.

He could sense her stretching her spirit, luxuriating in the widened pool of darkness.

'Would you rather be the shadow of a warlord' – he paused – 'or a prince of daemons?'

She laughed, like a man gurgling on his last breath. *'What shall we do? You have already gained the notice of Khorne.'*

'To win Cadia, I can be no mere mortal – tell your fellow shades that. Keen the crimson chorus when I reave through the Cadians. Call the bloodletters to feast, and draw the eye of our master. Let him know that if he gives me the power, I will deliver him the Black Legion.'

'It will take a great sacrifice to elevate you, Urkanthos. And Khorne will not be pleased if this... noctilith monstrosity does the red work for you.'

'Then,' said Urkanthos, 'we will have to ensure it does not.'

* * *

Humming, vibrating, *singing.* That's what the fortress was doing. *Singing.*

Morkath felt it deep in her blackstone-sheathed bones. One day out from Cadia, the weapons systems were awakening. Arcane energies in the depths of the fortress cycled into vibrancy. Not the portions she had tamed for the Warmaster – the crewed section with its stretched webs of flesh and tumorous growths. No, there the intelligence of the fortress was soporific, as if drugged. This resonance came from down deep in the wild fortress, where ancient corridors twisted and realigned like dreaming serpents. Where Morkath could place her hand against the wall and feel it thrumming with sentience that was not sentience.

The parts of the fortress she had spent her entire, unnaturally extended life trying to comprehend. For her Warmaster, for her father.

They were all in the council chamber, paying a final homage to their master, filling the stale air with their manifested thoughts.

Korda, with his calligraphic plotting, today spooling tight with tension. Skyrak, surrounded by his noxious psychic cloud. Krom Gat, the wheels running in forward and reverse, like spool-tape on a machine, replaying his argument for leading the assault on Cadia over and over in his mind. Urkanthos, his thoughts different today, as if each splash of blood were tainted by drops of ink twisting and diffusing amidst the red.

Only Zaraphiston was absent – perhaps in study or communion with the warp.

'Within a day, we shall approach Cadia,' rumbled the Warmaster. 'And the first phase will begin. You have all been following at my heels like hounds, asking me for your roles, and now you will have them.'

Korda's mental brush paused, the gears in Krom Gat's mind ceased turning. Skyrak's cloud of worry thickened until Morkath could barely see him.

'Urkanthos,' said the Warmaster. 'I am relieving you of fleet command.'

'But, Warmaster...'

'I will command the Black Fleet. You will strike ahead with a demi-fleet and storm the orbital defence platforms above Cadia. I do not wish this station damaged as it prepares to fire.'

Morkath could see the dark ink spreading in his thoughts. He did not like this duty, and they did not expect him to.

'It will be done, Warmaster.'

'Korda.' The Warmaster's head turned only slightly, fixing the Slaaneshi with his eyes. 'You–'

Morkath knew what the Warmaster was to say next. She could see it forming in his orderly mind. He would task Devram Korda with surrounding the stranded forces once the fortress cities were destroyed, Skyrak with unleashing plagues on the scattered defenders – and most crucially, order Krom Gat to use his warp engines to demolish the pylons.

But he did not get the chance.

The blackstone doors flew open, a psychic blast punching through them like a gale and slamming them back on their hinges. Zaraphiston, the winds of the warp swirling about him, strode into the chamber. For a moment Morkath saw his consciousness at work – wheels of runes and sigils, ever-turning and shifting. Deep in his hood, his eyes burned with witchfire.

'They come,' he said, in a multitude of voices. 'A battle-barge, driving straight for the *Will of Eternity*. Escorts have engaged, but it has diverted all power to its void fields and engines.'

'Estimated interception time?' asked the Warmaster.

'Forty minutes. I see souls aboard. Warriors. Stinking of fear and rage. The prow has Fenrisian runes.'

'Warmaster,' said Urkanthos. 'Let me engage them. They will attempt to board us. I can meet their boarding parties with my Hounds.'

'No.'

'Then what are we supposed to do?'

'*You* are supposed to do nothing,' growled the Warmaster. 'Except what I have ordered.'

'And the Wolves?' asked Zaraphiston.

For a moment, the Warmaster said nothing. Morkath worried the council would consider it a moment of indecision, but from his mental orbits, she knew he was calculating.

'I was once a Wolf,' he answered. 'And I know how to make them howl.'

'Assault boats! Ten minutes!' roared the Space Wolf, as he stalked through the troopers milling on the hangar deck. 'Ten minutes, warriors of Cadia!'

'Throne, he's loud,' whispered Vemmis, shaking his head and cinching his helmet tighter.

Sark knew what he meant. Despite the protective ear caps of her helmet, the auditory assault of his voice was almost painful.

They were prepping gear, settling packs and testing stablights. Fiddling with the gold-tinged goggles fixed to their helmets – meant to prevent blindness in the intense light of zero-atmosphere.

Down the hangar, machine-priests sang binharic hymns over a skitarii complement, pouring noxious emission-incense from pipes sprouting from their backs.

Space Marines assembled in squads throughout the chamber, performing pre-battle rituals. The idea was that if the demigods spread out among the ten assault boats, one destroyed craft would not kill the entire force.

The deck shuddered beneath them. Soft, at first, then hard enough to rattle their teeth.

Sark dropped a cartridge she was trying to force into the shot-gun's loading port.

'Damned thing. Don't know why I couldn't just have my frek-king lasgun.'

'It's a boarding action, we're going to get close,' said Vemmis. 'Talk to the grenadiers, they were only allowed to bring flechette rounds for their launchers.'

The deck under them lurched hard enough Sark had to grab the sleeve of Vemmis' tunic for support.

'Was that a hit?' she asked. She'd never been in a void war, and the claustrophobia of it didn't suit her. 'Are we taking fire?'

Vemmis shook his head. Before transferring to the 13th he'd done two years in Battlefleet Cadia. 'No, that's *us* firing. The big bang like a low-speed vehicle crash? That's a full broadside. Those ones that start with a low rumble then get violent are a plasma projector battery.'

'What's getting hit like, then?'

'You'll know it.'

The decking jumped up at them with a sound like a sledge-hammer striking a tank glacis, folding Sark's legs at the knee and sending Vemmis sprawling onto his face.

The primary lights went out, replaced by red emergency floods. Sark and her squad scrambled to get to their feet, the goggles making them clumsy in the low light.

'*That* was a hit,' Vemmis said. He reached a hand up, and Sark hauled him to his feet, shocked by the sheer dead weight of the promethium-gelatine in his flamer tanks.

'On your feet!' Sergeant Kvec called. 'Zeta Squad! Line up and prepare to board. No loaded weapons until you get in the boat. That means you, Sark.'

She stopped loading the shotgun – no harm in having a few in the tube – and shuffled up into position. She put a hand on Vemmis' shoulder and took a fistful of his uniform blouse. Felt the man behind do the same for her.

Yellow dome lights on the bulkhead hatch spun, throwing splashes of amber across their faces. Sirens whooped.

She kissed her fingers and pressed them to the picture of Saint Gerstahl.

'Rebreathers, up!'

Sark fumbled her rebreather up from around her neck and fastened it over her mouth. Punched it active and felt it suck to her face, sealing with her helmet and goggles. She drew her first heavy breath, tasting the rubbarine tinge in the recycled air.

'You're damned lucky,' said Kvec through the squad comm-bead. 'You're some of the only Cadians alive to ride to combat in an Astartes battle-barge.'

Ahead, the bulkhead hatches retracted into the floor, the atmosphere change between the two compartments washing them with a twisting cloud of fog as the warm hangar met the chill of the void-adjacent flight deck.

Their compartment held two Shark assault boats and a Caestus assault ram. Sark felt a prickle of fear as she looked at the dagger-like craft, knowing their thin hulls would be the only thing separating her from the icy void.

Another hit, knocking her helmet against Vemmis' tanks. She heard a murmur in her vox and realised someone had forgotten to mute and was praying.

'Emperor of Man, overseer of all things right,

Whose powers none can resist,

Save and deliver us…'

She was about to join in when the voice came across the hangar's auditory hailers, booming through the cavernous space over the crowds of milling Guardsmen, skitarii and demigod Space Marines.

'*Angels of the Emperor, soldiers of Cadia and servants of the Machine God, hear me! I am Jarl Sven Bloodhowl, of the Firehowlers.*'

A scatter of keening howls answered, as the Space Wolves made their enthusiasm known.

'*Today, my warriors, we sail into the songs. We shall be swallowed by the dread beast and cut our way through to its belly. A deed so valorous, it will be a thing of sagas. A tale told at fires.*'

Cheers greeted that. They began to shuffle towards the boats. Sark looked over her shoulder and saw Bloodhowl – she supposed it was Bloodhowl – standing on a stack of Munitorum containers with a vox-unit in hand, so the crowd could make him out.

'*Within moments, brothers, we...*'

'Ah, Throne!' Vemmis said.

'Something wrong?' That was Kvec.

'My teeth, they hurt. And my sinuses...'

All at once Sark felt it. The molars she'd had filled last year, coming alive as if they were being drilled all over again. An enormous pressure in her head.

Something tickled her under the chin, just below the rebreather, and with her free hand she tried to sweep it away.

She realised it was her own identity-tags, floating.

Was the flight deck low-gravity?

'*Unlike any venture before this,*' Bloodhowl continued, '*we serve together, strive together...*'

The laud-hailers went to static. Half of them blew, like the synchronous *boom* of a hundred war drums struck at once.

'Vemmis, is this normal?'

Pain in her finger. She let go of Vemmis' sleeve. Saw a jumping spark of static electricity flash as she let go.

'Up there,' Kvec said. 'Clouds.'

She saw Bloodhowl looking towards the vault of the hangar

ceiling before she looked up herself, at first confused by the growing pool of shadows above.

It was a thunder-cloud, roiling and spreading. Each tendril twisting out in a spiral like a hurricane, with arcs of purple lightning jumping from end to end.

Then with an intensity that might have flash-blinded her if not for the goggles, a pillar of electric fire slammed down to the deck. It fried troops where it landed, sending bolts of writhing warp-infused lightning chaining out into the tight-packed assault force.

Around the chamber, what laud-hailers remained began to wail with a chorus of the damned, the voices of things that clawed at ships' hulls and pressed at Geller fields when they crossed the empyrean.

But more terrifying was the being that emerged from the torrent of electric warpfire – no, it was *formed* of the electricity, coming into being amongst them with its black armour still glowing with corposant flame even as the massive gauntlet spat a stream of glowing rounds into the packed ranks.

She saw the power claw twice the span of a man's shoulders. The sword long as an autocannon. A face that had leered in the nightmares of every Cadian child.

They were supposed to be attacking the Despoiler.

But the Despoiler had come to *them*.

Sven Bloodhowl stood atop the crag of ammunition containers he'd climbed to address his sword-brothers. Noble was he in aspect, and fierce in mind.

And from this place aloft, standing above the heads of his war-host, did he see the arch-foe come out of the lightning. He came like a grim from the tales told on solstice night. Tales where the skjald must bite his own tongue after telling them, or risk attracting the hate which he has just invoked by speaking its name.

Ezekyle Abaddon. Warlord of the Eye. Carving the air with a sword that howled for souls.

His witchfire killed nigh a hundred men. Bones seared black. Blood turned to ash. Those behind fell to pieces at the wide arc of fire from his gauntlet. A weapon that had pierced the heart of Sanguinius and half-slain the Emperor now slew Bloodhowl's band.

On each side stood two Havocs, reaper chaincannons cycling. When they spoke, tongues of flame jetted three feet from their barrels. They earned their name that day, the reapers. For the tight-packed forces of the Emperor stood like a grain field ripe for the harvest, and they fell in great deltas of blood and ruin with each sweeping burst of the guns.

Noble Bloodhowl roared his fury and fired his bolt pistol at the foes, but it was naught but his pride speaking. The range was too long, and he could already see the folly in firing back.

Guardsmen and skitarii had been instructed, by him no less, not to load their weapons until boarding the void craft. And so Bloodhowl saw Cadians raise empty lasguns and be sliced down. Machine-soldiers worked at speed to toggle their devastating but stubborn weapons into function. Only the Adeptus Astartes fired back – but the crowd was so thick the bolter shells killed their own before they ever reached the Warmaster. Shots exploded amid flee-ing Guardsmen and knocked away steel craniums. Even those flying true appeared to turn aside rather than hit Abaddon – like snow flying with a change of wind.

The arch-foe waded into those still alive, stepping over the broken corpses already cut down.

Bloodhowl saw a Blood Claw of his pack strike at Abaddon with a chainsword. The Warmaster caught the blade with the Talon, snapped it, then tore away the arm that wielded the weapon. Half the Blood Claw's ribcage came with it.

Hakkondir, the man had been called. Bloodhowl would remember his name. Brave Hakkondir, challenging the Master of the Black Legion.

Transfixed, Bloodhowl was, in awe and astonishment. Abaddon cut into the press, and a dozen died. Even those two feet from the tip of the blade split in half with the violent shock of its passage through air. As though the spirit of the sword carried forth from its length and could cut on its own.

And then he beheld the boldest warrior of all.

A Cadian, a human woman, with a painting of a saint on the back of her helm.

She walked towards the Despoiler, firing a crude mechanical pump gun.

Firing, racking. Firing, racking.

Shouldering away troops who tried to run past her, holding the weapon high so as to not hit anyone when she fired.

She stepped into the gore-slick fan of violence the Warmaster and his Havocs had created, exiting the wall of fleeing men, and raised her shotgun directly at the face of a foe ten thousand years old.

She fired. And incredibly the scattershot did not turn aside but scored the Despoiler's armour. A bright crimson line marked his cheek.

She racked, fired again.

Nothing happened. She appeared to be pushing the pump-action of the weapon. It would not move.

Astartes, it was said, knew no fear.

Neither did this woman, this Cadian, as the ancient foe cut her through the shoulder with his writhing sword, carving her from neck to hip so she fell away in two pieces.

Even greater than the Blood Claw's death did this rile Bloodhowl. To see such heroism slain with one disdainful sweep could not go unanswered, and he keyed the jets of his jump pack.

Yet as he rose, a hand clamped his pauldron.

'My jarl,' spoke Kregga Longtooth, oldest of his Bloodguard and the wisest of his council. 'He attacks because he fears our purpose. They sacrifice themselves so we can continue.'

A Skyclaw pack leaped into the air, their contrails all twisting and engines aglow, the promise of glory on their lips. The Havocs diced them in the air with their chainguns, bullets the size of his gauntleted finger shattering the bodies of his warriors so they fell to the deck as carcasses of meat and metal.

Only one reached Abaddon. The arch-heretic impaled the incoming Skyclaw on his great sword, before ripping the body off with the Talon and throwing it aside. Then he whirled to meet the Blood Claws, smashing into them with his broad shoulder pauldron and sweeping low, severing five legs with a single strike.

'Leave them to their *wyrd*,' Longtooth said. 'Do not let them be slain for nothing.'

Bloodhowl cut his jump engines. Dropped to his ceramite boots.

'Assault boats!' he bellowed. 'Get in the assault boats! Do not fight them. All who survive, alight to the Blackstone Fortress!'

He leapt down among the crowd. Grabbed a running Guardsman with flamer tanks and shoved him towards the transports.

'Board and fire engines! With haste!'

Already two assault boats had lifted. One in panic, its front hatch still open. Those inside scrambled to find a manual override before they breached the hangar and died in the void.

Sven Bloodhowl had never run from a fight. He walked instead, shouting, encouraging, letting it be seen that he himself stepped onto one of the assault boats and held the door for those that were close enough.

More wanted to get on the ship than could be taken. Behind their matt-green helmets, he could see the hulking shoulders and trophy rack of Abaddon approaching, sword keening an unholy hymn from its multitudinous mouths, crimson light bathing his face from within the armour.

Then Bloodhowl seized the hatch's interior handle and closed it, yelling over the protesting moan of its stressed hydraulics that it was time to be away.

As they lifted, the Wolf Lord got a glimpse of Ezekyle Abaddon in the thick of the fight. Death in armour. Daemonic energies boiling about him. Cutting the life-threads of every mortal who came close. Engaging nine Astartes at once, from Chapters so mixed there was not two among them with the same heraldry.

One he killed with his daemon blade.

Another he speared through with Horus' talons, then blew the body off with the gauntlet's bolter.

On his left, a Blood Claw with a revving chainsword stepped in past the probing tip of his twelve-foot sword and its sea of faces. For a bare instant it looked as though the young Firehowler might land a blow destined to be chanted of in the sagas, but the Despoiler punched forward with the hilt of his weapon and rammed the barbed handguard through the Blood Claw's cranium like an awl.

When Abaddon swept the sword sideways to parry another blow, he ripped the Blood Claw's head from his neck with a tearing of flesh and stretching of tendons.

And in looking, Bloodhowl kenned a truth he had never known before.

This galaxy was full of those who called themselves warmasters. But this, this was a true master of war.

The Astartes stood firm, but their blades broke on him, and he murdered them like livestock before the column of lightning slammed down around him once again, and he was gone.

Yet he must have left something behind. For as the assault boat broke shipboard atmosphere and banked around on its heading, the flight deck of the hangar bay exploded into space with an expanding ball of flame that caused Bloodhowl to think of naught but the Fire Breather, the great wolf-mawed volcano on Fenris.

He touched his pauldron, putting fingers to the heraldic device of the mountain he carried on his shoulder.

'You go as Firehowlers must, brothers – in flames.'

And he knew, as his craft zipped towards the hulking darkness of the Blackstone Fortress, that he would soon join them.

EIGHT

Urkanthos could see Cadia.

A small blue dot glowing amongst the wreckage of Naval engagements, no bigger than the iris of a terrified man.

'Scan for incoming threats,' he ordered. 'If the strike fleet will have opposition, I want to know.'

He was in an ill temper, despite the homecoming.

Part of him rejoiced to be back on the bridge of the *Atrocity*. The Desecrator-class battleship had served as his home, chapel and personal vessel since the Gothic War.

Yet when he boarded, he was no longer hailed as Lord Ravager.

'Lord,' said a flayed man, cables interknit with his shining, exposed muscles. 'I sense a ship incoming. Fast.'

'From Cadia?'

'No, lord,' the sensor operator said. His back muscles contracted as he took in more data, experiencing feedback from the ship's beam array as if it were from his own nervous system. 'Approaching from spinward. Escort size. Aft-port quadrant, one-hundred-sixty degrees at minus thirty void-fathoms. Coming up under us in three minutes.'

'Three minutes?' Urkanthos checked the chart. 'Not possible. That is far too fast. Give me speed and ship composition. Identify it.

Weapons station, give me a firing solution. Tell the starboard hangar bay to prep squadrons Agony and Barbarius to launch as a screen.'

The sensorman's red lips trembled at being asked to do more. 'Calculating.'

Urkanthos didn't like it. He had already been through one ambush, an Imperial demi-fleet that had jumped their spearhead when they passed through the outer belt of floating void-wreckage that cut through the Cadian System. A graveyard of shipwrecks and debris, formed throughout millennia of the Long War, which was ideal for hiding a fleet.

The Iron Graveyard, the Cadians called it.

The desperate Imperials had damaged or destroyed just under ten per cent of his force, but that meant little – Abaddon's naval doctrine was to keep the junk-ships, cultist transports and armed inter-system clippers as an outer screen to cushion any blow.

They had lost vessels, but none they could not afford to lose. Urkanthos had not even stopped. Abaddon could deal with it in his following fleet, Urkanthos' destiny lay on Cadia.

Yet given the Cadians' fanaticism, he would not put it past them to deploy meltdown-ships. Strip an old craft down and run it into the fleet, then redline the reactor to take a few vessels with them.

Savages.

'I...' said the sensorman. His lidless eyes flicked back and forth, unsure.

'What? Keep me waiting, you'll be down to bones.'

'Composition is unknown metal. Faster than any Imperial vessel. Xenos, but not aeldari. It is... noctilith.'

'Blackstone?'

'Our spectromantic sensor bombardment has returned a density suggesting some blackstone, yes.' The sensorman swallowed, the Adam's apple bobbing in his meaty throat. 'It has noctilith aboard, or in its composition. Yet I sense no souls aboard.'

Urkanthos put his clawed gauntlets on the command rail and smiled beneath his grimacing mask. He had been on the raiding fleets in the tenth raid of the Long War. Landed on the worlds they'd scoured to capture research samples of the noctilith and tear down every edifice made from it. Knew how the Black Legion sorcerers hated the thrumming charge of the stone's negative energy.

And he'd seen the glyphs on the temples there, the interlocking lines, circles and angles of an antique race. An artificial race that, while dead, still walked. A race without souls.

'It is xenos,' he said. 'A vessel of the undying legions.'

'I have a firing solution,' burbled a weapons officer, his physical body long since liquefied until it was nothing but pink froth that filled his void-suit, animated by spirit and bubbling in his helmet as he spoke. 'Standing by for order.'

Abaddon wanted to destroy the pylons, worrying they would disrupt the warp cannon. After he'd returned from his raid, the Warmaster had tasked Krom Gat with demolishing the fields of null-stone, lest the servants of the False Emperor discover how to amplify their warp-nullifying effects.

Knowledge the Imperials did not possess, but a xenos might.

Khorne will not be pleased if this… noctilith monstrosity does the red work for you.

Urkanthos did not know if the whisper came from his memory, or the tall shadow that stretched out before him. He was increasingly unsure.

But if the fortress failed, it would be a ground invasion. Invasion meant bloodshed. And flowing blood filled the cup of power.

'Let it go,' he said.

'Lord?' questioned the sensorman.

'The Warmaster has given us narrow orders,' said Urkanthos. 'We are not cleared to engage xenos vessels. Should we risk pulling new forces into this war? I think not.'

Urkanthos watched the dart of the vessel pass beneath them in a streaking meteoric line, a needle heading towards the blue iris of Cadia.

Do your work well, little dead thing, he thought.

Behind his shoulder, he could hear Gore-mouth give a wet laugh.

'Another checkpoint? Are you joking?'

Munitorum-Sergeant Lazlo Kennik had just about had it with this groxshit. Ever since that big send-off at the lift-fields that morning, the streets had been a mess. Normal traffic, yes, but heretic insurgents had also detonated two body-bombs in the press of troops, and now the streets were full of provosts conducting vehicle searches and diverting traffic.

All of them officious badge-polishers like this provost-sergeant.

'We're on special assignment,' Kennik said, speaking into the vox-speaker set into the window. 'No stops, no searches. High-value cargo. Let us through.'

He thumped a fist against the inside of his Taurox's armaglass windscreen, where the passes were secured in a plastek sleeve.

'No good,' the sergeant said. His voice came in thin through the bulky unit. 'Archenemy bombed the street ahead. Weakened the roadway, no heavy vehicles. You need to divert.'

He stepped back and stretched one arm out left, waving in circles with the other arm indicating they should turn.

Throne, Kennik hated provosts.

But their armoured Taurox was heavy, even though it was a lighter Munitorum model built for traversing city streets, with armaglass cab windows and tyres rather than tracks.

'Frekk… What do you think?' Kennik asked, twisting around to look at his security in the cargo bay.

Virdenze looked out the starboard firing slit, his shotgun cradled in his hands. 'We're behind schedule already, sarge, I don't want to get flogged when we get to the mint.'

'Just take the diversion,' said Tavon, from the opposite side of the crew bay, shotgun across his knees. 'We don't want to fall through the frekking street.'

Ahead of him, a heavy Munitorum cab-hauler made a reluctant turn.

Kennik sighed and waved an acknowledgement, backed up slightly to gain turn clearance, then executed a wide left turn to follow the hauler down the street.

'Aw frekk,' he moaned.

'What?'

'It's a funnel street.'

Funnels were traps for the enemy. Trick streets that were twice as wide at one end than they were on the other, so attackers were mashed together as they advanced, and vehicles had little room to manoeuvre. Already there wasn't enough clearance for the hauler ahead to open its doors, and Kennik was fast running out of room himself.

Behind him, another hauler pulled in.

'Frekking perfect. Idiots. One of these haulers gets wedged and we'll all be stuck.'

'I've got a bad fe–'

Kennik heard the rev of acceleration behind him right before the jolting impact. A hit that wasn't hard enough to do more than throw him into his harness as the Taurox rocked forward into the bumper of the lead hauler.

'Shit!' he yelled, working the gear shift. 'Crazy sons of–'

Then the roll door of the hauler ahead came up, and Kennik knew he was in trouble.

The gunman inside wore mismatched Cadian fatigues, as did the two on either side training lasguns at his windscreen.

But it was the central figure that kept Kennik's attention, because of what he carried. The gunman stepped from the hauler's bed onto the hood of the pinned Taurox, and thumped his weapon's vented barrel on Kennik's windscreen.

Knock, knock, knock.

Kennik raised his hands off the steering wheel.

'I'm disengaging the hatch lock,' he said.

'The hells, sarge?'

'You want to argue with this meltagun?' he said, reaching for the hatch release.

Virdenze and Tavon heard the lock disengage, and raised their shotguns. Throne, but they'd at least take one or two with them.

But the double doors of the rear hatch cracked only wide enough for a hand to throw in the gas grenade.

One minute later, after Karle Petzen had executed the last crewman with his silenced stubber and flushed the cab's ventilation, Salvar Ghent ducked into the Taurox, a rebreather clamped to his mouth.

No sense being careless.

'Locker key?' Ghent asked.

'Here,' said one shooter, tearing a fob off one body and tossing it across the cab. Ghent caught it and threaded it into the lock of the safe affixed to the floor.

'Roadblock worked,' observed Petzen, as he dragged the driver's slumping corpse from behind the wheel. 'Thought we might have to push harder.'

'That's what's great about Cadia,' Ghent answered. 'Everyone follows orders.'

'We get them?' asked Petzen.

Ghent opened the safe to reveal three cylinders of heavy industrial steel etched with document negatives. He checked the values: fifty per cent, seventy per cent and ninety per cent ration cards.

'We're back in the printing business, friends,' said Ghent. 'Karle, get us off the street.'

Petzen was already putting the Taurox into gear.

As he drove, he used a pocket kerchief to wipe the Munitorum-sergeant's blood off the windscreen.

NINE

'They shouldn't have done it,' said Darvus, 'Stetzen RO is our airfield, they had no right.'

'That's how it goes, Lahon.'

Hanna Keztral checked her flight plan, made a course adjustment to keep them on true. Eased back on their airspeed, the craggy foothills of the Rossvar Mountains slipping beneath them. 'You know how it is. They needed a table, we were nearly done, they bumped us. Combat pilots get priority seating in the mess, it's tradition.'

'*We're* combat pilots.' Darvus chambered his rear-facing heavy stubber for emphasis. 'We're armed. We take fire. *Deadeye* is a frekking Avenger. A noble machine. Not a glorified ferry service like a Valkyrie. Unarmed support pilots, my arse.'

The Valk pilots had been from the Howling 119th, and Keztral still remembered the face their captain had made when Darvus retorted that their Avenger mounted a weapon.

'*A defensive weapon,*' he'd sneered.

'Don't let it get to you. Time to target?'

'Eh.' She heard the shuffle of maps and rasp of a flight calculator's card-paper wheel. 'Ninety-three minutes.'

'Okay.'

'It just chaffs me, is all. Stetzen RO is our place. Can't they read?

R-O. Reconnaissance and Observation. They're guests. Hells, the Navy flyers treat us better, and they're not even Cadians. That doesn't bother you?'

'I'm just trying to enjoy the flight, Lay.' Keztral shifted, trying to relieve the nerve pain in her right buttock. They'd been up an hour, their fourth flight in the last two days. 'This might be the last clear day we get. Don't let the Howling Arseholes ruin it.'

'True,' he said, laughing. 'I'll shut up now.'

That was the way with them. Keztral thinking, Darvus speaking. Part of it was their respective roles. As armament operator, Darvus didn't have much to do until they got to the target, and tended to fill the time by talking. Part of it was the privacy of the aircraft, which was one of the only places you could speak on Cadia without being in earshot of a superior officer.

But there was a mystical part, too. A sort of mind-connection. Because Darvus had been right. It *did* bother her. The whole thing. The way the Valk pilots had swaggered into their mess like they'd inherited it from a rich uncle. How the captain had spoken to them. The fact that Kraf Air Command had opened Stetzen to the Valks and the Navy flyers, so they had to jostle for hangar space and ground crews. It had been deadly, too. A flight of observation Valks from the 89th had come back from a long patrol the other day, only to find traffic on the runway so stacked up they'd run out of fuel before getting their shot at the landing pad. One poor crew had their engines cut while waiting, and the Valk had fallen three hundred feet directly on its chin.

Only the crew chief survived, and he'd been taken away rip-taped to a spineboard with bones poking through both shins.

But Keztral wasn't the type to complain. Which was fortunate, because Darvus had a dead-on knack for voicing the frustrations she tried to push to the back of her mind. A thing he mostly did when they were in the privacy of the open sky.

Given that they flew back to back, facing different directions and unable to see each other, it often felt like he was her subconscious as well as her armament operator.

'It is beautiful up here today,' said Darvus. 'Visibility's great for the rig.'

Keztral clicked her helmet mic once to acknowledge. They were at eighteen thousand feet and steady, blue skies for miles with little wisps of cirrus clouds on the horizon. One of the best flying days of her life, which is why she'd wanted Darvus to shut up.

They'd taken off from Stetzen without much waiting, streaking out past Kraf's northern defensive wall. Keztral had kept it low as they passed by the outwall habs of Salgorah – the illegal slumtown outside the defensive wall where she'd spent her childhood. With a ten-knot wind, hab-kids were on the rooftops, flying kites made from plastek ration wrappers and skewer sticks from unlicensed food carts. They were low enough to see a few of the kites dancing and circling – they were war kites, their strings coated with glue and broken glass to cut the lines or rip the plastek skins of their rivals.

She executed a slow barrel roll as she passed, so they knew who she was. She'd been the district kite-war champion at age ten when the recruiters had come and offered her a place in the aviation academy. Some general had seen vid-clips of the tournament, and was impressed by her natural command of aerodynamics.

Every few months, some of the kids at the missionary-run academy there would send her mail. She'd post back a thank-you, along with a box of combat-fired bullet casings for the cadets to use as good luck charms.

They'd made their turn north, then west, briefly glimpsing the defences of the inner Beta Curtain Wall. Gained altitude to avoid the howling wind shears that knifed through the Rossvar Mountains, passing above the snow-capped peaks as the gales tore great plumes of ice crystals off their summits. Fan-tails of snow, sparkling in the air.

'Gorgeous,' she said, even though it'd been three minutes since Darvus last spoke. 'Cadia feels worth fighting for today, doesn't it?'

'Feels like that every day, the commissar tells m–'

Keztral cut him off. 'Target. Target. Target.'

'What? Where?'

'Port-forward quadrant. Ten o'clock. About twelve miles out. Are those ours? A few units were coming back through the pass to reinforce Kraf, right?'

'They were.' Maps crinkled. 'No. No. That shouldn't be them. That was the Twenty-Second Armoured, they'd be kicking a bigger dust trail.'

'How long are we from hitting target area?'

'Sixty-seven minutes.'

'Is that the Archenemy column we're supposed to pict? How the hells did they get so close?'

'You want to go in?'

'Affirmative. Prime the pict-rig.'

'You sure? If we waste two spools of film on one of our own, the squadron commander...'

'Whoever the frekk they are, they're not supposed to be there. Even if it's one of ours high command will want to know where they are. If they're friendly, they're lost and disoriented or maybe erroneously marked as destroyed. If they're ours maybe the Valks at Stetzen can lift them out, get them behind the walls of Kraf.'

Keztral stood *Deadeye* nearly on one wing, rolling over before straightening out on a shallow descent towards the column of troops.

'Copy, priming the spools. You want the wing vid-picters as well?'

'Yep. We're eating the whole grox today, nose to tail.'

They grunted together, both feeling the G-forces of the turn and dive. Dropping altitude fast, gaining speed.

Keztral cut perpendicular to the column, leading it to the rear so she could bank around in a quick dive along its length. The sun, a muted ball of fire through her tinted visor, slid from one side of her canopy to the other. Friend or foe, she guessed the column was heading towards the mountains, and it'd be better to swoop down on it from the rear and get the element of surprise. Angle it right, and she'd come down out of the afternoon sun.

'Armament out,' she said.

A clunk beneath her, so big she could feel it through the pedals. The picter rig dropping beneath the nose.

'Run out, affirmative.'

An air pocket jarred them, rattling their teeth.

'Throne! Watch it, the lenses! Can we slow it down?'

'Sorry! No cloud cover up here today, got to do it fast before they spot us.'

The column, like a line of marching insects, ripped by their right-hand side. Keztral kicked up the speed, hurtling away from the troops before banking around to line up on them. She nudged the stick left and right, the black column of men and vehicles slipping from side to side in her canopy before the dust cloud of troops moving en masse settled into the midline of the Avenger's nose.

She treated the column as if she were approaching a runway – though no one in their right mind would approach a runway this steep, or this fast.

'Test cycle,' said Darvus.

A churning *thunk-thunk-thunk* tapped the base of Keztral's seat. She could feel it in her aching sciatic nerve.

'Looking goo– *Agg.*'

Darvus swallowed the word. The Gs were getting to him.

Hard dive, world rushing up to meet them.

A thousand miles per hour.

'Six seconds to target,' she grunted.

Eleven hundred miles.

Altimeter dropping.

Keztral felt the weight on her chest, heavy, like a body were lying on her.

'Five... seconds.'

Lock tone. Blaring alarms. Red lights on her instrument panel. A hunter-killer missile rushed past, their speed too much for its tracking system.

'Four,' she choked, vision tunnelling. Peripherals getting dark.

Eight hundred feet.

The wings groaned. Keztral eased back for fear of ripping them off.

Orange tracers zipped over them in lashing ropes. Too high. They were going fast, hard to lead. Flak detonations sounded behind, a clack as shrapnel hit their right wing. It stuck there, glowing like a coal.

Two hundred feet.

'Three, levelling.'

She hauled back on the stick, the pressure on her easing, making her feel drunk and weightless. Sucked a deep breath of air.

Then punched the ramjet. The blast of acceleration slammed her back into her chair hard enough to knock half a breath from her lungs.

'Two,' she shouted over the sound of gunfire.

They were level, the column racing up, disappearing below the lip of her canopy, into her blind spot.

'Cycling. Priming picter. Lenses open.'

'One.'

'Target acquired. Firing, firing, firing.'

Keztral felt the buzz through the cockpit, the clunk-zip of the lenses spinning like a rotary cannon.

She clenched her teeth, willing her hands to keep it steady.

Tracers everywhere. A sleet-like gale of them. Orange. Pink. Bright white streaks of plasma and crimson beams of multi-laser fire.

A sparkling yellow hornet arced directly into her vision and Keztral instinctively ducked to one side.

Whap.

It connected like a loose stone thrown into a groundcar's windscreen. Left a spiderweb pockmark the size of a thumbprint in her forward canopy.

Heavy stubber round. The column was firing everything they had.

'We might have to break.'

'Halfway there,' said Darvus. 'Hold on.'

A krak missile rushed up through her vision diagonally, leaving a gauzy trail that washed over the cockpit as they sped through it. A chorus of pinging impacts – small-arms fire flattening against their armoured underbelly. A lascannon beam knifed across them, so close it scorched a charcoal line across the casing of the starboard engine.

Lock tone.

Keztral slammed her thumb on the stick's fire button and chaff flares tore out around them, spirals of hot white fire intermixed with the reflective confetti of metal sheets. The missile detonated behind, kicking their rear up and dipping them lower as Keztral slewed upward to arrest the dive.

'Almost,' said Darvus, pulling the word out.

Ahead, spark-shells leapt skyward from an armoured vehicle, bursting into clouds of thick crimson. Blooming flowers of smoke wreathed one tank after another, obscuring the column. Foiling the picters.

'They're popping smoke,' Keztral said, slamming the pedals left and banking into the turn. 'We're gone.'

She jammed the accelerator and raced out low, slipping in and out of lock tones as they scrambled towards the cover of the Rossvar Mountains.

'Hey, Hanna?' said Darvus, 'I don't think they were friendly.'

* * *

Kell opened the door and took the briefcase from its Kasrkin escort, keyed the twelve-digit security code into its top and dropped it on a side table.

He kept listening as he removed the intelligence dossier and paged through it.

'It's required by law, you see,' the young priest said. 'To ensure the spiritual health of the leadership, the Lord Castellan must meet with his personal confessor at least twice per monthly cycle.'

'Yes,' Creed grunted. He was scanning a report on the Kasr Halig theatre as he spoke. 'That's what got you in the door. Because the Ecclesiarchy would make an almighty screech if I didn't.'

'So...' The confessor shifted. He was a sleek-looking man, a Cadian with sincere features, whose combat-regulation hairstyle was greying at the temples. 'Do you have anything to confess?'

'I confess,' said Creed, looking up from his report, 'that I have nothing to confess.'

He tossed the report on an ever-growing pile.

'How old are you, Confessor...?'

'Turantius, lord. And I am forty-six.'

'Young for such high office. What are your qualifications?'

'I was dean of practical theology at the Upper Divinity Schola, Kasr Halig Cathedral Complex. I inherited the office after the previous confessor to the Lord Castellan, God-Emperor rest him, was killed when the Volscani attacked Governor Porelska's command Leviathan at Tyrok Fields.'

'Aha,' said Creed. 'And you were next in line.'

Kell looked up to read the priest's body language.

'No, lord, next in line was Archbishop Stokkmas, then Cardinal Loquetho, then Abbot Mannfred Gabel. Sadly they, too, were on the governor's Leviathan.' The man shifted, pulling the hem of his red robes down his crossed legs. 'The office then fell to the most senior member of the faculty at the Upper Divinity Schola – and unfortunately, I am the only faculty member still living.'

Creed seemed amused by this. 'How did you manage that?'

'I was on a lecture tour of the trenches. Speaking on the subject of holding on to spiritual meaning during crisis.' He ignored Creed's bark of laughter. 'It is quite a practicable area of study for soldiers. If you wish, I do believe I could help you.'

'I do believe you can, confessor.' The Lord Castellan stood and drew up close to the priest, leaning in conspiratorially. 'Provided you have the right qualifications.'

'Ah, yes. Yes. What qualifications do you need?'

'Can you do this?' Creed raised his index finger, as if to tell the confessor to be silent. When the man hesitated, he urged: 'Go on.'

Turantius raised his finger, brow furrowed.

'Now go like this.' Creed bent his finger, as if beckoning to the ceiling.

Turantius shadowed, a sheepish smile on his face.

'Good, perfect.' Creed guided the man towards the door, opened it for him. 'Now this man here is Corporal Kacza. Corporal, the confessor has agreed to help us. I want you to take him to the northern citadel battlements and issue him a lasgun.'

Turantius opened his mouth to protest, and Creed thumped him on the chest with an open hand.

'Now listen, confessor. What I need from you is this.' He pointed at the wall, as if indicating the far distance. 'You take that lasgun, and point it out towards the horizon. And when you see the enemy you...'

Creed raised his finger and waggled it.

'But...'

'I don't need prayers. And I don't need practical theology or, Throne save us, a search for meaning. I especially don't need you wasting my time. What I need are bodies on the walls with weapons in their hands.'

He pushed the confessor out.

'God-Emperor be with you,' he said. And closed the door.

'Did you enjoy yourself?' Kell said.

'I think I rather did, yes. What's in the case?'

'We have a problem.'

'*A* problem? You've solved all but one now, have you? You're quite a wonder.'

'Aerial recon detected a heretic column past the western Ross-var, moving south in strength. Analysts are still going over the picts, but by matching banner patterns they've tentatively identified it as the Volscani Forty-Fourth, the Linebreakers. By the picts it looks like they have medium-to-heavy infantry. Cavalry squadrons. Light armour.'

'That's not possible. It's a misidentification. Last we heard the Volscani Forty-Fourth was about to be encircled north of Kasr Vark.'

'That's the thing, it looks like when the Sixty-First Interior were ordered to ditch their vehicles and pull out to Kraf by air, they never destroyed their transports. So the Volscani co-opted their Chimeras and slipped the net.'

Creed put the web of his hand to his brow, then took a breath and massaged his eyes with his fingers. 'They're headed for Kraf?'

'Via the Delvian Cleave.'

'How many?'

'Hard to say. Intelligence says maybe two to three divisions. Twenty-five thousand, maybe thirty?'

'And the Twenty-Fourth Interior has three thousand. Throne. I'd never have sent Barathus there if I'd known he'd get hit in force. Those poor bastards are too green for this.' Creed uncorked a crystal decanter of amasec and poured four fingers' worth. 'We can't spare reinforcements from Kraf. Not with the Astartes and Sororitas leaving us out to dry. And that pass has to remain in our hands, Jarran, *has to.* Can we give them air support? Artillery?'

'Difficult given the terrain. Wind shears in the Rossvar make close air support impractical. Same with artillery. We'd probably hit ours as much as theirs. And there's no flanking the Volscani from behind, either. Those Vark units are committed.'

Creed nodded.

'I thought…' Kell paused. 'I thought you'd like to contact him yourself. Personally. To tell him.'

'Barathus did want a fight,' said Creed, and gestured for his personal vox.

By the time Kell brought the handset, Creed had already drained the tumbler.

Castellan Mordlied felt his pride swell as he looked upon the procession.

Four hooded Chapter-serfs preceded the march, chanting praises to He Who Sits Upon the Throne of Terra. A dirge for a god that had transcended death. Praise for the light that showed the way.

They walked in a cross formation, the one in front carrying a reliquary mounted on a staff: the skull and ribcage of Brother-Saint Deristan inlaid into a golden crusading shield. Those on the wings, the serfs forming the arms of the cross, swung burning censers that spiced the air with synth-myrrh and burning coal. The one at the back held up a crumbling psalter, each page large as a flak jacket's chestplate, open to the 'Hymn of Immaculate Rage'.

On the parapet, the Guardsmen of Cadia parted to let the serfs through. A few made the sign of the aquila, heads bowed. Others recoiled at the odour of mortification and gland-sweat coming off the sinister figures.

They reached the fire-step of the parapet and turned left, walking the perimeter of the rampart. Sanctifying the space where combat would be joined.

The Black Templars came behind, power armour clanking and hissing as they moved. Marshal Amalrich stood in the vanguard with his command squad, Mordlied alongside hoisting the banner of the crusade.

Behind them, the whole strength of the Cruxis Crusade marched in close order, swords drawn and held at guard. The chains that bound their weapons to their gauntlets clattering against ceramite. Unhelmed Initiates walked the flanks, shouting for the lesser men of Cadia to make way. Announcing the names of each battle-brother, and reciting his deeds.

Here comes Lancorion, slayer of xenos.

Look upon Gwitech, who holed a traitor Land Raider with his meltagun.

Gaze, mortal soldiers of Cadia, on those who are vowed to be your salvation, and bring the exquisite wrath of the Most Excellent God-Emperor to your foes.

Amalrich reached the parapet and raised a fist.

The column stopped as one, still as a line of armoured vehicles halted on a road.

Mordlied tried to follow his master's gaze, to discern his thoughts.

The Martyr's Rampart was a triangular ravelin, one of the outlying demi-fortresses in the Kasr Kraf defensive system. Seven storeys high, it lay a mile outside Kraf's outer Alpha Curtain Wall, in the artificially levelled plain meant to serve as a massive kill-zone, where attackers would fall in their millions to the Kraf defensive batteries.

'A question, Brother Mordlied,' the Marshal said, placing one hand on the parapet. He was tall enough that the fire-step was not necessary, and he merely rested one foot upon the rockcrete walkway. 'Why do they call this the Martyr's Rampart?'

Mordlied was not meant to know the answer, but a Marshal could never stoop so far as to speak to a Guardsman.

'You.' Mordlied pointed to a Cadian officer with a gauntleted finger.

Mordlied had picked the man because he seemed self-possessed, but once singled out the human took a step back. 'Why did they deem this the Rampart of Martyrs? Who was martyred here?'

'I...' the man stammered. 'I... I...'

'Do you have a problem with your voice? Are you wounded?'

'No, lord, I–'

'I am not a lord,' corrected Mordlied. 'I am a mere servant of the Emperor. You may address me as honoured brother.'

The Cadian captain swallowed, adjusted his cap. 'Honoured brother. We are not aware of any specific martyr, though Saint Maretcza was said to have fallen in this region.'

Mordlied held his gaze on the captain to show, via his impassive helm, that this was insufficient.

'We, ah, we assume it is figurative,' he added with haste. He swept a hand behind them, at the high walls of the fortress city a mile distant. 'Our duty is to delay the enemy, establish an enfilading crossfire with the other outer bastions, and prevent the traitors establishing artillery batteries within range of the outer curtain wall. But it is assumed we will be surrounded, in which case we are to fire into the enemy's rear as they attack the fortress... until we are overwhelmed. That is why it is the Martyr's Rampart. We are the martyrs.'

Mordlied turned to his Marshal, already seeing the expression of grim approval on his face.

'It will do,' said Marshal Amalrich. 'Plant it.'

Mordlied grasped the banner-pole in two hands, raised it high, and plunged it down – driving it deep into a seam between the rockcrete slabs.

Then he let it go, flying in the wind off the plain, and turned to his brothers.

'We have chosen our ground!' Amalrich shouted, arms raised towards the heavens. 'What shall we defend it till?'

'Till death!' they chanted back, raising swords in the twilight. 'Till death!'

TEN

After twenty-four hours at the Delvian Cleave, Marda Hellsker knew, in her heart of hearts, that Ursarkar frekking Creed had played them.

It was a good defensive position, for sure. A pass through the Rossvar built into a narrow canyon, its inner walls honeycombed with multistorey bunkers and weapon emplacements. The roadway itself was wide enough for ten Leman Russ tanks to drive abreast, and now that the last column of evacuees had come through, it had been dotted with dragon's teeth – networks of pyramidal rockcrete tank obstacles – and steel I-beams welded into massive caltrops.

They had hardened their positions, made ready.

But that didn't change the fact that they'd been played. No one was coming here.

Vox signals were difficult this high in the mountains, but what they'd gleaned was that everyone expected a landing near Kraf, and soon. And no idiot – even one touched by the Ruinous Powers – would be stupid enough to land troops on the other side of a mountain from the combat sector.

They were a blocking force. Static defence. They'd lose more from the cold than enemy fire. As she supervised M Company digging foxholes in the roadway, she reflected that the ring and scrape of trench spades on frozen earth was the sound of her hopes being buried.

'Have you seen the colonel?' she asked a passing lieutenant.

When he turned, she realised it was Manvar Pesk, leader of A Company's engineer section. He'd torn a piece of bedroll to swaddle the lower half of his face. Such uniform modifications were usually not condoned, but Barathus ordered that they be tolerated provided they did not obscure rank or unit markings.

'No, sir. Anything I can help with?' He stepped close, pulled his blanket down to show a grin. 'Or are you just wanting a few minutes inside that warm command bunker?'

'Just wondering about the status of our winter uniforms. The ranks keep asking.'

'Shouldn't wonder,' Pesk said, putting his hands under his armpits. 'Why don't you inspect the wall casements? It's about ten degrees warmer up there with no wind chill. I can take over here.'

'No,' she said, nodding towards M Company. 'If they have to be out here, I should be too. Don't want them to think command section's sitting by the brazier while–'

'*Cadian Twenty-Fourth, Cadian Twenty-Fourth,*' blared a laud-hailer. The sound echoed around the rockcrete canyon. '*This is a general call. Assemble on the roadway trench-line for orders. Current pickets and lookouts, stay on-duty. All others, assemble in company formations.*'

For ten minutes, troopers streamed out of steel bunker doors and scrambled out of foxholes. Sergeants shouted milling soldiers into ranks. Officers did headcounts.

Hellsker caught sight of Barathus heading out from the parade bunker, his long single-breasted coat flapping in the wind knifing through the Delvian Cleave. His signals officer, Renkla, lugged a master vox and a portable laud-hailer mounted on a collapsible tripod.

'Colonel,' she said, falling into step beside him. 'Have you heard something? About our uniforms?'

'No, not yet.' Barathus climbed up the loose mound of dirt they'd thrown up digging the foxholes. His boots sank in the unstable ground. 'Here.' He indicated to Renkla. 'Set it up here.'

'It's cold, sir, and–'

'It's about to get a lot hotter, Marda, trust me.' He took the handset Renkla offered and gave it an experimental click, hearing the portable laud-hailer pop.

Sergeants called attention. Three thousand pairs of boots snapped together.

Hellsker stood at the foot of the dirt mound, facing the regiment. Watching Barathus in her peripheral vision.

Barathus nodded, brought the handpiece to his mouth. 'Sons and daughters of Cadia, at ease!'

When they hesitated, he added: 'Go on, move your feet, keep the blood pumping.'

Wind blew through, setting off a burbling hiss in the laud-hailer. Barathus let it pass. The troopers shuffled their feet, blew in hands.

'Troopers of the Twenty-Fourth,' he began. 'I'll keep this brief before you all freeze. I know our service in the war has been a disappointment to you. In honesty, it's been a disappointment to me. Not because of any action by you... but because of our inaction. The fact that we have trained our whole lives to defend this world, to see that sacred duty fall to others. It has been hard, and you have been patient. Throne! Have we all been patient.'

Barathus licked his lips.

'One hour ago, I spoke personally to Lord Castellan Creed.'

That got their attention. Even the most recalcitrant troopers, those upset at being dragged into the cold, looked up.

'He told me to extend his personal regards to every one of you, and expressed his full confidence in this regiment to fulfil the difficult task he has set for us.'

Hellsker abandoned any pretence of iron will and turned to look at Barathus. Normally an executive officer should always face the regiment, but who cared? No one was looking anywhere but at the colonel anyway.

'Lord Castellan Creed informed me that a large enemy force is headed this way. Up through the western pass, towards the Delvian Cleave. Largely infantry, with light armoured vehicles and fast-attack cavalry elements. Neither of which we have. Estimate is they're twenty-thousand strong at least, perhaps as large as thirty. Ten of them for every one of us.'

There was excited talking then, expressions of... what? Fear? Elation? Both? Ten to one was impossible odds – a Cadian's dream. But that was so many. *So many.*

'It's the Volscani,' Barathus said, shutting the babbling down. 'The traitors of Tyrok, who murdered Governor Porelska. They are tough fighters. Cadian-trained, so they know our tactics, and determined as all hell. Creed thinks they intend to force the pass, then march on the western walls of Kraf. If that's true, they will batter this position until they either get through, or choke the pass with their dead.'

He paused. Let them imagine that. Hellsker noticed that he was digging for something in his pocket.

'Our orders are to stand against their assault. To the last las-cell. To the last grenade. To the last trench and last trooper. With entrenching tools, if we have to. Creed asks that of each one of you, personally. He has told me that this pass is vital to the coming war, but due to the situation at Kraf, we cannot be reinforced. Air support will be minimal. We alone guard this pass, he is *trusting us* to guard this pass.'

Barathus pulled an object from his pocket, unfolding it with his clumsy leather-gloved hands. At first, Hellsker thought it was a map, but a flash of blue ink let her know it was a piece of paper torn out of a memo book.

'Some of you know,' said Barathus, 'that I occasionally torture my officers' mess with poetry.'

Laughter rippled through the troopers.

'Sadly true. And when I received these momentous orders from Creed, I could not help but pen a few lines. And while I know they are no equal to our great war poets like Dubyankha or Nictu, I hope you will indulge me.'

Barathus sniffed, smoothed the page.

Hellsker was close enough to see the shine of tears in the old man's eyes.

'*This is not a foxhole,*' he said. '*This is the rich earth of my world.*

> *Dirt I threw in handfuls on the coffins of troopers that*
> *came before me.*
> *Those who stood in the ranks on the bastion wall, lasgun*
> *in hand,*
> *And told the Eye that it could not have our future.*
> *This is not a foxhole, this is my world.*
>
> *This is not a foxhole, it is my home.*
> *The place I have shared with my comrades, eating, laughing,*
> *A hole that does not feel empty, for we fill it with light*
> *and courage,*
> *And where I have seen them pass into the Emperor's light.*
> *This is not a foxhole, this is my home.*
>
> *This is not a foxhole, it is my fortress.*
> *It is home, world, a kasr I have dug with my own hands,*
> *A legacy that was bequeathed to me, to meet the enemy*
> *blade first,*
> *As we have always, and I will not leave it, not surren-*
> *der it,*

*Not take one step back, for I have dug my fortress and
will hold it.
For this is not a foxhole – this is a grave.'*

Barathus folded the notes, his hands shaking from emotion.

Hellsker could feel adrenaline zinging through her. It had been
a good poem, or at least, a poem for the moment. But she could
feel herself being pulled between the excitement of battle and the
dread press of mortality.

The regiment was stunned, balanced on a knife between elation
and melancholy. Hellsker could feel it. What he said next would
be critical.

'I...' said Barathus, then put the back of his hand to his mouth.
'I think...'

A boom of thunder ripped through the sky. The colonel – and
everyone else – looked up to see the wing lights of Marauder bomb-
ers streaking overhead, likely on an attack run to hit the Volscani
before they disappeared into the foothills of the pass.

But the sky was also dark enough that they saw the fires in it.
Not the infected-bruise pulse of the Eye of Terror, but circular infer-
nos in orange and red.

Troopers milled and talked, fell out of ranks. A nervousness joined
the mix of raw emotion.

'It's the orbital defence platforms,' Hellsker said. 'They're under
siege.'

'Holy Terra.' Barathus raised the hand-unit to his mouth, depressed
the button. 'This is it. It's started.'

It was the wrong note, a poor ending. Ominous.

Hellsker didn't know the right words for the moment, no one
could put language to such an event, but before she knew it, she'd
taken a step forward at attention and shouted:

'Twenty-Four, in the war!'

A ragged response came. Eyes on her.

'I can't hear you, Two-Four!' she mocked. 'And neither can those Volscani bastards! You think they're going to quake at half-arsed calls like that? I want you to yell so the Despoiler picks it up in orbit! Try it again. Twenty-Four, in the war!'

'TWENTY-FOUR IN THE WAR!'

Then, they quieted, because the sky was going dark.

The Eye of Terror, eternally glowing with its unhallowed light, began to shrink where it touched the southern horizon.

At first, Hellsker thought it was a sign – that the Emperor had reached out and snuffed the blasphemous wound in space.

But slowly, gradually as a moonrise, they realised what it was.

It was an eclipse.

A cyclopean vessel blocked the wicked light, its sharp edges becoming more defined as it came over the curved shape of the planet and rose in the sky.

An eight-pointed star floated above Cadia, so large Hellsker could not even block it out with a hand.

The Despoiler had come to Cadia.

PHASE THREE

BOMBARDMENT

ONE

'See me, Khorne! See me!'

Urkanthos could feel warm blood through his armour. Splashing, spattering. It flowed in gouts and fan-tails that arced high in the half-gravity of the defence platforms.

When they came down, it appeared as if it were raining jewels on his armoured skin.

Turning his black armour red.

His nerves sang. Free from pain. Exquisite with joy.

For Urkanthos could sense the slit-pupilled eye of his god upon him. Gloried in the rush of sacred adrenaline banging through his veins. Each hammer-blow of his twin hearts coursed the vitae around his body so it was a living temple to the god of life, war and slaughter.

'Look here! Look what I have brought you. Look on the hot, wet springs I call forth from their bodies.'

He mauled through a squad of Naval breachers with his broad chainaxe, and thanked his patron for the gifts offered him this day.

They had expected to attack the defence platforms, but three cruisers had tried to forestall him. With skill and fortune he'd granted them the chill of void-death. Fired his Hounds of Abaddon aboard to make an abattoir of their corridors while screaming his name, so the Lord of Slaughter would hear them and see his servant Urkanthos.

Now he was on the defence platform, and Gore-mouth ululated with the rest of her shades. A chorus that terrified the humans as he ripped through them.

A knot of Cadians harassed his left flank, red daggers of their las-beams glancing off his armour and cooking the gore that sheeted him. One raised a meltagun, the haze of gas discharge already leaking from its vented barrel.

'Artesia!' he snapped, sweeping his power claw towards the troopers. They were beneath his notice. Fodder to satiate the daemon.

Gore-mouth streaked across the floor, Urkanthos' shadow stretching long, sprouting clawed talons and a mouth that left a smear of blood across the deck as it keened: *'Yes. Yes. Yes. Warm. Wet. Salt. Warm. Wet.'*

The darkness spilled up the Cadians' barricade and they fell, shade-claws opening arteries and slitting tendons with the precision of a fine scalpel – wounds no bigger than the thickness of a shadow.

The meltagun fell to the deck, bisected. Pyrum-petrol gas leaked from its severed cable.

Urkanthos sensed the deaths more than saw them. He was entranced by an oncoming rush of bullgryns, slab-shields thrust forward in a moving wall. Shock mauls raised.

His vision was red now. The crimson of blood-madness. Urkanthos saw not their armour, nor their skin, nor bone. He saw the hulking abhumans as though they were animated circulatory systems, nets of arteries and veins and capillary deltas like topographical maps of riverways that walked and moved.

He blinked and his vision returned. With a bellow of glee that filled his chest, he rushed for them, meeting their force with his own.

'Khorne!' he challenged. 'Fix your eye, Khorne!'

Two ogryns flew backwards, the strength of his charge cracking their thick shields and launching them into the low-gravity air as they flailed with broken arms. He buried his chainaxe into the shoulder of another, sawing through its barrel ribcage and glorying in the red that fountained from its severed throat.

'*Khorne!*'

A maul impacted his head, delivering a shock that blinked his vision white like a flash of lightning. He twisted towards the attacker and buried his fanged mouth into the bullgryn's exposed throat. He locked his teeth into the flesh, feeling the abhuman's gun-barrel-thick artery pulse on his tongue.

Then he bit down and tore the spouting pipe free.

'*See my gift!*' he said, words lost in the chunk of flesh.

He grabbed the head of the next ogryn and twisted, popping it free. The blast of the dying ogryn's grenadier gauntlet tore into his thigh, but he cared not.

Urkanthos could feel the change. Blood-power swelling inside him, stirring a deep well within his twin hearts, which now beat like war drums. Ecstasy flooded through him, as though a portal had opened in his soul and the empyrean were rushing in like a fresh-tapped promethium well gouting fuel towards the sky.

His tongue felt too big for his mouth, and he opened his fanged maw to let the rubbery, ribbon-like appendage tumble forth – its ends splitting in a flare of beautiful agony, splattering hot vitae to the deck before it healed.

Gore-mouth keened, laughing. '*More, master! Slay more!*'

With a creak of bone, like a tree sawing itself in a night gale, his left hand began to stretch and distort. Finger bones pushed into the hard ceramite of his power claw, fusing and combining with the blades, the claw's casing thickening to a chitinous organic shell.

His toes curled and burst forth from his boots, hooked nails crimping the steel deck. Two great boils ached on his forehead, and he knew the stubs of horns were about to erupt.

Ascension. He had achieved ascension.

But to complete it, the blood must continue to flow.

Urkanthos brought another bullgryn down with a swipe of his hooked foot. Stomped its head to paste while he gutted another with his new claw, pulling him apart so the innards stretched.

'*More,*' he snuffled, snout-like mouth smeared with red like a porcine rooting in a corpse. The bullgryns were slain, and he could feel the power ebbing, his bones shortening. '*Blood must flow! Blood must flow!*'

Ahead, a crew of Naval gunners worked an ordnance battery, trying to get a shot at the Black Fleet vessels hoving into view.

He rushed forward, hungry for change, leaping into the air to crush the first...

He did not come down.

White-hot lance-fire stripped the shield out of the gun-port window to his left, smashed through the void field, melted the gun and its crew into slag that spattered orange-incandescent to sizzle on the bulkheads and deck.

And through the hole bored in the defensive platform, the void came in. Freezing and empty, vacuuming out the oxygen and atmosphere. Stealing what little gravity the platform possessed.

There was a moment of gale-force winds, equipment smashing into walls and pillars, the few living Guardsmen – even one unlucky Berzerker – were ripped into the empty expanse of high orbit and scattered tumbling over the blue-green ball of Cadia. They clawed the air as they passed, their screams silent in the airless chamber.

Urkanthos grabbed a support pillar, crimping it with his taloned grip, and held on.

Frost rimed the steel. Void-cold chilled the wet cloak of crimson on his armour and turned it to a layer of red ice.

The blood, frozen and suspended in air, no longer flowed.

And Urkanthos felt the ecstasy leave him – and the eye of his patron move elsewhere.

At dawn, a new star graced Cadia's sky.

It was broad and dark, four times the size of a harvest moon, like a great black spider crawling across the vault of heaven.

Scuttling, slowly, towards Kasr Kraf.

Creed toured the defences. Nodding at troopers, adjusting uniforms and slapping shoulder plates. Shouting when he needed to – mostly at the officers, in order to further endear himself to the ranks. Told them that Cadian resolve could not be broken, and that they must be ready to meet the Archenemy with all their training and strength.

He gave short speeches, led chants of 'Cadia stands!' that appeared thinner and more rote with each hour the Blackstone Fortress slid inexorably towards Kasr Kraf.

The mood was dark. He hadn't needed to tell anyone that the orbital defence platforms had fallen within four hours – even in daylight, they could see the meteor shower of debris and the ring-fires of the ravaged stations.

'A bit like us, don't you think?' he said to Kell, staring upward as they boarded his personal Valkyrie.

'What, sir?'

'The defence platforms. Overrun, afire, broken… Gradually being pulled down.'

'Yes, sir. They are all that,' Kell affirmed. He knew Creed had intended it as a sardonic quip, but his usual twist of sarcasm was not there. 'Yet they stay up. Just like us.'

The Valk lifted off the bastion's landing pad, the door still open so Creed could look out onto the city. As they rose, lines of khaki-clad Shock Troops went to the wall, like mound-insects marshalling to defend their queen.

Kell slid shut the communication hatch between the cockpit and crew bay. Found a seat across from Creed, buckled himself in and put on the over-ear headset of the crew bay's internal vox. He flashed Creed four fingers.

Valks were loud enough that two seats away, no one would be able to hear them. And the Kasrkin honour guard didn't need to be told not to listen.

Creed keyed his own headset to line four. 'What?'

'You've been off since this morning. Feels like your heart isn't in it.'

Creed looked out the door as the Valk banked, down at the inner parade grounds and support airfields just within the defensive wall.

'That report from Magos Klarn this morning,' Kell continued, hearing himself in the headset, 'you never showed it to me.'

Creed shifted, looked up at the vox switchboard to make sure only two lights were illuminated – the ones corresponding to their seats.

'Magos Klarn officially informed me that the test-firing of the null-array has failed. We are advised not to factor it in when calculating our defensive posture.'

'I thought so. When you don't show me, it's usually bad.'

'No matter how much we drill, no matter how high we raise morale or throw up the walls, it means nothing. We can't defend against an orbital strike from that warp cannon. It'll pass through Kraf's void shields like they're nothing but a soap bubble. Without that null-array...'

Creed swept a hand out at the Alpha Curtain Wall, indicating the Valkyries ferrying Kasrkin squads to the battlements, the lines of transport Chimeras and the artillery towers looming behind. 'This is all useless. It's over. Naval planners are already reading power surges in the fortress. They give us a few hours until the first salvo.'

Kell let out a long breath. 'So where do you want to be for it, sir? Not at high command.'

'No!' Creed burst into a chuckle and shook his head, his face reddening. The first genuine laugh Kell had seen all day. 'No, no. I'm not spending my final hours among those frekkers – they'll rub it in my face, right up until we get obliterated… We'll go back to the regiment. I want to be with the Eighth at the end.'

'Yes, sir.' Kell toggled the vox connection to link to the cockpit. 'Captain Klass, we have an itinerary change. We're headed for Kraf Citadel, Kriegan Gates, Bastion Seven.'

'Going home, colour sergeant?' asked the pilot.

'We're going home.'

Morkath's skin prickled with the rising power of the fortress. She could feel the swelling generation of it. Artery-cables sizzled with empyric energy. Skeletal dynamos coiled with spools of blood-iron wire hazed the air with manifestations. She could even feel it buzzing in her noctilith teeth. Snaps of warp-discharge, like static electricity, sparked between them each time she opened her mouth to speak.

'I have awoken the empyric regulators,' said Prozus Ghael, captain of the *Will of Eternity*. 'Warp-beam is cycling up to full charge.'

Ghael was a former Imperial Navy officer, brought to the light of the Eye when his ship had been lost in the warp, its Geller field collapsing. He'd sacrificed his crew in order to make a pact with the daemons clawing aboard his vessel. Swore to give his ship to Abaddon should he be allowed to live. A shameful surrender to fear.

Morkath could see that fear clawing at him now, quite literally. During his two centuries of service in the warp, the negative thought pattern had metastasised into a minor daemon that gripped on to his shoulders and gnawed at the base of his skull. Its slick, prehensile tail wrapped his throat, choking him with panic.

His whole being was driven by fear.

Fear of Abaddon, fear of the very ship he commanded – her mother fortress, the *Will of Eternity*.

'She will be ready,' Morkath countered. 'I have reshaped the power channels and pacified the vessel's spirit. All approaches from the power core to the weapon system have been freshly recolonised and charged with warp energy.'

'Its charge was depleted during the engagement at emergence,' Ghael warned. 'And that discharge was only at half-power. Regardless of what the fortress witch claims, we do not have full control of this vessel. Each time the weapon fires, we must realign the focusing rings. That can take days, perhaps even a week. We must be sure.'

The Warmaster sat on his noctilith throne, listening to the debate. To a mortal's eye, he appeared as a statue, but Morkath could see the armillary sphere of thoughts turning around his head. Each planetoid left a wake of fire, so elliptical haloes of flame whirled and died around his brow.

Above their heads, suspended in the observation port like a convex sky of water and land, was Cadia. In the strange directional relations of void craft, the bridge party was standing upside down, looking up in order to glance at the enemy world below.

Ghael was still talking, venting his worries about the fortress, when the Warmaster cut him off. 'If we do not fire now, captain, when do we fire?'

Even the thought-daemon gripping on to Ghael winced at the Warmaster's tone. 'We will fire… at the optimal time, Warmaster.'

Devram Korda, standing by, gave a cruel chuckle.

'And when would that be?' the Warmaster asked.

'I don't know. Perhaps another two days?'

It was then that Morkath saw why Abaddon had marked Ghael as the man for this role. He'd wanted to hand the fortress to a conservative and risk-averse commander, the better to guard against it being squandered or, worse, used against him. Yet that fear also meant that if the Warmaster wanted a course of action, Ghael would not stand in his way.

'Dravura.' The Warmaster turned towards Morkath, and she saw his hidden favour in how his brow relaxed. 'Care of the fortress is your task. Is it ready for what we are about to ask of it?'

For days, Morkath had been in the depths of the fortress. Walking its labyrinth. Meditating in the shifting corridors and lipless whispers of its wild interior. Communing with those parts that remained untamed, its blackstone not yet charged with warp energy like the inhabited spaces – and as always, she found those sections to be the most alive. By colonising the fortress, she knew, she was killing it.

That was her task, to kill her mother to win her father.

'It is ready,' Morkath said. 'The warp energy emitting from the core is pure and strong, and the channelling will hold.'

The Warmaster cast his eyes towards the planet above. 'We shall unleash the fortress. Obtain a firing solution on Kasr Kraf. Cadia's fall begins today.'

A pair of weapons operators on the bridge lit up their consoles, hands dancing as they moved data-plugs and threw switches. They were less corrupted, less wired into their places than those on a traditional vessel of the Black Fleet. They spoke to acolyte-engineers through throat vox-units, clicking like insects between words, overlapping each other.

'Firing chamber – *click* – two, stand by for acti – *click* – vation and–'

'Focusing – *click* – array, assemble rings for orbital – *click* – strike, range three-hundred-sixteen miles, that is three-one-six mil–'

'Abaddon!' The voice tore through the air of the bridge like a chainsword. 'Warmaster, I require a judgement! I...'

The Warmaster's look checked the new arrival mid-stride, his fury draining under Abaddon's gaze.

It was Urkanthos – yet not Urkanthos. His voice was different, sliding in and out of an animal growl that hadn't been present before. A sound that chilled Morkath's stomach.

She beheld a man changed. Already, Urkanthos had been as far from an Astartes as an Astartes was from a human. Now he was a step beyond.

One of his mask's horns remained metal, while the other had become a curling outgrowth of his cranium. His Khornate skull mask had cracked and fallen away, revealing spine teeth and a lolling ribbon-like tongue, forked and probing. Talons thick as bayonet blades curled from his ceramite boots, and one arm had stretched into a cruel parody of a lightning claw, armoured with red chitin.

His right eye was human – the left, a golden yellow, the black pupil set vertically like a feline's.

But it was when Morkath looked at him with the blackstone eye that her breath caught. For she could not make out his thoughts. His brain had changed – no longer even transhuman. Only the needle-like pain of the Butcher's Nails still framed him.

Korda stepped forward, a note of jocularity in his voice. 'Urkanthos! I had heard tell of your good fortune. Congratulations, brother. Question, what shall we call you now? Urkanthos Half-Prince?'

Urkanthos roared, the deep inhuman rumble of a leonine, and sprung for Korda.

Morkath barely avoided being trampled as he stormed forward, his chainaxe raised and keening.

Korda's sword slithered free from its sheath and clanged against the axe. The resulting sound was so loud that a bridge crewman nearby fell to his knees howling, blood trickling from punctured eardrums.

Urkanthos swiped with his daemonic left hand, mauling furrows into Korda's breastplate. In response the Slaaneshi grabbed Urkanthos in a grapple, pistoning a bladed kneecap into his side.

Without Morkath's thought-scanning, the duel would be like watching two serpents strike each other – each blow too quick for mortal eyes.

The warlords fell, crushing two sensor officers who were tethered to their stations and could not flee. Morkath heard their skeletons grind beneath the weight of the titans.

But despite their great speed, they could only land a few blows before the Warmaster came.

'Enough!' With the Talon of Horus, Abaddon gripped Urkanthos around his swollen waist, his right gauntlet simultaneously holding Korda by the collar of his gorget. 'Enough, cease this!'

He lifted Urkanthos into the air, where the half-daemon struggled like a caught feline. In his right hand, Korda hissed and lashed out, both too deep in adrenaline to heed.

'I SAID, ENOUGH!'

His voice was so deep, so tinged with the depths of the warp, it rattled decking and caused a cogitator's cathode ray to blow outward in a fountain of sparks.

The Warmaster lifted Korda and slammed him onto the deck. Morkath saw the Slaaneshi lord's calligraphic thoughtstream go blank a moment as his head bounced off the back of his armour's power pack.

Korda raised his hands, open, to show he was done.

Then the Warmaster turned to Urkanthos, still lashing and hissing. His snarls no longer resembled the words of an Astartes but the feral chorus of the warp. Bridge lights flickered at the tirade.

The Warmaster slapped Urkanthos with an open gauntlet. Forehand then backhand. Each blow sounded like a shotgun blast as it connected with the mutated head.

'I am Abaddon of the Black Legion. Your Warmaster.' He struck Urkanthos again, and from his thoughts, boiling with arcane sigils of command, Morkath knew it was not Urkanthos he was speaking to, but whatever beings had taken him as a vessel. 'I am favoured of your master, Khorne, and I order your silence!'

Urkanthos shook his head, snuffling. His eyes squeezed shut, then opened again. Blood poured from scalp lacerations opened by the beating. He'd bitten his own tongue, and it hung half-attached and twitching.

'Are you easy now, Urkanthos?' Abaddon asked, his tone no different than if he had asked the current ship heading.

'Korda,' choked Urkanthos, tongue already knitting back together. 'I was ascending. The eye of Khorne on me. His ship fired. *Fired* on me, Abaddon. He must have a spy. He interrupted my change. Do you expect me not to strike him after this betrayal?'

'My ship did not know you were there. And I was not personally in command.'

'As Lord Ravager I have access to the communication logs, Korda.' Urkanthos' voice dipped low, into the animal growl of the warp. *'I know you directed the* **Slaughtered Saint** *to hit the defence platform.'*

'Because it was being fired upon.' Korda rolled his eyes. Morkath could see his thoughts moving quickly, the ink sketching, frantic, rather than forming them in loops and sweeps. Lying. 'Did my fleet not have clearance to return fire on the platforms when attacked, Warmaster?'

'You did, but not on the western side,' said Abaddon. 'That was set out for our boarding parties.'

'There, that is it. He admits it. Let me kill him. Let me unleash my Hounds on his host.'

'No.' The Warmaster shook him, rattling his head back and forth. 'You two travelled to the heart of the Eye together. Do not throw away oaths and comradeship for this nonsense.'

'...the western side, relative to what?' asked Korda. 'Western relative to the fleet's void-position, or western relative to Cadia's northern pole?'

The Warmaster looked down at him then, slowly, his gaze tearing from the Lord Ravager to settle on Korda. 'Maybe I *should* let him kill you.'

'Yes, yes!' shouted Urkanthos. The Warmaster ignored him.

'We will speak of your punishment later, Korda. I will have to think of a sufficiently agonising penance. As for you, Urkanthos...'

The Khornate half-daemon stilled, listening.

'Tell me something you want.'

Above Urkanthos' head, Morkath could see blood pooling and spreading. And for a bare instant she thought his shadow flickered, moving in a way that did not match him.

Urkanthos craned his head, looking up at the planetary sphere hanging above them.

'Give me Cadia. If we land, let it be me who delivers it to you. Give me and my Hounds a mandate to wade in Imperial blood.'

Morkath held her breath, watching the orbit of her father's thoughts slow and still. His decision would echo with consequence. Should the warp cannon fail, and a ground invasion be called for, giving Urkanthos a licence to storm Cadia would be tantamount to sanctioning his ascension. It could completely unbalance the Chosen.

Abaddon looked the half-daemon in the eyes.

'You shall have it.'

TWO

Inside the walls of Kasr Kraf, every head looked skyward as the weapon reached its crescendo. The heart of it fizzled and sparked. Arcs of filthy lightning burst jagged from its epicentre, striking out towards roiling atmospheric clouds that it lit up like festival lanterns – charging the water molecules with pure warp energy so they rained black, tarry pus.

Inside Kraf, the defenders could smell burned sugar and rotting meat. With the instinctual understanding of a soldier-society, they knew there was nowhere to go. Reserve units were sheltering underground, but the entire garrison could not do so – for that would leave the city open to traditional assault.

On Alpha Curtain Wall North, Servantus Glave, reassigned from deep patrol duty along with the whole Kasrkin 27th, darkened the tint on his helmet lenses. His eyes were still adjusting to the above-ground light, and the weapon's glare was too much for him as he leaned out of the gun-deck's firing slit, staring upward.

When he could take it no more, he ducked inside. He pulled the glove off his right hand and flexed it, thinking of all his father had done to put him here, on the front line.

In his mid-spire apartment, Yann Rovetske sat in a window seat, back braced against one side and his feet on the other. He smoked a lho-stick laced with grinweed, hoping that the weapon would not make all his work moot.

The Empty Man, who briefed him in his dreams, had said nothing about this terror weapon.

He glanced at the lead-lined toolbox in the room's corner.

At least if the city died, he would be rid of it.

Salvar Ghent, for his part, decided to spend his last hours underground watching ration cards run off the new plates. If they died, they died.

If they didn't, he wanted these cards to hit the street in time for the siege rationing.

At Stetzen Airfield, all flights were grounded for fear the weapon's firing might impact flight conditions. Keztral and Darvus gathered with the rest of the pilots and maintenance crews on the blacktop runway. Minutes before, they'd been sheltering in place inside a bunker, as ordered, until someone said 'frekk it' and they trickled outside.

As the hissing, spitting energy ball started to brighten, Darvus offered Keztral a handshake.

'Frekk that, get over here.' She hooked the shorter man around the neck with one arm and hauled him into her side, rapping his flight helmet twice with her free hand. 'Thanks for flying with me, yeah?'

'Yeah.'

He was about to say more, but the sky split in two.

Magos Klarn decided not to watch, despite his curiosity about the operating mechanics and energy tolerances of the heretic weapon.

He'd allowed himself to consider it for exactly three point nine seconds. Tried to imagine the blissful act of data-collection being his last experience before being taken offline.

Except, he had failed. And should he have any hope of receiving the Omnissiah's forgiving grace, he would need to do penance before the end. So in a monumental act of self-mortification, he denied his internal programmatic drive to study and catalogue. Instead, he descended to the null-array. The site of his failure would be his tomb.

Yet, if he had hoped this retreat would rein in his curiosity, he was gravely mistaken.

He found his sentries dead on the steps.

Two Sicarian infiltrators, deactivated by a massive energy discharge that had cooked their neural circuitry and burst their eye-lenses outward.

Klarn flattened himself against a wall, sliding into the shadows. He keyed his threat-alert grid active for movement and heat, volkite pistol held low as his scanner net blanketed the environment around him.

He sent a ping to his Sicarian guard detail, but received nothing back. Stalking crablike to the entrance of the null chamber, he picked up an anomalous hum. Data-scrubbers inspected and systematised it, identified part of the waveforms as the vibrational acoustics of his array devices.

Sabotage.

Keying his combat array live, he spun around the corner, weapons covering the room – raised like a crustacean in a threat display.

There was no threat. Whatever had been here had come and gone. Sicarian bodies lay segmented and burned, armament mounts sheared through by a weapons system unknown to him.

And his work, his fastidious work, was ruined.

Cogitator banks had been roughly moved about the room, rewired, in places even gutted and overturned. One power rerouter had been completely cannibalised for cables that had been plugged into a dangerously unshielded plasma reactor, passed through a vibration regulator, and threaded through the subterranean pylons

Klarn had studied for most of his radically extended lifetime. Other pieces of equipment he did not recognise at all, nor understand how he would control them without instrument panels or mecha-dendrite inputs.

The logic was bizarre, unorthodox – *alien.*

Trazyn the Infinite, Overlord of Solemnace, Archaeovist of the Prismatic Galleries and recorder of histories, stared out of a crack in his dimensional oubliette wanting ever so badly to explain where the tech-priest had gone wrong.

And he had been wrong. So very, very wrong.

Indeed, upon discovering Klarn's work on the anti-empyric nexus he had hoped to fix the tech-priest's follies with subtlety – rerouting a power channel here, inserting a fractal algorithm there. Nudging events from the shadows. After all, should these humans detect the paternal hand of the necrontyr on their shoulder, they would start hunting for an internal threat. Perhaps even bring in the Novamarines.

That would not be good.

Because Trazyn had been to the hollow interior of Thanatos, cradle of the Celestial Orrery. And in consulting its light-sculpture that perfectly mirrored the known galaxy, he had seen the crimson stain spreading across the stars. An infection, as though the cosmos were about to go into septic shock.

A wound that was about to engulf Cadia.

For while the humans liked to call this dimensional transit point an eye, that was not strictly accurate. It was a puncture, a stab wound in the skin of the universe.

Long ago, when the necrontyr fought beings that supped from the empyric dimension, master crypteks had fortified this place with countermeasures against the realm of madness. A cosmic suture to keep this wound from tearing open.

A suture that the Tomb-Killer, Abaddon, wanted to cut with shears.

But not today.

'What the frekk just happened?' Creed removed the cigar from his mouth, and Kell saw that he'd bitten it through.

For a moment after the fortress discharged, all had been impossible light and a sound like a thundering waterfall – but now, Cadia's sky was clear.

Shockwaves of warp energy boiled away like vapour above Kasr Kraf. Part of the empyric discharge seemed almost solid – the ghosts of fractal geometric shapes stuttering in and out of visibility – but the warp-beam had not come through.

'Was that a test firing?' Creed asked. His eyes darted back and forth. 'Or a malfunction? Could we be that Throne-damned lucky?'

Kell shook his head. 'Don't know, general.'

It had been hard for both of them, he knew. Neither had expected to live, yet neither could do what they wished – say last words, offer a final salute, thank each other for a lifetime of service. To do so would betray their fatalism to the regiment, and Creed would not ruin his men's spirit, even if he was about to destroy their bodies.

'Dispatch, colour sergeant.' The vox-lieutenant, a boy from the 88th, was barely out of the schola. Kormachen, Kell thought his name was. 'Coded vermilion, it's urgent, sir.'

Kell took the slate, raised his eyebrows to acknowledge the salute, and flicked his head to dismiss the man.

'Well? Don't keep me wai–'

'It's from Magos Klarn,' said Kell, breaching protocol by cutting his commander off. 'He says the null-array is active.'

'It's working?'

'Not only working, but stable. He suggested psykers may experience some discomfort.'

'Well they can damn well get used to it!' Creed said, shouting with exuberance. 'You hear that, troopers? We're back in it! The Mechanicus is shielding our arses and that big spokewheel can't do frekk-all to us. He wants Cadia to kneel. What do you say to him?'

'Cadia stands!' Kormachen shouted.

They took it up as a chant, over and over. Spreading from wall to wall, bastion to bastion, into the airfields and marshalling grounds they guarded. In the armoured reserve, tankers banged spanners on armoured hulls in time with the shout.

'*Ca-dia stands! Ca-dia stands!*'

It echoed through streets and alleys in the fortress city. Civilians in the manufactoria repeated it as they crimped Earthshaker shells closed and stacked boxes. Munitorum supply drivers heard it and leaned on vehicle horns to join the din.

In high command, they abandoned their chart tables and topographic displays, pounding fists on armaglass windows as they chanted.

Troopers heard it in the deep bunker shelters, the call reverberating through the walls until they too took it up. They grabbed handfuls of each other's tunics and jumped as they did so, pushing and pulling, words deafening in the enclosed spaces.

They chanted until the first lance strike hit the void shield like a hammer, rocking the energy canopy so hard it rippled. Sending a percussive bang through Kraf that the defenders felt in their stomachs.

The siege had begun.

THREE

'What does it feel like?' Colonel Barathus asked. 'Different than you thought?'

He had to lean close to make himself heard, gripping her shoulder with a claw-like hand in his excitement.

'Yes.' Hellsker lowered the monoculars. She squinted with her naked eyes, then blinked away the cold and nestled them back in the rubbarine cups. In the black tunnel, she could see a smear of vehicle smoke and the insectile figures of the enemy.

She was about to answer the colonel, tell him she hadn't thought one way or another about how it might feel to see the enemy, but her opportunity to tell that lie was cut off by the metallic *boom* of the three-barrelled Earthshaker battery beneath their feet.

Her tunnel vision rocked, and when she steadied it, she saw the dirty puff of an airburst above the clambering enemy. Some stopped moving.

'On target,' called the artillery officer to their left, peering, like them, out the fire-control bunker's vision slit. He snarled in concentration and keyed his hand-vox again. 'We've got it zeroed. Survivors moving. I see light armour. Salamander scout vehicle, looks like some Chimeras behind. Reel it in one point and a quarter-degree left, grid square green-two-zero.'

They'd been firing for four hours. Ever since Barathus had got a signal from the spotter team he'd sent up Rossvar's Dagger. The Dagger was a sheer peak climbing two thousand feet above the Delvian Cleave, so steep the artillery observers – all of them mountain lads, who'd grown up on the Northern Massif and had scored well during the 24th's alpine wargames – had needed to ascend with ropes and crampons. There was a desolate little pillbox up there, clinging like a wasp nest to the side of the cliff face, just below the natural cloud layer.

Due to their height, the observers could see two miles further than the heavy artillery emplacements on the northern end of the cleave. But Earthshakers didn't have to see things to kill them. So shortly after Barathus' speech, they'd started dropping long parabolas of fire down the slopes, past the point where the ridges and natural grade of the mountain interrupted their vision, to ravage the Volscani all morning.

That was the irony, really. Cadia was being pounded from orbit almost without answer, yet down here, in the grey saw teeth of the Rossvar, it was the opposite.

But now they could see the enemy. And Marda Hellsker would have to live up to the legacy of family and the expectations of training. She touched her uncle's sword, sending up a prayer for strength. Absently, she thought she should check the engraved wooden box in her footlocker, where she kept his plasma pistol. Sitting in the cold was bad for the coils.

Not that she'd warm it up – she'd never even touched the thing. The mere thought of it summoned the ghost-smell of burned flesh in her nostrils.

'Fire,' said the artillery officer, and the floor rumbled again.

'I remember the first time I saw the enemy,' said Barathus, this time switching to their in-helmet command vox-band. 'On Saga-this. First time I'd been off Cadia. Agri-world given over mostly to grain. Big rolling fields of it, from horizon to horizon. An enemy tank column was burning its way through. And I wondered what poor bastards were assigned to stop them. When I realised it was us – me, a seventeen-year-old cadet lieutenant and my Whiteshield company – I about shat my uniform.'

'And did you?' Hellsker asked.

'Shit myself?'

'Stop them.'

'We did.' He paused, raised his magnoculars. 'But I had a realisation. I wasn't up to it. Not up to stopping them. Just like you aren't.'

'The hells I'm not,' she hissed. Hellsker dropped her magnoculars, stared him down, breath misting. She felt light-headed, the adrenal hit from the insult rushing into a system starved of oxygen by the altitude. 'What do you think you're doing telling me that? What, the others get a poem, I get a running down? I should–'

'Relax, Marda.' Barathus raised a hand. 'I'm telling you this because I respect you. And this is the most important thing you need to understand as an officer.'

He glanced back over his shoulder, at the side gun-port looking above the floor of the cleave, at the troopers fortifying the foxholes and trenches.

'What I mean is, no one is up for this. Not you, not me, not Lord Castellan frekking Creed. War isn't natural. Nothing second nature about standing in a hole, holding it as the las-fire screams in. People aren't built for it mentally. It rips us up. So to survive, to do what needs to be done and stop them' – he pointed at the distant column of enemies – 'we have to become someone else. High command does most of the work for us. They put us in uniforms and regulate our haircuts. Give us titles based on our role in the machine – lieutenant, sergeant, gunner, pilot. Tell us how we're part of a great institution full of traditions and bravery. Fill our eyes with films of great deeds. To bury that person we are, and make us into the tools we need to be. But the last step you have to take yourself, Marda. You need to step into that other person who would stand when Marda Hellsker would run. Who will trade the lives of men and women she cares about for yards of dirt she's never seen before, and never will again. Who will manipulate people who trust her to take actions that will end in bloody ruin, and call it leadership.'

'Colonel…'

'We're about to face the enemy, and you need to find that person. Put it on like an Astartes donning his battle plate, because without it, you won't get through this.'

She stared at him, mind reeling. This was recidivist talk. Discussing Cadia as if its culture and traditions were some grand conspiracy to dupe its population into giving up their lives.

But… it was true, wasn't it? She could feel it.

'Just do one thing. Don't lose the person you are now. Remember her. Hold her close and keep her secret so you can find her when this is all over. Because if you don't, if you become the armour… Well, that's how you get someone like Ursarkar frekking Creed.'

'Yes, sir, I understand, sir.'

'No, you don't, not yet.' He snorted. 'You know what I saw on Sagathis?'

'Sir?'

'Children playing. Playing in the streets. I didn't know children did that. Here, they would've already been–'

He cocked his ear.

'Do you hear…?' he asked.

She did. A high, irregular whistle, like a military band member failing to hit a top note on a flute.

'I–'

'Incoming!' the artillery captain shouted into his handset.

A flash like heat lightning blinked in the gun slit, and the front of the bunker slammed inward at Hellsker.

The world went searchlight-white, and she knew nothing but the hot tang of blood on her tongue.

Morkath knew that when the Warmaster was truly angry, he got quiet. Indeed, the more furious he became, the more still he appeared.

Now, he was like a moon, unmoving and cold. Even his thoughts had almost frozen into a regimented ticking, like the precise movement of a fine chrono.

Around him, the mutated outgrowths Morkath had used to tame the bridge were all motion. Overcharged with empyric energy from the weapon's firing, they twitched and flexed. A wall of grey-pink lungs inflated and deflated. Fingers emerging from the ceiling waved like anemones. Fine hairs raised on the shivering skin that covered half of the Warmaster's throne.

Abaddon asked no questions, elicited no explanation for why the warp-beam had failed.

Instead, he said, 'We will initiate the contingency. Korda, inform the Legion and commence bombardment. Priority targets are enemy strongpoints around the designated landing zones. And keep fire on Kasr Kraf – do not allow them to sally and strike our planetfall sites.'

'Abaddon… Warmaster,' slurred Urkanthos, the daemon part of him unable to contain its eager glee. 'You *promised me Cadia.* Name me commander and–'

'You are ahead of yourself, Urkanthos. We bombard to reduce the enemy's defences and pin their forces down while we secure landing zones and objectives. Once the enemy stronghold is cut off – then you may march for Kraf.'

'I wish to *land now,* and–'

'Do not forget your pledges, Urkanthos. Whatever half of you remains mortal is still my man. I suggest you use this time to prepare your forces. As we have already discovered, these corpse worshippers have proven more resourceful than we expected – but not more than we planned for.'

The Warmaster stepped up to the great double doors of the bridge. Two hulking mutants, chained to the wall, bowed their bone-plated heads and dragged the doors open for him.

'Korda, I want to hear a full bombardment in ten minutes. I expect a progress report on the marshalling within an hour. Morkath!'

She ran to his side as he swept out the door, into his sound-proofed mapping chamber.

Inside, incense curled up from a yellowed ritual bowl made from an aeldari skull. A flayed skin-map covered one wall, an inked version of the Kraf combat zone on its goose-fleshed surface. Abaddon stared at it.

'I am sorry, Warmaster, there was no malfunction in the fortress, I can feel it, I...'

'Apologies mean nothing. They have deployed a countermeasure.' The Warmaster swept two fingers over the tattooed spires of the Elysion Fields, setting the ink swirling. 'They've discovered how to harness Cadia's pylon network. It surprises me, given your knowledge of the noctilith, that you could not detect that.'

'I can explain.'

'Explanations are a waste of my time, find me a solution. Or I will have you down on the surface, leading a cultist attack.'

'You cannot allow Urkanthos to lead the assault on Kraf.'

He did not deign to respond; instead, he swept a hand over a marker of troops and herded them towards a pass in the Rossvar Mountains.

'Warmaster, if Urkanthos ascends, your careful balancing of patronage will be upset. I can no longer fully read his thoughts.'

'I know he cannot achieve daemonhood. Why else would I have ordered Korda to fire on him?'

Morkath blinked, stunned. 'But if Korda reveals...'

'Korda can keep his mouth shut and take a beating when it suits his purposes. No sense hiding it from you, you'll probably see it in his thoughts before long. Watch him, Morkath, ensure he does not intend to use that information against me.'

'Yes, Warmaster. But Urkanthos is already half-ascended. If he completes it, there will be an internal struggle.'

The Warmaster stroked the map's shivering skin, conjuring an Iron Warriors glyph amid the Elysion Fields. 'Cadia will be a slaughter, no matter what we do now. If I disallow him from landing, my motives for doing so will be obvious and he will rebel – we do not need a faction-war right now. Particularly one where the Hounds of Abaddon are following a newly ascended prince.'

He paused and snorted.

'No, we cannot hold Urkanthos back. We must assume the fool will rise to daemonhood, though I cannot tell you how many times I've warned him against those gifts. I know more than can be written, Morkath, about the temptation to become a monster in order to achieve my ends. I've seen where it leads.'

Morkath saw her Warmaster's thoughts tumbling, like dice thrown in a wager-game. 'You are taking a gamble. You will give Urkanthos combat, but only the most dangerous.'

Abaddon twisted his fingers before Kraf, summoning a Khornate rune on the killing plains of the eastern gate. 'Urkanthos wishes to give us Cadia, so we will let him. He and his Hounds can go into the meat-grinder of Kasr Kraf. Urkanthos is too bloodthirsty. He mistakenly equates victory at Kraf as victory on Cadia. It is indeed the worst combat we will face, but the point is only to neutralise resistance so that we can demolish the pylons. Kraf is a key objective, and likely the most glorious one. It is an ideal situation. He will give us victory there...'

'...or he will die.'

'If we are fortunate, he will reduce the enemy greatly before falling.'

'Warmaster, my instincts say the nullification field is controlled from within Kraf. If Urkanthos takes it offline, we could fire the warp cannon on Kraf while he is still inside. The Lord Ravager is a useful tool, but we could sacrifice him if it gives us Cadia.'

Morkath saw the thoughts wheeling about Abaddon's head, their colours going dark purple and black. The same colour as his eyes as he looked at her, a lupine smile on his lips.

'You see what you can accomplish when you focus on the solution, rather than the problem?'

In number six torpedo tube of the Slaaneshi vessel the *Slaughtered Saint*, a deity sat in darkness, waiting to fall to earth.

Warbringer, its name was. And for nine generations the Valshak clan of gun-deck two had worshipped it. Their bloody handprints were on its casing now, mixed with the cremated remains of family members who had not lived to see the momentous day of its loading. Prayers had been scratched on its panelling.

As the tube's muzzle door rolled away, letting the cold of the void settle into the tube, the three-hundred-ton weapon ascended weightless, off the tube skids.

Red warning lights flashed along its casing, winking once.

Twice.

Three times…

Fire blossomed at the torpedo's rear, lighting the black tube orange for a nanosecond before *Warbringer* raced forward.

For a brief moment, stars wheeled and turned, the proud *Slaughtered Saint* visible behind, then *Warbringer* plunged towards the blue-green planet below, juddering as it entered the upper atmosphere.

Vibrations quivered through it, explosive bolts detonated and the first-stage engine dropped behind, searing incandescent white in the mesosphere. The warhead and second-stage drove downward, stabilising.

Warbringer burst through the lower atmosphere, into the clear skies of Cadia.

And it was not alone. As it streaked towards earth, aerial pollutants running streaks on its nose cone, it joined the contrails and ordnance lines of others like it.

The pencil streaks of drop pods, orange flares at the base where they'd superheated in the atmosphere. Barrage bombs and short-burn torpedoes. Cluster ordnance, spinning like tops as their altitude indicators triggered and they threw cyclonic spirals of grenade-sized bomblets onto the target area. Seeker torpedoes, their engines firing to redirect them into diagonal flight paths towards their strike zones.

Defensive fire slashed up at them. Bursts of flak. Interception lasers fired blind in grid-patterns, detonating warheads and slicing rocket engines from payloads, so both halves tumbled in opposite directions. Chaff-artillery detonating to fill the air with reflective discs and filaments that fouled the sensors of homing ordnance. Invisible jamming signals that turned guided munitions into unguided ones.

The second-stage engine shelved, falling onto the Kraf Plain, while the warhead took its terminal dive.

Falling fast, quicker than a human eye could follow. The flashing blue of a skyshield filling its forward arc. Beyond that, cliffs of reinforced rockcrete bristling with artillery.

Nose-cone sensors detected the buzz of a field. Staggered breaching-charges on its upper warhead fired – *wham, wham* – holing the skyshield then void shield one right after another. Opening a channel for a tenth of a second.

'Holy frekking Throne,' said Creed, peering through his magnoculars.

The windows of high command rattled, and Kell knew someone had taken a big hit. 'Sir?'

'Kasr Stark is gone.'

Creed left the magnocular tripod at the window and went to his desk map, marking an X over what was once a city of ten million.

Kell peered through the magnocular to see for himself. Stark was not burning, it had vanished. Secondary explosions still threw gouts of earth and debris skyward, spires collapsing like felled trees as their foundations gave way. Fires were starting, giving off acrid black smoke.

Then, the haze of destruction – the particulate matter of a destroyed city, of atomised stone, metal, flesh and blood – settled enough that it hid the scene.

'All Secundus under bombardment,' mused Creed. 'Drop pods spotted to our north, Titans pushing in on our east, and a heavy ordnance concentration on Kraf's southern defences.'

'Is the picture clear, sir?'

'No, I need eyes out there. Order all Kraf squadrons to scramble.'

Boots on blacktop. Crews shouting. A runway control officer with sergeant's stripes waved two neon gesture sticks and screamed to make himself heard above the throaty howl of engines.

Stetzen Airfield bounced in Keztral's vision as she ran. Everything was noise. To her left, air-defence bastions tore up the sky. Above, the skyshield and void field blossomed with hits that echoed like thunder off the walls of Kraf Citadel. She could actually feel the ionised, flash-heated air from the laser batteries with every breath.

Stetzen had been their home field for the entire war. She and Darvus had flown dozens of missions – probably hundreds – from its four intersecting runways. They'd gone up three times a day, sometimes. Combat operations at an active airbase, even a smaller recon and observation field like Stetzen, were always chaos.

But this, this was something else.

She, Darvus and *Deadeye*'s ground crew crossed the field amoeba-like, gripping handfuls of each other's uniforms to avoid getting separated in the turmoil of three full squadrons deploying all at once.

'No!' shouted Darvus, waving with his free arm. 'No, no, no, no, no!'

Keztral looked, and shouted a warning out of sheer horror. Across the airfield, a human wail briefly eclipsed that of the raid sirens.

A Valkyrie, confused by the unfamiliar field, had lifted vertically on its vector-thrust nozzles and banked left across the runway – unaware of the Navy Lightning streaking towards it on a short take-off, engines flared.

Darvus threw himself down, dragging Keztral with him.

She threw an arm over the back of her head, wishing she'd already put on her flight helmet.

For a gut-twisting moment she couldn't see the Lightning, the black hull of the Valk completely eclipsing it. Through the Valk's open hatch, she spotted a door gunner – mouth open, hugging his heavy bolter mount like it was his mother.

With a shriek of vector-thrust the Valk gunned its nozzles and climbed out in a nose-down diagonal, the flames of one nozzle washing over the Lightning's wing as it streaked by beneath it.

The Lightning ripped past, nose already raised, and climbed into the air.

Keztral shaded her eyes and saw the Valk, wobbling but undamaged. The manoeuvre had thrown the terrified door gunner out, and he dangled on his tether, kicking fifty feet above the runway. A crew chief started hauling him in like a fish.

Keztral felt something wet and warm on her sleeve, and realised her assistant mechanic had vomited.

'Frekking Navy air controllers aren't talking to the Militarum ones,' said Darvus.

'Then let's get across the runway before another taxis up,' Keztral said, pulling him to his feet.

They reached *Deadeye* within one minute, breathing hard. Stetzen was all frekked up. Runway Beta was blocked by a Marauder with an engine-start failure. Servitors and ground crews were hooking up a tow vehicle to drag it onto the grassy median.

'Do final checks while I mount,' Keztral said, buckling on her helmet. She grabbed the ladder, hauling herself up.

'Vest! Vest!' chirped Navella, her chief mechanic.

'Shit!'

Keztral hopped down, ripping at the yellow retro-reflective vest they were required to wear on the runway.

'It's twisted on your webbing,' said Navella, trying to untangle the vest from her straps and oxygen hose. 'You're going to break something. Here, let me–'

'Dammit!' Keztral yanked upwards.

'Take off window, five minutes!' warned Darvus.

'Just stand back.' Keztral batted Navella away and drew the serrated survival knife from her calf sheath. She wormed it beneath the vest, then sliced outward with one sawing cut. 'Okay, pull now.' It came free.

One minute later, she was buckled in. Navella slapped her helmet twice, ducking to get clear of the shutting canopy.

'Stetzen tower, Stetzen tower,' voxed Keztral. 'This is Avenger *Deadeye*, Eighty-Ninth Recon, tail number one-twenty-two, requesting an extension on our take-off window.'

'Deadeye, *this is tower. Thirty-second extension granted. Can you stack up on runway alpha in one minute forty?*'

Keztral saw Navella give the all-clear wave. Checked their taxi path to the queue of aircraft. 'Affirmative, tower. We'll be there.'

'Frekking Throne,' said Darvus. 'It's going to be tight.'

'*Language,* Deadeye,' responded tower.

They barely made it.

For all the disorder on the runways, things were starting to flow. Swarms of Valkyries lifted and headed west, looking like clouds of insects in the dawn. Clearing the northern flight corridor for the non-vector-thrust aircraft.

Within ten minutes, *Deadeye* was in the air, Keztral bracing for the uncomfortable whole-body buzz vibration of passing through the void shield.

'Will you look at that?' said Darvus.

Keztral had been watching her instruments, knowing that while the void shield was barely visible from afar, it became a nearly opaque haze when passing through.

Outside her canopy were more aircraft than she'd ever seen in the air – or on the ground for that matter.

Clouds of Valks. Wide Marauder formations. Lightning wings flying in wedges. Blocky Thunderbolts, viffing in sideways from their dedicated Navy airfield two districts over.

They had to fly close, grouped in a long ribbon in the mile-wide air corridor prearranged with the defensive batteries. To either side, lasers shimmered through the sky, and Keztral could hear the supersonic crack of passing artillery shells. Above them, flak detonated with such regularity it formed an artificial cloud-bank, raining slivers of shrapnel on them as they flew.

At first, Keztral thought the long trail of aircraft looked like a flock of migratory avians – but then the image hit her.

The kite festival. When every child in Salgorah outhab would put three or four scrap kites in the air each, tying the strings to long sticks to keep them all up at once. Those days when the sky could only be glimpsed between the translucent glow of plastek film, as if the heavens had become a glassaic window.

'All aircraft, Kraf Sector. This is Colonel Strekka of the Howling Hundred-and-Nineteenth. As you know – or maybe you don't – I have command over this north-east corridor.'

'Love that voice,' said Darvus.

Keztral smiled.

Strekka came in vox-distorted, yet they could still discern his famous baritone drawl. The joke went that more than one aviator had fallen in love with Strekka over the vox, then immediately out of love upon seeing his grox-slab face.

'I'll make this quick. Just wanted to let you know that there are currently eleven full squadrons above Kraf Sector, plus six demi-squadrons. That makes this the largest single-sector deployment of combat aircraft in the history of Cadia – meaning once we contact the enemy, it will be the largest in-atmosphere aerial engagement in planetary history.'

He clicked off, letting that information sit.

Keztral scanned the grouping of aircraft, letting the immensity of it wash over her.

Each Valkyrie she could see had five crew, plus twelve passengers if transport-loaded. Lightnings and Thunderbolts were single seat. Avengers double. Each Marauder bomber had five to six crew.

How many people were in this formation? Thousands, easily. Each one with parents, a past, memories of childhood and the academy – things they were prepared to gamble in order to protect this world.

'Just getting in the air without a fatality is a testament to your skill and the God-Emperor's grace. He's up here with us, I can feel it, and it's with His divine will that we'll strike the Archenemy landing grounds. Tie up their air assets and stop them from assaulting Kraf. Basically, find the enemy and frekk 'em up. Keep your formations tight in the corridor but watch your distance between aircraft. We don't want friendly fire or collision casualties. One last thing. When we engage, it's going to be hot, so don't feel shy asking for help. Let's show these heretic bastards Cadia doesn't just stand – it flies.'

'Find the enemy and frekk 'em up.' Darvus laughed. 'Hanna, I'm officially calling off my grudge with the Hundred-and-Nineteenth.'

'They're off the shit list?'

'That is correct,' Darvus said, in a mock officious tone. 'I, Lieutenant Lahon Darvus, in my capacity of Grudgemaster-General and Keeper of The Shit List, officially announce that the Cadian Hundred-and-Nineteenth Squadron is off– Frekk! Contact! Contact!'

A Marauder two hundred feet above them burst into flame and fell from the sky. Finger-sized debris caught in the airstream, spattering Keztral's cockpit with rattling impacts as the bomber dropped down on their right, splitting into two as it tumbled.

A sleek black shape, wings pinned back and nose aflame, darted past from above to below. Too fast to identify.

'Bats!' screamed someone on their squadron band. *'Bats! Bats! Bats!'*

The Air Battle of the Kraf Plain had begun.

FOUR

In high command's underground strategium, Creed leaned over the massive holo-table, blowing cigar smoke through the projection. Through the door, they could hear a constant babble of voices as officers shouted at each other, took vox-reports and tried to fix enemy movements.

'General,' said Kell. He offered a glass that Creed took without looking.

'Operator, have we had a holo-update yet? No? Should be soon, eh?' Creed tilted the glass to his lips, then paused. Sniffed it. 'Colour sergeant, this is water.'

'Yes, sir,' Kell responded. 'Hydration is important.'

'The only water I want in this glass should be frozen and floating in amasec,' Creed said, holding it out for Kell to take back. 'Preferably floating about two, oh, three inches off the bottom.'

Kell made no move.

'Oh, very well.' Creed rolled his eyes and drank the water down, grimacing. 'Kell's as bad as my personal medicae. Wants me to have a strong heart and a clean liver.'

The tactical officers laughed, but there was no warmth in it. Too much tension.

With a flicker, the holo-table blinked, changed.

'Oh, there we are,' Creed said. 'Quadrant officers, updates. Cardinal points, starting north and going chrono-wise.'

The holo showed the Kraf battle sector, the kasr at its centre, surrounded by its two concentric rings of curtain walls. Alpha Curtain was the outer wall, which girdled nearly all of Kraf Plain and stretched far out east, while Beta Curtain was the inner wall, standing five miles off the citadel walls of the fortress city itself.

There were so many units on the holo it was nearly impossible to read – so Creed had sliced it like a pie, assigning each cardinal direction to a different tactician for monitoring and updates.

'Northern quadrant,' snapped one officer. 'Has had a report from Wolf Lord Orven Highfell. The Iron Warriors have landed drop-citadels outside Kasr Jark, here and here.'

He indicated, stretching out two fingers in a V at the spires that had blinked into existence on the edge of the plain.

'Strange. If it were me, I'd have dropped them closer to Kraf, used them to stage siege elements and create a forward base for bombard artillery.'

'They could be trying to cut us off from Kasr Jark and the *Sword of Defiance*,' the tactician guessed. 'Separate us from our Astartes forces? The Dark Angels are tearing up the enemy landers. Observation teams report the *Defiance* has destroyed at least two large drop-ships and damaged another.'

'Perhaps they don't know how small those Adeptus Astartes contingents are.' Creed ran a hand over his mouth. Kell could hear the scrape of his bristle. 'Doesn't make sense otherwise – they can't be trying to control the Elysion Fields, the pylons make it useless as a landing ground. We'll keep a pin in that grenade, see how the situation develops. Not like the sons of Russ or the Lion will take orders from us anyway. Enquire if they want air support. Next?'

'Eastern quadrant has major activity,' said the tactician. Her dark eyes and skin reflected the data-slate. She was pressing the micro-bead into her ear with one hand, and scrolling through a slate with the other. 'Multiple landing sites, large air engagement in the north-east air corridor, Titan contacts by Baroness Vardus and her lances. Reports are still coming in and some have already proven erroneous. Strictly speaking it's a mess, general. Suggest we move on and give it a few minutes for the situation to clarify.'

'Very well.' Creed nodded. 'South?'

'Holding, though they're under heavy orbital bombardment. It seems like the enemy–'

'Crash report!' interrupted the northern quadrant officer. 'Dread-claw landing, north Alpha Curtain Wall. Enemy disembarking.'

The young man looked at Creed, sweat on his brow.

'Heretic Astartes, general. They're on the wall.'

Servantus Glave wished he were still underground. He was a tunnel fighter. Used to the cramped corridors, not the vaulted ceilings of the northern Alpha Curtain's heavy gun-deck. Underground you could control fields of fire.

And nothing came smashing through the wall.

The warning klaxons hadn't even cranked to full scream when the impacts shook the gun-deck.

Glave went down on his side, the ceramic shell of his carapace armour scraping on the rockcrete with a hollow sound, jamming the bottom edge of the breastplate into his ribs.

Muscle memory and training had him on his feet before the regular infantry around him. While they tried to drag themselves up, hands locked on their lasrifles, Glave dropped his volley gun and pushed up with his hands, only retrieving the weapon once he was on his feet.

His hand ached as he hefted the volley gun and snapped the servo-arm to his rig.

Check surroundings. Report threats.

He quick-scanned the gun-deck. Took in the vaulted ceiling fifteen storeys above his head. The guns – all the size of hab-blocks, set on 'vanishing' carriages that raised the massive artillery up to the gun-ports then dropped them back to the floor after they discharged, to shield them from fire. The ammunition-hauler vehicles that queued up to the cargo cranes that loaded the train-car-sized ordnance into the smoking breeches of the guns. Elsewhere, wobbling Sentinels used the clamps of their gripping arms to remove any burned-out block cells powering the las-arrays, and bring in fresh ones.

Someone in authority – someone who knew what they were doing, for a change – had posted Glave and his deep patrol down here. Knew they were tunnel-fighters, and thought they'd be better here than on the wall.

But it was hard to understand what was going on here, even when they *weren't* getting hit. Despite the sonic dampener fields around the guns, and a personal dampener clipped to his webbing, Glave's heads-up display was reading decibel levels so intense they'd cause hearing loss and heart arrhythmias within days. It felt like being pounded in the break zone of a stormy coast.

'Up! Up!' Sergeant Veskaj shouted through the vox. He raised his hellgun.

Glave saw it then, above. A ring of rockcrete in the outer wall, glowing white-hot and crumbling as it burned with enough heat to separate atoms.

Melta array. Enemy lander, boarding them like a ship.

Assess the situation, keep scanning.

Glave snapped his head back the other way, making sure they weren't focusing too much on the trouble they could see, and missing the trouble they couldn't. That was a danger of full helmets: tunnel vision.

There was another ring behind them, ten storeys up. Fusing and spitting. Nestled between two guns to shield it from fire.

He barely registered it when both rings blew out with a percussive *bang,* blasting crumbled masonry outward into the cordite-hazed air of the gun-deck. Hunks of rock tumbled into the gunners and ammunition-gangs below.

But not all of them fell. A few dropped and rose, defying physics. Pairing off in ones and twos that…

'Raptors!' yelled Veskaj. Through his dampener, Glave could hear the shriek of the sergeant's hellgun. 'Move to gun seventeen, defensive–'

'No, belay! Belay!' Glave contradicted, running the other direction. 'They're behind us at gun fifteen. We're closer, move!'

'Do it!' Veskaj said. 'Follow Glave. Form on fifteen!'

They ran. In Glave's heads-up display, a counter labelled *FEET UNTIL EFFECTIVE RANGE* counted down as they pounded across the deck.

That was the Kasrkin way. High situational awareness. Flexibility. Subsuming the ego in service of lethality and survivability. Where the Tempestus Scions were doctrinaire and rigid, the Kasrkin prided themselves on adaptability and trust. Veskaj would have no ego about being contradicted. Fire-team Gamma would think nothing of pivoting to follow the observation of its special weapons operator.

FEET UNTIL EFFECTIVE RANGE: 103

And a good thing. Because the horrors were already upon the gunners.

There were two. Black-armoured. Diving and screeching. The piercing screams of their helmet vox-emitters penetrating Glave's personal dampener and stabbing into his ears with such painful intensity that the sound broke up in his right ear, turning into a crackle like vox static.

FEET UNTIL EFFECTIVE RANGE: 56

One made a swooping pass on the gunners, mangling two with his chainsword. Firing a bolt into the windscreen of an ammunition hauler that spiderwebbed the glass and painted it with the driver's blood. So fast. Difficult to see. Nothing but a blur. Only when it briefly reached its apex did it slow enough for him to notice that it had a helm reworked into a dragon's open maw, a barbed tongue emerging from its mouth.

But it was the other that grabbed Glave's attention.

It had broken off, slamming feet first into the barrel of the massive artillery piece, its boot-clamps rooting it in place.

This one had a helmet so incongruously terrible Glave would remember it for the rest of his life. It was nothing but an open mouth, like the gaping hinged jaw of a carnivorous plant, ringed with teeth.

And it had a meltagun.

FEET UNTIL EFFECTIVE RANGE: 20

Glave put on a burst of speed.

For as its teammate dived and wheeled and killed on the gunners' platform, the maw-headed Raptor lowered the cylindrical nose of its weapon and began cooking the rotating hydraulic joint that allowed the cannon to ratchet into firing position.

'The guns!' shouted Okkun. 'They're trying to spike the guns!'

FEET UNTIL EFFECTIVE RANGE: 0

'Fire!' Veskaj shouted. 'Fire! Fire!'

Glave stopped hard, set his feet, and answered the shrieks of the Raptors with the scream of his volley gun.

Above, the void field sheltering the Martyr's Rampart puckered inward with another hit. The field stretched like a medicae's elastacine glove, slowing the orbital missile enough that Mordlied could see it clearly before it burst through and tumbled end over end, detonating on the outer glacis three hundred yards to his left.

The warhead scooped a chunk out of the sloped wall. Not enough to bring it down, but enough to create a scree slope of loose rubble that besiegers would find easier to climb than the smooth rampart.

The first of the enemy were coming. Groups of cultists trying the walls, organised into forlorn hopes that made piteous attempts to storm the breaches. Masked, tattooed men and women chanting as they came.

They cared not, it seemed, that the Martyr's Rampart remained under orbital bombardment.

'Order Squad Cruciform there,' said Marshal Amalrich, still poised on the fire-step. 'And Brother Lagraine with his heavy bolter. They are not to take one step backwards.'

'It will be done, Marshal,' said Brother Zalthean, stepping back out of earshot to transmit the orders.

Mordlied saw one storming party coming in on his right and lowered his bolt pistol, tracked a running man, then fired. The bolt caught him in the shoulder, cratering his ribcage and killing two other men with the shrapnel.

'They are gathering out there,' said Amalrich, gesturing out past the smoke. 'The masters of these wretched creatures. I can–'

A high-explosive artillery round ripped through the void shield and detonated directly overhead, and the Marshal paused the conversation as the shockwave whomped down on them, hot shrapnel ticking off their power armour.

'I can see a banner,' he continued, raising his voice to be heard over the screams of the Cadian wounded. 'There. You see? Crimson, with a black device.'

Mordlied looked. 'A skull with a twisted tongue, lord. The so-called Covenant of the True Name. Lorgar's filth.'

'Word Bearers,' the Marshal growled. 'That explains the chanting.'

A lance beam slashed down to their right, dissolving a section of wall eighty yards wide. Cadians on the outer edges of the impact zone rolled and ran, their uniforms combusting into flame. An ammunition store blew, throwing a nova cannon as long as a hab-block off the wall in a cartwheel.

It came to rest across the dry moat outside the rampart, like a log fallen across a stream. Though it still glowed forge-hot, several cultists tried to clamber across. A Black Templar, his armour scoured silver and right arm amputated by the lance strike, levelled his boltgun off-handed and butchered them.

Mordlied looked at the sky, like a man sensing a sprinkle of rain. 'This void shield should be offering more protection, Marshal. I am concerned. The defences may fail.'

'*We* are the defences. And we will not fail.'

Incoming fire streaked in from the marshalling enemy. Scarlet lascannon beams and the flash of scrap artillery mounted on repurposed cargo haulers.

'Lord,' said a voice. For a bare moment, Mordlied tried to isolate the sound in his helm's vox-system, checking volume. But then he looked down and realised it was a human standing below his sight-line, the officer he had spoken to.

'I am not a lord,' Mordlied repeated. 'Did we not discuss this?'

'That was Captain Teska, sir,' said the officer. 'He is dead. I am Captain Voyht.'

Mordlied narrowed his eyes, and saw that indeed this trooper was new. It was a female, with half her head swaddled in a bandage, the spot over one covered eye sopped with blood. She held a vox-receiver in one hand, its coiled wire leading to the backpack unit of a signalman. 'Indeed, captain, please proceed.'

'New orders,' she shouted. 'We're to pull back to the curtain wall.'

'Why?'

'This position is indefensible. The seismic shock of the bombardment has unseated the void-shield emitters, it's wavering between fifteen and forty-eight per cent capacity. We're going to be pounded to death before they even encircle us. You're to come with us, and assist our fighting withdrawal.'

A battle cannon round arced above them, and the captain and her signalman flinched, flattening themselves against the parapet.

'We are not part of your command structure,' Mordlied answered. He did not need to consult the Marshal on this. 'Nor subject to any of your general orders.'

'This comes direct from Creed, he honourably requests you to redeploy on the Alpha Curtain Wall, southern quadrant. You'll do more good there. His words, sir.'

'He wishes us to retreat?' Amalrich broke in, his eyes still on the battlefield, but no longer pretending not to listen.

'They are calling it a redeployment, Marshal.'

'Let us leave the twisting tongues to the Word Bearers. It is a retreat. And we shall not do it. This is the Martyr's Rampart, brother, not the Redeployment Rampart or the Tactical With-drawal Rampart. Not the Coward's Rampart. It was built to stand, and stand we shall until we can stand no more.'

'But...' said the captain. 'The Lord Castellan...'

'Tell the Lord Castellan, we have taken our vow, and we shall keep it,' said Mordlied. 'Go if your commander says you must, we shall hold this rampart.'

'With respect,' she said, 'it's becoming a pile of rubble.'

'Then we will sanctify this rubble with our blood. We shall defend each brick to the last, and turn it into relics you will venerate in your cathedrals for generations. Go – we shall offer what covering fire we can.'

Then Mordlied turned towards the battle, located a target, and put a round through a hulking abhuman that was using all three of its arms to climb up the scree slope.

Over the wall, the chants rose. Mordlied could see a dark figure in amongst the rabble, a third taller than the hunched, cowed masses of cultists, contorting as he read from books that chittered and flapped around him like crows about a corpse.

The Marshal gripped his power sword from its place embedded in the wall and twisted it free of the rockcrete.

'Lift the banner, Mordlied. Let us show these heretics who we are.'

'Dorn!' roared Mordlied, and lifted the dragon-tailed banner high.

Below them, the unclean horde quailed at the sight of the long pennant, and Mordlied's hearts swelled. The Cruxis Banner had lain for a day and a night on the lap of the Emperor Himself, and though the unclean did not know this, they sensed its power.

'For the Emperor and Dorn!'

The voice of their demagogue, and his surging flood tide of congregants, sucked up the little assault parties before the wall the way a large, fast-moving wave draws in the breakers that roll before it.

Bolt-shells exploded among them, scything through ink-marked flesh and turning bone to shrapnel. A plasma blast scorched down from the wall, its white-blue starfire incinerating four cultists before the Dark Apostle flicked a finger and blocked the tunnel of light with one of his avian tomes.

From his black-dripping mouth, the Heretic Astartes said a blasphemous name that could only be pronounced with his serpent tongue, and the Black Templar's plasma gun overloaded, burning the brother where he stood.

The wave of flesh spilled into the moat, filling it with their bodies, as they surged up the scree slopes. Ink-dark clouds eclipsed the sun, casting the rampart in shadow.

'Burn them!' called Amalrich, and the burning pilot lights of flamers ignited along the wall, flickering like candles against the encroaching darkness.

And as the Cadians withdrew, evacuating through the back gate into the long, crater-marked kill-zone separating the rampart from the curtain wall, the Black Templars anointed their enemy with sacred fire.

An ancient, crimson-smeared drop pod punched into the earth of Cadia like a comet thrown by a vengeful deity.

It contained only one man – though whether he was still a man was an open question.

Urkanthos did not wait for the hatches to unfold. He kicked one open, the percussive crunch of the blow sounding like two ground-cars colliding, followed by the tortured squeal of tearing servos as he forced the door open with his weight.

The descent jets meant to cushion the pod's landing had not fully cycled down, so when he waded into the battlefield he did so through a shin-deep blossom of rocket fire.

A wounded Seraphim was the only one who witnessed the moment Urkanthos, the Conqueror of Davorsa, first touched Cadian soil.

The favoured warlord of Khorne took a deep breath of enemy atmosphere, then watched in amusement as the fallen corpse bride tried to raise her bolt pistol.

'You may try, prayer-witch. I will give you this.'

She made a good effort, but the rotary cannon had taken her right arm and sheared off one of her jump-pack engines. Grievously injured from the fall, unable to prop herself up with her missing arm and kilted oddly on the bulky jump pack, she struggled like an overturned beetle. Sparks flickered in the gorget of her powered armour, underlighting her face and indicating malfunction. Her shoulder blades were almost certainly crushed. He could hear the bones grinding as she lifted the heavy weapon.

She fired, and the mass-reactive round ploughed the dirt two feet to his right. With a howl of pain she pulled the trigger again, but her shoulder had lost strength and the shot went no further than an infant could throw a ball. She was praying, stuttering a cate-chism from lips painted scarlet from internal injuries.

'A noble effort,' he rumbled.

Urkanthos walked to her, and saw on her face the horror his approaching form brought. Her chin began to quiver, either from fear or the chill of blood loss.

Korda had called him Half-Prince. A christening that enraged him, for it was true. He was half-ascended. Bones too long for his flesh. Nerves not gliding correctly and joints out of place. So much of his new body was like the wings of a moth fresh from a chrysalis, folded and slick, awaiting the warm sun to dry it so that it could stretch.

It hurt to move. Hurt even worse than the Butcher's Nails. As he strode towards her, blood sweated from his skin in little ruby beads that streaked down like raindrops.

'You followed your witch-leader, your canoness to destruction. I admire this. And you did great slaughter in the eyes of the Blood God before you discovered what was in those lifters, and were slaughtered in turn. Thus, you have twice-worshipped him despite your condemnations.'

Indeed, the flying canoness – Genevieve, the daemonic whispers told him – and her entourage had wreaked havoc on the initial landing parties until they'd flown into the largest lander and found the behemoth that waited within.

The Lord of Skulls had made a fascinating ruin of her body, even though only one of its rotary cannon rounds had struck her. At least two dozen more prayer-witches had fallen in their flight away.

He could see the agony on the wounded Sister's features, and for a moment he felt a strange kinship with this false angel brought to ground. They were united in pain.

Perhaps that is why he paid her the honour of approaching, why he knelt down and crushed her pistol in his crustacean claw. Took her shivering chin between the fingers of his natural arm, swollen too large for a gauntlet.

'Golden God of Mankind,' she said, 'shield my S-Sisters and guard thy shrine. Gift me one moment of strength, so I might strik-k-k–'

She started to hitch, her spasming head tugging at his fingers as something vital in her chest started to fail.

'I do not care about *your shrine,*' said Urkanthos, in a voice that spoke half in, half out of the materium. 'I do not care about your Sisters or your God-Emperor. I am here for only two things – *blood, and skulls.* And you will give me both.'

The sun shone behind him, and his shadow pooled on the Sister. It began to stretch, its edges unfolding into claws and quills.

'*Not just blood,*' whispered the daemon, Gore-mouth, and from the horror on the Battle Sister's face, Urkanthos knew she could hear it too. '*The right blood. Sanctified blood. Blood stolen from the Corpse-God so that we might reanoint His temple.*'

It was why, of all the dropzones, Urkanthos had chosen this one. He would draw the eye of Khorne with unholy slaughter, and be the Half-Prince no more.

The Sister's pupils dilated, taking on the glassy, wide shine of brain-death Urkanthos had seen so many times over the last ten millennia. A fresh well of blood spilled over her bottom lip and ran down her chin in a ribbon. She was looking through him, eyes wobbling left to right, as if beholding something behind his back. Her single hand, relieved of the weight of the pistol, fought the encumbering, joint-frozen armour and rose, as if reaching out.

It was so eerily real that Urkanthos himself looked over his shoulder, seeing only the smoking drop pod and field of landers unloading their war engines.

'*There is nothing,*' hissed the daemon. '*A death-hallucination. The crimson god grows impatient.*'

Urkanthos realised the Sister was trying to speak and, curious, he loosened his grip.

'S-saint,' she mewled. Weak at first, then louder, gaining strength, speaking, then calling, then shrieking in ecstasy. 'Saint! Saint! Saint!'

Urkanthos tightened his grip and wrenched the head off. It came away from the traumatised vertebrae with a tearing pop.

Then, still kneeling, he reached backwards and fixed it on his skull-rack, so the other corpse brides could see it when he came for them.

He turned towards the Shrine of St Morrican.

A temple he would make his own, painted with gore and built on a foundation of skulls.

A foundation that would begin with the dead woman, who called in vain for her saint.

Keztral was supposed to be pict-capturing the enemy landings up north, around the crashed Dark Angels cruiser *Sword of Defiance*. Cutting north-west along the Rossvar Mountains. Getting good shots of the massing attack on the wreck so Kraf Command could estimate enemy troop strengths and identify Traitor Legions.

That wasn't happening. She was way off her flight plan, out of the air corridor, amid the crossfire of orbital bombardment and air defence fire.

Running for her life.

'Break! Break!' screamed Darvus. 'It's on us again!'

Lock tone.

Keztral slammed the stick left and then forward, rolling them over into a dive. Heard the shotgun bang of Darvus deploying chaff flares.

It was a risky manoeuvre, the little buzz-fighter on their tail was nimble, made for sky-dancing through a dogfight, but Keztral bet it couldn't dive like her Avenger.

Deadeye plunged, the lock tone shutting off as the missile strayed towards the flares, banging harmlessly to their upper portside.

In the top of her canopy the buzz-fighter zipped by ahead of her on its weird, curving flight path, the three fins of its tail assembly spinning like the teeth of an industrial bore-tool. So small, she doubted there was a pilot inside.

It didn't need one.

For the packs of traitor aircraft hunting and killing through the skies were, nearly all of them, warp engines. Machines animated through wicked rituals of binding and sacrifice. Things more animal than aircraft. Airframes with pilots melded into them, becoming the heart of a raging, infected nervous system.

That was not common knowledge. But pilots were briefed on enemy aircraft variants, their capabilities and silhouettes.

Even now, pulling out of the dive, she watched the buzz-fighter move like an insect towards a Marauder bomber. It pulled a barrel roll, spinning like a top as it loosed unguided micro-rockets in a volley that missed the lumbering bomber's tail. Then, dodging improbably through its streams of answering turret fire, the fighter jinked in an impossible sideways diagonal to bring it into collision range.

It detonated, blasting itself into a cone of flak-shrapnel that scythed through the Marauder, sending it on a lazy path down, engines aflame.

'Suicide craft!' Keztral called. 'Darvus, don't let those buzzers get close.'

'I'm more worried about getting back in the corridor. A las-array nearly sliced our tail off a second ago. I don't want to get downed by our own groundfire, Hanna.'

'Copy,' she said, pulling a tight turn. As if to punctuate Darvus' point, a flak shell burst a few points starboard off her nose, rattling the left wing with splinters of hot steel.

'No damage, too far off.'

Darvus was right, they needed to get back into the safe airspace. But by turning around, they were going into the thick of the battle. Plunging into the air corridor like a sewing needle that had pulled away to tighten a stitch before once again pushing into cloth.

And the safe corridor was anything but.

Combat raged through the airspace. Disorganised. Mad. Contrails twisting together like loose yarn left to tangle in a box. Dogfights thundered at multiple altitudes, from the ceiling heights of the Lightnings' upper limits to down just above the heads of the disembarking heretics.

The vox was no less disordered. A hundred inter-wing conversations overlapped as pilots fought and died. Keztral narrowed their vox-link to only the closest aircraft.

'Sword Leader, it's on me! It's on me!'

'Sword Six, this is Sword Leader. I see you. Keep jinking around I'll be there in ten seconds.'

'Sword Leader, where are you? I'm out of chaff, it's–'

A hollow bang on the line, like a fifty-year-old ration tin exploding from the internal pressure of rot.

A Navy Lightning tumbled past, one wing nothing but an amputated stub of ragged metal. To her extreme right, a Valkyrie of the 119th loosed a hunter-killer that streaked upward on its purplish smoke and burst a Hell Blade interceptor, shredding it into a cough of debris. A Thunderbolt crossed her canopy view in a steep angle, running from autocannon fire, only to be slammed out of the air by a Heldrake that intercepted it claws first like a raptor diving on a kill.

'Shit!' She twisted briefly to watch the enemy engine fall with the heavy fighter, talons crumpling its cockpit as the reptilian head savaged one stuttering engine.

'Holy Throne,' said Darvus. 'They're trying to bail. It's eating–'

'Don't think about it. Find me a line to the target.'

'Affirmative.'

'Howl Squadron, Howl Squadron,' she said, sending a spike pulse on the Valkyrie band. 'This is Spyglass Three, we're breaking northwest to *Sword of Defiance* and would like some cover.'

'Confirm, Spyglass Three, send location and altitude.'

'Take us lower,' said Darvus. 'Combat looks less intense down– Frekk!'

Keztral nosed down. 'What?'

'Debris. Missile I think.'

She saw what he meant. They'd been relatively high before, when they'd broken out of the corridor running from the buzz-fighter. Now that they were in the lower altitudes, steel was raining from the sky. Aircraft parts. Burning wrecks. Ordnance, its fuel expended without finding a target and now dropping like miniature bombs. Something clinked off her right wing like a handful of thrown gravel, and she realised it was spent autocannon casings.

Then there were the chutes. A whole quilt of them, thick enough that she found it difficult to thread them. Each one with a pilot dangling in the sky.

'We're better off outside the damned corridor,' she said. 'Suck a handful of debris or a chute into our engine and we're going down. Can you–'

'Still waiting on that fix, Spyglass. Where–'

She heard Darvus stiffen just before he screamed: 'Evade, Hanna! Five o'clock high!'

Keztral slammed the air brake, punching the floor pedals hard to yaw the craft left and slide out of their expected flight line.

The dragon plunged past them, wings folded and claws extended.

Keztral barely had time to let out her breath before the brass wings sliced outward, arresting the Heldrake's descent. It flapped to gain altitude, trying to come up behind them.

'Spyglass?'

There wasn't much Keztral could do besides bank and ram the daemon engine. She'd committed to the dive. Try to recover now, and she'd bleed so much momentum the more agile Drake would have them for sure. G-forces stretched at her cheeks.

If the Avenger had had a gatling cannon rather than a picter, she might've been able to bank hard and wing the creature with a burst.

Instead, all she could do was bank hard left, standing on her wing tip as she zipped back out of the corridor and into the storm of groundfire.

Maybe it wouldn't follow them. Maybe...

'Spyglass, you've exited the corridor, don't–'

Autocannon tracers spewed below them in a line, like the dot-dashes on a vox telegraph. They glowed a sick, poisoned green.

Keztral pulled a hard-right bank and punched the throttle forward to max, burning away, angling low to the north-west.

'Spyglass Three! Spyglass Three!' the vox blurted. *'We can't do you any good out there, you're way off flight plan and we don't have the fuel to chase you.'*

Behind her, she heard an unfamiliar industrial chatter and worried the engine had thrown a turbofan – but no, it was just a sound she hadn't heard since training.

Darvus was firing the heavy stubber. Harassing the Heldrake as it pursued.

'Never mind,' she said, dipping even lower, to two hundred feet. Close enough she could see individual infantry along Kraf's outer defensive works. Red pen-lines of las-fire dazzled across the turf. 'I've got an idea.'

An airburst shell from Kraf boomed ahead of them, close enough for the shockwave to rattle them in their seats.

'Why are we going low?' Darvus let off another burst. 'Diving is its preferred attack pattern.'

'It won't dare.' She punched her feet on the pedals, yawing the aircraft so it rotated like a wavering compass needle to fly a zigzag evasive pattern. 'This low and it risks missing us and hitting the ground. It also takes us below Kraf's defensive fire.'

Another splash of autocannon rounds whickered by. One punched a hole through their left wing as big around as a bracelet. Steam bled from the hit.

Keztral reached for the vox-controls above her, throwing frequency toggles. Checked the map grid secured to the cockpit wall with rubbarine loops.

'Spyglass Three to ground. Spyglass to ground,' she broadcast. 'Distress, distress. Enemy bat in pursuit at grid beta-seven-niner, request groundfire.'

Keztral's seat kicked sideways, her flight helmet knocking the canopy's side panel with a hollow *crack*. She eased off the throttle and saw a stream of tracers drum the air ahead of them.

'Armour, no penetration,' said Darvus, over the chattering stubber. 'It's lining up on us.'

'*Spyglass,*' a harsh voice cut in. '*Deploy flares.*'

Keztral stamped her thumbs on the countermeasure buttons so hard it hurt.

Fan-tails of smoke and firebug sparks leapt up to her left and right.

And in an instant, the air was full of fire.

'Major. Major Hellsker. Major Hellsker, sir.'

Hellsker saw a wandering light. She felt drugged, heavy, like the time she'd broken her shoulder at the academy and the school medicae had overprescribed obscurine.

She dragged at her eyelids, trying to remember how her facial muscles worked.

'Who's in charge?' said another voice.

'She is, I think,' said the first voice. That was Dakaj, their chief medicae.

What happened? They'd been in the artillery observation tower, seen the enemy, then…

Who's in charge?

She is, I think.

Her brain lit up like a vox that'd had a loose wire reconnected, runes flaring and dial needles bouncing.

Her eyes flew open, then contracted again as she squinted into the lens of a stablight.

'Major?' asked Dakaj. 'How do you feel?'

'Barathus.' She sat up. 'What happened to Colonel Barathus?'

Dakaj looked at the other trooper, his orderly Suvane, the other voice.

'Barathus,' she insisted.

Her words came out slurred. Wet. It sounded like she'd said *Baratshush.* She put a hand to her lips and found blood. Her mouth was slopping with it, along with the rockcrete grit that dusted her fatigues and lodged between her flak vest and uniform blouse.

Hellsker spat into her hand and found it wasn't grit – it was teeth. Her tongue probed her gumline and found nothing but raw, swollen flesh where her right-hand molars used to be.

Rockcrete debris and rebar lay all around her, and from the numeral three stencilled on the wall, she realised she was still in the artillery citadel – but several floors down from where she'd been. She could see broken pillars and sky above.

'There was a hit,' said Dakaj. 'Orbital strike, we think, or a high-altitude guided bomb. Took the top three levels off the northside wall bunkers. Knocked out half our outward-facing heavy artillery. You're lucky to be alive. Damn lucky. The blast threw you into the far corner, to the part of the room that didn't collapse. The saints watch over you, Marda Hell–'

'I know I'm alive, where's Barathus?'

Dakaj took a deep breath. 'Somewhere in the rubble. We'd try to dig him out, but it might destabilise the pile and cause more damage. We've found one foot so far.'

'And his cap,' said Suvane, holding it out, as if this were helpful.

Barathus' cap. That sergeant's patrol cap he always wore. As if it made the courtly man more of a soldier's soldier. Part of the costume of command. The mask he had to wear to fulfil his duty, because he was not strong enough to do it himself.

'Do you have headache, nausea?' asked Dakaj.

'No. Well, yes. Here...' She reached.

'You have a beauty of a lump. Now do you see why I'm always telling you frekk-stubborn officers to wear your helmets?'

'I guess,' said Hellsker, taking the colonel's patrol cap. 'Yes, good advice.'

There was something tucked in the patrol cap's headband. At first she thought it was a prayer card or letter from home. But when she slid it out, she found it was his poem.

She folded the paper and put it in her pocket, then swung her legs off the cot.

'How long was I out?'

'Twenty-two minutes. I think you were knocked cold, but no sign of concu–'

'You have a vox?'

'The rescue team has one,' said Suvane.

'Good.' Hellsker stood, running a hand through her scalp-tight braids. Brushing the grit out of her hair. She turned to the orderly, looked him in the eyes. 'Tell the vox-officer to get on it. General signal. I want every section officer in the command room in fifteen minutes. Captains and above.'

'Which command room?' he asked. 'The colonel's?'

'No,' Hellsker said, sliding the patrol cap onto her head. 'It's my command room now.'

Glave ducked behind the sandbag wall right as it blew inward, the bolt-shell punching out a section he could probably stick his fist through.

The sandbags deflated and slumped at the hit, causing the wall to slouch and fill in the damaged portion. That was the beauty of sandbags, and why Cadia's southern deserts and beaches had been systematically stripped to bare rock over the course of seven millennia.

'It's coming for us,' barked Sergeant Veskaj. 'Eleven o'clock.'

Veskaj fired, the crack-zip of his shots splitting through the humid, smoky gloom. He fired shoulder-on to the heretic, a stance Glave had never used in combat before.

Fighting cultists and heretic light infantry, you came at the enemy chest-on, taking advantage of the carapace armour's ballistic protection. Face them sideways, and you risked taking a las-round in the join in the side of the breastplate – safer to be shot directly in the chest.

But the incoming fire was bolt-rounds, explosive, and you wanted to present a slim side-profile with your shoulder guard presented – in hopes that if you took a hit, it would glance off like a round hitting sloped tank armour.

Glave threw his left shoulder forward, raised his volley gun over the sandbag emplacement and let off another stream, causing the diving Raptor to break off its attack run and circle back into the vaults, chased by darts of las-light.

That was Glave's role right now – suppressing fire. Worry less about hitting the heretic bastards than keeping them unbalanced. Let the others try and get kill shots.

He and Fire-team Gamma had the advantage of reach for now – their hellguns had almost twice the effective range of a bolt pistol – and they weren't about to give that up by advancing. Especially when the engineers had so politely built them hard points in the event of a wall breach.

It was a game of stab-and-retreat. The Raptors would try to land and sabotage the guns, Gamma Squad would chop enough fire their way to dissuade them, and the heretics would go aloft again.

Except Fire-team Gamma had done their job a bit too well. With the gun crew dead, the Raptors had decided to clear the Kasrkin threatening them before continuing their mission.

The heretics were cagey, cautious. Probably because they were thinly disbursed on the wall. One- and two-man demolition teams. To his right, Glave could see another pair perched atop a volcano lance, weathering a storm of las-fire that swirled around them like snow in howling wind.

If there had been five of them, no doubt they would've charged Gamma and butchered them, but this pair weren't willing to risk it with only two.

That was fine with Glave. Hardened and confident as he was, he still didn't fancy tangling with a Heretic Assault Marine on the ground, much less one that could fly.

Where had that bastard gone, anyway?

'Deck two command, two command,' said Luzal. He had the hand-set of his vox pressed to his mouth and ear, hellgun ready in the other hand, its barrel supported by the sandbags. 'Two jump pack Astartes on gun fifteen, sabotage in progress. We are holding. Also on guns sixteen and thirteen, I–'

A shattering bang echoed through the shadowed vaults above.

The halogen floodlights around them, the glow-globes on the poles, the running lights of the floor...

All of them went dark.

'Frekk,' said Stitcher Kristan. 'At least it's only the ones on this position.'

To their right, gun sixteen was still pooled in light. It was not much help. Indeed, it only ensured no one could develop proper night vision.

'Everyone, shhhhhh,' purred Veskaj. 'No stablights, no flares. Helmet lenses only. Cover anything that glows. We're changing position. Move left. Slow, slow and quiet.'

They crouched, backs hunched and weapons low.

Glave could hear his breath in the rebreather. Heavy and strong, panting with adrenaline. Could they hear him? God-Emperor protect if they could hear him.

He drew a slow breath, counting to four on the inhale. Holding it for four. Breathing out for four.

He kept it up as they slid into the dark, making no sound but the occasional squeak of a scuffing boot.

Inhale four. Hold for four. Let it go for four.

His helmet's starlight lenses could see little of the surrounding world. They were light-enhancers, and there was not much light here. Paired with the cavernous emptiness of the space, there was little he could make out apart from the four crouched men and endless blackness.

Only the glow of...

'Luzal,' he hissed on the squad micro-bead. 'Your dials.'

'What?'

'Your vox-unit isn't shrouded. Your dials are–'

Two blazing eyes erupted out of the darkness above them – the blue-flamed irises of jump pack engines igniting only feet above their bent heads. Framing a giant that hovered two feet off the deck.

Luzal screamed as a barbed gauntlet lifted him in the air, blood spouting from a severed artery in his throat.

The fallen demigod used the kicking vox-operator as a shield as its other hand discharged its bolt pistol – *wham, wham* – into Okkun as the pointman raised his carbine. Okkun's chestplate cratered and his head exploded into gristle, leaving his lower palate and tongue perversely exposed.

Glave threw himself on his back to stay clear of the monster's reach, sighted his volley gun.

'Fire!' yelled Veskaj.

Glave smashed the trigger, holding it down. The move made his hand ache, but that was more than equal payment for the violence he unleashed.

The volley gun was at near point-blank range. Impossible to miss, even with one shot.

Glave got more than one. More than ten. He burned the power arrays in his volley gun. Cooked the barrel. Sprayed out so much sixty-megathule las-fire that he could feel the power pack heating his carapace backplate.

The beam gutted the Raptor, punching in below where its breastplate ended in a leering mouth, then slicing upward like an industrial cutter through the torso. Heat-resistant ablative armour spalled away in beads, servos fried and caught fire. Even through his rebreather, Glave could smell an odour like spoiled meat and cogitator parts cooking over an open fire. The right engine of the jump pack cut out.

Glave ripped the beam upward through the head, from face grille to crown.

The Raptor slumped over in the air, the remaining jump engine driving it face first into the deck, where it lay still.

'Throne,' Glave cursed. 'Holy Throne.'

He stood, looking at the fallen beast.

You better put a bayonet in the Despoiler himself.

He'd *killed* it. He, Servantus Glave, had killed a Heretic Astartes.

Let them argue he was unfit *now.* He'd destroyed a ten-thousand-year enemy of humanity in close combat. People got their names on walls for that. They made statues of you for that.

'Glave,' said Veskaj. 'Let's go, there's still another one.'

You better put a bayonet in the Despoiler himself.

'Glave, shake it off, let's move out.'

Put a bayonet in the Despoiler.

'Maybe I will,' said Glave. 'Maybe I actually will.'

FIVE

Deadeye tore the sky over the aegis defence line, the row of shields and emplacements flashing below Keztral in the space of a breath.

Orange tracer fire zipped behind her from below, the work of quad-gun automated turrets pouring explosive shells at the Drake.

The Avenger shook, bucked, and Keztral didn't know if she was being hit by the groundfire or the Heldrake behind her. In her peripheral vision, she spotted the bright-red glare of an Icarus lascannon.

'It's hit!' shouted Darvus. 'It's breaking off. Looks like it's climbing high and away.'

'Thank the frekking Throne,' she breathed. 'But we've been chased right out of the combat area. And we're low enough on fuel we're going to have to land with an empty tank and full negative spools.'

'Well… What's that?'

'What?'

'On the horizon. That smoke-cloud.'

Keztral checked her map. 'It's not tasked to anyone.'

'We should take a look. That's a weird cloud. And big. Like an armoured column.'

Keztral examined the map. Scoped the damage on the left delta wing. 'Are you sure we have enough fuel? Can you confirm it on the flight calculator?'

Keztral waited, hearing the scrape of the card-paper wheel.

'It'll be tight, but we can make it.'

They were quiet as they flew towards the cloud. Keztral watched their fuel and listened to the engines, constantly glancing over to check if there was any change to the hole through their left wing. Darvus scanned the clouds for the jagged wings of the Heldrake.

She could tell by the sound of the heavy stubber traversing back and forth, sounding like a dead tree limb creaking in a gale.

'That's it,' she said. 'I see it. Throne, it's big.'

'What is it?'

'I...' She paused. 'I don't know. There are some spires. Run out the picters, we need to record this.'

They were already low, already screaming in hot. Too dangerous to climb for altitude now.

'Ten seconds,' Keztral called. 'Increasing throttle, set lenses for high-speed shutter.'

'Affirmative, you see what we're driving at?'

Keztral leaned forward in the seat, squinting. 'The silhouettes are weird. Five seconds.'

She felt the forward camera drop, her seat rumbling as it started to cycle.

'Four.'

She saw the column now. A cavalcade of monsters. A madman's dream rendered in steel and iron, forges stoked with unholy light.

'Three.'

'Watch out for those pylons.'

She made an adjustment. Got ready to hit the target line.

'Tw–'

'The Drake!' Darvus yelled. 'He's on us. Frekking saints, I don't know where it came from.'

Behind her, she heard the buzz-chatter of the heavy stubber.

'Should I break?'

'No!' Darvus fired another half-belt. 'Get the picts!'

'Fire armament.'

Keztral hit her override buttons, triggering the cylinder. Below her, the spinning *clunk-clunk-clunk* of the rotary picter melded with the kick of autocannon rounds drumming the Avenger.

She couldn't look back. Wouldn't be able to, beyond her seat-back. Couldn't evade, either, not with the pict-array running.

But she could tell Darvus was giving the Drake hell from the way its autocannon bursts kept wavering off-centre. Green tracers splashed around them in parabolas, connecting when they slashed down across them but unable to hold on them in a way–

Two big jolts. They rattled her head forward and made her neck ache. She saw smoke streaming from their right engine. Cotton white, at first, then oily black.

And she could hear the whistle of outside air. A hole in the canopy.

'Darvus?' She wrestled the controls. Tried to prevent the stuttering right engine from dropping out. She could see flames licking in the well of the turbofan. Needles dipped. Losing altitude. 'Darvus, are you hit?'

Darvus didn't answer, but the heavy stubber kept chattering.

'I didn't hear about it,' said Sergeant Menschzak. 'And we're not supposed to let anyone get close without written orders.'

The Munitorum worker frowned, unsure. 'I… I have one of those, I think. Yes, here you are. It's in the work order.'

He set down his toolbox and took the clipboard from under his arm, leafing through thin forms on cheap pink carbon-copy paper.

Menschzak sighed, letting his lascarbine hang across his chest. Here they were, his whole squad, on guard duty to control access to the mechanisms of Beta Curtain Wall Gate West.

What a waste.

As he paged through the Munitorum work order, trying to cross-reference the poor copies and verify the stamps, he could feel the reverberation of the wall under his boots.

Rumour had it there was major combat on Alpha Curtain Wall North. Heavy bombardment and enemy movements in view of the South. The East, he knew, was bracing for a massed attack. They'd whiled away the last few hours listening to vox-feeds from the aerial battle brewing out there.

Hells, the troopers in observation units with their big scopes and rangefinders said even the Delvian Cleave was getting hit.

But here on the Beta Curtain Wall West? Nothing. Not apart from the orbital strikes that were happening all over. Hells, they were doing preventative maintenance.

'Why now?' Menschzak asked. 'The time for this work should've been a week ago.'

The Munitorum civilian shuffled his feet. Nervous, no doubt, that they might not allow him to finish his assigned task. 'It's a standard maintenance cycle. You can see it on the form. Today is the date it comes due. Every six months we have to inspect the gate's operation and apply lubricants.'

'You couldn't have done it earlier?'

He shook his head. 'I'm not responsible for that. They give me the work order and I do it. I have to follow orders.'

'And I have orders to keep people away,' Menschzak replied.

'Quite so, yes, quite so.' The worker dipped his head in deference. 'But imagine if the enemy came and it refused to close, due to not having performed proper maintenance rites?'

'How long?'

'Two hours at most, then I'm gone.'

Menschzak handed back the clipboard. 'You have ninety minutes. And you need to open the toolbox.'

'Do I look like a heretic recidivist?'

'You have to follow orders, so do I,' Menschzak said, a note of annoyance in his voice. 'There's been a new wave of bomb attacks today. One hit an airfield fuel depot. They told me I have to ask, so I have to ask.'

The Munitorum worker shrugged, and clicked open the toolbox, holding it out at arm's length.

Menschzak leaned over the box, looking at the rack of phials. 'They smell bad.'

'They are bad, I'm supposed to wear a gas hood applying it. Highly caustic, eats away rust. You might not want to lean so close, the stoppers are only so effective.'

Menschzak backed off a step. 'Just hurry. Our commissar makes her rounds in two hours, I don't want to have to explain.'

'You won't,' said the worker, weaving through the squad.

Within five minutes, Yann Rovetske had secured a descent line to the wall top above Beta Curtain Wall West. Donning his gas hood and rubbarine gauntlets, he clipped the automated ascent/descent reel on his harness to the rope and carefully rappelled to the top hinge, toolbox slung over his shoulder.

The gate was large. Twelve storeys. Big enough that when the wind came down off the Rossvar Mountains it created a gale-blast wind tunnel through the open gates.

They were open now, to permit the free movement of troops if necessary for a sally or raid, and the air tunnel pulled Rovetske away from the hinge for a moment, despite the fact that he'd sheltered in the V of the open gate.

He pinwheeled one arm, reaching out with a maintenance climbing axe to hook the edge of the hinge and pull himself closer. Secured himself in place with a magnet-line.

'Please,' he said. 'Do not harm me. I am a servant, and you have greater purpose.'

With one shaking hand, he reached down and withdrew a phial, uncorking it with his gloved thumb and using his other hand to fit it in the rear chamber of an industrial point-sprayer with its long, needle-thin tube, like the ones tank crews used to apply oil and unguents to out-of-reach areas.

In the tube, the primordial being bubbled.

'Shhhhh, shhhhhhh,' he whispered. 'Be easy. It is not time. Patience, patience.'

The hinge was ten feet tall, and for a moment he worried the contents of the phial was not enough. But as he worked his way down the hinge, it was clear there was more than enough. Where he squeezed the pus-like substance, it sizzled and curdled with delight, dripping down the joins Rovetske tried his best to fill.

Then, so slowly that he believed it his imagination at first, it began to retreat. More gel than liquid in the open air, it crawled and oozed against gravity to slip into the depths of the metalwork and spread itself over the loops and pins of the enormous hinge.

When he was done, Rovetske jettisoned the tube and let it fall – the *ping* of the phial ejecting cutting through the rush of the wind.

It spun away, disappearing below. The interior of the curtain walls was practically a refuse dump, and it would not be noticed.

He whispered a prayer as he loaded the next phial, sweating despite the piercing claws of the wind.

Rovetske did not like touching it. In fact, his whole body was screaming that he should take the case of phials off his shoulder, hold it at arm's length, and drop it into the heap below. But over his shoulder, he could feel the Empty Man watching him. Supervising his work. Yet the eyes were no longer the empty black of the void. Instead, the irises swirled with the cloudy, oil-slick rainbow of the empyrean that he'd seen in the sky every night of his life.

It made his skin prickle. Pressure in his sinuses.

He continued his work, the thing he had been training for ever since the Empty Man had come to him as he slept, at the age of ten, saying it had a job for him. A small thing, that would be greatly rewarded.

The packet of powder was exactly where the Empty Man had said he'd find it. Behind a loose brick in the garden. And his uncle's steaming pot of laq-tea was unattended, just as he had said it would be.

That night, the mortuarians had taken his uncle out the front door, lying beneath a silk banner of the Rovetske Trading House. And little Yann had a dream so delicious, he'd never forgotten it. A dream where he had power. Power over himself, mostly, but that gave him power over others. And for the youngest, ignored son of a trading house with no martial tradition that was no small thing.

Yann had always been good at convincing people. Parlour tricks and illusions came easily to him. He could convince his mother and father to do nearly anything he wanted, and he manipulated with easy confidence.

Yet this dream showed him a future where he could gain followers and talk women into bed with the slightest effort. But what interested him most was it showed him how to lie. Not merely deceive, but change reality. To give a man a coin, tell him it was a confection, and watch as he tried to eat it. An ability to reshape what others saw simply because this short young man was so trustworthy, they believed him over their own eyes. The power of suggestion, weaponised.

Just as the sergeant had looked at the blank stack of paper and seen a work order.

Ultimate power.

Ping. Another capsule ejecting.

The sound brought Rovetske back to himself, and he found that he was drooling on his Munitorum uniform.

He reached back for the tubes and found the case empty.

For an instant, he panicked – then realised he was at the bottom southward hinge.

The last hinge.

Had he... not remembered the task? Become so subsumed in the work that he'd finished in a meditative trance? But that would mean he had descended the wall, ascended it again, resecured his line on the opposite side and done it all again.

Five hinges, he could not recall.

No matter – it was time to be gone.

He ditched his gloves down the side of the wall, in case they'd been contaminated. Scrambled back up and packed away his line and descent kit. Checked his chrono.

Fifty minutes. He'd lost fifty minutes.

True to his word, he was gone before the commissar made her rounds.

Zaraphiston's eyes, rolled backwards in his head, looked like the blank orbs of a blind man. His lips moved like those of a sleeper whispering in dreams.

Ordinarily Zaraphiston screened his thoughts in Morkath's presence, knowing either by instinct or wisdom that she could see the impressionistic splashes of his conscious and unconscious mind. But now, he let her see. Allowed her to glimpse the image of two staring eyes that floated above his shoulders like insect wings, the uncanny colours of the warp boiling across the irises.

Then his natural eyes rolled forward, and the ghost irises vanished.

'It is done. I apologise for the interruption, Warmaster.'

'If you deliver what you have promised, there is no need for apology.'

It was an intelligence council, a meeting of Abaddon's inner circle within the inner circle – with only three participants besides the Warmaster himself. Zaraphiston as Lord Deceiver, the Alpha Legion spymaster Cacadius Siron to provide operational briefings, and Morkath to monitor proceedings.

'We had been discussing the specialist vox-centres.' Siron tapped a pale finger, ungauntleted, on several points marked around Kasr Kraf. His incongruously gentle touch caused the shackled map-abhuman to shudder. 'They will serve as artillery spotters inside the city, calling targets and directing fire. Your units are in position to execute?'

Zaraphiston pulled his hood up, hiding his inky eyes. 'They are. And the first wave of strikes has already begun – martyr bombings targeting infrastructure and other soft targets. They will continue to pull forces away from the walls. But as you know, that is prelude.'

The Warmaster nodded. 'The Raptor attack on the northern curtain wall. How goes that?'

'Heavy resistance.' Siron ducked his head to one side, lips pulling up in an expression of managed distaste. His thoughts manifested as a tarot layout, played in solitaire, columns reshuffling as new cards were revealed and played. 'But it's Cadia. There will always be heavy resistance. If there were not, I'd suspect an ambush. We are achieving our objective there, shielding Krom Gat and his Iron Warriors. But the raiding force are paying for it, and it's possible the guns will come back online. May I once again float reinforcing them? Another Dreadclaw sortie and we could–'

'No.' Abaddon shook his head. 'I have already committed all I am prepared to lose. No more. What about Gat?'

Morkath could see how much the abandonment of his Raptors troubled Siron. His mind shuffled columns back and forth. Turned another card, hoping it would open up a new line of thought. It didn't, and he dismissed the problem and moved on.

'Gat's endeavour is proceeding well. With Kraf's long-range artillery embattled, he's disembarking without issue. The only difficulty are the Wolves. The Ironwolves have dug in at Kasr Jark. The city itself is ruins, but with enough promethium in the underground reserves to supply their vehicles. That may complicate Gat's mission.'

'He has his fortress citadels.' Zaraphiston spoke with vinegar, his eyes once again looking elsewhere in time and space. 'And his machines.'

'Largely unarmed construction and demolition engines that cannot work well under fire. Mere tanks can't do what we're asking of Gat. He's clear-cutting a forest made of xenos stone, where the smallest pylons are the size of a hab-tower. He is up to the challenge, but hard opposition makes progress slow.'

'The bitch-pups of Russ.' The Warmaster snarled. 'Always in the most inconvenient place. Are we at least keeping the sons of the Lion bottled in their crashed cruiser?'

'We are,' said Siron, then paused. 'Though...'

'Though?'

'The Hounds of Abaddon are taking monumental casualties, and they haven't breached the hull.'

'We always knew the Dark Angels would not die easy. They never do.'

'Skyrak wants to unleash an orbital plague bombardment from the *Terminus Est*. It might be more efficient than taking it by storm.' Siron sucked air through his teeth. 'Though I had hoped to salvage the ship's cogitators.'

'Urkanthos will not like it,' said the Warmaster. 'We do not want to set our Khornates against our Nurgle contingent.'

'He's not with them,' said Zaraphiston. 'He is gorging himself on Sororitas blood at the Shrine of St Morrican.'

'Strange,' said the Warmaster. And Morkath felt her father's well-hidden disquiet as much as saw it. 'What else?'

'Southern attack is ahead of schedule. Only this far southern ravelin is holding out. There are Astartes there. We are keeping them pinned and bypassing. The Volscani are meeting resistance in the Rossvar, but we predict they'll force the pass in the next twelve hours. Legio Vulcanum are moving on the outer curtain wall in the east... Anything else?'

'The fortress is still unable to fire,' Morkath cut in, knowing that if she let any more demigods speak she would never get a word in edgeways. 'And I am getting strange monitoring readings. Things are... shifting. Realigning. Power from the deep fortress seems to be interrupted.'

The Warmaster turned towards her. 'I have heard a report that may interest you – Siron?'

'We had an observation sighting after the battle with the *Firemane's Fang*. Half a dozen ships, boarding craft, were seen entering fortress orbit and heading coreward. We dispatched interceptor craft that destroyed two, but that leaves several unaccounted for.'

'You think we have saboteurs.' Morkath could hear the horror in her own voice. 'Why was I not told?'

'I thought it was your job to know about the fortress?' Zaraphiston hissed. 'Or is that beyond your ken, noctilith child?'

Morkath's blackstone teeth pressed together. 'This is not a traditional void craft. It is not a built object, it's a living thing we have saddled and pretended is a ship. All our bridges and consoles are a mere overlay so we can tell it where to go and coax power into its warp cannon. There are no sensors to tell of breaches to–'

'Enough,' the Warmaster snapped. 'Morkath, we will speak in private. We are adjourned.'

Morkath waited as the others left, staring at her hands. Too furious and embarrassed to see their thoughts. She did not want to see what gloating images Zaraphiston had chosen to show her.

When the door closed, Abaddon stood, picked up a silver carafe and poured a goblet full of water. He passed it to her between his thumb and forefinger, as though it were a miniscule glass of liquor.

'Drink this.'

Morkath knew an order when she heard it. It could be poison, and she would still drink. He was her Warmaster, and so much more.

'You urged me to fire,' he said, as she finished the water in one long draught. 'And I listened. That action damaged the *Will of Eternity*, which is irreplaceable–'

'I could not know about the countermeas–'

'Do not interrupt me.' The Warmaster did not raise his voice; Morkath heard the quiet creak of the silver carafe as his bare hand tightened around it, denting the metal. 'You have disappointed me, Dravura. After all the favour I have shown. All the freedom I have given you. Perhaps it is my fault. That my belief in you was misplaced.'

Her father's thoughts darkened, not with rage but sadness. Regret. A deep anger, but directed internally.

'No, lord.' She was on her knees before her brain told her body to do so. 'You have done nothing wrong. I have failed you. The fortress resists me. I have done my best. You will find no lack of will or study, no sloth, but it is a heavy task. The fortress is ancient and deep, it does not think like a mortal, even a demigod. But I can do it. I *will* do it.'

She took the edge of his tabard and pressed it to her forehead, but he did not turn to face her. Tears leaked from her eyes, stinging the red flesh around the noctilith eye that had never properly healed – her body constantly trying to reject it.

'I want to believe you, Dravura. And yet, you have consistently failed to deliver on your promises. To the Legion, to me. You did not even know there were vermin loose in the fortress.'

'I will try harder.'

'That, I do not doubt. But I question whether you are equal to the task. Perhaps I should simply keep you a true cup-bearer, a creature who watches and tells me the thoughts of others. You are no demigod, and perhaps I should not expect you to display the loyalty of one.'

Morkath felt his hand on the back of her head, and her breath caught. Hearing her voice, the sound of snot in her nostrils, made Morkath hate herself more than even his soft condemnation. With revulsion, she realised that she was indeed acting like an arming thrall, not a captain of war. Her love for the Warmaster had made her pathetic in his eyes.

She swallowed. Mastered herself. Raised her head to look at him.

'I am no demigod, Warmaster, but your demigods were being murdered by this fortress until I came to you. I have channelled warp energy through more of this blackstone than all of your sorcerers combined. I have made you master of this relic. You set out to find me because you failed to control the last fortress – corrupted it with a daemon in hopes of binding it, yet instead made it feral. Good for nothing but to trade to the Red Corsairs. All these wonders I have done out of loyalty to you. What would you have me do? How shall I prove myself?'

She kept her tone even, aware that he could – perhaps even should – murder her for these words. And she saw the thought pass his conscious, flaring like a match-head. Quick images of how she would die. Raked through with the Talon of Horus. Strangled in the grip of one powerful hand. His fist closing around her head and mashing her cranium into the table edge until her brains were dashed out.

He knew what he was showing her.

And she saw those possible futures snuffed out as the Warmaster remembered the sight of her as a scrawny child, emerging from the darkness.

So instead Abaddon knelt, like he had the first time they met, and stretched out his hand.

'Find the vermin, Dravura,' he whispered, his thoughts a kaleidoscope of promises. She saw herself, standing beside his throne. Sitting among the Chosen. Cleaning the blood off his armour as he returned from battle, his hand laid paternally on her shaven head. 'Find the vermin and exterminate them. Then I will hold you in the highest regard.'

'I will do it,' she said, taking his hand. It still dwarfed her own, as though she were a child. 'I will bleed the stars if you ask me to.'

Abaddon withdrew his callused fist.

'Let us start with Cadia.'

Archenemy troopers swarmed over *Deadeye*'s carcass, dancing close to prod and examine the fallen Avenger before the roiling flames drove them back again.

It hurt Keztral, seeing the aircraft like that. Knowing what was inside. Seeing them gather around it like a bonfire in the early dusk.

She watched through her magnoculars from a quarter-mile away, jammed in a drain culvert beneath a raised roadway. The pipe was barely wider than a sewer access cover, meant to prevent a nearby stream from overflowing the road during the heavy spring rains.

It was so narrow she'd had to shove the precious bundle into it first before concealing herself inside.

'Darvus,' she whispered.

They'd got the picts. At least she thought they had. The pass had been a good one given their lack of time and the fact they were taking fire. She'd come diagonally across the disembarking column of machinery knowing it was the one pass they'd get.

Darvus firing at the Drake the entire time. Stoic, brave. Focused entirely on stinging the flyer as much as he could with his little needle of a weapon. Trying to put that needle in the beast's eye.

He'd stung it, she was sure. So had the groundfire of its own troops. She didn't know which actually brought the Drake down, but she liked to think it was Darvus.

Yet it had stung them too, as had the anti-air from below.

The ailerons and one elevator froze, preventing them from turning back to Kraf. The port-side engine caught fire. Needles on her promethium tanks dropped to nil. System pressure started to give out, the flight stick loose in her hands in a way that spoke of broken cabling. She was lucky the steering answered at all.

'Darvus!' she'd yelled.

She could hear him, but couldn't make out the words. Taking wheezy breaths. The man who was her subconscious hindbrain had gone silent.

Keztral had nursed another thirty seconds out of the starboard engine, then brought it in for a glide, coming at the dark-green fields of Cadia with her flaps all feathered out to bleed momentum. The undercarriage had taken a hit and failed to drop the landing gear. Thank the Emperor there was enough pressure left to run in the rotary picter and at least create a smooth surface for a belly landing.

She knew before she hit it would be a bad setdown.

She didn't know how bad.

The initial impact whiplashed her back and forth in her restraints, bruising her chest against the straps and snapping her head forward then back. It was like being in a forty-mile-an-hour groundcar crash, with the same crunch of steel.

Keztral had hit it on a downslope, thank the Throne, but that meant they slid.

Down the hill, their left wing connected with the burned wreck of a Leman Russ and sheared off, slewing the whole aircraft so it started to go down sideways. When it hit the bottom of the hill, the canopy rose up and folded over onto the remaining wing, and for a sickening moment Keztral thought they'd both be crushed, before it slammed back down.

She'd known she'd have to work fast. There was a lot to do, and enemies would be on them any minute.

Her hands slapped release catches, tore away her restraint harness.

'Darvus!' she'd said. 'Lahon, are you all right?'

Below the floor of her cockpit was a survival bag. Laspistol, rations, a locator beacon and a square of cameleoline, all nestled inside a backpack.

She scooped it up and pulled the emergency canopy release, grateful the hydraulics had not broken.

Keztral scrambled out on the wing, pressing her hands on the hot metal of the fuselage to keep upright.

'Darvus! Darvus, are you–'

Darvus gave a strangled answer.

He was still alive, though only in the most pedantic sense.

Lahon Darvus' head lolled to one side, looking at her with one violet eye.

The other was squashed, the brow drooping down over it, deformed by the gory funnel-shaped wound that had drilled down through the fibre layers of his helmet and into his brain.

'Throne,' Keztral gagged. 'Oh Holy Throne. No.'

Darvus still breathed in a light wheeze. The remaining eye blinked sluggishly, motes of broken glass from his helmet's shattered visor caught in his eyelash. One hand lay on the control panel, index finger crooked and twitching.

At first, Keztral thought Darvus was beckoning her closer, but then she realised what he was doing.

He was shooting.

Darvus, horrendously wounded, had used his last conscious control of his body to keep his finger depressing the heavy stubber's trigger. It would be locked on it still, had the crash not jarred it loose.

'I'm sorry, Lahon. Throne. I'm sorry. We're safe, don't worry. We're safe.'

She slipped her own flight glove in the twitching hand and held it. The metronome pulse of the trigger finger turned to light pressure as he squeezed back.

Darvus let out a long, relaxed breath.

Keztral was still holding his hand when she pressed the laspistol barrel below his chin and pulled the trigger.

She didn't bother with the second survival pack under Darvus' body. She wouldn't be able to carry redundant supplies along with the most important cargo.

The armoured housing containing the pict-film spools had bent shut – she'd needed to use the access hatch in the cockpit to pull the two heavy cylinders out and slide them into the special drum-shaped leather housings in the survival pack.

Keztral could already hear engines on the horizon when she dropped the incendiary grenade into the open cockpit and ran. She didn't wait to see the firework burst of the grenade, bright starbursts leaping upward followed by the chalky contrails of phosphorus, bright in the gathering dusk.

The stream and oncoming dark had saved her, allowing her to move concealed and leaving no tracks until she reached the culvert.

Now, huddled behind the cameleoline tarp, she watched the enemy inspect and prod the pyre of Lahon Darvus, a man who'd flown nearly two hundred missions with her. Who'd been so defensive of his honour, so proud of the heavy stubber he'd died manning.

And behind her was the pack, carrying the spools of film he'd died for.

Film that showed huge construction vehicles, mining variants with diamond-tipped saws and drills. Each testing their equipment by chewing into a pylon. Another lay nearby, felled like a great tree.

The pipe rumbled, its water jumping as a convoy of Archenemy troops passed above her on the elevated road.

Keztral stowed the magnoculars and huddled fully behind the cameleoline tarp, a sector map held in her hands, and a red-beamed stablight in her teeth.

She was north of Kraf. Past the defensive lines, somewhere on the road to Kasr Jark.

On the edge of the pylon grounds of the Elysion Fields.

SIX

'High command is concerned,' said Logistar-General Conskavan Raik. He did it with a shy smile, as if sorry to bother Creed with the news. 'They worry about the course of the war.'

'We all worry about the course of the war,' added Supreme Commissar Zabine. Then sneered at the glass of chilled leolac Kell offered her. 'No.'

'I'll have caffeine, if you don't mind,' Raik said, but lost interest when Kell pointed him towards a service cart.

Kell didn't serve civilians.

'Air marshal?' Kell asked.

'Nothing, get out of my face,' snapped Ravn Shrowd. It was his first cabinet meeting of the war, the first of Creed's tenure, as a matter of fact. He'd spent the time in his control centre, his neural augmetics connected to a theatre map of the air war and his trademark pipe between his teeth. 'I lost machines today, Creed. A great many machines that cannot be replaced. Worse, I lost pilots and airfields.'

'We've all had our losses, Ravn. It's been a long day. They hit us hard and–'

'I know how frekking hard they hit us!' Ravn Shrowd slammed his palm on the desk, making Raik jump. He leapt to his feet, tearing the pipe out of his teeth. 'You're a good ground commander, Creed, but you don't know the first frekking thing about running an air war! It was wasteful, what you did. Wasteful and reckless. You sent my pilots out there to die like some Throne-damned Militarum wave attack!'

Creed nodded. 'It was a gamble. Smash them flat, first thing. Destabilise the landings. And sometimes gambles don't pay out, that's frekking war.'

Raik leaned back from the thundering argument. Zabine brushed her uniform, letting the two save face by choosing not to witness this breakdown in military bearing. But Kell knew this was how Creed liked things. Shrowd wasn't holding back. Nothing careful or hidden. The exchange was loud, angry, profane – but honest.

'If it was a bet, it was a bad one, a damn bad one.' Shrowd pointed at the map of Kraf on the desk, indicating flight paths. 'Too many planes in the air at once. Too few held back for defence. Not enough room to manoeuvre in the fire corridors. And when they engaged and started letting off their ordnance and burning fuel, what do you think happened? They all turned around to refuel and rearm at the same Throne-damned time! We had stack-ups at every airfield across Kraf, planes circling in spiral queues at seven different altitudes, most of them without armament, laid out like game birds for the Drakes. And that was before a saboteur destroyed the fuel terminal at Stetzen.'

Creed nodded understanding, palms held up. 'All right, Ravn. All right, you're ri–'

'Thank frekk for the Valkyries and their vertical landings! If they hadn't been able to rearm and protect the columns, every poor bastard flying today would be lying in pieces all over the Kraf Plain.'

'You're right,' repeated Creed.

'I know I'm right.'

'You've broken your pipe,' Creed added.

Shrowd looked down at his pipe, only then noticing that he'd stabbed it so hard into the map that the stem had snapped.

'Frekk!' he barked in frustration, then flung the bowl against the wall. 'Frekking thing. Ah well, I have another one anyway.'

He slumped down in the leather chair and fished an identical pipe out of his rumpled uniform pocket. Brow dark, he began filling the bowl with shredded kolak weed.

'You are entirely right,' said Creed. 'I should have consulted you, and will in the future. I made a lot of decisions quickly, perhaps too quickly. But that is a consequence of *some* in high command insisting this war was already in its closing stages and sending out demobilisation orders.'

He turned towards the others.

'That is not fair,' chided Raik.

'It is,' said Zabine. 'It is an oversimplification, but fair. There's enough blame for us all to have a slice.'

'Well let's not sit here wallowing,' Shrowd said, holding out his pipe as Kell came around with a lit match. 'How bad is it, Creed?'

'Not as good as I'd like, not as terrible as I'd feared.' Creed gestured for the sector map.

Kell shook the match out, grabbed a map tube and spread out a tactical grid of the Kraf Defensive Sector.

'Things are quiet in the west so far, apart from the Delvian Cleave, which is seeing some action. Heretic landings here north of Kraf, the Iron Warriors. Not sure what that's about yet. Both Astartes enclaves in the north holding out, and I understand that Highfell and his Wolves have sallied to try and dislodge the Iron Warriors. The enemy elements besieging the Shrine of St Morrican are here in the east, and of course, the ongoing air engagement.'

'Call that mess off,' Shrowd said. 'We need to keep our air assets for interceptor roles and bombing forward siege-works. We've lost air superiority in this battlespace, nothing for that now.'

'As you say,' Creed said. 'South here, we've had to abandon the outer works due to bombardment. Except this one.'

He tapped a finger.

'Who is that?' asked Raik.

'The Templars,' Zabine said, craning her neck. 'Not fulfilling much of a tactical role there, are they?'

'None of them are.' Creed puffed his cigar. 'Sure, they're giving the Archenemy hell, causing casualties and tying down forces for now – but soon the Despoiler will rally everyone to the gates of Kraf and all those outposts will be stranded. Normally I'd say they could harry the back line, besiege the besiegers, but there's not enough of them. Even if the Kasr Myrak garrison could stage a breakout and support them, there would still be too few of them and too many enemies.' Creed shook his head. 'We're too spread out.'

'Any progress on the north wall?' asked Raik.

'Still hunting out the Raptors, but they don't seem to be reinforcing. I like that, it suggests the Archenemy doesn't have limitless numbers and attrition might be viable. We should batten down for a siege...'

Creed's eyes bounced back and forth, a movement Kell knew meant he was reconsidering.

'Why does he do it, though?' Creed asked.

'You're being obtuse, Ursarkar,' Shrowd said, puffing at his pipe. 'Why does who do what?'

'The Despoiler. We're a problem for him. We control his access to realspace. But given the Naval situation we can't stop him right now – yet he's focusing on us when he could bypass us and strike for Terra. He even tried to destroy us with minimal troop commitment with the blackstone.'

Zabine tutted, as if the answer were obvious. 'Abaddon hates us. His deep enmity towards Cadia has turned to obsession. Lord Castellan, this is basic academy-level history.'

'Maybe. Maybe. Perhaps that's it, he's just done with us. But I can't shake the sense that he wants something here. That we're not seeing this right.'

Creed's cigar end floated over the map of Kraf, sliding towards the mass of enemy landings in the north. Around the fortress citadels of the Iron Warriors on the edge of the Elysion–

'We need to discuss the ration allotment,' interrupted Raik. 'We're headed towards critical stage. If you plan for a siege, as seems likely, it will be even more crucial.'

Creed blinked, his eyes refocusing on the cabinet.

'Yes,' he said. 'Wait, *critical?* What do you mean, critical? We just reduced the ration.'

'Well…' Raik shrugged, as if Creed's gaze made him rethink his wording. 'A critical stage is now on the horizon. In the medium term. A number of ration distribution centres within Kraf have run out of stock before all the district cards have been filled. They've had to send people home hungry.'

'Embezzlement?' guessed Zabine. 'Shooting a clerk or two usually works.'

'It's gone far beyond simple corruption, supreme commissar.' Raik took a square of card from his jacket pocket and laid it on the desk. 'Far beyond.'

'What is that?' asked Zabine.

She and Shrowd stared, brows wrinkling.

'A ration card, lords,' Kell said patiently. 'Civilians and discharges use them to gain their food.'

'Oh yes,' said Zabine. 'Yes, I had an uncle who was released after he lost both his legs, he used to wear it around his neck. But ninety per cent… Isn't that rather high?'

'It is,' confirmed Raik. 'And we found two thousand like it. A group of Kasrkin ran into a counterfeiting operation stamping the things out. Not long after the press was destroyed, an armoured vehicle transporting plates disappeared. This printing corresponds to the subtle differences on those plates. But we cannot simply disallow the cards, that would slow distribution to a crawl. Nor can we change the plates now.'

'How much does this reduce our ration store?' asked Creed.

'Significantly.' Raik's fingers danced absently on a data-slate. 'By an extra thirty to forty per cent over a month, possibly.'

'I want it stopped. Raik, handle that.'

'With pleasure, Lord Castellan – though we'll have to cut the ration, of course. A further ten per cent?'

'Is it necessary?' Creed lowered his gaze.

'Unless you want to run out of food.'

Creed sighed. 'I'll announce it on my next broadcast.'

'No!' A horrified exclamation jumped from every mouth in the room, even Kell's.

'You can't do that,' said Zabine. 'Very unwise.'

'Inadvisable,' added Shrowd. 'When Porelska, Throne rest him, cut the rations, he never made an announcement.'

'My distribution centres will be mobbed.' Raik's white gloves squeezed his data-slate. 'The rationers killed.'

'Here's what we'll do,' said Zabine. 'Gradually reduce the ration. Drop it by two or three per cent a day, slowly enough that no one notices...'

'A dastardly suggestion,' said Creed. He'd gone stormy. 'The people of Cadia are sacrificing for this war, and they should know why. I'll tell them why. We're in this together, and I'll not starve them in the dark. If they must have less carb-loaf and proteyn, they'll know about it. They will appreciate the honesty – it'll be a damn sight better than what they got before.'

Kell waited until he'd ushered the cabinet out and closed the door before speaking.

'You can't tell them you've cut the ration.'

'Not you too, Kell. You of all people–'

'I of all people should know. My family had rationers. You grew up in the regiment. Don't announce it and they'll assume the distributors skimmed it, or there's just less to go around, or that their district warehouse was hit by a shell. Cadians are used to weathering misery, and while they won't like it, they'll get on. But if you get on that vox and tell them *you* did it, that Lord Castellan Creed knowingly and proudly took bread out of their mouths, they'll turn against you. And we can't have that during a siege.'

'It's dishonest. Bad leadership. As commander of the Eighth, I always–'

'With respect, you're not a frekking colonel any more, sir. You are leading a planet. A planet under attack where you are the central symbol of resistance. We cannot have that image tarnished with grubby politics. Don't undermine yourself.'

'Don't lecture me on... You're in no position...' Creed ripped his cigar out of his mouth and pointed at Kell. His fingers shook as he held the stub between index and middle finger.

Kell stood his ground.

'Throne damn it.' Creed collapsed into the wingback chair behind the desk. 'Bring me the frekking line-vox, I'll tell Raik.'

'No announcement?' Kell asked, bringing the rotary vox, picking up the handset and spinning the wheel to dial the extension.

'No announcement.' He puffed his cigar, realised it had gone out, and lobbed it across the room. 'Frekk!'

The dragon-tailed banner of the Cruxis Crusade waved above the Martyr's Rampart, its steel-woven silk lifting on the superheated backwash of ignited promethium.

'Burn them!' howled Marshal Amalrich. 'Incinerate them! Scour them from these stones where martyrs walked!'

Two brothers stood on either side of their wall section, washing the glacis with chemical fire. Heretic infantry screamed and blackened, flames roiling over their skin and igniting their ragged uniforms and ritual clothes. Others behind them, out of the flamers' range, gagged as the inferno ate up the available oxygen, and tumbled into the moat, clutching their throats.

Heretics burned with the same orange of Cadia's setting sun, which glinted off the tides of blades and armour so the whole battle seemed a rolling lake of flame.

Mordlied found a Word Bearer amongst the press of bodies, wading through the flesh of its followers as it discharged its bolter at the battlements of the rampart, staggering one of the flamer-brothers. Each shot from its massive weapon caused the worshippers around it to recoil, clutching bleeding eardrums.

From his vantage above, the crowd seemed to ripple around the Word Bearer like a pond disturbed by a rock.

Mordlied lined up his bolt pistol and pulled the trigger for a three-round burst. One round painted the Heretic Astartes' armour with the viscera of an unlucky follower, while the next two smashed into its boltgun, cracking the casing and magazine so the fat shells spilled out of it.

The Word Bearer's head snapped around, tracking the attack. Then in a blink it leapt the moat, ritual dagger in hand, scaling the sloped glacis of the rampart by sinking the hooked weapon into the rockcrete. Its unholy shouts pounded Mordlied backwards as if the words themselves held concussive force.

The fallen Astartes reared up over the parapet like a monster from the deep, a rune-inscribed grenade clutched in one hand.

Amalrich took the traitor in two cuts.

The first severed the arm with the grenade, dropping it down the slope where the amputated limb rolled into the moat.

The second cut passed through both thighs, so the heretic's torso followed the disembodied limb in its descending tumble.

A moment later, the wash of the grenade discharge atomised them both.

'Not one step back, Cruxis!' Amalrich intoned. 'For the honour of Dorn and under the ever-watching eyes of the Emperor, not one step b–'

Explosive impacts tore across Amalrich's breastplate, punching through his tabard and throwing the broken wings of his personal device into the air in pieces.

The stream of fire cut across Mordlied's vision and he heard a sound like a tank being holed.

There was rockcrete under his palms, but he could not see it. Green threads danced before his vision.

A hit. Heavy bolter, probably.

He ripped off his helm and found himself staring at his gauntleted hand, lying empty on the rockcrete.

The banner. *The banner.*

The pole lay four feet from his right hand, the sacred silk of it lying limp against the ground. Ground polluted by traitor blood.

Howling in rage and shame, he snatched it up and hoisted it high.

'Penance!' he lamented. 'My Marshal, I demand penance!'

He balled his fist, and struck himself across the jaw. It produced a meaty *thunk,* like a farmer clubbing a grox to death.

Amalrich had not fallen, still he bellowed his defiance at the crashing waves of attackers. When he turned, the heaving mass of them in their black robes, lit by strobes of muzzle flash, made it seem he had an ocean of rolling lava at his back.

When the Marshal saw the banner, his face fell. His eyes bored into Mordlied.

Mordlied struck himself a second time.

'Brother Devraine,' called Mordlied's lord and master.

'Yes, Marshal.'

'Please give Brother-Castellan Mordlied your chainsword, and relieve him of the dragon-tailed banner. The honour has become too heavy for him.'

'Yes, Marshal.'

Devraine revved the chainsword's blade to cut the links securing it to his wrist, then offered it hilt first.

As if in a dream, Mordlied handed over the relic he had carried for nine years.

'I am sorry, Mordlied,' Devraine said under his breath.

'Carry it high, brother,' Mordlied answered. 'Where all can see.'

Then he revved the gifted chainsword, gave something between a war-shout and a prayer, and dashed towards a knot of bronze-masked cultists who had surmounted the wall.

His first blow cleaved one man in two, shoulder to ribs. His next bashed the pommel deep into a cranial brainpan. With his free gauntlet, he seized a heretic by the throat and hurled him down the outer wall into a climbing party of his fellows.

Rage could be a great driver in war. Rage against the enemy, rage against oneself.

And Mordlied had rage to spare as the shadow of the dragon-tailed banner, cast by the setting sun and the fires of a sanctified battle-field, waved over his armour and his soul.

Night came early in the Rossvar Mountains. Tall crags began to block the sun starting at 1400 hours, casting the Delvian Cleave into cool shadow. It was often a relief after four hours of baking sun, the high altitude making the solar radiation more damaging since – this high up – the thinner atmosphere provided less shield-ing. Around 1000 hours the sun would hit them square, pleasantly warm at first after the freezing night, but by noon the roadbed and rocks of the cleave were hot enough you could feel the glow of it on a bare hand. The medicaes had even treated a few light burns from troopers picking up metal equipment laid out carelessly in the heat.

Thus when the burning glare of the sun dipped below the mountain range, there was an hour of blessed relief before the bone-deep cold of the night set in. Before wisps of cloud drifted through like mist, leaving men and equipment slick with dew. Before the dew turned to frost and the wind rushed through the cleave like the shockwave of an atomic blast.

It was, Hellsker realised as another detonation lit the horizon like heat lightning, a morbid comparison. The orbital round that had hit them had been only moderately large. Not nuclear. A kinetic round that had punched straight through one side of the outer defences and impacted the roadway, blasting a hole in the network of tank traps but inflicting no casualties.

'Well.' Hellsker stopped at the edge of a foxhole in the roadbed, looking down the Delvian Cleave towards the enemy. It was full dark, and not much to see. 'We survived the first day.'

'Day's not over yet, major,' said Sergeant Ravura. They were all walking in a hunched half-crouch, like their spines were bent from decades of carrying burdens. He pulled out a canteen. 'Water?'

She nodded her thanks and accepted, letting the ice-cold liquid temporarily deaden the throb in her gums and jaw. She'd turned down painkillers, wanting to stay sharp.

'Best not drink too much, ma'am,' he said. 'I have that detail melting snow to supplement our store, but...'

'But it's cold as a Valhallan cocktail out here,' she finished, handing it back. 'When do you think they'll melt enough to fill the supply tanks?'

'Never. Not with our rate of consumption. But we can keep a seventy per cent water ration for now. I'm having them move the operation inside. Not enough sun to do it natural.'

Hellsker nodded and pulled down the brim of the colonel's patrol cap. She'd taken Ravura for her command squad, part of a general shake-up she'd laid out at the officer's meeting. She'd also brought over Corporal Udza, because she had a good hand for the dials, but retained Barathus' standard bearer, Zaarun Rivelle, who'd served with the colonel for years and had fought with her uncle against the tyranids. Removing him would've been scandal, so now he stood beside her, the regimental banner stowed in two cylindrical carrying cases on his back.

To make room, she'd dropped Sergeant Dolethe into Ravura's role as company sergeant and sent the plasma gunner Cajca into a special weapons squad – mostly because she didn't want the volatile weapon near her. In his place she'd brought the sardonic Corporal Lek with his grenade launcher, which she prized for its versatility.

Those replacements might cost her down the road. Dolethe in particular hadn't liked it, though she thought a few days as a line soldier would remind him what he was missing in the command section.

Then, there was her other big move.

'Captain Pesk,' she called, not loud. She let the foxhole-to-foxhole whisper network spread the call where it needed to go.

Four foxholes away, a figure rose up from the black shadow of the road and waved a swaddled hand. 'Here, major.'

She waved him over.

Pesk climbed out and ran to her in a squat-crouch. As he crossed, Hellsker listened to the eternal rolling boom of artillery on the Kraf side of the cleave, like a distant storm.

To her left, on the northern side, the gun mounts on the remaining defensive bastion opened up with a gut-pounding crash. They fired into darkness, at suspected enemy congregating points. The shockwave of their discharge rippled through the ground, sending curls of dust into the air.

'Yes, major.'

'Let's go where we can straighten up.' Hellsker stepped a few paces away from her command squad, behind one of the sandbag bunkers they'd built to house the autocannon and heavy bolter teams. She unbent her spine, hands on the small of her back, then stamped her feet to keep the blood moving. 'Are we ready?'

'You haven't come to tell us the winter uniforms came in, then?'

For a moment, Hellsker nearly said she'd pass a word up the chain of command – then remembered she was the top of that chain. 'I haven't heard anything, no. Took a peek out the back with the big observation scope, things look hot around Kraf. My guess is that sending us coats and gloves is far down on their priority list.'

'Should I tell the troopers that?'

She thought about it. 'No. Not yet. How are you faring up here with the new assignment?'

'If they hit us, Alpha Company is ready. We've got the foxholes manned, a good kill-zone laid out with the heavy weapons. And... thank you for taking my suggestion on moving weapons company forward. They've ranged out their fire arcs with dummy rounds and screwed in their minimum and maximum angles so they don't drop on us.'

'Good. What about our little surprises?'

'In the holes with us. I had engineers ready in the blockhouses either side, but the cold looked like it had got into their demolition charges, so I pulled them for now. That's our biggest problem, temperature.' Pesk blew on his hands and rubbed them. Hellsker saw he'd fashioned mittens out of an extra pair of socks. 'It's not just cold up here, it's humid and cold. Mist gets into equipment and freezes. Could we get a rotation going? Every few hours send troopers and their kit into one of the wall-bunkers to warm up?'

'I don't see why... What?'

Pesk held a finger to his lips. A gesture Hellsker would've found insubordinate if his eyes were anywhere near her. But they were down and to the left, staring at nothing. As if trying to identify...

She heard it. Behind the rolling thunder of the battle behind them and the crash-scrape of the cleave's Earthshaker batteries being reloaded.

An engine. More than one.

On the other side of the bunker, she heard the automated quad-cannons set in the lower tiers of the bastions start to spit fire. Las-cannon batteries sizzled shots.

Behind them, a hollow *tonk-tonk-tonk-tonk* – like a man beating on an empty ration can – rang out as the mortars of weapons company let loose.

Hellsker looked around the corner of the bunker in time to see the sodium flares pop on their downward arc, burning with chemical brightness as they floated to earth on miniature parachutes.

Casting the oncoming monster in weird pools of black and white, like a pict negative.

'Frekk!' Hellsker shouted.

Before she'd thought about it, she was out from behind the sandbag emplacement, waving her arms at her command squad to get their attention.

'Armour! Armour!' she shouted. But a discharge from the Earthshakers split the air and they didn't hear.

A dazzling lance of red zipped over her head. Another drilled into the sandbags behind her and started a spot fire, penetrating the first layer of cover and amputating the leg of an autocannon loader. He howled.

A multi-laser, she thought, her brain sludgy from sudden adrenaline. *That was a frekking multi-laser.*

'Get down!' she said, grabbing Ravura and shoving him towards a foxhole. 'All of you, get low and stay low.'

'Throne!' the sergeant said, hand dropping to his laspistol. 'Is it on?'

They hadn't heard it, the zip of the multi-lasers difficult to distinguish at range from the background noise of bombardment. Or perhaps the flares had deployed close enough to mar their night vision.

But then the monster spoke and they heard.

Ahead of them, a rockcrete pyramid disintegrated. The blast sent an I-beam tank trap dancing across the roadway like a thrown jack until it snarled in another trap and pushed it ten feet with an ear-twisting screech of metal on rockcrete.

Lek dropped into a roll and disappeared into the closest ditch. Rivelle slithered after him. Udza clambered and dropped, careful of her bulky vox.

Hellsker jumped down, regretting it when she felt the jarring impact on her knees. 'Periscope,' she hissed. 'Does anyone have a...'

They passed it down the line. It was tight in the hole, body-to-body. These were four-man foxholes, and with Hellsker's command squad packing themselves inside the crowding was atrocious, especially with everyone crouching to stay below ground level.

But she took the scope and played it over the edge of the hole.

The flares had burned down to nothing but drifting candles, guttering as they floated to earth. Defence turrets still chattered and shrieked, tracer rounds flying in crossfire patterns, but she couldn't see the behemoth.

Then another round of hollow discharges behind her. Another line of pops and sizzles as flares illuminated the mouth of the Delvian Cleave.

And she saw it. High silhouette. Slab armour. A barrel cannon she could climb inside with ease. Two sponsons broiling the night air as it charged forward, sweeping back and forth so the iron tank traps ahead of it melted like ice left in the sun and rockcrete pyramid obstacles crumbled under its thermal assault.

'What is it, sir?' asked Udza.

'A frekking Demolisher,' she breathed back.

The big cannon on the Demolisher's turret thumped, slamming backwards so hard the vehicle rocked on its tracks.

Fire-wash prickled the back of Hellsker's neck as the massive tank round connected. She turned to see it had dead-eyed the emplacement she and Pesk had sheltered behind. It had blown apart and collapsed, nothing but a mound of sand and duckboard, stained with the blood of the heavy weapons troopers. Autocannon rounds cooked off in a box, like firecrackers in a can. *Pock-pock-pock.*

The heavy weapons behind were firing now. Filling the air above them with streams of tracers and the air with sound. The industrial hammer of heavy bolters. Rhythmic double-thud of autocannons. More hollow clanks of mortar tubes discharging.

'Stop!' she shouted at Udza. 'Tell them to stop. They're going to burn all their ammunition before the wave shows up. Anti-armour weapons *only.*'

In the periscope she saw rounds flattening and sparking off the Demolisher.

'Heavy teams, heavy teams.' Udza spoke into her over-mouth vox-mic, pushing her helmet down with one hand to try and hear herself amid the din. 'Unless you are anti-armour, cease fire. Repeat. Anti-infantry teams, cease fire. Don't blow your belts on this one.'

The Demolisher ignored the incoming fire, moving contemptuously side-on to the heavy bolter and autocannon nests. Rotating its sponsons to melt more tank traps, cannon traversing to line up another shot.

Hellsker could see the hides of flayed men stretched across it. Crimson splashed across them as lascannon turrets – expecting a slower attack and unable to reposition fast enough – stitched the roadway behind it.

'Down! Down!' Hellsker yelled. Some idiot had clawed up out of the foxholes and was going towards the damned thing.

Pesk, she realised. It was Pesk. She could see his swaddled head and hands. Tried to scream out for him to get back in the ground before the tank put him under the dirt permanently. Saw him crouch and yank something on a bundle.

The Demolisher didn't notice, it was still carving a path through the tank obstacles. Pesk was behind it, on an angle. But the vehicle was making crazy arcs and reverses, driving in circles to avoid being hit. He was out of its fire arc for its weapons now, except...

The cupola hatch popped open, its armaglass viewports winking in the sodium light. A tri-dome helmet and gas hood appeared. Red-stained hands gripped the fire handles on the pintle-mounted heavy stubber and swung it around at the engineer.

Hellsker dropped the periscope and grabbed Udza's lasgun from where she'd propped it up against the dirt wall. Squeezed off a distressingly inaccurate spray of fire.

Two or three others had the same idea. The tank commander ducked involuntarily in his hatch, the stubber angling upward as his weight dragged its trigger end down so the burst of fire went into the sky.

Pesk rammed the bundle onto the rear of the Demolisher and ran, leaving it stuck there by the magnet plate he'd activated. Red light winking.

He sprinted for the foxholes, head low as the red light blinked faster and faster until it was a steady burn.

Pesk didn't make it to the holes. He threw himself down in a foetal ball.

The demolition charge was faulty from cold. It half detonated – but that was enough.

The directed blast stove in the back panel of the Demolisher's armour plating. Smashed the engine. Sent red-hot shrapnel chunks the size of wine corks ricocheting through the interior.

Fuel tanks went up, flames blowing the armaglass outward and leaping from every hatch and viewport. Fire licked out of the Demolisher cannon's barrel like a burning tongue.

Two troopers clawed out and dragged Pesk bodily into the foxhole before the ammo blew.

When it did, it sent a rolling fireball thirty feet into the air, the gas pods of the multi-meltas touching off half a second before the shells.

At the roar of the explosion, Hellsker suddenly realised she'd never put on her helmet. She slammed it down over the patrol cap, buckling it under her chin with shaking fingers as she looked back into the periscope.

In the wash of orange fire, Hellsker could see the shapes of low hulls coming at speed.

The Demolisher wasn't supposed to punch through, it was to clear the way for an armoured-fist attack.

Hellsker didn't bother relaying the order to Udza. She just grabbed the handset on the side of the vox, slammed the transmission rocker, and yelled: 'Chimera assault! Chimera assault! Make ready and prepare to repel.'

She let the rocker go, then pressed it again and added:

'Cadia stands!'

SEVEN

Rising through the spiral stair and onto the viewing deck of the central spire, one thought occurred to Genevieve before all others:

Throne, it's beautiful.

From the wraparound balcony of the bell-tower, the whole of the shrine lay splayed below them like a vision of Terra.

Every window glowed, every arch and courtyard radiating a golden light. The shrine was like a luminous ship floating in a dark sea.

Glassaic windows sparkled, their mosaics of multicoloured panes bright like the pages of illuminated manuscripts. In one courtyard, a line of ghost-lights twisted and writhed in the dark, the faraway drone of a chant rising up from it. The monks in the worshipful quarter were walking its great labyrinth in meditation, each carrying a candle as they prayed for the Emperor's salvation.

Yet along the defensive walls were other lights. Brief flickers and stabs of bolter fire. Arrowhead muzzle flares cast by the wall cannons. Fountains of shooting sparks and burning trails fizzing in an interior cloister, as an Exorcist tank chorus raised a great *te deum,* their organs launching a missile fusillade into the surrounding dark.

Where the sacred missiles fell, they swept the ground in a pounding wash of cleansing fire – illuminating the swarm of sable-armoured forms that lurked in the night.

Hounds of Abaddon. Barbarians at the gate.

'It's magnificent, isn't it?' said Eleanor.

She stood at the balcony rail, looking down on the combat. Butter-yellow light gleamed off her polished black armour. At her right hand stood Arch-Deacon Mendazus, his ancient back bent under the weight of his towering mitre.

'Less magnificent when you're down on the walls,' Genevieve answered. 'They are already pressing us, and it's only the first day. Our Sisters need support.'

The arch-deacon thumped the marble with his crook. 'Perhaps if you had not squandered your Seraphim attacking their landing zones, we would not be so hard-pressed. Humility, that is what you always lacked.'

'I have lost fully half of my host today, your grace. I am well humbled. I could not have known there would be traitor engines in such number, and if you continue to speak to me like I'm still a girl in schola–'

'My apologies,' Eleanor cut her off, then touched the comm-bead on her right ear. 'Northern defence canton – a storming party of heretics is on the wall top. Dominion reserve, advance and purify.'

'Impertinent,' Mendazus muttered.

'The arch-deacon is correct, Genevieve. Had you not spent them, your Seraphim could be a mobile reserve, reinforcing faltering lines and countering enemy breakthroughs. Had you listened when I forbad–'

'I am your sister, not your subordinate. You cannot forbid me from anything.'

'Yes,' said Eleanor. 'It's quite a problem.'

'She is your Sister in Vow,' Mendazus chided. 'Blood means nothing. A lesson I should not have to repeat at your age.'

'I need no reminder of what I mean to my sister.'

Genevieve looked out into the fiery dark, her jaw tight.

Would Eleanor, with all her cool intelligence, understand what she had meant? She must. Subtlety had never been Genevieve's strong suit. Since their childhood, Mendazus had set them against each other, with Eleanor ever the victor. Greater with blades, greater in faith, and a natural leader. Perfect in all things – a natural choice for canoness.

Genevieve might have stayed a Seraphim, had it not been for the prophecy of Cardinal Subara – long dead now – who insisted that Katherine had come to him in a vision and said the twin girls in the Schola of St Morrican must be raised and installed as canonesses.

Mendazus had been deeply unhappy with that – he and Subara never got along.

And so Eleanor received the prestigious position as defender and administrator of the shrine, and Genevieve martial custody of the Ecclesiarchy lands around it.

'In any case,' said Eleanor, breaking the silence, 'let us not bicker as our Sisters martyr themselves. I requested you for a reason.'

'Which is?'

Eleanor wrote an order on a strip of parchment, handed it to a messenger with a jump pack. 'For Sister Superior Anastasia. New targeting coordinates for her Exorcists.'

When the Seraphim leapt over the balcony, her pack flaring to boost her towards the west, Genevieve felt a stab of envy. She wished more than anything to fly away.

'The Archenemy is pressing us hard,' Eleanor said. 'As you say, casualties are mounting, and it is only the first day. Soon we will not have the strength to fully defend the walls.'

'What is your plan?'

Eleanor looked at her, and the light played on her unblemished skin. The soft, smooth face of a woman who led her Sisters from the rear. 'Do you have your key?'

Genevieve's spine went icy. One hand rose to her chest, where the lump of iron hung. 'No.'

'You do not have it, or you will not do it?' sneered Mendazus.

'I… You cannot be serious. Not those monsters.'

'We cannot afford to spend our strength fighting these Heretic Astartes. Not if we have three super-heavy daemon engines joining the siege. This half-prince they howl about is reducing us in order for his effigies to finish the job. We must hit them, reduce their numbers without reducing ours. That means the Hermitage of the Pit.'

'A practical and fitting solution, Eleanor,' Mendazus said. 'The mind of a true canoness is a wonder to behold.'

Eleanor took something from her belt and held it out.

It was a key. Data-coded and bearing the skull-marked 'I' of the Adeptus Ministorum.

'If it comes to it, unleash them, Sister. Show these dwellers of the Eye what a hell we can make for them.'

'Tell me we are not that desperate.'

'You dare reject this duty?' Mendazus crowed.

'I have never rejected a duty. But why not you, Eleanor? After all, you have that.' Genevieve nodded at the machine standing behind her sister, looming like a shadow.

A relic Paragon warsuit, inlaid with gold.

It knelt on one armoured knee, as if in prayer. Empty pilot's chamber dipped low and its great cruciform blade set tip down on the flagstones. The left arm mounted a heavy flamer, protected by a tilting shield as large as a man. Purity seals puckered the surface, thick as a bowl of roses.

'Don't be absurd,' said Mendazus. 'She must command the defence. And it is a relic meant to guard the shrine. It cannot be risked unless it is absolutely necessary.'

'You and your Seraphim are faster moving,' Eleanor explained, raising the key in prompting. 'The arch-deacon is going into vigil. He will pray it is not needed.'

Perhaps she would die on the walls, Genevieve thought, and she would not have to venture to the Hermitage of the Pit.

As Genevieve accepted the key, its gene-mark recognised her.

The skull's eye sockets flared red.

EIGHT

Hellsker looked at the glowing face of her chrono, its ticking hands and numbers green with the light of radium paint.

It was comforting, that colour. It reminded her of being behind a lasgun sight during night exercises as a cadet. A time when the fury of combat was a future to be looked forward to, not a present to be dealt with.

Looking at the chrono gave her something to do as they huddled in the foxhole, waiting. Listening to the growl of tank engines echoing off the walls of the Delvian Cleave, split only by the tattoo-beat of the bastion's automated quad-guns and slash of lascannon fire.

She depressed the clacker on the vox. 'Steady, stay down. Don't look. Let the heavy weapons handle it.'

Ahead of them a Chimera exploded, painting the sky orange. Its low turret thumped along the ground like a wagon wheel, skipping over the foxhole directly to their right.

'Steady,' she said. 'It's going to work. Those frekkers won't know what hit them.'

Frekkers? Where had that come from? She wasn't much for profanity; her father didn't believe in it. Was it a stress reaction, a worry that this strategy she'd devised – her changes to Barathus' defensive deployment – was foolhardy?

Or was this the other one, the dark stranger Barathus had told her she must create?

Behind her, the autocannons and heavy bolters opened up. Tracers cracked above in chains of orange and gold light. Needle-lances of multi-melta fire answered, along with wavering bursts of heavy bolter shells.

'Almost,' she said into the handset. 'Stay calm. Remember. Let them pass. Let them show us their arses.'

The ground vibrated beneath her, bits of dirt sliding as the oncoming tracks rumbled through the ground. A small lip of the broken roadway, a fist-sized chunk hanging above the dirt wall of the foxhole, broke away and thumped her in the shoulder pad. Metal crunched and screeched on rockcrete as slab hulls bashed tank traps aside or dragged them across the paving.

Beneath her the dirt seemed to soften, shaken out of its hard-packed walls. One hand sank into the earth like it were flour. A heavy bolter hammered so close overhead that her helmet's audio bafflers clicked active, dampening it.

Her chrono clicked midnight.

The first day. They'd survived the first day.

With a belching roar the Chimera was above them. Thirty-eight tons of steel lurching forward and down on her as if it were a block-house ceiling caving in. She shoved her face into the dirt. Beside her, the veteran Rivelle involuntarily whimpered, his hand gripping the tubes of the battle standard.

Down the line, voices screamed in pain.

Then the down-angle of the Chimera's front track hit the back of the foxhole and caught, levering the rest of the machine's armoured bulk up onto the other side. Likely only a small bump inside the vehicle, but an instant of all-consuming terror in the confines of the foxhole.

Hellsker ground her teeth. Would the foxhole be narrow enough?

Would the Chimera be too heavily aft-loaded, and topple backwards into the hole, crushing them? Her chest burned, her body forgetting to breathe.

Then the belly of the vehicle slithered over them close enough to touch, and it was clear.

When Hellsker finally drew in another breath, it was heavy with exhaust-stink. She coughed, cleared her throat, and depressed the transmit rocker.

'Now! Now! Now!'

They rose up without a shout – she'd insisted on that. Total surprise. No battle cries, no cheers.

Let the weapons speak for you, she'd said.

Hellsker hauled herself up by the crumbling lip of the foxhole. Came to a crouch so only her tri-dome helmet would be visible.

The first wave of Chimeras had passed them. One had ploughed into an autocannon emplacement, its turret whickering fire at the fleeing heavy weapon team. Two more were repositioning to drop their ramps.

'Flares!' Hellsker hissed into the vox handset.

Beyond the tanks, a soft *pook-pook-pook* sound echoed off the canyon walls.

Down the line, one tank was frantically reversing, trying to back out of the foxhole it had plunged nose down in when the roadway collapsed.

Across the roadway, she could see troopers levelling the long tubes she'd ordered placed at the bottom of the foxholes.

Trooper Miklaj lifted his and set it down on the rockcrete lip. Flipped the blast shield out to cover the boxy tracker unit, so the debris blowback of firing didn't scratch its lenses or foil the sensitive internals.

Harsh sodium light bloomed in the air, starbursts of chemical burn washing the cleave wall to wall in contrasts of black and white.

'Fire!' she said, drawing her sword and levelling it towards the enemy.

There was no need for the order. They'd been instructed to shoot when the flares lit.

Orange-white tongues of fire flicked out the back of the launchers. Half a breath later the missiles jumped free of the tubes, fins snapping into place and secondary engines igniting to streak them towards the enemy transports. The distinctive *whoosh* of their passage through the air overlapped much like the gauzy contrails of grey smoke that followed them, stitching a cross-hatch pattern in the air.

The first krak missile smashed high into a Chimera's side, boring deep between the upper hull and detonating just below the track guard. Sparks leapt skyward, throwing the guard spinning like an autumn leaf while the severed tank tracks clattered to the ground.

Another missile glanced off the top of a turret and spun away, bursting against the wall of the cleave in a cough of scattered masonry. Other shots she couldn't make out, but there was smoke on the roadway, and flame, and the confused lancing of panicked las-fire from the loopholes in the Chimeras' sides. To her left, a turret fitted with a heavy flamer blurted burning promethium into the night, confused about where it had been hit from.

Beside her, Miklaj had waited. The Chimera in front of them was lowering its ramp. Hellsker could see the black helmets of the Volscani revealing themselves as the hatch came down on its hydraulics.

She gripped Miklaj's bicep below the launcher's shoulder rest. 'Fire, fire!'

'No.' He shook her hand off, a stunning rebuke of authority. If someone had seen, she might have to punish him. But...

But she was transfixed by the dropping ramp. The slow reveal of the Volscani with their gas-hooded faces. Eye-lenses shining in the flare-light. Cadian-style flak armour defaced with symbols of Chaos. Weapons...

Miklaj stamped the firing stud and sent a missile barrelling towards the opening hatch. It zipped in right above the lip and whammed into the chest of the lead Volscani, embedding in his ribcage and throwing him backwards, arms out.

Then it blew.

It had been a frag, not a krak. That's why he'd waited. Twists of shrapnel blew through the Chimera in a cloud of gore, plinking off the inside of the troop bay with a rattle like coins shaken in a can. Volscani screamed, rolled. Corporal Lek raised his grenade launcher and arced a frag in behind it, to catch anything that was still moving.

Four Chimeras were still active. Trying to manoeuvre around to engage their rear ambush. A Chimera turret, afire from the glancing krak hit, traversed around towards them and unleashed a stream of las with a sound like a low note played on a bass viol.

Hellsker ducked. It flashed past her and sketched a line of fire across the foxhole to her left, slicing through a trooper as he reloaded his missile launcher.

'Whiteshields!' she yelled into the vox handpiece. 'Now! Now!'

They came from the bunker hatches in the walls. Dashing out onto the roadway of the cleave, bent double to avoid fire. Gripping hand grenades and lasrifles, one boy – no more than sixteen – holding his helmet on with one hand.

It was a ruthless decision, ordering them to do this. But necessary. The regular troops were needed to hold the roadway. Whiteshield auxiliaries were good at this work. The kind that required enthusiasm and daring but not as much skill. Barathus had wanted to put them in the forward defensive trenches to absorb fire, or stash them in bunker positions in the honeycomb walls.

But this, letting them fall on the wounded tanks like scavengers, would give them more confidence.

Yet she hated herself for it.

A spray of heavy bolter tracers tore into one squad, ripping two Whiteshields apart and leaving another on the ground, frantically trying to pick himself up with an arm that was no longer there. Bright streams of multi-laser fire slit two cadets open like the passage of a razor.

Then the Whiteshields were on the tanks. Firing lascarbines and shoving grenades into viewing hatches.

The stalled Chimera – the one hit in the track – started dropping its ramp. A Whiteshield named Cazla slammed herself against the side of the hull and blind-fired her lasrifle into the crew bay on full-auto as her partner tossed a frag grenade in.

He'd thrown the grenade too early after pulling the pin, but it didn't matter. It only gave the panicking enemy time to unlatch the big double doors on the top of the transport and start clambering out before the frag tore them to pieces.

Through the smoke, Hellsker saw Cadet-Lieutenant Zander and his mob scrambling up onto the flamer tank. Four had been caught by the awful weapon as they came on and were rolling on the ground, their comrades futilely trying to beat out the chemically accelerated fire consuming them.

A Volscani commander in a padded tanker helmet rose out of the turret hatch, bolt pistol in hand, but he hadn't realised how many conscripts were on his vehicle – or how close they were. Zander grabbed the crewman's wrist and forced the bolt pistol away, then jammed the muzzle of his laspistol just below the man's collarbone and fired twice.

Zander and his squad mates dragged the body free, the commander's uniform glowing orange with embers where he had been shot, and dropped two grenades down the turret's cupola hatch.

'Close it!' Zander said, his high voice raw in the smoke from the turret's still-dripping flamer, and Hellsker realised one of his forearms had been scorched from touching the hot metal. 'Close the frekking thing!'

They tried to slam it shut, but hands shot upwards and pushed back, desperate. Hellsker could hear the banging of panicked enemy troopers inside the vehicle as they tried to batter down the rear and top hatches.

They didn't realise the Whiteshields were holding them shut.

Zander threw himself chest first onto the hatch, pressing it down with his weight until nothing but pinched fingers emerged.

Whump.

A hollow, muffled sound.

The banging stopped.

Whiteshields cheered and whooped. One stood on a burned-out hull and raised his lasgun high.

'Major,' said Udza, hand on her helmet's audio output unit. 'We're reporting clear. Enemy tanks neutralised.'

But Hellsker could barely hear the vox-woman above the drum of quad-cannons. The bastion defensive guns were active again – and as soon as she'd processed it, the searing lash-crack of lasgun fire joined it. That would be the troops in the forward trenches, hunkering down until now, engaging a new oncoming target.

'The hells is that?' asked Lek.

'That's what we knew would happen,' Hellsker said, turning and peering past the fire of the forward trench-line. Beyond it, and beyond the wrecked Demolisher, she could see more armoured hulls in the darkness. This time moving slow and steady, with infantry peering around from behind, disembarked and using them as cover. 'Another wave. More careful this time. They've learned their lesson.'

'Unfurl the colours, sir?' asked Zaarun Rivelle.

'Let them fly, Zaarun,' she said. 'They know we're here now. So let the bastards know who's about to kill them.'

Rivelle snapped the pole together with practised hands, and raised the standard. A plain battle standard, with a sun in a starburst.

Standard issue, not much inspiring apart from the *XXIV* stitched on its reverse side.

'Twenty-Four, in the war!' she shouted.

'Twenty-Four in the war!' the echo came.

And they were. The question was for how long.

PHASE FOUR

THE WEEK OF BLOOD

ONE

Excerpted from *Creed at Cadia: A Strategic Reassessment*, by General Dabatha Ravi (Chief of Operations, Cadian Second Army Group). Unredacted edition, with thirty-four full-plate illustrations. Held in the Inquisitorial collection at the Fortress-Library of Vespis.

> *Historical treatments of the Fall of Cadia – and most particularly Creed's role as commander – generally gloss over the seven-day period between the Black Legion's initial planetfall and their forces reaching the inner bastions of Kasr Kraf. The most popular versions of the narrative generally put the most focus on the first day of combat – the landings around the Elysion Fields, the breach of the eastern curtain wall, the assault on the northern citadel defences and the all-out attack on the Shrine of St Morrican, to name a few theatres – then jump rather abruptly to the later events.*
>
> *This is for a number of reasons, but two stand out above all others:*
>
> *First, given the number of battlefields and forces involved, it is difficult to establish a narrative through-line. The fighting itself was confused, with whole units unable to tell*

their part in it as a result of being wiped out. This is to a certain extent not the fault of historians, but of history itself as a discipline. War is an experience fraught with so much disorder that it is difficult to capture the scope of it in language. The historian's role is to communicate with clarity, and in an engagement like the eight-day struggle for Kraf Plain, clarity is nearly impossible.

The second reason, I believe, is a reluctance to engage with difficult questions about Lord Castellan Ursarkar Creed and his weaknesses as a commander. Most histories of Cadia are written by Cadians, and given what was to ultimately happen, there is a fear among us of stepping on the old man's grave.

But the truth is this: the Battle of Kraf Plain must be included in any strategic assessment of Creed, since it was during this engagement that his weaknesses and limitations as a commander came most to the fore. And it was the period where he was most disliked, and even reviled, by those serving under him – feelings that have shifted or been intentionally sanitised due to later events. Creed lost at Kraf Plain, frequently in a decisive and ignominious fashion. And I witnessed this first-hand as a junior tactical officer at the Kraf Command war room.

Perhaps it is best to put it plain, and avoid accusations of concealing my bias: I did not like Ursarkar E. Creed.

I was not alone in this. Indeed, the Lord Castellan was often most popular among those who never met him in person. While serving at Creed's holo-table, I thought him boorish, a problematic drinker, often dismissive of subordinates' advice, and extremely reckless. At times, I suspected he was being handled by his frankly sinister adjutant, Colour Sergeant Kell, who loomed behind him like a shadow.

I admit that for a time I personally blamed the Lord Castellan for the loss of our home world.

It was only in a review of surviving documents that I developed a much deeper and more nuanced appreciation of the stresses and difficulties Creed was under during that crucial period. And while I do not believe Creed performed well over the course of those eight crucial days, I am at a loss to name someone who might have performed better.

Creed, I now realise, had been dealt a catastrophically bad hand. Forced into the position as Lord Castellan, Creed had never trained or been prepared for the many roles he took on. While a brilliant commander at the divisional level, he was now effectively the head of a crusade in addition to being a wartime planetary governor. Never given time to fully set up a general staff, Creed found it nearly impossible to find senior officers he was confident delegating tasks to – fuelling his instinct to take on everything himself. Moreover, the high command cabinet representatives, elites who remained loyal to the murdered Porelska, treated the low-born Creed with hostility and suspicion. This led to him too often dismissing their advice and following his own instinct, as in the disastrous aerial engagement on the day of the landings.

Moreover, he inherited a theatre of war where his favoured military tactics – aggressive manoeuvre warfare and combined-arms assaults – were not an option. He did not know where the forces of Chaos would land, or in what strength. And he quickly discovered what every warmaster has learned before or since: that the allied forces of the Adeptus Astartes, Imperial Navy and Adepta Sororitas are not so much a unified command structure but a loose coalition.

At the time, standing around the recaff pot at Kraf Command, we junior tactical officers – every one of us, in the folly of youth, thinking ourselves Macharius reborn – often asked why Creed did not simply order the Sororitas and Astartes to abandon their spread-out positions and rally at Kraf. But Creed did not have that authority, nor the long personal relationships with allied forces that could compel it to happen. It is frankly a miracle he was able to so effectively enlist the genius Magos Klarn and give him enough support to complete his null-array, and keep such good relations with the Knights of House Raven and Astartes remnants under Lieutenant A'shar of the Raven Guard.

Creed's talents lay in charisma, inspirational leadership and tactical cunning – of which there are countless examples.

Where he fell short was in the administrative realm, where generals of crusade rank must be well versed in logistics and planning, and the diplomatic realm, where he would significantly improve with practice.

Though let us not get ahead of ourselves. As for now, the situation was this: by the end of the first day, Chaos forces had killed millions in the bombardment, reduced the continent's defences, and besieged every major force in the Kraf District.

An armoured column of traitor Rhinos and Baneblades had broken through the eastern outer curtain wall and rushed into Kraf Plain. There were traitors on the northern outer curtain wall. And the vaunted aerial forces based at Kasr Kraf had been badly mauled due to an inadvisable mass-deployment. Volscani battered at the Delvian Cleave.

And worse was yet to come.

* * *

'Kraf Station, Kraf Station,' she said, pressing the broadcast button and leaning into the goose-necked pickup mic. 'Kraf Station, this is Major Marda Hellsker, acting commander of the Twenty-Fourth Interior Guard. I am transmitting from the high-gain vox-station at Rossvar Mountain Strongpoint Beta-Seven-Nine. The Delvian Cleave.'

She released the button and watched the burning red light next to it cut out.

Static fuzz answered. Not loud, but a hiss like the sizzle of grox-bacon.

It was almost the only light in the room, that burning red eye. She found it comforting. Without it, the vox-room – high in the north wall and buried in rockcrete – was completely dark. Just her and the static.

Hellsker checked the glowing hands of her chrono, reading just past 0600. If it was accurate, that was. A deep crack bisected the crystal dome.

She ached all over. Her cranium throbbed from the discharge of so many missile launchers at close proximity. Scabby blood marked her lip from where she'd thrown herself flat to avoid a fan of heavy bolter fire and mashed her face onto the rockcrete. Her first attempt to broadcast had failed not due to equipment, but because she hadn't hydrated in seven hours, and her voice refused to work.

She was still getting used to speaking around the missing teeth.

Hellsker took a swallow from the numbing water of the canteen, still half-frozen from hours of fighting in the wind shear of the cleave. It could not be far above freezing in the vox-bunker, but it felt sweltering to her. She pulled the blanket-scarf away from her throat.

Decided she'd waited long enough.

She set her fingers on the broadcast button, bringing back the strangely comforting light of the burning red eye.

'Kraf Station, I don't know if you're receiving. I'm broadcasting in the blind. Repeat, this is Major Hellsker of the Twenty-Fourth at the Delvian Cleave, transmitting in the blind. If you can hear me, I can't hear you. I am making a daily report, as per orders.'

She took a breath, centred her thoughts.

'We were hit hard at midnight. Armoured infantry. Our observers up the mountain saw them marshalling, so we had time to prepare. They have Chimeras, a few Leman Russ patterns, all with markings of the Hundred-and-Sixty-First Mechanised Shock.'

Another breath.

'Three waves in all. Two armour, one infantry. Armoured units were mostly mechanised infantry. We repulsed them, but most importantly the roadway is now choked with wrecks, making further armoured assaults untenable. Several enemy Chimeras had functioning heavy bolters and multi-laser turrets. We've stripped those and repurposed them. Any relatively intact vehicles we've repositioned with an old Trojan support tank we found, and sandbagged around them to make them part of our defensive lines. Ironic, really. Volscani took them from the Hundred-and-Sixty-First and turned them on us, then we captured them and turned them back on the Volscani.'

She caught the digression, her report slipping away from professional brevity. This was not a confessional.

'They broke off the attacks at dawn. Seems they fear our citadel artillery pieces, and are keeping out of sight during the day. We're using the time to repair and refit. I'm formally requesting a resupply of lasgun cells, heavy bolter ammunition, but more than anything winter uniforms. We are taking cold casualties. Our observers think there might be snow in the next few days.'

She crinkled a page of notebook paper, squinting at it in the red light. She couldn't see what was written there, just the black of her dark fingers against the white paper.

'I have troopers and units to mention in dispatches. All of J Company, our cadets, deserve recognition. They engaged the first wave of tanks and destroyed them with hand grenades, despite casualties. Sniper Zadoc Plyn had nine confirmed kills, according to his squad, and was instrumental in repulsing the infantry assault. Oh, and Manvar Pesk, captain of our A Company engineering section, destroyed a Demolisher with a demolition charge, and fought on despite being wounded.'

Wounded was perhaps too light a word. After the first wave, Hellsker had insisted Pesk go to the infirmary, but he'd refused. Though his body appeared unmarked, his left ear was bleeding from a burst eardrum, and it was clear he had a splitting headache. One eye occasionally floated off-centre. She suspected internal damage from the shockwave.

But he'd insisted, so she let him. Part of her worried, though, she was allowing Pesk to kill himself in order to make her own job easier.

'This is Major Hellsker,' she said. 'Acting commander of the Twenty-Fourth Interior, signing off.'

She let the button go.

The red light went off.

Hellsker eased herself onto the cot she'd had brought to the vox-room, moving aside her pack and personal bag to lie down.

Which was when she noticed the wooden presentation box beneath it, and paused.

It would have been useful last night. Additional firepower. Perhaps even disabled one of the Chimeras before it could fire on the cadets.

Slowly she reached out and unclasped the locking hook.

Lifted the lid far enough to see the gleam of metal beneath, and catch the barest scent of ozone.

In her mind's eye, she saw crisped skin, coming off a man's hand like a lady's long gloves.

Then snapped the box lid shut, and pushed the box away.

When it was securely placed in a fireproof locker, she was finally able to sleep.

It was a grim situation report. One of the worst Kell had ever seen.

Traitor Titans had broken through the Alpha Curtain Wall in the east. House Raven and Cadian engineers were detonating bridges to slow Legio Vulcanum's progress. The northern Alpha Curtain Wall was still a frekked-up mess. Basic foodstuffs depleting at an alarming rate, with two ration riots in the manufactorum districts.

Kell flipped the scan-proof cover onto the situation report and nodded to the Kasrkin detail that had delivered the folio. 'Thank you, dismissed.'

The sergeant – a man with a bionic jaw on the right side – nodded, hesitated. 'Colour sergeant...'

'Yes, trooper?'

'May I see the Lord Castellan?' The sergeant's violet eyes flicked to the closed double doors behind Kell.

'Why?'

The Kasrkin shifted. 'Fighting on the northern wall. First deployment of elite units in the siege. Heretic Astartes. My company wants in. Hard to walk around guarding paperwork when there's enemy to be killed, colour sergeant.'

Kell nodded. 'You're Thirteenth Kasrkin, Second Battalion, C Company?'

'Alpha Squad, Fire-team Ziggurat, yes, colour sergeant.'

'Well, the Lord Castellan is in a strategic planning conclave. No promises, but I'll pass the request and see if we can arrange a rotation.'

'Thank you, colour sergeant,' the sergeant said, snapping an open-handed salute. 'Cadia stands.'

'Cadia stands, and Ziggurat with it.'

The guard detail left, smiles tugging at their mouths.

Kell waited for them to go.

'Cadia stands,' he mused, using his biometric key to open the double doors, and slipping through before anyone could steal a glance inside.

Ursarkar Creed, Lord Castellan of Cadia and Supreme Commander of the Defence Forces, lay snoring on the camp-bed behind his desk.

Kell shut the door, easing the handle to avoid the noise of the bolt. Creed slept little, and woke easily. Part of the hard-living approach he'd had ever since they were cadets together, and only exacerbated from a lifetime in combat zones.

Even as a cadet, in what passed for childhood on Cadia, Creed had been an inveterate insomniac. Staying up late reading strategic treatises by torchlight and occasionally raiding the instructors' liquor cabinets.

Living like that was hard on a body, even one filled with such indominable spirit. For years, a parade of medicaes had told Creed to get more sleep, regular exercise, to stop drinking and keep a better diet. And they didn't know about the regimen of caffeine pills, since the commander – so babyish in some habits – hated even the smell of brewed recaff.

He'd been up for four days straight when Kell decided to slip him the powder. Crushed sedative, the kind that reacted the least with alcohol. Still, he'd had to be careful of the dosing given the amount of Arkady Pride Creed had taken on board.

The desk was piled high with maps. Star charts. Data-slates concerning both Cadia, and planets in multiple systems. Kell wasn't sure what that was about. The Lord Castellan's diary lay amid it all, open to a page of shaky writing.

Kell leaned down and pressed two fingers against Creed's wrist, feeling the pulse. He didn't like drugging the commander, had only done it twice before – but for the good of both Cadia and the Imperium, Creed needed to sleep.

Ever since the academy, Kell had sensed Creed was the planet's hope. That he would live, and die, for Cadia. Indeed, Kell had no illusions that both of their lives would end defending their home.

'But by enemy fire,' he muttered into his mug of recaff, as he took a sip. 'Not by working yourself to death, you brilliant idiot.'

'I can hear you, you know.'

'What I get for talking.'

Creed shook his head, eyes still shut. 'The glow-globes. They started buzzing a little. Need to get that fixed. How long have I been down?'

'Five hours.'

'Throne damn it, I feel worse than before. Sleeping always reminds me how frekking tired I am.'

'Want more time?'

Creed sighed, shadowed his eyes with a hand. 'Why don't you read me the briefing sheet, tell me how frekked we are, then I'll get up and wash out my mouth. It's damned dry.'

'The amasec. You need to cut back. We don't want it to get as bad as that time at Tyrok.'

'No,' Creed snorted. 'No, we don't. How bad is it?'

'Eastern line has fallen.'

'Expected but unwelcome.'

'Supplies in Kraf low. Ration riots. Wolves are attacking Krom Gat at the edge of Elysion. Sons of the Lion and Sororitas still holding. Northern wall contested. Southern under stress.'

'So we need a miracle.'

'How big of one?'

'I don't know,' Creed mused. 'The Emperor and I aren't currently on speaking terms.'

Then his brow furrowed, whether against the headache of the downers or in thought, Kell was not sure.

'The southern wall?' he asked. 'Are the frekking Templars still there?'

* * *

Penance through slaughter.

Absolution by bloodshed.

Sublime forgiveness, earned with violence.

'Strike me!' Mordlied roared at the tide of heretics. 'Strike me!'

He wielded the chainsword two-handed, eye-lenses streaked with dripping lines of heretic blood. He swept a wide arc, separating two cultist heads. Grabbed a mutant by the shoulder and cut its throat. Saw a Word Bearer advancing upon him with a rune-inscribed blade raised, and stepped inside the traitor's guard to barge him backwards with a shoulder pauldron before slashing the chainblade up like a pendulum into the heretic's groin.

Whirling teeth shrieked on armour as he guided it to the joint, boring through the tough undersuit between groin guard and cuisses.

'Come on!' he roared.

The Word Bearer brought the inscribed sword down and it glanced off his helmet, jarring his neck with a spike of mortifying pain that salved his conscience.

Then the heretic fell, his leg severed, and Mordlied reversed the chainblade to bury it point down in the fallen traitor's breastplate, splitting the vellum tome chained to the Traitor Space Marine's chest, sending the shredded pages flying amidst the fountain of blood.

Mordlied looked up the rampart, searching for his master.

Marshal Amalrich saw, and turned his face away. Refusing to see Mordlied's deed.

Beside the Marshal stood Brother Jephreth with the dragon-tailed banner. The third to carry it at the Martyr's Rampart. Devraine had fallen last night to a Venomcrawler's autocannon, honourably slain as Mordlied should have been.

He had fallen to his knees among the endless tide of bodies climbing up the ruined bastion, propping the banner so it would not fall, shouting, 'Stand! Stand! Dorn!'

Mordlied had stepped forward to take it up before it fell, but Amalrich had locked eyes and pointed. 'Not you – He has judged you wanting.'

Jephreth had caught the banner instead.

At the burning shame of the memory Mordlied ripped his chainsword free. He drew his bolt pistol and dived once again into the mass of bodies, reaving and firing, burning away his turmoil in a welter of gore.

Mordlied did not know how he had failed the Emperor. Had he been vain and proud in his decades of bearing the banner of the Cruxis Crusade? Had his faith wavered? Perhaps he had become complacent, stopped trying. Secure in his triumphs and place at the Marshal's side. Too used to being a rallying symbol, forgetting his role was to smite the enemy in all his forms. Abhor the alien. Kill the mutant. Burn the–

And he knew. Knew what would prove his worthiness. The one target that would redeem him.

The sorcerer with the books.

Kill him, and he would carry the banner again. Slay the witch, and gain deliverance from this purgatory.

Wash away the stain of his weakness with the sorcerer's blood.

'For you, He On the Throne!' he sang in ecstatic fury, swinging his chainblade through a rank of grotesque-masked chattel. 'For you, Dorn!'

And Mordlied, bannerless, went to hunt a witch.

TWO

Excerpted from *Creed at Cadia: A Strategic Reassessment*, by General Dabatha Ravi.

> *With the areas between the two curtain walls now a combat zone, the Battle of Kraf Plain entered a new phase – one that, to a certain extent, favoured Creed's preferred tactics. Now given room to manoeuvre units and engage his armoured divisions, Creed launched a series of blistering counter-attacks against the heretic breakthrough in the east that threw whole units of traitors back against the ruins of the abandoned Alpha Curtain Wall.*
>
> *The armoured counter-punch destabilised the enemy – particularly its war engines – allowing the infantry to make a fighting retreat in good order. Coupled with heavy Kasrkin units arriving to assist in clearing the Heretic Astartes from the northern wall, the third day proved the most dynamic since the landings.*
>
> *And if things had turned out differently, this could have been a turning point. If the southern curtain wall had held, avoiding a two-front war. If the aerial defence*

batteries could've prevented more heretics from landing in good order. If Kraf Citadel had not, on that third day, been hit by the first wave of dive-bombing. If the slow, treading approach of Legio Vulcanum had not finally put the Kraf Plain into the range of their monstrous guns.

But it was not only external foes Creed had to contend with. Though low-level heretic attacks had hit Kraf since the start of the conflict, the true extent of the problem was about to become evident…

Up in the chapel tower of St Jaeneth of the Redoubt, the bell-ringer looked down a magnocular scope at the troops on the western wall. They looked, from above, like a stream trickling down off the wall and into the inner marshalling ground, marching down through the warren of streets.

He'd set the key loader just as the herald of the liberators had taught him. Did not keep the big vox-set on and broadcasting – he had no desire to be caught.

Holding the key codebook down with his clubbed fist, he picked up the receiver of the vox-set and toggled it live.

'Sending, sending. Voice of Wisdom Six sending. Acknowledge.'

In the earpiece of the receiver, he heard distorted words. At least, he thought they were words. Perhaps it was more like breathing, or sighing, a noise that slithered through the *ffffffffffssssss* of ambient static. Maybe not his masters at all, but the ghost of a signal broadcasting on the same frequency and coming through as crosstalk.

'Eeeehwaaa orrre. Eeeewaaa orrre.'

'This is uh, Voice of Wisdom Six. There are some troops moving here on the western citadel wall. Uh, looks like repositioning to the north and south defences.'

A sound in response, like whispering, and the smack of a wet mouth. The bell-ringer's insides went cold at the sound, and the skin of his hand tingled where he'd shaken it with the herald. Sweat popped on his forehead. He felt pressure in his sinuses.

Then all at once he knew what the voice was saying:

'Eeehwaaa orrre.'

We want more.

'I…' He looked down the mono-scope on its little tripod, lying on his belly against the cold flagstones of the bell-tower. Played the scope down across the inner courtyard. Found the bomb crater in the thin crosshair of the scope with its range tick marks. 'You dropped explosives in the marshalling ground yesterday. Inside number six Bastion West. It… it hit nothing. Two points east is a fuel depot.'

The line went dead. The vox's orange active light clicked off without him touching it.

An hour later, the flight of dive-bombers came.

And the fuel depot disappeared, cleansed by a leaping pillar of flame.

In the frigid tower, the bell-ringer was warmed by the heat.

'Is that hail?'

Hellsker peered out of the viewport meant for the Chimera's driver, across the top of the forward trenches and down into the black of the valley. Snow whipped and whirled in the dark, illuminated by the searchlights she'd finally deigned to use, even though it made the crews vulnerable to sniper fire. They stabbed through the blizzard, criss-crossing from the citadels and whatever lights still worked on the wall of Chimeras.

Sergeant Ravura pushed his knit cap back, pulled the micro-bead out of his ear and listened, quiet, to the sound coming out of the muffled night.

Thump-thump. Thud-clump-thump. Clap-thump-krrrch.

His brow furrowed. 'It's not footsteps. Maybe hail, but thankfully not on us.'

Hail was the only thing that made sense to Hellsker. It had been cold the last two nights. Bad enough the troops in the trenches had to rotate into the walls every few hours to warm up. Six troopers in D Company had lost toes to frostbite while repulsing the wave attacks of the night before, another nine had hypothermia and might be out several days.

Those casualties were nowhere near the worst they'd suffered. Both trench-lines had been overrun just before three in the morning, and Hellsker had been forced to become that other person again, what she thought of as the dark officer, and drop mortars short in order to drive the Volscani back.

Not everyone killed in the barrage had been a heretic, and she knew there were troopers who blamed her for that. Hells, she blamed the dark officer herself.

But they'd held it. Partially due to the wall of Chimera wrecks across the roadway, patched with sandbag heavy weapon emplacements between. The tanks with working heavy bolters faced forward, while others were sideways to employ their lasgun arrays. At each end, wrecks were installed hatch-outward as communication tunnels between the forward trenches and the throat of the cleave.

It got them through the night, but Hellsker wasn't sure it would hold again. High-altitude snow had started in the morning, and killed the cleave's greatest advantage – seeing the enemy mustering for attack, and targeting them with artillery fire.

'That's not hail,' snorted Lek.

'Belay that tone,' Ravura said. He'd grown increasingly irritated with the sardonic corporal. Tempers were fraying all around. 'No one asked you.'

'Oh, don't I know it.'

Hellsker cocked her head, listened to the odd noise. 'Okay, Lek. I'm asking. If it's not hail, what is it?'

Lek was quiet, as if judging whether he was sure enough. 'You're all kasr-born. Southerners. I'm a boy from agri-country. We don't get hail up there, but we do have equines. And that, sirs and mamzels, is the sound of hooves.'

Hellsker listened.

Thud-thudda-thud. Clack-slip. Thunka-thunka-thud-thunka.

Faster, thicker.

'Hooves,' Ravura mocked. 'What, they hit us with tanks and–'

'Shit,' said Hellsker. 'Regimental channel, Udza, *now.*'

'What?' said Ravura.

'Threat report mentioned Rough Riders.'

The vox-operator keyed a channel and handed over the set. Hellsker stamped the button hard enough to actually feel it through her numb fingers.

'Hellsker to all units, Hellsker to units, prepare fo–'

A searchlight on the Chimera to their right blew out in a cough of sparks, hit by a sniper's hard round.

'Cavalry! Cavalry! Flares thirty-second interval. Mortars at number two grid line. Throne damn it, everyone just fire into range markers two to three, chest height!'

Las-beams from the trenches lit the snow pink with their passage. Heavy bolters and heavy stubbers salvaged from the heretic wrecks lashed tracer fire into the blast of wind howling through the cleave.

Too late.

In the first bloom of flares she saw that her grid coordinates were far too hopeful. The heavy bolters firing too high, the artillery dropping long. The mortar barrage, split between flares and frags, wouldn't stop them.

The Volscani had got close in the storm, swaddled in white blankets and lances wound with cotton bandages to blend in with the snow. Probably they'd come unhorsed for stealth, then mounted just out of sight.

Their hoofbeats made a weird hollow sound as they thumped and slid on the frozen, powder-covered ground.

Thud-thudda-thud. Clack-slip. Thunka-thunka-thud-thunka.

Las-bolts drummed into the riders and stopped dead. They were heavy cavalry, with both mount and rider clad in carapace armour. Clawed hooves drummed the broken roadway, six to a beast, their genehanced, bionically augmented mounts snorting great plumes of steam into the winter air.

One rider caught a las-bolt under the arm. The force of it lifted him from the saddle and he slid away, the charging mount behind clattering over him and mashing his chest cavity. A monster equine exploded from a heavy bolter round, its front legs gone so it pitched forward, rolled over its master and bled out drumming its half-mechanical hooves in the snow. Mortars detonated in a line, throwing up cones of rockcrete and dirt. But the Volscani's heavy armour meant that few went down, and many of the animals who should've fallen instead continued on with great roses of blood staining their blanket camouflage. Ranks of stimm-phials in the mounts' thick necks hissed as they discharged a last burst of chemical courage.

'Fire!' Hellsker shouted, half into the vox and half hoping her voice would carry. 'Fire! Fire! Fire!'

Heedless of the fusillade, the riders leapt the first trench, coming down in a skid and scramble of hooked hooves before they went on, muscles bunching to clear the second.

A Cadian, standing to get a good shot at the underside of one beast, slammed backwards as a flying hoof stove his face in. Most simply lay on their backs, firing upward. A mount landed hard on the frozen roadway after the first jump, its leg splintering in a compound fracture, and slid thrashing and whinnying into a foxhole. Panicked shooting lit the walls as the beast bit and kicked in the confines of the hole.

One rider, unhorsed and riddled with las-fire, staggered forward and buried his lance in a foxhole. The shaped krak grenade on the end of the lance exploded, collapsing the earthen walls to bury the troopers inside.

Beside Hellsker, the Chimera's heavy bolter fired, drumming out shots that pounded her unprotected eardrums, venting gases that felt almost tropical in the frigid metal transport.

'Major!' said Lek, gesturing.

She jumped backwards away from the viewport.

Lek plugged his grenade launcher barrel into it and fired, not the *pook* of a frag grenade but the shotgun blast of a flechette round. He advanced the drum, fired again.

An explosion to their left. A lance-mounted krak grenade.

Impacts on the roof of the transport. Clatters and thumps. Screams.

'They're over!' yelled Ravura. He slapped the opening stud of the rear hatch with his elbow, already revving his chainsword and holding his laspistol high to clear the lip of the back hatch as it lowered.

Riders on the inner roadway. A sanctum not breached since the first night. They charged through, sabres drawn, cutting down on the Whiteshields that served as ammunition runners and water-carriers to support the line troopers in the tank walls and heavy weapons positions. Hellsker saw one – Mezcali, a cadet barely seventeen – drop a drum of heavy bolter ammunition and grab a rider's reins, trying to drag it down.

The rider chopped down at her, scoring her helmet and slicing bloody lines across her arms and knuckles, before the mount tossed its head and sent her flying and charged on.

The mortars, Hellsker realised. *They're trying for the mortars.*

'Udza!' Hellsker stepped out of the Chimera's hatch, firing her laspistol so scarlet darts lashed at the backs of the horsemen. 'Tell weapons company to down shells and prepare to repel with las-carbines. I–'

Something big and hard thumped her, sending her reeling, boots skidding on the icy roadway, so she careened out into the open courtyard behind the barricade.

A mount's flank, she realised. Another rider had come down off the tanks nearly on top of her and barged her aside in its haste. It rushed into the darkening interior of the cleave and dived into the developing massacre.

The dying light of the last sodium flare lit blood-slicked sabres as they rose and fell. Genehanced beasts reared and kicked, shattering ribcages with a sound like a boot stepping in the wet leaves of an autumn trail, and breaking the twigs beneath.

Troopers fired from the upper loopholes of the cleave honeycomb. Fire-teams sallied out the casement doors in knots of four and five, hunched and covering each other as they moved to eliminate threats and retrieve casualties. One trooper – Hellsker could not see who, apart from his gold-tinted goggles and engineer facings – grabbed a Whiteshield by the webbing and backed up, dragging him towards the casement door. The engineer kept his lascarbine braced at the shoulder and firing as he did it, the squealing Whiteshield painting a wide stripe of blood across the ice.

Twenty feet from her, Hellsker saw a horseman turn towards the pair and dig his heels into his mount, the beast's mane of phials hissing so its whole frame shuddered and eyes went wide. He lowered the explosive lance and shook his shoulder to seat it properly.

Almost leisurely preparing for the charge.

'Cadia!' Hellsker said, not knowing why she did so. 'Cadia! Cadia!'

Her laspistol seemed to fire on its own, peppering the repositioning heavy rider across his side and head. He reined in, armoured head swivelling towards her, harassed by her fire but uninjured.

'Get back! Get inside! He's going to try and blow open the casement.'

Her uncle's sword leapt from its sheath, power field spitting and hissing. Sparking blue as the blowing snowflakes hit it.

She realised her mistake.

The patrol cap was nondescript enough to avoid the crosshaired gaze of snipers. It did not mark her as an officer. But a power sword was a status symbol impossible to ignore.

Stupid.

With incredible speed the mount's clawed feet gripped the roadway and launched it nearly sideways. Within the time it took to fire two more shots it was on her, the ineffectual darts of her pistol sizzling on the heat-treated surface of the mount's carapace helm and skirts. Explosive lance gleaming red in the passage of her shots.

Useless. Frekking useless.

She should've dodged. Rolled. Anything but met the charge. But the dark officer had taken over with one mad thought: *How would it look if I killed this man?*

And instead of dodging, she jagged to one side and sliced for the beast's chest.

But the lancer was trained: a second before impact he drove spurs into the beast, swerving it right while leaning far over the other direction to redirect the lance.

Her uncle's sword connected with the lance in a pop of yellow sparks, and then she was on the ground, breath gone, sliding backwards along the icy road. Her jarred spine numb from the impact and the cold surface.

It was still going, embedded lance pushing her along, and for a moment she thought it would slam her into the Chimera barricade, breaking her neck.

Instead the beast slowed to a crawl. And as it lowered its head towards her, she saw that below its helm and hanging panels of neck armour, it was some kind of reptile. It snuffled, washing her with steaming, sulphur-vent breath. A long, sticky pink tongue – its twin tips punctured with sense organs the size of straws – flopped from the scaled monster's mouth and began to quest for the hot blood of her wound.

'*Hey, hey, nict,*' the rider said. He drove his heels in and whistled, trying to bring the beast back under his control. Then he shouted over his shoulder: '*Nict howlt, Braddau! Komandesti! Komandesti!*'

She'd studied her Volscani phrasebook. That meant 'officer'.

He was drawing a laspistol when the beast reached out with a claw and planted it on Hellsker's chest, pinning her hard enough she couldn't breathe.

Two other riders emerged from the snow-blind darkness. Congregating around her. Eye-lenses of their wraparound carapace helmets flat and dead as tarnished coins. One drew a laspistol.

She was going to die. On her first command. A failure. Pinned to the ground she was supposed to hold. Laspistol unable to penetrate...

Oxygen starvation made her pistol seem to weigh as much as a field pack, but still she dragged it up from the roadway. Her uncle's sword had dropped when the lance struck her, but the pistol was still in her hand.

And now, she was underneath the armoured skirts of the animal.

She pulled the trigger.

Red darts stabbed up through the beast's underside. It reared, screaming, throwing its rider and slapping out with one claw at the thing that had stung it.

Hellsker's laspistol flew away into the darkness, but the weight was off her chest now.

She yanked the lance free and rolled, scrambled to her feet with the lance in her hands.

A las-bolt flew past her left ear.

She swung the lance at the two riders still in the saddle.

They wheeled away, fearing the grenade at the tip. The wounded beast snarled at her and she thrust the tip at its open mouth, breaking teeth so it leaped backwards and trampled its fallen rider. He screamed, helm crumpling under its weight.

'Come on!' she screamed. 'Come on, you traitor bastards!'

They lowered their pistols.

But instead of the crack of a lasweapon, there was a hollow, throaty discharge.

The two riders were shredded, armour plates coming apart and misting the whirling snow with gore. Mounts reared, shaking their heads, carapace skirts peppered with iron darts the length of her index finger.

Lek stepped up on her left side and racked the grenade launcher again. His second flechette round fired low at the beast's unarmoured legs to splinter bone and break them down.

'Frekking Throne, major,' he said. 'Are you all right?'

'Marda,' Sergeant Ravura said, rank disappearing in the tension. 'Where are you hit?'

'Shoulder,' she said, rolling the muscle. 'I don't think it's too bad.'

'Hells, it would've been if you hadn't cut the tip off that lance. Never seen anything like it, sir, if you don't mind me saying so.' He held out her power sword, recovered from somewhere on the roadway.

Hellsker looked at him with dead eyes, uncomprehending, until she looked at the end of the lance she held.

There was no tip on the lance, nor a grenade. Just a clean-sheared cut where her power sword had sliced directly through it.

'Never mind,' she said, taking the sword and keying its activation stud. 'We're wasting time. Rally the reserves to the mortar pits. Make sure they don't spike the weapons.'

'Yes, major,' Udza said. 'Reserve Alpha-Beta, to mortar position. Repulse heretics, prioritise equipment and…'

'And sergeant,' she said.

'Yes, major?'

'When this is over, go to my quarters and get my plasma pistol.'

THREE

'Blood of the frekking Angel,' Creed blasphemed. 'It's all bad news, isn't it?'

Kell looked down the briefing slate. Tapped the scroll stud once, twice. 'Yes, general. A bleak assessment.'

Creed leaned over the theatre map on his private desk, looking at the heavy milkstone tokens marked with the insignia of each unit. The whole sector laid out like a game. 'We're losing, Kell. Full retreat to Kraf Citadel. Spilling a lot of enemy blood in doing it, true, but Abaddon doesn't care about how many bodies he leaves here. Attrition tactics only get us so far.'

'The Adeptus Astartes and Sororitas are still holding.'

'Who cares?' Creed leaned over the map, picked up a miniature Chimera marked with the livery of the 177th Mechanised Shock – reported destroyed – and tossed it aside. It tumbled off the table and dropped on the thick carpet. 'The Throne-damned Astartes and Battle Sisters are attracting attention, but they're all bottled. No damned use. None at all. The Order of our frekking Martyred Lady didn't stop the heretic war engines driving down on our eastern curtain wall. The damned Templars didn't prevent the southern wall from being breached. Arguably the Wolves are doing their part by mixing it up with the Iron Warriors, but even then I'd rather have them clearing the northern curtain wall. Who knows what the ever-loving-frekk the sons of the Lion are doing up north in their wrecked cruiser, though I suppose I should be grateful for the amount of fire they're putting into orbit.'

'Baroness Vardus has engaged the Titans of Legio Vulcanum,' said Kell, in counterpoint.

'And much luck to her.' Creed scratched a lucifer match across the smoking tray weighing the south-eastern part of the map down, and used it to relight his cigar. 'She's a woman with a dagger trying to beat an armoured swordsman. I respect the hell out of the baroness, but she has her limits.'

'We need to consider closing the Beta Curtain Walls. Protect the muster fields.'

'I don't need you to tell me that.'

'If we wait, we risk–'

'And if we shut them too early, we'll strand thousands of soldiers out there to be torn up by the heretics.'

Creed crossed his arms. Kell noticed he'd chewed his cigar end almost flat.

Kell looked down at the slate, scanning it for updates. Gave Creed his privacy. That was, he knew, how he could best be of use right now.

Ursarkar E. Creed did not mind losing soldiers. Indeed, he'd personally signed as many Martyrdom certificates as any commander the Cadian Eighth had had in its history. Ordering troopers to rend their flesh on the bayonets of the enemy, or crack their bones against a fortification wall, had never bothered him. Kell had printed the form letters to next of kin and watched Creed sign them without a hitch in his breath.

But this, *this* bothered him. Wasting lives. Troopers dead for no obvious benefit. Squandered. In Creed's estimation, if a soldier had to die, they should die for the benefit of the Imperium and security of Cadia. Shutting the gates now would not just condemn whole regiments to death, but a bad death. One where they would give up their lives in futility.

'Frekk!' he barked. 'Fine. Close them.'

'Right away?'

'Give them twelve hours. By nightfall tonight, they're shutting.'

'That might—'

'What?' Creed's head tilted to one side, his bulldog face even more sour-looking than usual. He took his ragged cigar out of his mouth and ditched it in the ashtray. 'That might what, Kell?'

''Cause a rout, general. If you set a deadline like that, they'll do anything they can to make it there. Abandon positions, break off contact. Drop lasguns and run to make it to the barbican.'

'We have plenty of lasguns. We need men to fire them. Tell the commissars no punishment if troopers come in missing equipment. And I mean that. Any execution for loss of kit needs to be explained to me *personally*. We'll…' Creed wiped a hand across his face. 'We'll designate some units to hold the enemy advance. At least they'll feel like the sacrifice is worth it.'

Kell nodded. 'Yes, sir. There is… There's one more thing.'

'There always is.'

'I'm to present this to you.'

Kell reached behind the stack of picts, scrolls and banded manuscript-reports on the document caddy and picked up a sword. He held it reverently, two fingers and a thumb gripping the pommel, the other hand holding the brass chape at the tip of the scabbard.

With a small bow, he presented it to Creed.

'What's that? What the frekk is this supposed to mean?'

From his voice, Kell knew that Creed recognised it.

'It's the power sword of Sergeant Lukas Bastonne, general. He fell in combat with a heretic sorcerer on the southern curtain wall.

Though the regiment will be keeping his medals, Colonel Devere asked that his sword be presented to you.'

'Well I don't want it. Send the frekking thing back with my condolences.'

'Sir,' Kell responded. There was an almost undetectable note of chiding to the word. 'Colonel Devere said it was in Sergeant Bastonne's final instructions that it go to you, to do with as you see fit. Perhaps in the regimental chapel, or the Museum of Resistance?'

Creed hesitated, reached for it – pulled his hand back as though the scabbarded blade were radiating forge-heat – then grabbed it halfway down the scabbard.

'Thank you, general.'

Kell looked up to find Creed standing, listless, the blade limp in his right hand.

Creed took three steps towards the sideboard with its nearly empty decanter of amasec, but instead collapsed into one of the leather chairs.

'Throne, Kell. Lukas Bastonne.'

Kell knew how he felt. They hadn't been close to Bastonne. They'd known him, of course. Creed had even dined with him privately when he presented him with the Star of Terra – Bastonne's second time receiving the Militarum's highest honour – after the Battle of Tyrok Fields. What had impressed Kell was how *solid* Bastonne had looked. Eternal. As if bullets could not touch him. The man from the recruitment posters and propaganda picts made flesh. Yet utterly unpretentious, despite that fame. In fact, while Creed revelled in his reputation, Bastonne's notoriety seemed to irritate him more than anything.

'This damned war,' Creed said, unsheathing the sword three inches to look at its stained blade. 'It's going to take the best of us, I think.'

Kell said nothing.

'Going to be hard for you to work up a propaganda broadcast

for tonight, isn't it? We have to tell Cadia its favourite son is dead. And I haven't given you much for the opening.'

Kell nodded. Each 'Flower of Cadia' broadcast began with upbeat news – an attack repulsed, a Baneblade that reported an unusually high kill count, a trooper going above and beyond. Kell was not above making it up, if need be, but the stories were better if they were true.

'Give me something good, Kell. Anything. One handhold on this cliff.'

Kell took a deep breath, scrolled. 'The Delvian Cleave is holding.'

'The cleave?' Creed's brow furrowed. 'Didn't we estimate a breakout there today?'

'Well we've been getting reports from the commander saying it's holding. Zero enemy penetration. Lots of requests for supplies, though.'

'Ignitio got the fight he wanted, then. At least one of us is putting up a good showing.'

'No.' Kell shook his head. 'Colonel Barathus was killed in action on landfall day. It's that major who was in here, Hellsker. She's apparently seen them through an armoured assault, two wave attacks and...' He chuckled. 'A cavalry charge.'

'Cavalry?' Creed laughed, shaking his head. He paused. 'Tall woman, recaff-colouring, black hair in a bun?'

'That's her.' Kell brought up a personnel file on his slate and turned it, so Creed could see the headshot-pict.

Creed raised his eyebrows. 'Isn't she related to someone?'

'Colonel Hellsker. The Twenty-Fourth's commander when they got wiped out and were refounded as an Interior. Supposedly killed fighting a carnifex hand to hand.'

'Stupid thing to do, but a good story.' He chewed a thumbnail, looking at the pict. 'She doesn't *look* like a hero.'

'No,' said Kell. 'Not enough scarring.'

Creed shrugged. 'Give it to the propaganda lads, see what they can make of it. Dress it up if they need to, buff up her after-action reports, add some facial wounds to the pict. Cadia lost a hero today, perhaps we can make another one.'

'Yes, general.'

'Well then.' Creed stood. 'Let's see what those foul junior tacticians have conjured up on the projection table this morning, shall we?'

FOUR

The rungs of the ladder were slick and cold, chill enough Keztral had to wear her flight gloves.

The pass wasn't high altitude, exactly, but the mountains still squeezed enough moisture out of passing cloud formations that everything was regularly drenched with light rain – which, combined with the wind funnelling through, dropped temperatures fast.

Another gale blasted by, tugging at her flight suit and making the watchtower lean on its guy wires. Girders creaked.

Her body ached. By her best calculation, she'd trekked upwards of ninety miles in four days.

She'd moved at night, mostly. Avoiding Archenemy patrols, keeping to high ground where she could keep a watch on traitor movements and get a signal for her vox. For a day, she'd even carried a rune-inscribed traitor helmet, reasoning that it changed her silhouette enough that she might be able to slip past enemy units if she kept her distance.

Bad idea. She ditched it – the thing gave her bad dreams.

Reaching the top deck of the watchtower, she drew her laspistol and pushed the hatch upward with the barrel, just in case it was occupied. It wasn't.

With a final grunt, she hauled herself onto the platform, paused for her mid-morning gulp of water, then opened her scope pouch to see how badly she was off course.

At first, she blinked to clear her eyes, as if confirming she wasn't hallucinating, then dialled back the scope magnification.

There were two spires on the other side of the ridge. Spires that shouldn't be there. Upturned arrowheads of metal, high as ten-storey citadel towers, bristling with weapons that lit the air with sizzling fusillades of energy spears and cannon discharge. Eight-pointed stars marked their walls, alongside sigils that made her throat tighten.

Two false pylons, just outside the field of real ones.

And before them, in the blocky maze of trenchworks, were the flash-stabs of bolters as humanoid figures traded fire. Some were silver and black, the others blue-grey.

Keztral sighted a tracked vehicle rolling over the trench-lines, throwing red lascannon beams into the earth. Bracing her elbows on the watchtower's parapet to avoid shaking, she dialled in on it with the scope. Full magnification, image enhance charged to maximum.

For a brief moment, before it slid away, she saw the rivet-studded image of a snarling wolf on the side.

The Ironwolves.

Her dead reckoning had been on-target after all.

Though engaged in furious combat, the Wolves were the closest allied force. And with the resources of the Astartes, they – unlike a front-line Militarum unit – would have air transport able to get her pict-spools back to Kraf.

She opened her pack, carefully extracting the high-gain portable vox. Settled the leather-padded cups of the headset around her ears and set the dials to the emergency channel. Consulted the code-book for the daily call-and-response keywords.

'Dastov's Kin, Dastov's Kin. Emergency band, all allied units. Dastov's Kin.'

She waited, hearing the pop and fizz of an open vox-line in a theatre where the atmosphere is being torn apart. After two minutes, she repeated the call.

A response. Hollow. Partial. Crosstalk from an adjacent channel.

'Last drop we– ... –hree points west. Should hit a– ... confirm target.'

It seemed to be calling coordinates, directing artillery or an airstrike. Far away? Hard to tell. She shifted the set's aerial, homed in on the signal. If it was a roving Kasrkin squad spotting targets for the Aeronautica, or an armoured artillery section, that would be almost as good as the Astartes – better, since they wouldn't be engaged in direct combat.

Keztral tried to identify the signal direction, searching the dial to find it again. Realised it came from Kraf.

After three minutes of fiddling, she nailed the correct band. It came through loud and clear. Cadian accent, with a slight Kraf lilt. Weird channel. Non-standard.

'Good hit. Confirm massive casualties. Next three salvoes, walk it back to the armoured pool. It–'

'Unidentified signal,' she said. 'Dastov's Kin, Dastov's Kin. Requesting aid. Can you identify your unit and position? I would like to move to you.'

Silence. Some kind of distortion on the band. Words, twisted and scratching, but unintelligible. Squelched to the point that they seemed inhuman.

'Unidentified signal,' she repeated, 'can you give me the daily code, your unit and position? Pilot down and seeking aid. Carrying vital intel.'

She waited. Three minutes. Four. Nothing.

It was forty minutes later, when she'd climbed down the tower and started back up the footpath towards the Wolves, that the vox bleeped again.

The unfamiliar channel.

'We hear you, Dastov's Kin. We answer Nestor's Sword. Kasrkin Long-Range Team Delta-Niner. Our signal triangulation has you in the Elysion Ridge. Come to point epsilon-grachii. The railhead. We'll be waiting to bring you home.'

Keztral knelt, stretching the map over her thigh. Consulted her codebook to translate the nonsense coordinates into usable ones. The point indicated was across the pass, maybe a day's walk.

'Praise the Emperor,' she breathed.

Yann Rovetske handed the handset back to the artillery spotter, and closed his codebook.

This spotter – there were so many of them, at least two dozen spread across the city – was just inside the northern citadel wall in an evacuated tower hab. One of Rovetske's star pupils, in fact. Background in civilian broadcasting. She'd managed to call long-range artillery into Kraf targets with such unerring accuracy the sector's aerial defences had been spraying the sky in grids, thinking an unseen observation aircraft was helping call the strikes.

One woman, Rovetske reflected, had not only killed thousands of Cadian lapdogs but persuaded them to waste whole lockers of Hydra ammunition, too.

'You did the right thing, calling me,' he said, pulling on his gloves.

'Have I done a service?' the spotter asked. He could see the eagerness on her face.

'Yes, though how big of one remains to be seen. Perhaps it's nothing, perhaps it will prove the key to our victory.'

'The Warmaster.' She licked her lips. 'Will he know that I delivered it? Will he know my name when the liberation comes?'

'He will know.' Rovetske smiled, enveloping her in his calming essence. 'He will know it just as I do, Adukah.'

'Thank you,' she said, blinking back tears. Believing.

In a detached, academic way, Rovetske realised he did not recall the woman's true name. The woman reminded him of Adukah Ventner, a rhetoric tutor from his youth, so he'd christened her such. It did not matter. He said a name, she wanted it to be her name, and the lie did the rest.

'I must go,' he said. There was a fanatic in Highsgate itching to strike his local las-cell manufactorum, and Rovetske had a body-bomb vest earmarked for him.

Then there was the other thing... The monumental thing.

'Keep the faith, Adukah,' he said, reaching out to touch the woman's cheek. 'You will be rewarded.'

FIVE

'Blood! Blood! *Blood!*'

It coated Urkanthos' armour, sticky and sweet. Cast dazzling arc patterns in the air as he cut through the Emperor's shrews. Crushing-in their cuirasses with backhand blows like thunderclaps. Piercing their helm domes with his teeth. Slashing throats so their wailing hymns gagged on blood.

The chapel's defensive force of corpse-brides was dead now, the outer gatehouse and the chapel within at his mercy.

He gave it none.

For within the chapel were not martial Sisters, but priests. Frail old men who chanted in their white robes, praying for deliverance and to smite him.

He'd taken his time about it. Blood pooled ankle-deep in the chapel, cascaded down the stairways to the crypt. Artesia leapt along walls, long-limbed and tinted crimson, drawing her shadow-talons across the robed hypocrites – slitting tendons at the back of the knee, opening arteries in the neck, bursting eyeballs.

They fell to their knees, screaming.

In a last futile act, they prayed to their dead god.

Urkanthos tore the arm off one and slashed it through the air in the sketched shape of a Khornate rune, spattering a tapestry of Saint Katherine with dots of blood in foul patterns. He tore the shaven head off another and mashed it on the altar, befouling an offering plate and filling a golden chalice with gore.

Before the altar stood their high priest. Thin and bent, his body slumped forward under the weight of his enormous spire-like hat. Spewing invective at him.

Urkanthos decided to dispatch him with a particular flourish.

With one long-taloned hand he grabbed the high priest and dragged him kicking to the altar. Incredibly, the old priest pulled a stub pistol from his robes, and fired point-blank until the chamber was empty – the slugs flattening on Urkanthos' armoured hide.

He threw the priest on the altar, smashed his fist through a glass reliquary holding the broken thigh-bone of a saint, and stabbed him to death with the sharp end of the sacred femur.

Urkanthos could feel the swell of warp energy about him. Thick and tacky like coagulating vitae. The presence of empyric entities, the eye of Khorne upon him.

'It is coming!' he bellowed, caring not as a Sister with a heavy bolter spanged shots off his crimson-glowing form. *'A blessing, I feel the blessing. Khorne, I offer these bloody humans to you!'*

His change, it might finally be his change. Urkanthos could feel the ether pregnant with power. And if not that, perhaps an influx of warp energy into the Lords of Skulls, which had been moving sluggishly into position at one-quarter power. If they came fully online, his transformation and ascendance would be assured...

Under the churning surface of the blood, things began to move. Elongated red arms broke the surface, pulling the Sister and her heavy bolter down. Conical skulls pushed their way through the blood that dripped from the walls, howling from needle-toothed maws as they were born into reality.

The skeletal corpse before him twitched, bloated, distorting.

Urkanthos plunged his hands into the broken chest and levered the ribcage beneath open like a cabinet.

The bloodletter clawed its way from the chest cavity, slick with arterial red. No bigger than a small child at first, it flopped newborn on the altar and began to grow. A stretched lung covered its head like a caul.

The gift given, warp energy drained from the ether, leaving it cold and empty.

'Daemons!' roared Urkanthos. 'Only more warp spawn. Damn you, Khorne! You ungrateful wretch. I defile this sanctuary for you! I have committed myself to murdering these Imperial fanatics for you. *And what do you give me?'*

He gripped one of the growing bloodletter's horns and wrenched its skull off, then heaved it into a corner.

'Daemons!'

'Urkanthos!' scolded Artesia.

He wheeled on the shadow-daemon. 'Why does he mock me? Why does the Blood God give me his leavings? You said he wished for sacred blood. We have given him sacred blood for days, yet I am still twisted and half-changed.'

'You have not given him enough. His eye has moved on.'

Urkanthos snarled, a sound like emergency brakes trying to stop a dropping mag-lift. 'Not enough? Not enough? *When will it be enough?'*

He gripped the Khorne rune on his armour and wrenched it off with a pop of rivets. Then he slammed it to the mosaic floor of the raised altar dais and stamped on it.

'I renounce you, Khorne! I renounce your fickle nature, your uncaring eye. You are the least and worst of gods, as useless as the Corpse-Emperor. Tzeentch deigns to bring his followers change. Nurgle is generous with his blessings. Even cursed Slaanesh does more for his devotees. You are filth! You are nothing!'

He spat a stream of bloody phlegm on the icon. Then he opened his arms in challenge and spoke to the sky, visible through the fractured dome of the chapel ceiling.

'Is your eye drawn to me now, little god? Do you like what you see? Why don't you come punish me? Are you unable to do even that?'

There was silence.

The bloodletters had moved on, sensing human flesh and eager to rend it.

Nothing moved in the defiled chapel, apart from the dripping of a hundred surfaces drenched in gore.

Artesia started to cackle.

'Now you mock me too? Even as your patron refuses to defend himself?'

'You think Khorne cares if you renounce him? If you abuse his icons and spit on them? He is a god, you half-mortal fool. Do what you will to his rune. Jump on it, crush it, piss on it. It's a piece of metal, and at the end of it he will still be a god and you will be a petty little half-mortal.'

She dissolved in laughter again.

'I renounce him, and he does not care? What kind of god is that?'

'Renounce what? You think he has your name in a book somewhere? No! You shed blood in his name and he blesses you – if others shed more blood, he blesses them.'

Urkanthos threw his arms towards the pools of coagulating gore. 'I have made this chapel an abattoir!'

'It is a planetary siege, fool. You kill too slow. Millions are butchered each hour. Massacre rules on this world, and you think this little siege will gain his eye?'

'You told me...'

'I told you to make a dramatic gesture, to spill gouts of blood. To make the vitae flow like a river broken its banks. This siege warfare is a trickle, not a flood tide. Khorne does not care about victory or

tactical objectives, he wants **carnage.** *And you cannot gain his attention battering your forces against walls.'*

'What am I to do then, if they will not fight me another way?'

Artesia said nothing, merely casting herself over a large bloodstain, writhing and splashing with the pleasure of it.

'What am I to do?'

'Have patience – and use the Lords of Skulls.'

'The western wall is breached,' Genevieve said. 'The gatehouse
chapel is fallen. Within a day, the outer defensive cloister will fall.
And the great super-heavy skull-machines have...'

The tower rocked and swayed with a hit. In the priestly quarter, a gout of flame roared skyward, the shockwave ripping out in
a gale of rockcrete dust and swirling parchment.

With a pang, Genevieve realised it had hit the scriptorium
centre. Millions of edicts, tactical treatises and illuminated hymnals
atomised.

In the distance, the super-heavy machines ground towards the
shrine.

Genevieve had caught so many blows on her left greave it
had almost been beaten to bare metal. Her tabards, despite their
flame-retardant qualities, were brown with scorch-marks. A flamer
blast had enveloped her, burning away the sacred parchments of
her purity seals and melting the wax.

One of her Seraphim worked to replace them as they spoke.

Her sister's armour, by contrast, gleamed with fresh lacquer.

'We have lost much,' Eleanor answered.

'You should have been there, on the wall,' Genevieve said. 'Perhaps
it would not have fallen if...'

'It would have fallen, and I would have with it. Then the strategic
and spiritual health of the most venerated Shrine of St Morrican
would be in your hands. And Emperor help us were that to happen.'

'Words,' said Genevieve. 'Words and commands, while I worship with deeds. You have Sisters singing in a choir when they could be on the walls.'

'We battle Neverborn here, sister, not some invading army. Faith is a strategic asset we cannot abandon. Without those choirs, and Arch-Deacon Mendazus' continuous liturgies in the Chapel of Morrican, you would have been overwhelmed.'

'Just like the two of you. Safe behind the walls saying prayers, while others–'

'He is martyred, Genevieve. A saint's death. He refused to stop saying the Recitations of the Holy Throne, even as the half-prince tore him to pieces.'

Genevieve gasped. 'That… That stubborn…'

'Stop. He raised us, Genevieve. Made us what we are.'

'No, he made us deny what we are.'

There would've been silence between them, if not for the pounding of cannon fire.

'Is that why you called me here? To tell me that?'

'It is time. To go to the Hermitage of the Pit. It cannot wait. Now that these so-called Lords of Skulls have our range, we cannot hold out more than a day.'

'No.'

A spiral of tracer fire whipped from one of the lumbering machines. It drilled into a bell-tower in the shrine cloister, decapitating it in a spray of brickwork.

'It is our only choice. Now that the arch-deacon is martyred, they will not take orders from any but one of us. Rally the damned, and unleash them on the heretics' flank. An armoured column will follow – perhaps we can get enough Retributors in range to destroy one or both war engines.'

'You are sending me to die.'

'It is an honour to be martyred in service of the Emperor. It was for Katherine, it was for the arch-deacon, and it will be for you and I, when the time comes.'

'Martyrdom is self-sacrifice. And you are sacrificing everyone but yourself.'

Eleanor coloured. 'As you so often remind me, your task is to attack, mine is to defend. So I release you to the attack, with my blessing.'

Eleanor turned back to her siege.

'That's all, sister? After thirty-five years of trying to make you care, of wanting to be something to you other than another Sister. This is where we leave it?'

Eleanor sighed. 'As Arch-Deacon Mendazus taught us, we are no more to each–'

'No,' Genevieve snapped. 'The old hypocrite is dead, and we don't have to pretend he was correct. We vow to treat all in our Order as if they were our sisters. Equally. But Mendazus, he always pushed you to treat me less. You knew how it hurt me, you just feared that any sign of affection, any warmth, would soil your Throne-damned holiness in his eyes.'

'Language!'

'Language, you say. Let's talk about language, *sister*. Yes. I said a blasphemy. But words left unsaid can be blasphemy too. If this is the last time, I'm not holding my tongue. All my life you have been ashamed of me. Treated me like some dark reflection, a warning of what would happen if you were less than flawless. Used me as a dupe to blame any failure on, while taking all the responsibility for yourself. Bathing in the approbation of that old, judgemental–'

'Don't you think it was hard living so close under his eye?' Eleanor snapped. 'Someone had to run the shrine commandery. Not all of us can go reiving through the air. You have no idea the freedom you enjoyed in being allowed to fail.'

'Fail.' Genevieve took a step back towards the balcony. 'Is that it? That is your valediction for me, sister? I am a failure.'

'No, that's not...' Eleanor looked away, shook her head. 'It does not matter. There is nothing I could say that would satisfy you, Genevieve.'

Genevieve laughed, a sharp snort through her nostrils. 'It was never your words that I wanted.'

She leapt off the balcony.

As she keyed her jump pack and rose towards the fight, she thought she heard Eleanor call her name.

SIX

'Careful!' shouted Hellsker, body tensing as a shower of rockcrete dust and chips scattered down from Cadet-Lieutenant Zander's boot. 'Angel's blood, the boy's going to kill himself.'

Sergeant Ravura shrugged, then winced. Last night, a piece of grenade shrapnel had sliced through the shoulder clasp of his flak vest, dropping the armour open and carving a nasty furrow across his shoulder blade. 'He wants to prove himself. You remember what being a Whiteshield was like.'

Zander clung to the side of the Delvian Cleave, a hundred and fifty feet up. Feet pressed against the side of a bunker position, hands gripping the inside of a firing slit. Edging sideways like a wounded arachnid towards where the big canister hung, its chute snagged on the protruding barrel of a quad autocannon mount.

'What do you think is inside?' asked Pesk. The engineer captain looked at her with the one eye that still responded. The other, covered with a bandage, was permanently dilated and rolled aimlessly. Pesk's condition had deteriorated since the first night when he'd blown the Demolisher, and Medicae Dakaj had privately told Hellsker he suspected a shockwave injury and progressive brain bleed. Pesk still insisted he could stay on the line.

'Our coats, finally?' guessed Lek.

'Lasgun cells,' wished Ravura. 'Or maybe some food.'

'Painkillers,' said Pesk, nearly wistful.

'Do you have a headache?' Hellsker snapped.

'No,' said Pesk, sheepish, looking at his boots.

'You're to inform me if you get a headache, Manvar.'

'Yes,' he said. 'Yes, of course.'

A shell streaked overhead, and detonated in the peaks above the cleave. They flinched as a trickle of rock cascaded down the wall to their left, and Zander gripped the firing slit, waiting for the tremor to subside. He took one more step and grasped the quad-gun's barrel for balance, then drew his combat knife and began sawing at the snared chute.

'Move away!' shouted Ravura. 'Stop looking up, morons, you want to get killed by the one damn resupply that hit the target?'

When they'd heard the approaching aircraft, they'd taken cover thinking it was an enemy raid. Those came, sometimes, but the cleave's wind shear, plus the Hydra and quad batteries, meant that airstrikes were a risky proposition for the Archenemy and bombs rarely fell on target.

Of course, neither did resupply packages. They'd spotted six exiting the Marauder's bomb bay. Two had drifted into the peaks, where Plyn and his alpine snipers were searching for them. Enemy fire had shredded another, and the other two had drifted to the Volscani.

Then there was this one.

'How long do you think–' started Udza, stepping forward.

'Watch out!' snapped Rivelle, putting out a protective augmetic hand to restrain the vox-operator.

The chute tore with a horrifying rip, the package plummeting in a spiral like a shot bird as the holed parachute tried to compensate.

It came away so quickly that a cord entangled Zander's arm, dragging him away from the wall.

'Throne!' squeaked Ravura, the big man's voice high in alarm.

Lievett Zander plunged from the wall, wind shear blustering through the chute, his arm cinched tight in the paracords and falling with the enormous case towards the hard roadway.

'Dakaj!' Hellsker shouted.

'Here!' the medicae said, rushing forward.

Everyone was running towards the impact point, so much that when the banging crash of the case hitting roadway and breaking open echoed through the Delvian Cleave, she couldn't see Zander.

Frekk, not Zander, she thought, shoving soldiers aside. Telling them to gangway. *Please not Zander. Not the kid who'd taken on the Chimeras for her. Please, God-Emperor, not...*

They parted, and she saw him covered in blood.

'Frekk!' shrieked Zander. 'Frekk, get it frekking off me!'

The cord had coiled his forearm like a serpent, biting so deep the blood ran. His fingers throbbed purple with trapped blood, the limb twisted in all the wrong ways.

Hellsker could see shards of bone piercing skin.

Dakaj skidded to a stop beside Zander, using kneepads to go directly from a run to a crouch. A pair of shears in his hand, working the blade between flesh and cord. Cutting through the entangling wire with meaty snaps.

'It hurts,' wailed Zander.

'Where?' said the orderly Suvane, frisking the cadet-lieutenant, looking for broken bones. 'Where does it hurt?'

'Everywhere,' said Zander. He sobbed. Bloody spittle ran from his mouth. 'Frekking everywhere.'

Some troopers were stunned, looking at the wounded White-shield officer.

Others were scrambling, gathering up the strewn bounty of the case.

'Food!' someone said. 'It's food! Thank the Throne.'

Hellsker's gaze was rooted to Zander.

Dakaj had finally snipped the cord free, and was wrapping the wound with compression bandages. 'Any other trauma?' he asked Suvane.

'No,' said the orderly, feeling Zander's ribcage and spine. He snapped the clasp on the officer's helmet and started lifting it free.

Then he stopped, shot a look into Dakaj's eyes.

The chief medicae caught the glance, and leaned back to see the base of Zander's skull, where the orderly's red-stained fingers were holding something in.

Dakaj bit his upper lip, touching his lower teeth to the edge of his black moustache, then looked at Hellsker and shook his head. The medicae's violet eyes, set deep within black rings of insomnia, were so hurt she could barely stand it.

He drew out a pain-dumbing syrette of obscurine and wedged it into the crook of the cadet-lieutenant's wounded arm.

Zander's face slackened, his red-wet lips opening in a relieved sigh, before sucking breath again.

'M-major,' he said. She came down close. 'What'd we get, major? Is it food?'

'Tin!' Hellsker turned and snapped her fingers. In the commotion of scavenging the container, not everyone had seen Zander's state. Ravura was bellowing at troopers to stop tearing into the cans, to show some discipline. 'Bring me one of those food tins. Let him have a taste.'

But when Cadet-Sergeant Vivek came close, a tin in her hand, Hellsker knew something was off. Disappointment and sorrow dragged at the young Whiteshield's features. A green smear was on her cracked, wind-burned lips. 'I'm sorry, major, it's... It's not... I don't know, it's spoiled.'

Behind the cadet-sergeant, troopers were spitting and hacking.

Hellsker dipped her fingers into the open tin, felt a cold, oily substance. It was thick and dark green on her fingers. And when she brought it to her face and inhaled, she knew instantly what it was. Had a sense memory so strong, she recognised it even through the scentless air of the mountain cold.

Those Munitorum bastards. Of all the Throne-damned things they could've sent. All the useless, stupid things to lose a man for.

'Major?' Zander asked. His voice had an edge of uncertainty to it. 'Major? Did I get us something good?'

The troopers were turning to her, quieting, confusion and concern on their blistered faces.

Don't show them, the dark officer said. *Don't show them how furious you are. If you do, the next time the enemy hits the cleave, they'll break. They can stand against the Archenemy, but if they realise their own have abandoned them, their resolve will crumple.*

You need to fix this, right now.

'Major? What flavour is it?'

'It's not food,' she said. 'It's better.'

He blinked twice. 'Better?'

'I told high command about you, Zander. About what you did on the first night. Mentioned in dispatches how you led the assault on the Chimeras. And they heard.'

'Mentioned… me? What flavour?'

'It's not food,' she said, dipping her fingers into the oil and drawing it out, holding it close so his failing eyes could see. 'It's Alpine Woodland Green Number Five. Paint.'

'Why would they…?'

She took his drooping chin, and held his head up. Then smeared the paint across his helmet, over the white stripe, then spooned another handful out of the container and wiped it down his shoulder pad.

'You're a Shock Trooper, son,' she said. 'A real, Throne-damned Shock Trooper. Congratulations.'

Zander breathed heavy in shock, hot air misting from his smiling mouth.

'You're all frekking Shock Troopers!' she said, standing and raising her voice. 'Pass that paint around, get rid of those ragged-arse stripes on your helmets. You're all promoted. There aren't any frekking Whiteshields in this regiment. Not any more.'

Hellsker slapped her paint-covered hand on Cadet-Sergeant Vivek's shoulder pad, obscuring the white field there. 'And you're acting lieutenant of J Company, Vivek.'

'Yes, major.' She nodded, scooping out a handful of paint and scrubbing it over her helmet stripe. 'Pass it around, J Company! Don't be greedy.'

'And someone vox the scouts,' Hellsker yelled. 'I want a situation report on those two containers. Whatever's in them, we want it!'

Whiteshields whooped, smiled. Huddled around tins of paint as they dipped hands in to messily slop over the shameful badges they'd worn for so long. They playfully socked each other's flak vests, saluted each other with green-stained fingers. Exchanged oaths of comradeship that billowed out with smoke in the frozen air.

'Good save,' said Ravura, under his breath. 'But I swear, if I find whatever slate-pushing son-of-a-civilian sent us this shipment, I'll twist their head around.'

Then the scream of a shell came overhead, joined by another, and another, overlapping like the howls of the damned, and Ravura yelled: 'Positions!'

A quad-gun started to drum, and former Whiteshields scuttled half-bent towards foxholes and emplacements.

Hellsker drew her uncle's plasma pistol, unused to its weight, and keyed the coils active. The vibration set her teeth on edge, and she thanked the Throne she hadn't had to fire it yet.

'Dakaj,' she said. 'Get Zander ins–'

But when she turned, the medic and his orderly were already gone, leaving Lievett Zander lying propped against the container.

He was already dead.

Trazyn the Infinite, Overlord of Solemnace and Archaeovist of the Prismatic Galleries, had a rising suspicion that he was in the wrong place at the wrong time.

After stabilising the null-array, he'd occupied himself with a site survey of the regions and environs of Kasr Kraf, obtaining a general sense of the geography and troop dispositions that had proved invaluable as he subsequently tracked and recorded the progress of the battle.

When the Black Legion's vehicle assault had met Creed's armoured regiments on the Kraf Plain, he'd been there to observe. As the Word Bearers punched through the outer curtain wall in the south, he'd managed to take sufficient notes and image-captures for a future display. And while he had been hard-pressed to visit every major event – after all, much of his time had to be spent tracking those battle-fronts bordering on the Elysion Fields – he'd at least dispatched a stealthy scarab swarm or two to collect image and motion-captures of regional engagements.

Yet now, at the very crux of the battle, he had chosen poorly.

Arch-Cryptek Sannet, hidden in orbit with Trazyn's personal vessel, the *Lord of Antiquity*, had just sent him an interstitial message. It told that Black Legion warp-constructs had breached the easternmost gate, and a furious combat was in progress just inside the Beta Curtain Wall, in front of the Jorus Redoubt.

The colonel of that bastion had left the gate open past the deadline, hoping to allow the Mordian Sable Guard and 707th Armoured Shock time to make the gate – and had instead triggered the closing procedure too late to keep the Chaos Space Marines out.

Now Militarum forces were attempting a major repulse under

the personal command of Supreme Commissar Zabine – who had taken command after a series of executions – supported by the Novamarines. Leman Russ variants were burning out their drive-trains trying to push the gates closed as Helbrutes shouldered them open. The most dramatic battle of the campaign so far.

And instead he was here.

'Curse the Dead Gods,' he swore, breaking the crypto-seal on the orbital image-capture scroll and panning through the chryso-prase projection floating before him. 'Damn, damn, damn. Sannet?'

'Yes, lord?'

'Your strategic projection algorithm has failed us. I suggest a full recoding.'

'Why, lord?'

'Why? Why? Dare you ask this after sending me that projection?' Trazyn, cautious not to be seen, stepped out of his hyperspace oubli-ette and gestured with open arms. 'They're *singing,* Sannet.'

Trazyn stood on the extreme western gate of the inner curtain wall, on the barrel of a disabled wall gun large as a hab-block. Normally it would be an exposed position, but the illusion emit-ter hanging around his hooded neck meant that his image refused to register on all but the most psychically attuned humans.

He stretched his arms out at the army of cultists that massed below the western gate.

An army of cultists that were, undoubtedly, singing.

They were down on all fours as if in supplication, bodies leaning side to side with the ethereal song, so that the multitude kneeling before the closed gates looked like a churning sea. Some stabbed or shot themselves at an unknown cue, joining the mounds of bodies that lay in patches amid the hysteric mob as wall guns blew great craters in the carpet of flesh. Whole lines died, refusing to stop the odd swaying and burbled keening, even as a heavy bolter calmly walked fire down the line, so each knew for horrible seconds that they were fated to die.

Mutated Astartes, their misshapen armour covered with robes, walked among them swinging censers that trailed pale yellow smoke.

'They are doing this,' said Trazyn. 'While at the eastern gate and Jorus Redoubt, a battle for the ages is taking place. Think of what acquisitions I am missing.'

I think you will recall that I predicted the breakthrough would come at the eastern gate,' responded Sannet, appending a glyph indicating a respectful tone with an undercurrent of resentment. *'All indications were that this would happen. It was your theory that cultist and Black Legion forces hooking in from the southern breach would assault the western gate.'*

'Sannet.'

'I recall you observing that the eastern gate attack was a feint, and that Abaddon-Who-Despoils is a strategic mastermind.'

'Abaddon the Despoiler. And yes, that is what I thought. But it's your fault for not talking me out of it. If you'd only made a more convincing case, I would not be stuck here watching whatever *this* is.'

'Yes, lord.'

Trazyn fell silent, mulling. If he was honest with himself – a practice he, through long experience, found neither enjoyable nor profitable – placing himself at the western gate had been his decision. Besides, it kept him far from the xenocidal savagery of the Novamarines, whom Trazyn had always found dull and bothersome, and were more likely than any other troops on Cadia to detect him.

And so he resigned himself to make do with whatever information his scarab swarms could record, and tried to find a pattern in the swaying. It was at least an interesting ritual to analyse, from a socio-ethnographic standpoint. To what purpose was this? To summon forth a warp entity? To beseech the gods of the false-dimension for success in an upcoming assault? Perhaps that was so – he could see Black Legion transports mustering behind the cultist horde.

'What are they singing?' he said.

'You would like a translation node? For what language?'

'Warp-chant of some kind. Run it through a filter to identify via diction and grammar.'

'Some meaning may be lost due to our inability to read empyric tonality, or warp–'

'Just the words.'

Sannet went quiet, and Trazyn was about to ask for a progress scry when the muddy, bubbling speech of the crowd started to resolve into intelligible phrases.

Father of Laughter, Beacon of Joy, Bearer of the Cup of Bliss, He-Who-Makes-Life, Fertile Mother, Generous One Who Gives Even the Enemy Rebirth...

'My apologies, lord. The filter must be malfunctioning and streaming out trash-glyphs, I will–'

'No,' said Trazyn, crouching and enhancing the images in his oculars. 'It's not trash-glyphs. It's the thirty-three-hundred names of the Empyric Godhead Nurgle.'

Trazyn cast his sensor-suite wide, reading for everything – aural anomaly, brainwave patterns, seismic–

'Sannet!'

'I detect it, lord. A structural disturbance within the wall, if it pleases you...'

'Huntmaster! Get me down there!' he said, his mag-locked feet pounding on the cannon barrel as he charged back to his hyperspace oubliette. 'Get me behind the walls, three hundred cubits back. On solid ground.'

As he dived into the pocket dimension, letting the little cylinder of extradimensional space slide closed, his aural sensors picked up the terrified wail of defenders within the wall.

'Quickly! Quickly!'

When the oubliette slid open again, he was at a standoff distance behind the massive gates, standing atop one of the autocannon bunkers and other defensive works that dotted either side of the gatehouse road. A network of weapons, meant to pour fire if the gates were ever breached.

They were not breached, they were not even *touched.*

Instead, they came apart.

Rust crawled at the cyclopean hinges. Metal pitting, twisting, browning and curling like leaves in a campfire.

The open oubliette was a window until he stepped through to make it a door, and Trazyn risked doing so only because it might allow him to focus an ocular scry.

What he saw on the blackening, ageing hinges were creatures swaying, dancing, *singing.*

He dialled back his chronosense and scryed in closer.

They were microscopic Nurgle daemons, a voracious, milling colony of them spread atop and within the gate hinges. They capered and sang, mated and excreted, multiplied and died en masse to become colonies for their gleeful descendants.

But most of all, they ate. Consumed each other with mouths of needle teeth, wiggling loose in decaying gums. They cannibalised the dead and gnawed their own fleshy limbs. And they ate the metal of the hinges so the thick steel became nothing more than a lattice web of darkened metal, creaking as the weight of the double doors began to pull, twist and shear the weakened structure. Behind the deteriorating pins, knuckles and hinge plates Trazyn could see the spreading colony eroding the thick rockcrete of the wall itself.

And Trazyn, who had lived sixty-five million years and seen civilisations rise, fall and turn to dust, knew exactly what this was: the power of aeons unleashed. These revolting beings were not eating the machinery, they were *ageing* it.

A growling rumble bellowed across the plain towards him, and he normalised his chronosense in time to realise it was a splitting crack – the top two hinges of the left-hand gate had split, and it leaned crazily out of the frame.

The troops under it had only a brief time to run before the bottom hinge twisted and sheared, and the slab-like gate forged from an adamantine-steel alloy came down like a broken tombstone.

Thick as a Leman Russ tank was long, it crumpled armoured vehicles and burst a fire-support platform in a puff of rockcrete dust.

Before the haze settled, the second gate came down. But on that side the nurgling colony had infected the door itself, and before separating from the wall structure it started to groan and bend like a sick man holding his stomach. When it fell, the bent end hammered into the earth like a bare hand trying to dig a grave.

The singing had ceased – only screams now, as thousands of cultists rushed through the open gate, firing stubbers and waving bone charms, many armed with nothing at all. They climbed the fallen gates as though they were ramps. Shot disoriented Cadians who were still stumbling from the wreckage, blinded by shock and the drifting clouds of dirt.

The Huntmaster stepped to his side, protectively raising his synaptic disintegrator.

It was not, Trazyn realised, a mere intervention from the so-called gods of the warp. He had just witnessed one of the most successful acts of sabotage in Imperial history.

To his left, a company of Baneblades leapt forward, crawling between the tracer fire of the bunkers and aegis lines, heavy bolters chattering and lascannons alight.

But even this overwhelming display of armoured might, Trazyn knew, could not meet the moment. Calculations spooled across the right side of his oculars, his strategic subsystems comparing the forces, terrain and combat postures of the various units; Sannet's reports of a sudden heat plume over the Black Legion transports idling outside the walls indicated one conclusion.

'This is the breakthrough attack, the true breakthrough attack!' he said, knowing the words would be lost in the pounding of battle. And amid the most desperate fight of that day, as millions of soldiers grappled in mortal struggle and munitions arced over his head, Trazyn raised clenched fists at the sky.

'I was right, Sannet, you hear me? I was right!'

'What the hells is happening out there?' Creed said.

The western sector officer – Ravi, Kell thought her name was – stammered.

'I-I don't know, general. The gates are open.'

'The gates are what?' Creed slammed his tumbler on the holo-table so hard, the image briefly flickered out. 'What do you mean *open*? They were reported closed on–'

'Sorry, general, sorry,' Ravi said, motioning for quiet as she pressed a hand to the augmetically implanted vox-hub that had replaced her right ear. 'Reports say it's…'

Ravi's eyes wavered, darting across the holo-table as if tracking a zigzagging insect before she looked up at Creed. 'General, I regret to inform you the western gate has fallen. Some kind of chemical attack. The passage is open and gates are inoperable. Baneblades of the Hundred-and-Thirteenth Death's Head Company have engaged but they've already depleted half their ammunition. Black Legion transports are preparing to storm.'

'So even if we retake the gate, we cannot hold it is what you're saying.'

'Yes, general.'

'So we're frekked.'

'That is an accurate assessment.'

Creed nodded, puffed his cigar. He cocked his head slightly as he did so, a sign Kell knew meant that he was mulling a difficult call.

'General,' said an officer. When Kell turned he saw the man wore the blue tabard and high collar of a Navy liaison, the gate symbol of Battlefleet Cadia pinned to his braid.

'He's thinking,' Kell interrupted. 'Give him a moment.'

'It can't wait, general,' he continued, speaking past Kell. 'We are getting power-surge readings from the heretic vessel *Terminus Est*, it has run out guns and is manoeuvring into a planetary bombardment position.'

'Targeting what?' Creed asked. His eyes were distant, their expression unreadable as they reflected the green holo-projection.

'Our ballistic cogitators indicate the *Sword of Defiance*.'

'Bad day for the Dark Angels too, then.' Creed sighed, tore his gaze from the projection map. 'Does anyone have good news?'

'The eastern gate is holding, Task Force Jorus Redoubt–'

'Doesn't matter a wet fart if we've lost the western gate. We'll have to pull the whole mess back to the citadel. Anything else? How are the sons of Russ doing?'

The northern quadrant officer snapped to attention. 'Wolf Lord Highfell reports their engagement with the Iron Warriors has entered a final phase, he expects to deliver victory in a day, perhaps two.'

'Well praise the Emperor for that. And the Templars – don't tell me, they're still at the damned Martyr's Rampart, yes? Yes. The Sisters?'

'Heretic super-heavy machines moving on them,' reported the eastern sector officer. 'We haven't had an update. Baroness Vardus estimates four days until Legio Vulcanum is in range of the citadel.'

Creed blew smoke out his nostrils so it wavered the table's holo-grid, then stepped back from the projector.

The tactical officers went to attention.

'Well,' he said, raising his eyebrows, 'didn't like running the damn war from in here anyway. Kell?'

'Lord Castellan?'

'Get the Valk's engines spinning, we're setting up a command post on the wall. This is now a citadel siege, and that's the kind of fight you don't organise inside a bunker. We'll need a vox-operator – you, what's your name?'

'It's Kormachen, sir, of the Eighty-Eighth.'

'You know the joke, Kormachen? That until you serve six months under me, I won't bother to learn your name.'

'I've heard it, sir.'

'Well it works in reverse too. Now that I've learned your name, you're not allowed to die. Don't make me learn some other damned voxman's name, Kormachen, you hear me?'

'Sir!'

'Now walk with me, Kormachen, I want to see this battle with my own eyes.'

Keztral entered the railyard carefully, quietly. Crouched beside walls with her laspistol held low.

She was going to meet friends, but this was Archenemy territory. Artillery detonations banged over the horizon, like some massive piledriver stamping the foundation for a new hab. *Wham-Wha-Wham-Wham-Wham.*

The sound echoed off the abandoned freight vans and stockhouses of the depot, hammering her in overlapping claps of sound that felt almost like they had weight. Jags of other industrial detonations – Astartes bolter fire, she assumed – punctuated the air at random intervals.

Keztral hurt all over. She'd used a third of the gauze and tape in her medical kit just binding up her bleeding feet. The canteen at her hip had been empty two days, with the water sources she passed too polluted to replenish it. In the mountain pass, she'd licked dew-slicked metal to rejuvenate her dried tongue and cracked lips.

Every pilot went through escape and evasion training, but she'd never been physically conditioned to walk this long across difficult terrain with a heavy pack. Worse than the pain was the sodden blanket of apathy that had descended over her. An acceptance that she probably had no control over her life or death.

It's almost over, she told herself. *You made it. Got to the coordinates – just don't get stupid and sloppy right at the end. This is still heretic country.*

Keztral peered out from the corner of the van, leading with the nose of her laspistol. She was low, sheltering behind the hard cover of its iron wheels, minimising her silhouette.

When she spotted the Kasrkin squad, kneeling in a circle, watching their quadrants, she sobbed, but was too dehydrated to actually weep.

In her long trek, she hadn't met a friendly face – not alive, anyway.

On day three, she'd passed a copse of poles hammered into the broken earth. Rebar scavenged from pulverised bunkers, mostly, but also flag-poles and the wicked iron stakes often sunk at the bottom of defensive ditches. They varied in length from knee-height to ten feet.

Atop each stood a Cadian head, canted at odd angles as if the heretics jamming them on had to negotiate around the spines or find weaker parts of the skull base. A few, still helmeted, had the spikes go completely through the cranium and lifted their helmets the way an officer raises his hat to a passing war widow. Others had runes carved into their cheeks and foreheads that seemed to deepen as she looked at them, as though they were not patterns but holes in the world. Holes leading to a dark place that drew her eyes, while her brain recoiled like a scalded child.

Those dead, defiled faces were the last companions she'd seen, not counting the civilian woman she'd come across just two hours before. The woman had been a shell-maker by her uniform and blackened fingertips, and pressed the head of a three-year-old boy to her chest. The boy lived, but bloody snot had dried in a crust over his upper lip.

She'd unbuckled her respirator so they could see her face, and tried to get them to come with her. Said that she was two hours from help, but the woman only cringed deeper into the corner. Keztral had even set a ration bar in front of the child and showed him the flight wings pinned to her suit. Said, 'Cadia, Cadia pilot,' and made swooping gestures with her hands. Next she tried, 'Creed? My boss.' She saluted in pantomime. 'Is Lord Castellan Creed.' She mimicked smoking a cigar. 'You know? Come with me, Creed's troopers will help you. Kasrkin. Big and tough.'

The child said only one thing: 'There are wild animals, we hear them.'

And by his mother's stare, Keztral knew they would not come. The mention of Kasrkin had made the woman close her eyes, her lips moving in prayer.

There are wild animals. And to them, she was one of the wild animals. Armoured beasts that swept into their habclave with their rebreather-masked faces, demolishing buildings with artillery and carving passages through interior walls with meltaguns. Hells, an animal wearing her uniform might've bombed their hab.

Keztral thought of the mother and child as she unbuckled one side of the rebreather and stepped out of the cover of the van, raising one hand in welcome.

They sighted her immediately. They were already crouching in a loose formation against a stockhouse wall, guarding their left flank with a stack of wooden crates. One had a volley gun on a bipod, resting on boxes labelled *FODDER*.

'Here,' she hissed. She checked her right and left down the tracks, making sure a sniper or Archenemy patrol wasn't going to catch her dashing to the waiting rescuers. 'Keztral, Eighty-Ninth Combat-Pict Recon, tail number one-twenty-two.'

The sergeant beckoned her.

She jogged to the next van, looked left and right.

Saw the sergeant's inviting wave.

And stopped.

She was being stupid, she knew it. She'd spoken to Kraf on the vox, and they were right where they said they'd be. Kasrkin, as promised. Why was she hesitating? They didn't call out to her, so what? Probably keeping a low profile, speaking only by encrypted vox-bead. Kasrkin were never exactly friendly.

Unless...

He waved again, not with urgency but incredible patience. And it hit her. That's the way she'd beckoned to the mother and child. That slow, *come here* gesture. Coaxing them, baiting them.

There are wild animals.

Keztral's neck hairs prickled against the collar of her flight suit. Is that what she'd been reduced to on her long, solo trek across the war-spoil of her home world? Timid prey, cringing in a corner, fearing a world infested with uncaring bringers of violence regardless of what flag they flew or god they worshipped? No longer able to tell hero from heretic? A rodent foaming with terror as it ran between the feet of two great canines that bit and rent each other, knowing that either could crush her under a clawed foot?

No, she was no rodent. She was a Cadian.

She stepped out, following the beckoning gesture, her boots crunching in the gravel of the trackway. Swallowed the rising gorge in her throat as the panic came again.

Then the Kasrkin with the volley gun turned his helm to look at her, to see what was taking so long.

She froze when she saw his left eye.

There was nothing remarkable about it, apart from the fact she could see it. Because there was a crater blasted through the face-plate of the helm, with its ragged plate-and-fibre interior edges stained rusty with gore.

338

A dead man's helmet. And once she noticed it, she registered other things. Like how the sergeant's shoulder markings were First Squad, Eighth Company, while the volley gunner was marked as Seventh Squad, Fourth Company. How their armour didn't quite fit. How the eye-lenses were dark, without the sheen of live optics.

The sergeant raised his laspistol, but he was hesitant and too slow.

Keztral didn't raise her pistol, she dropped her body into a crouch behind the lowered sights and tugged it up onto the fire-team. Kicked out three shots to keep their heads down and bolted back the way she'd come, blind-firing behind her. She broke right to put a van between her and the imposters as the first lines of white-clear hellgun beams sizzled past.

As she ran, she let out a hysterical bark of laughter as her brain processed what it had just witnessed. How a red dart from her laspistol's hotshot pack had stabbed straight into the join between the volley gunner's breastplate and helmet, pitching him back in an arc of crimson.

She'd just fired her first shots in anger, and killed her first enemy.

Hanna Keztral, kite-war champion of Salgorah slum, was a Throne-damned frekking Cadian soldier. True she was running from the enemy, and had only intended to cover her retreat, but she was fighting, she had a weapon.

A defensive weapon, the Valkyrie pilot sneered from the depths of her memory.

And that only made her laugh harder, so hard she feared it might choke her breathing and slow her down.

She glanced back, seeing the false Kasrkin rounding the van. There were four of them left. But they were slow and unused to the heavy carapace, the ill-fitted armour sliding around on their frames and making them clumsy. They ripped the helmets off to clear their vision.

Two fired on the run, their hellgun beams sparkling past her.

Real Kasrkin would've hit her three times by now.

She was still laughing about that when the shot slammed into her lower back, pitching her face first into the gravel of the tracks, one elbow going numb as it barked against the edge of the nearest freight van. She smelled burning uniform cloth. Hot liquid spilled down her thighs.

Spinal shot. Probably paralysed.

Keztral decided not to go down like prey. She sent orders to her legs, not knowing if they'd be followed, and rolled under the belly of the van, hearing shots spang off the wheels. She wormed her way through, her bulky backpack jostling and scraping against the rusted undercarriage. She made it to the other side and stripped the heavy pack off, noting with almost idle detachment the smoking hole bored in her vox-unit. No spinal shot at all. The powercell had burst, showering her legs with battery acid.

No calling for help now – if help was ever coming.

She ripped the pict-spool tube free of the pack and levered herself up into the open van. Squirmed back into the shadows in the rear corner. Her hotshot cell was out, but she had a spare in her webbing, plus an igniter.

It would take them a moment to find her.

She could hold them off with the pistol, and with the other hand, burn the negatives.

What it showed might be vital to the war effort, but her orders were clear: under no circumstances let the enemy know Cadia's reconnaissance capabilities.

Keztral set the igniter and negative tube on the rough board flooring. Fumbled the las-cell out of her webbing and tried, with shaking hands, to slot it into the pistol.

With a thump of boots on floorboards, the sergeant was in the freight van door. He'd not bothered to pull himself up, simply leaped.

Keztral snapped the cell into the laspistol, clicked the charge stud and pulled the trigger.

'For the Emperor!' she shouted.

Yet the laspistol said nothing. It displayed not a shot-counter rune, but the letters *ERR*.

Error.

A frekking dead cell. Of all the frekking times.

She hit the charge stud and tried again. Nothing.

The sergeant stripped off his helmet, letting it fall with a heavy *thump* on the floorboards. He smiled, but not by choice. Silver piercing rings pinned his mouth corners up below his eyes, exposing upper teeth serrated like a saw.

He keyed his looted chainsword to rev once, twice. On the third, he lunged and ripped it through the corner of a crate, filling the air with wood shavings and the smell of the timber yard.

Keztral scrambled backwards, negative-tube in her hand.

Outside, she could hear the other two with their strange bark-growl language. And more coming, howling.

'You know what we are?' said the sergeant. He breathed with a slurping sound, saliva flowing freely down his chin.

'Animals,' she said.

'Liberators,' the sergeant retorted. 'Here to free you from your officers, commissars, cardinals and False Emperor.'

She pointed the pistol and fired, knowing it would do no good.

His swipe hooked the gun in the body, teeth biting into the casing and throwing it into the ceiling, wrenching it out of her grip and dislocating her left index finger on the trigger-guard.

'Cadia stands.' Keztral raised the negative tube to defend herself. If she couldn't destroy it, maybe he would do it for her. 'Frekking swing, I'm tired of looking at you.'

And he did. He raised the chainsword so high it sparked off an iron band in the van's roof before he brought it down, and

Keztral – ears full of its howling – raised the precious pict-spools to take the hit.

The blow came with an explosion of splinters, blood and screams. Light blinded Keztral, and for a bare instant she thought she was meeting the Emperor.

But it wasn't the light of the Golden Throne, it was the harsh grey sun of Cadia pouring in from the fractured hole where something big had crashed in one side of the freight van and out the other, dragging the sergeant with it.

His fallen chainsword lay running on the decking, rattling back and forth.

Keztral dived for it, worrying if she didn't deactivate it, it would cut her. Then she heard the screaming outside, and couldn't help but look.

Wild animals, she thought.

The sergeant flopped, open-mouthed and neck broken, in the claws of a beast. Ten feet tall it was, and muscled. Hair sprouted from clawed feet and furred a bestial face.

His squad mates backpedalled, raising their hellguns on the creature and blasting shots that died in embers on the feral monster's armour or set spot fires on its hairy arms.

Corded muscles thick as Keztral's waist bunched and the monster threw the sergeant across the railyard, where he landed with a crunch of bone against the side of an engine.

The beast pounced on the closest false Kasrkin and sank conical fangs into his shoulder, then threw its head back and ripped the whole arm free, stretching the tendons.

When it turned on the last heretic, she saw the power pack of its armour, marked with red-and-black sawtooth designs and rattling with bone charms. Keztral thanked the Throne the beast's body blocked the carnage as it leapt onto the final armoured man, worried him against the ground, then lifted him in the air and slammed him with a crunch like a boot breaking an iced-over puddle.

Then it turned on *her.* Sniffing. Blowing through its blood-slick snout. For an instant she looked into the thing's yellow eyes, and had no doubt that the taint of the warp clung to it like the musk of blood and animal saliva it exuded.

Dumbly, she looked down at the chainsword, still running in her hand.

'I...' She tried to drop it, but her petrified hand wouldn't respond.

The animal came fast, low, lips peeling back from its gore-slicked teeth as it charged for–

The bolt-shell cracked through the air, and at once the beast stood as fully committed to stillness as it had been to action. It looked over its shoulder, growled and snuffled.

Then it was gone, loping on all fours into the twisted ruin of the railyard.

Keztral keyed off the chainsword and fell to her knees. Utterly exhausted.

She could barely react when the power-armoured warrior crossed into her vision, his bolter trained on the retreating monster.

When the bolter swung in her direction, bone charms and fur tails rattling on the warrior's armour, her hands were already raised.

'Friend,' she croaked.

'Name yourself,' barked the Astartes through his closed helm. She could barely understand his accent, all yawing vowels and clipped consonants. 'Identify.'

'Captain Hanna Keztral, Eighty-Ninth Combat-Pict Recon, tail number one-twenty-two.' She weakly raised the tube. 'I have intelligence.'

'What happened here?' he shouted. His plated finger rested on the trigger.

Keztral knew, somehow, that it was not an idle challenge. A

lifetime of living underneath the boots of soldiers and officers had taught her well when she should see and when she should not.

'A monster,' she said. 'A Traitor Space Marine went berserk. Turned on its own.'

'That is what you saw?'

'Yes.'

The angel of the Imperium removed his finger from the trigger and lowered his bolter. 'Then you are very fortunate I arrived, Hanna Keztral. I am Brother Stakkl of the Ironwolves, we have been monitoring your distress calls.'

She could only nod.

She would never in her life, not to her commander, her confessor or even herself, admit what she had seen.

That the colour and markings of the angel's armour were the same as the beast's.

SEVEN

'This is a bright day, my charges,' Deacon Vowtt intoned. 'A glorious day. Smell the fyceline and battle-smoke in the cloister. Feel the sting of rubble beneath your feet! This is the day of atonement, my flock. The sacred Order of Our Martyred Lady calls you to wash your sins clean with Archenemy blood.'

Genevieve was grateful for the cherubs buzzing overhead with their censers. The spicy scent of incense covered the man's stink.

'Can they move faster? Haste is paramount.'

Deacon Vowtt dipped his silver-headed aspergillum in the reservoir then lashed it back and forth in the air, splattering his flock with the unguent. 'Patience, Sister, patience. His vengeance cometh, and soon, but the damned cannot make haste. Better to position them before unleashing their zeal. Then they will move fast enough.'

He smiled at Genevieve with blackened teeth. His robes, once white, had gone yellow through decades of sweat stains. A pair of goggles hid his eyes – Vowtt lived in the dark, and even the weak light of wartime Cadia was too much for him.

Yet Vowtt was nothing next to his charges.

They came slowly, clad in rags and burial shrouds, moving as well as they could. A few – the fresher ones, with cords and stimm-injectors emerging from bruised surgical lesions or pink scar tissue – walked mostly upright. The older damned crawled and twist-hopped along, their skins necrotic from the damp crypts. Infected bulges marked them where muscles had swollen under wine-coloured skin, patches of dark mould colonising their flesh. Lolling mouths ran with salivary foam. One spasmed, jaw opening and closing in a *clack-clack-clack* until the teeth began to tumble out of receded gums.

'Feel the hot draughts, my flock. Sense the movement of the air! It is the winds of war, the breath of a city afire!'

Genevieve realised that he described how things *felt* because his flock wore hoods. Dead augmetic lenses, deactivated and dark as the deacon's own goggles, pierced the obscuring cloth. All had helmets or skullcaps bolted down over their lobotomised brains – the pacifier helm that kept them docile until the proper time.

Genevieve told herself that they deserved their fate. That they were heretics, traitors and deserters. The absolute worst Cadia had to offer.

Their arms ended in implant sockets, and from them hung electroflail spools or circular saws on cables. The sound of their dragging feet filled the cloister, second only to the heavy tread and piston-hiss of the Penitent Engines behind them.

Where the arco-flagellants were twisted perversions of flesh and machine, the heretics bound to the penitent devices were worse. The condemned hung slack in their nest of cables at the heart of the walking torture devices, fully exposed to enemy fire. Those in front had pendulum arms mounted with spinning saws or spiked flails, heavy flamers hardwired behind the brutal melee weapons. Further back were the Mortifier-pattern walkers, their unwilling pilots sealed in sarcophagi that at least had targeting arrays to help fire the heavy bolters.

Six hundred arco-flagellants and nigh fifty Penitent Engines.

They smelled of shame and death. A charnel reek undercut with embalming fluid.

One arco-flagellant caught her eye due to its straight-backed posture. It was a woman, with strong limbs and noble bearing, walking with a regality that belied her situation. A shroud covered her entire body, plastered to her due to the whipping gale raised by the firestorm ravaging the outer districts of the shrine.

When the noble flagellant stepped again, the shroud blew off one bare leg, and Genevieve saw the socket hook-ups for a suit of power armour, and a running stripe of fleur-de-lis tattoos.

She looked away, using the pretence to ask: 'How do I do this?'

Vowtt licked his lips and accepted a bronze casket from his servitor train. He kissed the lock before turning it, and opened the lid to reveal an instrument panel of coloured lights, two keyholes, and a perforated knob Genevieve realised was a vox microphone.

'Turn the keys and speak the word, and they will activate,' he said reverently. 'Their mind-impulse units will send them wild, straight towards the nearest enemy. Perhaps even confuse them into attacking one another. But don this medallion...' He reached into the casket and indicated a disc marked with the seal of the Adeptus Ministorum. 'And it will serve as a beacon. Where you go, they will follow.'

Genevieve lifted the medallion and put it around her neck. Then took the set of two keys from her belt and slotted them into the casket inputs.

'It is a momentous occasion,' Vowtt intoned. 'Only twice has the Hermitage flock been deployed on Cadia, once–'

'Let's get this over with,' Genevieve said, and turned both keys.

She flinched back as an electric shock stung her fingers, sparks leaping between the keys and her gloved hands. A hum filled the air. Electro-flails crackled and squealed like severed power lines, rigid throats moaned. A blue aurora briefly rippled above the mass of hoods.

Deacon Vowtt laughed, raising his arms at the manifestation, the dancing corposant flickering on his sallow features.

'Say the word!' he cried. 'Grant them peace in violence!'

Genevieve turned to her Seraphim – what was left of them. Only eighteen now, and none would be left after this charge. 'Get ready to fly, you know your patterns. Superior Navarette?'

'Yes, canoness.'

'Hold the banner high.' She opened her vox-link to the guard-house. 'Open the gates.'

Then, as she saw the portcullis grinding open, she turned back to the casket, pressed the INITIATE button and said:

'*Eviscerare!*'

Six hundred and fifty pairs of augmetic lenses snapped to crimson. And a noise like the pits of hell filled the Hermitage of the Pit.

'How is it not enough?' Urkanthos roared at the Warpsmith. 'How are we not through? We have given the daemon engines skulls, fuelled them, slaughtered our own cultists on their altars, and yet they move slowly!'

Before them, the two towering war engines ground towards the Shrine of St Morrican, the massive drums of fuel on their rear chassis bubbling with daemonic glee as the eighth-rank bloodletters inside banged another salvo into the walls of the shrine.

They had broken the outer walls this morning, with the two daemon engines crushing through the cloisters and minor chapels behind the defences. They blasted through the sacred city as they went, creating their own ramps of rockcrete debris as they advanced slowly on the inner wall of the shrine.

'They have made tremendous progress,' said Lotharn the Warpsmith, his mechadendrites snapping at each other in irritation. 'We will be in the shrine by tonight.'

'*Progress,*' Urkanthos growled, and the daemon voice slipped out, causing the Warpsmith to snap his head around. 'I don't want progress, I want to turn this shrine into an abattoir. They hide. They fire from concealment. Spring ambushes then demolish buildings to stymie us. They tease us.'

'The Lords of Skulls are slaughtering...'

'Not enough! Not–'

'Urkanthos.'

Urkanthos the Half-Prince quieted immediately, and turned.

A pillar of purple flame stood flickering behind him, a warp manifestation that triggered his Butcher's Nails to bite deep just by looking at it – though now, they only bit on the side of his skull that was still flesh.

'Warmaster,' Urkanthos bowed.

Abaddon stood in the flickering tongue of fire, image wavering as it rolled. *'Urkanthos, you asked me for Cadia. For Kraf. Yet you spend your forces against this mere shrine? The Black Legion is through the western gate. Possessed have covered the walls of the Jorus Redoubt in blood. Krom Gat and his Iron Warriors are near broken fighting against the Wolves, without support from you. Even your own Hounds throw themselves against the bastard spawn of the Lion, and you sit here grinding your daemon armies against a target of no significance.'*

'My god says that we must destroy the shrine if Kraf is to be taken.'

Abaddon was quiet. And even through the gulfs of space and the eddies of the warp, Urkanthos could feel the Warmaster's eyes. *'Khorne says that, or you say that? I am not sure if you should listen to either.'*

'We will have what we need by tonight.'

'Urkanthos,' whispered Artesia.

Abaddon flickered. *'I promised you command at Kraf, Urkanthos. Ensure you are there to take it.'*

'I will be, Warmaster. Rest assured that the honour of the–'

'Master!' Artesia warned.

There was screaming from the flank. The sound of saws and mad wailing. A roar of engines.

Across the plain, streaming out of the squat and quiet fortress, came a river of abomination. Tech-bastardised prisoners reworked into idiot berserks. Slashing the turf ahead of their running bodies with flails and saws, mangling themselves and each other, lost in agonised slaughter.

Lumbering torture racks fitted with spinning blades and gouting flamers, their pilots twisting in horror at their drug-spurred frenzy of ever-present violence.

A river that pounded with the hot coursing of unspilled blood. A horde of berserk violence even Khorne could not have imagined.

'Perhaps sooner,' Urkanthos purred. *'I must see to my work.'*

Urkanthos ran nearly half a mile – knuckles thumping the turf, leaping onto fallen hunks of wall, gliding short distances on his proto-wings – to the bounty of combat. Bashed through his own warriors to meet the charge.

'Stop them. Trap them. Murder them.'

A dart formation of Sororitas passed on his left, jump packs not carrying them in their usual arcs but burning in a straight flight.

Let them. Let them try the daemon engines. The slaughter was here.

The mad brain-dead fanatics of the False Emperor – corpse-animals serving a corpse-god – had plunged deep into the ranks of the blood-letters, driving a wedge in the force. Packs of his Hounds of Abaddon, the complement under his direct command, roved in tight units bringing down the lumbering punishment engines. Keening saws threw spirals of gore into the air. Electro-tentacles split bodies open to fling vitae towards the heavens. Daemons roamed in packs to hobble and murder the awful, beautiful things.

Even as he approached, he saw one of the detestable machines stumble and fall as a Berzerker champion cut its piston-tendons with a lightning claw, his packmates falling upon it to carve the steel arms from their housing and rip the unwilling pilot from her cradle.

He smelled the blood, the exultant vibration of slaughter, the way his own pounding hearts circulated his warp-changed vitae through his system, might soaring.

He felt the red eye of his god drift towards the field of honourable atrocity.

'*Now!*' whispered Artesia as her winged form flitted along the churning ranks of men and daemons beneath him. '*Call him now!*'

'*Khorne!*' he roared. '*Look here, you ungrateful god. Lord of the Skull Throne and God of Rage. See the gifts I give you!*'

He wrapped his wings and sped forward with the momentum of a stone lobbed by an ancient war machine. Crashed into a Penitent Engine with such force the condemned pilot's skeleton shattered and skin burst.

Artesia flitted and danced as though cast by firelight, slitting and gorging, singing. Calling more of her Neverborn kin to the field.

'*Khorne!*' Urkanthos swept his chainaxe through the air, cleaving four tech-horrors at chest level, marvelling that even bisected, the arms still flailed in the spasm of attack. '*King of Brass. Called Kharneth in the dark tongue. See the red offerings I bring you!*'

Promethium flames washed him, and Urkanthos reached out with his daemon claw and crumpled the attacking engine's flamer, letting the whirling saw snap and throw its blades as it met his carapace exoskeleton. Then he wrenched the mechanical limb free and smashed it into the pilot like a flail. Spun the dead appendage around, crushing electro-fanatics and daemons alike until he winged it sidearm at one of the Rhino transports that were now driving at top speed through the combat, ploughing through friend and foe alike.

'*Khoooorne!*' he howled at the sky. Burying his axe, he snatched up a lashing flagellant with one hand and a Khornate Berzerker with another, holding both towards the roiling crimson thunder-clouds gathering overhead. '*Bless me and I will give you Cadia! Bless me, and I will give you the Warmaster! I swear this to you on the only substance that matters.'*

He crushed both warriors, feeling the jewelled beads of their essence patter and spurt down upon him. Baptising him in salty heartblood. Vitae that had flowed in the family lines of both warriors, passed from time before time, their lines ending now in the grip of Urkanthos who was called the Half-Prince.

Half-Prince no longer.

Urkanthos' hearts pumped in glory and pride, then in exultation, and for a bare instant in panic as they hammered so hard he thought they might burst.

Then they did. His organs ruptured, spurting blood into the clean emptiness of his chest cavity, flooding the space between his organs.

'What?' he said, confused at the terminal pain.

'A prince of daemons does not need hearts,' she hissed, her dribbling mouth now cascading red.

But his hearts did not stop. Incredibly, impossibly, the disconnected and damaged organs continued to beat, coursing more vitae into his abdomen from a seemingly limitless dimension of red.

Urkanthos bellowed as his chest wall began to swell. Ribs cracked, reknit, cracked, reknit. Building themselves longer and thicker with each agonising transformation.

Beneath his feet, the ground split in chasms wide as his elongating arms, and when he looked down he realised the sides of them were not earth but meat, raw muscle that slid and bunched and bled with the seismic shock of his ascension.

'No! *Yes!* NO. NO. *Yes, Khorne, my master.* Please, no.'

Two voices within him, as his human soul tore in two. Immortal tearing away from the mortal, a god ripping free of its physical shell. He felt – actually felt – a small and neglected human part of him die in the creation of his new self. It slid out of him as though it were a placental afterbirth that had nourished the daemon in its foetal state, and was no longer needed. Pity he would not miss. His body a mere vessel.

But free will. It was the departure of free will that made his eyes go wide.

Especially as Artesia Gore-mouth leapt onto his back, burning her shadow-self onto his skin, crimson mouth laughing in his ear as she amalgamated into a part of him.

'Khorne!' she yelled. '*Khorne, I have brought this one to you! See my sacrifice, Crimson Emperor!*'

Urkanthos howled with the power, and the glory, and the horror. But most of all with the overpowering thirst for blood.

Through the smoke of the battlefield, over the heads of the enemy. Speeding above a lapping wave of red daemons they went. Leaving the atrocious struggle of damned and daemon behind them, hearing nothing but the keening of buzzsaws and hammer of heavy bolters. Then a percussive crunch as the armoured column slammed into the breach in the lines, Immolators laying a path of fire.

Genevieve had used Immolators before. Seen how they worked. Knew that as they drove through the enemy press at top speed, they would plough through the burning corpses, accumulating flame-crisped enemy dead on their glacis plates as if ploughing through a bank of snow.

They would make it, if she and her Seraphim did their part.

Genevieve held her blade point first as she flew, the coils of her plasma pistol thrumming in her left hand. 'To the closest one, with the rotary cannon. Keep it occupied until the Retributors punch through! For the Emperor and the honour of Saint Katherine! For sacrifice and sacred blood. For the blessed Saint Morrican and his shrine!'

A winged red thing dropped down upon them, black claws extended, but Superior Navarette raised her inferno pistol and vaporised it with a single shot, the mirage-waver of the beam exploding the daemon in a cloud of drifting cinders.

They had scrounged all the inferno and plasma pistols they could. Changing out their bolters for weapons with greater armour penetration. Even Genevieve had acquiesced, and had one of the relic melta-weapons holstered at her hip.

'*It's turning, canoness,*' warned Sister Arvum. Her intra-helm targeting and ballistic cogitator systems were the oldest and best-maintained of the flight.

Genevieve could see the heretic war engine pivoting. Crested head snapping around at an unnatural angle, body following slightly behind.

'*Rotary cannon cycling,*' Arvum said, an edge in her voice. '*Estimate incoming fire in four, three, tw–*'

'Break!' Genevieve ordered.

She twisted over in the wind, spiralling upward and to the left, corkscrewing through the sky in an evasive pattern. Ripping through the airstream as it hissed past her helm and snapped her robes. In the corner of her eye, she could see the others doing the same in the helm's formation grid, scattering like sparks of a firework.

Tracer fire rattled through the sky beneath them in a luminous chain, wavering through the air like a whip. Genevieve levelled out, teeth clenched so hard she thought they might crack, and only then looked at her squad indicators.

No casualties, praise the saints.

Sister Navarette came up on her right, keeping a safe standoff distance to avoid mid-air collision. Her banner was furled, electromagnetic wires stitched into the edges keeping it wrapped tight around the pole to aid aerodynamics.

'*Incoming!*' Navarette voxed, jinking right as more tracers slapped by.

'Hit!' a voice blurted in the helm-vox. 'Altitude loss. Descending. Overloading plasma pistol and initiating fuel purge. Grenades active. I will meet you at the Golden Throne, Sis–'

Genevieve felt the rocking sound wave of the detonation rather than heard it. Cast her eyes backwards to see the twisting cloud of blue-white fire blooming among the daemon tide an instant before it slipped from her view.

'Five seconds to target,' Arvum reported.

Genevieve's martyrdom indicator showed three dead.

Fifteen Seraphim left.

'Four seconds.'

The armoured column was lagging. Cross-chatter filled her command channel with exclamations about tracks and vehicles bogging down in daemon flesh.

'Three seconds.'

A ballistic warning chimed in Genevieve's helmet and she rolled over and cut her pack thrust, catching a glimpse of muzzle flash sparkling from the rotary cannon. She plunged at the shell-pocked earth, the crack-zip of passing rounds only dulled by the wind roaring around her helm. She cancelled a collision alarm as she whipped by Sister Galtana. Screams furred the vox-channel into ragged distortion.

She pirouetted, rolling over in the buffeting push-pull of terminal velocity, and fired her jump pack again. Two more martyrdom indicators in her helm.

Thirteen Seraphim left. Heretic abomination rising large in the tunnel vision of her helm. It had moved around on its tracks, repositioned. Flanged death mask tracking them.

An enormous cannon on its midsection rotated to face her. The bore of it was huge. Big enough for Genevieve to fly right inside.

'Two sec– Aaaaaaaggggghhhhh!'

Streaming gouts of red fountained from the belly gun, spraying through the air like the open gate of a dam. She'd fallen so far in her dive that the main body of it passed above her. She adjusted her trim and slipped out sideways to the left in a rising half-pipe arc, but a thick glop the size of a credit coin splatted across the back of her right vambrace.

Pain lit her wrist as if it had been branded with a hot iron. And were it not for her power-armoured gauntlet, she might have dropped her blessed blade. She flew on, cuffing the spatter away on the flapping left sleeve of her robe, partially through pain, and partially through the sense of defilement.

Blood, she thought. *It's boiling, warp-tainted blood.*

Her squad martyrdom indicator was more red than blue. How many left? Eight? Nine?

She had no time to count.

'Fight like the God-Emperor watches, Sisters!' she said, firing her engines to maximum and overcharging her plasma pistol. 'For He surely does!'

The engine's cleaver, large as a groundcar, rippled with bound warp corruption as though pulled from a field of cooling lava. Veins of fire pulsed through the charred, blackened surface.

She'd expected it to be clumsy, but when it moved, it moved *fast.*

The plan had depended on it being slow. That was their play. Approach on a vector where one engine screened them from the other's fire. Get inside its long-range weapons, where the big blade would be clumsy. Like a man trying to hit a bite-gnat with a sword.

Get behind it to damage the thing, and make it turn away from the armoured column.

But the titanic cleaver sliced through their gathered formation not once but twice as they flew past its hull, carving diagonally then across like a master duellist.

She felt impact as the weapon passed, and thought the blade had struck her. But it had merely been one of Sister Galtana's severed legs, spinning away like shrapnel.

Genevieve backed air and flipped, coming at the engine feet first. Her furnace-hot plasma pistol automatically fired to avoid melt-down, the blue-white tunnel of solar energy lancing into the crystal fuel tanks at the rear of the death-idol's chassis.

'Find cables and tanks. It runs on blood, so bleed the filthy warpson!'

Her five remaining Seraphim – Golden Throne, only five now – were already at work. Slashing cables that spurted and whipped through the air like live things. Firing on support chains so one of the huge crystal blood tanks, three times Genevieve's height, rocked free in its housing.

Maddened blood-daemons clambered onto their tracked temple-engine, leaping and snapping jaws. Throwing swords. One mass, climbing each other for height like swarming insects, seized Sister Devona by the ankle and dragged her down into their gnashing, clawing pack. They tore at each other as much as her, no unity in their hunger for blood.

Before she disappeared beneath, she fired both inferno pistols into the side of the weakened blood tank, rupturing the side in a burst of crystal – drowning the whole daemon mass in a rush of scalding gore.

'*Retributors disembarking!*' reported Navarette. She darted past on a diagonal. '*The monster isn't turning fast enough! It will see them.*'

'We'll do what we can,' said Genevieve, getting a toe-hold on an armour rune and using it to spring into a backward somersault, avoiding a swipe of the giant cleaver. She finished the manoeuvre with fists extended, a pistol in each, boring a hole in the engine's back armour with the inferno and unleashing a stream of plasma into the muscle beneath.

But she knew it was not enough. Even with the Retributors, it might not be enough. As soon as the squad fired their multi-meltas it would turn on them, and the tide of Neverborn would crash down on the infantry.

'Fuel warning,' said Sister Chalice. 'Four minutes at current usage. Less at full-burn.'

How foolish Eleanor had been. They could not take on a daemon engine of this size with jump infantry and heavy support squads. They needed their own war engine. A Knight. A Titan. A Baneblade tank.

A line of munitions screamed by her in a gale, like buckshot from a shotgun's muzzle. One caught Sister Buratina on the shoulder, exploding in a red wash of acid, gnawing her down to the ribcage and exposing a pitted skeleton from her breastbone up.

Another pattered off the Lord of Skulls, bouncing and rolling like a grenade.

But it was a skull.

It detonated, and the air shook with the daemon engine's fury.

Genevieve darted across the body of the hell-machine, raising her head to see what had...

The other daemon engine had sighted them. It was different, that one. Darker armour, like dried and clotted blood rather than fresh. More mutated, with the armour around its face breaking away like eggshell, exposing a round hooked mouth like a leech.

When they hit the rear of the first war engine, they had exposed themselves to the fire of a second.

A second war engine. Engines that were not machines, but daemons, subject to all the discord and jealousy of the Archenemy. In a flash, her unkind memory brought forth an image of the bloodletters tearing at each other as they fought over Sister Devona.

'Abandon attack!' she ordered. 'Break off!'

'Canoness?' Navarette answered.

'Charge the other engine. Sting it with anything you have. Draw its fire!'

'Understood, canoness!'

Four. Four Seraphim left. Not good for much but bait.

She would spend their lives to buy a war engine.

They opened throttles and sped at the mutated Lord of Skulls, pistols hissing and sizzling, Navarette singing the Hymn of Grateful Martyrdom.

'Oh see us, Glor'ous Emperor, Upon whose walls we die,

In glory thou willst shroud us, in golden caskets lie,

Bathed and washed in incense, and laid inside our tomb,

We know this day was fated, since e'er we left the womb.'

'Break!' Genevieve shouted.

Too late for Navarette. The skull took her in the breastplate, her last act being to trigger the banner's suspensor field, giving Sister Chalice time to dart around and snatch it out of the air.

But the arcing skull-grenades had largely passed by – detonating on the rear tanks of the abomination's fellow engine.

The Lord of Skulls bellowed like the whistle on a hell-bent rail engine. And when it backed tread and twisted its upper body housing to come about, the rotary cannon did so firing directly at the dark-blooded daemon engine.

High-calibre rounds tore into the engine's structure, blasting away one pauldron and clanging off the headcrest before the sucker-faced thing responded with another arcing rain of skulls.

'In position,' voxed Retributor Superior Laqiza. 'Opening fire for the Emperor, Katherine and Saint Morrican!'

Genevieve saw the melta-beams ignite as she powered clear. Two squads of Retributors were all that had made it through the slaughter. They stood in a clear space before the daemon engine, their low-slung weapons braced and hissing. Meltas running on continuous fire so heat made the sweat pour from them as they converged their dual beams to the same spot on the daemon engine.

'God-Emperor bless you, Superior Laqiza,' said Genevieve. 'I will see you at His side.'

'At His side!' she responded.

Then at the convergence of the melta-beams, a spot that hazed in wavering desert mirage as armour melted and ran liquid, a blue tongue of nuclear fire appeared.

'Reactor meltdown!' shouted Genevieve, turning over in the air and bolting for the shrine's inner wall. 'Get clear! Get clear!'

Behind her, the two bellowing daemon engines poured fire on one another, and to her left – out on the plain where daemon and damned had struggled – came a deeper and more threatening roar.

An enormous shape rose into the sky, beating the air with dark wings.

Larger than a Dreadnought, it was, and Genevieve was sure it had not been there when they had completed their overflight.

It came for them. Wings slashing through the air as if doing violence upon the very atmosphere of realspace.

'Fuel expended,' grunted Sister Chalice. *'Altitude loss imminent, canoness – I'm sorry, take the banner.'*

Genevieve reached down, adjusting her trim to get closer to the flapping triangular standard as Sister Chalice started to drop. Her gauntlet fingers brushed the pole, clamped on. 'Be easy, Sister, I've go–'

A white, brilliant flash filled the air around them, and Genevieve could suddenly taste the metal fillings in her molars.

And the rolling shockwave pitched her from the sky helpless as a fish jerked out of a clear lake.

'Oh Throne,' Eleanor whispered. 'Good God-Emperor on His Throne.'

'Yes, canoness,' Sacresant Superior Eugenia said, stepping to the balcony, her halberd tapping the flagstones. 'He is good.'

The initial explosion blasted outward in a hissing, rolling circle of dust and debris seventy feet high. Half-ruined cathedrals and scriptorums in the outer districts collapsed.

Behind her, the tower's glassaic rose window shattered, blowing pieces of coloured glass onto the singing choir, showering them in the ruined images of saints and miracles.

And the rolling mushroom cloud could barely form before the second war-effigy, already afire from within, detonated too.

It was not as violent – a munitions explosion rather than a reactor failure – but a few buildings ravaged by the first explosion collapsed in on themselves in a rolling crash of tumbling brickwork.

Including half the inner defensive wall.

'We cannot hold it.' Superior Eugenia looked down at the wall. 'We may have to consider repairs, or whether we will fortify the shrine itself.'

'Canoness Genevieve,' said Eleanor, into her vox-link. 'Genevieve, sister. Respond. I saw you fall short of the outer gate. State location.'

'A glorious martyrdom,' Eugenia said, raising her proud chin. The outer districts were burning, and it reflected on her dark skin. 'Have peace, canoness, our Sister is indeed at the Emperor's side.'

'She's not your sister, she's mine.'

'*–ster.*'

Words in the pain.

'*–enevie–*'

Genevieve's eyes came open like the rusty roll-shades on a hab-block. Slow and protesting, so resistant she could almost hear them squeal.

'*Sist–*'

She tried to lift her head, and found it nearly impossible. Only an inch from the ground before she had to let it crunch back into the rockcrete dust.

'*Genevi–*' Static. '*–are you?*'

For a moment she thought the immobility was from spinal trauma. At least, until she noticed the dim projections of her helm's display. Ghost targeting reticles flared and died, dancing back and forth before disappearing. Her left-side vision was nothing but diagnostic scroll, too dim to read, as if it had gone into hard reset.

On the right was the martyrdom indicator – now an entire block of red.

Not paralysed, but power *loss.* The worst fate of a power-armoured warrior. Vox out.

Her right arm was working, and she hit the emergency helmet seal and stripped the encumbering shell away.

Light hurt her dilated pupils. Flash-burned dust burned in her throat. She coughed, wishing her helm's hydration tube had been functional.

The left side of her power armour had not only seized up – the joints were jammed. Ablative ceramite layers, treated to resist heat, had taken the initial thermic discharge, but the servos had fused. It had entombed her leg in a half-bent position, her left arm frozen in the act of shielding her face.

She was trying to move, planting an elbow into the broken courtyard and dragging herself by inches, when the spawn of the warp came.

She saw a body red and slick, like muscle flayed of its skin. But there was nothing weak or sensitive about those ropy, unshielded slabs of anatomy. The taloned feet dug into the debris-strewn mosaic of the courtyard as it landed, fouling a saint's features and sending cracks through his beatific halo.

At first she thought the creature wore an iron helm, before she realised its face *was* the helm – the bone was the metal, and metal the bone. The thing's upper face was caged in a restraining brass muzzle shaped from the Blood God's rune.

What was once a trophy rack was now a row of spikes emerging from its powerful shoulders, the heads still spitted on them. And in a horrifying realisation, she recognised one of those heads.

Sister Heloise, one of her Seraphim, killed on the first day of the siege.

It held a broad, warp-forged axe flinted from obsidian, the kind of axe a primeval murderer might've used.

But it was the wings that were the most horrible. They were not flesh or metal, but shadow. Not wings at all, but a vast, inky cloud of night that took the *shape* of wings. Genevieve could see where it clung to the daemon's back in sticky masses, a symbiotic parasite grafted onto the warp creature.

A dozen dark eyelids opened along the wings, the eyes within regarding her with the sightless milky gaze of a boiled fish.

'I have killed your daemon engines,' Genevieve snarled. 'Broken your attack. Martyr me and I die in victory.'

She rolled over, pulled her plasma pistol from its holster, and pulled the trigger.

The coil failed with a spit of electrical discharge, heated to the point of burnout by the flash.

'I do not care about the Lords of Skulls.' The daemon took a step forward, the shadow-wings falling around it like a cloak. *'They were a means to an end. A tool for slaughter. Their daemonic essences have gone back to the true dimension, and the Warpsmiths will bind them again.'*

'You will not take the shrine.' Genevieve dropped the plasma pistol and unsheathed her blade, miraculously still at her hip. Held it point first towards the approaching horror.

'That is the problem with you corpse worshippers, you think that everything is about you. Think that we must want to spite you, to destroy your sacred relics and cathedrals. I spit on your shrine. It is meaningless to me. A pile of stones venerating a man you do not remember. But I do. I saw your Emperor with eyes of flesh, and I saw His feet of clay.'

Genevieve laughed. 'Then if this shrine is so Throne-damned insignificant, why have you beaten yourself against it?'

'I came here for blood, and you gave me blood. I should thank you.'
It took a step forward, and darted its pointed tail at her.

She parried, and the tail clanged off her blade like an iron spike. Planting one heel in the rubble, she pushed herself backwards. The daemon was coming at her, its corded barrel chest heaving as it huffed breath, the rage building.

'As for why I am here... We all serve a master, don't we? And while I care not if you banished my bound daemons – my god does. And Kharneth is not a being who takes vengeance lightly.'

It raised the axe, and Genevieve lashed out with her right arm, levering herself against the ground to roll.

The broad axehead slammed down beside her like a guillotine, scattering mosaic tiles. She leaned and slashed a wicked cut across the beast's red knuckles.

'Little bitch!' it roared, rocking its blade free from the ground. *'Before, this was only for my god. But now it is for me. I will slaughter you in sight of your Sisters. I will drag you by the hair to where they can see, to humiliate and ravage your corpse. Your skull will decorate my rack.'*

The slash came sideways in an arc, no way to dodge. It slit the air with a *hssssssssss...*

Then a sable blur slammed into the daemon from the side, and the hissing ended with the dull clang of a cathedral bell.

The daemon lord staggered from the force of the blow, feet sliding in the rubble, one hand clawing furrows in the tiles to arrest its skid.

Crouched protectively over Genevieve was a towering angel clad in black and gold, one leg thrown forward in a fighting stance. Her right arm was raised to eye level, elbow back, so the gleaming tip of her anointed blade – long as a tank barrel – tracked the daemon's every move. In her left was a tilting shield mounted on the outside of a heavy flamer, its surface so puckered with purity seals it resembled a bowl of roses.

Fresh lacquer gleamed on the warsuit's armoured shell.

The daemon Urkanthos raised his caged head, yellow eyes burning in the depths of the iron, and bellowed: *'She is mine!'*

'Wrong,' said Canoness Eleanor. 'She is *mine.'*

The daemon flew upon her like a mad feline. Spitting and mauling, shadow-wings stabbing out, axe swinging one moment, then jabbing with the spike at its summit.

The Paragon warsuit should have been no match for it.

But Eleanor was a cool, canny duellist, well drilled with the shield.

Instead of defending, she attacked with it. Bashed forward so the tilting shield met the daemon's caged skull with the clang of a forge.

He came on again and again, the combatants smashing into each other two or three times a second. Urkanthos screaming with the raw throat of a prehistoric lizard, Eleanor silent.

She kept the shield in a high guard, using the round notch in its outer edge to keep him within her sight as he circled, stepping to keep herself between the abomination and Genevieve. When they met with a crash and crumple of metal the sanctified blade darted like a scorpion's tail, and within moments a third of it was tacky with red.

With each contact, purity seals fell from her shield like tree blossoms in spring.

And with each strike, the aura around her brightened.

At first Genevieve thought it was her vision, blurred with pain – but no, her sister was *luminous.* Slippery as mercury and bright as a rank of votive candles.

He smashed into her once, twice, black claws scoring her warsuit, but she sidestepped the third so he overbalanced and charged past her. As he turned, jaw opening in a roar that exposed the furnace in his throat, Eleanor opened up with her shoulder-mounted storm bolters, chewing holes in his shadow-wings before snapping the shield outward and washing him with two quick bursts from the heavy flamer.

Then he was on her again, axe biting so deep in the shield that parts of it began to come away, the blade sinking into the flamer behind and raining promethium on the ground.

He dragged the shield down and thrust his tail at Eleanor's exposed head.

She snapped her head to one side, the tail's barb embedding itself four inches into the back of the pilot's cradle. A blast of storm bolter fire drove him clear, but the blow had opened a wound in her scalp that dyed her white bangs red and turned half her face into a mask of blood.

Eleanor's flamer was disabled; her shield cut ragged, with gashes clean through and a splintered bottom edge. It was the warsuit's arm now, more than the shield, that took the blows. Axe blows had shattered the storm bolter's magazine boxes. Still, she guarded Genevieve with her body.

'*You are dying, little one,*' growled Urkanthos. '*You cannot stand.*'

And instead of charging, he leapt into the air to rend with his clawed feet – tail wrapping around the shield-arm to trap it.

It was the moment Eleanor had waited for.

She wrenched down with her heavy flamer arm, yanking the daemon out of the air and slamming the meaty tail to earth. Then with blurring dexterity she reversed the long warblade and plunged it down like a dagger – spearing the thrashing tail and pinning it to the mosaic floor.

'Release!'

The warblade's power cable disengaged, and Eleanor turned and ran.

She scooped up Genevieve as she passed, the warsuit's empty right hand shovelling her off the ground and pinning her tightly to her chestplate with a violent slam, carrying her away with its clumping tread.

Eleanor saw the daemon clawing to snatch them, restrained by his pinned tail and roaring so low it rumbled Genevieve's organs.

'That was a relic sword!' Genevieve shouted. Her face, pinned to the breastplate, was eighteen inches from Eleanor's own. 'You're just going to leave it?'

'Relics can be lost defending assets of the shrine,' yelled Eleanor. 'And you are the shrine's greatest asset.'

'Never known you to run from a duel.'

'That was no duel,' answered Eleanor. 'It was an exorcism.'

Her eyes looked towards the shrine's final defensive wall, as if that explained the cryptic response. And it was only when Genevieve twisted around that she saw the burning trails reaching the top of their parabolic arc and turning to plunge down. And she knew that Eleanor's order to 'release' had not been for the cable, but for rank upon rank of Exorcists.

'Holy God-Emperor on His Golden damned Throne!' she said.

Eleanor didn't reproach her – she knew a prayer when she heard one.

Urkanthos seethed. He grasped the silver blade to withdraw it from his tail, but the thing was anathema to him and the mere touch of it seared his hand. When he had ascended, he thought it would be an end to pain, but the touch of this sword made the Butcher's Nails seem like the mere prick of a thorn.

'Urkanthos!' hissed Artesia, clinging to his shoulders.

'I know!'

'Urkanthos, look up.'

He did, and saw the arcing smoke trails, already starting to drop.

Necessity provided an answer, and inured him to the agony.

He picked up a fallen chunk of masonry and bashed it into the sword, knocking it from the stone and whipping his tail free.

Then he channelled his rage into motion as he leapt into the air, wings pumping as he ascended up and out of the courtyard, spiralling away as the first salvo of Exorcist missiles pounded down onto the arena of combat, bathing it in the fires of sanctified ordnance.

'*I swear I will slaughter those two,*' he snarled.

'*But first, Kasr Kraf.*'

'*Yes. First, Kasr Kraf.*'

EIGHT

They came for Salvar Ghent in the night.

The plan was to jump him while he was asleep, but even the snatch squad knew that was a foregone conclusion. No one within the citadel walls of Kasr Kraf was sleeping that night. Early on the morning of the seventh day, heretic guns had begun to hammer the fortress city. Shells the size of railcars smashed through the reinforced streets and detonated in underground bunkers. Artillery towers collapsed in on themselves, holed through by ordnance stamped with the names of dark gods. The toppling barrels of their guns blocked streets and crushed whole complexes of hab-bunkers. Special weapons teams made up of combat engineers, outfitted with meltas and Trojan armoured vehicles, worked round the clock to clear channels and allow the movement of troops and vehicles.

The result was not merely a din, but an endless roar of explosions and shivers. Buildings quaked, swayed and often collapsed. Citizens working in the manufactoria and Administratum scribes in the requisition and logistics halls had to stuff their ears with the foam plugs every Cadian carried beside their gas hood and mandatory helmet.

And no one was sleeping.

Perhaps it was because of that aural assault, the drumbeat of artillery, that they were able to get to him without a shot. At least, that was what he told himself as a solace.

He didn't like to think of all the resources he'd invested in the men guarding his quarters, whom the invaders had dispatched with snapped spines and knives jammed into windpipes.

A terrible, terrible waste.

They'd broken down the door with a shaped charge, come in crouched low, laser-targeters painting the dark walls of his dormitory chamber. Dragged three people out of his bed before realising that none of them were him.

No, he'd been at his night desk, reviewing the day's ledger.

'If you'd asked, I would have let you in,' he'd said, dropping the accounts in his automated incineration bin as the targeting beams snapped onto his chest.

He had not been surprised when they dragged him out from behind the desk, bound his hands, and put a bag on his head. Indeed, he'd always assumed it might end like this, and that sense only grew stronger as word filtered up his distribution chain that provosts were asking questions, and a few card-dealers had gone missing.

What *had* surprised him, though, was who had finally broken down the door.

Not the provosts, or even the Officio Prefectus – but fully outfitted Kasrkin, bearing the markings of the Cadian Eighth.

They asked him no questions, and that was fine, because he wouldn't have answered them. If questions came at all, they would come from someone whose lapels were weighed down with rank pins heavier than those of a captain. At least, that's what he assumed when he heard the Taurox doors slam closed, they fixed sound-mufflers over his ears, and the vehicle merely slowed for checkpoints, rather than stopped. Then it was out of the Taurox, with two soldiers hooking his elbows, and an hour of walking on polished floors.

You'll probably die today, Ghent thought to himself. *But what happens before then might prove interesting.*

Just how interesting was immediately clear when they removed the bag from his head.

It took his eyes a moment to adjust to the light. And another to register the surroundings. He was at a long table of burnished wood, set with the uncleared remains of a large meal. On the far wall stood a massive fireplace with two leather wing chairs facing it, and Militarum-issue chemical bricks glowing in the hearth.

And across from him, a man staring into his face with naked disdain.

'You know who I am?' the man said.

'I do,' responded Salvar Ghent. 'But do you know who I am?'

'Well enough to know you're a traitor,' said Jarran Kell.

He raised his right arm and set it on the table, the sledge-like immensity of his power fist resting on the wood with a heavy *clop.*

'You're a seditionist. An underminer. You've flooded this city with fake ration cards and requisition scrip that's depleted our stores and led to rioting. It's damaged our ability to defend this citadel when the enemy is at the gate.'

As if punctuating his point, a shell landed in the city outside, and a shiver ran through the room. Boneware dishes rattled on the tabletop.

'But what's worse is that you've entered the service of the enemy. Sold out your world and your people.'

'I don't follow you.'

'No,' sneered Kell. 'No, I suppose you *don't* follow me. You follow your dark master.'

'Unless my dark master is Imperial standard credits, I think you're mistaken.'

Kell flicked his eyes to the Kasrkin behind Ghent, and pain exploded in his head as a carapace-reinforced gauntlet backhanded him across the jaw.

'Next time you get smart with me it'll be this that hits you.'

One gun-barrel-thick finger of the power fist tapped the table.

'Now, tell me about the voxes.'

'What voxes?' he said, but when he felt the Kasrkin move behind him, he added in haste: 'I need specifics, I deal in a lot of voxes.'

'The big ones. The high-gain kind. Don't pretend, we've put it together. The men and women in the signal corps caught you because you got too damn confident. Thought you were too smart and could get away with turning off the encryption. We picked up a signal from a downed pilot, and while trying to fix her position, we heard you or one of yours giving her nonsense directions.'

'You're mad.' Ghent shook his head, laughing. The whole thing seemed incredibly comic to him. 'If you're going to shoot me, colour sergeant, do it for a crime I actually committed.'

'Once we'd identified the signal's vox-print once, we were able to intercept them and see the pattern. We couldn't break the cryptography, true, but we noted the pattern. A high-gain vox signal goes out on an unused channel, then the next ordnance lands closer to a military asset. Even before we stumbled across one of the artillery spotters nestled up in a disused watchtower, we were sure that was what was going on. The ration scrip in his pocket, though, that was sloppy. Paying your people in your own product. That's when we knew our investigation into the stolen printing plates and the anomalous signals were, in fact, one investigation.'

'Half the workers in Kraf are carrying bad scrip.'

'Tell us where your sleeper agents are located, or I'm going to hurt you, Salvar Ghent. And the prospect of that should scare you, since I'm not trained in torture. I have a tendency to go overboard.'

'I haven't done anything against the forces of Cad–'

'*Don't lie to me!*'

He brought down the power fist in a slam, cracking the table in a ragged split and upending several dishes. Splinters needled out of the polished surface. He hadn't even turned the power field on.

'Show him,' said Kell.

One Kasrkin grabbed his hair, forcing his head down to look at a data-slate.

It was a low-quality vid. Grainy and black-and-grey. Shot underground, and in low resolution to aid broadcast over the unencrypted image-bands favoured by provosts and the Administratum.

There was a man in Kasrkin carapace, standing up against the tile wall of an underground tunnel and squinting into the beam of a stablight. He wore no helm, exposing his freckled cheeks.

'*State your name and unit,*' said a voice off-screen. A voice much like Ghent's own.

'*Tolkerka, San,*' said the Kasrkin, shooting a vinegar look out of frame. It appeared this might've been the second take, and in the first he'd been less than cooperative. One cheek was broken, and an eye freshly black. '*Corporal, Thirty-Eighth Kasrkin.*'

Behind him, the hand tightened on his hair so tight his scalp creaked.

'*Should you have come down here, San Tolkerka?*'

'*Frekk you.*'

The laspistol shot hit San Tolkerka above his blackened eye, and he dropped leaving a dark splatter on the tile wall.

The frame panned right, to a woman in a provost's uniform.

'*State your name and unit.*'

The woman was Provost-Sergeant Layla Stind of Suppression Unit Six, Bastion South.

Then came Trooper Verezen Stowwer.

And Trooper Feyezal Annhema.

Each increasingly frightened. And each admitting that they shouldn't have come down there.

With each shot, the Kasrkin's hand got tighter and tighter, until Ghent thought his scalp might be tearing.

'We've seen enough,' sneered Kell.

'No.' Ghent smiled. 'I think they should see what I've done, don't you?'

The Kasrkin, not given a specific order, let the vid play.

And his armoured hand went so rigid, it nearly cracked the slate.

The film had cut, a static line showing the clumsy edit.

And now it showed the Space Marine.

It was a heretic. A traitor. Razor-honed spikes came off its armour. The face was a misshapen bag of bones, with teeth too big for its mouth and a single horn beginning to press its way through the right side of the forehead.

The heretic demigod pawed the floor, cursing in foul languages that made the screen fizz to static. It clawed at the man holding the picter, who stepped back in alarm.

But it was trapped. The entire tunnel had collapsed down upon it, pinning it to the floor.

A man stepped forward, his head out of frame. In his hands, he carried a meltagun on a sling. You could tell it was heavy and unfamiliar to him.

He turned towards the picter, and in a voice identical to the one before he said:

'To the traitors that use this broadcast band, I have a message. Don't. Frekking. Come down here.'

Then he turned and fired a shot into the heretic's head, melting its features and lighting the horn like a candle. When the creature still moved, he fired again, holding the beam on target until the thing liquefied.

The hand on his scalp loosened.

'You know of any traitors that kill Chaos Space Marines?' Ghent smiled again.

'I don't care how many heretics you've executed. You killed Cadians to achieve your ends.'

'Killed Cadians to achieve... Bit of the lasgun calling the helmet green, isn't it, Kell? How many Cadians have you and your boss killed? Hell of a lot more than four.'

'You call me Colour Sergeant Kell, filth.'

'No, it's a made-up term.'

Kell blinked, insubordination so unfamiliar to him that it temporarily stunned the man. 'Made up? I earned these stripes by–'

'Someone *gave you* those stripes because they thought you were useful. Basic leadership trick, really. You have ten followers and pay them all the same, but you have one that's marginally more competent than the others and might cause trouble, so you tell him he's a captain, or colour sergeant, or Grand High Frekk-Head or whatever, and say the others have to listen to him. Maybe you give him a shiny badge or nice pistol. Costs you nothing, and that man's now indebted to you. Even better, the other nine start thinking that if they play their cards right, when he dies *they* can be Grand High Frekk-Head. I didn't invent this, it's just how it works.'

Kell shook his head, grave. 'Who taught you such blasphemy?'

'The same as taught you, I just learned a different lesson. And what I learned was that I shouldn't throw my life away in return for a six-by-two plot some cadets lay a wreath on once a year.'

The power fist leapt off the desk, closing over Ghent's throat. Not enough to choke off his air, but hard enough to hurt. It felt like being pressed to death with cinderblocks.

'You're sick,' Kell said, his face inches from Ghent. The violet eyes were furious and exhausted, the teeth brown from ill-care. A warning crackle of lightning played over the back of the massive weapon.

Ghent fixed his eyes. Refused to flinch. His whole life he'd dealt with soldier boys who tried to intimidate him, and he knew that if he was here, it was for a reason.

'I'm done with you,' said Ghent. 'I want to speak to your boss.'

'He's at the front. The Lord Castellan doesn't speak to nothings like—'

'He's in that chair, by the fireplace.' Ghent motioned with his eyes. 'I smelled his cigars when I came in. Besides – I don't think you rate a table spread like this.'

The power fist tightened, cutting his air. 'Say that again, you piece of shit. Just try to...'

A shape, blurry, sat forward out of the chair. 'Kell.'

The power fist relaxed. Released him.

Lord Castellan Ursarkar Creed stood and sparked an igniter, relighting his cigar. 'All right, Mister Ghent, you wanted to talk? Let's talk.'

'You know Kell is right,' said Creed. 'I should line you up and shoot you just like you did those men.'

'But you won't.'

Creed sat at the head of the table, where Kell had been. The colour sergeant refilled the Lord Castellan's glass, while Ghent studied the lines of veins on the broad nose, and the puckered scar that ran from the stubbly hair to the opposite eyebrow.

The eyes, fractured violet, studied him back.

'Why won't I?'

'Because you need something from my network. Maybe you saw that video, and realised why you don't have an underground problem any more, even after pulling the deep patrols. You set this up like an interrogation to spook me into complying, but it's really a negotiation, isn't it?'

Creed puffed his cigar. 'Undo his cuffs. Pour him a drink.'

The Kasrkin undid his restraints, set a glass of amasec before him.

'You like the cigar?' asked Ghent, rubbing his wrists. 'It's one of mine.'

'I doubt that. This is from a very reputable shop behind the Varkor High Gate, by the Armoured Tactics College.'

'Yes, they probably sold them to you for two hundred credits per dozen, and said it was at-cost – but I guarantee they bought them for ninety.'

Creed grunted, non-committal. 'And you'd know how?'

'Who do you think supplies your very reputable shop? High command doesn't allocate much freight space for pleasure goods – they're too busy importing the things Cadians need to live, not what makes them want to live. Don't you think?'

'What I think, is that you are testament to a failure in the Cadian System,' said Creed, ashing his battered cigar.

'Because I've been allowed to exist, you mean?'

'No, because if Cadia can't find a use for a man with your abilities, that speaks pretty ill of our eye for talent. Hells, I've half a mind to make you supreme commissar.'

'Never wanted to wear a uniform. I don't like working with people.'

'Neither do I, thankfully Kell's quite good at it.'

'I have a man like that – Petzen. Provided he's still alive.'

Creed turned his head, indicating Kell should answer.

'Detained,' Kell rumbled. He still looked as though he might change his mind and beat Ghent's brains out against the table. But he wouldn't.

'Can you satisfy a curiosity of mine?' asked Ghent.

'Depends.'

'You don't write the speeches, do you?'

Creed barked a laugh. 'No. Frekk no. Kell does those. Fine job at it, too. Like I said, he's good with people.'

'He doesn't like me much.'

'Well.' Creed waved a hand through the smoke. 'He's an idealist, you know. Which is a damn good thing to have around, but I prefer a bit of flexibility.'

'And judging by the colour sergeant's expression, what you're asking me for doesn't square with his... rigidity. So what is it?'

'Two things. The first is supply. We're burning out las-cells at an incredible rate. Wearing through spare parts. My understanding is you can get those things – that you're the one who collects what falls through the hole in the Munitorum's pocket.'

'At what price?'

'No price.' Creed paused, as if waiting for him to understand. 'For free. A contribution to the war effort. Turn it all over, everything.'

'And if I do?'

'Well I won't leave you in a soundproof room with Kell, for one thing. But otherwise I'd ask yourself exactly what you have to gain holding out. Listen to that artillery, Mister Ghent. Do you think the enemy will strike a deal with you if those walls come down? What will that do to your profit margin?'

'And if you win? What will I get then?'

'Immunity, for one. Full pardon. You'll keep your dirty money – hells, I'll order the Administratum to launder it. Give you a Throne-damned official position as minister for contraband or whatever.'

'You really are desperate.'

Creed sat back, rubbing his forehead with a finger. 'You have no idea.'

Ghent thought for a moment.

'No government position, I don't like working for people. Business is no fun without autonomy.' Ghent lifted the amasec and tasted it. 'But if you're open to suggestions...'

'Give one.'

'Expansion,' said Ghent, as another artillery strike rattled the dishware. 'I've united the gangs in Kraf, but the other kasr syndicates are rooted too deep. After all this shit is done, your provosts hit the organisations in whatever cities remain, and my syndicate moves on their rackets. Consolidation would be good for both of us. You have a problem, no provosts mincing around in the back-alleys mucking up the trade, you just come to me and I'll sort it. You get me?'

'That's a big ask.'

'Can't grow up in the Imperium without wanting an empire. You want the keys to the warehouses or not?'

'Depends on what you have.'

'Have your man give mine a list of your needs, we'll have it.'

'Huh, I'll bet,' Creed said. 'The second part is confidential. But you need to level with me on the voxes. Did you supply anyone high-gain voxes, ones with a key loader and encryption?'

'No,' said Ghent. 'But I know the ones you mean. A week back, we caught a man in the tunnels with one. The item seemed hot, recidivism-hot, so we haven't tried to offload it.'

'We have a sabotage problem. Kell thinks you're part of it, but I don't. There's no profit motive. And I think you're smart enough to know that Chaos doesn't keep its side of bargains. Your people have a vox-thief network, otherwise you wouldn't be so good at dodging our patrols. And you know where the scum hides – I want you to hunt down those artillery spotters and end them.'

'I'll need money, for bribes. And for paying bounties to anyone who brings one of the voxes in.'

'You'll supply those yourself. Call it an investment.'

'All right. Is that all?'

'One more thing.' Creed puffed, his eyes on the broken table. 'You united the gangs in Kraf?'

'My predecessor did most of the early work, but yes.'

'How?' Creed's eyes slid to him, and for the first time Ghent saw the man's vulnerability and frustration. A man struggling against forces far bigger than even his formidable will. 'What did you say? How did you convince them to come together?'

Ghent sighed, clicked his tongue. 'Okay, here.'

He gestured for Creed to lean in. The Lord Castellan, eager, did so.

Ghent's slap took him full across the face, rocking Creed backwards into his chair, a red handprint across one cheek.

Kell was on him in half a second, hand seizing his lapel, power fist drawn back to pulverise him.

'Wait,' said Creed, stilling the sergeant. 'If he'd wanted to kill me, Kell, he'd have grabbed a knife from the table. Hit me with a glass. Whatever.'

But when Creed looked at him, Ghent saw the fury there.

'If you're making some kind of point,' the Lord Castellan said, clenching and unclenching his fists, 'you'd better explain it.'

'Are you dead?' Ghent asked. 'Hurt badly?'

'Of course not.'

'Well, that's what I do,' said Ghent, looking at Creed rather than the furious Kell. 'I slap the bastards, then I ask them if they're dead.'

He raised his hand, fingers splayed. 'Because I hit you like this, see? Fingers all apart. The fingers are the gangs. If I hit you with just one, I'll break my finger. Hit you with all five spread apart, I might hurt your pride. But if I bring them all together.'

Ghent curled his hand into a tight fist.

'Now... now I'll do some damage.' He paused, cocked his head. 'Usually I hit someone with the fist then, but we can skip that part.'

'Good lesson. Vivid. Thank you.'

Kell let him go roughly, shoving him back into the chair.

'You asked,' Ghent said. 'Doesn't work unless it's a surprise. Sorry about the slap.'

'That's fine,' said Creed. 'I've got something much worse in store for you.'

Ghent breathed slow, wondering if he'd gone too far. Perhaps slapping a planetary governor, in front of his men no less, had not been the wisest choice.

So when Creed placed the parcel, with its wax-sealed envelope and two silver double-eagle pins in front of him, his brow furrowed in uncharacteristic confusion.

'The hell is this?'

'A certificate of impressment. Plus rank pins of a colonel in the citizen's militia.'

'No,' Ghent said, hoping his face didn't carry the revulsion so evident in his voice. 'I told you, I never wanted a damn uniform.'

'Too bad,' smiled Creed, with naked vindictiveness. 'Congratu-lations, Colonel Ghent, you're the Grand High Frekk-Head now.'

PHASE FIVE

THE KRIEGAN GATES

ONE

'Think, my allies, of the fist. Strike an enemy with an open hand, and his pride may be hurt – but he will not be killed. Strike him with a finger extended, and that finger will be broken. But hit the enemy with the closed fist, comrades and allies – with the fingers knitted together, supporting one another – do that and you can deal some damage.

Five forces fight on Cadia Secundus.
The might of the Astra Militarum.
The strength of the noble Astartes.
The wisdom and skill of the Mechanicus.
The holy zeal of the Adepta Sororitas
And the Aeronautica Imperialis, warrior-angels in our skies.

Yet too long have we fought separately. We have slapped the Despoiler, not struck him a blow.

We must close the fist. And we will close it at Kraf Cita-del, where walls already weather enemy assault. Cadia stands, allies. But unless it stands united, it will not stand for long.'

– The so-called 'Kriegan Muster',
as recalled by General Dabatha Ravi.

Excerpted from *Creed at Cadia: A Strategic Reassessment*, by General Dabatha Ravi.

> *Later, when historians tried to impart it with a sense of grandiosity, it would be called the Kriegan Muster. But that title is deceiving, as at the time it was unclear whether the enemy's primary attack would centre on the golden vaults of the Kriegan Gates. While it is true that within twenty-four hours of the broadcast, intelligence determination hardened that the gates would be the target, debate remained hot in my own tactical staff that this would prove a bluff.*
>
> *Indeed, those of us who had taken against the Lord Castellan privately cursed him for playing his cards too early. With our staff committed to a posting at the Kriegan Gates – a redeployment that used incredible amounts of resources, and caused huge disruption to our work – there were murmurs that the Archenemy build-up we watched through our field magnoculars would be another stratagem. If so, not only would our forces be badly positioned, but the whole high command tactical room would be forced to move once again, too. Indeed, if the enemy knew Creed was there, would that not incentivise them to hit another location?*
>
> *Better, they reasoned, to stay within the citadel bunker and move to the front when it was certain where the attack would coalesce.*

Others griped that by so clearly planting his banner at the Kriegan Gates, Creed was inviting attack – intentionally exposing himself to fire in a risky gambit to force the Archenemy into attacking the strongest point. In retrospect, I believe this faction to have been correct, though they did not intend it as a compliment. By their minds, Creed was risking the sort of decapitation strike the Black Legion is known for, and as we will see, they were not entirely wrong.

But let us not belabour the point. Creed bet large on the Kriegan Gates, and as the next forty-eight hours passed, it was increasingly clear that he had placed his chips wisely.

What also became clear during the lead-up to the Chaos assault was Creed's talent for personal command. Previous chapters have discussed the Lord Castellan's history of service as a colonel, and how that background ill-prepared him for the combined-arms warfare and political considerations of theatre command. But what we have not discussed was how that same history gave him a common touch with the rank troopers that is often so lacking in those of field grade.

Much has been made of Creed's symbolic refusal to look at the enemy, how he kept his back turned to them as a gesture of belittlement and disdain. Let me be plain: this is true, but only to a point.

Having drawn duty as Creed's roving tactical attaché during these visits to the front lines, I witnessed his conduct there in person. While the legends are not untrue, I believe his behaviour was more calculated.

Like all charismatic leaders, Creed had a theatrical streak. And given his often prickly nature in private, it is my belief that his bluff performances as a soldiers' soldier were in fact that – performances. The man we saw in the citadel war room was an intelligent but dysfunctional man who seemed ill at ease with people, and prone to fits of anger or melancholy. Yet Creed's public persona was bold and wry, often with a bawdy sense of humour and encyclopaedic knowledge of barracks-room profanities. He would borrow lasguns to fire at the enemy, lead the troops in trench songs with frankly shocking lyrics, and come bearing 'gifts' that were invariably boxes of frag grenades seconded from a resupply column.

Colour Sergeant Kell also transformed during these front-line visits. The man we had known in the war room had been soft-spoken and diplomatic. As much a valet as a regimental colour sergeant, known for observing rather than speaking.

Yet with a power fist shrouding his right arm, a shoulder-mounted amplifier barking his orders at inhuman levels, and the colours of the Cadian Eighth flying overhead, he seemed to grow to twice his height. During one particular visit, I realised halfway through that an ogryn had joined the circle around Creed – but Kell's presence meant that I only noticed the hulking abhuman when we were ready to leave.

I got the sense that both were playing a role, but also that it was a role they enjoyed. Indeed, it was not long before I began to suspect that Creed's decision to move high command to the front lines had as much to do with his personal tastes as its strategic necessity.

I think, in other words, that he liked it. That the abstraction and stress of the war room with its holo-grids – where whole regiments were blocks of light and *nothing more – was not good for him. He needed to put on the public face he had cultivated and reconnect with the combat troops. The immediacy of battlefield command appealed to him.*

They were, after all, his people in a way those of us in the tactical corps were not.

And if it was a role, he performed it brilliantly for days on end.

But while this change in tone boosted the morale at the Kriegan Gates, it also began to draw in the previously scattered allies of the Cadian Defence Forces.

For while it is true that the so-called 'Kriegan Muster Speech' was a rhetorical triumph and no doubt inspired confidence (see Appendix 7 for my own recollection of the text), other factors played a key role.

First was the imminent danger to Kasr Kraf, which scared the far-flung allied forces into converging. While battles still raged in Cadia Primus – including the full complement of the Titan Legions, unable to reposition to Secundus – Kraf was clearly the enemy objective. The rapid collapse on the Kriegan Plain and fall of the outer and inner curtain walls no doubt spurred allies like the Adepta Sororitas and Adeptus Astartes into moving to reinforce, having previously been too wrapped up in their own objectives.

But the enemy mastery of the skies played a large role too. Orbital bombardment of the Sword of Defiance *had finally driven the Dark Angels from their stubborn defence of the strike cruiser. The Ironwolves – now victorious over the Iron Warriors – were also feeling the strain of fleet bombardment. And the spectacular detonation of two daemon engines had rendered the Shrine of St Morrican indefensible.*

Put simply: Kraf was the only safe place to shelter.

While its vertical shields had largely failed, leaving it open to dirt-side artillery, it still had functioning skyshields and horizontal fields. This made it the only point on Secundus that could not be struck from space.

But Creed's second message – sent encrypted and point-broadcast to commanders, rather than distributed wide – also contained a veiled threat. What the Lord Castellan referred to as a 'slap'.

It said that Valkyries of the 119th would arrive to extract allied forces within eighteen hours, but after that there would be no flights. While this was explained as a reality of diminishing air power, his assertion to also cut off non-Militarum vox-relays and cease the daily threat briefings to commanders – again cast as wartime necessity – threatened to leave the allies both blind and voiceless in enemy territory.

Tactically, they had no choice but to comply.

'We haven't received acknowledgments,' said Kell. His colours were planted in a stand, and he pursued Creed across the wall with a data-slate.

'I know,' he responded, voice barely audible above the artillery.

'Not one. Not the Templars, not the Sororitas, not even–'

'*I know.* You don't have to keep telling me, I have eyes, Kell. Valkyries are sent, we should know who's coming back soon… if any.'

Kell snorted, looking down the wall top. They were within the dispersion field of the command centre, their talk screened by dampeners – but it paid to be careful.

'You think I shouldn't have listened to him, don't you?' mumbled Creed, pressing a pair of magnoculars to his face and scanning the horizon.

'No,' Kell growled. 'I think you should have shot him. I can't begin to fathom why you didn't. Sir.'

'Am I not destroying my enemy, if I make him my ally?' He turned to Kell with a wry smile, and Kell almost hit the man. Creed must've read the expression because he raised his eyebrows and turned back to his magnoculars. 'I suppose not.'

'Allies can become enemies again, dead is permanent.'

Creed was quiet long enough that Kell raised his own lenses, thinking the exchange over.

'You remember that canine our supply sergeant had on Vestilla Prime?'

'What?'

'That cyber-mastiff that... what-was-his-name had – Sergeant Svanteg – from Delta Company?' Creed held a hand up at waist height. 'Big bastard, sharp teeth, bionic leg?'

'I was in the field hospital for most of Vestilla. Took a slug for you while we were storming that old bottling plant.'

'Right, yes, right. Well anyway, Svanteg had this awful beast of a mastiff. Got it from a fighting ring, I think. Nobody liked the thing, and it hated everyone but Svanteg, but it was spectacular at keeping the lizard-vermin from eating the grain stock. Then one day, a cadet-commissar decided to run a surprise inspection and the mutt nearly took his hand off. Commissar Nabari was forced to shoot the ugly thing.'

'The cadet or the canine?' asked Kell facetiously.

Creed shot him a look of affectionate frustration before looking back into his magnoculars. 'Anyway, you know what happened after that? The damned lizards got into the grain store. Ate their fill, shat it full of toxins, we had half the regiment on sick call every morning for a month. Pretty soon, even the commissar was missing that mean, ugly old mastiff. You see the analogy?'

'Yes. What I don't see are any acknowledgements.'

'Bah.' Creed sniffed. 'Valkyries are out for pickup. Maybe they didn't get the message. Warp distortion's playing hell with the vox-lines. Or maybe–'

'Sighting!' yelled a trooper to their right. She was crouching behind a massive monocular scope, its black lens wide as a battle-cannon barrel. 'Armoured column, crossing inner curtain wall at point six-three-oh-echo.'

'More hostiles,' Kell said. 'We should tell the Basilisks to have anti-armour shells ready.'

'Maybe,' Creed said, squinting. Kell saw him lower the magnoculars, judge distance, adjust the focus and raise them again.

'There!' said Creed, shooting a finger out towards the horizon. 'Right there, at the inner wall.'

'Iron Warriors remnants?' Kell scanned and adjusted, trying to find the flash of metal.

'No,' said Creed. 'It's the frekking Ironwolves!'

Hanna Keztral held on to the Predator's hull for dear life. The rumble of the tank's motor and jarring, wobbling movement of the chassis had pounded her entire body into numbness.

It had been a full day of driving – engines at full shriek – to get here. And due to some Astartes code, they had not allowed her to ride inside the transports. Which left little option but to use her kit's paracord and D-clip to secure her webbing to a handlebar on the Predator and hang on. If there had been an engagement, she would've been paste.

Still, under the circumstances, she was glad to be on an Iron-wolves Predator – the Dark Angels in the column, having evacuated the *Sword of Defiance* when it literally began to fall apart around them, seemed far less friendly.

The Wolves were trying to use speed to slip back into Kraf Cita-del and avoid any entanglements. There was discussion of waiting for the Valkyries to evacuate them – but the Ironwolves refused to leave their precious armoured vehicles, and decided to seek a breakthrough.

The question had become where the breakthrough should happen – most major gates, after all, had already been sealed and were under active siege.

All but one.

'Pilot,' she heard in her helmet. It was the Wolf in the tank cupola, his gauntleted hands fastened around the grips of a storm bolter. 'My lord Highfell wishes you to swear again that you know where you are going.'

'I do,' she said. Though she knew she wouldn't like what she'd see when she arrived.

She was right.

Enemy artillery and chemical fires had pounded Salgorah District to the point that Keztral lost her bearings in the habclave of her birth. The rooftops she'd flown kites from were burned or collapsed, stained strange colours by the discharge of chemical explosives.

Towers had fallen. Courtyards filled in with rubble. Only when she glimpsed a half-collapsed pillar in the shape of an angel – part of the chapel where she had been anointed and registered into the service rolls as a babe in arms – did she find what she was looking for.

It was called River Run because during the rainy season, those living in the citadel opened the water gate and the street became a rushing stream. As a child, she'd played in the evacuated water, taking strips of cast-off plastek foam packing and sledding down the street's steep grade, propelled by rushing waste water.

When they were tired, they'd go to Gandolpa's String Cart, which made the best spicy carb-strings in the district.

She considered telling the Space Marine about this, but realised she didn't know what words to use.

'It's called River Run,' she thought. *That's what you say, Hanna. Simple. 'This is River Run, because in the rainy season it becomes a river.'*

But that was wrong. It *was* called River Run. Just as this *was* called Salgorah, where once lived a man named Gandolpa and a girl named Hanna Keztral.

Keztral felt the disconnection as it happened, an almost physical sensation of dizzy ache.

As a pilot, she had lived her life in the near-term. Revelling in immediacy, letting the rush of speed and focus keep her in an eternal present. A privileging of the *now* above the *then,* a life where she was a pilot of the Aeronautica, not a frightened little girl using scabbed-over fingers to build kites out of trash.

That separation had held when Salgorah was a physical realm she had to keep at mental distance. A place that existed at great remove. A place her colleagues might see on a passing overflight and think: *Is that trash heap where Keztral is from?*

Not *is* from, *was* from.

Salgorah was no longer there. And she felt the onrush of memories, memories of a place that now existed only in her mind, subsume her sense of the immediate. She had never wanted to go home again, and now she never would.

When the tanks drove up River Run there were no children and no string-carts. Instead, abandoned tents littered the roadside. Bundles of belongings lay discarded, pots and pans spilling from a plastek bag, a sewing basket blown open by the wind, so tangles of ribbon blew like pennants from its top. There were children's lasguns carved from scrap wood, and a fabric doll with its helmet made from a cast-off mess-kit cup – limbs wrapped in white paper where a child had dressed its pretend wounds.

A few bodies lay by the roadside. They were wrapped in stained winding-sheets and laid shoulder to shoulder in clusters of two and three. Meagre belongings and stubby, burned-out candles clustered around their heads.

Family groups.

She realised it was a displacement camp, set up around the water gate. The whole population of Salgorah had gathered at the only entrance to Kraf they knew, clamouring to be let inside.

At some point, they had been – but they'd been forced to leave everything. A pile of clothing near the wall marked where they'd been told to strip, lest they bring lice into the citadel. Tangles of fluff drifted through the air, carried by the breeze, and it wasn't until some snagged on her flight suit that Keztral realised it was hair.

Her memory flashed back to her academy entrance, the feel of a buzz-cutter on her skull. Long twists of curly copper hair falling into her lap.

They'd been shorn like livestock before entering.

The Ironwolves' treads shredded the encampment as they went up River Run, towards the gate.

For a panicked instant she thought it was blocked, but no – as they got close, she saw the camouflage netting concealing the entrance. A troop of Kasrkin stood guard behind the gauzy material.

'Our gratitude, pilot,' the Space Marine in the turret said. 'Jarl Highfell has made contact with the guards – you have steered us true through the maelstrom. And in return, we shall save your world.'

Keztral looked up at a sky empty of kites.

Even if they saved Cadia, her world was already gone.

'Are you moving me?' Genevieve asked.

'Yes.' Eleanor leaned down over the stretcher as it floated on its repulsor lifts. A Hospitaller stood at each end. 'Rest. You can sleep.'

Genevieve's lips trembled, blue-grey with trauma. The flash-burns of the detonation had been awful, far more serious than they seemed from the outside.

When they had pulled the armour off her left arm and leg, parts of her skin had come with it. One side of her scalp was burned clean, and she was lucky to have retained vision in her natural left eye – though Eleanor detected the cloudy mist of a cataract.

They had given her obscurine for the pain. And in the depths of the drug she'd told strange stories about the trophy rack emerging from the daemon's shoulders. She said that one of the heads there was Sister Heloise, of her Seraphim, who spoke to her.

'Canoness,' said Sister Eugenia. 'The relics are loaded and away.'

'And the bell?' she asked.

'The Sky Talon pilot says her craft should be able to airlift it within twenty minutes.'

'Airlift?' asked Genevieve. 'Are you removing the relics from the sanctum? You can't, sister, we've strived so…'

'Shhhhhhh,' said Eleanor, placing a bare hand over Genevieve's gauntlets, which rested in a sign of the aquila on her chest – the way one would lay a corpse for burial. 'The blasphemer was right. The shrine is only stones. It can be rebuilt.'

'But the relics, the altarpieces, the frescoes…'

'I have what is important to me.'

Genevieve closed her eyes as if lulled by the bobbing of the repulsor field, until she heard the howling of an engine.

'Where are we going?'

The downwash of the Valkyrie's vector nozzles sent the Sisters' robes flying as it came down on the pad, settling neatly at an angle, the two rear landing struts touching ferrocrete before the nose.

A side door rolled back. Within, the Valkyrie's crew chief – his lower face covered in a rebreather and his webbing secured to the ceiling by a tether – looked out at Eleanor. He was crouching down, almost casual, his arms resting on his knees as if he'd been waiting for them.

He looked at Eleanor and raised a fist.

'We have sworn to defend Cadia,' Eleanor said, raising her closed gauntlet. 'And as you say, sister – deeds, not words.'

'Marshal.' Mordlied knelt at the foot of his lord, his helmet placed before him in supplication. One lens remained cracked from the heavy bolter strike. 'I have made atonement. Slain the enemy sorcerer. You have granted my request to posthumously ennoble Neophyte Descares as an Initiate. But I petition you once again. Please restore to me the honour of the crusade banner if Brother Maltheus falls.'

Marshal Amalrich did not look at him. He stared over the hill of rubble that now served as the fire-step of the Martyr's Rampart. Waiting for the Archenemy to come take the blasted ruin from them again.

'I will not,' Amalrich said. 'Let us hear no more about it.'

'Why not?' he spat. And the moment the words left his mouth, shame wormed its way into Mordlied's stomach like a corkscrew.

'When you ask such a thing, you prove your contrition is not true. Forgiveness and redemption are not contractual. No good deed can erase a failure in faith. The Emperor knows your secret sin, yet you cannot admit it or perhaps even see it. And that is why not.'

'You have heard the call from Cadia, Marshal? We are invited to muster at the Kriegan Gates.'

'I have heard it, how have you?'

Mordlied did not speak for a moment, ashamed. 'You never removed me from the command channel, lord.'

'I will do so,' Amalrich said, keying the power field live on his sword. 'This is our position. Our vow. And we will not abandon it.

The enemy comes, Mordlied, and the Emperor calls. Get off your knees, and let the Cadians worry about Cadia.'

She was sitting on an ammunition crate and spooning breakfast gruel into her mouth when he found her.

'Captain Keztral? Hanna Keztral?'

The lieutenant was a few years younger than her – twenty-one, possibly twenty-two – and had the sallow, slightly flabby look people get when they spend a lot of time on void craft. His blue Naval uniform had yellow facings, and markings from an air wing she didn't recognise. He wasn't looking at her, but calling generally, as if he'd been told where she was but not what she looked like.

She let her arm, exhausted from the mere act of eating, drop the tin spoon into her porridge with a plop.

'Yes, what is it?'

'Ah, there you...' he began, trailing off upon seeing her.

Keztral's return had not been triumphant, nor formal. After turning over her pict-tubes she'd endured six hours of debriefing, most of it standing up. What she'd seen, where she'd gone down, how she'd contacted the Wolves. What, if anything, she thought was going on in the picts she'd taken. Four men from Kraf Air Command had just sat, filling the room with their lho-stick smoke, and asking question after question.

They had not reciprocated. None had even given their names. Every time she'd asked the status of Stetzen Airfield, the 89th Combat-Pict Recon, or whether she'd fly again, they said the same thing: *That is not currently relevant.*

When it was done, she'd only had the energy to eat a starch-bar and crawl onto one of the cots in the unassigned persons hall, waiting for orders. She hadn't even changed clothes.

'No salute, lieutenant?' she asked, voice dripping with irony.

In her torn and bloodstained flight suit, she barely looked like a human being, much less a superior officer.

'Well, due to Navy rank structure, we're technically the same grade, but if you want one, I'll oblige you.'

The lieutenant offered a collegial salute. He did it Naval style, with the palm facing in, and after a moment she responded with the palm-out Militarum standard, not bothering to rise. They were both casual gestures, the kind a sergeant would've bawled her out for as a cadet.

'Do they want me back for more questions? Can I finish breakfast?'

'No, sir,' the lieutenant said. 'I mean, no questions. And you can bring the chow if you like. But I have a groundcar pulled around and we have to move it soon so... Pardon, but have you seen a medicae, ma'am? You're limping.'

She had seen a medicae on arrival, for all of five minutes. He'd wound bandages around her feet then moved on to a trooper with a forehead laceration.

'My boots are full of blood.'

'I can get you new ones,' he said, opening the door of the open-topped utility groundcar. 'I'm Lieutenant Sobin. I'm your new ground coordinator. Anything like that you need, I'll handle.'

She climbed in, gingerly, and sat. 'A new flight suit?'

'Sure. Yesterday I would've said no good, but something freed up in the supply line and things are flowing again. They're practically giving lasguns and helmets away – literally if you count the new civilian militia.' He climbed in and slapped the driver on the shoulder. 'Sergeant Pavel?'

The groundcar jerked into motion and turned onto a gravel roadway, tyres crunching the stones.

'I want to go back to Stetzen, if possible,' she said, half shouting over the open-top's engine. 'Back to the Eighty-Ninth Combat-Pict. Request a transfer or–'

'Sorry, can't do it. Stetzen got hit bad on the first day of the air war. It's been evacuated. You're assigned to Ramstead now. The Eighty-Ninth functionally doesn't exist, just like my outfit, the Scarus Two-Hundred-and-Thirty-Third Naval Airlift. Your boy Creed really skazzed us on that first day.'

'He's not my boy.'

'Sorry. Anyway, whole theatre is a mess. We've got pilots without aircraft, aircraft without pilots, ground crew with a pilot but no aircraft. Gunners without pilots… You get the idea. It's all catch as catch can now, matching up crews and equipment however we're able. Cadian locals in Navy aircraft, vice versa. My wing was transport logistics. Void-to-ground stuff. Supersonic delivery boys, really. Now I'm with you.' He paused to slide a pair of solar-tint glasses onto his face, the wide-lensed, stylised kind Navy flyers wore. A stamped aquila rested its claws on the bridge of the nose, and its outstretched wings formed the upper frame. 'Some poor bastards are flying airframes they've never clocked hours in before. Kraf Air Command's just smashing units together to cover losses and keep us flying. We're both Squadron Three-Nine-Nine (A) now.'

'What's the "A" stand for?'

'Amalgamated.'

She said nothing, put a hand to her brow to block the sun. After so long in the battle-smoke and briefing rooms, her eyes weren't adjusting.

'Hey, it's pretty bright today, you want some tints, captain? We've got plenty considering the number of unclaimed footlockers at base.'

Sobin held out a folded pair of tint glasses, matching his own.

She took the hand off her brow and accepted them gratefully. They helped, and she decided she didn't completely dislike Lieutenant Sobin after all.

'Thanks,' she said.

'Least I could do, considering the citation.'

'Citation?'

'They didn't tell you? You're getting written up.'

Frekk. She closed her eyes. One of the four men yesterday had been a commissar. 'For aircraft loss?'

'What? No, I mean you're getting cited for valour.' He dug in his jacket, extracted an envelope. 'I'm guessing that's what this is.'

Keztral took it, stunned at how heavy it was. After a moment of dumb staring, she could only say: 'That's the seal of Air Marshal Shrowd.'

Keztral cracked it open, ran her eyes down the page.

For all those who read these present bearings, note that CAPTAIN HANNA KEZTRAL of 399th Squadron (Amalgamated) and LIEUTEN-ANT LAHON DARVUS of 89th Combat-Pict Recon (deceased) have this day been awarded the BLACK SHIELD OF CADIA, the highest award for gallantry in support of combat...

'Frekking sons of cowards,' she snarled. For a moment, she wanted to crumple the paper and throw it from the groundcar, but it would feel too much like spitting on Darvus' memory.

'What's wrong? It seemed like some big deal.'

'It's a non-combat award. For conspicuous valour *while in support of combat operations.*'

'What? That doesn't make any sense. You're a combat pilot in a combat unit. Hells, you were shot down. And doesn't an observation Avenger mount a weapon?'

'A defensive weapon. And no, though I fly in a warzone, it's still considered support. I'm not rated for offensive aircraft.'

'That's a shame,' said Sobin. 'Because you've got one.'

'What?' she said. Distantly, she noticed the groundcar had lurched to a stop.

He pointed past her shoulder, and she turned.

Then scrambled to her feet, holding the groundcar's roll bar for support.

'Three-Nine-Nine is a strike outfit,' said Sobin. 'Air-to-ground specialty. And there's your mount.'

'Throne,' she breathed. 'God-Emperor, look at it.'

'It's a little battered. She's a patched-up Navy model, and the backseat's a servitor not a gunner. There might be kind of a smell. But it's the best we can do for now.'

Keztral looked over the aircraft, from the swept-down wings with their vector engines to the blocky tail. It was in grey Navy drab, its canopy open and waiting.

And under the nose, in the place *Deadeye*'s picter-array sat, were the gleaming barrels of a rotary bolt cannon.

'What's its name?'

'Doesn't have one. You got one in mind, sir?'

'*War-Kite*,' she whispered, then turned. 'When do we fly?'

The Kriegan Gates.

Servantus Glave couldn't help but crane his head to look at the golden underside as they passed beneath it. Above him, on the interior of the massive structure, were gleaming bas-reliefs of battles past. Glorious campaigns on foreign worlds, heroes of the past. Files of tri-dome helmets and Kantrael-pattern lasguns. Generals in full dress uniform, holding models of planets they had liberated. A chronicle of resistance against the Despoiler.

Put a bayonet in the Despoiler himself.

That voice had got stronger. Throughout his battles on the northern Alpha Curtain Wall, the fightback against the Raptors, and the tide of warp-evils that had come after. They had been putrid things, lithe and sinuous with razor claws. Moving in a way that entranced and repelled. Thankfully, most of his contact with them had been through firing slits in the thick wall, but that was only partial protection.

Their perfumed smell was hard to describe, like drinking wine only to find it was not fully fermented, but still rotting mash. When he looked at them, *thought* about them, Glave got the horrid sensation of flower petals lightly brushing his skin – at first with the softness of a spring bloom, but the more he paid attention to it, the more those invisible blossoms crinkled and withered into the scratching of a desiccated flower.

He felt the sensation returning and shook the memory off with the mantra.

Put a bayonet in the Despoiler.

The words must be saint-spoken and Emperor-sent, because they had seen him through the fights in the wall, the fallback to the Beta wall, and now the breakthrough battles in the retreat to Kraf. As Kasrkin, they'd served as outriders, bouncing along the flank in a stripped-down Taurox scouting for threats – then speeding away as Glave poured into them with the pintle-mounted storm bolter.

With that mantra he had gunned down monsters and whispering those words he'd fired on Heretic Astartes – until his kill count rested, by his own reckoning, at three. Granted, it was hard to tell in combat who shot who, but Glave knew it in his soul.

Was that improbable, that one Guardsman would kill three mutated, transhuman monsters? No, it was not improbable – it was *miraculous*. And miracles by definition defied belief.

Similarly, he and the rest of Fire-team Gamma should have died a thousand times by now, but they hadn't. Another sign of divine favour.

Sergeant Veskaj was still alive, as – incredibly – was Stitcher Kristan. The rest of Fire-team Gamma were new faces, peeled off from remnant squads. They were not important, none of them.

They were all there to deliver him to the point where he could, in turn, deliver Cadia.

Because Glave was on a mission from the Golden Throne, and the front lines of a siege were the perfect place to fulfil that sacred assignment.

He, Servantus Glave of the 27th Kasrkin, would kill Abaddon the Despoiler.

TWO

Urkanthos entered the chamber shrouded in night, his long shadow-wings wrapped around him like a cloak.

The fortress' air ran cold, often only a few degrees above freezing. Yet as he came, he brought the hot stickiness of the charnel house with him. A tangy abattoir reek like the final, panicked breaths of livestock who have just smelled the gore and seen the cleaving-axe.

The Warmaster's Chosen recoiled with the force of his presence, or at least, what Chosen remained. Krom Gat's chair sat empty, the Lord of the Undivided slain by the savage sons of Russ.

As the daemon passed, the warp-infused blackstone of the doorway crawled closer, as if drawn to him as water is drawn downhill by gravity.

Out of the corner of Morkath's eye, even the Warmaster's thoughts slowed in their motion, the zodiac reshuffling as planets rose and fell, so many of them tainted furious red.

Only Zaraphiston the Seer smiled. And he alone kept his back to the daemon prince once named Urkanthos.

'*Warmaster,*' the ascended lord said, the thought-speech desynchronised from the movement of his caged jaw. He gave a courtly bow, holding his shadow-cloak behind him in one hand so the Chosen could glimpse the red muscle underneath. '*Fellow brothers.*'

Then his head came up, and Morkath could see yellow eyes burning in the rune-stamped cage of his helmet.

Thought-reader, he said. *That explains why he tolerates you. How many know of that, I wonder?*

He did not say it with his lips, nor did she read it with her mind. He *sent* it as a telepathic spike that pierced her language centre with a sensation of being stabbed through the skull.

Morkath gasped – for he no longer had thoughts.

No mortal brain operated beneath the skull. Urkanthos was pure warp manifestation now. No mere meat-vessel channelling the ether gods, but part of the empyric pantheon itself.

'Urkanthos,' rumbled the Warmaster. 'Or do you name yourself differently now?'

'Though I have risen to a prince of daemons, I am still Urkanthos to my friends.'

'Are we friends, then?' said the Warmaster. 'Your brothers fight across Cadia, your own warband unsupported by their commander as they struggled with the sons of the Lion. And yet you – without telling this chamber – have slaughtered the Emperor's fanatics to bribe your way to ascension. I ask, thing-that-was-Urkanthos, is this the behaviour of a friend?'

'It is the behaviour of one who knows what is required for victory,' hissed Urkanthos. *'That is what you have taught me, Warmaster. To do what is necessary. And an ascension was necessary to take Kraf.'*

'We have gambled much on this battle, Urkanthos. This final siege of Cadia. And I will not have you trading it to your red god.'

'I fight for no god. I fight for you.'

'Fight to own me, perhaps. I wonder if you are the same Urkanthos who was my axe in the whirl of the Eye, who forsook petty gods to follow a greater path.'

'Why would you say this, Ezekyle? All I have done is become a greater warrior that can be used in your crusade.'

'We do not fight crusades, Urkanthos,' he said, shaking his head. 'That is what *they* do. Launch blind crusades for their god. It is why the warp hungers for them, because they are looking for a master. I wanted you to be your own ruler.'

Urkanthos stepped forward, clawed feet digging into the black-stone. His stride was so long he stepped over the table to stand before the Warmaster, and Morkath could not help but shrink back.

'*You abuse me. Level charges of disloyalty. Claim I am not yours–*'

'You were never mine, I am claiming that you are not your own.'

'*It is folly.*' Urkanthos spread his stance wide, and Morkath realised it was only the raised noctilith throne that forced him to look up at the Warmaster. If her father climbed down, he would be level with the smouldering rune of Khorne branded on the daemon's chest.

Abaddon did not speak for a moment, letting Urkanthos stand in this position of humility.

'You have broken the covenant of this chamber, Urkanthos. To bring no being here with you. No warriors, no slaves and no daemons. Yet a warp-parasite rests on your back. It is not the first time.'

'*I do not know what you mean.*'

'Your bloody-mouthed god has given you many gifts, Urkanthos. But lying was not one of them. Though you may be an ennobled lord of the warp, you forget that I am the Warmaster of Chaos. And though I care not for titles the warp gods give them to me, and among those is commander of daemons.'

It was only then that Morkath saw the ripples of warp energy drawing back through the noctilith floor, withdrawing like the sea before a tidal wave and collecting under the blackstone throne.

'*Ezekyle, what is this mock–*'

'**TELL ME YOUR NAME!**'

The words howled forth from the depths of the warp, coming

from the Warmaster's bottomless mouth in a chorus of voices that sounded like nothing more than atmosphere tearing out of a holed ship.

It washed over Urkanthos in a tide, and as it struck him the black shadow-cloak leapt up in full extension to reveal his wings, their leathery darkness seizing and quaking like the creature were being electrocuted. Pale, misty eyes blinked in shock and pain, and it keened with the sound of a drill bit on steel.

'Arteeeeesssssssiiaaaaaa of the mooouths of goooore!'

'Begone, warp-shade. Out of my ship. And never again enter.'

It was the most horrible thing Morkath had ever seen. Deep-sunk talons ripped free. Shadowy leech mouths, full of rings of hooked bone teeth detached, vomiting blood. The shade pulled itself upward, stretching and tearing, and the white eyes receded into the empty dark eyelids to become bleeding mouths.

The shade was not part of Urkanthos, but grafted onto him. A psychic parasite.

The Khornate lord bowed in pain, muscles bunching. Bellowed at the floor so loud his helm cracked. So loud Morkath had to cover her ears or become deaf.

Then the shade flapped upwards into the haunted vaults of the fortress and there was quiet.

Urkanthos panted, snuffled. Blood poured from his nose-less nostrils.

'I am the Warmaster of Chaos. More powerful than any thrall-daemon. You say you are a prince, but a prince is not a king. Do you understand me?'

'I... I do. Thank you for the lesson, Warmaster. And for ridding me of that creature.'

It was difficult to hear Urkanthos through the blood flowing from his mouth. Morkath did not need to see the daemon prince's thoughts to know his fury. The yellow eyes spoke of murder.

'I believe that I have made you a promise. And like all promises I make, it still stands. Do you wish to lead the attack on Kraf?'

'I do, Warmaster. The others have put Cadia on the altar, and I will slaughter it.'

'Go and do so.'

Urkanthos turned and strode from the chamber, bleeding freely from the delta of craters left along his spine and shoulders.

And though he did not turn, Morkath heard his voice – again, meant only for her.

You see how he treats his friends, Fortress Child. Imagine how he treats his creations.

When the chamber was empty, the Warmaster dismissed her with a single order.

'I could not read his thoughts, Warmaster. It–'

'You cannot read Urkanthos, who will soon either destabilise the Chosen or die. You cannot read Zaraphiston. Krom Gat is slain by the Wolves. Your usefulness grows meagre here. It is past time for you to find the vermin.'

Forces gathered at the Kriegan Gates. The finest troopers of Cadia plus multiple allied Guard regiments, under the strategic eye of what was certainly the greatest Lord Castellan in two millennia. Formations of tanks and armoured vehicles. Squadrons of aircraft. Two commanderies of the Adepta Sororitas. A baronial household of House Raven fighting a rearguard action. An unheard-of alliance of the Space Wolves and Dark Angels, alongside scratch companies of Astartes from two dozen Chapters. And as if that were not enough, a full war cohort of skitarii.

Perhaps the most interesting and varied assemblage of Imperial forces that had ever defended a single city, hardening their strongpoints for what was sure to be one of the most momentous fights in the history of the Cadian Gate.

And already, the forces of the Black Legion were hammering the breastworks and aegis lines thrown up before the thirty-storey-high bastion that guarded the way into Cadia. Hunting packs of Maulerfiends. Raptor harassing assaults. Insectile war engines so bristling with limbs and weapon-mounts they defied any categorisation.

One would think that such a bounty would cheer Trazyn, but he stared out of the oubliette with frustration. His towering stature meant that he saw directly over the helmets of the Cadian 33rd's second trench-line.

'I am like Warden Zaddir at the feasting table, Sannet. It is agonising.'

'That comparison is a bit... dramatic.'

'It is dramatic because it is from the dramas,' Trazyn snapped. Though even in his defensiveness, he knew Sannet had a point. The Royal Warden Zaddir, as the old plays told it, had tried to betray the Mephrit during the flesh times. In punishment, they had sewn his mouth shut and forced him to attend lavish feasts as he starved. 'Hyperbole or not, I hate sitting here looking at so many possible acquisitions. And these fools are going to throw them away.'

Trazyn's vocal actuators emitted a series of chiding clicks as he shook his head. Down the line, a Heldrake flock had dived down to immolate two squads of the Cadian Ninth. It had been like that for two days, dive and burn, hammer and retreat. The Hounds of Abaddon slamming the aegis lines like a storm tide. Softening them up with each wave.

'If you step out of our shooting hide you will be seen,' said the Huntmaster. 'The game will detect your scent.'

The old deathmark sat cross-legged on the floor of the hyperspace oubliette, his synaptic disintegrator broken down and floating in a layout as he inspected each part.

'Allow me the luxury to lament, game warden. To watch history when one could participate is no easy thing.'

'Should we decide to bag a specimen, though...' The Huntmaster took the focusing tube of his disintegrator and mimed blowing through it, despite having no breath. 'I can oblige you.'

'*Surely you are not thinking of taking an active hand, lord archaeovist? You have already tipped the scale once. And to risk doing so twice could never be worth the possible cons–*'

'No, no,' Trazyn answered, with an affected weariness. 'I suppose not.'

'Wisest to let nature take its course,' the Huntmaster agreed.

'Yes… I'll only interfere if the human position gets very desperate, or if it will amuse me.'

It was good, Trazyn thought, to set parameters.

'How long can Cadian forces hold the gate?' asked Orven Highfell.

Creed pursed his lips around the cigar, considering his answer.

Kell found himself shuffling his feet in discomfort. Creed was making the Wolf Lord of the Ironwolves Great Company – not to mention the other worthies – wait, and it was all Kell could do not to nudge him.

Usually the tallest man in any room, Kell was still unused to the sheer size of the Space Marines as they clustered around the holo-projection table. Creed never appeared intimidated in the presence of the revered Adeptus Astartes, but Kell – even after a career as glorious as any in the Guard – could not help but feel a little like a boy of seven, dressed in a cadet uniform and sitting at the adults' table during the Restsoul Day Feast.

Highfell, it was said, had seen the legendary days of Horus' betrayal. And now he stood in their command bunker looking out on Kraf's northern muster field.

They'd pulled the command section back from the top of the Kriegan Gates the day before, when it was clear the position was too exposed to enemy artillery and airstrikes. That hadn't been planned in advance – a Basilisk-sized round had dropped directly onto the top of the wall, so close that it had killed an entire section of logistics staff and spattered stone debris across the heat-flash bubble of Creed's refractor field.

Creed hadn't even been wearing it at the time. He hated the weight of the humming, buzzing thing around his neck – said it gave him a headache – and the dumb bastard would've been killed if he'd walked ten feet to his left. But, Emperor be praised, he'd been leaning right over it, scrutinising the holo-table. They'd managed to evacuate Creed before the enemy battery zeroed their follow-up shot.

Holo-table, staff and Creed's personal Kasrkin detail withdrew to a fortified passage in thirty seconds, closing the stairwell blast door just ahead of a direct hit.

Afterward, Kell had given him a rare dressing-down in private – at least, as much as he could given the difference in rank – and the triangular field projector was hanging once again atop Creed's breastplate.

'How long can we hold?' Creed mused, pulling the cigar from his lips and blowing a stream of smoke that wavered the holo. 'Hold for what, exactly? That's the question.'

'A little obtuse,' said Lieutenant A'shar. The Raven Guard's armour was covered in purity seals, only partially patched and reconsecrated from the vicious fighting at the Jorus Redoubt. Half his languid face lay flat, a cheekbone broken. 'We have a plan, I assume?'

'We do,' said Creed. 'Though some forces in-system are trying to disengage and join us here, our problem is we don't know when reinforcements from the rest of the Imperium will arrive – if they're coming at all. Who knows if our distress signal was heard? But we have one other option.'

He withdrew a data-key and slotted it into the holo-table's input port. When he turned it, a number of new markers flickered into being on the projection. Each listed a facility name and list of units.

'What you're seeing is the most closely guarded secret on Cadia. Something not even high command has been aware of, though it has not gone unnoticed.'

Logistar-General Raik bent close and read the unit designations, with an acid tone. 'Eleventh Kasrkin Air Assault, Two-Hundred-and-Eighty-Second Shock Infantry, Ninety-First Heavy Ordnance Battery… Why Ursarkar, it's the "lost" reserve units.'

'They weren't lost, Conskavan. I knew where they were. These facilities are what's known as Salvation outposts, deep-cover bunkers constructed thousands of years ago, to allow a planetary commander to keep a reserve army in their back pocket – one that could emerge when the time was right. If you've heard the old Cadian myth of the Army Under the Mountain, ready to roll out when Cadia needs it most – well, that's a folklore distortion of this reality.'

'And it is time for them to heed the war-drums, and pounce on the traitors as their backs are turned.' Highfell smiled, bearing a grin that was more lupine than Kell remembered.

'Exactly. That's our play – we will allow the Archenemy to draw up siege forces outside the Kriegan Gates, then smash him from the rear with the nearest Salvation units, fresh from their holdsafes in the Rossvar. They are the hammer of the Emperor, we are the anvil.'

'To besiege the besiegers,' said Master Korahael. He alone of the Space Marines still wore his helm. 'When can they be activated?'

'That's the tricky part. Timing. To trap the Archenemy forces, we cannot reveal the reserve too early. Our foes must be fully committed and dug-in, unable to suddenly manoeuvre out of the trap. I estimate if we activated them now, it would take at least twenty-four to thirty-six hours for the closest three regiments to receive orders, deploy from their positions, and fight their way to our aid. But we must not show our hand too early – the enemy does not yet have real siege elements in place. No heavy artillery, heavy armour or troops massing in the numbers needed. Once they commit, we can activate.'

'I would not think of this as a traditional siege,' Canoness Eleanor said. 'They are led by the ascended daemon they call Urkanthos with nearly limitless troops at his disposal. And the Despoiler is restless for victory.'

Creed nodded. 'Do you wish to brief them, Inquisitor Daverna?'

The Inquisitorial legate – her scalp marked by a sutured cut that looked quite fetching, Kell thought – nodded. 'Our intelligence profiles suggest he is the Despoiler's closest and most devoted warlord. A member of his inner circle. No doubt he has been tasked with storming Kraf and destroying the null-array. We assume this is some type of reward or boon granted to him, a sought-after honour for his loyalty.'

'You may find,' Korahael cautioned through his helm grille, 'that loyalty in the Black Legion does not mean what you suppose.'

'That's what we're hoping,' Creed said, pointing at Korahael before retracting the finger, concerned he might cause offence in the gesture. 'Currently this siege appears exclusive to Urkanthos and his warband. If we destroy him, will the others fall to bickering over who gets the glory of taking us down? Thanks to Lord Highfell, Krom Gat is already slain. The Archenemy might have limitless troops, Canoness Eleanor, but his command echelon is getting emptier by the day.'

'According to debriefs with our allies in the Adeptus Astartes,' Daverna nodded towards the demigods, 'the Black Legion is no Cadian battalion with a clear chain of command. It's a group of rival warbands that have coalesced around charismatic leaders. Personal loyalty is everything. Front-line troops revere the Despoiler, but their bonds of fealty tie them to direct commanders, who have in turn pledged to the Master of the Black Legion. Break down his command structure, and the Despoiler will lose command-and-control. Great waves of troops are only an advantage if you can direct them.'

Eleanor nodded. 'Let us discuss this delaying action, then.'

'Yes, let's,' Creed said. 'Officer, adjust the focus of the table. I think the last hit on the skyshield misaligned it.'

When the tech dialled in the image, Creed held out his hand for the long table stylus.

'A classic defence-in-depth operation,' he said. 'Fifteen companies of the Cadian Thirty-Third Infantry are here, manning the aegis lines before the Kriegan Gates. I've also supported them with the Ninth, largely heavy weapons companies.'

Creed reached with the arm-length stylus and pointed to a fan-spread of troop blocks marked *33* with the letters *A* through *I,* messily superimposed over the maze of trenches. The images clipped through each other. 'We've dug in a group of Leman Russ patterns from the Two-Hundred-and-Ninety-Second Armoured as static firing positions, hull down behind the earthworks but able to reverse out in case of a pullback. That will get messy, though. Hard to manoeuvre groups of tanks in reverse through a choke point. We've issued the crews incendiaries with orders to ditch and burn at the slightest hint of a traffic snarl. Tanks we can replace from the armoured stores, but able crews are in short supply.'

'How long do you expect it to hold?' asked Highfell, stroking his long beard.

'The Thirty-Third are crack troops. And I have informed Colonel Deshane he must repulse the enemy for as long as possible while we prepare. The Thirty-Third loves him, and if he asks, they'll do it.'

Kell could hear the hedging, the veiled worry under Creed's bluster.

'That is not a number,' said Korahael. 'How long will he hold. Hours? Days?'

'Two days, at current casualty rates, one if Urkanthos is reinforced. The hope is to reduce the Hounds of Abaddon before they create a breach. Because the real war of attrition isn't here.' Creed tapped the aegis lines before the gate, then moved the long stylus into the warren of streets behind the gate. 'It's here. Behind the Kriegan Barbican and within the outer ring of Kraf's civilian habs. They were purpose-built to funnel attackers into ambushes. I have some surprises awaiting there for when the barbican falls – including three fresh regiments of Kasrkin. They know this district and its alleyways inside out. There are false streets that lead to dead ends, courtyards we've sealed off with steel portcullises to create kill-boxes. Hells, half the street signs have been changed around so they can't be followed. House-to-house fighting where every hab is a hardened bunker. It's going to be bad for the Hounds, especially with their combat doctrine. We'll break them into small groups and annihilate them. Add another twenty-four hours of delay. But that's still not the endgame.'

He slapped the tip of the stylus on the open space just ahead of his new command bastion, behind the warren of streets.

'The northern muster field. Here's where it will be decided. Whatever remains of the traitor assault, with luck even Urkanthos himself, will break through and strike the Cadian Eighth, under my personal command. Our plan will be to encircle and destroy – they will be taking enfilading fire from both flanks, courtesy of the wall guns sectioning off this muster field. Canoness Eleanor, if you would do my troopers the honour of deploying in their centre before the command bastion, I'm sure they would appreciate both your firepower and calming presence. Master Korahael, given that you have been operating with the Ironwolves, I had hoped your Fourth Company would deploy with them on the right. And Lieutenant A'shar, your demi-company on the left.'

'Armour?' asked Highfell. 'I mean besides ours.'

'I have some partial regiments we can throw into the flanks,' sighed Creed. 'But many have to be positioned at the other gates in case of a simultaneous assault or hardened push elsewhere. They're devilish exposed on this open field. I'll commit some, though in the main this will be an infantry brawl.'

'What about the Mechanicus?' growled Korahael. 'I do not see your Magos Klarn here.'

'Magos Klarn has requested that his skitarii maniple deploy within the Egressium Gate, at the foot of the command bastion, guarding the passages to the null-array. I agreed. The Knights of House Raven, sadly, are engaged elsewhere.'

Creed turned a crank, advancing the holo-projection eastward, where giants roamed.

'Baroness Vardus has successfully delayed the advance of Legio Vulcanum in the east, at great cost to her household. But Vulcanum is still nearly in range of the citadel. There is a very, very large Warlord-class with them which she cannot realistically stop.'

'What if we commit air support?' asked Highfell. 'The largest beasts are still prey to raptors.'

Creed blew air out through his lips, as if leaking cigar smoke though his stub lay cold in an ashtray. 'Already committed, I green-lit a series of strike packages suggested by Air Marshal Shrowd. And I am pleased to report that the Valkyries of the Howling Hundred-and-Nineteenth have managed to disable the tainted behemoth.'

'When can they be back here to support our own operations?' asked Eleanor.

'They won't be. The Hundred-and-Nineteenth consisted of only a dozen operational machines when Colonel Strekka volunteered for the strike. It was a martyrdom mission. He personally took the Warlord offline by diving his aircraft into the Titan's command room.'

Silence.

'The Hundred-and-Nineteenth effectively no longer exists. Apart from aircraft and crews grounded due to damage, it is non-operational.

I've transferred all active crews to the Eighth support wing – I ordered them destroyed, so I'll take in the survivors.'

'We have awarded the slain crewmen the Iron Gate, First Class,' said Kell. 'And Clavin Strekka the Star of Terra.'

'Our air support situation has not improved, then,' Korahael mused. Kell was amazed by the master's seemingly endless pessimism. 'We have scratch companies of Space Marines fighting under scratch companies of air wings, and civilian militias holding the gates. When is this madness to begin?'

'The preparations should be complete in the next twelve hours. The Salvation bunkers can be notified and set to roll open within four to six hours' notice of Urkanthos committing his forces. That should provide plenty of time to–'

But out before the Kriegan Gates, an ink-dark bolt of lightning slammed the ground.

It rent the sky in two, as if cracking reality and exposing the void beyond. Darkness rushed from it, covering the sky. All along the walls and through the fortified city, spotter lights snapped on to search for targets, then went orange and died – powercells sapped.

The holo-table in front of them blinked like a man falling asleep under sedation, then went dark.

'With respect, Lord Castellan,' said Odric A'shar. 'I do not think we have twelve hours.'

THREE

Sable lightning slammed Urkanthos into the burnt planetary crust of Cadia, the etheric teleportation burrowing through the hill of corpses heaped before the Kriegan Gates. It blew Cadian and cultist bodies aside as it struck, their mouths and eye sockets briefly alight with warpfire, jaws working in a silent chant.

When it struck topsoil, it fused the earth to glass for fifty feet in every direction.

Urkanthos knelt buried underneath the charnel heap, breathing the atmosphere he'd sworn to burn. Feeling the trickle of spilled vitae running down the corpse mound like light rain dribbling through a forest canopy.

'Master,' said Artesia, and he could feel the chill shade of her slipping through the hot darkness, fed by the blood. She settled on his shoulders and he let her bite. *'It is time to show them your glory. All of them – above and below.'*

His taloned feet hammered down, bunched shoulder muscles heaving upward so the corpses, still jittering in their electrified spasms, tumbled away from his rising form.

As he broke air, he pulled his axe free, scattering bodies. He stretched his tree-trunk limbs and shadow wings wide.

'Blood!' he bellowed. For he knew nothing else to say. *'Bloooooood!'*

And in a micro-instant of cognition, a thing sensed and known rather than seen, he knew that the corpses around him with their burning eye sockets and gaping warpfire mouths were not randomly seizing with the electrical strike.

No, their mouths were opening and closing, trying to speak with empty lungs and tongues that snapped sparks and glowed with the energy of the true reality.

Blood, the dead mouthed. *Blood. Blood. Blood.*

Around him, his Hounds of Abaddon took up the cry in a chant, not screeching or howling, but deep and bass-filled as a war-horn.

Blood. Blood. Blood.

Until the word had no meaning, only a driving sound that was near a weapon in itself.

Urkanthos made no speech. Rallied no troops and told them no plan. There was no need.

He promised them the only thing they desired.

'You will have blood!'

And then he was bounding across the battlefield, crawling three-limbed over heaps of Cadian and Khornate dead, a bulwark of the slain heaped in front of the murderous wall guns of the Kriegan Gates. They were but obstacles. Cold blood. Tacky and coagulated. Displeasing to him and his god.

No, not his god. To *him.*

For as Urkanthos tore towards the Kriegan Gates, smelling blood and crushing skulls beneath his feet, his oneness with Khorne came upon him like a violent storm. He had not been mortal for aeons, yet now he was so much more and less than he had been. Before he had used the warp like a ship catches the wind in its sail to propel its keel through the water. No more. Now he was the wind.

He was a part of Khorne himself.

A dazzling barrage of energy beams lanced from the walls, stinging his skin and punching clean holes through the Hounds around him. Arcing shells cracked open above them, showering burning chemicals that warped armour and scalded flesh.

Lascannons. Volcano lances. Incendiary phosphor shells.

Things that burned and cauterised. Incinerated warriors and left behind smears of greasy ash.

Weapons that shed no blood.

It enraged Urkanthos. That the enemy, these *pathetic* fleshbags which existed only as offerings to him, had stolen from him the substance of worship. That each drop of blood burned to carcinogenic, invisible particles was one Khorne would never taste.

He dived into the aegis line, kicking aside a shield emplacement and impaling the soldier behind it on his foot's long fore-claws. A dug-in Hellhound spewed fire at him point-blank, immolating a squad of Cadian infantry in its panicked discharge of the inferno cannon. Urkanthos sliced out with his axe and severed the turret from the tank's chassis as if striking the head from a man, then roared in indignant fury as the severed promethium lines ignited and filled the vehicle with flame.

No blood. *No blood.*

He sunk his taloned hand into the yielding steel of the wreck and levered himself over it in a jump, landing on three men in the communication trench, their ruptured insides bursting from their skins like he'd crushed rotten fruit. The rest of the squad scrambled backwards, peppering him with panicked snap-shots. He unhinged his jaw and spewed a torrent of pins and razors that rent them, stripping one side of them down to the bone and painting the trench with a fan-tail of gore.

The magic of taking what should be within, and bringing it without. Of exposing a thing down to its barest components.

His Hounds surged over the aegis line behind him, chainaxes keening songs of praise to the Taker of Skulls. Each bolt-pistol discharge throwing vitae that sanctified the air and blessed the earth when it fell like rain.

The momentary relief of the violence soothed him before a yellow dart sliced into the trench to his left, and Artesia barely had time to cloak him with her wings before the defences around him ignited in nuclear fire.

Hounds died, flash-burned to ash by the superheated air or lifted into the sky as living warriors and falling to earth as dead statues fused inside their armour.

In the past, Urkanthos had been driven deeper to rage-madness at the loss of his brothers. The precious Hounds who had followed him since the day they'd turned on the False Emperor. Each kill he'd made after suffering a loss like this one had been a lamentation, an expression of anguish, grief channelled through his axe.

Now he cared not. He was not one of them, and they were the worst kind of fools to look at him as their leader rather than their harvester. Each was a tool that helped spill more of the carmine promethium that fuelled his blazing fire – and who would, as they fell, spill their own contribution to his magnificence.

But burned they were wasted. Stolen from him.

'*Artillery!*' he howled, both yelling the order and forcing it upon the minds of his war-engines and up to the ships. '*Explosives here!*'

And as he darted towards the Stormsword super-heavy that had immolated his men, the first barrage began to fall among the retreating Cadians and the Berzerkers that hacked at them.

High-explosive rounds built to maim and disembowel flayed Cadians and Hounds alike with brass shrapnel. Airbursts coughed down cones of rusty spikes that nailed flesh to dirt and flakboard walls.

The Stormsword tried to back off, stinging him with twin streams of lascannon fire. Ground shuddered and spat beneath him, and he realised he was galloping across a strip of landmines. But his muscles were swollen hard with the fresh infusion of slaughter and he barely felt the detonations.

Axe blade met tank glacis, and in the moment before the strike, Gore-mouth sliced her wings in on either side of the weapon, scoring guide cuts in the steel that the butcher blade cracked open. The armour crumpled inward like a groundcar hitting a lumen-pole at full speed, the front of the super-heavy tank collapsing in a V-shaped gouge.

Urkanthos felt the driver, hull gunner and loader crushed between the front and outer bulkhead. Felt a pleasant sparkle of pain on his side as the gunner manning the dual heavy bolters on his left held down the trigger in an unthinking spasm as shattered ribs punctured his organs.

Deep inside, shells began to roll loose. Crew screamed.

Urkanthos did not wait. He leapt straight upward, Artesia beating her shadow-wings to propel him the last leap to the golden wall of the Kriegan Gates, where he sank his axe deep and began to climb.

'Blow the gates!' he bellowed, as a salvo of orbital fire threw debris into the air behind him, pulverising the sacrifices he had brought Khorne. *'Raptors, to me.'*

Climbing upward. Claw. Axe. Claw. Axe. Claw. Axe.

Gold plating and stone rubble rained on him with every smashing handhold.

Defenders on the wall's fighting parapet. Spitting down at him with las-fire. Shoulder-fired krak missiles streaking by, tickling him with their cotton-twists of contrail. Artesia batted the ordnance away with semi-corporeal flicks so they went tumbling and careening towards the ground.

'Blood! Blood! Blood!'

One slammed into his shoulder and detonated. And it was like boiling water had scalded him across his back. He howled with the pain, but it turned to elation as he saw his own hot blood splash the golden bas-reliefs of human ancestors. Baptising them with what was within, just as he would their descendants on the wall top.

He clawed up three more handholds and grabbed a macro-cannon protruding from the wall face. Laughing, he wrapped the barrel under one arm and levered it down like a wrestler breaking a limb – pushing with all his atrocity-fuelled strength as stone cracked and rebar strained like ligaments.

The artillery piece – barrel, breech, firing platform and all – came out of the wall, carrying a square of rockcrete with it. Panicked artillery troopers tumbled screaming into the air and dropped twenty storeys to the slaughter pit of the melee below.

Then Urkanthos swung inside to the sounds of wailing, and the banquet of red, sticky delights began.

Westol had his accident during Hellsker's time at the Hostile Environment Training School on Prosan – the first time she'd lost a trooper under her command.

Prosan was a blasted world in the Cadian System, supposedly spoiled in a long-ago war. Cooked hardpan flats and craggy mountains of volcanic glass. Drifting rad-storms that could blow up without warning. They had to wear fully sealed environment suits just to complete the daily formation marches and mock battles. It was what she'd imagined a world would be like in the wake of an Exterminatus.

Westol was a special weapons operator. A veteran. Dependable.

Far more dependable than the twenty-one-year-old Hellsker, who was fresh out of the St Gethsemane Infantry College, and building command hours to take the Captaincy exam.

Perhaps it was those years of service that had killed him. Westol, nearly forty, boasted that he'd fought in three warzones and never suffered an overheat. He lavished his weapon with preventative maintenance, often obtaining passes to continue cleaning its coils and praying to the machine spirit long past lights-out. He knew how heavy to go on the trigger.

But all three combat stripes on his sleeve came from temperate zones. Prosan was different, and his muscle memory did not adjust to the reality of its baking atmosphere.

His plasma gun failed him their second day, as they lay on the rim of a volcanic crater, firing at the mobile target servitors buzzing around the floor of the caldera below.

Hellsker sprinted to him as soon as she saw the vent of blue-white flare, an image that licked and twirled like flame but was there-and-gone in the same way as a lightning strike.

She got to him fast enough to see the plastek and rubbarine suit still running and bubbling like liquid on his raw red underskin. His face was charred on one side, and it cracked, revealing pink underneath as he screamed.

He was rolling, beating at the suit hardening on him. Teeth on the right side of his mouth had cracked in the heat discharge. He threw off his heavy rubberine gloves, which were smoking. His lovingly maintained plasma gun lay in the rocky soil, spitting liquid solar fire from its burst pipe coils that fried the earth.

Hellsker saw it just before it happened. Westol, insensate, rolled over the rim of the crater in his panic and pain. Only when his legs slid into space did he try to grab hold of the edge.

It would've been kinder to let him fall. But Hellsker didn't want to lose a man. Especially not as good a man as Westol. That was not what a good officer did.

She grabbed his reaching bare hands.

'I have you, Westol! I have you.'

But to her horror, Westol still fell, the skin of his hands and arms stripping away as though he were wearing a lady's pair of long evening gloves and was sliding out of them.

And leaving Hellsker with empty sleeves, marked with the skull-and-gate tattoos of a Cadian veteran.

For that reason, she'd been grateful that after calling for her uncle's plasma pistol, she had not yet found cause to use it. The day Cadet-Lieutenant Zander fell had been the last frontal assault – the enemy seemed to have lost the taste for it. Instead, they'd launched a series of sabotage operations and flanking manoeuvres. Volscani sappers conducted night raids on the bastion walls, trying to blow their way in and spike the guns that cost them so heavily on each approach. They conducted fire-and-move artillery strikes with field guns limbered to the back of their equine monsters. Artillery crews had spotted several large cargo haulers pulling into the valley where the Archenemy staged their attacks – clearly, they were stocking up for a big push.

Then for the last two days, it had been mountain war. Two units of Volscani pioneer companies had managed to hook around and find a line of ascent up the northern face of Rossvar's Dagger.

If it had not been for the artillery observers who had been living in the observation post since their arrival – and the warning they voxed before the Volscani butchered them – the pioneers might've seized the heights above the cleave and rained las-fire and grenades on the forces guarding the roadway.

As it was, Sergeant Plyn and his snipers had caught them on the rock face, slowing them long enough for Captain Cyung and his alpine company to respond.

But now, Cyung was stationed up there permanently, in case of a repeat. Which meant fewer lasguns on the roadway barricade when the cargo haulers came.

Not as a supply convoy – but as a weapon.

'The wheels!' Hellsker shouted into the vox-amplifier, standing like a tank commander in the open hatch of a dead Chimera. 'Not the driver, target the wheels!'

Tall and wide as a two-storey bunker hab, long as a train car, the huge vehicle barrelled towards them, engines growling with prome-thium hunger. Las-fire spanged off the slab-panels welded to the driver's windscreen. A multi-laser sketched a burning orange line across the grille, popping one of the headlumens it had kept doused so they didn't see it coming.

Heavy bolter shells chewed roadway and popped the front tyres. A missile landed short and skipped across the rockcrete like a stone on a lake, missing the vehicle entirely. The machine hurtled on towards them on the wheel rims, sparks fountaining on either side.

The trenches would be no impediment. They were mere grave-ditches now. Collapsed and stuffed with enemy dead.

Hellsker's hands shook as she raised the plasma pistol, thumb sliding the charge dial forward. Felt her tongue retreat into a knot in her throat as the gun began to hum in her fist like a living thing. When she'd taken it out of the case after receiving it at her uncle's flag ceremony – the only time she'd done so, until the cleave – she'd been so afraid of it she'd assembled it with the coil in backwards.

The hauler was nearly in pistol range. Autocannon rounds punched through the improvised armour of the crew bay, and in response it blasted its horns in defiance, filthy steam pouring from its chimney vents.

Hellsker laid her finger on the trigger. Watched each coil flare in turn from neon blue to overcook white. *Tick-tick-tick-tick-tick.*

'Sir!' Ravura said, tugging her sleeve. 'Sir, we should withdraw!'

'Not now.' She took a breath, held it, tried to control the shake of both hand and pistol.

A red warning rune winked on, a keening tone nearly covered by another air-horn wail from the hauler.

Hellsker slammed her finger all the way down.

White-hot solar energy lanced from the pistol. The recoil of the discharge was massive, and the shot climbed higher than she'd anticipated, striking the fender just above the right wheel, spalling away plasteel that dropped molten and hardened in the cold air.

Only because the overcharge stream was so long was she able

to walk it down to liquefy the three-deep metal wheel rims on its right side.

It hit the trenches already canting to one side, the shallow ditch making it heel over like an equine with a broken leg. Stressed metal groaned as the driver's cab rolled over, the momentum of the cargo container behind crushing the crew compartment against the ground as it tried to follow, then itself wallowed sideways with a double *wham-wham* as the whole smoking vehicle rolled onto its side, then its roof.

'Engineers!' Hellsker voxed over the cheers and applause. 'Secure that! It has improvised ordnance. Disable it before it–'

Hellsker was never able to finish the order. Over the cheers she heard the hammer of quad-guns and crew weapons high up in the bunker walls shooting at something now screened by the bulk of the crashed hauler.

Vox bleats sounded in her micro-bead.

'Approach! Grid nine-two-alpha–'

'Throne, it's another o–'

'–ifferent angle of approach.'

'Frekk! It's under my field of fire, can't get a bea–'

Hellsker only saw it just as it came around the head of the wrecked hauler.

Another cargo vehicle, cutting not right at them but diagonally across the mouth of the cleave towards the undamaged southern artillery barbican. This hauler was not only armoured, but also covered with wire-mesh nets that held barrels and cylinder bundles to its body.

Tube charges.

'Vehicle bomb!' Hellsker barked into her micro-bead. She was already swinging down the tank hatch and hauling it closed. Dropping so fast she accidentally booted Udza – standing below so Hellsker could use the wired handset – in the cheek. 'Cover! Cover! Cover!'

The blast wave lifted the front of the Chimera hulk into the air, tilting it backwards onto its rear track angle before dropping it back down with the swaying jolt.

Hellsker disentangled herself from the heap of struggling bodies that was her command squad. Someone was swearing about a limb fracture. She ignored it and looked out the driver's slit.

A five-storey hole – bigger than any artillery strike – had been carved out of the southern barbican. Rockcrete had shelved away into a scree slope, the interior floors of the hive-bunker defences exposed.

In one compartment, an artillery crew continued to work the gun carriage of their heavy mortar, their hyper-focus of loading and firing unaffected by the damage. One floor down, a shell-shocked trooper stumbled towards the light. His uniform jacket had been torn right off his back by the blast, and a scalp injury covered his face in blood as if he wore a red veil.

He stepped unthinkingly off the edge and dropped four casements down onto the scree.

Where the boots of a Volscani storming party trampled him.

'Twenty-Four!' Hellsker said into her micro-bead. She slammed the hatch stud at the back of the Chimera. 'Move to repel, southern barbican. Clear it room by room – and fix bayonets!'

The Archenemy was inside – and it was a blade fight now.

She drew her power sword and stoked the plasma coils to a humming brightness.

Had Trazyn been around Creed's command table, discussing the vulnerabilities of Abaddon's command structure, he would've found the present situation darkly humorous.

After all, Creed had made a similar gamble by posting the Cadian 33rd Infantry before the Kriegan Gates. Famed for their resolve, it was well known that the unit's high morale was due to the inspirational leadership of their long-time commander, Colonel Vikkam Deshane.

So when the Raptor pack dived down on the fighting platform of the Krieg Barbican, murdering his command squad and plucking the colonel into the air, the regiment lost its most crucial asset.

Still, the 33rd might have held. Fought to avenge their beloved officer.

But the Raptors knew their art, and their art was terror.

They did not kill Vikkam Deshane. Not immediately.

First they dangled him above the trenches by his arms, kicking and twisting like a prey-rodent, their vox-pickups amplifying his sobbing, pleading final words.

When they were sure the whole regiment was watching, they began to tear Deshane apart. Dropping his blood like rain. Letting pieces of him fall across the trenches. Each agonised moment broadcast and recorded so his screams continued long after he was nothing but a red skeleton.

Then, Chaos fleet guns pounded down onto the combat in a fresh barrage – killing Chaos Space Marines and Guardsmen alike.

The 33rd broke. Not in the well-ordered fighting retreat that characterised the withdrawal across the Kraf Plains, but a full rout. Dropping lasguns and stripping equipment. Abandoning trenches and vehicles. The Cadian Ninth, their heavy-weapon stations now unsupported by infantry, followed.

Berzerkers sawed into their backs as they ran. Caught them with bolt-fire as they clambered out of trenches and ran across open ground, stripping helmets and armour in an attempt to get to the few open slab-hatches that would take them through the wall. None opened to them.

Trazyn shook his hooded head, clicking. 'They have breaching charges on the gates. It's over here, Huntmaster, take us to the next line.'

Behind him, his personal deathmark closed the oubliette and prepared to translate inside Kraf Citadel.

Servantus Glave looked out of the firing slit in the third-floor bunker hab, and saw the Kriegan Gates bow inward as the breaching explosives blew.

'They held,' he said. 'Throne, they actually held.'

'Don't be so sure,' said Sergeant Veskaj, bending down to put his head next to Glave. 'Look.'

The doors were opening, slowly propelled by crowds of tiny, black-armoured figures at their base. Countless squads of Traitor Space Marines manually pushing the cyclopean doors inward foot by foot.

Hundreds of Black Legion troops poured in, like a dam gate releasing floodwaters. Raptors zipped through, breaking off in packs towards predetermined targets. Insectile war machines and daemon engines ground forward, heedless of mashing their own troops beneath their tracks.

That was when Creed's surprise fired. Two full armoured regiments lined up, their cannons pre-zeroed to the Kriegan Gates. Valkyries hovering, ready to loose ordnance.

'Fire,' said Stitcher Kristan. 'Fire, you bastards. Fi–'

Blast-shock pounded backwards through the Kraf outhabs, the sound ricocheting through the alleyways in successive claps that deafened troopers not wearing their helmets with their audio-baffling.

Earthshaker shells. Melta-shells from heavy mortars. Valkyries sent Hellstrike missiles streaking down into the mass, the rear of their under-wing rocket pods flaring in spiral patterns as they loosed orange-glowing parabolas of destruction down on the leading edge of the Hounds of Abaddon.

And ahead of that, a full regiment of Kasrkin crewing bunkers and casements, their hellguns filling the air so thick with white lasers it burned an after-image into Glave's eyes even through the tinted lenses of his helm.

'Frekking Throne!' he swore, blinking the purple streaks out of his vision.

'God-Emperor,' said Kristan. 'They're still coming.'

Glave looked back, and the medicae had been right. Hundreds of Heretic Astartes had simply disappeared, vaporised or immolated into char. Yet more came, tearing through the snowdrift-high ashes of their dead and shouting their war cry: 'Blood! Blood! Blood!'

'To positions.' Sergeant Veskaj reached back and clicked his hell-gun's reactor online. It spun up with a *pwweeeeee*. 'You know what to do. Kill as many as possible.'

'It's what I was born to do, sarge,' responded Glave.

He raised his newly issued meltagun and kissed the aquila crest on the frame.

It was not a bayonet, but if Abaddon came, it would do.

Around Creed's holo-projector, tactical officers shouted updates and reports – navigating data-slates and flipping clamp-bound intelligence binders with one hand, the other pushing their micro-beads deeper in their ears. A dozen messenger-skulls hovered like buzzing insects above a pond, awaiting answers to their queries. To one side, a Mechanicus tech-priest chanted binharic code-prayers as his mechadendrite finger-cabling attempted to stabilise the image on the overloaded holo-table. Ahead, a shell arced over the outhabs and landed just ahead of the Sororitas formation marshalling in front of the command bastion.

Faces were grim. Word had gone out to the Salvation bunkers, but vox-nets had been mangled badly, and the Valkyries dispatched to hand-deliver orders were being preyed upon by Drakes. Creed's error on Zero Day coming back to bite them again.

Thirty-six hours, Kell thought. *We have to hold them thirty-six hours.*

He tried to calm himself by immersing into the familiar chorus of an active strategium, a mix of murmuring voices and artillery fire.

'Second Kasrkin reporting hard contact, hand-to-hand fighting, casualties significant.'

'–Mordian Forty-Fourth Steelhearts now engaged, initial losses–'

'–large daemon among the gun-crews in wall-section Citadel-North, they–'

'–we're seeing a total breakdown among Thirty-Third units on the wall, they're abandoning positions–'

'You.' Creed pointed to the last tactical officer. 'Ravi, is it? What are you saying about the Thirty-Third?'

'Full retreat, sir.' Ravi, unlike the others, did not hold her ear as she worked. One had been replaced by an inbuilt augmetic. 'We thought it was just a pullback from the trenches, abandoning positions that couldn't be held. Fighting withdrawal. It's not. They're running. Full flight away from the gate along the wall and out into the streets.'

'If they're not defending the wall, that means there will be more breaches. And we can't funnel them into the outhab warrens properly.'

'No, sir.'

'Kell?' he asked. 'The orders.'

Kell did not need to ask what orders he meant. 'Sir?'

'It's time,' Creed said, holding out an expectant hand. 'Hurry, Jarran. Now, please.'

Kell pulled the two plasteel scroll-caskets from beneath his breastplate, where they'd rested ever since the sobering night he'd presented Creed with Lukas Bastonne's sword.

'General,' he said, handing them to his commander.

Creed stepped close to the junior-grade tactician and spoke low. 'Take these – listen to me, Ravi, eyes on mine, this is important. Take them yourself. No servo-skulls. No transmission. Do it in person. Take my Valkyrie and a fire-team of Kasrkin. One goes to

Air Marshal Shrowd. The other to Logistar-General Raik, who may have further orders for you. Do not open them, and do not let anyone but those two open them. No one. Not even the goddamned risen Emperor Himself, you understand?'

'Yes, sir, but my station...'

'I will put someone on your station. Go now. With speed.'

She ran.

'You, son,' Creed gestured. 'With the bionic throat. You stand in for her. Keep your eye on that wall as...' He trailed off.

'Frekk!' Creed exclaimed, tugging at his finger. 'Dumb frekking son of–'

Kell stepped in. 'What is it, general?'

'Forgot to put my seal on the damned caskets.' He pressed his signet ring into Kell's hand. 'Catch her, Kell, don't let her get on the Valk without stamping them.'

Real panic gripped Kell's throat. He should've noticed. Should've absolutely noticed. But the babble of the strategium and lack of sleep was making him sloppy. If they went out unsigned, Shrowd and Raik might not know the orders were serious. Might think they were enemy disinformation and leak them to intelligence. Hand them to Inquisitor Talia frekking Daverna. Then they'd all be against a wall.

He took off at a run, grabbing the vox-officer Kormachen and dragging him along.

'Ping the Valk, tell it not to take off until we've seen Ravi. Absolutely *do not lift,* understand?' He switched on his chest-mounted vox-hailer. 'Ravi! Tactical Officer Ravi, halt where you are. We have further order–'

On the communication bridge to the Valkyrie platform, he saw her nutwood skin and black hair flash as she turned around, as if unsure she'd heard correctly.

'Ravi come–'

The explosion threw him forward, the thunderclap *bang* of it slapping his eardrums so his hearing turned to a whining tone of tinnitus.

He was on his knees. Would've fallen except for the colours of the Cadian Eighth, which held him partially upright. Kormachen was rolling, holding his arm.

Creed. Oh Throne. The Lord Castellan.

The crater on the bastion's command deck was twenty feet across. A direct hit. Where tactical officers once circled a command table was now just a hole in the rockcrete, punctured by twisted plasteel rebar.

A junior tactical officer lay to one side, her impeccably pressed ivory command uniform unmarked despite the fact that her lower half in its blue trousers lay shoved against the opposite parapet. Two messenger-skulls wiggled drunkenly through the air, unharmed apart from the blast hooking their wire message-cages together.

'Ursarkar!' Kell shouted, forgetting in his panic the proper mode of address. 'Ursarkar!'

He tossed the colours of the Eighth to a stunned orderly and plunged into the shell hole. His bootheels slid in the loose scree and he went down on his back, slithering into the cone. 'Ursarkar!'

He saw a uniform sleeve emerging from a rubble pile and ignited his power fist, using the limb's artificial strength to lift a shelved piece of rockcrete the size of a hatch off it. The limb rolled free and he saw the gold braid and red facings of a Naval attaché.

Nearby was a piece of fabric, stained grey by atomised rock, but when Kell brushed it clean he saw it was the red robe of the tech-priest.

'Ursarkar!'

A noise answered. Coughing.

He found Creed below a piece of rockcrete the size of a coffin-lid. The Lord Castellan was dusted grey as a ghost, his hands over his face. He'd only survived because the crushed housing of the holo-table had taken the weight of the falling slab.

'Medicae! Medicae here!' Kell shouted, letting the slab fall aside and kneeling. 'Ursarkar, Ur– General, sir. Are you hit?'

Creed moaned, sat up.

'General, are you–'

'I can't see, Kell. I can't bloody see.'

'Don't try to move, sir – frekking medicae, Throne damn it! Where–'

The section medicae slid down beside them, his butterfly zip-kit already open. 'What do we have, how is he?'

'I'm f–' Creed started.

'He says he can't see.'

'Concussion blindness,' the medicae said, clicking on a handheld stablight. 'Sir, if you could put your hands down.'

'I–' Creed started, then coughed out chalky dust. His face was covered in the rockcrete powder, with clean trails in the pattern of his fingers.

'Sir, don't speak,' said Kell, putting a hand on Creed's shoulder. 'Concussion blindness, that can be temporary, right? Shell shock.'

'Could be.' The medicae upended a canteen over the Lord Castellan's head to wash away the debris and shined his light in Creed's squinting eyes. 'But it could also be detached retinas, trauma to the brain's visual centre, even internal damage from the pressure change. I–'

Creed slapped the stablight out of the medicae's hand.

'Will you frekking sons-of-deserters listen? It's not frekking concussion blindness, it's this Throne-damned frekking thing!' He thumped the triangular refractor field on his chest. 'Bastard flashed like a photon grenade when it went off. I told you I don't like these things, Kell.'

'You're better off than the rest of the command section,' Kell said.

Creed looked around. 'Oh shit. They got damn close, didn't they?'

'Too close,' said Kell, turning towards the crater rim. 'Kormachen?'

'Sir?' The vox-officer looked down, he was pressing one arm against his chest, with the other hand on the vox-receiver built into his helmet.

'Are you wounded, Kormachen?'

'No, colour sergeant, just an arm fracture. I'll be fine.'

'Raise that damned Militia Colonel Ghent, ask him what he's doing about those artillery spotters.'

'Actually, he's on the vox now, sir – he says it's locked in.'

It was the first one that had been the most difficult, Salvar Ghent reflected. But that was always the case, wasn't it? The first credit you stole, the first sexual conquest, the first murder – you had to get over that initial one before you had confidence and momentum.

This was the same way. At first, with only two of the specialist voxes, they hadn't been able to triangulate the signals when they picked them up. Both vox-operators would scan up and down the bandwidth before they hit on a signal, then they'd both tune to it and wait, hoping they'd catch a request for a strike, and there would be a second follow-up message acknowledging the hit or walking the second barrage closer to target.

But with two voxes, they only caught the direction of the broadcast – meaning that even when they dispatched their teams of triggermen the search parties had to comb half a district top to bottom.

Finally, they staked out a likely target – an airfield against the citadel wall – and waited. It took them three searches and three separate broadcasts, but they found the woman at the top of a chimney-stack in an abandoned manufactorum, camped out on an internal maintenance catwalk.

Then they had three voxes – and things became easy. They got momentum. Learned the broadcast patterns and types of places the spotters liked to hide.

Trigger teams fanned out all over Kraf, embedding themselves in districts and waiting for a call to bring them coordinates.

They shoulder-barged doors in hab-blocks, climbed up weather-monitoring towers, kicked down the sheet metal walls of rooftop sheds. Each time they ended it with a blistering hammer of shots from their short pattern auto-carbines, the kind with drum magazines that were easy to hide under a cloak.

Each time, they got another vox. And their citywide interception net became larger and more tightly webbed, able to catch the really cunning fish.

Like this one.

'Eeeehwaaah oooreee. Eeeewaaah ooooreee,' the vox hissed.

The bell-ringer put the magnocular scope up to his eye, the broad form of his back hunched over the specialist vox. His positioning was brilliant. A north-western bell-tower that had a clear view west all the way out to the curtain wall, but could still see the northern citadel martialling ground through a screen of gun towers.

He put the magnocular down, and reached for the receiver, and Ghent distantly observed that he had a clubbed hand.

'Is that why you didn't change your broadcast channel?' he asked. 'Is it hard for you with the one hand?'

The bell-ringer's hand froze over the receiver, then relaxed.

'It's you,' he said, turning. 'For a minute I thought...'

His words trailed off when he turned around. Whomever he'd expected to see, it was not Ghent in his rumpled officer's greatcoat and slicked hair, a pair of aquilas shining at his throat.

'It was a lot of trouble finding you, did you know that?' Ghent said. 'Good spot you have here. We expected whoever was dropping ordnance up north was in the northern district. It stands to reason, right? You shouldn't be able to see the northern muster fields from here, at least not normally. But then we remembered that melta torpedo yesterday. Punched right through the skyshield.

Dud, supposedly, but still brought down the Hydra flak tower that was blocking the line of sight between here and the muster field.'

The bell-ringer's throat worked, the knot there bobbing.

'*Eeeeeh waaaaah ooooreee…*' the vox bleated.

'Shh, sweetheart.' Ghent looked at the vox with a finger to his lips. 'We'll get to you in a moment… I'm dealing with your greedy friend here.'

The bell-ringer was still frozen, his hand clamping and unclamping above the vox-receiver.

'That's how we sniffed you out – you got greedy. Didn't change frequencies. You could taste that big score, that next artillery hit right out of your reach. I always warn my people about that. It's what gets you caught. Too much thinking about the end result, and you stop being careful. And suddenly, someone you really don't want to see is standing in your door.'

'I've killed him,' the bell-ringer croaked. 'That oppressive bastard Creed. He pretended he was different, but he still sent men like me to menial labour, called us civilian scum and lied to our faces while cutting our rations. I've killed him for the liberator Abaddon, and in revenge for a million Cadian children weeping due to empty bellies.'

As he spoke, the bell-ringer's hand drifted towards the vox-set.

'If you were hungry,' said Ghent, steeling himself to move. 'You should've come to me.'

The bell-ringer was fast. Snatching the stub pistol up from the floor with a strength that came from hauling one-handed on bell ropes for two decades. He rose up from the floor, snarling with brown teeth.

Ghent didn't draw, he just stepped aside.

The triggerman behind him already had his autogun levelled, held in a hip-shooting position found in no Cadian drill manual, but ruinously effective at short range.

Solid slugs the size of a fingertip chopped into the bell-ringer, tearing his robes and driving him backwards as his muscles spasmed from the trauma. His stubber discharged a single shot that flattened against the cathedral bell above, tolling out a final note as he fell backwards through the window arch where he'd looked down upon the soldiers of Cadia like a vengeful god.

Ghent did not bother to look where the bell-ringer fell. He merely crossed the tower and scooped up the vox-receiver, waiting for the last of the reverberations to die away before hitting the transmit rocker.

'Hello, hello,' he said. 'Are you still there? Confirm.'

'*Eeeeeh waaaaaah ooooreee...*'

'And you're going to get it, my friend. Much more.'

He reached out and slammed the key loader switches to neutral, dropping the channel encryption.

'Kraf Air Command, I know you're listening. Triangulate this signal. Fix origination point outside Kraf as ground target, we narrowed it down to sector...' He snapped his fingers, gestured.

A woman with one of the illicit voxes on her back shuffled into the room, showing him a map.

'We put it in sector six-gamma-three, happy hunting.'

The squealing, breathy voice at the other end of the broadcast fell silent, as if stopping in the middle of an inhalation.

He hated to admit it, but Ghent was having fun.

Ten minutes later, *War-Kite* dropped in on the approach.

They were right where air command said they were going to be. Three spite engines that had once been super-heavy artillery. Webs of spongy flesh stretched across their armoured hulls. Big, snail-like bulges humped over the chassis, enormous cannons of bone and metal angled out like a telescope from an observatory.

They'd slipped out from under the camouflage netting that had hidden them for days. Trying to run on their tracks and stubby anchor-legs that pushed them along like tortoises.

War-Kite wavered as it came in, the targets sliding back and forth through Keztral's targeting reticle as she lined up the bulbous shells.

'Take it slow, Kite-One,' counselled Ragnal. *'We'll keep the bats off your pass, save fuel for the climb out.'*

'Incoming on your nine, Rag, half a mile, he's on you.'

'Thanks, Vikka, I'll lead him on, you tag him out.'

'Affirm.'

Her escorts. She had dedicated escorts now. Lieutenants Steren Ragnal and Vikkalyn Mak. Both Navy, both mounted in Thunder-bolts – and both extremely deadly against Chaos interceptors.

'On the line,' Keztral said. She eased back the throttle and placed her finger on the stick's main trigger, feeling the shivering vibra-tion through her feet as the bolt cannon – so much heavier and faster than the picter rig – rotated in preparation.

In her peripheral vision, a burning wreck fell from the sky.

'Got him,' said Mak. *'Locust down.'*

Groundfire streaked up, green and orange. A few bursts of multi-laser fire. Minor impacts – heavy bolter rounds, maybe – clattered off the bottom of one armoured wing. Nothing serious, most Arch-enemy troops were throwing themselves at Kraf.

A lock tone. She punched the countermeasures and flare-fires blossomed around her wings. Two rockets zipped below her cockpit, seeking the already disappearing heat bloom.

'Firing in three,' she said. 'Two.'

The abominations were coming up fast now, a thousand feet out. Her altimeter read two hundred feet.

'One.'

War-Kite fired its first shots in anger.

The discharge rattled the cockpit hard enough she had to set her teeth. Behind, she heard a *click-click* as Darvus' identity tags swung back and forth into the back of the heavy stubber – she'd hung them around the servitor's neck.

Bright yellow barrel flare stabbed out from below the nose of the aircraft like a dragon breathing fire – Throne, it had to be twenty feet long. Smoke like trailing cloud streaked by either side of her canopy. The noise was like the sky tearing in half.

Plutonium-cored anti-armour bolt-shells ripped into the dome of the lead spite engine at a rate of twenty per second. It stoved the shell in, pulped the unnatural flesh beneath, threw a debris cone that peppered the next engine with flaming metal and viscera. Keztral pulled up, dragging the stream of punishment into the second engine, and this time added ribbons of crimson from her lascannons that over-penetrated and carried into the third engine.

It was already burning when she swept her bolt cannon over it and scythed through a bulbous outgrowth that looked disturbingly like a head.

'Good pass!' she yelled.

'Good hit, Kite-One, now up! Up! Drakes inbound. Remember, don't get screwed, get altitude. Do the crime, then climb, climb, climb!'

Ragnal liked mnemonic devices. An annoying but useful trait.

Keztral banked hard over and rolled out right, then turned over on her other wing to confuse any Heldrake dive-killers, punching her throttle forward to climb out steep.

Air command had learned a lot about how to operate against Drakes since Day Zero. Or at least, anyone still alive had. They dived and turned like raptors, but climbed like pregnant groxes. If you wanted to live, you spent as little time at low altitude as possible – but make a speedy ascent and get on top of them and most of the time you could spend a leisurely seven or eight seconds securing a hard lock before wrecking them with a hunter-killer.

Out the left side of her canopy, she saw the charcoal-black and coal-orange of a fireball rolling skyward as one of the spite-engines cooked its ammunition.

'*That's first blood for you, isn't it, Keztral?*' asked Mak.

'But not the last,' she answered.

In her crew mirror, she could see the pale-skinned servitor, its mouth sewn shut and Darvus' identity tags around its cable-laced neck.

'I have enough for another pass,' she said. 'Let's find a new target.'

FOUR

Cracks of bolt-fire echoed from the rubble in ones and twos. Bright daggers of flame lighting the matt-black of the crusaders' armour.

Mordlied knelt before Amalrich, placing his helm on his knee.

'Marshal,' he said, his voice soft.

Amalrich looked out over what was once the Martyr's Rampart.

Its corners and lines were shapeless debris now, no block of masonry sitting neatly on the other. Flamers had burned the fire-step black, melta-shots had made rivers of liquid stone that had cooled and hardened like lava flows. Corpses, human and otherwise, lay scorched to disarticulated bone or fused into the very rock.

'Send Squad Purgatos to the foot of the rampart,' Amalrich said to his herald. 'They think they can withdraw and rest. We will provoke another attack.'

The Marshal's tabard was charred brown, his great sword nicked and battered.

'Marshal,' repeated Mordlied.

'I heard you.'

'I have discovered our sin. It has come to me in a vision.'

'You are mistaken.' The Marshal looked down upon him with clouded brow. 'You mean you have discovered *your* sin. It is with you that your vision–'

'Every one of our brothers who has carried the banner has died. How many hands has it passed through? Nine? Ten? It is true I was the first, and I lost honour by dropping the banner – but it is a judgement not on me, but the whole crusade.'

Amalrich's gauntlet drifted from the hilt of his sword, settling on the beaded rosary that hung at his waist. His fingers rubbed the charm at the end of the loop – a reliquary containing the finger bone of Saint Xanda.

'What could we have done to displease the Emperor? Look at these defences. We swore to hold here in the face of hell. We have done so. To suggest otherwise dishonours the memory of our brothers.'

'That is pride speaking, Marshal. And pride is a sin. We have held our own vows above the work set before us. Listen.'

Amalrich did so. Even in the slack of the fighting, they could hear the pound and roll of explosions far to the north.

'Kasr Kraf requested our aid, and we refused. Our pride has led us astray, and the Emperor has judged us for it. We have fallen to the stubbornness of our gene-father, Dorn. But there is still time to redeem ourselves – Creed still calls for us, and we have one working Thunderhawk.'

'That is not possible – we are committed by our own words. We made a sacred vow to defend this rampart, before the Emperor and with our hands on holy relics.'

'Marshal, this is a ruin. It has not been a rampart for a long while – and we did not vow to defend a ruin.'

As Mordlied looked up, his head still bowed but eyes raised, he saw Amalrich's mouth tighten. The two surviving members of his command squad turned their heads, almost imperceptibly, to await their master's response.

'Tell me,' said Amalrich, 'about this vision.'

* * *

He did not need to sleep for the dreams now. When the Empty Man wanted him to sleep, he slept. No matter what he was doing.

His eyelids were pink and puffy, there was a bad scrape on his forehead. When the last dream came, he had been walking up a flight of stairs to make a check on one of his artillery spotters. So many of them had fallen silent, and he wanted to know why.

Consciousness vanished in an eye-blink. In mid-stride.

When he awoke, he was face down on the steps, his head bleeding and one of his molars knocked loose. He'd slid ten feet down on his face.

And he stayed there, face down, because boots were slapping past him as men ascended the stairs. One trod on Rovetske's hand and he had to bite his cheek to keep from shouting. Lingering echoes from the Empty Man told him to stay down, to let them pass him like the corpse the killers thought he was. There were, after all, so many dead in this city. No one gave bodies a second glance apart from looting them.

He heard the bang of a door, a blister of autogun fire. And then he stopped his breath as the boots descended again.

One paused to pat the pockets of Rovetske's Administratum uniform, looking for ammunition or lho-sticks. And for a brief moment of panic, Rovetske thought how cold the night was and how the man must feel his body heat.

'*I am cold,*' he whispered, so low it was barely audible. No louder than two fingers rubbing against one another. '*I am dead flesh, and have nothing worth falling behind for.*'

The hand stopped mid-frisk and withdrew.

Rovetske waited a long time after the footsteps disappeared down the stairwell.

His agent was dead. The specialist vox with its key loader and codebook gone.

At least he knew what was happening to them. Gunned down by death-squads, hunted like animals, which was after all always how the Imperium treated humans.

Despite the investment of time and effort to deploy the network, and the hours he'd spent personally training the spotters, Rovetske could not bring himself to be too upset. An operation like that was always going to have an expiration date, and the agents themselves were expendable.

Already the Empty Man had entrusted him with a new purpose. One far more targeted.

For in the dream the cloudy eyes of the Empty Man had shown him where he would find the object. Where it had landed, and where it was to be delivered.

The most difficult thing was manpower. His network of agents had been significantly reduced by the campaign of assassination, and the vehicle and body-bombers had a natural attrition rate.

He made contact with a saboteur cell he'd seeded in the tunnel and sewer maintenance department of the Administratum. Work crews like that were useful, since even the local gangs that haunted the underground tended to let them pass unmolested. No one wanted a tunnel collapsing on their heads, after all.

The object was exactly where the Empty Man said it would be. It looked as it had when the warp-roiled irises had burned the image into his brain.

It had smashed through the city, taken out a building, buried itself in the street. Its outer casing still glowed with heat when they found it, the beams of their industrial stablights playing through the smoke curling from its metal exterior.

'Throne!' said the foreman, his heresy forgotten in his shock. 'Is that...?'

'Don't think about what it is,' said Rovetske. 'Just get the jacks under it, raise it. And get the repulsor sled here.'

'We're... going to move it? How? It's too big. We can't even manoeuvre–'

'It will be all right,' Rovetske said, injecting empathic will into his words. 'I have all in hand. We do not need to move the whole assembly, just this part.'

The foreman's tight shoulders relaxed, and he nodded. 'All in hand, sir.'

'Good boy.' Rovetske knelt and opened his toolbox, selecting the bolt-fastener he'd seen in his vision.

His last thought was that the steel tool was cold, but then he blinked and his eyelids refused to open.

On the backs of his shut lids, blooming like the violet of a warp storm in the dark Cadian sky, were the Empty Man's eyes. Far away, he heard the sound of the tool ratcheting again and again.

Krrrrrt. Krrrrt. Krrrrt.

When he awoke, it was because of the pain in his fingers.

They were bleeding, the nails ragged and broken. And he realised that they had been used along with the bolt ratchet to manually extract the screws in the object. Their flesh was tender and bruised.

Which is why it hurt so much to strangle the foreman. He was a big man, after all, with a muscular neck. Rovetske tasted blood where the hulking worker had struck him in the mouth. He'd had to put his knees on the barrel chest to keep him forced down while he killed him.

The rest of the crew were already dead, slumped over jacks and lifting equipment. Bloodstained tools from his kit lay scattered on the tunnel floor, as if they had calmly continued working as he'd bludgeoned them one by one.

The foreman though, he was smarter, stronger, more resistant.

But he was also turning purple, foaming at the mouth.

They couldn't live, the Empty Man said from behind his lids. The words came as he blinked, like a strange dot-dash military code. *They have served their purpose to the Despoiler.*

And knowing it was true, Rovetske leaned his body weight down on his hands until the foreman stopped moving.

He was shaky and weak when he arose, but that did not matter. The can of promethium was not heavy, and it became lighter the more he splashed on the big cylinder and the bodies that lay around it.

The object on the repulsor sled, marked with bloody fingerprints where he'd twisted and pulled out the bolts with his own hands, moved easily on its cushion of anti-grav field as he slid it away from the flames. He moved it carefully, so very carefully, whispering soothing prayers to its machine spirit.

One had to be cautious with such a thing, after all. The cousin of this god-munition had levelled Kasr Stark.

And it would not do for the inner warhead-shrine to detonate while on the sled.

At least, not until it had arrived at its intended place of apotheosis.

In the chamber Yann Rovetske saw in the flickering, nearly imperceptible darkness of an eye-blink.

When the rage and bloodlust built high enough, war stopped being war.

Defeat enough enemies, and it was a fight not a battle. A personal struggle of self against the foe. Less an exercise in strategy, in objectives secured or ground taken, than a need to act one's internal emotions upon the adversary.

Push beyond that, and the fight became a harvest. So much blood swelling Urkanthos' muscles and hardening his hide that the concept of individual victories and struggles became too abstract. The enemy was no more than wheat to be scythed. Grapes to be trampled. And he entered a state where he would no more remember killing a specific opponent than he could recall cutting a single stalk of grain.

That was the level Urkanthos had reached when he burst through the exterior wall of the Kriegan Gates and dived into the ranks of livestock on the other side.

That's what they were: livestock. Receptacles for vitae. Inside the cage of his helm, his yellow, vertically slit eyes peeled away their skins and muscle so all he perceived were pulsing circulatory systems branching away from hearts the way root systems fan out of a plant bulb.

And in cutting them, rupturing those veins and tearing open arteries so their quick-beating hearts spilled more libations for the Lord of Battle, Urkanthos cared not if one came from Mordian or another was a Kasrkin in heavy armour. Even those ensconced in the thick hulls of tanks were merely blood within a metal shell. Hellgun beams and bolt impacts prickled harmlessly on his bone-hard skin. And when a new regiment threw itself at him in a disorganised wave, he was halfway through their ranks before noticing that these hearts were strong, but also small and young – a full regiment of Whiteshield conscripts.

He drove a wedge into the ranks, into the warren of streets behind where his daemon sight picked up hearts pulsing and thumping in the buildings – terror-fast, like prey animals in the presence of the predator.

They meant to trap him. Funnel his Hounds into alleys and kill-zones. He could see ambushes set up at corners, weapon-teams manning bunkers, humans crouching or lying in a mistaken belief they could hide from him.

He charged into the main thoroughfare, across a belt of landmines that stung his flanks. Plunged a hand into a bunker hab's second floor and ripped the wall out, casting four men into the street and scooping another into his mouth, where his teeth punched through thick carapace armour.

'*Into the streets!*' he yelled. '*My Hounds, track them, find them, kill them!*'

And behind him came the Hounds of Abaddon – already bloodied and reduced by the breakthrough, following him because they worshipped slaughter, and he was its embodiment.

Let the Cadians spring their ambushes. Let them butcher the Hounds of Abaddon. It was simply more blood for the altar.

Urkanthos, prince of daemons, ran ape-like on his knuckles through the streets and into the gory celebration that would follow.

'Holy Terra!' Sergeant Veskaj swore. 'What was that?'

Glave saw it too. Big and crimson, a blur that rushed past the loophole hatch, too fast and close for him to get a proper look.

'I don't know, but it's big,' he answered. 'Heavies will deal with it. As for us...'

He could hear the madman howls and chainswords of the approaching Berzerker pack and unshrouded his meltagun, sticking the barrel through the stepped-back loophole that ran the length of the bunker hab.

He didn't have to wait long. Glave had barely finished muttering the Benediction to Peace and Invocation of Violence when a rush of beetle-black armour filled the street below.

'Let them get further in,' said Veskaj. 'Steady... steady...'

The spirit moved him, Glave pulled the trigger, and two Chaos Space Marines melted.

'Damn your eyes, Glave!' Veskaj poured fire from his hellgun down into the mass.

Amber runes on Glave's meltagun blinked, requesting he wait until gas build-up allowed another shot. While waiting, he triggered a frag grenade and pushed it out the slit. By the time it exploded with a dull *wumpf* and a rattle of shrapnel on ceramite, his meltagun was already at the loophole again.

Another Berzerker fell, legs incinerated and hip joints fused.

Still it clawed across the ground towards the bunker even as its companions ran it over.

'On the stairs!' Stitcher Kristan warned. He was watching their backs with a hellpistol. Below, one of the trip-mines they'd rigged discharged with a cough of directional pellets and a harsh screech of shrapnel on armour plate.

They were on the second floor already. Fast, so fast.

Glave spun, advancing towards the door with the meltagun already angled to sweep the stairs. On the indicator, amber block-runes counted their way upwards to full charge. One amber. Two. Three.

He saw an empty landing below. Nearly full ch–

The stairwell wall broke inward as the transhuman madman rammed through the wall rather than turning the corner. It put the heretic nearly at the top of the flight, close enough that he swung his chainaxe at Stitcher Kristan and buried it in the rockcrete doorway as the medicae flinched backwards. Red smoke jetted from a helm grille bristling with ivory teeth.

'*Blood!*' it howled.

Green rune.

The melta-beam liquefied the Traitor Space Marine from eye-lenses to hips, his massive disconnected parts – the legs still pumping in a run – rolling down the stairs and leaving the chainaxe buried in the doorway.

'They're climbing the building!'

Screams from the firing slit. Sergeant Veskaj howling as a spiked gauntlet punched through the narrow window to grab him and force a bolt pistol into his chest.

It discharged, and the screams stopped.

Glave swivelled with his meltagun, but the assailant at the vision slit was already gone, letting the sergeant's corpse drop on the floor.

'Stairs again!' shouted Stitcher Kristan.

Glave spun back. The legless Berzerker he'd seen below was trying to scramble up the stairs towards them, shouting blasphemies.

Glave vaporised it, leaving another pool of liquid armour slag hardening on the stairs.

'Three floors,' said Kristan.

'What?' Glave snapped.

'No legs. It had no legs, but it clawed up three floors trying to kill us.'

Glave thought about that, then swept the beam of his meltagun along the rockcrete stairs, eating away at the grey stone and metal supports beneath.

'Well the next one will have to jump for us.'

For days, Morkath had assumed the enemy was clever. Evasive. One step ahead of her. That the Wolves of Fenris were such skilled trackers and wildsmen that they could expertly navigate even the untamed, fathomless depths of her mother.

She was wrong.

For near a week Morkath had plumbed the known areas of her fortress. Pushed enough warp energy into her nodeshrine to grow an amniotic sac connected to the nervous system of semi-organic warp channels grown into the holes in the blackstone.

Once it was ready, she'd crawled inside the tight confines of the womb and filled it with the warp-conductive fluid medium that blocked out the noise and movement of the outer world and let her mind wander.

She passed her internal eye through the vessels and arteries of the skin and nerve-bundles she'd grown through the warp-charged stone. Opened rheumy eyes set in walls and ceilings and floors. Read the thoughts of maintenance-slaves so catatonic with the terror of their thralldom that their memories were near blank. A Fenrisian might have walked past them, barging one aside and breaking its shoulder, and ten minutes later it might not have remembered the event.

Twice she gathered her strength and sent a pulse through the nervous system that awakened the imperative cantrip she'd psychically grafted into the minds of the chattel. For two hours in each instance, they stopped all but the most vital tasks and searched for the invaders.

Once they found a Guardsman, separated and alone. A frail mortal who Morkath could capture for psy-vivisection, slicing and peeling until she could retrace his steps and find the rest of the vermin.

But the fortress slaves were half-feral even without the imperative cantrip activated. And once that switch was thrown, there was little she could do to restrain them. By the time she secured a mag-lev transport and directed it to the nearest stable chamber, the thralls had chewed him to little more than a skeletal marionette.

We really should be feeding them more, she thought.

Thankfully, Cadians made good helmets – the brain was intact.

Few of the Warmaster's brotherhood had retained a functioning omophagea organ. For reasons that remained unknown, the touch of the true universe appeared to either send it into maladjusted overdrive or wither it entirely. But she knew Cacadius Siron, the Warmaster's intelligence chief, was one of the few whose gene-seed was healthy enough to practise the old art.

Morkath could not help but watch, fascinated, as Siron's full lips chewed the Cadian's grey matter.

'Lost,' Siron proclaimed, as if judging the quality of a steak. 'In the terror of flight. He did not know where he was headed.'

'How was he separated from the others?'

'Not separated, severed. I see fortress doors opening and closing.

Chambers twisting. He was with the Wolves. One said...' He concentrated, lined brow furrowing.

'Yes?'

'A Wolf said the fortress was letting them through. Or baiting them into a trap. They do not know which. It was allowing them passage through the wild deep. Places we have not charged with the warp.'

'Could the fortress be bringing them to us?'

'That is what he thought, but the Wolves did not believe so. They believe, sorry, *believed,* it wanted them there. Except then came a door. A door that cycled, like an airlock. Only one at a time could step through. He went through between others – but when he stepped through... Strange.'

'Describe it to me. I will know.'

'He stepped out of the door and saw them on the other side of a crystal wall. But they couldn't see him. And he was... at an odd angle. Looking at the bottom of their shoes. As if the airlock chamber had moved like the cylinder of a stub revolver, depositing him in a neighbouring room. He banged his hand numb on the wall, hearing them ask where he had gone, but they could not hear him. Then they walked... They walked up the wall like insects, footsteps echoing strangely. Rising higher and higher in the limitless cyclopean chamber until their stablights no longer played on the crystal wall.'

'And then he ran?'

'No... Then another door opened, and he followed it. He followed it for two days until he heard voices, and thought he'd found the Wolves again. But it was your thought-thralls.' He shrugged. 'Then they ate him. Was that helpful?'

'It was,' she said, sucking air over her blackstone teeth. 'Now I know why I have been unable to find the Wolves.'

'Do you?' he asked. It was with a disarming casualness, almost conversational. And before Morkath caught herself, she almost betrayed too much to the spymaster. She had almost called the fortress *my mother*.

'The fortress has been hiding them from me. Directing the vermin away from the reformatted and warp-treated parts of its body I can see, guiding them to a place it wants them to go. The *Will of Eternity* is aiding its own sabotage.'

'And this pitiful mortal, what purpose in breaking it off from the group?'

'A decoy. It knows I am searching. We must be getting close, and it's trying to divert the search to another sector of the fortress. It broke off the least valuable one. The one that it considered disposable. That is why I know the fortress is using him, otherwise he would not have survived alone.'

'It is treating us like an infection. Like parasites. Trying to purge us.'

Morkath could say nothing to this, because she knew it was true. Her mother fortress had rejected her entirely.

'Do you know that crystal chamber? The revolver cylinder?' As Siron asked, he brought up a wire-frame schematic of the known areas of the fortress. Purple warp-blooms blossomed over the areas she had charged with empyric force. 'He was discovered here, yes?'

'Close, here, in the outer drive chamber. But I doubt the fortress is letting saboteurs into its motive array. There are several cylinder-chambers like you described...'

'But how many within two days' walk?'

'One,' she said, pointing. 'Here. One entrance leads to four branching pathways.'

'Do any lead to critical systems?'

'None that avoid chambers we've inhabited. They'll be spotted. Except... What's this? This red spot?'

'Dead chamber,' said Siron. 'Backfire from when we used the weapon. It vented strangely and burned away our organic additions. It was marked for you to recolonise.'

'Gods of the warp, that chamber's the only buffer between the deep fortress and the port-side shields.'

'Summon a mag-lev, I'll get a team.' He swivelled away from the schematic, raising a hand to his ear. 'Cell Vega-Two. Meet the Fortress Child at mag-egress point...'

'Seven.'

'...seven. Full tactical loadout, expect contact with Space Wolves boarding party and various Imperial auxiliaries. Bring melta weapons for blackstone-breaching. Consider the fortress hostile.'

Morkath opened her mind to the roiling Chaos of the true dimension and slammed her hands onto her mother's bulkhead. In doing so, she both called a mag-lev and pumped the fortress full of the poison she felt at her betrayal.

Around the hatch, the blackstone underneath the layer of webbed flesh moaned as the dermal surface ran to wet pink. Ivory horns emerged from the nascent gums, surrounding the mag-lev hatch with a prickling maw of hooked teeth.

Morkath hoped it hurt her. Like she had her daughter.

The Cadians had sprung their trap, and now Urkanthos ravaged it.

He raked his claws through hab-bunkers as though they were made of sponge. Artesia screeched in delight as her razor-edged shadows flowed into firing slits and decapitated Kasrkin in sprays of gore. A squadron of Sentinels ambushed his flank, stinging his ribs with lascannon fire, and he fought them like a grown man battling children. One he knocked flat with a backhand, crumpling its cockpit with the blow. With his axe he slew the second, driving the blade into the body like he would a skull and leaving it there – keeping his hands free to grab the third, rip open its armoured panelling with his teeth, and pulverise the pilot with a butt of his caged head.

'Prince!' Artesia whispered. *'Prince, look upon your host. We have been lost in slaughter too long. The Hounds have sacrificed too much.'*

The orbits and solar variances of this physical world meant little to Urkanthos now – still less the arbitrary division of those gravitational forces. Yet as he looked through the red tunnel of his vision and saw the Blackstone Fortress rising above the eastern horizon, he realised how long he'd revelled in butchery.

He could see the evidence of it in the blood.

So much vitae. An amount that made focusing difficult. Now that he'd slowed his violence, it was impossible to sense anything but the blood. The same way a rotting corpse drove out every smell in a room, the arterial bounty overcame all.

Urkanthos saw the world as blood on darkness, all moving slow. He knew walls only due to the splatters upon them. Saw his Hounds moving in their thick coats of gore, the fluid, underwater speed of their blows flinging arcs of crimson in the air. Pools of red describing casualties in the upper floors of the bunkers. The Baneblade *Vicanthrus* rolling over a squad of Guardsmen – bursting them like skins of wine – as they tried to escape a collapsing building.

At the end of the street, three Berzerkers were flying apart. Rounds from a heavy weapon detonated inside them, so limbs tumbled and breastplates blossomed open to show wet outlines of shattered ribs and pulsing organs.

There were so few left of his Hounds. He had led them into these streets knowing they would be an abattoir for both friend and foe, but he had never imagined such a price. For each dead Kasrkin, they had to blast open plasteel doors, carve through casements. Brave overlapping fields of fire from murderous heavy weapon squads as well as the plasma and melta beams that curdled and cooked the blood with their passing. As Scourgemaster of the Black Fleet and leader of the Hounds, he had always known that in a stand-up fight he would lose one Berzerker for every fifty Guardsmen slain – a hundred, if the thing was done right.

But these Kasrkin, they were themselves warriors of the blood. He had never seen their like outside the hated, unenlightened Chapters of the Adeptus Astartes. As his daemon-sight flew, he saw a wounded Kasrkin discharging a hellgun point-blank into a Berzerker's lower abdomen – his bayonet broken on the power armour. A sergeant with a power sword counter-charged against a whole file of Lazcare's pack, taking down one with his plasma pistol before a chainaxe split him shoulder to hip.

Several streets over, a line of bunker habs four blocks long lifted into the air in a curtain of flame, tearing apart forty warriors from Pergaza's contingent. The mortals had contested the buildings until the Khornates stormed it, then triggered pre-rigged explosives. The Cadians had baited his warriors inside then sacrificed their own lives to annihilate them.

'*Count our dead to theirs,*' he said to Artesia, and she flashed off his shoulders and circled. '*How steep is the butcher's bill?*'

'*One Hound for every thirty mortal dead, master! They are standing unto death, bringing your warriors with them into the blood-sleep.*'

'*And they say the Adeptus Astartes know no fear. Even the Corpse-Emperor's sons do not throw away their lives with such wantonness. One Hound for every thirty. It is unthinkable. Perverse.*'

'*And yet,*' hissed Artesia, clamping back on to his shoulders and whispering in his ears with bloody-lipped mouths that opened on each wing. '*The problem is also the solution. Look at the streets.*'

He looked, and saw the rivers. A literal floodtide of blood, deep as a human hand, flowing down the rockcrete streets and lapping in dead-end courtyards. Warriors splashed gouts of it as they ran, sent great deltas of it in the air when they fell.

'*Call your kin,*' said Urkanthos.

'*This close to the antipathy-broadcaster they may not come. The bloodletters fear it, the thing we are here to destroy. Their minds recoil at the vibrations of emptiness it projects within the city.*'

'*Then call something with no mind.*'

Urkanthos knelt in the street, planting both hands into the tide of carnage. Heedless of the blizzard of las-fire that burned the air around him neon and blackened the muscles of his exposed back. So swelled was he with the power of the ritual offerings, he did not even feel it. If he let some of that power out, he would still have enough to break Cadia in two.

'*Come,*' he bade. '*Come and run and feast. Push your muzzles deep into the foe and slake your thirst.*'

The blood stilled, mirror-smooth. Surface going tacky and dark like a wound drying before a scab.

Then Artesia gave a low whistle, like a huntsman, and the skin of the blood began to stretch and distort like a membrane. Beasts pawed at the underside, thrusting blunt snouts against the elastic surface and stretching it so their rolling eyes were visible through the gore portal's distorted surface. Thin sounds of baying and snuffling came from a place far outside reality.

Then a claw ripped through, and the membrane popped like a blister.

Out of the hand-deep blood came creatures bigger than a human, scrabbling and snapping, huge heads emerging just before muscular shoulders that levered their bodies out of the rivers and pools of crimson. They barked and growled, shook themselves so droplets flew from their scaled hides and the Khornate runes on their heavy collars flew back and forth.

And then with a mere thought from the arch-daemon who had become their master, they charged.

The interior portcullis gate of the muster field dented inward with the force of the daemon's might. Behind it, even through the stuttering fizz of the inner void shield, Creed could hear the howl of fleshless throats. The portcullis took another hammer-blow.

Across the muster field, behind the firing slits and crenellated slabs of an aegis line hastily thrown up between ferrocrete bunkers and redoubts, the Cadian Eighth waited.

'Steady,' he said, into the handset connected to Kell's laud-hailer. They'd taken a position on the central redoubt, quad lascannon batteries positioned on either side. 'They're coming through any minute now. Remember that at your back is the last free city on Cadia. At your front are your comrades in the Kasrkin, who have sacrificed themselves to thin the enemy and absorb their strength. Supporting you are the Sisters of Our Martyred Lady and the Whiteshields of the Hundred-and-Eleventh, who look at you for an example of what a soldier of Cadia should be. On our flanks are the mighty Adeptus Astartes and armoured war machines of our world and that of Vostroya. No regiment in the history of the Emperor's Imperial Guard can boast of such an honoured position. And we will acquit ourselves in a way that shows reverence and thanks for this moment.'

He clicked off.

'What's taking the big red bastard so long?' Creed mumbled. 'I'm running out of speech.'

'He'll be through soon enough,' Kell responded.

'Took him three hours to get this far into the city when I thought I had at least two days – now he's making us wait for it.'

That was putting it almost too simply, Kell thought. The abomination Urkanthos had taken them off-guard. Creed had expected a greater gathering of forces. Swarms of spider-legged death-engines. Warp rituals. A heavier reliance on armour.

But most crucially, he hadn't expected the 33rd to rout. Troops were not in place or fully briefed on their roles. Chains of command and lines of communication hadn't been established. The forces here on the marshalling ground had been hastily shouted together through laud-hailers and a pen-and-paper map.

And up in the Rossvar, the first Salvation forces were starting to emerge – far enough away and on such a short timeline they might as well be on the Eastern Fringe.

The 111th Conscripts had been a stopgap measure, the only infantry unit ready to deploy. And Creed had never planned to use the Cadian Eighth to absorb the breakout before it hit the heavier troops – but there was no one else he trusted to do it.

Another blow rocked the portcullis.

'At least the Kasrkin did their job,' Kell said.

'They did, poor devils.'

'Do you want me to take over the speech?'

'No, Kell, just get the colours up, make sure the warpson daemon-frekkers can see them. I'll just fall back on the old reliable words.'

'Yes, general.'

The portcullis exploded outward, not with the force of a daemon, but blown clear of its hinges with high explosive.

Through the haze came the hulking chassis of a Baneblade, its hull-mounted Demolisher cannon smoking from blowing open the gate. The vehicle's three hundred and six tons of bulk squeezed through the arch like the iron fortress it so very much was. Skulls decorated the sharpened pieces of rebar welded to its cupola and track guards. A flayed man was chained to its front – extra limbs sewn onto him to make the eight-pointed star of Chaos.

The tank fired, the round dropping short and to their right, fountaining debris three storeys high. It ground towards them, the heavy machine moving slow.

'Frekk,' said Creed. Then raised the handset and clicked it on, saying what he always did when there seemed nothing else appropriate. 'Cadia stands!'

'Cadia stands!' the Eighth Regiment echoed, ragged, nervous. Pre-battle jitters. Even veterans got them.

Kell opened his hailer. 'I can't hear you, Eighth! And if I can't hear you the Emperor on His Golden Throne sure as frekk can't hear you! Again for the Emperor, Cadia and the Lord Castellan! One, two, three–'

'Cadia stands!' they shouted. Together now, with determination.

'Are they going to take this line from us?'

'No!'

'Who's going to stop them?'

'The Eighth!'

'Who?'

'*The Eighth!*'

The first Baneblade shell hit the aegis line, stoving in a bunker like a field cook breaks a barrelhead to get biscuits. A Basilisk battery answered, dropping a line of ordnance on the mammoth armoured vehicle.

It drove through as if they were paint shells on a training ground.

From behind it poured spawn of the warp, low, muscular things that moved with a jackal-like cunning. Tasting the air with bifurcated tongues, their spined neck-frills presenting and folding like the fans of aristocratic ladies.

The wall cracked and split in two places around the central gate. One a breaching charge that threw a debris cone thirty yards, another the hacking, splitting assault of an axe the size of a Sentinel.

More daemons poured from the breaches, the thump of long-range shells and lascannons unable to do more than gouge holes in the approaching mass. The quad-guns around them lit, splitting the air with a screeching zip of fire.

Chain-weapons revved, Berzerkers pounding out of the gate. Far more than Kell had expected, given the hours of punishment the Kasrkin had inflicted. A cold feeling, like a bayonet wound, lanced through his intestines.

'Call it,' Creed said.

Kell planted one foot on the forward lip of the redoubt and drew his power sword. The colours of the Eighth a splash of proud crimson, charcoal, gold and white amid the drab khaki and green of the regimental lines. He judged the forward rank of the enemy attack, eyeing the range.

'Cadian Eighth!' he yelled. 'On my mark… fire!'

Las-bolts filled the air, massing so thick that troopers gasped and snapped down shade-visors against the glare, hot neon ghost-images burned on their vision. Each fusillade came so thick it made troopers cough as the bars of energy zipped through the pollution-choked air of Kraf – filled with emissions from weeks of troop movements – baking the ambient hydrocarbons into ozone.

The lead ranks of the daemon horde pitched and rolled, the canid monstrosities savaged under the assault. Carcasses mounted and dissolved, like a wall made of ice, as they melted into blood-laced ectoplasm. As they were blasted apart, the exposure of their perverse internal anatomy – like nothing living, or that could live – made Kell draw breath through his teeth.

The smell of cooking warpflesh, carried on the backwash wind of the las-discharge, nearly made him vomit.

Within the ranks of immaterial hounds, Berzerkers in black armour charged ahead heedless of their char-severed limbs and armour plating pierced in two dozen places – until they fell.

High and clear notes cut the battlefield from behind Kell, and an arc of Exorcist rockets plunged down into the stagnating enemy charge. Earthshaker shells dropped in curtains, lighting flash-cones of high-explosive fire that threw separated pieces of daemons into the air where they dissolved before falling to earth.

On the right, a pack of flesh hounds made a break around a low bunker and lunged at Ninth Company's line – but a quad-gun caught them in the open and misted a few, leaving only two that a flame trooper met with a hose of promethium fire.

'Keep pouring!' Kell roared. 'Make the warp spawn think about it before charging again!'

'Kormachen.' Creed gestured. 'See there, Fourth Company? There's a natural divot in the ground running diagonal to their position. Tell them to get a heavy bolter down it, they're going to use it to move up.'

Kormachen nodded, opened a channel. 'Creed to Fourth, Creed to Fourth. You have a geological vulnerability, low cleft in earth at number seven-six aegis shield. Deploy support, recommend heavy bolt, confirm – wait, sorry.' He paused, switched his channel. 'Yes, I hear you, company master, go ahead.'

Creed looked at Kormachen, the young vox-officer's brow furrowed.

'Lord Castellan, Company Master Korahael and Wolf Lord Highfell have requested to hook into the right flank in order to assist repulsing the attack.'

'Kindly request them *not to,* Kormachen. We can't practise defence-in-depth if we don't have any depth. Besides–'

The wall shattered, and Urkanthos, daemon prince of the Lord of Battle, darted onto the field, making his play for the Cadian lines.

'–if they're waiting for gaps in our lines,' Creed continued, 'they may not have to wait long.'

Volscani everywhere. White flare of her plasma pistol lighting up the eye-lenses of their gas hoods like she'd shone a stablight into a warren full of vermin. Smell of charred flesh in her nostrils, choking. Hellsker coughed as she hacked into them. Slamming her blade down over and over on helmets and shoulder pads, jamming the point into gas hoods to fracture lenses and blind heretic eyes. Beating aside bayonets and smashing the basket hilt into faces.

Ordinarily her power sword would have sheared through the rifle barrels. Melted through traitor skulls as though they were no more than mud. But sometime in the last hour of combat – she didn't know when – the generator had taken a hit and the cutting sheath of the power field winked out. She kept battering at them with it anyway, using the now-blunt cutting edge to stun them. Ramming the point into vulnerable areas. Not so much a sword as a heavy metal bar.

Hellsker was a good swordswoman. Better than good. Back at the academy she'd fenced heavy sabre competitively, and in her graduating year missed a spot at the northern hemisphere championships by a single point. But this was like no bout she'd encountered on the mat. The honeycomb bunkers were narrow and dark, chambers no bigger than the dwelling room of a mid-sized bunker hab.

The only thing she could compare it to was a brawl she'd got in as a cadet, when a gang from a rival academy jumped them in a claustrophobic drinking-cellar in Kasr Tyrok. Like that one, this melee was a blur of uniforms, fought nearly chest to chest.

Throne knew where the command squad was. Volscani had broken through on three levels, and she'd charged up the stairs thinking the others had been behind her. For a moment the dark officer had come unbidden, called out by the sounds of combat and the urgency of the defence.

And that dark officer wanted to kill.

She'd only lived this long because both sides were terminally short of ammunition.

A Volscani grenadier came at her, broad and muscular, his flak vest buckled over bare flesh covered in runic scars. He pointed a laspistol with one hand, and raised a ritual trench club in the other, its skull-faced head covered in tacky blood and hair.

Hellsker chopped down on his wrist with her sword, sending his laspistol to the ferrocrete floor with a crack of bone. She followed up the swing by shoulder-barging him in the chest, knocking him backwards and stealing some of the force when his club deflected off the backward edge of her helmet with a hollow clunk-scrape.

She drove the pommel of her sword up into the grenadier's jaw and saw his face deform with the wet sound of an egg cracking. Bone ground on bone. He tried to raise his club again, but she'd sent him sprawling straight back into his advancing squad, and the club tangled in a forest of bayonets and stumbling enemies.

'Command!' she yelled into her vox-bead. 'Command, on me, second level!'

She'd got ahead of them. Dangerous place to be.

Hellsker shoved off of the grenadier and fired her plasma pistol. She shot low, not bothering to raise it more than hip level. He howled as his legs vanished in a tunnel of light and two other heretics fell behind him, cut down at the knees. The bodies entangled the enemies rushing in through the bunker's interior hatch, stemming them a moment.

Behind them a Volscani sergeant was shoving and jeering, revving his chainsword. He pulled a heretic trooper out of the way and lunged for Hellsker.

'Volscan conquers!' he bellowed.

She parried the chainblade in an explosion of sparks, the spinning saw teeth rattling on her blade and numbing her arm with the vibration. It circled and came again, overhand this time, and the blow might've landed if he hadn't contacted the low ceiling and given her a moment to leap backwards.

But the dodge slammed her back foot into an unexpected object, a bulky heavy thing that turned her graceful retreat into a sideways stagger, and she came down sideways, throwing her sword-arm out to break her fall.

For a thin instant, she thought she'd caught herself on the sword-tip and might stay upright. But the blade's purchase slipped and she went down, the basket hilt slamming onto the ground hard enough to send a bone-deep ache through her limb like an electric bolt. Her plasma pistol skidded from her grip.

God-Emperor, she prayed, as the sergeant swept towards her, drawing back his chainblade for a decapitating strike. *Don't let me have broken my frekking arm.*

There was no way her parry could stop the chainsword. Her numb right arm couldn't muster the proper strength, and with the field dead, the sword had nowhere near the weight necessary to stop a wide cut.

'Volscan conquers!' He swung.

She threw up the guard anyway, felt the impact, and shrieked as the chewing teeth of the blade sawed into her face on her right eyebrow and cheekbone, filling her world with noise and her nose with the hot smell of plasteel saw teeth friction-burning her skull's orbital. Hooked blades tickling her eyelashes with their furious passage.

The noise ended.

Yet she lived.

Hellsker pushed with her blade, shoving the chainsword out of her face with a wet, sucking as the teeth came free from her brow. The hooked blades had stopped, jittering and twitching in their tracks as they failed to rotate, jammed against her uncle's sword.

His sword, which was buried halfway through the chainblade's body, stuck fast like a mythical weapon sunk into an anvil.

She didn't understand until a blue shimmer danced up the blade and it sunk a quarter-inch deeper into the chainblade's frame. An intermittent flash of power field, there and gone like a strobe light, lit the sergeant's bronze-skull face mask, revealing his confusion as he tugged at his broken weapon.

Hellsker hauled backwards on her trapped sword and kicked for his elbow, hearing a meaty *thwack* of boot sole striking muscle and a grunt of pain.

The fall. She'd struck the sword's hilt on the ground during her fall, and that had restarted the field.

She smacked the power sword's generator with the heel of her palm, producing an anaemic aurora that allowed her to draw the blade free of the weapon and plunge it into the sergeant's stomach, where it lodged, its brief flicker of energy spent.

The sergeant fell on her, pinning her to the deck with his weight as she tried to wrestle her blade free.

Hellsker pushed up with her knees, hauling at the sword with her right hand while desperately pounding it with her left. But the rest of the squad was on her. Stomping and stabbing down with bayonets. Gas hoods looking down with blank fury.

'Cadia sta–' she tried to say.

A spike bayonet found her shoulder, the frostbitten cold of it like no pain she'd ever felt. A boot cracked into her ribs. More blows fell, but the sergeant had been a big man and his slab muscles absorbed most of the violence as she rolled him back and forth, using him as a shield. There were a dozen of them. Impossible to fight.

'Cadia stan–'

Her defiant last words were cut off when an object battered her face. It was heavy and curved in sleek lines, power cables running along its length. It smashed down on her once, twice, its force spent on the lip of her helmet but striking hard enough that she felt a crunch in her nose.

She grabbed for it, hoping to get her thumb in the trigger-guard and fire it, where it would easily hit one of the assailants.

Her gloved hand gripped and fumbled. She let go of the sword and trapped the pistol with the other. Found the trigger and mashed it down.

It was only when she saw the blue-white solar glow that she realised it was her uncle's pistol.

Throne, of course she'd go like this. After years of feeling the gravity of fate emanating from the weapon, of course it would be the thing to kill her.

She didn't let go.

'Cadia stands!' she said, as the pistol began to vibrate, the coils already radiating heat through her thick gloves.

The one holding it realised too late what was going on. And even then, his Volscani packmates were huddled so close around him that when he tried to leap backwards to get the weapon clear, the crowd wouldn't allow it.

Hellsker pulled the sergeant's body over her so she didn't see the overheat. Still, the light of it blazed in through her closed eyelids when the hammer-on-anvil sound came, followed by the fizzing hiss of the coils rupturing.

And all those scary screams.

She didn't escape, not fully. Heat flash-burned the back of her left forearm, cooking away her heat-resistant tunic sleeve so that the check pattern of its thread seared into her flesh from elbow to wrist. The top of her tri-dome helmet partially melted, and might've caught her hair alight if not for the patrol cap crushed under it. When she unbuckled it and stripped the hot ceramic shell off, she saw why her micro-bead hadn't worked – the Volscani with the trench club had knocked the battery housing cube on the back of it clean off so it dangled by wires.

Hellsker was climbing out from under the sergeant, beating the spot-fires off her uniform, when Ravura charged in, pistol first.

'Sergeant,' she croaked.

'Martyrs of Cadia!' he swore, seeing her emerge from the pile of charred Volscani corpses. She must have looked bad, because she saw he'd pulled his pistol aside – nearly shot her.

'Hold,' she coughed, staggering to the hatch and closing it to prevent a new assault. 'Get the squad up here. Secure–'

'Major, we have to go. They've broken through below us. We're surrounded top and bottom. We need to get out, either down-compartment to fight it out room by room, or to the mortar emplacement for a last stand.'

'That bad? Where's the squad?'

Behind Ravura, in the next compartment, she heard the deep boom of Lek's grenade launcher.

Ravura shook his head. 'I'm with Lek. No one's seen Rivelle – last saw him one compartment down, using the colours like a spear. We tried to follow you but got cut off by a storming party, only Udza made it past.'

'Udza?' she asked.

Then Hellsker looked down, and saw the blocky thing she'd stumbled on that had nearly killed her. Udza was face down on the floor, crushed under the awkward weight of her master vox. An exit wound had taken the back half of her helmet off.

Hellsker grabbed the handset on Udza's vox for the last time, pressed the rocker.

'Hellsker to Twenty-Four. Hellsker to Twenty-Four. Pull back to defensive positions. Meet me at the firebase. Cadia stands, and we will too.'

The Raptors came from nowhere.

Straight out of the sky, their jagged shapes silhouetted against the gore-coloured clouds. Screeching with such force it roiled Kell's insides and made him clamp his jaw.

'Keep the bastards away from the Lord Castellan!' he bellowed, stepping up to the command bastion's firing step to replace a man who'd just fallen in two pieces, blown apart by a bolt-shell. 'Cadia stands!'

The Raptor who'd hit the unfortunate trooper was one of three that had made it to the command platoon. Two had come apart in mid-dive, torn to pieces when a Hydra flak battery got a bead on them. A third fell while massacring its way through a heavy weapons squad, when a quick-thinking autocannon gunner swung his weapon around and pounded its breastplate in, at the tragic cost of his neighbouring crew, who fell to the shrapnel of heavy rounds meeting ceramite.

Two had made it within pistol-shot of Creed. Their intentions were obvious – kill the Lord Castellan, and rip the motor out of the Imperial meat-grinder chewing through the Chaos assault.

'Surround them, choke them!' he bellowed through his vox-amplifier.

Three storeys below, Cadians threw themselves at the giants, firing blizzards of las-bolts that needled the monsters' armour with scorch-marks. One tried to lift itself clear, bolt pistol pointing towards Creed's command centre, and was dragged down as Shock Troopers leapt onto him like the landing skids of an evacuation Valkyrie, howling in pain as the barbed armour carved their flesh and the fire of the jump jets cooked them.

But they dragged him down, preventing the behemoth from rising even as they fell two and three at a time to the frustrated slashes of his chainsword.

'Gangway! Gangway!' a trooper shouted, shoving aside the milling crowd and raising a plasma gun.

'Let the gunner through!' Kell ordered.

The weapons trooper hefted the big gun with its side grip and raised it high, crescent butt plate pressed tight to his shoulder and coils casting a wavering underwater light across his scarred face.

The point-blank shot vaporised the Raptor's head and right pauldron, the arm with the bolt pistol falling to the earth.

To Kell's right, the final Raptor broke through the press of bodies, lightning claws boiling with void-tainted power fields as they vivisected a dozen men in three strokes. It came on shrieking, half-blind from the stabbing of mortal bayonets. Straight at the only colourful symbol it could find to orient itself in the pounding, pulling tidal sea of Cadian uniforms.

It was heading straight for the banner of the Cadian Eighth.

'Take it down!' Kell drew his power sword.

Cadians smashed against it as it barrelled its way through, firing and cutting. Bayonets and swords broke away in its ceramite shell as it passed. The armoured beast bristled with snapped-off blades. It swiped aside files of troopers, their blood boiling from the touch of the lightning claws and sizzling in the air. Talons sank into the ferrocrete side of the bastion as it came up the angled tower wall at Kell, piggish eyes glaring. The serrated, tarnished gold horn it had instead of a mouth howled so loud the tower shuddered beneath him. Kell thought his ears might be bleeding. Troopers next to him flinched away, their downward fire ceasing under the sonic assault.

Kell didn't wince; instead, he drew his sword back, aiming along the tip. Judging the moment. Hoping the thing had taken enough fire to slow it.

The Raptor's jump pack flared, propelling it up the tower, scythe talons reaching out ahead of it to impale him.

Kell smashed the banner of the Cadian Eighth down, the field around his power fist lighting yellow as it met the lurid warp field of the lightning claws. It was a blocking strike, slamming down on the talons to drive them into the ferrocrete face of the bastion and trapping them there.

His sword plunged at the Raptor's upturned face, driving in hard just behind the breastbone and down into the thing's corrupted hearts.

For a second it thrashed and scrambled, a fish on a line, but troopers either side of Kell pressed their lasguns to its mutated head point-blank and pulled triggers until it stopped moving.

The ceramite made a rusty, groaning sound as the body slid back down the face of the redoubt.

'Took care of it, did you?' Creed said when Kell walked back to the command table. Kell doubted the Lord Castellan had even looked up from the map during the assassination attempt.

'Our Kasrkin detachment caught another group coming from the west, they eliminated them with heavy losses.'

'Good,' said Creed, then mumbled, 'Not the losses of course, too many of those recently.'

Kell looked at the sterile, crease-marked surface of the map with its coloured wooden blocks and spots of cigar ash, noting the growing pile of markers placed to the side – units eliminated. After the first hour, when the horde of daemon hounds broke on the disciplined fire of the Cadian Eighth, they'd pulled Creed back to the command bastion. Mobile skyshield generators now hummed at the corners of the fighting top.

'We've made the blood daemon pay dearly.'

'Doesn't matter if we don't stop him,' Creed said. 'I can buy time with the lives of our soldiers, but we're running out of lives to spend. Stop that,' he snapped at an aide. 'Where are you going with that? The Twenty-Second Vostroyan Armoured Hussars–'

'Are gone, general. The traitor Baneblade and its war engines.'

Creed looked up at the battlefield, passing a hand over the back of his shaven scalp. 'Ah, yes, I see. Well, that's just the point, isn't it? With the daemon and Berzerker attacks pinning us in place, we don't have the breathing space to take on the war machines.' He gestured to the half-circle of units on the table, surrounded by red blocks. 'We're like a seawall holding back the ocean, but that's all we can do. If I split off fire from holding back the tide of heretic infantry, they'll overwhelm the lines. But while we don't, the heavy elements are blowing holes in our centre. And now we're fully committed, apart from the Sororitas commanderies and skitarii, but they're meant to hold the centre if there's a breakthrough. I'd have sent the damned Ironwolves in as a spearhead, but they're all that's holding the right flank together.'

Kell's vision drifted over the map, then out to the battlefield.

Lieutenant A'shar on the left flank, his mismatched Company of Brothers battling a spearhead of daemons.

On the right, the Ironwolves and Dark Angels, such strange bedfellows, pounding at the Berzerker forces, trying to drive towards the murderous traitor Baneblade and its complement of crab-legged cyber-daemons.

And in the centre, the great daemon prince, smashing at their lines again and again. Weathering every barrage. Standing alone each time the smoke cleared. Swooping back to rally forces for another push.

Already, the ranks of the Eighth were thin enough in the centre that Battle Sisters were beginning to take shots at daemons who'd penetrated the line.

'Companies B and C are going to break,' said Kell. 'They've taken too much punishment. We've already had to patch their lines with the conscripts. And that Baneblade – we can't seem to crack it, no matter what we throw.'

'The Sisters will hold,' countered Creed.

'General,' a tactical officer said, a quaver in his voice. 'Report heavy ordnance landing on eastern citadel wall, north of the Drakkon Gate. It's the Warlord Titan, sir, *Vessel of Damnation* – it's operable again.'

'Shit,' Creed growled. 'Can we get a Throne-damned break?'

'Incoming aircraft,' shouted the Aeronautica subaltern, raising her hand for attention.

'Ours?'

'Unclear,' she said. 'Not responding to request for identity codes. Their vox may be out. It came in from the south, through the shield. Low over the city. It's...'

Engines screamed overhead, and Kell instinctively jumped to Creed's side, ready to shield him with his body. An aircraft ripped over them, its wounded airframe pouring out a smear of grey-black smoke, engines dying like a lho-stick igniter short on promethium.

Creed shook Kell off, and looked up.

'I'll be damned,' he said. 'Took them long enough.'

Esteemed Thunderhawk gunship *Tabernacle of St Sawan* had scorned both gravity and the guns of the enemy for over five thousand years. Now, it made its final defiant stand against both.

Red warning lights splashed across the troop cabin, shining dull on the scarred black armour of all that was left of the Cruxis Crusade. Twenty-one battle-brothers and six Neophytes, secure in their restraint racks and muttering prayers to the God-Emperor, begging Him to forgive their pride.

The cabin jostled hard from a hit, heaving upward. Power-armoured joints whined as they absorbed the blow. Turbofan engines, usually quiet and well ordered, gave a stuttering scream. An alarming sound, but not as alarming as when one engine cut out entirely and the cacophony came only from the port side. Candles, fallen from the relic shrine at the rear corner, rolled back and forth across the deck.

Mordlied held tight, one gauntlet clamped to an overhead handle and facing the closed forward ramp of the gunship. Above him, his enhanced senses could hear the Techmarine pilot reading out failing systems and fuel inefficiencies.

They were going down. But that was as it should be. This was a mission of penance.

And none would be more penitent than he.

'I should not have allowed this,' said Amalrich, in his private vox-channel. 'I regret it even now. We have not even a Chaplain to–'

'Dvraine conducted the proper rituals,' Mordlied snapped. 'If the crusade lives beyond this day, he can be anointed and ordained. His actions will be retroactively sanctified in the eyes of the Emperor.'

'Tell me true, Mordlied. You had the vision?'

'I did.'

Amalrich made no answer.

Armour plating rattled with hits. The cabin lights briefly grew bright with the power surge of an energy weapons discharge. And still, Amalrich said nothing.

Mordlied knew the rebuke had stung.

It was for such speaking out of turn that Mordlied stood here now, at this doorway to death. Indeed, why he had requested to be here. One could not speak to a Marshal in the way that he had, at least not without punishment and ostracisation. To tell a brother of Amalrich's rank that he was wrong, and do so in front of the rest of the crusade, was a violation beyond thinking.

Unless, that was, those words were guided by the Emperor. Spoken not in insubordination, but prophecy.

And there was a role, a social function, that dealt with brothers who did something so brave and foolish. Who said the things to authority that others could not. Divinely inspired speakers of truth who needed to be heeded, but also to then die.

'Go with the God-Emperor, and do not make me regret this.'

Then he cut the channel.

Hydraulics hissed and light poured into the cabin, the pilots dropping the forward hatch as *St Sawan* was still incoming. Giving them an escape route should the craft go down hard.

'Cruxis Crusade!' Amalrich roared. 'Dismount and assume storming formation.'

Red figures, thick as pilgrims at a shrine, blurred past twenty feet below. Clawed arms reached up. Heretics in black armour discharged pistols. Bolt-fire whipped through the open door and sparked off the ceiling of the crew bay.

The heavy bolters on either side of the hatch ripped to life, mincing two channels in the heretic tide. One last rocket streaked off a wing, smashing into a daemon engine fifty feet away and overturning it, the monstrous red torso liquefied and the mechanical spider-legs beneath it spasming, crushing daemon hounds in its death throes.

The nose made a final dip and the great assault craft touched down with a bone-jarring impact, cabin shaking as it entered a slide on its fuselage, following the channel it had made in the dead. Daemon and traitor bodies mounded up before the partially dropped hatch as though it were a dozer blade, crushed under *St Sawan*'s final descent.

Mordlied let go of his handhold and took the banner of the Cruxis Crusade from the rack on the ceiling, pointing it forward like a spear as he emerged.

He was up the half-dropped ramp before the craft had stopped sliding, the first to emerge from the belly of the gunship.

Mordlied planted one ancient ceramite boot on the edge of the hatch and stopped there, letting the heretics see him a moment – dragon-tailed banner unspooling in a tainted wind, letting the foe know what had befallen them as, in his other hand, he raised the enormous blade towards the daemon prince ravaging the lines of the Cadian Eighth.

'For penance,' he intoned. 'For blessed Dorn! For Cadia – and for the Emperor!'

Then Mordlied, invested in the Armour of Faith and wielding the Black Sword, leapt into the heart of hell and brought it the vengeance of the Emperor's Champion.

But as he did it, he knew that he was damned.

For his oaths to the Marshal were weighed with falsehood – he had seen no vision.

'Nearly, master, nearly!' hissed Artesia. *'Do not throw away your one chance in haste.'*

Urkanthos gripped the earth of the marshalling ground with his taloned fingers, pawing, tearing up clumps of dirt and rock. His claws shredded the squad of mortals he'd eviscerated only minutes before.

He'd been waiting, gathering his strength. Glorying in the blood-letting of the multi-hour slaughter and taking skulls where he could do so in safety – if only to relieve the urge to slay. It wracked him like the pains of a mortal illness. His muscles bulged and expanded, steel-hard hide stretching like an infected limb. So much vitae filling him, the life force thundering through his skull.

Daemonhood, he had thought, would mean being free of the Butcher's Nails. An end to the pain and irritation of kill-compulsion, an ability to slow down and enjoy the deaths. To carve his bloody victories in celebration rather than relief.

But this, this was worse.

Yet Gore-mouth was right. If he charged before the line was broken, before he was fully swollen with power, they would most assuredly kill him. So the Hounds of Abaddon broke through, and he followed behind to kill the cut-off mortal soldiers.

Another red wave hit him, and he felt saw-tooth bone ridges emerging from his vertebrae, the skin first tenting then splitting. He roared, the sound of a lion in the darkness, and raised his head to see what had tortured him so.

He saw the Baneblade *Vicanthrus* roll over a trench, its heavy bolter sponsons on either side firing down the length of the dirt channel to kill men by the dozens. Its main cannon fired, bucking back in its housing, and a ferrocrete bunker burst like a skull taking a bullet, the tank round boring a small hole below the gun slit and blowing the back out in a spray of debris that flayed another eleven troopers.

Urkanthos snorted, blood running hot from his nostrils. His vision was crimson, unable to differentiate friend from foe. Blood from blood.

Then, the black figure stepped into view.

He alone stood apart, dark as polished jet, carrying a banner and a hand-and-a-half sword that he used to chop through the roiling mass of daemons and Berzerkers. Warp-things quailed at the dragon-tailed banner in his hand, fearing to look at its painful emanations.

White light, hateful in Urkanthos' sight, burned from the warrior and his flag.

Behind him, his weak crusader brothers attacked the Baneblade, the dim muzzle flare of their bolters doing nothing to its armoured skin.

And at the sight of the haloed figure, Urkanthos could no longer restrain the kill-urge.

He bellowed and slashed his own daemons and warriors aside, smashing a path towards the sable knight.

Who arrogantly sank the banner upright in the ground, took his dark-bladed sword in both hands, and prepared to meet the charge.

Head down and heedless the prince of daemons came on, flattening troops beneath his feet, carving through daemons so they howled and dis-apparated, misty soul-essences breathed into the caged snout of their oncoming lord. Waving an obsidian axe as deep black as his own blade.

Mordlied's vision blinked and stuttered. The arch-daemon. Burning brazier. The daemon, now closer. Skulls. The face of the monster. A brush of white-feathered wings.

Eyes. The most cool and determined eyes he had ever seen.

An axe. A voice.

He swung upward, the Black Sword meeting the daemon's down-swinging axe with force he did not know he had in his body, even encased in the relic armour.

A white flash, flat and terrible as lightning, filled the air between them – and when Mordlied could see, the daemon had not been driven back. It still loomed above him, but the daemonic axe had shattered – its obsidian shards lodging in the daemon's flesh like thorns.

It roared in deep-throated agony and pleasurable rage.

Then it swung the haft of the axe down, and Mordlied felt his insides break.

Amalrich cut his way to the spot where banner and Champion had fallen, four of his best Sword Brethren forming a spearhead to reach the site of the duel.

To recover the armour and sword. To recover the Champion if he still lived.

'Mordlied!' he yelled, frantic in his concern and anger. 'Brother Mordlied, do you live?'

Mordlied lay where he'd fallen on the grass of the marshalling field. In the same spot he'd met the daemon prince and broken its infernal weapon. And where the same prince of hell had bludgeoned and smashed and stomped him lifeless before braying like his infernal hounds and tearing towards the front line.

One hand still gripped the hilt of the Black Sword, and the other fist held the fallen crusade banner across his chest so it did not touch the ground. Still, the daemons did not want to go near him.

'Helm,' said Mordlied. 'Remove it.'

Amalrich undid the seals, and lifted the old relic helm free. Blood had pooled inside.

'Father Dorn,' he intoned, seeing the damage.

The Armour of Faith had not buckled nor dented. Had not even scratched under the assault. A cruel miracle.

Cruel because within the armour, Mordlied's body had been crushed. Each joint had smashed inward due to the unyielding plate, pauldrons and breastplate driven together. Helm bashed down so it pressed on the gorget, compressing the vertebrae together like a derailed train.

Far off towards the front line, the daemon roared. But this must be done, the armour and sword could not be lost.

'I was false,' whispered Mordlied. 'Marshal... I saw no vision...'

Amalrich's blood ran cold, and his fingers, which had cradled the wounded Champion's head so gently, began to press down. 'You have dishonoured us then. Dishonoured this armour and–'

'...until I approached the daemon. Then I saw it. And a voice. It spoke to me.'

Amalrich relaxed his grip. 'Sigismund. You saw Sigismund, as the Champions do.'

'No, not him. She said I had done well to bring us here. She quoted... Saint Sawan...'

He paused to take a series of short breaths. Sips of air.

'She said the greatest... act of... faith... of love for humanity...'

'Is self-sacrifice.'

Amalrich finished the quote, because Mordlied's lips had gone cold, and spoke no more.

'That one truly is magnificent,' Trazyn observed. 'Not rare, true. But he has a certain... vitality.'

Blood lashed through the air as the Berzerker champion broke the Cadian line, leading his squad deep into the human ranks.

His axe, double-headed and on a haft seven feet long, killed the Cadians two and three at a stroke. It tore open veteran troopers of the Eighth and fresh conscripts of the 111th alike, their rent carcasses steaming in the cold air. As he crested the aegis line, he bellowed his supremacy at the quailing conscripts in the back line, the muscles on his unarmoured arms as thick as the soldiers' waists. And if he broke through, the hulking red monster behind him would most assuredly do so too.

'It's a shame, really – Huntmaster?'

'I have range,' the deathmark hissed with relief. He had been so patient, ferrying Trazyn around Cadia in his hyperspace oubliette. Ever staring at his back, longing for a quarry.

'The big one in front, please,' Trazyn said, raising two fingers.

The Huntmaster raised the long barrel of his synaptic disintegrator and settled his cyclops ocular behind the sight. Ghost-lights built in the leptonic chamber as he adjusted the beam emitter to maximum focus. The tip of the weapon barely breached the oubliette, hardly visible. A Cadian trooper standing three feet away, smoking a lho-stick with shaky fingers, did not even turn his head.

A quarter-mile away, a flickering emerald halo played around the champion's horned helmet as he dived into the conscripts.

Trazyn dropped the two fingers.

Nothing happened.

Trazyn's vocal actuator ground, lights flaring in irritation.

'Don't rush me,' murmured the Huntmaster. 'This is an art.'

Normally, Trazyn would never have brooked insolence, but he was a being who respected skill. Before biotransference, Trazyn had traded the Huntmaster's phaeron a full decurion of warriors and several dangerous artefacts in return for the extraordinary being. His fealty secured. And for millennia he'd done exemplary work bagging big-game specimens for the gallery – though obsession had marked him in recent years. Since awakening, he saw the galaxy as an eternal hunting ground, and every enemy as one of the great trophy-beasts he'd tracked across savannahs and through hostile rainforests.

So, Trazyn did not rush him.

Ziiiip-crack. Pale green smoke ghosted from the barrel, no more than a minor lho-puff from the trooper. The boy jumped and turned, but the barrel was gone, its thin, invisible beam already slashing across the battlefield.

In the distance-enhanced view of his oculars, Trazyn watched the Khornate champion fall. He was a tough one. Most humans died outright when the beam entered their craniums and flooded their nerve systems with a shredding floodtide of subatomic particles.

This one simply fell to his knees as if suffering a massive stroke, hands opening and closing so his great chainaxe dropped to the dirt. Cadian conscripts immediately swarmed him, stabbing down with bayonets.

'Mmmmmm,' the Huntmaster sneered. 'Not a clean kill, let me have another.'

'Best not, I think. At least not from this shooting hide.'

'What about the big one?'

At first Trazyn thought he meant the daemon prince – but then a target indicator winked politely at the edge of his visual field, and he turned to look at the enormous Chaos-corrupted Baneblade that had driven up over the ruins of a bunker, and plunged headlong into the back lines of the Cadian Eighth. A force of Black Templars moved on its flank, support weapons making little progress.

'A beast so large, warden, well – I doubt even you could take it in one shot.'

'It might require three or four,' he mused.

'How close can you get us to it?'

'Without danger? A hundred standard cubits. With danger, close enough to kick.'

Trazyn opened a dimensional pocket, letting a silver stream of mindshackle nano-scarabs scuttle over his turning hand. He had only brought one swarm of the constructs, and it was not a small thing to deploy them. But that vehicle was quite troublesome, and perhaps it would be better if it turned its guns in a more productive direction.

The little canoptek insects looked up at him, tiny heads cocking one way then the other.

'Seems a pity to destroy a thing so useful – close enough to kick, please.'

There had been no blood. NO BLOOD.

When he'd broken the mortal in the black armour, smashed him like a man stamps on scuttling vermin and watches them twitch in their agonies, the blood had stayed on the inside.

He had killed it, yet it gave him nothing.

While taking from him the great weapon he'd been granted. An adze-axe forged from the black hearts of murderers who had killed before humans had even been fully human. Primaeval hate and vengeance hammered into cutting stone.

He did not need it, in truth.

Urkanthos was more weapon than anything he could wield.

But he could wait no longer – and his Hounds, though nearly expended, had got him close enough.

He smashed through the Cadian Eighth and into the troops beyond. Small, weak troopers with white stripes on their helmets. Urkanthos sent them flying with each sweep of his arms, picked one up and bit through its midsection, pulling the stringy insides out as he ripped the lower half from his teeth and heaved it into the mass.

They were delightfully sticky and warm. Nearly unarmoured. Young, vital blood, offered up for the feasting.

Artesia darted and slashed, singing scream-hymns with her bloody mouths that burst eardrums and stopped hearts. Yet the small troopers kept coming, so much so that Urkanthos had to remind himself to drive on rather than be lost in the joy of the red festival.

Finally, he was unleashing the power.

Cannon shells and explosive bolts detonated against his hide, their shrapnel scything down the Cadians but harming him not at all.

A Leman Russ Exterminator pattern surged towards him, drilling out autocannon and heavy bolt-fire. From the cupola, a commander fired a pintle-mounted storm bolter, as if the sheer volume of fire could stop him.

He grabbed the vehicle under its chassis and flipped it over, then put a fist through the belly and ripped out its engine.

Then in a rush of feral excitement he leapt past the dead vehicle and out of the conscript mass. His talons met polished black ceramite now, the armour of the Battle Sisters.

They sang as he cut them down. Clear, bright voices challenging the shrieking battle-notes of Artesia's ode to the Blood King. Poetry of the Golden Throne trying to drown out that of the Throne of Skulls. Intoxicating, their blood was. Slick and rich with righteousness. Wine-like blood. All the better because he needed to work for it.

Blood everywhere. *Blood* on the ground. *Blood* in his mouth. Not slaking his thirst. No, no, no, but the salty *blood* making it greater.

A *blood* Sister stepped up wielding a *blood* sword and he grabbed her with a hand and *blood* crushed her, wringing out the form so *bloodbloodblood* spilled on the earth. Heavy *blood* bolters scored his *blood* flesh, rounds flattening against *blood* his iron skin. And he wished they'd break through. Wished they'd spill his *bloodbloodblood* wanted to feel his red warm vitae on his skin mixing with the *bloodbloodblood* already covering him. Why were they not *blood* taking it? What *blood* must he do for them to wound him? He wanted to bleed *bloodbloodblood* on the field of *blood* and release the madness contained within.

He raged with fury at their inability to hurt him. Pouncing and striking. Ripping open their bodies and smearing it on himself.

'*My prince!*' Gore-mouth yelled. '*Do not let the slaughter-madness take you. The null-array! Remember the null-array!*'

'Celestians!' called Eleanor. She had prepared her countercharge, judged its moment perfectly. The beast Urkanthos was insensate, given over entirely to slaughter. 'It is a mad beast we shall put down today. Filth of a false god. Your Sisters have sacrificed themselves to destroy this creature, who will join them?'

'I will!' shouted Sister Galatea, ever first to the melee. She lowered her halberd to emphasise her point. 'Drive it to the heart. Send it to hell.'

Others echoed down the line, all ready to fulfil their vows. To undo the shame of the Chandry Mission, and defend Cadia as their Order had promised. To kill a prince of Chaos.

'I will, canoness,' whispered Celestian Sacresant Eugenia, slapping the panel shut on Eleanor's jump pack and keying the activation. Eleanor could feel the heavy machine kick-rumble to life, the vents blowing warm air out their wing-like flutes to clear the pipes.

'I will,' said a voice in her micro-bead, broken. Nearly inaudible.

Eleanor looked down the line, trying to find the source of the voice.

At first, she thought the two Seraphim were bringing a wounded Battle Sister back from the line, taking her to the Hospitaller. But that made no sense. The remaining Seraphim – those who had been unable to join Genevieve in her attack on the heretic engines – were part of the counter-attack force.

It was only when she saw the mother-of-pearl mosaic on the ornate jump pack, of Saint Katherine dying at the hands of the Witch-Cult of Mnestteus, that she knew what was about to happen.

'No,' she said.

'Yes, Eleanor.'

Genevieve could barely walk. Without the support of the armour, she wouldn't have been able to bear her own weight. Her face white as a winding-sheet, lips pale and bloodless. Sweat plastered hair to her forehead. Each movement was stiff, and made with clamped teeth.

Eleanor remembered the burns.

One of Genevieve's Seraphim put her sword in her hand, helping fix her fingers around the hilt.

'Genevieve, you can't.' Eleanor tried to key her jump pack, but it was still warming up. 'Why must you do th–'

'Need I say why?' Genevieve asked, accepting the charred Seraphim banner in her other hand.

'No.'

'If you want to help...' Genevieve said, snapping her helm visor closed. '*Pray for me, Eleanor.*'

Then she rocketed upward with her two Seraphim, towards the Lord of Massacres.

'What is happening, what the frekk is happening?' Creed slammed his palm on the map, punctuating each word. 'I need updates. Frekking eyes-on updates.'

Kell was looking through his magnoculars, calm where the other mobile strategium staff were rattled. He'd been the target of mid-battle rages before.

'Urkanthos engaged a Black Templar. Hard to see, not sure what went on there, and it appears to have goaded the beast towards our lines.'

'Give me that.' Creed wrested the magnoculars away, cuffed sweat off his eyes and looked into them. 'Throne, he's through the Eighth, through the conscripts, into the damned Battle Sisters.'

'One of the canonesses is engaging,' Kell observed, pointing out the arc of contrail streaking towards the daemon prince. 'No,' he corrected himself. 'Now it seems both are.'

When Creed lowered the magnoculars, Kell knew the expression he saw there. Heartsickness. Anger. The dislocated, ill feeling Creed got whenever he wasn't in control.

'They're going to die, Kell.'

'I think so, general.'

'Without leadership the Sororitas defence will come apart. Hells, with leadership it might. Alert the skitarii, tell them to be ready for a charge.'

'Yes, general,' snapped Kormachen.

'And all of you!' he shouted, wheeling on the command staff. 'Sidearms! Carbines! Helmets! Every frekking one of you get a weapon and get downstairs in front of the tunnel entrance – we'll throw rocks at the big bastard if we have to. You hear me?'

'Yes, general,' the troopers answered. The tactical staff stood stunned.

Kell opened his vox-hailer channel and shouted. 'Weapons, helmets, battle ready. Your Lord Castellan orders it, you hear me?'

'Yes, sir!' they shouted.

'So go!'

Kell felt a tug on his sleeve. It was the Lord Castellan.

Creed patted the two hellpistols holstered at his waist, murmured: 'Are these loaded?'

'Yes, sir, I saw to it.'

'Good, good,' he nodded, heading towards the stairs. He turned in the doorway, eyebrows raised in humour. 'Wouldn't want to face off against a daemon colossus without a working hellpistol, would I?'

Her jump pack was as broken as she was. It kept fizzling and reigniting, causing her to dip and weave. One bank of nozzles going out, then the other. At one point both cut at once and she dropped far enough that a chainsword clanged off her kneecap, packs of daemon hounds leaping and snapping at her toes.

Then the last of her Seraphim, Desult and Chendrava, caught her, lifting her higher until the relic pack's power core flared again, sending her hurtling towards the beast.

'Allow us to deliver you, canoness,' said Chendrava.

'Bless you,' she said to her Sisters, sword pointing towards the daemon's heart.

He saw her. Eyes burning in the cage that encased his horned head. Body slicked with charnel gore.

The daemon was heedless of the combat around him. Genevieve saw the last of the Hounds of Abaddon falling to bolters and multi-melta fire – his entire host destroyed – yet he paid no heed. They had got him as far as he'd needed.

He had made the Egressium Gate, and if he breached it, the null-array lay open to him.

'Katherine!' shouted Genevieve, through her helm's laud-hailer. 'Strike for the Blood of Saint Katherine!'

Below her, the commandery cheered and yelled ecstatic thanks as she met the daemon and he raised his claws to meet her.

Movement was pain, and strength was agony. Yet Genevieve used the jump pack to her advantage, weaving up and out of the first blows.

He was not aiming for her. Instead, his sweeping, overlong arms slapped Desult and Chendrava to the turf, the incandescent beams of their inferno pistols washing across his red-purple hide with no more harm than milk.

In Genevieve's helm display, their casualty indicators winked martyrdom red.

But her sword also found flesh, cleaving into his body, opening a puckered gash across the eight-pointed star branded into his chest, which felt not so much like muscle as a bundle of steel cabling.

The beast Urkanthos roared and recoiled, stung. Genevieve pressed her attack, knowing her life was measured in moments, in individual cuts and lunges, her body failing like her pack. She could not move her left leg. Blood pooled in the soles of her sabatons. Each movement lit her burned left side with itching, screaming torment.

Nearly done, she told herself. The pain could last no more than a few seconds. Her weariness would be gone. Oblivion in the Emperor's light awaited.

'Katherine, give me strength!' she said, hacking into the beast's cage-mask. Iron and brass flew aside like shrapnel, glowing orange where she'd carved it away. 'Let me finish it!'

Her blade sank into his recoiling shoulder, hewed one of the spikes from his skull rack. Scattered claws from a talon raised in defence.

Then the daemon belly-laughed and she knew that she'd been baited, overcommitting to her attack.

It had not been a stagger backwards, it had been a retreat. And with the quickness of a feline he pounced forward and the defensive hand became an engulfing one that closed around her from pelvis to throat, trapping her sword-arm between his knobby helmet-sized knuckles and tree-trunk thumb.

Her blade flailed strengthless, slapping his fingers with its flat.

He squeezed with his thumb, and the arm broke at the elbow joint with a wet crack.

'God-Emperor, I give this death to you.'

Urkanthos squeezed, and Genevieve heard her power armour groan as it started to give.

Eleanor swept towards the daemon. Her golden blade, the duplicate of Genevieve's own, plunging lance-straight towards the daemon's heart.

She was not the air-warrior Genevieve was. On the sparring mat, Eleanor was the superior fencer, and for a brief instant she saw her sister's face at twelve years old, looking up hurt as she'd battered her down once again. But Eleanor's blade mastery was all poise and balance, move and counter-move.

One could not fight that way with a turbofan-powered jump pack blasting one towards combat. To win Genevieve's salvation, Eleanor decided she would become like her sister.

The beast's head snapped towards her as she came, faster than such a big thing should be able to move. One vilely twisted hand rising to block her assault.

She rolled right and darted past the hand, planning to drive her sword into his throat.

But then a black, leathery curtain flashed up from his shoulder and engulfed her right arm. The strange substance, corporeal and non-corporeal, pulled her blow as its bleeding, laughing mouths reached barbed tongues out to taste her flesh.

She landed on the daemon's chest, poised upon the thing, grabbing on to its cage-mask for leverage as she pulled at her trapped blade, feet planted on the steely surface of its pectoral muscle.

And nearly face to face with Genevieve.

She was caught, the same way a bird-keeper takes a starlark in the hand, pinning its wings.

Eleanor could see her sister's face purpling as the daemon crushed her.

Eleanor thought again of the starlark, and what would happen should that bird-keeper start to squeeze. How it would kick and scratch, its beak pecking with what little strength remained. Imagined the pathetic sound of its hollow bones crackling just before Urkanthos wrung his fist and she heard the sound for real.

It was worse than she imagined.

'Genevieve!' Eleanor screamed, but why she did so made no sense to her.

The distended face with its bulging eyes and grey tongue was not her sister. Could not possibly have ever been. Everything about Genevieve that Eleanor had known, had been infuriated by, and had loved was absent. As though she had witnessed the death of a sister and the birth of a stranger.

She ripped her blade away from the shadow and plunged it deep into Urkanthos' chest, directly between her feet. He must not have expected that – though saints knew why not – because his reaction came far too late.

The sword grated on a shoulder blade, split sinew and muscle, plunging down, down, to the centre, nearly to the heart.

And perhaps Urkanthos was not wrong to have moved too late, because when he grasped her and tore her away like a clawing kitten, she left the sword behind, the last eight inches of its blade protruding from his clavicle.

Eleanor reached for her inferno pistol, but he shook her so the weapon fell from nerveless fingers, then flung her to the turf so she landed flat on her jump pack with a gristly popping sound. Exquisite pain radiated from her lower back down both legs, and her head – which had whiplashed backwards to crack against her jump pack – lolled to one side. Neither the damaged servos nor her traumatised muscles could support its weight.

She tried to rise, but the bone-deep ache through her spinal column refused. Medical alerts in her helm's preysight blinked nonsensical messages.

She blinked them clear, because they were obscuring her view of Genevieve's body.

It lay next to her, one hand outflung, gauntlet still clenched around her sword.

Eleanor reached for the sword, the twin of her own, and closed her hand around the hilt.

Not to pick it up, for she had not the strength, but so she could hold it with Genevieve.

Her hand found her sister's just as the beast's gnarled fist came down, pounding Eleanor into the earth of Cadia.

The world they'd failed to defend.

FIVE

+Do not speak! No verbal, no vox. Psychic communication only!+ Morkath broadcasted, resonating the thought through the warp-veined noctilith around them. The empyric polarisation was weak – the chamber on the frontier of the tamed fortress was due to be reconsecrated.

So her thought did not carry much force.

Siron and his strike team did not need to be told, but the fortress-slaves she'd called up to join them – former Naval voidsmen – were still trying to communicate verbally and getting spooked. To them, her internal voice was but one among a babbling mob that choked the vox-waves.

'Tahw si gnineppah? Tahw si gnineppah?!' said one, on the edge of panic.

Siron stepped forward and twisted the voidsman's head around with an easy wrench to get their attention, then put a black-armoured finger to his helmet grille.

'Hhhhhhhhhhhhhhhhhhhhhssssss,' he exhaled.

His meaning was clear, though the verbalisation emerged in reverse. The very phenomenon that had caused the brief outbreak of existential terror.

The fortress was fighting them now, Morkath was sure of it.

Intentionally stalling and delaying, using misdirection and fright to stymie the team as they made their way to the port-side power junction. One chamber back, it had attacked their sense of perspective. What was near seemed far away, and what was close appeared distant. Before that, they'd felt gravity tugging them towards the ceiling and had crossed a chamber where darkness and light were reversed, and their shadows too bright to look upon.

Indeed, steps from the mag-lev transport, a voidsman had suffered a sudden delusion that his comrades had been replaced with shape-shifting aliens, and killed three of his squad mates in a burst of autogun fire.

But the most unsettling thing was how the fortress thrummed. Veins of warp-flow licked through the faults and channels in the blackstone, drawing all the empyric energy in one direction.

Bleeding it towards the centre. Letting the organic growths Morkath seeded in the vaults go dry and powdery. And as those bulbus growths withered, so did her ability to reach through the fortress.

Every few minutes, the chambers jostled with the violence of the energy transfer. The fortress contorting, seizing, the wild noctilith reasserting itself.

Powering the weapon, she realised. Her father was preparing to fire again, and he had not told her.

Was this a punishment? An incentivisation? Had he finally lost patience with her?

+Which way?+ enquired Siron. The team had switched off their voxes an hour ago when they'd been bombarded with gibberish crash-alerts from what claimed to be the command room.

+A moment,+ she sent, then knelt and swept a hand through the ashen organic debris that blew across the floor, trying to find a pustule, a tentacle – anything.

There. A thick, branching vein, still pulsing with a mix of warp force and electrical energy, bursting up through the blackstone like a root jungle system emerging through rockcrete. She closed her eyes, feeling its throb in her hand, and let her vision follow it.

She raced down through the floor, forking and twisting through the untamed fortress and into fire. Fire and blackness. It was the weapons battery portion of the power coupling, feeding energy from deep reactor chambers to a fire-control station above the port-side defensive batteries.

Then slashing it out into space in the form of las-fire.

Energy streams in the vein were running two ways. Those going to the las-battery powered the defensive countermeasures, while the electricity running the other way carried words. Status reports. A message as if coming from underwater.

'–still receiving fire. Regular torpedo and missile spreads, but the waves are coming too fast for us to get them all. Gods of the warp, port-side control, we need more power. Primary batteries will burn out at this rate of intercepting fire, we need the secondary batteries online if– Brace! Brace!'

The chamber shivered, and the voice dipped out for a moment.

+We're under attack,+ Morkath transmitted to Siron. +A battery talking to port-side control. Fleet action. We just took a hit.+

Siron's helm snapped towards her. +The crash alerts, the gibberish from the command room. It was a call to general quarters. Battle-fleet Cadia has decided to stop lurking and come for us while all eyes are on Kraf.+

+They can't possibly win, can they?+

Siron shook his head. +Destroy us? No. But crippling the *Will of Eternity* would be a victory in itself. Stranding it in Cadia's orbit means we cannot bring it to Terra.+

+They will make no headway against our shields,+ Morkath thought.

+Provided we have shields. Perhaps this was the object of the sabotage all along? The Wolves have signalled their allies. If that is an energy cable, can you follow it back to the junction?+

+Yes. Though if they think even unshielded we will fall to torpedo volleys, they won't–+

'Port-side control and central control! Something big's happening out here!'

+We need to go,+ Morkath said.

'One penetration!' shouted the weapons officer from his cradle. His sewn-shut eyes flickered as he scrolled the data feeds projected on his inner-vision. 'Two, three. Damage only structural, grand admiral.'

'Three shield penetrations with a fifty-torpedo volley,' Grand Admiral Kozchokan said, thumping a fist on the arm of his command throne. 'We're wasting ourselves here.'

Through the viewport of the forward bridge, he saw a tunnel of light red as a dying star lance out and hole a Dictator-class cruiser, boring through its launch bays and refracting out the other side.

The wounded cruiser's engines cut, and it started to yaw and roll. Not dead yet, but it soon would be.

'Is that the *Imperator Dominant*?' Kozchokan asked, refusing to hide his deepening depression. 'Or the *Spirit of Mordian*?'

'The *Dominant*, grand admiral.'

That was the second battle cruiser to be floundering in the void, not to mention the *Strike for Macharia!*, which had taken a critical lance-hit and exploded, lost with all hands.

'Break it off,' he said. 'Vox Creed that we tried. I'm not going to smash my fleet to pieces trying to–'

'Warp emergence! Warp emergence!' shouted an officer at sensor control. 'Coming on the starboard bow. Close, close, close. It's going to catch us in the wake and roll us. Prepare for displacement.'

'General alert!' shouted engineering. 'You heard him, send the call to brace for roll.'

Kozchokan signalled his throne-servitors with frantic gestures until they keyed his descent protocols, the throne moving forward and down the stepped tiers of the command cathedral on its articulated arm so he could get close to the sensor officer.

'What the hells is this, lieutenant? Roll us? We're a Throne-damned Retribution-class battleship, who the devil is going to roll us?'

'It's big, sir – biggest emergence signature I've ever seen.'

'Archenemy reinforcements?'

'Most probably, sir.'

Outside, another cruiser ruptured and split, the two halves spinning in opposite directions glowing with internal fires.

'Hells,' Grand Admiral Kozchokan swore. 'We've been evading the bastards for weeks and Creed brought us right into their net. Weapons! Run out starboard batteries. On their realspace translation we give them all we've got.'

'Sir,' the weapons chief acknowledged. 'Bridge to starboard fire control. Load and run out all weapons and prepare to fire on transmitted coordinates. Aim six degrees low and fire on order. Do not wait for complete visual on target. Wait too long and the roll will break our firing solution. Repeat, we need to volley *before* full emergence.'

'Communications? Signal fleet. I want torpedoes in the void as soon as the initial bow wave passes, heading towards emergence point. Further waves may scatter them, but if it's as big as signals says it is, some will find the mark.'

'Sir, sending orders now.'

'It's coming through,' signals reported. 'Throne of Terra, it's bigger than the damned fortress.'

The first bow-wave hit the *Righteous Tyrant*, a rolling surge of empyric energy that glimmered in the void and lifted the massive battleship before settling it again.

'Emergence in twenty, nineteen…'

'Tell me when ready.'

'Broadside ready, grand admiral,' replied the weapon's chief.

'...threat recognition fixing a silhouette... thirteen... twelve...'

Grand Admiral Kozchokan opened a wide personal frequency. 'Kozchokan to all ships. It has been the honour of my life to have commanded you, whether you hail from Battlefleet Cadia, Scarus or otherwise. Remember, we die in the skies of our fortress world. Hold fast, do your duty. We'll meet the Emperor with our heads held high.'

'...three, two...'

'Fire broadside,' Kozchokan ordered.

'Aye, admiral, f–'

'Hold fire!' shouted signals, holding the blocky headphones over his ears. 'Hold! Hold! Hold!'

'Signals! What are you–'

The signals officer spun around in his rotating chair, eyes wide, hands still clamped over the headphones. 'Sir – it's the *Phalanx*!'

Hard rounds ripped through the sandbags above her head, popping holes in the bags so the silica cascaded down. The stream made a gritty hiss as it fell on Hellsker's tri-dome helmet.

She blind-fired her laspistol over the sandbag wall, and heard an answering knock as autogun rounds thumped into the rapidly deflating emplacement and drummed the flakboard backstop.

They were in the mortar pit, the little sandbag keep at the end of the cleave they'd built up as the last point of resistance. But it was melting under the relentless storm of infantry fire coming in from the roadway, and now that the Volscani had captured at least half of the wall-bunkers there was also fire coming from above. Snaps of las flitting between the tops of the cleave suggested an enemy storming party had gained the top of one canyon side, and were in a vicious firefight with the pioneers and snipers.

Soon, the squads holding the wall chambers directly on either side of them would fall – fighting there was already hand to hand – and they'd be gutted with enfilading fire from above.

'Ready? Pull!' Ravura shouted to the fire-team lined up below the step. Each yanked the pin on a frag grenade and let the spoon fly open. 'One, two, three… throw!'

They heaved all at once, not even waiting for the volley to explode before they dipped hands in ammunition boxes to fish out the next volley. Down the cleave, the grenades detonated in a series of percussive thumps.

'You're short,' said Corporal Gevzette. She knelt, staring down her periscope eyepiece. A wire connected the monocular to the T-shaped visual array sprouting from her backpack – specialist kit salvaged from her heavy-mortar position. She was the last of the bastion gunners, her comrades overwhelmed and killed at their stations when the Volscani breached the wall bunkers. 'Backstopped on a pillbox, mostly. Aim four degrees to the right next time – there's a group lurking in a doorway.'

Ten steps behind, two troopers from the weapons company, Mestven and Tzai, were loading the last functional mortar. The tube was broken – its bipod snapped in half and the mounting bent from when one of the cavalry mounts had trodden on it – but they'd propped it up in a cradle of sandbags to keep it operable. Tzai sighted and called the shot, since he'd taken a las-bolt through the shoulder and only had one operating arm. Mestven, one hand swaddled in a blanket, reseated the scalding metal tube after each volley before dropping in another round on Tzai's order.

And along the sandbag redoubt, troopers snapped shots at the Volscani that leaned out from behind the half-ruined heavy bolter nests and revetments that had repelled them for so long.

Lek ran up, his head low. 'Got a report, major.'

'How many left?'

'We have fifty-six troopers here, including wounded. Maybe another thirty in the walls, but they're not going to hold long.'

'Officers?'

'Pesk, since the engineers have been operating here, plus Lieutenant Tovla from G Company. One of the non-responsive wounded might be Captain Jelak, but… his face.'

'What about the colours? Has anyone seen Rivelle?'

'I do,' said Gevzette, adjusting her periscope eyepiece. 'He's out there. On the eleven, just before the wall of wrecks.'

She pointed the direction and held the eyepiece out for Hellsker.

Hellsker wasn't used to the device. The world seemed to wobble and stretch as the wind shook the T-shaped aerial with its binocular picters. Las-bolts sizzled past, fouling her vision.

'Focus ring's on the front,' said Gevzette.

Hellsker found it, then wished she hadn't.

On top of the burned-out wall of transports stood a Volscani trooper. Big man, either a sergeant or grenadier, both arms replaced with augmetics shaped into bird claws.

He was waving the colours of the Cadian 24th Interior.

They were nothing special, as colours. A standard white flag with gold tassels on the fringe and a haloed skull on either side, with the numbers *XXIV* in one corner and a pathetically small list of battle-honours.

But the white standard had a new red stripe – from the blood of Zaarun Rivelle, whose head had been jammed on the top of the pole.

Zaarun Rivelle, the old veteran. Who'd stood by her shoulder throughout, always offering his steady resolve. Following every order as though she'd been an old campaigner, rather than a green major whose previous operations had been sweeping up warp-touched rebels. The one trooper, even more than Ravura with his slightly paternal manner, to have treated her like a real Shock Trooper.

Hellsker's skin went cold, her whole body numb, as if her soul had retreated into herself and her flesh were only a shell. A bunker under siege.

She knew this feeling. Knew it from the day she'd missed that final point in the sector fencing championships. The time, at the age of four, she'd been pulled screaming off the carousel at the muster faire because she'd refused to get off the plastek Leman Russ when the ride was over. But most of all, she knew it from when she'd opened her assignment orders and saw her posting listed as *The Honourable 24th Interior Guard, Kasr Kraf*.

It was shame. Naked, exposed shame. Every Cadian's horror – to meet a challenge, be found wanting, and still be alive.

And there were few things as shameful as losing the regiment's colours.

'Ravura?' she asked.

'Sir?' He paused while reaching into a grenade box.

'How long will this position be viable? A no-groxshit assessment, please.'

Ravura tilted his head, as if in apology. 'Twenty minutes?'

'Do we have a working flamer?'

'One of the engineers, Eveza, has a bit of a tank left, I think.'

Hellsker keyed her comm-bead. It was a new helmet, stripped off a casualty.

'Hellsker to Twenty-Four, they have our standard. Killed Rivelle, stuck his head on it. I won't lie, we're not long for this. But if this is our hour of sacrifice, I won't do it cowering. That's no death for a Shock Trooper. I'm going over the top in two minutes, and anyone who wants to follow me will be welcome. Those that stay due to preference or wounds – resist how you can. Burn our codebooks and kill as many as possible before they take you.'

She swallowed.

'We can't recapture the colours. They'll just take it off our corpses again. So our objective is to burn them. This will be close assault. Get bayonets and trench spades. Grenades and demolition charges if you have them. Anything that fires. Two minutes begins now. Our signal word will be *Rivelle*.'

'Major?' It was Pesk, limping. He carried a bundle of charges, his slack face questioning. 'May I join?'

Hellsker looked him up and down. Sighed. 'Yes, Manvar, you can. But please let someone else throw those. You're… incapacitated.'

'I thought we could c-c-cast them out as our opening salvo. Clear the way a bit.'

'That would be good.'

'And I thought I could take a look at your sword,' he said, putting his palms out. 'And do what I can.'

Two minutes passed so quickly, Hellsker wished she'd given herself five. But by that time, they would've been overrun – the Volscani were so close now that when they threw the four demolition charges, the bundles landed on helmets rather than roadway.

Explosions tore through the Delvian Cleave, the pounding discharges overlapping each other as they echoed back and forth. Rockcrete chunks, handfuls of earth and enemy body parts rained down on the sandbag redoubt.

Lek arced smoke grenades over the parapet, one after the other – *pook, pook, pook* – their casings already split along a seam and weeping indigo smoke as they fell.

'Rivelle!' Hellsker yelled. 'Rivelle!'

She was first down from the redoubt, boots slipping on the bloody roadway, half-turning her ankle on a Volscani breastplate that had been blown right off its owner.

'Rivelle!' she shouted, as she put her head down and charged. 'Twenty-Four, in the war!'

Las-fire zipped and slashed past her, stabbing from the inky miasma. She shouted 'Rivelle!' again and it ended in a painful cough as an autogun slug flattened against the left-breast panel of her flak vest, knocking the breath out of her.

She kept charging, advancing – attacking for the first time in this damned, useless battle where they'd ground themselves to gore to stop the enemy. Where they'd stood without any support, and despite all they'd done, the heretics were still going to break through.

Where their only recognition, if even that, would be a line on a field report. *CADIAN 24th (INTERIOR) – NO REPORT, ASSUMED LOST.*

A shape staggered out of the obscuring smoke. Wounded Volscani trooper, concussed by the charges and holding a throat wound.

Hellsker chopped her power sword into his side, feeling the blade sink deep before she wrenched it free. Pesk hadn't fixed it, the field still brightened and faded like the garish neon lights of the Tyrok red-light districts, but the cutting field was strongest along the blade, and it never fully went out. But she had to put her arm into it.

'Twenty-Four,' she yelled, lowering her laspistol to cut down a shell-shocked Volscani who blundered towards her voice. 'Follow me!'

And they did. They were into the enemy now, those still shaken by the violence of the demolition-charge volley. Heretics that had thrown themselves flat were trying to rise, and find fallen lasguns and pistols. She saw the artillery spotter Gevzette, her backpack discarded, raise a trench spade and chop down as though it were an axe, sinking it in the back of a Volscani's neck as he was on his hands and knees. A Volscani came for her with his bayonet, but Ravura intercepted him with a textbook rifle parry – knocking the enemy's lasgun aside with a dull crack of the barrels connecting before sinking his bayonet into the heretic's guts.

Gevzette picked up the dead trooper's fallen lasrifle and pushed on.

'Keep moving!' shouted Hellsker. 'Don't get bogged down!'

The smoke would only linger a few seconds, and already the deep indigo was fading to a sky blue. She could see wisps of white and grey twisting in it, marbling the air as though they were amidst a sky criss-crossed with contrails.

'I got it!' Lek snapped. 'I see them!' He raised his grenade launcher and banged a flechette round into a knot of heretics emerging from one of the side bunkers, shredding them before he dashed into the carnage, vaulting a low rockcrete revetment before racking his launcher and firing another frag point-blank into the chamber.

That was his job. His and Eveza with her flamer. To keep the side chambers temporarily suppressed so the attack couldn't be hit in the flank. Both were terminally short of ammunition, Lek's bandolier flopping empty on his chest.

But it was working. God-Emperor, it was working.

Footsteps in the smoke, scratchy on the grit of the roadway.

Hellsker lunged when it was only a shadow, her blade-tip ripping into the canvas of a gas hood.

Impact. Pain. The heretic soldier had come bayonet first and lodged the triangular spike into her right shoulder pad, burying the tip half an inch into the meat of her upper arm.

The trooper fell but the rifle stuck, dragging at her sword-arm so she had to turn and blaze two shots at the squad charging in behind him to keep them at bay.

'Ravura!' she shouted, but the sergeant was already with her, grabbing the rifle barrel with one meaty fist and yanking it free before he wheeled to clash with another enemy.

Hellsker met the charge, firing and cutting. Smashed her sword hilt into a face. Carved into a leg. She pulled the trigger on her laspistol until it no longer fired, then threw it into a file of reinforcing Volscani and instead used her off-hand as a weapon, grasping a rifle barrel and dragging the trooper behind it onto her blade.

'We need to keep moving,' Ravura said, grabbing her sleeve. 'They'll–'

Then another flurry of las-fire cut through the smoke. Intense, panicked shooting now. Escalating. A storm of incoming shots like a string of burning firecrackers where individual shots became impossible to distinguish.

Red bars of incoming fire dismantled the Volscani coming towards them, cutting the troopers down with treacherous shots to their backs. A round passed by Hellsker's eyes, between her head and Ravura's, and dazzled her enough not to see the shots that put him down, leaving scorch-marks on the earcup of his helmet and blowing his lasrifle into scattered pieces.

Hellsker huddled down, making herself small.

A tight grouping of darts slammed into the spotter Gevzette, drilling her multiple times along with the enemy trooper she'd locked rifles with. Both went down together, flames marking the through-and-through wounds dotting their bodies.

Sparks leapt from hits on Eveza's flamer tank – once, twice – then daggers of flame leapt from the top nozzles and the big dual-cylinders went, immolating three men.

She looked back to see the scratch mortar crew, Mestven and Tzai, trying to pull Pesk down into cover. The engineer stood with his back to the blizzard of fire, staring back towards the abandoned sandbag firebase.

He raised his arms, as if in praise.

'Ravura,' she said, shaking him.

'I'm all right,' he said. 'Just rang my bell a bit. Help me get up.'

'Twenty-Four!' she yelled in her comm-bead. 'Get up, Twenty-Four! One last push. Give me one minute of fight, just one last minute.'

She dragged herself up and threw herself into the thinning smoke. Leaping bodies, cutting at human shapes that melted away beneath her blows. Dodging and retreating. Incredibly evasive. Gone the moment she seemed to reach them even though the smoke was thinning. Her feet tangled in the strap of a fallen rifle and she almost fell, wheezing as her lungs rebelled against the chalky foulness of the air.

It was only when she broke free of the powder-blue cloud that she realised the Volscani were running. Not retreating, but in full rout.

They'd dropped weapons. Were stripping helmets and webbing as they sprinted away. One tripped over a piece of rubble with a snap of bone and fell full-length, scrabbling for a pistol.

Hellsker grabbed for a discarded rifle on the roadway as the Volscani's gun cleared his holster – but instead of pointing it at Hellsker, he jammed the barrel under his chin and pulled the trigger.

And it was quiet. The Delvian Cleave, burned and ruined, littered with bodies and rubble, had no sound apart from crackling flames on one of the barrier Chimeras and the fading voices of the enemy.

'Major?' asked Ravura.

'Shhh.'

Hellsker sheathed her sword and staggered forward to the dead trooper, taking the laspistol from his cold grip. She went forward slow, gun held two-handed.

'It has to be a ruse,' the sergeant hissed via the micro-bead.

Hellsker nodded, approaching the Chimera barricade. Looked for traps in the back hatch of a vehicle before ducking inside to peer out the driver's slit.

Volscani were fleeing down the road in droves. Two thousand of them at least.

'What the frekk?' she hissed.

'Major,' said Ravura. 'Look.'

When she turned, she saw that he held the regimental colours, a look of puzzlement on his face. 'Did we scare them, do you think? Do–'

'Did you see her? She was magnificent!'

Hellsker ducked out of the Chimera, and saw the ragged voice belonged to Pesk.

He was held between Mestven and Tzai, his face nearly blue from the smoke grenade, hair half-burned away.

Hellsker reflected at how she'd once thought Pesk was handsome, with that sly smile and clever mind. But this was a different man, and a different mind, entirely. Rail thin, with a face unable to make the mischievous expressions she knew so well.

Now the grin was one of beatific madness.

'He's hit bad, major,' said Tzai. 'Spinal. We tried to pull him down but...'

'I saw it,' she said.

'You saw it?' Pesk cackled. 'Wasn't she incredible? I've never seen anything like it.'

'The major chased them off, she did,' said Ravura, more exhausted than celebratory. 'Scared them right down the valley.'

'No, not the major, the *angel*. She was behind us. Came out of the sky. Armoured in gold and her arms outstretched, like they are in the glassaic. Doves soared around her, I could see her light shining through her wings. She promised she would come.' He stopped and grinned at the sky, head lolling backwards as a wave of pain took him. 'You saw her, didn't you, Mestven? You must have. She shone so bright.'

Hellsker glanced at Mestven; he shrugged and shook his head.

Tzai looked at the road.

'You saw her?'

'There was a lot of smoke,' said Hellsker. 'And we were looking at the enemy.'

'What do you mean you didn't see her?!' Pesk shouted, yanking at the arms holding him. Voice breaking. 'She filled the sky! The whole frekking sky!'

Hellsker looked back along the length of the cleave to the other end of the bunker canyon – there was nothing in the sky. Nothing but scab-red clouds, building over Kasr Kraf.

Too late.

Kell knew it the moment they sallied out of the command bastion's bottom level and saw the carnage around the Egressium Gate. The Sisters had tried to hold there. Tried valiantly even without their canonesses – but there was no stopping the daemon.

He'd smashed through the lines, battering down the Celestian Sacresants so their broken shields lay atop their crushed bodies. Halberds scattered the ground, hafts snapped and blade-tips blunted on him. Amid the red-and-black robes lay the khaki uniforms of the 111th Whiteshields, slain to a man. On either side of the gate, lascannon crews slouched over their weapons and firing positions, dead at their controls.

Screams sounded from within the throat of the Egressium Gate tunnel.

'We're going down,' said Creed, drawing his pistol and waving for the headquarters platoon to follow. 'Come on. Kasrkin with special weapons up front. If anything bigger than me comes at us, fire at it.'

'It's no good having a general down there,' murmured Kell. 'Let's stay back.'

'No good having a general anywhere now.' Creed checked his hellpistol load. 'Generalship isn't going to win a damned thing if he destroys that null-array. They could just use the fortress to wipe us out. Best use of me is as another infantry officer. Now stop fussing and come on.'

They found the first skitarii bodies fifty yards down, some mangled and broken, others wandering aimless and cogitator-dead, smashed but not killed in the daemon's rampaging descent.

'Look at this,' breathed Kormachen. 'How could we possibly kill a thing that can do this?'

Creed opened his mouth to answer, but deep below a seismic rumble – like the city being ground in a mortar and pestle – echoed up through the Egressium tunnel.

'We may not have to,' he said, as the walls began to shake.

'Down! Deep breath!' Kell said, throwing Creed into the wall just as the throat of the tunnel lit orange and the coursing fireball ripped through the air, sucking the oxygen out before it, so that barefaced command staff began choking, caught between breaths.

Kormachen fell to his knees, hands on his throat.

Kell saw the flames consume him just before the refractor field fired, and the world turned milky white.

'Eleanor? Eleanor, are you there?'

'I'm here, sister.'

'I can't see you. It was dark, and I was alone.'

'You are not alone any more. I do not think we will ever be alone, now that we are with the Emperor.'

'But where is the Emperor's light? I cannot imagine this is correct. Can this be death? Martyrs are to spend eternity at the side of He-on-Terra. I was taught that it was so, and I told others such. Were we wrong?'

'That is not possible.'

'But it's so empty here. Not merely dead, but like it never lived.'

'Do not say such things, Genevieve. We are simply in perdition. The transitional plane, a place of quiet.'

'It is not quiet, I hear a hum.'

'A hum?'

'Listen.'

'You are right, but I do not hear it, I feel it. I would say in my teeth, but...'

'...but you cannot feel your teeth. It's a strange sensation, isn't it? Not having a tongue resting in my mouth, touching the back of my teeth. It is like experiencing null-gravity for the first time.'

'But I have felt this before.'

'Where?'

'At Kraf, when I first arrived. There was a... I can't describe. An unpleasant resonance. One of the troopers said it was the null-array.

That the psykers did not like it, and that it made everyone feel off. That–'

'Eleanor...'

'I was discomforted by it, I–'

'Eleanor, it has stopped.'

'Eleanor.'

'Yes, sister?'

'That was not me.'

'Genevieve.'

'And that was not you.'

'Begone, daemon! Voice in the dark. In the name of the Emperor and Saint Katherine I banish thee. With my annunciation of faith, I banish thee. With each banner that waves before the Eternity Gate, I stab thy heart!'

'These are worthy words. I bow to you, Eleanor, and to you, Genevieve. Twice-fold sisters, bound in blood and vow. You have served the Emperor well – but death need not be the end of service.'

'It may be a ruse, Eleanor – the warp speaks with many voices.'

'Who are you? Unborn devil or martyred saint?'

'I am no daemon, but many fear me. I am no martyr, for death cannot claim me. I am a thing both wondrous and terrible, and I will not tell you not to be afraid. No soul knows what I am, for even I do not know. But I am duty and faith, word and deed, and if you wish to serve the Emperor, come with me.'

'Heavenly Throne, the light!'

'It's so bright. Do we go, sister?'

'Together.'

'Come. There is much that we must do. You are my steady hands and my messengers. And you shall rally my armies.'

Eleanor opened eyelids of skin and flesh, and regarded the world with eyes of fire. Her ocular augmetic, a clumsy imperfect thing, was gone.

She floated free in the vacuum of space, the green flicker of a Geller field around her and the golden prow of a ship at her front. The warp lapped against it, sluggish and becalmed.

Before her was the crystal viewport of a command bridge, and through it she could see the faces of Sisters, looking out at her with wonder.

Eleanor knew their faces. Could recite their names. So much of the world was now open to her, though she needed no miracle to know them.

For the majority of her life, she had carried a book inscribed with the name of every Sister on this ship – the ill-fated cathedral-frigate *Fire of Saint Ozynia*, which to the eternal shame of the Order, had diverted to liberate the shrine world of Chandry before coming to Cadia's aid. Dogma held that the Emperor had punished them for this arrogance, and they were lost in the warp.

They had not been lost, they had been saved. Saved for this moment, when Cadia needed them most.

In the crystal, Eleanor saw herself as they saw her – an avenging angel encased in burnished gold, eyes flaring with white light too bright to look upon. Purity seals floating ghost-like in the void.

And a golden blade stretched out pointing the way – to Cadia.

Genevieve did not know where she awoke.

Cyclopean vaults stretched into empty darkness above, their spaces yawing and cold. The black walls had an uncanny shine to them, as if the spectrum-shifted light did not reflect correctly.

She had no idea where it might be.

She knew it was not the empty place, and she knew it was not Cadia.

Which is strange, because there were so many Cadians here.

Cadians from every regiment, and every specialty of warfare. Standing in exhibition lines displaying uniform variations. At attention next to floating grids of their kit contents. Frozen in the act of disembarking from Chimeras or fast-roping down from hovering Valkyries.

Some were old, very old, wearing the antique blade shields that had been common before the hardened shoulder pads now in use. Tactical kit Genevieve had only seen in the oldest statuary.

In addition to where she was, she didn't know *when* she was. There was a staleness, an expired feel to the world she had never felt before.

But she did know her task.

She came on the bell step by step, its bullet-scarred surface emerging from the gloom.

Dead Sisters lay around it, their blood running crimson down the iron surface.

And as she approached it, she heard the noise.

A soft *pat-pat-pat* of fluid.

Blood ran down the iron surface of the bell like the first drops of icicles melting on the eaves of a hab. Drip. Drip-drip.

Jewelled drops of red, sparkling in the half-light, met the upturned forehead of a slain Battle Sister and stained her pale skin with splashes of crimson.

Pat. Pat-pat.

It was running freely now, the blood of the faithful sacrificed to preserve the relic. Below, in the shadow of the iron skirts, she saw a Sister frozen for centuries in the instant of death finally let out her final breath.

Genevieve put her hands to the warm surface of the bell and pushed.

It moved a hand's breadth at first. A sway. Its mace-like clapper shifting.

When it swung back to her, she gripped the bell's lower edge and pulled down with the strength of her power armour, flinging droplets of blood that spattered the floor and faces of the stasis-locked troopers. Sizzling and spitting on force fields.

'Cadia, Sisters!' she shouted. 'Cadia!'

And the clapper of the bell struck.

Clang.

In the bowl of the massive instrument, she heard the echo of a second bell – from the Shrine of St Morrican, an entire galaxy away.

One.

Genevieve caught the backswing, using it to lift her up off her feet, before she used her body weight to drag it down again.

Clang.

Two.

Only after he'd torn the null-array to pieces did Urkanthos understand how powerful the arcane device had been.

The half-metal soldiers of the Mechanicus had put up little resistance. Crushed under pounding fists, eviscerated on his talons, their mortified flesh slit and severed with Artesia's scalpel-like wings. Pitiable little creatures pretending they no longer had blood, and that this somehow cheated Khorne of his due.

Blood mixed with promethium crude still pleased the Lord of Carnage. A skull was still a skull, despite being refashioned of steel.

Even their magos could not stand against the rushing force of a daemon unleashed.

None hurt him as much as the flying prayer-witch, whose sword still pierced his collarbone and chest, needling at him like a splinter in a foot. The pain ignorable until he twisted and it made itself known.

Then he was in the final chamber, surrounded by the roots of deep-sunk pylons wired with arcane cogitator-banks and the copper cabling of broadcast antennae. Xenos technology, awful to look upon with his warp-shaded eyes, perversely mixed with human creations.

Within the chamber, his blood rage slipped its last chain.

The emanation of the pylons vibrated through him, bone-deep, like the tremor of an earthquake. Like he was a chainaxe cranked to full rotational speed. And all at once he realised why the daemons had been so hesitant to charge the muster field. Why the intelligent bloodletters would not come, and only the vitae-mad flesh hounds answered his summons. They were little more than animals, able to be bidden with a whistle and driven forward unthinking. Urkanthos, so swollen with mortal bloodshed, had more weight in the physical plain and did not feel the effects of the null-array in the same way as the hounds. The hounds that had become subtly slower and weaker as they moved towards the Egressium Gate. Whining and loping, heads low, at times even seeming to shy away from the charge.

Poor, blood-starved devils. Whining and snapping as they returned to the warp, their bodies dissolving so fast into ectoplasm even their skulls did not remain.

Only among the pylons did he feel it. How it nearly shook his warp-essence apart, threatening to shatter him. Pulsing under his skin and rattling his long teeth together until they began to pop one by one in powdery explosions, dusting his mouth with chalky bonemeal.

Artesia howled in his ear: *'Destroy it! Smash it! Make it stop!'*

Whatever it was had been anathema to beings like him. And only when he'd torn it down and bathed in the cleansing, glorious flames of the explosion did he fully feel his supremacy over the physical world.

It was as if he had lived his whole existence wearing shackles and weights – iron balls manacled to each limb, and heavy chains across his shoulders. And with the annihilation of the array, those unnatural constraints had fallen away.

Urkanthos realised he had never experienced daemonhood without the restraining influence of the Cadian pylons or that of the

Blackstone Fortress – which he now knew to be the same. That eight-pointed obsidian star in the sky was no expression of the Chaos gods, but the antithesis of it.

And he was free.

Urkanthos disdained the Egressium Gate, half-collapsed in the explosion. Instead he drove directly upward from the pit below Kasr Kraf, Artesia's wings driving him towards the surface until he hit tunnel rock and cracked through, the mound of his shoulders driving up through the layers of rockcrete and soil. Finding as he did so that the very earth of Cadia was full of human bones, every inch of it a mass grave, so when he erupted amidst the lines of the Cadian Eighth, the broken soil around him released a cascade of dirty skulls that rolled and clattered towards the ragged Guardsmen who'd stood against him.

'*Cadia is fallen!*' he crowed, glorying in how the insectile mortals, the little bloodspots, ran from him. '*I have brought it to the altar, and tied it for the slaughter. Your skulls–*'

Then pain flared deep in his chest, the prayer-witch's blade lighting up inside him like a hot iron.

He hissed, clawed at the hilt, scratching furrows in his own flesh.

'She is coming!' a voice sang. 'She is coming! She is coming!'

At first, he thought it was Artesia, speaking into his ear from her bloody mouths, but this was no daemon voice.

He saw a brightness in his peripheral vision – on his skull rack – and reached back to wrench the object free.

The thing burned in his hand like a coal, hot and searing.

It was the head of the prayer-witch, taken on planetfall day when he'd landed outside the Shrine of St Morrican. And for the first time, he looked in puzzlement at the fresh, pink skin – the incorruptible flesh that had not decayed, and escaped combat, fire and the explosion of the null-array without a single mark.

'She is coming!' the head sang in triumph. White light burned through its eyes and shone from the open mouth as it spoke. 'She is coming! She is coming!'

Around him, the bodies of the slain Battle Sisters rustled. Jaws moving. Dead throats producing a sound like wind through tall grass.

'She is coming. She is coming. She is coming.'

Urkanthos saw his enormous shadow lengthen, as though a new sun had come up above the horizon.

Artesia screamed, a harsh terror-sound that came from her many mouths and echoed across both realspace and empyrean.

Her burrowing claws tore out of his shoulders and scrabbled down his arm, trying to shelter within his shadow before bolting off into the sky without a word to her master.

Urkanthos turned, and saw what came.

'Go! Go!' Creed roared, running out of the blasted throat of the Egressium Gate. He waved troopers towards the rearing daemon, who had turned his awful face towards them.

Above, they could see the purple billows in the clouds – the Blackstone Fortress preparing to fire on the unprotected city. Nothing to do about that.

Kell shouted at a platoon of retreating troopers, calling them back to the fight via the blare of his vox-amplifier. 'You there! You're going to let that warpson take our world? You have missile launchers, use them! If that doesn't work, use frekking lasguns, if that's not enough you have bayonets!'

Las-fire cracked past. Reinforcing groups of cultists and a fresh force of Black Legionnaires had flooded into the marshalling ground, ready to keep them pinned until the fortress could do its work.

'Get your guns and fire!' yelled Creed. 'Form up, right now. Cadia stands, and even if it doesn't, the Eighth stands. Because we're the frekking Eighth Regiment, you understand? We are Cadia.'

'The Emperor protects,' murmured a staff officer, kissing a talisman for courage.

'The Emperor?' sneered Creed. 'Frekk, son, that Throne-bound bastard isn't here. I don't want to hear any groxshit about the Emperor protecting frekking anyone. That's your job.'

Slack-jawed, the staff officer stared at him. Creed ripped the man's laspistol out of its holster and shoved it into his stomach. The officer didn't respond, looking past him at the horizon.

'Take it!' shouted Creed, jamming the barrel into the man's stomach. 'Take it, you useless–'

'Ursarkar,' Kell said, restraining the commander with a hand. 'Ursarkar, don't. The morale. You're losing composure it–'

Creed wheeled at him, and the expression on his face made Kell stop. At first, it was anger, but then an odd, pained grimace crossed his features.

'General,' said Kell, concerned. 'General, are you wounded?'

'No, Kell,' he responded. 'I'm smiling.'

Creed inclined his head, and Kell turned to see what the commander looked at.

She came out of the sky on alabaster wings, burnished golden armour clean and bright, reflecting the white light that surrounded her.

From half a mile away, Kell paradoxically could still see her face – set in an expression of fierce serenity. An expression that said the punishment she was about to deliver was as inevitable as it was just.

'Celestine!' yelled the few living Battle Sisters, raising their hands in ecstasy. 'The Living Saint comes! We are witness to a miracle.'

And she was not alone.

It was only when she streaked over their heads like an arrow that Kell realised the rings of haloed light behind her were not emanations of her holy form, but the engine-flare of landing craft.

'Reinforcements,' said Creed. 'That's my kind of frekking miracle.'

* * *

Daemons ran from the corpse-bride as she came at Urkanthos, parting like a warren of rodents pursued by a viper. Painful light panicked them, so they mounded each other as they fled, the scaled forms of the flesh hounds writhing three deep in places as they tried to escape the searing burn of her aura.

Behind her, landing craft set down hard on the body-strewn ground of the muster field, explosive bolts blowing their front ramps open so swarms of Battle Sisters emerged, the bolters in their hands nearly as dangerous as the prayers they intoned.

She slammed down in front of Urkanthos, landing with a graceful touch of her sabatons, which somehow transmitted incredible force, as though the planet jumped, electrified at her touch.

'You must be the Corpse-Saint,' Urkanthos chuckled, giving a bow. *'I have heard of you. But you come too late.'*

She said nothing, the fierce burn of her halo flaring as she lowered her mirrored blade in a challenge. Around her, crimson roses sprouted and bloomed in the eye sockets of the unearthed skulls that lay around her feet.

'Have you nothing to say? No sermon?'

'You are not worth my words.'

Her sword flashed around in an overhand cut, dazzling the air with reflections, the light piercing into his eyes.

Urkanthos met the blade with his talons and the discharge of a thunderclap. He shouted, hand scalded where his claws had met the white-hot edge of the weapon, and cut in with his other hand, swiping out to grab her wing and tear it off.

But she leapt skyward, outside his reach in a flash and suspended in air, then dived down inside his guard and grabbed a handhold on his mask, wrenching his head upward with strength unbelievable given her size.

Screaming pain lanced through his face as the silver blade stabbed down through his mask – smooth as a needle – and pierced the orbit of his left eye. Blood and ichor poured down from the burst organ, and he roared, slapping out with his big hands.

She was gone like smoke. Back in the air, shining like a figure in a cathedral window.

'You think you can kill me by piercing an eye?' he snarled. The jelly orb had already begun reknitting itself.

'No,' said a voice behind him. 'But it let me come up on your blind side.'

Hot agony speared deep in his chest, the blessed blade in his shoulder driving the last eight inches into his body, so the tip pierced his monstrous heart.

Daemons felt sensations so exquisite, mortals could not comprehend them. And this was the most exquisite pain Urkanthos had felt in ten thousand years.

It staggered him. He bent over gripping his chest like a man suffering cardiac arrest, thinking that it was not supposed to be this way. That he had conquered Cadia. Delivered it to Warmaster Abaddon and the God of Blood.

But as the sword pulled free of his chest, he roared skyward at the pain, and saw the glowing ember of the Blackstone Fortress in the sky.

Abaddon, he realised in that moment, had played him for a fool. Made him trade his loyal Hounds to open a city the Warmaster would obliterate from orbit – with him still inside.

In some ways, a welcome revelation.

For when Urkanthos whirled to see who had stabbed him, and saw the twin prayer-witch Sisters resurrected, with the corpse-god's light pouring from their eyes and swords in their hands, he at least had some perspective to salve the onrush of fear.

'Enjoy your victory,' he snarled. *'Abaddon will make it brief. And I will see your souls in the warp.'*

Then, the shining blades fell on him. Hacking, stabbing, severing, slitting, piercing, burning. Shedding no blood as they cut him apart.

And Urkanthos, Ascended Prince of Chaos and former Lord Ravager of the Black Fleet, for the first time felt his essence banished into the deranged vortex of the empyrean.

Where his long scream of anguish was but one among many.

The first Space Wolf hit Morkath and the team from an ambush position in the castellum gate, lunging out of a toothed alcove to splash bolt-fire into the flank of Cell Vega-Two. One round caught Siron's breastplate and detonated, marring his winged-skull heraldry. Another round crushed in a strike-brother's helmet, pulping his brains. His thoughts simply disappeared, leaving not even a psychic echo.

Vega-Two returned fire, spanging shots off his armour and blistering the corner he hid behind.

Morkath did not shoot, she gestured – reaching out to the fang-lined maw of the alcove so the fleshworked walls slammed shut on the Space Marine, piercing his armour and holding him in place.

It did not kill him, he was too hardy, but it immobilised him enough that Siron could put a bolt pistol to his head and finish the kill.

'Ahead!' said the team scout, before opening up down the main passage. Mass-reactive shells streaked down the corridor like flares, casting rings of light that rushed down the walls and into the open chamber beyond.

The Wolves were there. Only nineteen of them now, plus a few Cadians, but enough to do the damage required. They were within running distance of the power coupling, carving their way through the daemons and the mind-slaved crew Morkath had compelled to stop them, even if they needed to pin the Wolves down with the weight of their bodies.

Siron slapped one brother on the pauldron and pointed at the retreating Wolves. The Space Marine hefted a reaper autocannon and poured fire at them with the distinctive one-two-one-two chugging fire of the weapon. A round tore a Wolf in two and made three others duck behind a pipe assembly. One fortunate shot slammed into the leader's back and, while it deflected into the wall, pitched him onto his face.

Around them, the fortress rocked with another hit. They had seen the *Phalanx*, the colossal starship which served as fortress-monastery for the Imperial Fists Chapter, out of a viewport window in the previous chamber, and no doubt the Wolves had too. Both sides knew what was at stake.

'Can you shut the doors?' Siron shouted at her.

Morkath planted her hands on the rebuilt floor, on either side of a pipe rapidly turning into a sheath of bone, and cast her essence through the spongy marrow within to find hatches, doors, anything.

There. A slide-door, big as a Baneblade, between the Wolves and the coupling.

She pushed her will towards the doorway and told the parasitic flesh-mechanisms to close.

It began sliding shut before the fortress blocked her, vibrating at some frequency that shivered the warpflesh and sapped its strength. She could no longer command the door.

And the resonance, the stubborn resistance, backfired down the pipe and into her.

Morkath's blackstone teeth picked up the vibration and seemed to twist in her gums, her heavy stone eye rolling in her head, straining its nerve attachments. Noctilith bone sheathed in her frame ground, stabbing at her.

The fortress howled in agonised fury and Morkath realised only halfway through the scream it was not the fortress, but her own mouth.

Siron ripped her off the pipe, breaking the connection.

An orange-flamed bolt-shell streaked past her face and into the wall, and Siron threw her behind his bulk to return fire with his bolt pistol.

It was a Space Marine that had not been standing there before. A black-armoured creature of hate with heraldic devices of bones and flame – images of the infernal – a halo of fire circling his head.

More appeared in the chamber, stepping out of wavering curtains of smokeless flame that rippled once and went out. They carved up the daemons and drummed suppressive fire onto the Havoc with the reaper autocannon.

Siron met the closest one with his power fist, the hell-spawned ghost ripping into the intelligence chief's armour with a flaming chainsword before Siron vaporised it with the melta under his combi-bolter. The thing disappeared in a sizzle of fire.

The Legion of the Damned. The closest thing the Imperials had to daemons.

'Morkath!' Siron yelled, dragging out a power sword to meet another ghostly combatant. 'Vox the Warmaster! Tell him *Devicus.*'

'I...'

'Just do it!' He ripped an object off his belt and threw it into the chamber, a red rune winking as it fell.

Morkath reached out with her mind, the way she was not supposed to. Used her closeness to the Warmaster to search for him, seeking out his brilliant, unmistakable presence in the disordered mental riot of all who lived upon the fortress.

He was on the bridge. Morkath saw him. Their connection was strong.

She mustered all her strength into a word she'd never heard.

DEVICUS.

The canister flared like a falling star, and erupted in a strike of fuchsia lightning as if it had shattered reality like a rock through a window.

It was a teleport homer.

And out of the broken rent in realspace, through the howling portal, came Morkath's father.

Drach'nyen, the End of Empires, slashed wide, bisecting a Fenrisian Long Fang along with the three daemons he'd been battling. The Talon of Horus howled like a tortured soul, then pulverised two Cadians and drilled through another Space Wolf's helm.

Further down the chamber, she saw the Wolves' leader slow his run and turn with a grimace – no, not a grimace. He was laughing. Tossing his head, as if this were all a great joke.

He passed an object to his companion, a Wolf even older than he was, then threw away his empty bolt pistol and took his enormous chainsword in two hands.

'Sven Bloodhowl,' said Siron, shaking the ash of a slain warp-ghost off his power sword. 'Come, we have to get close. Assis–'

'No!' Morkath shouted. 'Bloodhowl gave something to the other Wolf, it's a diversion, he–'

There was no point, she realised, in explaining herself. Instead she reached out to her father's mind, warning him of the danger. Not to engage the Wolf Lord.

Too late.

Bloodhowl keyed his jump pack and bounded towards the Warmaster, storm bolter rounds from the Talon sparking off his power armour and tearing his flame-embroidered cape to tatters.

He came down on Abaddon with his whirling chainblade, swinging onto the Warmaster's upraised daemon sword.

But the Space Wolf pulled the blow, cutting his pack early so he slammed to the decking just ahead of the Warmaster, thrusting the chewing blade forward into Abaddon's breastplate in an attempt to stagger him.

It did not work. The teeth of the sword dug into the Warmaster's breastplate, but he was not moved. Instead, the Talon of Horus smashed across the Wolf Lord's face with a slap of energy discharge.

The daemon blade followed, carving into Bloodhowl's back as he spun away, breaking open his armour's reactor and shearing through the jump pack. One barrel-like jet thruster fell away, clanging on the deck.

The Warmaster, seeing the Fenrisian career sideways, crushed the chainblade under his foot, and left the lesser creatures to deal with the unarmed Space Marine.

And continued towards his goal.

But Bloodhowl shook his head, cuffed blood away from his mouth and licked red lips.

Then laughed.

He unfastened one gauntlet and threw it at the Warmaster's back, hitting him in the pauldron with a heavy clang of metal on metal.

The Warmaster stopped. Turned.

'Please, Warmaster!' Morkath begged, as they rushed forward. But there were too many daemons and deck crew in the way. 'Do not be baited.'

Bloodhowl threw his other gauntlet, and this time Abaddon batted it from the air, fuming.

The Wolf Lord threw his arms out wide.

Abaddon leapt on him, hacking and clawing, infuriated by the ineffectual pounding of Bloodhowl's bare fists as the Space Wolf threw himself at the Warmaster, heedless of the weapons scything into his body. Laughing as he punched Abaddon's stone-hard face.

Laughing at the absurdity. Laughing because he knew no other way to die. Laughing, because an explosion had just torn through the power couplings in the distance, severed cables spewing fountains of white sparks into the ceiling vaults before the overload burst the crystal view-wheel above, venting fire into space.

He was still laughing, mortally wounded, as Abaddon vanished in another jagged break of lightning. And when she realised Siron had also disappeared into a clap of empty air.

Morkath heard the hollow slam of the port-side void shield collapsing.

She had only begun to run for cover, triggering bulkheads and opening armoured hatches, when the first volley from the *Phalanx* crashed into the *Will of Eternity*. It took her off her feet, but she was running again in the seconds before the second impact, with enough time to seal a hatch before her world went dark, and she was imprisoned in a sepulchre of alien black stone.

PHASE SIX

ELYSION FIELDS

ONE

The Valkyrie's thrust nozzles still wavered the air of the landing pad when Creed stepped out, ignoring the red-carpeted mounting stairs the Kasrkin sergeant had placed below the hatch for his use.

'Kell,' he said. 'Remind me never to ride in one of these things again.'

'Yes, sir,' Kell said, holding out a briefing slate. 'I will remember, general.'

'Don't give me that tone.' Creed took the slate and scanned it. 'You know I can't take you everywhere. The Eighth took a mauling and you're the damned colour sergeant, your place was here consolidating and rebuilding. Unless you want to let someone else carry that banner?'

Kell said nothing.

'Didn't think so. Anyway, you wouldn't have been able to do much. We got chased up and down by a few locusts. Nothing the interceptors couldn't take care of.' He sighed, handed back the data-slate as they walked towards the upper spire of Kraf Command. 'I'm tired, just summarise. Give me the executive digest.'

'Archenemy fleet's been driven to the other side of the world. The *Phalanx* and the remainder of the fleet have control over Kraf's skies. The *Will of Eternity* appears to have suffered critical damage and become inoperable, but seems to be far enough out that orbital decay isn't going to drop it on top of us.'

'Well thank the Throne for that. Do we have teams aboard assessing salvage?'

'Yes, Kasrkin with experience on the defence platforms–'

'Back when those existed.' Creed nodded at some Mordian Sable Guard who made the sign of the aquila at him. 'What is this about the Mechanicus fleet? Was that part of Tor Garadon's contingent with the *Phalanx*?'

'No, that's… different. Canoness Sylvania and her group were lost in the warp, their ship sabotaged by a traitor and becalmed. The Saint led her to the *Phalanx*, as she tells it. And the Legion of the Damned led the *Phalanx* to Cadia. Cawl just seems to have… shown up.'

'Have you ever felt,' Creed said, nodding at a trooper who held the door of his office open, 'like we're the corner pocket on a tilted bill-yard table? Everyone just seems to keep rolling towards us.'

'Fortunate for us, then.'

'Maybe.' Creed looked at the map. 'Lot more to work with now, isn't it?'

There were so many more markers on it. The units Creed had kept in reserve, locked away in remote postings and the hidden Salvation outposts planted in strategic areas had started to emerge. Over the past two days he'd been all over Cadia, giving orders and passing out activation codes. The most important, those he needed to promote or give privileged orders to, he'd insisted on visiting in person.

But things had not gone so smoothly. For some vaults, the massive doors failed to open, trapping the units inside. Avalanches had covered escape points, or troopers had fallen to infighting and ill-discipline from going too long without orders. Others were emerging in enemy-held areas and facing annihilation.

For the majority, though, the opening doors were a glorious

moment of catharsis. Troops held back and half-mad from inactivity emerging to chase the enemy from sectors where they were already fleeing. Mop-up operations and pursuits. Relieving besieged garrisons that welcomed the new arrivals with almost the same ecstatic joy Celestine had conjured.

But it had been a near thing, and the thought that it had almost been too late – that Urkanthos or the fortress could have, indeed probably *should have,* wiped them out – preyed on his mind. Any way you cut it, Creed had waited too late. There was such a thing as too much nerve, and under any conventional military campaign it would've been a blunder.

Indeed, Creed himself seemed a little miffed that they'd been saved by literal divine intervention – but it did not pay to look a gift Chimera in the engine block.

'Could the archmagos dominus be here because of his interest in the Blackstone Fortress?'

Kell shrugged. 'Don't ask me to try and get inside that head.'

'Who's first on the agenda?'

'Inquisitor Talia Daverna, she's been waiting outside for quite a while.'

'How long?'

'Two days, on and off.'

Creed winced. 'Better start with her.'

Talia Daverna sat before the desk, refusing to be intimidated by Creed's looming. One of the few people since the start of the invasion that had managed that feat.

'I'm not going to circle around it, Ursarkar, I don't think either of us have time for that.'

'So don't circle.' He took a sip of his amasec.

'I've picked up anomalous troop movements. Assets that are not where they're supposed to be.'

'The Salvation outposts. Our reserves. You knew about that, one of the few who did.'

'Not the outposts,' she snapped, each word spoken through clenched teeth. She rose to her feet, hands tented on the map across from Creed, towering over him. 'Now, Lord Castellan, you're going to sit down, remember that I am the frekking Inquisition, and tell me the truth.'

Kell's stomach dropped out. Daverna's change in demeanour came so fast, he hadn't seen it coming.

'I think I prefer to stand.'

'Sit. Down.'

Creed jerked his head sideways, and Kell brought him a chair. He sat.

'My sources say there are anomalous movements. Secret orders. Fields being cleared–'

'The new airfields, you mean?'

'You Throne-damned know I don't mean the new airfields. I've lived my entire life on Cadia, you think I don't know the difference between a dirt airfield and a surface-to-space embarkation field?'

Creed said nothing.

'Tell me it's not what I think. That it's not what it absolutely looks like.'

'It's not.'

'You know that can't happen. You got the same briefing every Lord Castellan receives. Hells, I gave it to you myself. There are certain contingencies in place in case Cadia is ever *in extremis diabolus,* and you know very well what they are.'

'I know the plans. And no, they are not what you think. I should have briefed you, I apologise. Here's the truth. We know that the war is not done here, but there's no guarantee the next battle will be in the Kraf region. It could be back on Cadia Primus, Tertius – hells, it could be up in orbit or on the Blackstone Fortress for all we know. That might even be preferable. So we need low-void transports for repositioning purposes. Better to take troops up and into orbit, then back down halfway around the planet, than try to fly atmospherically. Faster, and it avoids the swarms of terrestrial enemy fighter craft. Or we can get up into the ships to assist them in void war, that's all it is, Talia.'

'Are you lying to me, Creed?'

'I have no talent for lying, you know that.'

'Any contact with warp entities this extreme, on any planet, would require mass troop purges or sector sterilisations from orbit. Indeed, it's amazing that in its history, Cadia has never needed to execute that before. But we've also never had daemon manifestations this widespread before. We are already looking at the need for quarantine and selective mass-executions, at the very least. But if warp entities continue manifesting as they have been, the Extremis Protocols must be followed.'

Creed snorted. 'General virus bombing? We defeat the Despoiler and you wipe us all out from orbit, you mean? Ruin the finest fortress world of the Imperium, and the recruiting base for the hardest assault infantry in the Militarum?'

'We have to think about the big picture. The world would be resettled. There are more Cadians off-planet than on these days anyway. Generations of troop musters have ensured that. And we wouldn't be running the risk of exporting tainted soldiers to every battle sector across the Imperial domain.'

'You'd seriously do that?'

'No.' Daverna blinked. 'No, not me personally. I've had massdaemon contact too, you know. If it happens, I'll be on the ground with the rest of the poor bastards. But if it needs to be done, it must be done. You understand that if it reaches that point, you cannot have… contingencies.'

Kell felt hot inside his uniform. He'd known about the Extremis

Protocols, of course. Had been there when Creed was briefed, though then it seemed like a ghoulish theoretical, with none of the weight it now carried. A prearranged plan known only to the Lord Castellan and Inquisitorial legate, plus their closest staff for continuity purposes. He recalled how foolishly privileged he'd felt knowing such a deep secret.

'I need to hear you say it, Ursarkar. The words need to come out of your mouth, so I know you understand.'

Creed bowed his head, ran a hand over the stubble at the base of his skull. Mumbled.

'Louder. So you can't claim a miscommunication. Look me in the eyes when you say it.'

Creed closed his eyes, shook his head. Opened them again, and met her gaze.

'No evacuation,' he said.

Hellsker sat in the wooden chair at Kraf Command, feeling out of place.

It was warm, first off. Uncomfortably warm. She'd only been stationed in the Delvian Cleave around two weeks, but in that time she hadn't experienced a temperature more than ten degrees above the freeze point, and her command style put her mostly on the roadway, in the wind.

Everyone was clean, too. With well-pressed uniforms, fairly crackling with starch.

She'd once looked like that.

Technically, she knew the process to go through in order to look like that again. Just like she knew how to sleep on top of a bed rack, rather than underneath it as she had finally done last night, unable to settle for fear that an orbital strike might collapse the building on her as she slept.

The Cadian 46th Armoured Shock had relieved them the day before – coming out of an obscure holdfast in the Rossvar.

So rattled had her remaining troops been that they'd almost opened fire on the lead Salamander scout vehicle, thinking the Volscani had somehow got behind them.

The 46th had orders to take position on the cleave, allow the 24th to rest and resupply, and for Hellsker to go directly to Kraf Command.

'Throne of Terra,' the lieutenant-colonel of the 46th Shock had said, looking at her bedraggled troopers and the burned-out roadway. 'Looks like your people need a rest. Call them down from the walls, we'll take over.'

Hellsker had been embarrassed to tell him that the troops on the roadway were it – on paper, the 24th Cadian Interior Guard contained three thousand troopers. But in reality, it was now an under-strength platoon.

'Next,' the desk-colonel said.

Hellsker was staring at her scuffed boots, one sewn together with gum-glue after the toe cap had been torn open by a piece of shrapnel. Didn't realise he'd meant her until he repeated the summons with a sharper edge.

'*Next.*'

'Sorry,' she said, springing from the chair, and coming to attention before the desk with a snap of boots. 'I'm here to see the Lord Castellan.'

'You and everyone else, trooper,' the colonel said, not looking up from the lined and columned schedule book spread out before him. 'And I must say...'

He raised his eyes to Hellsker, hard and flinty. She could see he had an augmetic hand that looked like it had gone in a blast injury, plus a bionic eye that flowed seamlessly into a forehead plate where part of his skull had been replaced.

'People who *do* get ushered in to see the Lord Castellan of Cadia, Supreme Commander of the Defence Forces and Hero of Tyrok, usually make more of an effort in their uniform and comportment. You're not on the damned aegis line now, you know.'

Hellsker felt a flicker of shame at her appearance. Embarrassment at her ragged patrol cap stained with blood, her scuffed boots, the trousers with holes run in the knees. Rank chevrons removed, because they'd shone too much during the night fighting. Sweat stains showing on the underarms of her greatcoat. But it was only the smallest flicker, like a lho-stick igniter sparking but refusing to light.

'My apologies, sir. I have been on the line and not been issued another uniform. There is a shortage, and I was unable to have this one laundered. No excuse, colonel. I do have an appointment.'

'Been through it, have you?'

'I think everyone has, sir.'

'Damn right, it's been hell around here.' He picked up a stylus, pointing it at a column of names. 'You have an appointment? Name, rank and unit.'

'Hellsker, Marda. Major, Twenty-Fourth Cadian Interior.'

The stylus stopped halfway down the column of names. She noticed the tip was shaking.

The colonel set the stylus down, and looked back up into her face. His natural eye was huge, the mouth below the thin moustache slightly open.

He stood quickly, chair squeaking on the marble behind him.

'Major Hellsker,' he said. 'I apologise fully and completely for my manner. It has been, ah, a trying few weeks at Kraf Command. So many people coming through, you know. Plus the shelling. Not' – he corrected himself – 'that it is in any way comparable to your service. The stress has made me snappy. I would take it as a personal favour if you did not bring it up when you speak to the Lord Castellan.'

Hellsker looked left and right. Spooked. Heads were turning towards her. Officers whispering.

'Uh, no, of course not, colonel. Sir.'

'I'll buzz you right in.' He hit a button on the desk. 'The eleven-thirty appointment is here, a little early.'

'Thank you... sir?'

The inner door to Creed's office opened twenty feet behind the desk, and she started walking towards it. Slowly, tentatively, looking over her shoulder at the outer wardroom with its long table, where everyone seemed to be looking at her.

'Major Hellsker, everyone!' said the desk colonel, clapping. 'Of the Twenty-Fourth Cadian.'

And then they all started to clap. And nod. And smile at her. A few whooped.

'Pardon me, major,' said a Kasrkin trooper, stepping forward from the guard detail, hellgun slung across his chest.

'Corporal?' She held up her hands, in case he wanted to wand her and pat her down.

'I wondered if you would be good enough to sign this for me?' He held out a card and a stylus.

'Oh,' she said, taking it. 'Is it a visitation card? Some kind of official–'

'It's for me, my name is Varrek?'

'I mean if it's a base pass or requisition, you really need your commanding officer to–'

She looked down at the square of glossy card-paper and stopped.

It was a lho-card. The kind that came in packs of smokes, with notable Cadian officers and Imperial heroes inside. She'd collected them as a cadet.

But she'd never had this one.

This one had her face on it.

'What the *frekk?*' she said.

'Quite a welcome,' said Creed. 'A true hero of Cadia.'

'Pardon me, lord, but... how did this happen?' Hellsker held up a crumpled handbill with her officer's intake photo on it. It had still been in her hand when Kell had extracted her from the milling crowd of officers and closed the door.

'Your vox-reports,' puffed Creed. 'They were quite exciting. And they came steadily at a time when we couldn't seem to win. The Commissariat thought they were useful.'

'I don't have this scar.'

'There's some artistic licence.' Creed waved a hand, as if it were no matter. 'To be frank I was sure you'd have known about it before now. We put updates on you through all the airwaves, and it's amazing no one recognised you in the common billet, by insignia alone – though judging by your uniform maybe not.'

'I don't deserve this.'

She saw movement on her flank – Kell offering her a tall glass of amasec.

'Who cares? The Commissariat wanted a figure to raise morale, and they picked you. And it did raise morale – so it's immaterial whether you deserve it or not. Though if you want my personal opinion, you do.'

Creed raised his glass in a silent toast, then drank.

'Did… did you want me here to do a propaganda tour?'

'The Lord Castellan has a mission for you,' said Kell. 'One for which you are very suited.'

'It relates to the orders I gave Barathus,' said Creed. 'About the importance of holding the cleave.'

The two went silent, as if she was supposed to say something.

'My lord…' Hellsker started.

'You can call me sir or general.'

'Sir… Colonel Barathus never confided in me the strategic purpose of the mission.'

Another pause, and Creed barked a laugh. 'You mean you fought that tenaciously without knowing why?'

'Yes, sir.'

'You're a better soldier than I thought.'

'Why is it so crucial?'

'Because the Delvian Clea– Kell?'

Kell waved his hands, made a throat-cutting gesture. Then pointed to the chair and tapped his ear. Mouthed a four-syllable word she couldn't make out.

Creed made a frustrated grunt, but nodded.

Was the Lord Castellan worrying his personal office was bugged? Who the hells would have the capability to tap Creed's communications?

Belatedly, she made the four-syllable word out: *Inquisitor.*

When Hellsker was a cadet, they'd done exercises learning to escape from a Valkyrie that crashed in water. They'd been strapped into jump seats of a weighted facsimile aircraft that flipped over on a hinge and submerged in a pool upside down. Their task had been to undo the buckles and straps, and swim out the door before they drowned. Then do it again, and again, until the movements came naturally.

The feel of the water pouring into the open doors of the train-ing craft, rapidly rising to submerge her face, was a sensation she'd never forgotten. That's how she felt now, as if she'd been suddenly submerged in an unnatural and dangerous environment.

'Thank you for handing me those maps, Kell,' the Lord Castel-lan said.

Kell had handed him no maps. It was a ruse to cover the brief silence.

'We needed the Delvian Cleave,' Creed said, leaning over the sector map, and finding the cleave with his finger, 'because it's our main movement channel across the western Rossvar. There are troops emerging there, from the sanctuaries, which are needed at Kraf. But it's more than that.'

'Do you need access to the sea?'

'Yes, that's part of it. First phase will be ensuring that the cleave stays open so that reinforcements can reach the Kraf battle sector, but what we really need is a grass space port here.'

He tapped the lowland beyond the cleave. 'We have assets in space with nowhere to land. And we may need to do an orbital lift of our forces to the other continents. We don't know where the Despoiler will strike next.'

Hellsker sat back. 'Are you saying it isn't over?'

'Not nearly.' Creed shook his head. 'The Archenemy has one last push in them, I can feel it. The Kraf area is too wrecked to pitch out an improvised landing field. But beyond the Rossvar, well there's been less fighting, but it's enemy territory.'

'Your task is to cross the Rossvar with the Twenty-Fourth Cadian, leave a force at the Delvian Cleave to hold it, and clear a zone in preparation for its possible use as a ground-to-orbit port,' said Kell.

'I... It's impossible. General, I don't think you realise that the Twenty-Fourth Interior is destroyed. We're a platoon unit.'

'Not on paper, you aren't.'

'We're wiped out,' she snapped, no longer letting shame and awe restrain her. 'Combat ineffective. Paper isn't reality.'

'Ahh,' Creed said, sitting on the corner of his desk, and beckoning towards Kell. 'See that's the beauty of being Lord Castellan. When I sign a paper, it becomes reality.'

Kell passed a writing board, clipped with a seal-laden parchment.

'This is a special order of reorganisation,' he said, picking up a stylus and scratching his signature. 'That tasks two remnant units – the Ninety-First Infantry and the Nine-Hundred-and-Twenty-Second Combat Engineers to immediately report to the Delvian Cleave, where they will join the fresh troops of the Forty-Sixth Armoured Shock. There, they will form an amalgamated unit under the banner of the Twenty-Fourth Cadian Shock Troops, under your command.'

'That's a regimental-sized unit, sir, I'm only a major.'

'Not any more,' Creed said, stuffing the orders in a message tube and holding it out. 'Your command, Colonel Hellsker.'

'I… but… sir.'

'What?'

'I'm flattered, but I can't do this. I'm exhausted. And I'm an infantry officer – not even that, an Interior Guard trooper. The Forty-Sixth Armoured Shock is a mechanised regiment, mounted infantry and battle tanks. I don't know a damn thing about commanding armour, I've only been an executive officer for an engineering regiment. This is combined arms. Maybe I could head the Nine-Hundred-and-Twenty-Second section, and you could find someone else to take overall command?'

'You're scared of failing,' said Creed. 'Good, I wouldn't trust you if you were too confident about it. And you want to know why you – well, here it is. I don't care if you know which end of a Leman Russ points towards the enemy, you have a fine armoured commander to handle that for you. And these troopers are going to be thrilled to serve under the woman who held the Delvian Cleave.'

'We got lucky. I made mistakes, lots of mistakes. Everything went wrong. I took three thousand troopers into that canyon and I have just under forty left standing.'

'But they were *standing,* Marda. That's the Throne-damned point. You held them together. They didn't break. You did what Cadians do, we stand. To the last trooper. You made mistakes, so the frekk what? You think I haven't made mistake after mistake in this invasion? I lost the air war on Zero Day because I thought I knew better than my air marshal. I put the wrong man in command of the Kriegan Gates. And we're all standing here because I got so lucky a frekking angel saved me when I was too stubborn to use my reserves. And my mistakes killed a hell of a lot more than three thousand troopers. You think I'm not tired, that I don't want to give it up and just sleep for a while?'

Hellsker looked down, the shame returning.

'You hung on at the cleave until your last las-cell. You didn't frek-king run then, so don't start now.'

She accepted the message tube.

'Thank you, sir. I will do my best.'

'Stand up, colonel.'

She did, at attention, as Creed took a pair of rank chevrons from Kell and pinned them to her collar. 'You might want to get supply to requisition you a new uniform. Just a suggestion.'

'Yes, sir, I tried. But they had none to spare.'

'Kell will give you a requisition order on my stationery. Give it to the desk colonel, he'll get you straightened out. Probably give you the one off his back.'

Then as they laughed, Creed did something so unexpected it made her stiffen.

He took her by the shoulders and leaned in, and for a moment she thought he was about to plant kisses on her cheeks the way families did in the far south.

But he didn't; he whispered, nearly beyond hearing.

'It's not a lifting field,' he said, so close she could feel the prickle of his stubble and the smell of amasec on his breath. 'It's an evacuation point. If things go wrong, secure the ships. Save as many as possible. Kell has a package for you. If the worst happens, get it to the person whose name is on it. Guard it with your life. Tell no one about this.'

She nodded. 'Yes, sir.'

Creed stepped back and patted her shoulders. 'Any other kit you need? Sidearm?'

'No, sir, I managed to get a hellpistol. If you could requisition me a new power sword, that would be helpful. The generator on mine needs a rebuild.'

'No time for that,' said Creed, pursing his lips. He hesitated, then stepped over to a credenza against the wall, brushing aside scrolls and rolled maps, unearthing a scabbarded blade and presenting it to her. 'Here, try that one. Had it lying around.'

She saw Colour Sergeant Kell tense.

'Thank you, lord.' She took it, marvelling at the ornate basket hilt with its image of the Cadian Gate. Pulled the blade from the scabbard, feeling how easily it moved. 'It's...'

'You'll get used to the weight,' Creed said. 'Mind, you're a colonel now. You should be fighting with a map, a vox and a pointed finger. If you get in range to use those weapons, it usually means you've frekked up bad. I haven't fired a shot this whole war, not really.'

'Lord, I can't accept this.'

'You already have.'

'It's the sword of Lukas Bastonne, sir.'

'Yes,' Creed said. 'And tomorrow, no matter how many heretics you run through, it will still be the sword of Lukas Bastonne. I'm not giving it to you, I'm entrusting you with it. In fact, I'm entrusting you with quite a lot. When you're done with that blade, find someone trustworthy to take it up – now get out of here, I'm busy.'

She saluted.

The sword seemed heavier than when he'd given it to her.

But the package Kell handed her, wrapped in a weatherproof plastek seal-bag, was light.

By weight and feel, she knew it was a book.

'And that,' said Archmagos Dominus Belisarius Cawl, 'was how I proved the hypothesis.'

The Kraf council room was silent, and Kell took the moment to wonder again at how much things had changed since the initial war council in this chamber.

One wall had an enormous crack running floor to ceiling, hastily patched with rockcrete and rebar. The holo-table in the centre no longer functioned. But it was the faces that'd had the greatest turnover.

Gone were Sven Bloodhowl, Magos Klarn and Supreme Commissar Zabine – no one had seen her since Jorus Redoubt. Amalrich's bannerman had changed. Canoness Eleanor was not present – now a soul-servant of the Living Saint, who had declined her invitation in order to minister to the dead. She'd insisted to Creed that they burn the Cadian martyrs, purify them with flame, and he had finally relented – she was presiding over the funeral pyres as millions of Imperial casualties fed the flames.

The entirety of the Kraf battle sector smelled of burning corpses.

Baroness Vardus was present, but looked physically changed. Painfully thin and haggard, her proud Knights badly damaged by the combat with Legio Vulcanum. Kell had heard she'd initiated a reactor overload – trying to take Vulcanum's Warlord Titan with her – when the Imperial Fists had swept in and turned the tide of the battle.

And there were the new faces. Tor Garadon of the Imperial Fists and Canoness Sylvania in Eleanor's vacated seat. Captain Ruis Tracinto had arrived, from Kasr Partox, along with his Fifth Company of the Crimson Fists. Baron Ryevan from House Taranis, who'd slipped out of Solar Mariatus with the 51st Armoured.

But none so strange as the archmagos in the centre.

'Any questions?' Cawl asked the silent ring of commanders.

'Yes,' said Tor Garadon. 'Was that supposed to make sense?'

'Agreed,' said Wolf Lord Highfell. 'Please explain again.'

'What aspect do you find obscure, exactly?' answered Cawl, a hint of buzzing annoyance in his vocals. 'The sections concerning the Eriad System? The mathematical proofs? Empyric polarity? Perhaps I can repeat the binharic sections if you did not–'

'None of us speak binharic,' said Creed.

'I do,' said Baron Ryevan. 'On Mars, it's considered a necessary part of cultural literacy.'

'Oh, excellent,' said Logistar-General Raik, rolling his eyes. 'Can we get a translation?'

'I would,' said Cawl, 'but few words fully translate to High Gothic. To appreciate the meaning, you truly have to hear it in the original language. You see, ten thousand years ago–'

'For the sake of the Motive Force,' said Baron Ryevan. 'It's not that hard to understand. The archmagos dominus was on Eriad Six investigating ancient noctilith chambers. There, deep below the surface, he discovered the ruins of a pylon network similar to that of Cadia, destroyed when the Despoiler had bombarded the world during the Fourth Black Crusade. Cross-referencing archaeologica surveys of pylon-like structures across the Gate, he found half a dozen more examples of pylon worlds destroyed by the Black Fleet.'

'Yes, I got that part,' said Canoness Sylvania. 'What's the significance? Is Abaddon quarrying the blackstone, building a weapon?'

'Augmenting his Blackstone Fortress,' said Tor Garadon. 'He's already shown extreme interest in the fleet assets and their tactical–'

'No, no, no!' Cawl rapped the stone with the butt of his axe in irritation. 'The pylons aren't his weapon, they're our weapon. Don't you understand? We've always thought the Eye of Terror was the warp pushing into our reality. An incursion. But it's the other way around. Realspace is falling into the warp, and these negatively polarised pylons are the thing holding the galaxy together.'

Garadon sneered at the interruption, his heavy brow casting his eyes in shadow.

Cawl sighed, and two mechadendrites slid out of the bulbous hive in his midsection to straighten his robes. They nipped at each other before retracting.

'I always forget how much you unaugmented like analogies. Think of the Eye of Terror like a wound. And the wound has been partially sutured shut. Well, as the skin moves it puts stress on the sutures, but they hold, and while they hold the wound can heal.

Except for the part left open. Now imagine if you cut the sutures – the wound tears open, correct?'

'Yes,' said Creed. 'What you're saying is that the Eye of Terror used to be larger, and whatever ancient race built these pylons, these anti-warp-charged–'

'Reductive to call it anti-warp, but continue.'

'–they managed to limit the Eye's size, pen it into this area of the galaxy. What we know as the Cadian Gate isn't random. Someone constructed it this way.'

'Yes. And Cadia is the linchpin of that chain of planets. The keystone that holds the others up. There are more pylons here than any other place in the galaxy.'

Creed slumped. 'That's why there's never been a major warp-spawn incursion, isn't it? The pylons were holding it back.'

'In theory,' said Cawl. 'But the pylons are also weakening – as the Despoiler destroyed fields across the galaxy, the stress upon those on Cadia has become greater. Looking at the data of the late Magos Klarn, it seems their resonance has weakened even in the past decade.'

'That would explain why the Legion of the Damned have taken positions out in the pylon field up north,' Garadon said. 'Seems like they've known all along.'

'The Elysion Fields,' said Creed. 'It's the densest pylon field on Cadia. And...'

'I have something on that!' exclaimed Air Marshal Shrowd, nearly always quiet in these conferences.

'Yes?'

'We had an observation pilot take some pict-captures. They were late coming in, since she was downed and had to find her way back. They showed an unusual armoured column at the edge of Elysion – demolition vehicles. War engines with saws and drills. In her pics, they were demolishing a pylon.'

'They've already started cutting the network,' said Inquisitor Daverna. 'That's why the empyric horrors manifested so heavily at the Siege of Kraf. They've further weakened the effectiveness.'

'But if I am given leave,' said Cawl, three of his hands raising their index fingers in unison, 'it is possible I may be able to stabilise the network – or even magnify it, as Klarn did.'

'Lord Castellan,' said Shrowd. 'Request leave to attend to this. I'll get updated information on their location and, if possible, put together a strike package.'

'Do it,' Creed said. 'I think the rest of us should discuss a general marshal at the Elysion Fields. It's logically the next target, and Kraf has been reduced enough that it cannot withstand another siege anyway. Give me deployment estimates – how fast can we reposition and prepare defences there? And how many troops can you each commit? What–'

–are our troop dispositions and who should deploy in which sector? Kell, call up to the strategium, have them bring up an Elysion map, the biggest they have.

The voice echoed from above. Not a thing heard by the ear, but one felt in the mind. An overheard conversation seventy-two floors above, in the heart of the enemy's command chamber.

One he could still hear, even though he was deep underground, in front of the steel blast doors that marked the east gate of Kraf Citadel's central munitions bunker.

Yann Rovetske undid a strap on the repulsor cradle to access the warhead control system. Opened the panel so the cogitator chips and nests of blue, red and yellow wire spilled out.

He sensed his powers had increased. Each time the warp eyes opened and looked through him, they left a portion of their power behind. As if the roiling cosmic colour-shifts of the iris had flowed into him.

When he looked at things now, he saw the colours bleeding and shooting through each other, as though they were seen through a prism that kept turning.

It was nearly impossible to tell blue wires from red, or red wires from yellow, but he knew. Knew by touch. Yet it was a touch of his mind not his hands, much like he did not hear the voices from above with his ears.

Baroness Vardus, what is the current fighting strength of House Raven?

The Kasrkin team lying around the chamber had been easy to kill. Determined, strong, faithful to their corpse-god even unto death.

That is what made them so simple to influence. The Imperium preached about the strength of the mind, the fortress of faith, but that only made them more susceptible. When Rovetske told them what they must do, he'd told them to do it in the name of the God-Emperor of Mankind. And all that determined faith, the life-long indoctrination to give all for the Emperor, meant that when they turned their guns on each other, they did so with an unswerving determination and not an ounce of doubt.

And now he was here, the warhead nearly primed. This close to the magazine, it would level the entire citadel. Kill every member of Creed's little war council. A decapitation strike that would make Tyrok Fields fade into memory.

He bit through wires, stripping them with his teeth. Uncaring of how the copper spools inside cut his gums. The taste of blood was not new. At some point during the day-and-a-half journey, he'd had a vision and bit off a chunk of his tongue. When he'd spat it out upon awakening, he'd seen it was the size of the tip of his little finger.

Rovetske joined blue to yellow. Red to blue. Gripped the L-shaped range-finding cogitator board and ripped it out.

Grabbed the arming cylinder, twisted it, and plunged it in so the lights on the ordnance board winked on.

Rovetske muttered a prayer, taking the ignition system's signal wire and stretching the full width of his arms to get the dangling, stripped wire to the power supply.

'Step away,' said the voice. 'Raise your hands, turn around, and step away. Slow.'

Rovetske turned his head around so far it hurt, his vertebrae grating as his chin passed behind his shoulder.

That made it hard to breathe, his trachea had twisted closed, so he rotated his body to face the man while keeping him locked in his eyes.

The speaker was short, wearing a rumpled Cadian officer's greatcoat with silver pins on the collar, his black hair slicked back. He held a compact autopistol low, as if he expected not to use it.

'Step away. Right now.' He raised a miniature vox, depressing the clapper. 'Petzen, I found a way through. He's here.'

There was no way for him to join the wires. Not without being shot. So long, at least, as this man lived. But he would not live for long. He dropped the wire.

'Shoot me,' said Rovetske, enunciating through his swollen mouth, 'and you'll trigger this melta-torpedo. We'll all go up like at Kasr Stark. No, my friend, you do not want to shoot me. Not me.'

'Take your hand off the panel,' said the short man. 'And step away. Not telling you again.'

'Put the gun barrel in your mouth,' said Rovetske. 'See how it tastes. Does it taste like gun oil and powder? You won't pull the trigger. It's just to see. Just curiosity.'

The man's pistol raised, then settled its sights on Rovetske's chest.

'Oh, you are good,' said Rovetske, clapping. 'So good. You are syndicate, yes?'

A prismatic shine passed over his eyes, the image of the man bubbling and flowing.

'Salvar Ghent,' he said. 'That is your name. Saalvaaaar Ghent.

You own Kasr Kraf. What are you doing working for these insects, Salvar? Wearing their symbols. You never wanted that. And you don't want to shoot me.'

'Last warning.'

Rovetske stepped closer to the torpedo, poured more will into his words.

'When this goes off,' he said, 'it will be the greatest revenge upon Cadia that has ever been devised. A lifetime of stealing from these high-born bastards, of subverting their society, of living outside their broken system, could not be as delicious as destroying the system itself.'

Salvar Ghent lowered his gun, took a step forward.

'And we can escape, you and I. Can you conceive of how grateful the Warmaster will be? How much power he will give you? Unimaginable. A dirty little criminal empire is nothing against that. You could be one of the greatest men in the Warmaster's army, a chief among chiefs, a demigod.'

Ghent took another step forward. 'A demigod?'

'Abaddon's favourite. Legions under your command. Working for the most powerful being in the galaxy. What do you say to that?'

Yann Rovetske smiled with bloody teeth.

The first bullet slammed into his hip, spinning him around so the rest of the burst passed through his bicep before punching into his chest wall and then drumming his back as he fell, his slack face pressed against the cold steel of the warhead.

He left a wide bloodstain as he slid down the casing and fell in a heap below it. He could feel the repulsor field of the sled prickling his arm hair, making it stand on end.

Salvar Ghent leaned over him, crouching, elbows on his knees and pistol loose in his grip. His impassive features were no easier to decipher up close.

'I appreciate your offer, but I'll tell you the same thing I told Creed – I don't like working for people.'

Ghent lowered the pistol to his face, and for the first time in days, the eye that stared through Yann Rovetske was not full of colour, but empty darkness.

Until the muzzle flash.

She awoke screaming. Screaming because she saw his face.

'Father!'

Sitting straight up from unconsciousness, sweat cold on her skin. Breeze stirring her hair.

Blackstone all around her.

Wind was not common in the fortress. And it was a moment before she could track down the source of the noise – a cracked hatch that had been partially blocked by debris. It was not wind, but the fortress' atmosphere draining away, rushing through the micro-crack.

'Father,' she said, pulling her arms around herself.

Again, her mind replayed the shattered reality of his teleport. The Warmaster who she loved disappearing into the ether.

She did not have the courage to move. She was on the chamber ceiling, rocking back and forth as the inorganic objects remained on the floor. Nothing but corpses accompanied her, each one decaying in a chronology separate from the others.

A Cadian was nearly fresh, limbs stiffening in rigor mortis as his fatigues stirred in the atmospheric depressurisation. A nearby Space Wolf was skeletal – bones already brown and corrosion weeping from the bolts of his power armour. To her immediate left was a pile of dust and nutrient salts, identifiable as a body only due to its shape and the rusted eight-pointed medallion lying just below the shape of the head.

'Why did you leave me? I did what you asked. What kind of father leaves his daughter to die?'

Except, she hadn't died. And the Warmaster must have known that she would not.

And had she really done as he asked? She had found the Wolves, but not quickly enough to save the power coupling. The fortress, her great gift to him, was stricken.

'It is a punishment,' she said, understanding. 'You are punishing me. Leaving me here to teach me a lesson. To sort out my mess.'

And she would do so. Repair the fortress, increase her bond, and show she could be the daughter he wanted her to be.

But if he wanted her, why leave? Why no word or gesture, not even a glance as he killed the Wolves she discovered on his orders. And now, he had abandoned her in an empty shell of tomb-rock.

But then again, no father was perfect.

It was the crystal patch she worked on first. Found a web of warp-flesh and carved it away with her knife, letting her well of power flow into it as she laid it on the whistling micro-crack. The hiss of escaping atmosphere died, and the Cadian's uniform stopped stirring.

And in that work, as her father's work always did, she was reminded that he was harsh because of his high regard for her. Coddling would make her weak and foolish. She must earn his affection, and in doing so she was made more capable. A greater, more powerful being.

So when the hatch opened of its own accord, the fortress beckoning her into its wild depths, she went without fear.

For there she travelled to enact her father's will.

And it was there that she first heard his voice.

TWO

'Almost,' chided Cawl. 'Patient now, little thing. Patient, patient. Two skull lengths ahead. Thirty-five degree sinister pivot. Now down – no, too far, one degree up – there. Increase ultraviolet spectrum. Yes. Image coming through well. One inch forward. One more...'

His alert pinged: *Four seconds into exploration.*

Inside the noospheric data-cloak of his vision, he looked through the micro-skull's eyes. Mapping algorithm splashing out through the weaving tunnel that corkscrewed through the pylon. To Cawl, the rushing yellow wire-frame pulsed out ahead like brain signals travelling through synapses, his secondary consciousness scrubbing the return data to look for patterns.

He saw the data-net of the mapping algorithm flow out into a wider cavern. He'd made it.

Four seconds into exploration.

'Go, go now! Into the cavern, quickly.'

It zipped forward, clipping one of its teeth off on the underside of the tunnel in haste. Out into the dark, into the interior of the megalithic structure. A cavern that contained...

Static.

'Cack!' swore Belisarius Cawl, ripping the broadcast cable out of his temple's access-port and casting it to the floor. 'Useless blasted thing. Always the same, Qvo. Six seconds in, and we lose signal. It's like the damned universe has a mem-glitch, like reality isn't programmed correctly in there. How many probe-skulls remain?'

'*Nine,*' squawked Qvo. '*Nine skulls remain operational. Two non-operational. Twenty-three not answering sign–*'

'I know they're not answering the signal, they're in here.'

Cawl slapped an augmetic hand against the black surface of the pylon's base.

He'd expected the dull clank of metal on stone, as if he'd struck a slab of marble or volcanic basalt. What you might predict from a piece of stone big around as a hab-block that stood twenty storeys in the air and another ten beneath the surface.

But that was not the sound that it made. This made a reverberating *boom,* like a deep temple drum.

Cawl's threat-centre jumped at the sound, the claws of his servo-crawler scuttling him away to a safe distance, beweaponed arms emerging from his robes, arc scourge sparking and fusion welders set to maximum burn.

The stomach-lurching *thump* echoed through the cavern, across the other pylon bases, which stood at semi-regular intervals, some sunken or tilted like funerary obelisks in an antique chapel yard. Each four-sided slab reached to the cavern ceiling, so the ghostly place appeared like a hall of pillars.

'Damned thing,' he growled, and hauled back to strike it again before thinking better of it and pulling the blow. A pattern-analysis alert blinked in his vision, a polite intrusion by his secondary consciousness that had remained data-scrubbing even as his primary mind had enacted combat programs. 'Well... hello.'

The results were as exciting as they were maddening. With his pattern-divination tool still active when he'd struck the pylon, it had mapped the resonance of the sound – and found that the answers from across the cavern had been no echo. Each pylon had boomed with the same reverberation simultaneously.

'But what does that *mean*?' he yelled at the blank darkness of the stone. 'You're all connected. Fine. I know that. Some of you are damaged, degrading, but how to activate your function? What's the medium for communication linking you with your network across such vast gulfs of space? Some kind of quantum entanglement?'

'Yes, that's broadly correct.'

'Excellent, and if that is broadly correct then…' Cawl stopped, feeling his cheek muscles twist up inside his rebreather as he turned. 'Ah, Veilwalker. You finally deign to show your faceless orb here after–'

Cawl stopped when he saw the xenos. Or rather, when he realised the xenos was not the one he'd expected. Tall, statuesque and hunched. Emerald light burning from a thorax reactor and a scalloped hood shadowing two balefire eyes.

Again, combat protocols engaged, target-auguries slamming down on his vision. His long body wound around like a centipede changing direction, dancing back and forth to make himself harder to hit, weapons raised.

'Pardon me, archmagos dominus, I did not mean to break your concentration. I am Trazyn the Infinite, Overlord of Solemnace, Archaeovist of the Prismatic Galleries and–'

'Abomination!' Cawl hissed, sending a thought-impulse to six Kataphron Breachers, which swung their weapons around, joining his target net. 'Move and I'll take whatever blasphemous, unliving echo of the Motive Force you still possess. There is an entire maniple of skitarii topside. I have you, xenos filth.'

'So disappointing.' The giant leaned on his glowing staff. '*Abomination,* always abomination. Do you know how often I have been addressed thus? Given your fluency in High and Low Gothic, Linguatechnis, binharic and various dialects of Cant Mechanicus, I thought you might find a more novel descriptor.'

'It is an accurate descriptor. *Abomination* (noun): a loathsome, repulsive, hateful or disgusting thing. Derived from the archaic High Gothic, *ab homine*, "away from mankind".'

'A shallow linguistic interpretation. Quoted verbatim. And partially in error.'

'Partially?' Cawl recalibrated his arc scourge to full power and rage-scanned bibliographic directories. 'You are ignorant of our language and its nuances.'

'I think you will find that *ab homine* is a debased folk etymology, on which your current understanding of the word rests – i.e. repellent, abhorrent, etcetera. *Abomination* is derived from the archaic High Gothic word *abominationem*, itself the past participle stem of *abominari*, meaning "to shun as an ill omen". See: *ab* (away from) and *omin* (omen or augury). Understood in this way, you are correct about its description of me, as the fact that I am choosing to speak to you is, in fact, an extremely ill omen.'

'It is common usage,' Cawl shot back, still scrolling through his lexigraphic database for loopholes.

'Common usage is acceptable – if one wishes to be common.'

Cawl smiled, banished the scrawl of text. 'Who is quoting now? That is *War in Heaven*, is it not?'

'You have read it?'

'I own a copy.' An incomplete copy, but the xenos didn't have to know that.

'Now that is more in keeping with the Belisarius Cawl I had heard stories of. I doubt Magos Klarn had an appreciation for necrontyr drama.'

Cawl snorted. It made a windy sound in his rebreather. 'Klarn was a nincompoop.'

'Yes, I had to build the entire null-array for him. His understanding of the pariah matrix was significantly poorer than yours.'

'Why does that not seem like a compliment?' Cawl paused his

data collection program mid-cycle, no longer interested in where the necron might have emerged from. '*You* built the null-array?'

'I had hoped to guide him, but time was short, and he was quite hopeless. He didn't know half what you do.'

'Ha! Ha-ha! I knew it. Knew that jumped-up enginseer couldn't have done it.' He slapped the pylon again, setting off another echoing bang. 'Three days carving away at this thing and no progress. Felt ridiculous that Klarn figured it out so quickly. You said, creature, that you know the pylons?'

'I was present when they were installed. Or at least that is how my engrammatic banks have encoded the experience.'

'They are necrontyr make, then?' Cawl asked, hating the eagerness in his voice.

'Yes.'

'To hold back the Eye of Terror?'

'And far more besides. Will you accept a schematic packet?'

'Ha! And let in a jokaero code-virus or whatever you're planning? I think not, Lord Trazyn. Why, after all, should you help me and the Imperium?'

'Two reasons. First, because I feel as though our continued relationship might be fruitful. I am a collector of very old and very unique things – and suspicions tell me you could be a source of both. Second, because this planet is about to be overwhelmed by the Despoiler. And after that, the galaxy. Do you know why they call him that name?'

'*Despoil* is an Old Gallic verb, meaning to–'

'Because he *despoils*. And I have a great many things I do not wish to be despoiled. Things I have spent a great deal of time and effort assembling. So, we have common cause – now, do you want my aid?'

Cawl crunched data, built if/then logic charts. Thought about it.

'Or do you want to continue cutting away at this resonance amplifier, thinking it's the control node?'

'Oh, very well...' Cawl sighed, drumming the claw tines of his servo-crawlers on the floor.

The alien stepped forward.

'No, no! Ah, ah, ah.' He raised his weapons, keying the Breachers to inch forward in threat. 'Not a step, or you will be atomised. Here is how we shall accomplish this. You direct me, while I do the work.'

'I will have to move.'

'And why is that?'

'As I said, this is a resonance amplifier.' He pointed a long skeletal finger. 'The control node is that way. That is what we need to bring into alignment if the matrix is to fulfil its intended purpose.'

'To hold back the Eye of Terror,' Cawl said.

'No,' said Trazyn the Infinite. 'To seal it like a tomb.'

The chamber shivered, dust drifting down through the beams of the dig-site lumens, and for a micro-cycle Cawl thought the necron had triggered some ancient device.

Then the vox-alert came in on his transponder.

'We don't have much time,' said Cawl. 'Archenemy landers are inbound. The *Phalanx* has started its bombardment.'

'You humans,' Trazyn clicked, shaking his head. 'Always in a rush.'

'Crash alert, general!' the new communications officer said. She was a captain, and given that they were in a semi-permanent field headquarters, had an entire team working the master vox, along with a bank of cogitators compiling plot data from the mobile modar and scatter-beam return stations around the perimeter of the Elysion Fields.

'Landers?' asked Creed. 'Are they the landers from the southern pole?'

The communications officer waved for more time, pressing her clamshell earphones to the sides of her modified cutaway helmet, listening.

Kell drifted close to see for himself. For the last three days, they'd been on the move. Getting everyone out of Kraf, fortifying the Elysion Fields, developing a plan to hold. Dropping prefabricated bunkers and installing aegis lines. Hopping all over two continents in Creed's personal Valkyrie, rallying troops from the Salvation outposts and telling them to muster at the Elysion Fields within days – a hundred miles worth of marching or driving, for some of them. They'd already received vox-reports of traffic jams on the roads coming in, clashes with Archenemy forces and logistical frekk-ups.

But two hours ago, they'd received a sighting report of small craft exiting the Archenemy fleet's hangars in a swarm, entering low orbit.

Abaddon was coming.

Meaning when the reinforcements arrived, they'd probably attack the enemy rear more than anything. If they weren't completely exhausted by the relentless forced march.

'Confirmed,' the comms officer said. 'Should be on-screen soon.'

'Coming from which direction?' asked Creed.

'Everywhere,' she said, turning a slate-display on its pivot.

A pulse-wave rippled out from the centre of the screen, lighting up masses of green contacts as it passed by them. When they faded, and another pulse expanded outward, they were closer.

Communications staff started to shout, turn dials, their voxes lighting up with reports.

'Drop pod strike in the east, near the remnants of Legio Vulcanum,' said one officer, 'reports of red-armoured Traitor Space Marines – initial sightings suggest Crimson Slaughter. Looks like an initial force to secure a landing zone.'

'They'll be trying to take the Pestrak Gap along with Vulcanum then, come in on our eastern line.' Creed waved his cigar. 'Not unexpected. We knew the Titans would be reinforced. Baroness Vardus and the Hundred-and-Eighty-Fifth Heavy Armour will take care of them. If necessary, Korahael and his Astartes reaction force can bolster the defence.'

'Incoming northern line,' broke in another operator, sweat beading her upper lip. 'Booking in low, heavy transports. I am informing the Sororitas.'

She threw switches, adjusted a toggle. 'Eighth HQ to canoness, Eighth to canoness. You've got incoming Archenemy forces. Report lift-vehicles with daemon engines clamped below. Expect contact in twenty minutes. Prepare to repulse, God-Emperor be with you and–'

'I have landers touching down south of us! Inside the Kraf curtain wall, armoured vehicles disembarking. Black and gold. Estimate one hour until contact.'

'Abaddon,' sneered Creed. He met Kell's eyes. 'Heading for our southern line, of course. We made it personal for him.'

'Are we ready, general?' Kell asked.

'I don't think we have a choice but to be.' Creed cracked his neck and looked down at his paper map on the camp table. 'Tell the Astartes reaction force they may be needed on multiple fronts. We at least have the mountains hemming in our western flank.'

'General,' warned the chief communications officer. 'We have squad- and company-level orbital transports screaming in low west, just above the Rossvar. Looks like a close deployment, using the cover of the valleys as marshalling grounds. Commodore Trevaux requests leave to commence prearranged bombardment pattern.'

'Go.'

'*Phalanx*,' said the communications chief. 'You are weapons free and cleared to bombard on sector grids beta-three to beta-niner. Danger close authorised. Fire, fire, fire. Fire, fire, fire.'

'Someone get that frekking Cawl on the vox,' Creed said. 'I want a situation report. If we're all dying to buy him time, I want to know he's getting close to finishing.'

Supersonic booms split the horizon to their north-west, and over the side of the parapet, Kell saw the grey saw teeth of the Rossvar disappear behind a curtain of orange flame streaked with the neon pillars of lance hits. A creeping bombardment thirty miles long.

The *Phalanx* unleashed.

'Frekking Throne,' swore Creed, raising his hand to guard his eyes against flying grit as the first shockwave blew past them. He stepped away from the staff to stand beside Kell. 'Maybe we'll just blow the damned planet up ourselves, eh? Don't give Abaddon the satisfaction.'

'Don't joke about that,' muttered Kell. 'We'll stop him here. If not, we'll go to the tunnels. Cadia stands.'

'And if it can't any more, and I can't give the order... Kell, you know what to do. I'm not sure I'll be able to say the word.'

Kell nodded. 'I'll save you from that. Might as well, I've saved you from everything else over the years.'

Creed raised a hand and thumped Kell on the nape of the neck, one of the only places he could feel it in the heavy carapace armour. 'I'm glad you're here, Jarran. At the end.'

'General?' said the communications chief, holding out a corded handset. 'I've raised the archmagos.'

Creed took it and yelled.

'*–the frekk is going on down there, Cawl? I need a status report.*'

'We are making progress, Lord Castellan. We have successfully brought the control node online, and are about to entangle it with the two nearest pylons.'

Cawl's mechadendrite hive writhed and buzzed with activity, adjusting equipment and slamming a cable into one of the inscrutable bore-holes in the surface of the control node.

'*Two pylons? Only two?*'

'Once the initial matrix is built and running, we should be able to bring more pylons online exponentially – then bring their empyric polarity into concert.'

'How long? Large-scale traitor attack incoming.'

Cawl dipped a finger into one of the emerald-green holographic tablets that floated projected in the air, sketching a necron rune that brought the control node to a vibrating hum. 'Three days? I believe we can get the network to full power then.'

'Too long. Assume you have thirty-six hours at most. That may be an overestimate.' Creed paused. *'And who's "we"?'*

Cawl looked over his shoulder at the xenos giant, who stood half-hidden in the shadow of a pylon, surrounded by the weapons of the Breachers. He'd plucked a servo-skull out of the air and was turning it over in his hands, death-mask head tilted to one side as he examined it. The suspensor engine buzzed in irritation, trying to escape.

'I… ah, I mean the royal *we,* Lord Castellan. We the defenders of Cadia. We the Imperium. We're all on the same side, aren't we?'

At the side of the cavern, Trazyn tore the skull's data-projection lens from its orbit with a dusty *crack,* and tossed the empty skull behind him.

'What are you doing?' mouthed Cawl, covering the vox handset with one hand and throwing the others up in indignation.

'This is unique wiring,' he said, as if Cawl was being deeply unreasonable. He ran a palm-emitter over the component. 'Unique to the forge world of Magnax before it was lost in the Heresy. The same filaments and focusing lenses used in las-impulsors. Far too good to be repurposed in a servo-skull.'

'Put it back.'

The alien's impassive death mask tilted to one side, and Cawl swore the metal mouth curled up at the edges. Then the necron flicked his necrodermis hand as if performing an act of prestidigitation and the component vanished into a hole in reality. He opened his empty hands, innocent. 'I lost it.'

Cawl bit off the shout that was rising in his throat, his hands raising in fists. Realised Creed had said something else.

'I'm sorry, Lord Castellan... Transmission break, can you repeat that last part?'

'You said we're all on the same side. I certainly hope so.'

One thousand feet of altitude.

High cloud cover, slate grey, underlit orange from the fires.

Kasr Kraf was burning.

They'd said it was mostly abandoned when the Black Legion came in, and Keztral hoped that was true. Hoped that the civic evacuation had included the ones who'd waited at the water gate, banging their fists on it until they were bloody, and shed everything they owned to gain safety.

Even their hair.

There had been a massive explosion, Keztral heard. A detonation that had started deep in the caverns below the citadel and torn the inner fortress city apart. Flung the main spire upward like a rocket that failed to launch and crashed back to the landing pad.

Now it burned like a bonfire on tithe-muster night. Those fires, traditional on the evening before a regiment shipped out from Cadia, always cracked and popped in strange ways as troopers threw low-grade explosives into them – pieces of flares, scratch-made fireworks made of paper and gunpowder, once even a belt of autogun ammunition.

That's what this looked like. It burned, but it also exploded as ammunition bunkers and shell lockers touched off. Sparks fountained from random buildings and tongues of fire licked and died, their detonations banging over the Kraf Plain a moment after the fires erupted.

She hoped that the Archenemy had lost troops to it. More than they could afford.

'Making attack run,' she said, sucking breath through her rebreather. She'd been having lung problems lately. A tightness in her chest. Shallow breaths, like her uniform was too tight. Probably all the smoke. Everywhere on Cadia was choked with it now. 'Keep me covered.'

'*Commence attack run, Kite-One.*' Ragnal's voice was tense. They'd been jumped by a flight of Heldrakes as they'd come in over the Rossvar. He'd taken some hits. '*No Drakes incoming.*'

'*They're all attacking the Eighth and the southern perimeter,*' added Mak. '*Plenty down there to dissuade you – be careful.*'

Keztral nosed down, coming out of the lower wisps of cloud where they'd lurked, screened from the enemy but still able to see out.

It was like descending into a hailstorm.

The armoured column below her was two miles wide, and four long. Like a carpet of swarming insects scuttling over the carcass of a dead man.

But the dead man was the Kraf Plain, rising to the foothills of the volcanic bowl of the Elysion Fields.

Tracer rounds sprayed heavenward. Shooting stars falling upward. Sparkling balls of exploding flak, whipping dashes of pulse-fired lascannons. So much fire from below, the smoke of the discharges started to wreathe the targets.

She came in steep, more like a dive-bomber than a strafing craft. This kind of fire made traditional attack runs impossible, she'd be knocked out of the sky if she got that low and approached so flat.

Keztral unleashed her payload at five hundred feet, firing bolt cannon and lascannons at once. Stamping a palm on the RELEASE ALL stud and hearing the six bombs let go, *War-Kite* seeming to jump in the sky with the sudden unburdening.

She didn't wait to see how they landed. Just went wing over and climbed out back into the shelter of the clouds. Seeing the dirty-yellow reflection of the detonation as she came up into the bank.

A hit. Always a hit – it was impossible to miss the column.

But she also knew that it didn't matter. Even if every bomb hit a separate vehicle. If her lascannons stabbed through three hulls each, and each one of those hundreds of bolt-cannon rounds had felled a motorvator block, Abaddon would still have enough troops to kill every trooper on the Elysion Fields.

+Where is the child?+ the voice shouted. +I need the child.+

The Warmaster was often quiet. Quieter than most men would expect – but when he was loud, he was authority itself. That was what surprised her about the voice. It was frantic. Fraught with worry.

Yet there was no mistaking it as his voice.

Morkath believed the fortress was dying.

Though that would mean it had once lived, and she was unsure if that was the right word. Dwelling on it, she thought that many words she had once known the meaning of had become alien since the *Will of Eternity* broke under the guns of the *Phalanx*.

Morkath thought she knew what space was. And time. Distance and proportion. She walked for hours and ran her hand along mile-long bas-reliefs.

Yet always down.

Down, down, down.

Into the depths of the fortress.

Morkath had come to accept that she had never controlled this place. Not truly. And she never knew the alien intelligence, much less had any special relationship with it. She was merely the most successful microbe in the bacterial infection that colonised it. Given a chance to rid itself of them, the fortress took it. Yet that was likely no more than a convenient circumstance. A shortcut. For Morkath was convinced that the fortress could simply have waited millennia until the infection had run its course, and Abaddon and his servants burned themselves out.

Though that might be ascribing a consciousness, an intentionality, that was incorrect.

Morkath did not know what consciousness meant any more either. It was possible her mental self had become entangled with the blackstone – or had been for as long as she could recall.

She never interacted with the noctilith itself. Whatever kinship Morkath had once had with the fortress was through the flesh-work and energy channels she'd formed within it. Charging up the blackstone like a battery or magnet, aligning its polarity with the warp.

But that polarity was reversed now. She could feel it. Feel the reverberation in her noctilith eye and sheathed bones. A tuning-fork ringing that was not merely audible but so clear she could almost sense its sonic fields.

It hurt. Gods of the empyrean, it hurt. Her implanted eye itched uncontrollably, the flesh around it hot and puffy. Two of her blackstone teeth had come loose. As if this place, and her own components, had become anathema.

Only by drawing deep from the warp could she still the muscle spasms and bone-pains as her body tried to reject the parts of it that were now utterly foreign.

Yet every hour, the resonance grew stronger. As if the fortress was responding, attuning, to another force. It was healing, too. Each broken spar slowly fusing back together like snapped bone. A process that would be too slow to notice if she did not now exist inside the strange time envelope of the noctilith, where aeons passed in seconds and a breath lasted a full lifespan.

Abaddon had always known about the pylons. Indeed, her father's Crimson Path had depended on neutralising their negating effect on the warp. The fact that the *Will of Eternity* was made of the same noctilith that formed Cadia's pylons was never but a curiosity to Morkath. The idea that one could act on the other, apart from the violence of the warp cannon, never occurred to her – it was as absurd as the sympathetic magic practised on feral worlds, like wrapping a twig with human hair and snapping it to break a bone.

Yet it was happening, she could feel it. Whatever was occurring on the surface had formed links with this never-living, broken organism that she wandered alone.

At times, the fortress showed her a window – which was impossible, since she only seemed to go deeper within. Every one hundred and two minutes standard, it orbited past the Elysion Fields and she saw a battle was going on. Without doubt, a battle larger than any ever fought.

It appeared like a dirty smear, a district-wide forest fire trailing smoke halfway across the continent. Incredibly, she could see the las-fire even from near orbit, where it looked like pulsing banks of red in the smoke.

She continued walking, listening for her father's voice. Wandering among the warp ghosts that flickered through the passageways.

It was the warp energy bleeding off. Psychic impressions, embedded in the blackstone through its centuries of habitation, being purged. They moved stuttering and quick like poor pict-capture reels. A man walked down the corridor, holding his bleeding side. Two cultists nailed a below-decks thrall to a bulkhead. An Imperial voidsman crew from long, long ago – the Gothic War or earlier – fired a gun that no longer existed.

+Come, child,+ said the Warmaster. +Come!+

And she ran, for his voice was close.

The fortress was trying to keep her separate from her father. A last cruel act. She sprinted towards his voice, throwing her mind against the corridors and chambers like an echo.

+ My Warmaster, I am here!+

She discovered him in a great vaulted chapel, its floors and ceilings riven by cracks. A shattered altar stood at one end.

He was kneeling as a ragged, inhuman wretch crawled towards him, and he reached out a hand to her.

+Morkath,+ he said, before the image faded.

She dropped to her knees and put her hand to the place where he'd knelt. All this time, the eternity of these days of walking, she had thought he was calling her out of the dark. Instead, it was only a memory-wraith.

Morkath lay on the place where her father had first extended his hand to her, stroking the floor as she felt the last of that moment bleed away into the ether. She opened her mind to draw it deep, the last scent of a departed relative, a smell left on a scarf or bottle of cologne.

+Swear you will find her. We need the fortress child, everything depends on it.+

Another psychic echo of the Warmaster. Strong and close – perhaps only a few chambers away.

Dravura Morkath pushed herself up and staggered towards her father's voice.

Her father, who needed her.

THREE

'We fight at Elysion. We stand at Elysion. This war shall be decided among ancient pylons that have stood for ten millennia, and aegis lines set up this morning. Yet the fight is not only at the Elysion Fields. People of Cadia and those who aid us – now is the time to stand and meet the enemy. Wherever you are, that is your Elysion Fields. Every street must become a battlezone. Take action. Cadia stands, and on this day – wherever we are – we stand united.'

– Ursarkar E. Creed, 'The Address from the Elysion Fields', partial recording by Denska Kazelle, held in Cadian High Command Archive, Special Section 9: Audio and Visual Relics of Lost Cadia.

Excerpted from *Creed at Cadia: A Strategic Reassessment,* by General Dabatha Ravi.

And so, we come to the end.

Given the exhaustive treatment this volume has given other engagements during the final war for Cadia, the first-time reader will be surprised to learn that Ursarkar E. Creed's most famous battle gets such spare mention.

But since this volume is a detailed strategic history of Creed's battles rather than simple hagiography, I confess to working under certain practical constraints.

Namely, the documentation of the Battle for the Elysion Fields is extremely spare, and difficult to reconstruct. As discussed in Chapter 12, while a systematic method of recording and archiving vox traffic and general orders was in effect at the beginning of the conflict, this effort deteriorated as the war dragged on. Archival recordings made by the Commissariat largely perished with Cadia, and even Creed's celebrated vox-addresses have needed to be recalled from memory. The only existing clips that survive come from Corporal Denska Kazelle, an audiophile vox-operator who illicitly modified her unit to record on slug-spools. Even then, the recordings are of poor quality and only two are complete.

In addition, first-hand accounts of the Elysion Fields are rare, and those that exist are fragmentary. Those who survived were largely reserve soldiers stationed in the Salvation outposts, who arrived in time to attack the enemy's rear rather than participating in the central combat within the pylons.

The few surviving line soldiers tend to offer conflicting and unsatisfactory accounts. So intense was the combat that the battlefield was almost entirely engulfed in smoke, to the point that rebreathers were necessary merely to stay alive. Rolling banks of las-fire could be seen even from the Phalanx. The pylon forests, too, played their part, meaning individual troopers rarely had the line of sight necessary to take in the wider strategic picture.

I have had little success persuading the few surviving commanders to talk, and most are posted to active *battle-fronts. The hallowed brothers of the Adeptus Astartes have, of course, returned my enquiries unread.*

I myself was not present, having been seconded to supporting a complex logistical operation under Logistar-General Conskavan Raik.

From my own studies, I believe it is unlikely Creed was able to actively maintain command-and-control. He laid the plan, delegated each sector to commanders, and then let them fight it out as they saw fit. The Adeptus Astartes, so difficult to control in a standard rank structure, were turned into a mobile reserve that could deploy at their own discretion. Given circumstances, it was a good plan.

Creed's military objective remains a subject of speculation. Mechanicus elements gathering in the tunnels suggest an attempt at a technological solution, and rumours abound of tech-rituals performed in the caverns. While I personally believe this was an attempt to build a larger and more decisive null-array than the one at Kasr Kraf, this is only speculation on my part so I will not elaborate. Already too many wild folkloric stories have attached themselves to this battle – everything from personal combats, to phantom soldiers, to Astartes devolving into ravening beasts – and while these may be fine for prayer-primers and cheap trench novels, they cannot be taken seriously.

What we factually know is this:

The first wave of Archenemy landers came from the west, over the Rossvar and through the curtain bombardment laid down by the Phalanx. While an estimated half of these landers did not make it through the orbital fire, those that did unleashed a force of cultists in battalion-strength which swarmed into the pylon fields and into the guns of the Cadian Ninth Shock Infantry.

Disgraced at having run at the Kriegan Gates, when they had followed the 33rd into rout, the Cadian Ninth fought to wipe away the stain of shame.

But their heroic stand cost them, since by nightfall on the first day, the traitors and their Word Bearers demagogues had all but overrun the western lines. When the Cadian 75th and 403rd Armoured reached the earthworks as a relief force, they had to assault their own trench networks in order to take defensive positions against the next wave.

The Cadian Ninth Shock Infantry was, to a soldier, killed in action.

Circumstances were equally grim on the eastern front.

There in the Pestrak Gap, the fallen god-machines of Legio Vulcanum met the shield-wall of Baroness Vardus of Raven and the Knights of House Taranis.

While such a grouping of Titans would have made a tempting target for the Phalanx's bombardment, events in the north and west meant the ship could not properly allocate fire to this sector. By the time it was freed up to do so, combat had been joined in the gap itself, and any bombardment would have buried both sides in an avalanche.

Due to the chivalric deed-records of House Raven and Taranis, we know an unusual amount of detail regarding this sector. It appears the baroness held her line until midday on the first day, when the first major strike by the Crimson Slaughter Traitor Space Marines pushed back the 185th and plunged her Knights from a fire-support role into the heart of combat.

Her machine mortally wounded and fellow Knights fallen, Vardus entered single combat with the Reaver

Furioso Rex – *a mount twice her weight – and felled it before her own reactor went critical.*

A general retreat by the 185th was only avoided when the Dark Angels Fourth Company and Crimson Fists Fifth reinforced the line, providing infantry support that the super-heavies of the 185th had previously lacked. The front stabilised, the fighting continued into the second day.

Only in the north did the line hold entirely steady, as the Order of Our Martyred Lady formed an impenetrable shield against the slaughter-machines and daemon engines of the Warpsmiths. Seraphim flights proved decisive, as the large war machines had difficulty switching between tactics necessary to repulse aerial assault while also executing the anti-bombardment movements meant to avoid Exorcist barrages. These daemon engines, many of them demolishing vehicles intended to clear-cut the pylons, never reached the fields themselves.

Only there, whether by faith or consummate tactics by the Living Saint, was the traitor host stopped cold.

But it was the southern line that was the most difficult ground to hold. With no mountains hemming it in, the southern edge of the Elysion Fields provided the enemy their largest area to muster – including behind the cover of the curtain wall of Kasr Kraf. It was also the simplest to attack from the air, and had the most fallen pylons, providing cover for an enemy advance. All around, a tough tactical position.

Which in my estimation, is why the Lord Castellan chose it for himself.

'Stop, Twenty-First, *stop.*'

Creed shouted it into the vox.

Kell bellowed through the laud-hailer, his voice hoarse from two days shouting over the constant slash of lasguns and roar of bolters. *'Twenty-One commissars! Do your work! Keep them in their positions!'*

For two days, the Eighth had held firm, the 21st at their back. Through rolling artillery bombardments, Heldrakes yanking troopers from their trenches, and the grinding battering-ram combat of Militarum infantry against the fallen demigods of the Black Legion.

The massive traitor column had largely been transports, meant to overrun their lines before disembarking their metal-cased killers.

Yet Creed was no Whiteshield cadet-lieutenant who'd quail under the shock assault of Rhinos and Land Raiders. He'd had time to prepare.

The Black Legion had marshalled the armoured assault in the south because it appeared ideal – open ground to disembark in force, and pylon ruins to screen their approach.

If it had been a heavy infantry assault, that might've worked. But it wasn't – it was armour. And all those fallen blackstone obelisks created excellent choke points to control the avenues of assault.

Each space between pylons held anti-tank mines and wide ditches. Sandbag and aegis strongpoints with lascannon and missile launcher teams with overlapping fields of fire. Ideal grids for ground-attack aircraft and pre-ranged artillery.

And every tank that was wrecked in those choke points made them narrower. Now they were traffic jams of burning wreckage, with collections of burned-down chassis collapsed from heat, their blackened skeletal shells no taller than Guardsmen.

The ones that managed to break through did no better.

Creed had taken every Kasrkin he could find, loaded them with anti-armour capability, and let them loose to roam the front in Valkyries looking for breakouts.

Whole squads of Black Legion died by their hands. The Valks

would immobilise or hole the vehicle with a missile as the fire-team bailed out on ropes or grav-chutes to kill passengers as they emerged – the Valk circling the stricken vehicle nose down to clean up any notable threats or chase down runners. Then, despite steep casualties, the Kasrkin would mount up and do it again.

That's when it turned into an infantry fight – the space behind the choke points nothing but a field of empty transports.

The line had held for two days. At least, until minutes ago when the command vox squalled a message from the colonel of the 21st Cadian Heavy Bombardment.

'Throne, we're overrun! Black-eyed fiends in the trenches. They're wrong, twisted. They're chewing me from the inside.'

'Frekk!' Creed grabbed a data-slate, watching the feed of a forward pict-setup mounted high on a pylon.

The vid-feed was green and blurry, but it was clear the troops were running. Abandoning the artillery positions that had helped keep this stalemate going.

He watched as a commissar at the lower edge of the screen banged shots into the fleeing mass, but it was no good. They were collapsing like a sand dune trampled on by a battalion – little rivulets running first, then a total shift as they shelved away and bolted.

'Idiots!' Creed threw down the slate and mounted the firing step, waving his hands towards the first troopers that emerged from the haze of battle smoke. 'You'll kill us all! Slacken the fire and they'll be on us. We can't recover once they're in amongst us! Frekking fools!'

He didn't call them cowards, Kell noticed. No trooper could be a coward that endured what they had over the last two days. There had been no sleep, no rest, not even any space between waves. Everyone wore rebreathers due to the ultra-ionised air from the las-volleys. Even Creed had finally consented to use one. An hour before, a traitor column had got behind their positions.

'Back to your trenches!' Kell roared in support. A few troopers turned, faltering. 'Will you run in front of your comrades? Can you live with that shame? The eyes of your Lord Castellan are on you!'

But then they looked above him, at the arc lightning snapping at the inner dome of the skyshield – and ran.

'Oh frekk,' Kell said, as he turned. 'General.'

Clouds gathered above their heads, collecting on the inner dome of the skyshield. Red-flared and spiralling, like the wound left by the hooked mandibles of a parasitic worm.

'Is that what I thin–'

Lightning shattered the world like mirror glass, splitting air, earth and flesh into shards. Troopers Kell had campaigned with for twenty years fell apart like paper dolls cut to confetti.

'It's done, Ursarkar.' Kell keyed his comm-bead. 'Stryker Two – Dust, dust, dust!'

'What the frekk does that me–'

The Valkyrie on the pad behind them cycled its turbofans from still to full, keening like a lost soul. Daggers of flame stabbed from the thrust nozzles on its wing tips, bringing it to three feet of hover.

It had just dropped its ramp when the behemoths emerged from the lightning, weapons firing.

A Cadian trooper came apart, his top half detonated by a storm bolter round. His squad mate thrust at the attacker with her bayonet, only to have cross-sections of her lasgun clatter to the duckboard flooring as a lightning claw slashed through it. She had time to blink before she, too, fell to pieces. A rush of flames tore down the trench, immolating half a squad. Autocannon rounds blasted through the bank of vox-stations and scatter-beam plotters, blowing out their logic boards so they burned with an acrid stink, throwing the operators from their stations.

The comms-chief pulled a hellpistol – an ornate family

heirloom – and got off a shot before storm bolter rounds burst her skull and most of one shoulder. Her wire-coil micro-bead suddenly fell and bounced on its webbing mount, an ear still attached.

Golden balls of light streaked towards Kell, flashing bright white on Creed's refractor field, bursting into firefly embers. A diagonal line that seemed to go everywhere apart from where Kell stood.

Except he couldn't stand any more. One knee gave out, strengthless.

The echoing report of the bolt-shell only registered in his ears after he started to fall.

'Kell!' Creed yelled. He was at Kell's shoulder, dragging him up.

And that's when the pain arrived. Scathing agony from knee to groin. Both excruciating and numb at the same time. He saw a glow of white bone in the ruin of red that was once his joint. The knee-cap had been blown off entirely, and his entire trouser leg all the way up to his groin armour peppered with shrapnel.

Red stains were welling into the fabric like ink spilled on a table-cloth; he could see it spreading in the weave of the fabric as they grew from speckles to splotches.

Out of the pyre smoke of their burned troopers came an image he knew from propaganda picts and intelligence reports. A silhouette impossible to miss. A claw hooked like that of the aquila hanging around Kell's neck, a sword tall as two men. Trophy racks and a topknot.

'Grraaah!' Kell howled, shoving Creed off. 'Go, Ursarkar! Get the frekk out of here.'

'No, I–'

'Go!'

The Kasrkin from the Valkyrie grabbed Creed, dragged him back-wards, shielding him with their bodies, hellguns raised and drilling slashes of fire towards the oncoming foe.

Abaddon, the monster of the Eye, who had haunted Kell's night-mares since childhood, came on like a charging cargo hauler. He raised his great claw and hammered a burst of fire into the retreating Kasrkin, butchering two of them.

They closed ranks as they went up the ramp, the Valk already starting to rise.

Kell planted the standard of the Cadian Eighth and hauled himself up with it, taking one shuffling step to get between his commander and the oncoming nightmare. It occurred to him that he should've sent the standard on the Valkyrie – no chance now.

'Kell, we'll get the Valk to fire, we'll–'

'I save you,' Kell grunted into his micro-bead. He drew his power sword. 'You save Cadia.'

Abaddon was more terrible than he'd imagined. Moving so fast. His smell, like the penumbral forges of the warp. Sulphur and spice. An aura like the sizzling stillness before a thunderhead broke into violence. Blood-spattered armour, big as a mountain. Ghost-flickers of awful things circling his head.

Yet his face was so appalling because it was still so human. No horns or spikes, just a sneering marble bust.

'Jarran,' Creed said in his comm-bead, barely audible over the scream of the ascending vector-thrust engines. It wasn't the voice of the Lord Castellan, but that of the directionless orphan he'd met so many years ago. 'Thank you, my brother.'

Kell thrust out with his sword, the energy field seeming to gutter in the presence of the Warmaster of Chaos. He lost his balance, knee buckling, but the thrust plunged towards the unprotected face, its mouth open in a black maw of anger.

Then his sword fell, dropping to the ground on the arm that held it.

With a guillotine chop, the daemon blade had severed it, and in another instant Kell was off his feet.

The Despoiler held him in his massive claw, two finger-scythes arcing over each shoulder and the thumb slicing into his lower ribs and pressing on his back, to pin him inside a cage of pain. Slicing razors, crawling with corposant lightning, pressed down through armour and flesh.

He locked his power fist around the battle standard, refused to let it drop.

'Cadia stands.'

'But you can't. And I *will* kill him,' the Despoiler said. His voice was deep and rich, laden with a passion Kell did not expect. 'In the meantime, he will watch you die as he runs. And your death will be a dishonour.'

Kell could feel his ribs creaking under the pressure. Blood was in his mouth. It was hard to get breath.

'You're slaying me with the same gauntlet that killed an angel and touched the Emperor,' he choked. 'How is that a dishonour?'

The noble face turned down in fury. 'I am no failure like Horus.'

'If he's such a failure, why do you dress like him, eh? Tell me th– Ccccchhhhhkkk...'

Pressure. Bones popped and ground. Kell felt his vertebrae wrung apart. The nightmare did not crush him so much as it kneaded his body like clay before throwing him into the dirt.

A cruel inverse of the old creation myths, where a god moulded humans from earth – Kell lay there a man unmade and cast to the soil, his head lolling forward, awkward on his broken neck.

He could see the blood spreading across his chest from where the five talons had cut him. It soaked into the fabric, bright scarlet, each line of blood growing fat and wide.

Blooming. The pattern blooming on his chest, as the world faded to nothing but that vibrant, living colour.

Red.

Red like the fireworks in the victory celebrations.

Red like the flowers in his mother's garden.

Red like the scarlet chrysanthus.

Like the Flower of Cadia.

'I think I hit him.'

Lord Castellan Ursarkar E. Creed, general of Cadian forces, stared out of the Valkyrie's side door at the battle below.

'What?' he said.

'The Despoiler, lord,' repeated Servantus Glave, patting the volley gun slung across his chest. 'As we extracted you. I think I hit him, maybe wounded him even.'

'Oh. Good for you.'

He looked vacant, not at all like Servantus Glave had expected. Stitcher Kristan had checked him out as they lifted, but he wasn't wounded.

'I'm going to kill him, sir. You'll see,' Glave whispered, stepping close. 'Don't you worry, you'll be glad of me by the time this is done. We're going to the tunnels? Well, we're tunnel fighters, the Stitcher and me. Deep patrol.'

Creed did not respond, and Glave worried he'd pushed things too far, become over-familiar.

'Cadia stands,' he added.

'United,' answered Creed, not looking at Glave.

'Sorry, sir?'

'Cadia stands united. That's what Kell intended. He writes the speeches, you know – *wrote* the speeches, I mean. I just say them. That was his big idea after the Battle of Tyrok. Neither of us are from the good families, first Lord Castellan ever without known parentage. He thought it was a time to level things, break down stratifications, get everyone's shoulder behind the stone. So that's what I was supposed to say: Cadia. Stands. United. Three beats like that, boom-boom-boom, to make sure the point hit home. And that's what I said. Cadia. Stands...'

Creed looked at him for the first time, and Glave saw how tired he looked.

'And then... the frekking mic went out.' Creed laughed. 'That's all anyone heard, "Cadia stands" – they all missed the last part. And there was this tremendous roar like nothing I've ever heard. My ears rang for half a day afterward, and Kell had to shout when he leaned in to say, "Well, looks like the Emperor wrote that one."'

'He certainly did, general. The Emperor speaks. That's how I know we're going to win.'

'What exactly makes you so confident?' Creed asked, raising those faded-violet eyes.

'You do, sir.'

'Oh, right. Of course.'

'Way I figure it, if you can stand, we can all stand.'

Creed nodded, bouncing his head a bit, looking at the battle below. At the shattering volleys of las-fire and roiling combats. At arrowhead deltas of Traitor Space Marines, beetle-black, forcing their way into the Elysion Fields.

A pylon took a hit and fell, shattering into parts and flattening an artillery firebase full of Basilisks.

'Approaching the caves, Lord Castellan,' the pilot said. *'Best to close the side hatch to minimise pressure differential.'*

Creed drew in a breath, thumped Glave on the shoulder pad, and reached up for the inter-cabin vox. 'You stay close to me, corporal. I need a tunnel fighter. And if you want to kill the Despoiler, I'll give you your shot.'

He clicked the handset.

'Pilot?'

'Sir?'

'Negative on going into the caverns. Land at the mouth. I'm not hiding in a hole while my troopers face the enemy.'

'Yes, sir. Cadia stands, sir.'

'Frekking right it does,' he said, and cut the connection.

When the Valk touched down, he came off the ramp before it had fully lowered, arms clasped behind him and coat flying. He had a fresh cigar in his mouth, unlit. Glave thought it might be his last one.

The troopers at the tunnel mouth looked spooked, their eyes wide. No wonder, since the noises coming from the front were awful.

They were from the Eighth, a special urban assault section by their patches. Good candidates for tunnel fighting.

'Troopers of Cadia, whose world is this?' Creed called.

But he was too quiet, used to the amplifying presence of his colour sergeant, and only the closest murmured an answer.

'Lord,' said a commissar, apologetically offering him a magna-horn.

Creed raised it to his mouth. 'I said, soldiers of Cadia, whose frekking world is this? The Despoiler's world, or our world?!'

'Our world!'

'And whose tunnels are these?'

'Our tunnels!'

'We're the rearguard. Me and you. Our job is to make them pay for every bloody inch. Now when the traitors come, are you going to run, or are you going to stand?'

By their cheers, Glave knew they would stand.

+Where is my child?+ the Warmaster demanded. He was furious, fit to murder. +I have extended this deadline several times. And now you have lost the work.+

It was an old imprint, and it was difficult for Morkath to read more than outlines in the smeared, impressionistic images. The Warmaster wasn't wearing his armour, yet he still intimidated the other Chaos Space Marine as they circled the table. The surgical table was real, as were the medical instruments around the room, though all were shrouded with plastek sheeting, noctilith dust lying heavy in every wrinkle.

+My Lord Abaddon.+

+I am Warmaster now.+

+Warmaster… You do not appreciate the difficulty of these operations. The surgeries, the subdermal implants. The untested marrying of noctilith to human flesh—+

The Warmaster ceased his predatory circling, and laid his fists on the empty surgical table – in her physical reality, Morkath saw where the pressure of his bare knuckles had dimpled the metal.

+I do not appreciate? Let me illuminate what *you* do not appreciate, master Apothecary. You do not appreciate the resources I have put into this project. Nor the favours I have called in. Nor the manpower cost of raiding the Black Ships for psyker children. You do not appreciate what artefacts I had to trade in order to get you those damned consultations with the drukhari flesh-wych. And nothing to show for it but tortured bodies out the airlock. Then you succeed and… what… you *lose* the child?+

+Don't you see this is a success? An incredible success. I did not even realise the subject had survived, yet she scrabbled off the slab and into the corridor. And when I chased her, the fleshwork doors slammed in my face and she turned the fortress-thralls against me. She can *speak* to the corrupted fortress, Warmaster. The control we've striven for. No more channelling daemons into the noctilith to try and subdue it, trading one malign intelligence for another, we have a purpose-built control device that can itself be controlled.+

+A child. One that has escaped with the components we need in order to make another.+

+A child who will grow, and can be recaptured. She is frightened. New to transhuman rebirth. Even our own neophytes go mad for a time.+

The Warmaster stepped towards Morkath, and as the milky haze of his features solidified, the expression of concern on his face broke whatever the shadowy Apothecary had given her for a heart.

The Warmaster raised a hand to his comm-link.

+Urkanthos,+ he said. +Round up your Hounds. A hunting pack. We are going deep in the fortress.+

As he faded, Morkath stood in his dissolving psychic imprint.

Abaddon had always told her that she was a feral child, raised by a cult in the depths of the fortress. That she belonged to the blackstone, was perhaps even its creation.

Those were lies.

He'd fashioned her. A human key ground out of flesh and bone, purpose-made to unlock the fortress and assist his great work to blaze the Crimson Path, break Cadia and bring faithless Terra to its knees. The *Will of Eternity* was so valuable because he could domesticate it – he had traded the other to Huron Blackheart because it was ungovernable, the daemon channelled into it too wild.

Abaddon had created her, as his father Horus had created him.

Where is my child?

The words were undeniable: he had claimed her as his own.

Had he left her here intentionally to learn this truth? Was that the only way he could confess to her what she had known all along?

'If so, then I am here, father,' she whispered. 'And though your lies sting, I will show you that I am a worthy daughter – and I will show you how much you need me.'

Dravura Morkath, the Fortress Child, went to salvage her father's dream.

Deep within the synapse-tunnels of the noctilith control node, Belisarius Cawl discovered a new reality.

For so very long, he had delved into the fringes of human science. Pushed the borders of arcane research to depths that none had since that hack Arkhan Land.

Yet his mapping programmatics were still uncovering functions of the pylons. Beam-emission points. Focusing chambers. Particle anomalies that suggested these great megalithic structures had not so much been built as shaped, like the aeldari did with their bone-constructs. Except where wraithbone was psychically attuned, this stone's warp signature was inert. Indeed, properly calibrated, its signature was negative – like an empyric black hole.

Over the last forty hours, two parts of his tripartite consciousness had aligned the network to that negative polarity.

Meanwhile, his third consciousness was humouring the necron with conversation.

'What I mean, dear archmagos,' said Trazyn, in the fourth hour of this lecture, 'is that the Imperium cannot be fully appreciated from a human perspective, or even a *transhuman* one.'

'I see.'

'After all, what is the Imperium? Because humans and human-adjacent beings refer to it as a single thing, a monolithic structure. Yet any cursory analysis will tell you there are *many* Imperiums – your Mechanicus, the Inquisition, the Administratum, individual planets, etcetera. Alliances between these are at best nominal and–'

'Do you hear that?' Cawl asked.

'What, the combat? Yes, my scarab swarms have been keeping abreast of it. Your Lord Castellan is managing a fighting retreat through the tunnels–'

'He's not *my* lord. That entirely misunderstands the relationship.'

'As I said, lots of *little* Imperiums–'

'Are they close?' Cawl broke his secondary consciousness away from the node mid-cycle, using it to plot auguries for threats.

It was then he discovered the cache of martial updates waiting patiently in his PENDING file.

Oh, Omnissiah, the skitarii maniple. For a full day they'd been battling alongside Creed in the tunnels, but he'd frozen alerts to keep focus. The tech-warriors were largely inoperable now, their beautiful forms broken by Black Legionnaires and Abaddon's Terminator vanguard – spearheading an onrushing flood of empyric horrors.

Nearly here. He sent a mental command to the ranks of electro-priests and combat servitors waiting silent in the nodal cavern. The Breachers hemming the obnoxious xenos in turned on their tracks and faced their weapons the other way, ready to receive targets.

'Indeed they are close – on the other side of the cavern. Do not be concerned, should it come to it I will defend us while you continue the work.'

'Defend us? You don't even have a ranged weapon.'

'My dear archmagos, I am an Overlord of the Nihilakh Dynasty. I do not need a ranged weapon – I point at things and they die.'

Cawl was about to argue the absurdity of this claim, but at that moment a wall of the cavern collapsed in a roar of obliterated rock strata.

And hell surged through.

Trazyn felt a certain regret when the Black Legion tore into the electro-priests, bolt-rounds and the lashing cages of electrical discharge crossing in a spectacular display.

After all, the attack interrupted such a stimulating conversation.

It was so rare these days to meet a being of wide perspective – someone fit to discuss the nature of the universe with. He'd been starved for conversation ever since that mountain had dropped onto poor Orikan.

Indeed, in a remote corner of his neural spooling, he had been continually working on what he would acquire from this expedition should he need to effect an exit. Events appeared to be reaching a conclusion, and while playing saviour had been amusing, one way or another his role would soon be finished. And given the aid he'd delivered, no one could possibly begrudge him one or two little souvenirs on the way out.

Like an archmagos dominus that was such good conversation, for instance. Cawl was unusually bright, for an augmented human – and given that he was a mere ten millennia old, Trazyn enjoyed his youthful vigour.

Yet he banished all thoughts of Cawl when he saw the specimen that strode through the electro-priests, throwing bodies ahead of his blows.

Trazyn took it all in.

The way his topknot flew as the snarling head snapped back and forth. How the hot blue snap of the priests' energy bolts danced between the poles of his trophy rack.

The specimen broke through the back line of the priests, one pale-fleshed worshipper impaled on his daemon blade, the dying priest pawing at a black gauntlet as sparks jumped from his brass-capped fingers.

Abaddon the Despoiler turned towards them. A walking relic of the Heresy. Able to be displayed in total, or disassembled for parts in the Warmaster display Trazyn had long dreamed of as a capstone to his Horus Heresy gallery.

Abaddon's statuesque brow furrowed in recognition, and he bellowed one furious word: 'Cawl!'

'Oh yes,' Trazyn muttered. 'What a centrepiece you would make.'

'Trazyn! He recognises me. He knows what we're doing. The electro-priests won't hold him, and the Breachers...'

'Do not be concerned,' he said, opening his dimensional appendices and extracting a tesseract labyrinth. 'I have brought a few useful odds and ends.'

He activated the labyrinth and threw it over the head of the Breachers as one vat-grown torso was pulped under the exquisite Talon of Horus. The labyrinth bounced twice, billowing prismatic strands of energy that played oil-slick rainbows across the dark of the cavern.

Tall silhouettes moved in the expanding dimensional rift.

Trazyn did hate to toss exhibits into destruction – but sometimes one had to trade an acquisition to collect a greater prize.

After all, one had to give in order to get.

With a performative sigh, he reached into the dimensional pocket and withdrew two more labyrinths, and keyed them to unfold.

Lieutenant-Commander Cerantes of the Ultramarines saw the charge coming towards him, and did not hesitate. He saw eight-pointed stars and skin banners. Horned helmets and warp mutation.

Golden eyes set upon black ceramite – a device he knew too well.

He raised his volkite pistol, inscribed with the device of the Five Hundred Worlds, and sent a shimmering heat ray into the chest of the closest black-armoured traitor. The Space Marine fell rolling in agony, joints and eye-lenses pouring smoke as the legionary burned from the inside out.

'Repel the Horusian traitors! Remember Calth!'

He swept his blade forward and his praetorians rushed into the enemy, blue armour bright even in the shadows. Thick breacher shields slammed into the ranks of black ceramite. Short-bladed gladii stabbed, twisted and stabbed again. His sergeant's legatine axe rose and fell in the targeted chops of a well-drilled warrior.

Traitor viscera spilled onto the black marble, steaming in the cold.

But which traitors were these? Cerantes wondered, as he signalled his two Contemptor Dreadnoughts to the ends of the line.

The traitors' iconography was unfamiliar, like no Legion he'd ever known. Perhaps the Word Bearers or World Eaters had taken on a new raiment for the engagement at Armatura, spurred on by a ritual purpose.

All he knew was that, by all means, he must hold this line – though he did not remember receiving the order, nor who had given it to him.

But the thought disappeared immediately – because before him stood the Warmaster.

A taloned gauntlet he knew by sight alone impaled one of his praetorians, sinking through his midsection and lifting him into the air before the inset storm bolter tore him off. Blood bathed the silhouette of the arch-traitor Horus.

But the armour was wrong, and the face – the face he knew.

'Ezekyle,' sneered Cerantes, locking eyes with the traitor.

Ezekyle Abaddon. With one hand he extended his gene-father's lightning claw in a beckoning gesture of challenge, and with the other, he raised his uncanny sword and rammed it point down into the blackstone floor – carving a gory wound not merely in the rock, but through the muscle of the universal plain.

Affronts to the Imperial Truth squirmed up from the gash like insects fleeing a punctured nest. Gibbering and screaming, they poured into the right side of the line and swarmed up the breacher shields, climbing one upon the other.

'When I drag you before the Emperor, brother, you will wish I had killed you for these crimes.'

Then Cerantes charged into the melee, and locked blades with the First Captain of the Sons of Horus.

'All pylon matrix arrays active!' Cawl buzzed in triumph, fully detaching his consciousness from the command node.

It was only then that his tri-layer consciousness scanned the chamber, his appraisal subsystem tagging up to two dozen unique forms of archeotech.

There were the Ultramarines, stolid and daring. A spearhead of green-armoured Salamanders in defunct heraldry. To his right, a regiment of Vostroyans clawed at the stone and vomited, stasis sickness overcoming them even as bolt-shells exploded among their ranks.

The unanswered fire might've broken them, but then long-las discharge ribboned overhead, originating from a group of cloaked snipers atop a ruined pylon. The Vostroyans rallied under the fire support, picked up their rifles and committed themselves.

Most incredible of all, a golden giant – a Blade Champion of the Custodian Guard – rushed into combat alongside the Ultramarines, weaving a flawless ka'tah through the bodies of his foes.

'Oh my.' Cawl glanced at the final labyrinth, still in the necron's grip. 'What's in the last one?'

Trazyn tapped his finger on the construct in a move that, in a human, Cawl would assume was pensiveness.

'I only wish to unleash this one if it is entirely necessary.'

Cawl looked out over the massive amount of ordnance flashing across the nodal chamber. Ten thousand years of killing machines and transhuman warriors tearing at each other in a locked melee.

'Whatever's in there – is it worse than any of that?'

'Much worse,' said Trazyn. 'Because if I let this specimen out, it will never, ever stop.'

FOUR

Glave handed Creed the canteen, and the Lord Castellan took a deep draught as they came around the corner.

He needed it. Creed had been shouting and bellowing his way down the tunnels, marking every step backwards with challenges and encouragement to the rearguard. Holding gateways and aegis redoubts until they were untenable, then ordering up a wave of demolition charges and grenades to toss behind them as they made a fighting withdrawal to the next position.

Glave had never seen anything like it. Creed had not put a hand on his hellpistols. Only ordered and encouraged, pointed and redirected. Fighting the battle with the Cadian Eighth as his weapon, and Glave at his back – hammering anything that merely *looked* at Creed with the chopping beam-fire of his volley gun.

He'd killed three more Traitor Space Marines, though most had been hit by far more las-fire than his own. Yet he knew the victories were solely his, and he could feel the light of the Emperor shining on him.

The Emperor who had put him at the side of His instrument, the Lord Castellan. Who would lead Glave to his ultimate fate as the slayer of a Warmaster.

But the Despoiler had done them one better. He'd let them retreat down the main tunnel leading to the pylon cavern then bottled them there. With Creed and his vanguard of Kasrkin contained, he'd taken a dead-end spur that ran alongside the cavern and demolished the common wall.

The Emperor never said things would be easy. And what they saw when they came into the main cavern certainly did not look easy.

'Frekking Throne,' Creed blasphemed.

What Glave saw made no sense. During the war for Cadia, he'd seen many forces working in combined-arms formations rare even in the hottest and largest warzones. Yet this was another thing entirely.

'How did the Vostroyans get down here, sir?' he wondered. 'Didn't we pass over them as we flew to the tunnels?'

'What worries me more is that there are no Ultramarines or Salamanders contingents I know of,' said Creed. 'Suppose I wasn't the only one with a reserve.'

Glave stared and adjusted the magnification on his lenses. The cavern, the bedrock of the world itself, was beginning to shake, rattling his vision. But at the far end of the line he made out a hulking Ultramarines Dreadnought fighting against two things that had once been its kin, but were now sin-twisted mockeries. A third traitor machine already lay smoking.

The royal-blue Dreadnought smashed a crackling power fist into one traitor machine, staggering it, then spun towards the second that had entangled its other arm in a ropy mass of barbed steel tentacles.

To Glave's shock, a golden blur flashed out from under the stricken Dreadnought's feet, sweeping etheric blue arcs that passed through the gripping feeler-cables, severing them from the traitor machine. The detached appendages constricted and shivered in death-spasms as the golden blur moved on to meet the renewed attack from the other enemy machine, which had recovered from the Dreadnought's blow and was bashing down with its power fist.

As the golden shape dodged aside and lunged to pierce the huge daemon engine, Glave saw it was a gilded human, taller even than a Space Marine, fighting back to back with the Dreadnought as if the two were equals. For a foolish moment he thought it was the Emperor Himself.

But no, it was a Custodian of Terra – like on the cathedral windows.

Glave stood fascinated as the gilded man dodged and parried, spun and cut, then leapt backwards more than his full height and vaulted off the Ultramarines Dreadnought's power reactor, body bent like a bow and his sword held two-handed and point down.

When the auric hero rode the falling traitor machine to the ground, its sword embedded deep in the corrupted face, Glave knew what this was.

'It's a miracle,' he breathed. 'The Emperor is risen! Troops of all battles have come to defend Cadia!'

'Whatever they are, I'll take them.' Creed snorted. 'Eighth, move up and take positions! Use pylon bases for cover, fall into any prepared positions you can! Fix bayonets, it's going to be fought close!'

Creed pointed towards a shape amidst the black tide of the enemy – a red topknot lost in a forest of spikes.

'That's our target. The Despoiler. We shoot our way through to him, got it?'

Glave keyed his volley gun to full power and locked it to the articulated arm on his chest armour.

He was about to enter the clash of heroes, a battle to break the world.

'Trazyn!' Cawl screamed, using machine-speech and his fluted vox-hailer at the same time. 'Whatever you're holding, we need it now!'

Tactical prediction auguries blared crimson in his vision. Warnings that the line was about to fall apart.

The last Helbrute standing had just torn down the Contemptor Dreadnought, liquefying its hull armour with a multi-melta blast before using the ragged stubs of its severed power scourge to shred the entombed pilot like a meat-grinder. Salamanders were dying at a rate of one every thirty seconds, even their mighty ceramite unequal to the task of warding blows from Abaddon's Terminator guard.

A pair of willowy dancers twice the height of a human, their scales mauve and gleaming with iridescence as they wheeled and kicked, swept through the Vostroyan ranks. The pair looked at none but each other, entranced as mirror reflections, as their palms met and legs spun, heedlessly slitting open the Guard troopers in an elegant massacre.

What soldiers were not bleeding out clawed at sores that opened in their flesh, slapping the suppurating wounds as slick-bodied flies teemed from a pock-holed mountain of sentient meat that now anchored the Chaos line.

Cawl lowered his solar atomiser and redirected power into the thermic focusing array, stripping his force field output to dangerous levels to get a sufficiently tight set of melta-waves. Angling high to avoid the troopers.

Released.

One dancer vanished in a wash of atomic radiation, its ectoplasm scalded to vapour in a fraction of an eye-blink.

The other dancer, still holding its partner's blistered hands, twisted around serpentinely and shrieked at Cawl – lipless mouth stretching in a snarl as its jaws, gums and spined fish-teeth forced their way forward.

It had no eyes. Instead, what Cawl had thought were closed eyelids feathered with lashes opened to reveal that they were yet more mouths, red tongues plump and ululating deep in the ocular cavities.

'Trazyn!' Cawl's atomiser was offline. Shield barely operable. He brought down his axe in a guard, slithering a defensive screen of mechadendrites out of his thorax hive. 'Do something, you useless abomination.'

Trazyn stepped to his side, raised a long necrodermis arm towards the warp creature, and pointed a finger.

The daemon tore through the Vostroyans, each of the four arms slashing and throwing, flinging their bodies aside like dolls. Troopers howled and moaned in ecstatic pain as they spun away, faces masked in the horrified confusion of sensory overload.

It came at them on all fours, long body writhing back and forth like a serpent, head disjointing at the neck and twisting all the way around so its gnashing spine-teeth would come at them from below, chewing their loins and bellies.

A green halo of balefire flickered around its awful face.

The head exploded, ichor bursting high enough to scatter in flecks across Cawl's robes, where his augmetic tertiary hand wiped it away with disgust.

The long, scaled body drummed the blackstone floor, muscles seizing so hard it broke its own bones. At least, until a skeletal figure emerged from a colourless split in reality and fired another particle beam into the secondary brain at the base of the spine.

'Was that adequate prey?' asked Trazyn.

The impossible marksman static-whispered a response Cawl could not decipher.

'Good hunting, warden. I will signal when I need you.' Trazyn raised a hand in dismissal, and the retainer stepped back into the breach in realspace.

'The tesseract,' Cawl snapped. 'Right now. I don't care what's inside. We need it.'

'Very well, but I'm warning you – you won't like it.'

* * *

'You will not reach Terra, Ezekyle. Nor Horus. Guilliman...' Lieutenant-Commander Cerantes had to push to say it. Push through the blood that was forcing its way up his throat. Force it with breath rendered feeble due to his punctured lungs. 'The primarch will stop you.'

'There are no more primarchs, brother,' said Abaddon. 'No Horus. That time is gone – yet the galaxy still burns.'

And in the face of the enemy, the betrayer, Cerantes thought he saw an expression of... what? Regret? Pain? No...

Another lance of pain ripped through his side as the First Captain of the Sons of Horus skewered his father's claw deeper into Cerantes, scraping ribs and rupturing organs.

And in that dimming moment of hyper focus, Cerantes understood that it was envy. The traitor envied him.

'It is kinder that I slay you in your ignorance,' said Ezekyle Abaddon.

Then he drew the daemon blade across Cerantes' throat, and the last sound the lieutenant-commander heard was a scream of overpowering rage and limitless anguish.

And a bellowing shout: 'Cadia stands!'

When he saw the Despoiler drop the Ultramarines captain and turn his way, Glave felt a chill wash over him.

Despite the distance, it seemed those glittering eyes, spheres of polished onyx, found him. Picked him right out of the line.

But it was not him – it was the Lord Castellan. Creed.

The king of devils and Warmaster of Chaos wanted Creed, and he was coming.

'Fall back,' said Creed, then raised his voice above the splintering crack of las-fire and zips of hellguns, the magna-horn to his lips. 'Fall back, group up! Make them cross the debris field!'

Heavy weapon fire on their position had blown out the side of one pylon, unleashing a wave of stone debris that swept down on two companies, making the space between them a no-man's-land of broken masonry and Cadian bodies. There was some sort of vibration in the walls, a hum that made his teeth hurt and sinuses pound. Cracks as wide as his finger were jagging up the pylons' surfaces, causing bits to flake off like plaster.

The whole cavern, in fact, had begun to shake. On the ceiling above, there was a *boom, boom, boom,* like artillery, or the tread of a Titan.

What was left of the rearguard made it to the top of the scree slope and began setting up positions amid the blackstone – stacking hunks of fallen noctilith to form low walls and rifle pits.

The Despoiler came for them. Faster than he looked. An avalanche given form.

He ripped aside the Ultramarines still standing in his path. Drove storm bolter rounds through the Vostroyans. Then the golden giant was on him, etheric blue sword describing its arcs and parabolas, scything aside daemons with every cut, reversal and plunge.

The Despoiler shattered the oncoming blade with a backhand sweep of his own, and Glave hoped the noble warrior might still tackle the arch-traitor or stab him with the broken blade.

But the gilded man fell, his shining helmet tumbling away from his body.

Killed in a single stroke.

To his right, feral howls bounced among the sound-amplifying angles of the cavern, and Glave saw loyalist Space Marines in the colours of Russ storm towards the Archenemy host. Some brandished bolters and chainswords, while others carried none. Glave saw long, muscular limbs unburdened of their armour. Fringes of grey and black hair. Wicked fangs bared from skulls that appeared elongated, hooked claws in place of gauntlets.

Some charged on all fours. A loping run, wrists bending back further than they should as the palms contacted the floor.

And as they tore towards the unholy forces, Glave thought he saw the markings of the Ironwolves, and even the great Wolf Lord Orven Highfell himself, waving his power axe among the mutated packs.

Then they smacked into the Archenemy with a meaty slap and all was lost in a blur of claws, teeth, fur and ectoplasm as inhumans tore into inhumans.

The Despoiler kept coming. Chopped down a Space Marine that clambered past the press of daemons. Fractured an Ironwolves helm with a stream of storm bolter fire.

The armoured nightmare broke free into the last bit of no-man's-land – and into the range of the Cadian lasguns.

'Eighth!' Creed bellowed. 'Fire!'

Air shimmered in bands of rainbow light, as though refracting through each molecule like a crystal.

And she found herself amidst hell.

Before her, a pouring horde of Chaos filth – Black Legion, Terminators, a septic outflow of minor daemons spilling across her vision from right to left. Among them waded larger evils – the lords of the warp stalking, capering and plodding. Bewinged and avian, slender and licentious, corpulent and smug – all of it awful.

A solid wall of las-fire drummed into it like a horizontal rainstorm. Beams so thick they overlapped and weaved like threads in a tapestry, so it was impossible to tell one shot from another.

Deep within the volley walked the silhouette of a figure in Terminator plate, pushing ahead against the wash of energy as though it were but a hard wind, and not a very cold one.

'Mamzel?' asked Tempestor Daraq, his hellgun shouldered and pointing. 'Are we cleared to engage?'

The Kappic Eagles were too disciplined to go weapons live without her order. Even now, one was vomiting from the daemonic miasma of the cavern, his weapon still shouldered at the ready.

He should've had his helmet on, not his parade beret. In fact, why *didn't* he have his helmet on? The air of Vladus Secondary was toxic, irradiated. And where was this? The interior of the cathedral Valeria had led them to? Where...

'No,' she whispered.

It came to her in a flash of images. Valeria. The ruined world. Her strike team, frozen. A hooded metal horror emerging from a tunnel of emerald light, bringing with it the howling of tomb winds. A bolt-shell exploding in Valeria's chest. Her eyes open, conscious in a dark gallery, as tiny legs scratched in the tissue of her brain...

She spun and raised her condemnor boltgun, pointing it in the face of Trazyn the Infinite.

'Abomination,' sneered Inquisitor Katarinya Greyfax.

'You see,' the xenos said to a tech-priest. 'Not very novel, is it?'

Greyfax didn't care what that meant. She pulled the trigger – or, she told her finger to pull the trigger.

It did not respond. And the itching in her mind grew to a fever pitch.

'I think you will find that the mindshackle prevents that,' said the xenos.

'How did you possibly– No, I don't care. Where are we? What is going on?'

The necron did not need to answer. Greyfax could hear the shouts, the cries of *'Cadia stands!'* and see the pylons.

'No...'

'Yes, I'm afraid.' Trazyn swept his long arms out wide. 'This is Cadia, indeed, the heart of the pylon matrix. And we are about to fulfil Valeria's great aim of using it to close the Eye of Terror. An ambition you so decisively cut short when you put a bolt-round in her chest.'

'And you expect me to fulfil that heretic's aim.' Greyfax turned and spat, her mouth unbearably dusty.

'I often find irony the best punishment, don't you?' He paused. 'Unless, of course, you would prefer it if Abaddon destroyed Cadia and caused a wound in the universal plain – that is an option.'

Greyfax let out a breath through her teeth, turned to the Kappic Eagles.

'Kill that detestable xenos,' she said experimentally. When none moved, she sighed. 'It was worth a try. Eagles! Fire-team formations, move and cover. I want containing fire on those daemons, do not let them reach the Cadians! Personal kill team, you're with me.'

And they moved, crouched forward and hunting. Letting loose the zip-crack of hellgun shots that slashed through the incorporeal forms – her own group heading towards the silhouette.

Even through the tinted lenses of his helmet, Glave could barely look at the fusillade of las-fire. Barrels along the rifle line blinking in strobe-patterns. Bars of energy streaking outward – so much brightness that his lenses had adjusted to maximum opacity, as if he were operating on desert hardpan or a high-altitude zone in snowblind conditions.

It looked like a firefight in night vision – the las-bolts overwhelming everything else, and the troopers firing them turning into glowing ghosts that only existed in the brief muzzle flashes of their weapons.

'Come on!' yelled Creed. 'Come on, come on! Put him down!'

All of them firing at the onrushing behemoth.

The Despoiler's armour now glowed with the energy absorption of three infantry companies' worth of laser barrage, the hot sparkle of heavy bolter and autocannon tracer rounds zipping and arcing through the mass.

The huge form barrelled through it, the hunched shells of the Bringers of Despair lumbering three steps behind.

'Keep it up!' shouted Creed.

A Terminator dropped, an autocannon round punching through

one knee and blowing a leg away. Lashing chains of green bolt-shells ripped through the hurricane of laser fire and into the Cadian line, half the shells contacting las-bolts and exploding in air before they reached the target.

Not everything hit the Despoiler – some flashed off the aura of daemonic entities that orbited him like fluttering, shrieking spirits. His great talon, outthrust, answered their fire with a stream of blazing stars that slaughtered an entire Kasrkin squad and detonated a plasma gun coil, so Glave saw the dying men silhouetted like shadow-puppets in front of a bloom of white starfire.

The barrage slackened, las-cells running dry. Ammunition belts feeding slack through receivers. Troopers shouted that they were empty, requested cover, fell back to find ammunition boxes or supply runners. A man to his left fumbled with his webbing for another box, dropped it, and vomited with the tension.

'Steady,' Creed cautioned. 'Krak grenades up. Anyone with demolition charges, make ready.'

Glave cut off his spiralling stream of volley-gun discharge. The power pack's internal reactor could produce as much energy as he needed – but keep the fire up too much, and he might burn out the cabling feeding the energy from the pack to the weapon. Already, he smelled the smoky tang of fried wiring.

The Despoiler still came. His armour was stripped of all gilding and ornamentation, black now with carbon-char rather than paint.

He came directly at him, fulfilling the fate that Glave had prayed for ever since he was a child.

'I will have you,' boomed the Despoiler, his armour still hissing with smoke. 'I will have you all, Cadians. I will have your bones and your blood, your screams and your useless prayers. I will have your lives and your world.'

And Glave, borne to that place by the Emperor, suddenly felt cold all over, as though he were already a corpse.

'Bayonets!' Creed called.

Along the line there was the whisper of steel drawing from scabbards, and the click of shaking hands affixing blades.

Glave took a breath, undid the top button of his uniform blouse, then raised his volley gun and took a step towards the Warmaster of Chaos.

And then, the sky fell.

She came like a meteor. Like a thunderbolt. Like a blazing comet that falls from heaven and makes the unenlightened weep in fear.

She came like the Emperor's vengeance manifest – for that was what she was.

Eleanor and Genevieve flew beside her, burning jets for altitude past the pointed tips of the Elysion pylons, out of the acrid smoke of the battlefield, and to the open skies – their engines twisting the contrails of the aircraft duelling above the combat zone.

Then they dropped hard, following in the wake of her light. The gold-tailed corona like a ship plunging through the atmosphere.

They did not know how the Living Saint knew where to strike – or indeed, how she determined that the vibration of the activated pylons had cracked the vault of the nodal cavern nearly to the point of collapse.

One did not ask a saint the whys and wherefores of a miracle – one simply offered their silent faith.

That faith was rewarded. For when they struck the earth, the ground broke rather than their bodies. Fractured like a sinkhole, with ragged shelves of granite and blackstone the size of fishing vessels crashing down onto the tight-packed host of Traitor Space Marines, daemons and corrupted war engines, killing traitors and faithful alike in the close-packed battle.

A column of dust and dirt poured down into the nodal cavern and billowed outward as it hit the floor.

And in the choking dust storm they landed – one-two-three – between the Cadian line and the Despoiler.

Their glow shone yellow in the drifting dirt of Cadia, all the more tangible as motes whirled around them like lightning insects.

'Ah, the masquerade saint,' the Despoiler sneered. 'Nothing but the dream of a dead thing on a living throne.'

'You strike with words because you dare not strike with blows. I am an angel of the Emperor and you fear me.'

'I knew an angel,' the Despoiler said, playing tendrils of energy around his gauntlet. And in the gulfs between the fingers, the Sisters thought they saw blood and heard the death-echo of a righteous being. 'And you are no angel.'

They flew at each other, the Despoiler and the Saint. Ardent Blade of Saint Katherine meeting Drach'nyen, echo of the first murder. Each strike reverberated through the nodal cavern, as two shards of pure anathema clashed together in a psycho-ecstatic onslaught.

With each blow of blade on blade, the daemonic visages of Drach'nyen howled as if scalded, the sound bouncing from pylon to pylon and tearing into the open sky above. And at each contact point, the pure silver of Katherine's crusader sword tarnished.

There was no contest between them. Abaddon wielded the Talon of Horus as well as the shard of ancient homicide, and even with the flames of righteousness flickering around her wing tips and the light of the Emperor streaming from her blank eyes, Celestine had but one weapon to his two.

But she had duty, and faith.

The Sisters swept in, pistols firing and swords crackling with the unleashed energy of the miraculous. Sparks dripped from blades as they cut down at the Despoiler, marking his armour and arresting his killing blows. Breaking off and circling to battle the winged, un-anatomical things that descended on them from the skies in an effort to put out their light.

And as they pressed their attack, the faith of the cheering Cadians swelling their muscles and causing light to shine from their open mouths, they saw the Warmaster of Chaos take a single step backwards.

They had forced him to retreat.

'Archmagos.' Trazyn juggled chrysoprase tablets, reading alignment grids and dimensional fissures. 'We have reached the critical stage. Either unleash the pariah matrix, or the planet shakes itself apart.'

'Then we activate!'

Cawl scuttled to a bank of cogitators and logic-banks at the centre of a cabling nest. Tapped out a consecrated cypher-mantra on a clackboard.

'Oh Omnissiah, one who brings us function, please bless and sanctify this befouled marriage of xenos architecture and sacred Mechanicus input devices. Judge us not for our trespasses into the labyrinth of forbidden knowl–'

'Archmagos!'

'Please just let the damn thing work,' he said, and pressed the ACTIVATE key.

Across the cavern, the temperature dropped. Warp beasts bellowed in horror as the air seemed full of static charge, black sparks jumping between metal objects as a new dimension pushed at the skin of reality.

No creature knew what was occurring save Trazyn and Cawl. Only that their exhalations ran fever-hot one breath, and in icy clouds the next. Troopers popped nosebleeds. Sinus headaches. Twenty-two unaugmented humans across the cavern dropped from strokes or sudden cardiac events.

Sanctioned psykers of the Cadian Eighth and sorcerers of the Black Legion, beings so completely unlike one another apart from one crucial quality, fell in seizure as their souls were ripped out of their mortal forms and commingled as they funnelled into the warp.

Snaps of arc lightning, black as the unstarred void, lashed between the bases of the pylons, throwing sparks of dark matter where they connected other noctilith.

Those that looked too closely at the strikes saw that they were no electrical discharge – but micro-fissures in the air and stone, through which an elsewhere place could briefly be seen.

To call it a dimension would be incorrect. The warp was a dimension. A mirror world of psychic reality where the twisted spawn of emotion and concepts played out their own mad lives. This was, if anything, the opposite of that. A place of un-life. Soulless emptiness that was vast and tangible, yet did not exist in the common way of meaning at all.

It was defined by what could not exist there – and what could not exist there was anything.

The black streams of anti-galaxy sparked and crawled up the pylons, up out of the caverns and into the Elysion Fields to coalesce at the pylons' tips, so from afar they appeared like a field of sorcerous grave-candles.

Three thousand feet above, Hanna Keztral was rolling *War-Kite* back and forth, the autocannon and las-beams of two Drakes streaking past her airframe. They had already splashed Ragnal, his Thunderbolt falling from the sky in a teardrop of flames. Mak hadn't reported after the last sortie. Keztral was alone, and thinking of her mother again. The way she'd sewn Keztral's gloves to her sleeves in winter so she wouldn't lose them because they were her only pair. How angry her mother, long dead, would be at these daemon-craft when they killed her little girl.

But then the Drakes gave tortured-metal squeals and peeled off, their long snouts bending around to bite and worry at themselves, tearing off armour plating and digging into internals like a bird with a parasite.

'What the hells?' she said, looking over her shoulder as they slipped out of her view.

Below her, the anthem of vibration reached an unbearable pitch. A noise so bone-deep wrong that combat on the surface stopped entirely. Black tendrils lashed free of the pylon points, smashing into each other and coiling into a spiral that in an eye-blink rammed through the atmosphere in a sonic boom so loud the soundwave radiated out across the atmosphere of the whole planet and lapped itself, echoing like a gunshot in an empty plaza.

And the streams of pariah energy drove straight for the Eye of Terror.

Dravura Morkath saw the beam lance by the *Will of Eternity* through the bridge crystal, the anti-psychic clap of its passage resonating through the blackstone so violently she fell in a seizure that nearly killed her.

When she regained her feet and wiped the foam from her mouth, she saw that it had lanced the Eye of Terror like a boil, bursting the convex skin of the dimensional tear so it collapsed in on itself.

And to her horror, she saw that the Great Eye – open since humanity had first looked into the skies of Terra and imagined gods in the stars – was starting to close.

'It's working!' Belisarius Cawl crowed, all four of his arms held up in triumph. The read-outs on his dataveil were strong, determinative. Internal numeral-crunchers worked the results over, cross-referenced them, controlling for environmental factors. Yes, there was only one conclusion. 'It's working, you abominable, filthy genius! We've done it, we've–'

But when he clicked the data-stream into natural vision, his celebration ceased.

Around the nodal chamber, warriors twisted in agony. Cadians and Vostroyans held their craniums, their sounds tracking in Cawl's auditory pattern-recognition as inhuman, like a newly born servitor before formatting, or livestock in the kill-paddock.

The activation seemed to have driven the Fenrisians, those with the mutant gene-seed strain Cawl was only too familiar with, completely feral. They swarmed up the body of a Bloodthirster, hacking and biting. The thing staggered, its flesh starting to melt as it lost its connection to the mortal plane. Its mouth dropped open in shock, the head of Orven Highfell rolling from its jaws as the Wolf Lord's body fell from its talons.

The daemons were dissolving. Vanishing in gouts of blue flame as they fled back to the immaterium. Coming apart like a shawl when a child pulls on its loose thread. Melting then sizzling away like ice cubes on a hot pan.

But the same fate had befallen the Legion of the Damned, who had pinned the Black Legion advance, ensuring it bogged down before reaching Creed. Wraith-warriors grew thin and insubstantial, their forms wavering like pict-reels projected from a weak bulb.

And the Saint. Cawl could see the Saint weakening.

Yet the Black Legion, warriors long before their infection by Chaos, needed no mystic connection to keep killing. They drove on, swamping the reeling Imperials. Throwing them back and crushing their bodies underfoot. Surrounding Celestine's twin attendants.

'Trazyn, is this normal? How long will this last? Can we–'

No answer came – and Cawl found that the abomination was gone.

'Extend that line right! Extend, damn it!' Creed shouted through the amplifier. With the Legion of the Damned dissolving, there was real worry they'd finally be flanked. 'Cadia stands!'

'General,' Glave pointed. 'The Saint, general.'

The combat before them had gone sour. Celestine's light was pale and dim, less like burnished gold, and more like a tarnished brass halo on a battered servo-skull. Her Geminae Superia were caught in the whirl of the melee, both sheeting blood from deep wounds as they rammed their swords downward two-handed, unable to strike otherwise in the press. Their forms, formerly bright and sharp, were dimming like the daemons and ethereal Space Marines.

And Glave knew why.

It was because of him. Because his faith had wavered. The Emperor had preserved Glave. Put him at the side of the Lord Castellan. Set the Despoiler in his path, even shown him the Living Saint.

Yet Glave had felt the weakness within him when he'd seen the Despoiler coming. Felt his resolve fail. And due to that, the God-Emperor who sat upon the Golden Throne had withdrawn the gifts He'd so generously given.

Glave saw he could be a Guardsman no longer. There was a time to step into line, to follow the shouts of officers, and there was time to hear the calls of the divine voice of Terra.

That moment came when the Despoiler slapped his razored gauntlet into the Saint with a percussive *bang* of energy like a transformer blowing, and her body – seeming suddenly very small – sprawled backwards with her arms flung wide.

Snarling with triumph, the Despoiler sliced the daemon sword out wide and blood arced in the stale air.

'Saint!' Glave shouted. And he was running before he consciously knew he would do so. Down the scree slope. Towards the Despoiler, keying his volley gun to a whining hum in preparation for the shot. A shot he knew had been set in motion ever since he'd been born, since the review board had leaned over him and given him his charge.

'Glave!' It was the Lord Castellan, but he did not listen. 'Glave, come back here! Frekk it – charge! Charge!'

Servantus Glave felt the world slide and lock into place as he strode towards his purpose, and met his destiny.

He didn't see the Traitor Space Marine who fired the shot. Didn't see the stray bolt-shell streaking in towards the Kasrkin line. And he only barely registered it when a las-bolt struck the shell mid-air, detonating it five feet above his head and two feet to the left.

The sting registered first, but he had been peppered with shrapnel before.

He kept running. At least, until his breath hitched on the welling blood, and his punctured airway swelled pencil-thin with inflammation.

In the next step, it was as though his leg did not exist. It simply folded under him, his heavy kit dragging him down. Glave might have fallen on his face had another trooper not barged past and twisted him mid-fall so he slammed down on his back, propped up awkwardly on his power pack.

Boots pounded past him, Kasrkin rushing into the boil with war-shouts and hellguns cracking. Glave let go of his volley gun and tried to loosen his carapace around his throat, but the clumsy gloves couldn't get purchase on the wet collar, and kept poking at the spongy ruin of his neck.

That couldn't be right. This was not what was supposed to happen. He'd seen the signs and heard the angels.

Someone fell next to him and slid, and for a moment Glave thought another casualty had joined him – but it was Stitcher Kristan going down hard on his kneepads, medi-kit already in hand.

'It's all right, trooper. Let me look at it.'

Glave felt the sting get worse as Stitcher's plastek-gloved fingers probed his neck. He swallowed blood to clear his mouth.

'Not supposed–' he said, then stopped to swallow more syrupy blood. 'Despoi...'

'It's all right,' Kristan whispered, removing his helm. Glave saw las-bolts stripe the air above the medicae's head. 'It's all right, corporal. No talking. Rest easy.'

Glave felt cold, but it was the look in Kristan's eyes that stopped him speaking as much as the order. It was a look of knowing. As if the medicae had heard this before as he looked into the faces of dying troopers, who said that this was not supposed to happen to them, that they'd gone to war thinking it would be the others that took the las-bolt, or got buried alive by an artillery barrage. That they were meant for greater things.

He had always imagined that at martyrdom he'd be greeted by the Emperor and surrounded with golden light. Yet instead he was cold, and instead of light, a deepening twilight was dimming his peripheral vision.

Servantus Glave, who had striven so hard to become a Kasrkin, did not feel like an elite soldier then. He felt like a young man wearing a costume, who had been raised to believe that the ugly profession of war was in fact a glorious crusade.

He had always thought his death would mean something. And in his bones settled an undeniable sense that he'd been tricked.

Distantly, he heard Kristan's voice.

'You did your duty, trooper. If you hadn't been out front, Creed would've taken that hit.'

Glave didn't know about that. Hadn't Creed been well behind him?

But the cold dark was closing in, and he didn't have the strength to question it. At least it was something.

And when Kristan lifted his vambrace and opened the port – the one leading directly to his vein – and pushed the plunger on the obscurine syringe, all he felt was gratitude.

'Be at peace, soldier of Cadia.'

For while there was no holy light waiting on the other side, at least the enfolding darkness was warm.

* * *

Greyfax gritted through the pressure.

That's what it felt like: pressure. Like an over-atmosphered module on a voidship, or diving deep into liquid sea, too fast, with a rebreather. She felt like she were being pressed to death with stones, like a vice around her temples were closing and the plates of her skull were about to slide loose.

Still, she reached out with the Will. Battering her psychic essence against the nearly physical force of the pylon emanations.

'Grraaaaaaaaaaggghhhhh!' she growled. Spittle dripped down her chin and onto her armour. Using her anger, the disdain that had always fuelled her to cross any boundary and go any distance.

This Imperium disgusted her. She had no idea what had been allowed to happen during her captivity in Trazyn's gallery, but clearly things had gone far off the rails. There were Space Marines of the Adeptus Astartes revelling in their fall to base mutation. Mechanicus worthies consenting to pollute themselves by partnership with heathen aliens. Hellfire spirits that were of the warp as much as the daemons they fought.

And worst of all was the false woman – Greyfax refused to call her a saint – her form encased in golden armour and razored wings flaring behind her. Light shining on her resolute features, both fine and strong with a blush of blood on the cheek, her lips wine purple.

A mesmerising face, Greyfax admitted, which was why the idolatrous soldiers had fallen for her.

But worst of all was that expression of serenity. As if this girl knew the galaxy and what it had to offer, as though a suit of power armour, an old sword, a pair of wings and a few mad visions showed her the true nature of the cosmos.

Even as she lay defeated and bleeding on the stones, her ceramite bodice carved open by Abaddon's blade, her sword upraised in both stoic defiance and the acceptance of martyrdom, she remained serene. Even as the Talon of Horus pinned her shoulder to the rock, ready for the execution stroke of the Despoiler's blade.

Never.

Greyfax would not let her have that death. This so-called saint would not be gaining immortality through the quills of hagiographers and chapel-cults. No. Greyfax would question her, get her on the stand, and expose her for what she was.

This heretic fraud was hers to break.

Locking her teeth, she slammed her will across the chamber like an open hand, gripping it around the Despoiler's cranium. Her psychic self feeling his marble-cold skin and the rough tickle of his topknot.

Then she *squeezed*. Channelled the pain and pressure of the environment from her own consciousness to his. Made her own agony and discomfort an attack as she forced him to feel it with her.

Greyfax was not a transhuman demigod. She had not fought across ten thousand years.

But Greyfax knew how to handle pain – and she bet she could bear it more than even a Warmaster of Chaos.

Across the cavern, Abaddon staggered, his spearing thrust with the daemon blade foiled as he rocked backwards, shaking his head.

Their connection broke, triggering a psychic snap-back that stung her like an ice pick to the eye.

The scowling face, unmarked and full of righteous anger, turned towards her.

'Away from her!' Greyfax snapped, raising her condemnor bolt-gun. 'She's mine.'

Trazyn watched from high in the nodal cavern, wreathed in the impossible cloak of the oubliette.

'That one,' he said, pointing at an enormous Chosen that had smashed into the skitarii lines and was grinding its way through to Belisarius Cawl.

The Huntmaster shouldered his synaptic disintegrator and took a sighting. Fiddled with knobs that were not there. Fired.

The Chosen dropped, cut down on Cawl's blind side as he hosed solar atomiser fire at a Black Legion squad.

'When do we take the alpha?' the Huntmaster asked, jutting his chin towards Abaddon. The Warmaster was now locked in a swirl of combat. He murdered Kasrkin with each blow. Ran them through, bashed helmets in with his pommel. Mauled them the way a lupine predator tears into a flock of wool-bearing livestock. 'I have a shot. The disintegrator will keep the damage internal, and he would still be fit for display.'

'No.' Trazyn sighed. 'What is a Warmaster without his mind? I'd rather have ten thousand injuries to his armour and person than kill a single cell inside that brain.'

The Kasrkin were dead now. The regular troops of the Eighth were falling back in good order, but disoriented by the smoke grenades they'd triggered to cover their withdrawal as they hooked arms under the Saint and dragged her from the killing field. By all accounts, the flock had retreated.

But the shepherd remained.

Down in the smoke, Creed moved forward, pistols drawn. He called, shouting. Rallying troops that were not there. In the high-frequency resonance of the chamber, Trazyn's auditory transducers could not make out his words – but by his mouth shape, he knew what the Lord Castellan said.

Cadia stands.

'Do you want that one?' said the Huntmaster. 'It's more recoverable.'

A Terminator breached out of the smoke, swinging its autocannon around at the general, but Creed dropped to one knee and slashed out with hellpistol fire that drilled into the brute's cracked eye-lens.

It fell.

Cadia stands.

Trazyn tilted his head. 'Perhaps he's worth considering.'

The Geminae Superia were gone now, disappearing under the weight of the Bringers of Despair. Celestine was lost somewhere in the smoke.

Greyfax had regrouped her Kappic Eagles and pushed on the Terminators still visible, unwilling to dive into a blind fight.

Cadia stands.

Abaddon surfaced in the smoke, only ten cubits from Creed. Slid with inexorable, impossible quiet towards the general. He crouched low, only the tips of his trophy rack cutting through the twists of artificial fog.

Closer, closer.

Creed twisting and turning.

Cadia stands.

'Lord,' warned the Huntmaster, disintegrator already raised and sighted.

Other Terminators converging on the general backed away, knowing that this one was for the Warmaster. There was a searchlight flitting in the cloud, maybe a lost Kasrkin or medicae searching for Creed.

Cadia stands.

'Lord?' The Huntmaster sent it as an interstitial message, unwilling to break his aim with sound vibration.

Abaddon, so close now that it seemed impossible Creed did not hear the servos, barrelled towards the small commander. The man who had held Cadia for longer than anyone anticipated. Who had kept the defence energised with speeches and front-line visits. Who had endured an attack more overwhelming and terrible than any other in Imperial history.

Creed finally spun, stabbing hellpistol shots into the face of a foe he'd spent a lifetime preparing to face as the two commanders finally joined an unequal combat.

'*Lord! You have to choos–*'

'Fire.'

The Huntmaster's particle beam stung the Despoiler's head just as he swept the Talon of Horus down on Creed.

Trazyn saw the general thrown to the side, one pistol sliced in two and dribbling acid from its powercell. Creed had blood on his uniform, spattering his face. One hand was a bloody mess.

The Despoiler swept the general up in his claw. Trazyn's measurement suite noted the power thrumming through it as it began to crush, slowly, as the Warmaster spoke to the choking commander.

'Fire, Huntmaster.'

'I don't need to, lord. Another predator's on the stalk.'

Behind Abaddon, the searchlight was growing closer, getting stronger.

And when it burst through the veil of smoke and stretched out its bloody wings, Trazyn realised it was not a searchlight at all, but the etheric glow of Saint Celestine's sword. She held it low, point upward, and it was lit end to end with curling fire.

Flames she extinguished by sinking the blade hilt-deep into the small of Abaddon's back.

It slid in below the power cylinder linked to the Talon of Horus, severed its power cable, passed up underneath the bottom of the breastplate, and lodged.

Trazyn could hear the Warmaster's roar even over the vibration of the pariah matrix.

Stitcher Kristan was sweeping his big stablight around the darkness when he heard the Kasrkin shouting that they'd found him.

Ursarkar E. Creed, Lord Castellan of Cadia, was trying to stand up when Kristan got there, with two Kasrkin forcing him down by his shoulders and murmuring reassurances.

Kristan slid down next to him and went to work assessing, charting wounds from his boots to the crown of his head.

'Lord Castellan, sir? Mind telling me what happened?'

'He's gone,' Creed coughed. 'Old spike-arse flashed out. Teleport anchors. Probably his last shot to get away before the pylons...' He coughed again, deep and rattling.

'I meant your injuries, sir.' Kristan took the Lord Castellan's left hand by the wrist and raised it, carefully turning the hand around to see the extent of the damage. Fingers flopped this way and that like broken candles, held on only by the barest scraps of skin.

'Can we save them?'

'The fingers? We can try.'

He sprayed a combined counterseptic-analgesic on the stumps and began to carefully clip each finger off, dropping each digit into his cold-storage pack in case they could be reattached.

Kristan wasn't hopeful of that, the wound was messy. Probably the Despoiler's lightning claw. An augmetic was more likely.

'Hurry up, man,' Creed griped. 'Hurry, I need to get back on the line. Just wind me up with bandages enough to walk. Painkillers too, if you've got them.'

'We won, sir. So let's just take it easy.'

'No, it's not over. Not by a long shot. The Despoiler, he said– Gaaaaaahhh!' Creed winced as Kristan probed his chest for rib fractures.

'What did the Despoiler say?'

The voice came over his shoulder, and Kristan could feel a static charge there, like standing near a dynamo. His arm and neck hairs prickled and rose.

Celestine. The Living Saint was standing at his shoulder. Kristan took a slow breath and kept working, fighting the urge to raise his eyes.

Creed's face was ashen from blood loss. His grey-black stubble stood out against sweat-slick cheeks. 'He said that he'd sealed our fate before he'd even come to Elysion. That he'd show us what true commitment could accomplish.'

'Sir?' a vox-officer interrupted. 'Transmission from the *Phalanx*. Line's heavily distorted, but I think I made it out.'

'The Archenemy fleet is moving in,' said Creed, both a guess and a certainty.

'Yes, sir, using the *Will of Eternity*'s wreck as a screen.'

'Not as a screen,' Creed said, forcing himself up. 'As a projectile. He's going to drop the Throne-damned thing on us.'

The impression-wraith of Captain Prozus Ghael was still seated in his command throne on the *Will of Eternity*'s bridge. He might be there forever.

He was fighting, clawing, trying to stay in the throne as ceramite gauntlets ripped him out of it, bloody cables slithering from his skin embeds as they pulled him away, his neck bending back, skull-port interfaces tethering him to his station.

Then a disembodied power sword cut the fibre bundle, and he was gone.

As much as they had disliked each other, Ghael had a strong connection to the fortress, and Morkath didn't relish the thought of the tormented centuries he would spend in her father's dungeon. The trauma of his removal would echo for a long time – and indeed, just as she thought that, the re-enactment restarted, as it had every few minutes since she'd found the bridge and started running her system assessment.

The looping thoughtform dissolved into telepathic steam as she sat in the command chair.

His ghost was the only thing even pretending to be alive there. She'd needed to remove the bodies of the crew from their terminals in order to properly assess the damage.

She alone had survived – and not only that, she'd succeeded. And as the *Vengeful Spirit* pulled into dock range of the wreck she once considered her mother, Morkath opened a hail.

'*Spirit*, this is the *Will*. Dravura Morkath transmitting. I'm requesting a private channelling or secure holo-projection. Connect me to the Warmaster.'

A voice answered, so overwhelmed by daemonic crosstalk it was almost impossible to parse. One of the communication-psykers, half-mad from the vibrations Morkath had been trying to shut out.

'I don't care,' she insisted, responding solely to the reply's tone. 'Tell him the Fortress Child wants to speak.'

Silence for six full minutes, then the projection-array fizzled, wisps of ozone drifting up from its ancient coils.

He stood before her then. The Warmaster.

Due to the projection-array's size – meant to communicate with an entire bridge crew rather than a single person – he loomed huge, the size of a Dreadnought.

Standing before him in flesh, Morkath had often felt like a child looking upon her parent – but now, she appeared like a canine beholding its master.

His image stuttered and rolled horizontally, sliding to the left and reappearing at the right before it fixed in place.

Abaddon greeted her with three words: '*You are alive.*'

'I am.' Morkath bowed. It was not the bow of a servant, but one of fealty. Its depth indicating respect for a mentor. 'And I continue your work.'

'*What work can you continue? The fortress is broken. Its utility wrecked. Good only for–*'

'The fortress can be repaired, Warmaster. It is not a machine that can be broken. It is an entity, and it is healing. With the proper structural guidance, and noctilith grafts, I believe it will become whole again.'

Morkath punched a set of commands into the throne, streaming the data she'd collected to the *Spirit*'s bridge.

'When Cadia is brought to heel, and the servants of the False Emperor scattered, we can repair it. We can yet still hammer the Imperial Palace flat under its guns.'

'Morkath, why did you do this?'

'Because it is my contribution, Warmaster. The service you wished me to perform, to salvage what others had ruined. Preserve this as your greatest weapon and flagship. To fulfil the reason you created me, and learn the truth you wished me to discover by leaving me here.'

He said nothing, and despite the indistinct image she knew he was overcome. There passed a flicker of emotion in his eyes, a break in his stoicism. In another being it would mean nothing, but for her creator Abaddon it revealed vast wells of buried affection.

'It is a gift of filial piety and love, from your most devoted daughter.'

'Morkath.'

'Do not call me that, I am not the Fortress Child. I am *your* child. Created by you to fulfil a purpose. I am under no illusion that we share blood, but you made me and raised me in your care. Kept me close. Just as your gene-father kept you close. There is no sense denying it.'

'You are mistaken.' He shook his head. *'I made you because when we put a daemon in the last fortress, it went mad. Became uncontrollable. I had to pass it to the Red Corsairs, bargain it away to get any benefit.'*

'I know. And though you did not care for me but as an object then, have I not proved myself? I know your heart. How you have grown to care for and rely on me. I am not sentimental. You need not be anyone you are not. Just acknowledge me as yours. Let me serve you, not as the Fortress Child, but as your own. Dravura Abaddon, Mistress of the Fortress. I will deliver you Terra.'

'*I have other plans for the fortress.*'

Out the viewport, the *Vengeful Spirit*'s prow slid past the docking clamps. The massive ram-head kissed the centre of the fortress with a grinding crunch that lurched her forward in the throne.

'What?'

'*You have done all you can, little servant. I see that and acknowledge it. And in your own way, you are giving me Cadia, for which I am grateful.*'

'Warmaster! Don't throw this fortress away.'

'*It is no longer of use to me.*'

The *Spirit*'s engines flared, turning the ship into a shadowed wedge in contrast to their bright corona. Morkath cast a look over her shoulder, at the stern viewscape, and saw the green-blue of Cadia – its mountains and streamers of battle-smoke – creeping closer.

'Let me off then. Convey me to the *Spirit*. We can salvage enough noctilith to create a resonant war council chamber. No one else knows the minds of your council. No one else knows *your* mind so intimately and completely.'

'*Yes,*' he answered. '*I allowed you close. Perhaps too close. A risk I must mitigate. You are a useful tool, but someone once told me a useful tool is worth sacrificing – do you recall who said that?*'

Morkath's shoulders dropped. It was done. She would not demean herself in his eyes by fighting it.

Morkath put her head in her hands, unable to look at him. 'Do one thing. Grant me my desire. Acknowledge me. Let me die with your name.'

'*No.*'

'Father!'

He leaned backwards, as if struck. The word had touched some pain in him she did not realise existed, but she didn't care. If she hurt him, so be it. He was not the one hurtling towards terminal orbit.

'*I am sorry, Morkath,*' he said. '*I have disappointed you.*'

Morkath blinked. She had never heard the Warmaster apologise – for anything. Within, she felt an old hope bloom. A moment bathed in his light.

'*But in my experience, that's what fathers do.*'

He cut the transmission, and her further hails were not answered.

She rotated the throne towards the stern, watching the incandescent burn of atmosphere lick at the viewport. Seeing the snow-capped mountains of Cadia grow until she could see its ridges and valleys like crags on the face of an old, bitter man.

He would not let her gracefully spiral into de-orbit. The Despoiler was pushing her straight down to the world below.

Morkath reached her consciousness through the stricken fortress in the moments before impact, flowing all of her soul out into the blackstone, so she did not have to die in the body he'd made for her.

'Do what you want, father,' she said, thoughts reverberating through the alien stone. 'But you cannot stop me from fulfilling my promise.'

And with her mind suffusing the stone, blazing like an asteroid, she broke the world for him.

PHASE SEVEN

EVACUATION

ONE

Cadia Tertius had always been the least-populated and wildest space on Cadia. A place where cadets did wilderness training and the majority of locally produced ammunition was manufactured. At its far northern edge, members of high command and the old military families had fine wilderness lodges where they hunted imported game and took children on gruelling multi-day mountain treks and summiting expeditions.

The kasrs and fortresses of Tertius were lightly garrisoned, and though they'd been subject to invasion by cultists, had believed their continent had once again got off relatively lightly, as it had in previous Archenemy invasions.

Within a second of the *Will of Eternity* striking it, Cadia Tertius functionally ceased to exist.

Half a world away – docked in protective anchor over the Elysion Fields – the Imperial fleet could not take readings directly from the impact site, and the Black Fleet itself was already regrouping for an attack on the *Phalanx*.

As a result, the one surviving witness to the initial formation of the strike zone was Arch-Cryptek Sannet in the *Lord of Antiquity*, who recorded the data from the ship's position in high orbit, sensor-cloaked and tethered to a dead orbital defence platform.

That data, specifying the size of the blackstone debris, its trajectory, speed and mass, remains cryptomantically sealed in the vaults of Solemnace.

Cawl's first indication that something had occurred was when the nodal net misaligned, its null-matrix failing in six dozen places as the pylons shifted under the micro-quakes running throughout the entire crust and mantle of Cadia.

The matrix went down like a hive city's power grid, parts of it snapping off while others continued unabated. Whole pylon sections flashed off and on again before the system became critically overtaxed and went dark.

At first, he thought it was an overload – that was before the seismic alarms turned his vision into a patchwork of environmental reports and crash alerts.

Then, he had no idea what had occurred. However, his later study of the impact zone, based on environmental effects and picts later taken by the *Iron Revenant*, suggested that the fortress remains were moving relatively slowly when the strike occurred. Had an asteroid the size of the *Will of Eternity* struck at the spot travelling a standard speed of twenty miles per second, a third of the planet would have calved and become a new moon.

Even so the devastation was monumental, melting a crater fifty miles deep and ejecting noctilith dust and particlised gypsum into the atmosphere. Larger pieces of debris streaked directly into space, or arced into the atmosphere and fell hundreds of miles away. Superheated by re-entry, they ignited forest fires and touched off prairie blazes across the southern grasslands of Cadia Secundus.

The initial blast wave hit Hanna Keztral as she rearmed and refuelled *War-Kite* at 399(A)'s temporary airfield south-west of Kasr

Kraf. While the Rossvar Mountains took the brunt of the hit, the blast funnelled through a saddle between two peaks and blew a sudden, violent crosswind perpendicular to the runway.

A Marauder bomber tumbled sideways on its final approach, wings folding and tearing away as the fuselage rolled like a barrel across the grass. Thank the Throne it was coming back with empty bomb bays and nearly out of fuel, because when it smashed into the prefab used as a missile bunker the small fire killed no one but the crew and an unfortunate ground team.

War-Kite, taxied next to the solidly built jet-grade promethium station, escaped damage – but Keztral watched as a whole corrugated metal hangar lifted in the wind and peeled away into bedsheet-sized pieces of shrapnel, guillotining into thirty-one pilots and crew who had gathered to shovel down a quick meal at the mess tent.

The first indication that Logistar-General Conskavan Raik had that anything was amiss was a sudden blare of vox interference. He had been on the horn with nearly every command on Cadia, and an untold number of fleet officers, for nearly four days straight. He'd taken to regularly chewing caffeine pills, and it made him jumpy and prone to tantrums – especially in the two days since he'd got a visit from Inquisitor Talia Daverna, who'd confiscated his vox traffic records, and grilled him for two hours over certain landing zones.

Deep in a Salvation bunker in the eastern Rossvar, one converted into a command centre after the planned demolition of Kraf, he had neither heard nor felt the blast wave.

'Atmospheric storms?' he shouted into his line-vox to the transmitting room. 'Nothing like that on the weather reports... Well, what bloody good are these meteorological analyses if they can't predict something like this? Yes, I realise that sending the signal by atmospheric bounce is impossible, but surely not every relay tower is down across the battle sector–'

Tactical Officer Dabatha Ravi put a report on his desk, tapped it twice, which was their signal for top priority.

'Hold on. Don't ring off, I'm not done with you.'

Raik rested the handset across his shoulder and read the report. It was printed on the back of a casualty list, the paper shortage even reaching high command now.

'Frekk!' he snapped, and threw the report away in disgust. It fluttered to the floor.

'Sir?' Ravi enquired, watching the logistar-general, far too well heeled to swear, grind the heels of his hands into his eyes.

'I'm sorry, Dabatha. Get that paper would you? We'll need it for the archives.' He pressed the handset back to his ear. 'Are you still there? No, forget that. I need a narrow-beam straight to the *Phalanx*, then have them relay it down to Elysion for the Lord Castellan. Initial message reads *Request Execute Chrysanthus*. You've got that? Yes. Chrysanthus, like the Flower of Cadia. Good, then do it now.'

He slammed the receiver down hard, then bit his thumbnail.

'So,' said Ravi. 'It's happening.'

'Yes – signal Shrowd and the Navy. Tell them to get the transports in position.'

'Before codeword confirmation, sir?'

'Let's hope that upstart's still alive to give codeword confirmation. So yes, send the troop boats. Then send word for my coat and personal trunk, as soon as we hear back, we're going to get on one.'

When a sonic boom shattered the sky, Marda Hellsker was still riding high off her first armoured assault.

The Volscani had been regrouping for another go at the Delvian Cleave when they'd hit them – the 46th Armoured Shock driving down out of the cleave with the 91st Shock Troops and 922nd Engineers in the troop bays of their Chimeras.

Hellsker had ridden front and centre in a command Salamander, pointing the sword of Lukas Bastonne towards their objective, the bloodied standard of the 24th Cadian Interior snapping over the vehicle cupola.

Lieutenant-Colonel Vastal of the 46th knew armoured warfare well, and the tank formations made figure-of-eight patterns as they came down the slope and into the west – surrounding and destroying Volscani remnants, herding them like sheepdogs driving livestock.

They'd made the landing site on the second day, with the 922nd Engineers laying out the loading zones with white spray paint and chemical tracklights. Marking arrows and approach paths, numbering the rubbarine landing pads they hauled off the cargo-8s and 16s that followed the armoured column.

Meanwhile Hellsker had got the 91st into a perimeter defence, bolstered by Basilisk firebases. A bulwark to hold the landing zone against the hordes of cultists that increasingly converged on this island of floodlights and work-squads in the middle of enemy territory. For days, they'd been trying her defences, and only getting bolder.

The 46th kept the road umbilical open, patrolling and fortifying the line of march for the few Kraf civilians who'd remained in the city, temporarily housed in the shelled-out hive-bunkers of the Delvian Cleave.

Despite the noise of the blast wave, Hellsker didn't think much of it. The sky-shattering noise of the *Phalanx*'s bombardment curtain at the Elysion Fields had been louder and longer, like close thunder that never stopped, and she assumed it was only another volley.

It was the tidal wave that let her know this was not an orbital barrage.

The first wave was half a mile high, swamping the oceanic naval base at Kasr Phen and coming to within sight of the landing zone. That first boiling wall of water left a carpet of buildings, ships and bodies in its wake like shells washed up on a seashore. One was a Dzant-class missile boat, a three-hundred-ton vessel that stood beached fully a mile inland.

The bodies had been stripped and rolled, their uniforms shredded off and skins abraded until it was impossible to tell if they were Imperial or traitor.

Worn down, she thought, like beach glass.

Thirty minutes later, another wave came – bigger, closer.

The ghost ship swept another two hundred yards towards their lines, heeling over on its side so she could see directly down the flapping hatches of its deck bays.

Where she saw smooth white cones nestling.

She lowered her magnoculars.

'Ravura? Call me up Pesk and the engineers. We need to move the landing zone.'

'But, colonel... we're established. We're under fire. Not heavy fire, but fire all the same. The waves can't possibly reach–'

'The waves don't have to reach!' She stabbed a finger at the ship. 'Those frekking missiles are *live*.'

'General! Lord Castellan, sir!'

The vox-officer ran up to them before they'd even registered that the sky was a different colour, or seen the battle tanks blown into the disordered pylons like collections of autumn leaves.

He held out the vox handset. 'It's Logistar-General Raik. He says, *Request Execute Chrysanthus*. Do you know what that means, sir?'

Stitcher Kristan was still working on Creed, had even helped him clamber over debris as they made their way up from the nodal cavern.

Creed stared at the sky. It was brown as brick dust, the low clouds tinged a muddy khaki, like the colour of his uniform. 'Maybe it's done. Maybe we could hold out.'

Dark shapes emerged from the smoke. Kasrkin and Kappic Eagles raised their hellguns, then lowered them, recognising the silhouettes of Space Marines.

'Lord Castellan.' It was Odric A'shar, lieutenant of the Raven Guard. 'We have indications from the fleet – they drove the Blackstone Fortress into the planet. Cadia Tertius is gone. South of here are wildfires, horizon to horizon. Coasts are being racked with tidal action – if *Chrysanthus* is an evacuation call, I suggest you make it. The Black Templars and Dark Angels have already made their own embarkation plans – will the Ironwolves…?'

He let the question hang until he saw Creed shake his head.

'No, I thought not. Where is Cawl? We will need his ships.'

'I don't think I can do it,' said Creed. 'If I say that word, it's over. After all the blood they've shed for me, I don't know if I can ask them to abandon Cadia.'

'Would you rather we all die?' asked Kristan. 'That we wait for the planet to break apart under our feet? We've stood long enough, the frekking planet broke before we did.'

Creed beckoned for the receiver, clicked the line open.

'Logistar-general?'

A delay, a squeal.

'Throne, so you are alive.'

'For now.'

'Are you going to call it? I don't think the planet will be habitable for more than a few hours.'

'I'm going to call it. Is everything ready?'

'It is. I've already sent them to positions. But we need the codeword if they're going to take off.'

'Thank you for working with me, Conskavan. You may not be a proper soldier, but for logistics you can't beat the Munitorum. And–'

A squeal on the vox.

'*Attention, all units. Negative Chrysanthus.*'

Not Field Marshal Raik. A woman's voice.

'*This is Inquisitorial Legate Talia Daverna of the Ordo Hereticus. Rosette number 9588/D7. I have Inquisitorial jurisdiction for this sector from an order dating to 897.M41, including override power. Negative on codeword Chrysanthus. This planet is under full quarantine due to spiritual pollution via overwhelming daemonic manifestation.*'

Kristan saw Creed look at A'shar, who hung his head, shaking it.

'*With the force of the God-Emperor's Holy Church and the Ordo Hereticus, I inform all Adepta Sororitas on Cadia that it is their sworn duty to ensure none escape this quarantine.*'

Kristan saw two Battle Sisters shift their postures to bring their bolters towards Creed. Not at him, but held low in his direction.

'*We have fought together for the Emperor. Now, let us serve Him by dying together as well. Furthermore I–*'

A black gauntlet snatched the handset from Creed, stretching the vox-cord up to its greatest extent and bringing it to a cruel mouth.

'Attention, all units. Disregard negative Chrysanthus order and quarantine restrictions. This was broadcast in error. Stand by for orders.'

'*Who dares contravene an Inquisitorial mandate? Identify yourself, broadcaster.*'

'This is Katarinya Greyfax of the Ordo Hereticus. Rosette number 7134/S3. I have Inquisitorial jurisdiction over this sector dating to before you were born, and declare your quarantine order null and void. Sororitas, you are not cleared to engage friendly forces. Logistar-general?'

'*Yes, inquisitor?*'

'All units – Chrysanthus, Chrysanthus, Chrysanthus. Get us off this rock.'

* * *

Belisarius Cawl was, in fact, planning to do just that when his temporal cogitator sensed a desynchronisation. A stasis field. Xenos-make, and powerful.

Not one that froze the subject in place, but one that held them apart from the outside timestream.

'My dear archmagos dominus,' murmured Trazyn. 'I do not think you will be needing that order-code you're drafting. I have instructed the *Lord of Antiquity* to fix a teleportation matrix on our position. I think it will be more comfortable for you than travelling via the hyperspace oubliette.'

'Are you kidnapping me, xenos? Taking me for your little collection?'

'It is not little, and no, I am not engaging in anything so base as kidnapping – consider it an invitation.'

'Can I refuse?'

'It is an obligatory invitation. After all, I have assisted your Imperial faction greatly in this endeavour, and lost exhibits because of it – I do not think I should walk away without just compensation. What poor hosts the Cadians would be if they did not let me take a small prize.'

Cawl scuttled sideways on his bladelike legs, as if backing to the side would help him gain advantage. 'Why me, though? If you are a collector of histories, then I am merely tangential to this affair.'

'You are interesting, though. Far older than some of your kind, and with a great deal of knowledge I can draw from – and besides, my cryptek Sannet has been examining your ship's collection of relics. I am especially interested in what is sealed in that big casket our spectromantic bombardments cannot penetrate. Besides...'

The alien raised a hand and let a ribbon of tiny silver insects swim and dance around the moving fingers.

'Once the mindshackle is in place, you would serve as an excellent partner in new acquisitions – perhaps even better than Valeria.'

'You do not want me.'

'Do I not? Why is that so?'

'Because I am not ripe yet. I have more to do, further things to accomplish. My significance and historical value would only grow. Take me in a century or two, when I am more accomplished, and the catch would be all the greater.'

'Ah,' Trazyn answered, and Cawl's vocal analytics caught the smallest twinge of good-natured irritation in the affect. 'I have heard this tale before, when I studied your Fah-ree Tales. "Eat me when I'm fatter," says the boy to the witch. "Let me cross the bridge, and devour my larger brother instead," says the littlest zoat. I know how this tale ends. With me pushed into an oven or thrown into a river. No, I do not think so.'

'But would you lose the things I am to make? I-I have a task. A great work, given by the Emperor Himself. Take me now, and I will refuse to create. That purpose will not be fulfilled – and you will lose out on a wealth of specimens even you could not imagine.'

'A trick. A tempting one, but a ruse.'

'Is it?' Cawl asked. And knowing he would be incinerated should it ever be revealed he'd done so, he ran the seal-unlocks on a data packet and scrubbed the most sensitive elements, running a standard censorium bot through it to kill all but the names and images. He broadcast it via data-drop into the alien's barely visible web of sensor-tendrils.

The xenos snatched it out of the air and, by some means Cawl could not fathom, simply opened the hololithic spread of binharic as a projection above his palm, reading it like a scroll.

Trazyn leaned close, one finger tapping his elongated chin with a dull *tick-tick-tick*. His finger rolled the digital scroll over faster and faster. Balefire eyes reflecting with the pattern of the digits, unlocking the mental thought-images and wire-frame schematics.

'What are these constructs called?' he enquired, without looking up.

'Primaris.'

'Indeed. And there are many?'

'More subtypes and patterns than even you could ever catch, not even with all of eternity.'

'Oh, dear archmagos, trust me – eternity is a long, long time.'

'Yes,' Cawl sighed. 'But in all that time, there will never be anything quite like Cadia. A historical event like this, well... It is very unfortunate, I admit, not to have a piece of it for your collection. Ah, but you don't want me. I'm a tertiary figure at best. Didn't even arrive until after the Siege of Kraf. No...'

Cawl looked pointedly out of the stasis bubble, at the command section standing around a vox-officer, speaking into the wired handset.

'You want a figure of significance. A central symbol of the battle, who embodies what happened here. One that will not be contributing any more to this galaxy... You want a man, for lack of a better term, who *is* Cadia.'

Trazyn followed his gaze, then looked back.

'Leave me be,' said Cawl. 'Do not touch my ship – and I will give you a whole new galaxy of things to play with.'

'Perhaps I *will* wait,' Trazyn said, and smiled with his metal death mask. 'And eat the next zoat.'

The sight of that smile gave Cawl the shivers.

Engines screamed over the Elysion Fields, Thunderhawk gunships in the yellow-gold livery of the Imperial Fists fighting apocalyptic windstorms to hot-drop into the battlezone. Whatever energy the pylons had channelled disturbed the air when it was let loose, and now alongside the legions of reappearing daemons, cyclone winds and squalls of ash-coated rain were sweeping the sector.

'Aboard! Aboard!' Creed shouted, waving his pistol towards the waiting gunship. 'Everyone away.'

At his feet, a Cadian corpse – two days dead – clawed up his trouser leg with a sudden daemonic animation, dead eyes cooking to cataract opacity with the warpfire manifesting within.

Creed shot it in the head, and Kristan put two more hellpistol rounds into the brainpan so it fountained empyric energy as it drummed the turf with its boots.

The dead were rising on Cadia, and given the millions that had perished during Abaddon's assault, they far outnumbered the living.

Creed had kept the Cadian Eighth on the Elysion Fields, covering the airlift. He could hear the zip-splinter of las-fire to his right, as D Company held the line against a punishing onslaught of puppet corpses and daemons made up entirely of quills.

Elsewhere, purpose-built landers were hauling troops skyward thousands at a time. Taking off in clear fields from touchdown pads with bright lights and neon paint marking the approach paths. But here the evacuation was a desperate mess.

There was no consistency in who was picking up who, and where they were going. There were small Navy landers, Imperial Fists Thunderhawks, Mechanicus explorator shuttles designed for skitarii away missions, with mobile labs and minimal life support. Nobody was working on the same vox-channels, much less flight pattern. Poor visibility due to the dust storms had caused multiple mid-air collisions.

And it was all piecemeal, a craft setting down, loading itself to bursting, then blasting up for another surface-to-orbital run. No plan of where to take soldiers of a certain regiment, Chapter, maniple or Sororitas commandery. Just whoever could fit, going wherever there was a free docking bay.

He didn't envy whoever was up there that would have to sort it all out. But Kristan assumed that wasn't Creed's problem any more.

'Come on!' He shoved a Mordian Sable Guard trooper towards

the open hatch. The woman ran past Odric A'shar, who backed into the Thunderhawk's bay, firing his bolt pistol.

'Are you coming, Lord Castellan?'

'No room, I'll take the next one.' He sketched a salute towards the Raven Guard Space Marine, and shoved Kristan forward with his injured hand. 'But my medicae can fit.'

'No, sir, you go.'

'Troopers in there need you. I'll take the next one.'

'There is no next one, sir. At least I don't think so.'

'Then I'll make sure you're off.' Creed thumped him in the shoulder, a playful punch with the side of his wounded hand. 'Go, I'll hold Cadia until the last.'

'We need you, sir. It's not over.'

Creed shook his head, raised his voice above the wind and gunfire. 'I'm done. I'm frekking tired, Stitch. I don't think I've got another battle in me. Besides, you know what they'll say. I'll be the Man Who Lost Cadia, and all this frekk.'

He threw a hand at the craft engines lighting the dust.

'You think I want to explain this to the Inquisition?'

'Cadia still believes in you, general.'

'And they'll keep believing if they don't see me get old. Or dragged across the coals. No – the Imperium likes its heroes dead. Cleaner for everyone. Means I can't frekk it up.'

He waved a hand at A'shar, who was gesturing that they needed to lift off.

'But, general, Cadia stands, sir.'

'And so will I, always, as long as no one's around to see me fall. Hey, you have a light?'

He reached his cigar out. It was stale and crushed nearly flat. Had been in his teeth for days.

Kristan ignited his wound-cauteriser wand, and touched it to the end, then ran towards the Thunderhawk.

Creed was still there, smoking, as the hatch closed.

Kristan, according to Imperial records, would be the last person to see Ursarkar E. Creed alive.

'Delta Company!' Hellsker shouted into the vox. It was on laud-hailer mode to cut through the sound of las-fire and engines. 'Make firing withdrawal twenty feet, keep the line firm. We've almost got this. You there, Second Armoured Company, just leave the Chimeras. Frekking leave them. Pilots say it's too heavy.'

She turned, looking at the embarkation line. Troops were filing forward, hands on each other's backs like they'd been caught in a cloud of blind-gas, heads down in the blowing gale. Shuffling into the bay of the last lifter.

It had been rough getting the big transports off the ground. They'd evacuated the site a mile further inland, the closest they could get to the foothills while still having a viable landing zone. But the ground was uneven, and the three transports could only set down one at a time.

And people kept coming. Streaming in from the Delvian Cleave with stories about how Creed and the Eighth were keeping the evacuation lines open through blood and grit.

Some were civilian, she saw. In work-gang uniforms. Others were pilots. Everyone that could get out of Kasr Kraf and from the surrounding fortresses.

A knot of troopers were huddling in the dirt, scooping earth into empty ammunition boxes with a trench spade. She was about to yell at them, get them back into line, when she saw a corporal break off and carry two of the boxes to the troopers shuffling towards the transport.

He went up and down the line with them as the evacuating troopers dipped hands into the boxes, filling pockets or dipping shell casings inside.

Taking bits of Cadia with them.

She saw one man, a tanker from the 46th, kneel and pull a strip of sandbag out of the dirt. He tied it roughly around a glass stopper bottle full of dirt and hung it from his neck, kissing the phial as he stepped onto the boarding ramp.

Her throat felt like she was trying to swallow a grenade. She wasn't prepared when she heard the words.

'Are you Hellsker? Are you in charge here?'

'Yes, sir, Colonel Hel...'

The needle pistol was big in her vision. A long, wicked barrel.

'Call it off.'

'What? Call what off?'

'The embarkation. Get on your frekking vox and tell the pilots to come out. This is an illegal operation.'

'I'm working under the authority of the Lord Castell–'

'I know whose authority you're working under.' The woman grabbed her by the flak vest and pulled her close, the needle pistol jamming into her unprotected throat. Her captor was huge, with broad shoulders, and clad in a tailored officer's coat. 'Inquisitor Daverna of high command. And I know all about you, *Major* Hellsker. How Creed favoured you, how he bribed you into this illegal action with a rank elevation. Call the pilots out. Tell them no lift.'

'These troopers have fought hard, they deserve–'

'These troopers will start developing signs of mutation within a month. Two months, and they'll be vessels for Neverborn or defecting to the Despoiler. Were you at Tyrok?'

'No.'

'Well I was. And I knew the Volscani. They were no worse than us Cadians, and they fell. Your troopers are not special, major. Our Imperium doesn't deal in exceptions.'

'Colonel, the final companies are embarking, I...' slurred Pesk. He stopped in his hitching walk, one shoulder higher than the other, his face half-slack. Lek was at his side.

'Are you all right, sir?' said Lek.

'The inquisitor wants us to stop the embarkation.'

Pesk took a hitching step forward. 'This is a misunderstanding, surel–'

'Mutation,' Daverna snarled.

'No, he's injured, he–'

The shot dropped Pesk on his back.

Lek grabbed Daverna's arm, tried to force the pistol up.

His hands were still holding her forearm when he fell to his knees, then onto his back. Two needle-darts protruded from his forehead.

There were shouts, scuffling. Troopers rushing towards them.

Daverna swung the pistol back to Hellsker. 'If your people try anything...'

'Stay back!' yelled Hellsker, her hands raised. 'Inquisitor, I'm going to key my micro-bead and tell them to stay back, all right?' She slowly, deliberately, changed frequencies to wide-band.

'Everyone, stay back,' she warned, then knelt in front of the pistol. 'Even you, Zadoc, listen up.'

'Tell them to send the pilots out.'

'Yes, I will. But you should get low, inquisitor.'

'What?'

'It's dangerous here. Active combat. Archenemy snipers in the zone. You could get hurt. We've lost two officers already. It would be a very natural thing to occur.'

'What the hells are you talking about? Get the pilots and–'

Talia Daverna's head exploded. A hotshot round at long range, flashing out from somewhere near the front line.

She toppled between the corpses of Pesk and Arun Lek, her body unrecognisable.

'Plyn?'

'Yes, colonel?'

'The inquisitor has been killed by a heretic sharpshooter.'

'Tragic. Should've kept low, sir, like you said.'

'Make a sweep for the assassin before you get on the transport, will you? He's a good shot, might be dangerous.'

Marda Hellsker scanned the horizon. Not to look for phantom sharpshooters, but because it might be her last chance to look upon Cadia. The world she'd lived for, and so many of them had died for.

There wasn't much left to see.

She nodded at the bodies of Manvar Pesk and Arun Lek.

'Carry them aboard. Leave her. She wanted to stay anyway.'

Sixty minutes later, drop-ship *Ascension of Saint Evocus* started lifting – and it was only then that Hellsker saw the enormity of what had been done to her world.

The dormant volcanoes of the eastern Rossvar had gone active, pyroclastic flows sweeping down across the Kraf Plain, where she could make out the blasted corpses of Legio Vulcanum Titans. To the south, half of Cadia Secundus was on fire, the forests and plains already nothing but grey ash shot with embers on its western side, and active yellow-white flame in the east.

Gouts of steam rose from the seas, and she realised they were boiling off. Past the Caducades Sea, an enormous trench had opened, and waterfalls were cascading down both sides of the undersea canyon towards the planet's mantle.

Throne, the planet was splitting. Continents ground against each other like teeth, a noise so cacophonous it rattled the ship's viewport until they pulled out into orbit and the soundwaves ceased travelling in the airless void of space.

Everyone aboard, if they could see, was gathering at the portholes. Watching their world die through badly polished windows no bigger than a soup bowl.

'The troops want you to say something,' said Ravura.

'Throne,' she breathed. 'What's there to say?'

'A eulogy, for Cadia.'

'We can find a priest.'

'There's no frekking priest, Marda. We've got you. And we're watching our world die. Just, anything. Something from the primer?'

Hellsker reached for her book, and realised it wasn't there. She'd offloaded it to make room for Creed's package.

She fished in her other pocket for a prayer card, a hymn. Whatever she could find so she didn't have to think up what to say over the slain and mangled carcass of her home world.

She found the piece of paper, and it seemed like the right thing.

Hellsker got up on a shell box filled with Cadian earth, called for silence. Only realised belatedly that the bagged corpses of Pesk, Lek and the others who'd died just before evacuation were arrayed before her. Lined up so the medicaes could add a handful of soil to their bags before they were jettisoned in void-burial.

The paper crinkled in her hands. It was torn, the ink had run. There was blood on it from a wound she didn't remember taking.

She cleared her throat, and started to read.

'*This is not…*' She stopped, voice shaking. She accepted a canteen and swallowed water. Forced herself to speak louder. To deliver it with strength, as a Cadian officer should.

As Barathus had.

'*This is not a foxhole,*' she began again, steadier this time. '*This is the rich earth of my world.*

Dirt I threw in handfuls on the coffins of troopers that came before me.'

Those who stood in the ranks on the bastion wall, lasgun in hand,
    And told the Eye that it could not have our future.
Crimson las-beams slashed in all directions. Bursting the bellies

of living corpses. Driving back warp spawn beyond the description of speech.

'Hold them, hold them! Cadia stands! Cadia stands to the last!'

There were only a handful of the Cadian Eighth left. They fought with their backs against a pylon, defending a redoubt of their own dead. Kneeling, eyes behind gunsights, pouring their last darts of fire into the cataclysm around them.

A greater daemon reared out of the mass, its two avian heads splitting the toxic air with a screech.

A Cadian trooper raised her missile launcher as her partner loaded the last round. He'd just closed the breech when a green las-shot spiked him under the chin, but he'd done his part, and the missile streaked its chalky parabola into the daemon's proud chest, blasting it open so the ribs gaped and the heart burned.

'Cadia stands!' yelled Creed, firing the last of his hellpistol. 'The Eighth stands!'

It was magnificent, Trazyn thought, as he drew out the tesseract labyrinth.

What a centrepiece it would make.

This is not a foxhole, this is my world.

This is not a foxhole, it is my home.

The place I have shared with my comrades, eating, laughing,

A hole that does not feel empty, for we fill it with light and courage,

Logistar-General Raik had been in high command the entirety of the war, ensuring that supply lines kept running. He'd only taken fire two or three times, had almost been in no danger at all, surrounded by the biggest walls and guns the kasrs could offer.

And now, he was going to die defenceless on this unarmed transport.

The Drake was all over them. They'd waited too long. In an unusual act of selflessness, he'd held the transport until every

Cadian in the Rossvar communications hub – from the chief of signals to the cooks and janitorial staff of the Administratum complex – were aboard.

Raik wished he were back in cargo, so he didn't have to see it in the cabin's big viewport wall. See the big dragons ripping at their panelling, blowing warpfire and blasting autocannons into the engine assemblies. Raik swallowed down vomit as one engine cut, and the craft started to dip. He buckled his harness.

The Drake kicked off and circled to the other engine, opened its maw.

The stream of tracers rattled through it, shredding plating along its spine and severing a secondary wing. For a moment the monster screamed, neck twisting around like a serpent as it beat its aerofoils for altitude.

Then the hunter-killer, engine sparkling like a purple firework, detonated in a concussive cough that lanced shrapnel through the warp engine.

It had started falling, and the evacuation craft gradually rising like a weak balloon, when the Avenger buzzed by. The fuselage had damage, its paint nearly stripped. Clearly, it had been through hell.

'Hail that pilot,' Raik said. 'Ask their name and status, and give them my thanks.'

'There's no need for thanks, transport,' echoed the response. 'This is Captain Hanna Keztral, in War-Kite, Ground-Attack Squadron Three-Nine-Nine (A).'

In her cockpit, Keztral dipped a gloved finger in the stream of blood running from her nose. She'd been pulling so many Gs in the last six hours it seemed to dribble all the time now.

She dabbed the bloody fingertip next to the other red-brown dots on her instrument panel. Nine smudges. One for each kill today.

She could hear the *tink-tink* of the identity tags behind her.

'I have Lieutenant Lahon Darvus as gunner. Write that down on any citation. D-A-R-V-U-S. We're low on ordnance and fuel, but keep ascending, we'll follow you up to scare off the bats.'

As Keztral turned into the sun, going almost vertical, she nursed more fuel into the turbofans to increase velocity in the thinner air.

'Captain Keztral,' the transport sent. *'What is your operational ceiling?'*

She switched off the vox, and fell in beside the drop-ship.

Inside the craft, Raik watched the Avenger keep pace with their steep climb. Breaking off and circling at times to look for enemies.

It was only when the sky started to turn black, and the twin turbofan engines cut out, that he realised the Avenger was an atmospheric fighter.

The aircraft tumbled back towards the red surface of Cadia, drifting like something light in the wind. Like a leaf, or a kite.

And where I have seen them pass into the Emperor's light.

This is not a foxhole, this is my home.
This is not a foxhole, it is my fortress.
It is home, world, a kasr I have dug with my own hands,

'Are you all right?' Kristan asked the trooper.

He was huddled up to a low window, looking at the ravaged planet. Thirty minutes ago, Kristan had decided he didn't want to see it any more.

'Just thinking,' the trooper sighed. He winced as Kristan removed his calf dressing, then his gaze wandered back to the porthole. 'It was a las-bolt. We were some of the last ones out of Kraf. Ran into Archenemy scouts coming the other way.'

'The rest of your people make it?'

The trooper shook his head. 'Good men, loyal.'

'We've all lost a lot.'

'Everything I worked for. I built so much, and it's gone.' The trooper slid a lho-stick out of a tight pack and put it between his lips.

'We'll have to rebuild it.' Kristan wound the dressing tight and tied it off. 'On the bright side, you've got lho-sticks. Lucky. Not many of those left. Plenty of troopers would pay a fortune for one. Hells, I know I would.'

'Really?' said Salvar Ghent, taking the tube of paper from his mouth and rolling it between his fingers. 'How much are you offering?'

A legacy that was bequeathed to me, to meet the enemy blade first,

As we have always, and I will not leave it, not surrender it,
   Not take one step back, for I have dug my fortress and will hold it.

On the bridge of the *Vengeful Spirit*, Ezekyle Abaddon sat in his command throne, watching Cadia break apart. He raised his goblet, fashioned from the skull of the clone-parody of his father, Horus, and drank the dark wine within.

Around him, warriors howled and raised weapons in celebration. Beat ceramite fists on breastplates. Danced. Two Khornates clanged their helms together to the beat of a victory chant. The deck ran with the blood of celebratory sacrifices.

They had done it. After ten thousand years, the gate of the False Emperor had broken open wide.

'It's happening,' said Zaraphiston. 'I can see it.'

As the Cadian fault widened, its gaping chasm yawing down the molten core, the void-space on either side of the rupturing planet began to tear and abrade.

Empyric energy poured through the void, spilling from a fracture that started in the sundered pylon fields of Cadia and extended impossibly into the emptiness beyond. A seismic fault in the skin of the universe, a fissure in realspace that stretched on and on into the dark heart of the Imperium.

Somehow, idly, a psychic message imprinted on his conscious. As if a thousand minds were thinking the same thing, all at once, sending an echo through the emboldened warp.

For this is not a foxhole, it whispered, *this is a grave.*

He did not know what it meant, and he did not care. For Cadia was broken, the Crimson Path laid, the Black Legion victorious and the kingdom of the False Emperor torn in two.

Ezekyle Abaddon took another drink – and let the galaxy burn.

ABOUT THE AUTHOR

Robert Rath is a freelance writer from Honolulu who
is currently based in Hong Kong. He is the author of the
Warhammer 40,000 novels *The Infinite and the Divine,*
Assassinorum: Kingmaker and *The Fall of Cadia,* and the
Warhammer Crime novella *Bleedout.* His short stories
include 'War in the Museum', 'Glory Flight', and the
Assassinorum tales 'Divine Sanction', 'Live Wire'
and 'Iron Sight'.

YOUR
NEXT READ

KRIEG
by Steve Lyons

The Death Korps of Krieg lay siege to a hive city on the outskirts of Warzone Octarius, desperately trying to prevent untold masses of orks and tyranids spilling out into the Imperium. How far will the ruthless Korpsmen go to achieve victory in a seemingly unwinnable war?

YOUR
NEXT READ

CREED: ASHES OF CADIA
by Jude Reid

Ursula Creed, Lord Castellan of the legendary Cadian armies, returns to the remains of their home world on a mission of the utmost importance.

YOUR NEXT READ

MINKA LESK: THE LAST WHITESHIELD
by Justin D Hill

Cadia has stood in grim defiance against the enemies of the Imperium for ten thousand years, an indomitable bulwark against the forces of Chaos… but now, the 13th Black Crusade has come, and there will be no victory. Here, Minka Lesk will be tested in the very fires of a world's destruction.